The Round-Dance of Water

D1612895

Sergey Kuznetsov

THE ROUND-DANCE
OF WATER

Translated from the Russian by Valeriya Yermishova

DALKEY ARCHIVE PRESS
Dallas / Dublin

Originally published in Russian by Astrel as *Хоровод воды* in 2012.

Translation copyright by Valeriya Yermishova, 2022.

First Dalkey Archive edition, 2022.

Library of Congress Cataloging-in-Publiication Data: Available.

Dalkey Archive Press acknowledges support from the Illinois Arts Council
Agency.

www.dalkeyarchive.com

Dallas / Dublin

Printed on permanent/durable acid-free paper

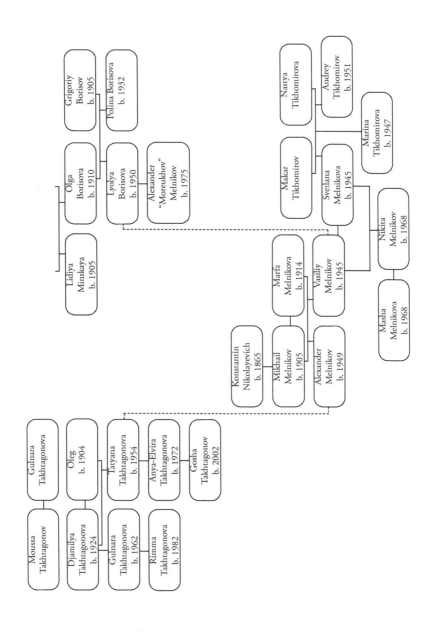

Grigoriy Borisov b. 1905

Polina Borisova b. 1932

Olga Borisova b. 1910

Lyolya Borisova b. 1950

Alexander "Moreukhov" Melnikov b. 1975

Lidiya Minskaya b. 1905

Nastya Tikhomirova

Andrey Tikhomirov b. 1951

Marina Tikhomirova b. 1947

Makar Tikhomirov

Svetlana Melnikova b. 1945

Marfa Melnikova b. 1914

Vasiliy Melnikov b. 1945

Nikita Melnikov b. 1968

Masha Melnikova b. 1968

Konstantin Nikolayevich b. 1865

Mikhail Melnikov b. 1905

Alexander Melnikov b. 1949

Gulnara Takhtagonova

Oleg b. 1904

Tatyana Takhtagonova b. 1954

Anya-Elvira Takhtagonova b. 1972

Gosha Takhtagonov b. 2002

Moussa Takhtagonov

Djamilya Takhtagonova b. 1924

Gulnara Takhtagonova b. 1962

Rimma Takhtagonova b. 1982

PROLOGUE
LIKE A FISH

(THE 2000s: THE FUNERAL)

There is no one more pompous than an old alkie.
Hellblazer

Many films start with a funeral,
you have to start somewhere,
and there's no better beginning than somebody's death.
Mara Malanova

Alexander Vasilyevich Borisov
A.k.a Moreukhov, born 1975

Nikita Vasilyevich Melnikov
Born 1968, Moreukhov's half-brother on his father side

Elvira Alexandrovna Takhtagonova
A.k.a Anya, born 1972, Nikita's and Moreukhov's cousin
on his father's side

Rimma Leonidovna Takhtagonova
Born 1982, Elvira's cousin on her mother's side

Masha Melnikova
Born 1968, Nikita's wife

1.

ALWAYS LIKE THIS

When my father died, says Moreukhov, I was completely sober. For the first time this year.

So much the better: two weeks ago, Alexander Melnikov's body would have vanished among the other corpses.

Blue and swollen, eaten away by fish, torn up by pincers, maimed by underwater snags. Bloated children's bodies like deformed midgets, rags of flesh floating among men's and women's decomposing hipbones. They stare with dead eyes—the ones that still have eyes. They rise up one after another, surface from the dark depths, and the current stirs their hair, which is indistinguishable from the rotting seaweed.

They swim toward him, reach for him, surround him. Fingers stripped of nails grab Moreukhov by the hands, blackened tongues playfully tickle his neck.

Mildew, slime, silt.

Mere retinue, all of them. Then the underwater gods come up: an old man with a long beard, scaly arms, and large, bulging eyes. Another one with a fish tail, coiled horns, and sticky frog fingers poking halfway out of the murky water and slapping it with webbed palms, dark splashes flying in the air. Behind him, another one rides a catfish, holding its barbels like reins. Another one, then another one.

Slimy, reeking of swamp and scales, they dive out of the blackness: fish mouths, toad eyes, droopy whiskers . . . they stretch out their hands, grasping, whisking you down to the seafloor, where darkness and blackness reign among roots, snags, rotten stumps, underwater monsters, slime, sticky embraces, the smell of fear, and the smell of your own vomit.

I'd have to bribe my way out, but have nothing to offer.

Okay. Corpses and water creatures. That's in the end. But what happened in the beginning?

In the beginning, there was a blackout. I can never remember except by accident. Red Label whiskey, I believe. A blonde whose name escapes me, something very funny. Everything was funny. Festive. After all, it was New Year's, Christmas, Old New Year's—the holidays, everyone out celebrating. The office plankton was making merry, drinking champagne right on the street.

So, in the beginning, it was champagne?

No, no. I don't like champagne. In the beginning, it was the usual— cheap cocktails, you know, in cans. A screwdriver or a gin and tonic. Sometimes a two-liter bottle of Ochakovo beer. I could keep this up for a long time—a week, two weeks, even a month. Until the money began to run out.

And then?

Then it was business as usual. I'd go up to the counter—you know, there's this little store by my building called On the Clearing, for some reason I always buy booze there . . . so I'd go up to the counter and instead of a gin and tonic, ask for over-thirty-proof vodka. Then the saleswoman would get a bottle out from somewhere, always with a different label and always at the same price. I'd take a few big gulps right there at the counter and wouldn't remember a thing afterward. Only, a few days later—sometimes a week, rarely more than that—I'd resurface in my own apartment. Face beaten to a pulp, torn knuckles, and at my bedside, Dimon and what's his name . . . Tiger Darkovich, I mean, Lev Markovich, my addiction specialist. Dimon always called for him. There'd be an IV, saline solution, and more water. And he would leave me pills, which I never took.

So, after two weeks, you'd get back to normal?

What do you mean, normal? What's normal about all this? Look at me—my hands are still shaking. My face is swollen, I'm missing a front tooth. Normal my ass. So in a nutshell, in two weeks, I was in almost the same state as before my bender. And I can't even remember my nightmares. That is to say, I don't want to remember them.

But were you sober on February 4th?

That's anybody's guess. It had only been a week. In theory, I was sober.

Good. And how did you find out about your father's death?

What do you mean, how did I find out? And why my father's? Maybe he's not my father. Maybe I made it all up. My patronymic is Vasilyevich, not Alexandrovich. Maybe my father's not Alexander, but Vasiliy Melnikov, his brother. And Uncle Sasha really is my uncle.

OK. So how did you find out about Uncle Sasha's death?

Why are you hounding me? How did I find out, how did I find out . . . Why are you interrogating me? Who are you?

Come to think of it, who am I?

I can say "Anya," I can say "Elvira," I can simply say "your sister."

The word "sister" doesn't need an explanation: a blood sister, a half-sister, a cousin. Simply a sister, the one you never saw in your childhood. A sister who didn't even know she had a brother.

To this day, I know almost nothing about you. I only try to imagine you—the man who once called my dead father his father. I try to imagine your life, your apartment, your benders and your demons, which are as repulsive and silly as the monsters on Andrey's computer.

I try to imagine Moreukhov lying on a sunken sofa in the middle of a ransacked room with his hand in his dirty underwear, watching a black-and-white movie made so long ago that, at this point in time, not only the famous director and lead actors, but most likely everyone down to the best boy is dead. And so Moreukhov stares at the pale shadows of these dead people while, at that very moment, on the other side of town, Alexander Melnikov grabs his chest, turns blue, gasps for breath, reaches for the phone, tries to inhale one last time, and opens his mouth convulsively like a fish caught on a hook and hauled to dry land, yanked out by an invisible line into the dry non-existence of death.

Moreukhov will learn about this and say: *When my father died, I was completely sober*, though he's not quite sure himself if he was sober or if Alexander Melnikov was in fact his father.

And Anya thinks spitefully: yet another lie. It's always like this with my father.

2.

MINE WILL DO WITHOUT IT

Alexander Melnikov's daughter officially became Anya at the age of sixteen. Before this, she was registered everywhere as Elvira. Her grandmother had insisted on it given her enduring eastern love of exotic names. However, her mom always called her Anya.

Anya is still angry with Grandmother Djamilya for not choosing a normal Tatar name. If she was called Zemfira, Zarema, or Alsu, she wouldn't have changed it. Or she could have given her a Russian name from the start. For instance, her mom had been Tatyana since birth and no big deal.

Then again, Anya, Elvira, Alsu—what difference does it make? Whatever her name is, you can see that she's Tatar—broad cheekbones, slanted eyes, Asian . . .

Grandma Djamilya was famous in her own right and, as Anya's mom used to tell her, it was only by accident that she didn't receive a medal for heroism in her day. She was a sniper who shot several hundred Germans. Of course, it would have been nice to recall the exact number, but it must have been hard to tell if she had killed or only wounded them.

Had power scopes been invented yet? If so, had they been available to Soviet snipers? Specifically, Grandma?

Grandma was slight and thin. It was hard to imagine her at war with a rifle in hand.

The other week, three-year-old Gosha fashioned a gun out of a hockey stick while out on a stroll, lay down in a snowbank and shot at pedestrians. Grandma must have also lain like this during all four years of the war. In the snow, in the mud, in the grass, in the rubble . . .

Grandma died two years ago—it's too late to ask her what happened back then. Maybe Mom knows? And Anya smiles picturing how she'll dumbfound mama Tanya from the threshold: *Mom, do you remember how many Germans Grandma killed?*

Still, Gosha will only be glad.

As always, Anya smiles when she thinks of her son. Not the anxious smile she was taught at IKEA, but a barely perceptible one with the corners of her lips. Her coworker, Zinka, accidentally catches her gaze:

"What are you smiling about? Getting ready to see Andrey again?"

Anya nods. Zinka comes closer and whispers:

"I picked out an amazing lingerie set at Nastka's. They're having a sale today and I convinced her to hold my size till Monday. I'll buy it with my advance. Gorgeous. Black and red, all trimmed with lace. My boobs look like this in it!" and Zinka gets carried away, holding her arms out almost a half-meter.

Anya giggles.

"Stop it," Zinka says. "Do you know how much it turns my guy on? Drop by Nastka's, pick something out for yourself."

Anya shrugs her shoulders:

"Mine will do without it."

"Oh Anya, you'll lose your man! They'll lure him away! You've got to hold on to a man like that with both hands! Of course, you're beautiful, men can't take their eyes off of you, but still . . ."

Ha! A beauty. Just a former athlete. A good figure, used to staying in shape. A cold shower and exercise every morning. Twenty-five minutes. Sit ups, bend overs toe-touches, pushups. Abs, ankle guards, lumbar region. Ever since she was on the school swim team. To start the day off right. Grandma didn't say for nothing, "No pain, no gain." Must be why no one can tell that Anya's thirty-three, why she still likes to look at herself in the mirror.

To hell with men—the most important thing is to like yourself.

To be honest, she would like it even more if men paid a little less attention to her.

For example, Mark Borisovich, their outlet manager, always follows her with his eyes. Anya knows that look and it doesn't bode well—especially if the management's looking. And it doesn't matter if she's working at a clothing market or a cozy boutique in a shopping mall. Though it never happened at IKEA—well, Swedes are a cold northern people, disciplined, thrifty, and so on. So Anya had three-years of peace and that was swell.

Mark Borisovich comes up to her, gives her a smarmy smile, and asks: "How's it going, Anechka?"

Zinka goes directly to her section, men's footwear. As if to say, I'm busy, you're on your own.

Zinka gets it too.

"Thank you, Mark Borisovich, everything's fine," Anya replies. "Not too many customers today, strangely enough. It being Friday and all."

"That's alright. They'll come by when they get out of work." He rubs his small palms together and reflexively tugs at his wedding band with his left middle finger. "And what are you doing after your shift today? Maybe we could go someplace? Drink a little coffee, listen to some music. And whatever."

Anya smiles her full IKEA smile.

"I'd be glad to, Mark Borisovich, but I can't. I have to pick up my son from daycare."

"Ah your son . . ." he grows instantly glum. "Maybe you can call your mother, ask her to pick him up?"

How attentive! He must have heard me talking on my cell phone, asking my mom to pick up Gosha and take him over to her place.

"Can't today, Mark Borisovich. Maybe another time."

"Another time sounds good," and he smiles his smarmy smile again. "Maybe next Friday? You never stop working, Anechka, you don't even relax properly."

That's true. Anya never stops working. It's been fifteen years and she's still a salesgirl.

Fifteen years of work experience, fifteen years of independent life—and all during the most horrific post-perestroika years.

Anya remembers: it was a difficult time.

She remembers: coupons, empty shelves, merchant tents, clothing markets, currency exchange booths, million-ruble price tags, the abbreviation units of exchange, currency revaluation, wholesale markets, indoor pavilions, shopping centers, the 1998 crisis, and empty shelves all over again.

Fifteen years as a salesgirl. What else could she do, become a killer? She didn't know how to shoot.

Unlike Grandma.

"Thank you, Mark Borisovich," Anya says. "Let's definitely grab a coffee sometime."

What can she do? Sooner or later, she'll have to say yes—to coffee, to music. And when the time comes for "whatever," she'll have no choice.

She doesn't want to lose her job—after all, it's six hundred dollars a month plus a bonus. Standard work hours, labor book. Shoe department in a shopping mall.

A good job, no worse than IKEA. And it pays better.

Tomorrow, on Saturday, Anya will go to pick up Gosha from her mother's house and he'll run to her. Anya will hug him and only then lift up her eyes.

Tatyana Takhtagonova sits in silence with her small hands crossed over her belly. It's as if her face has gone numb.

"Something happen?" Anya asks in a whisper, for some reason. Mama Tanya replies, also in a hushed tone, as if afraid that Gosha will overhear:

"Sasha died yesterday," and, after a pause, she adds: "Your father."

She falls silent again, because, really, what can you add? After the divorce, Anya saw her father three or four times, and as for what happened earlier, she doesn't remember, she was too young.

Uncle Sasha got divorced when I was seven and since then, hasn't exchanged a single word with my father. I saw Uncle Sasha at Grandpa's and Grandma's birthday parties. It was then that he told me I had a half-brother, my father's son from another woman, who was named Sasha, like him. At that point, I must have been twenty years old.

So I rarely saw Uncle Sasha, only a few times a year, and his daughter, Anya-Elvira—rarer still. But for some reason, I like to imagine her standing in her shoe store, talking to her manager, then, hugging her son in her mother's front hall and mouthing: "Something happen, Mom?"

And Gosha doesn't hear a thing as he saunters down the hall waving a shoehorn, shouting:

"Look at my pistol, Mom! Look, look!"

And I, Nikita Melnikov, gaze out the window of a taxi, sigh, and think: "I also would have liked a son like that."

3.

IT DOESN'T GET IN THE
WAY WHEN YOU KISS?

Nikita doesn't have children.

Nikita has a small business, a good apartment, a Toyota, and a wife, Masha, but no children.

He doesn't seem too worried about it.

At present, he's sitting on the edge of a hotel bed, the bed sheet so wet you could wring it out, his shirt and pants strewn somewhere on the floor with Dasha's dress. Meanwhile, Dasha's lying on her back in bed, her body turned slightly toward his, her plump arms thrown behind her head. She has short hair—only a few millimeters in length.

Drops of sweat glisten in her smoothly shaven armpits and on her breasts, hips, and belly. Nikita thinks there may even be a small puddle in her belly button.

Dasha smiles.

A smile, plump arms, a turn of the head.

In her ears—massive silver earrings. A pierced eyebrow and—as Nikita now knows—tongue.

That's Dasha. She's twenty-two.

In three years, Nikita will be forty.

He's thinking: *It didn't turn out too badly, huh?*

So Nikita also has a young lover. Her name is Dasha.

Dasha and Masha—sounds like a catchy rhyme. Nikita doesn't like it. To be honest, Nikita isn't sure he likes sitting on the edge of a hotel bed with a young woman he barely knows lying there. But what're you going to do—it just happened.

Three hours ago, Dasha came in to pick out an aquarium for some small agency. She said she worked as a secretary there. Zoya was supposed to have a meeting with her, but Zoya was late (either stuck in traffic or overslept, he'd have to clear that up later); anyway, Zoya wasn't there, Victor was also out at a client's office, so it had to be Nikita. It's a small company—about seven office staff in total. And only three of them work directly with clients.

So three hours ago, Nikita sat there trying not to ogle Dasha's breasts in her plunging dark dress, contemplating her hedgehog hair, annoyed that he was wasting time on this—the order was trivial, Zoya should have been talking to this girl!—fielding questions and getting more annoyed. *Are these authentic Indian statuettes? Are they from India, or are they locally made? Excuse me, I recognize these, and who is this? I believe the dancing Shiva is depicted somewhat differently in the canon.*

Nikita's parents are convinced he breeds pet fish. In reality, he buys the fish at Aquarium World on Novinsky Boulevard and his company merely designs and services the tanks. While other companies have a standard selection of decorative caravels and pirate treasures, Nikita's offers ethnic aquariums featuring exotic underwater cities, Chinese and Japanese pavilions, multi armed Indian gods, statues from Easter Island, and even sunken Russian churches (he even has expert certification that the churches are exact replicas of the ones submerged in the Rybinsk reservoir). Also, Roman ruins, Arabic minarets and Indian relics. Nikita doesn't know how Arabic minarets could have ended up on the sea floor, but they are popular with clients. They must see it as a prophecy of Islam's defeat in the clash of civilizations.

It's a surprisingly successful business. Nikita doesn't himself know why.

The young woman was clearly in no hurry and kept verifying prices and asking more and more questions. After a while, Nikita got hungry and started peeking at his watch, but Dasha didn't get the hint. Nikita sighed—the customer's always right, what can you do—and suggested they finish the meeting over lunch.

In the office lobby, Nikita handed the young woman a down jacket that had seen better days. When Dasha's arms slipped into the sleeves, she turned around to thank him. Their faces were suddenly very close and, for the first time, Nikita thought: *She's not bad, sexy. Only much too young.*

Nikita decided a long time ago that young girls weren't for him. Dumb, vacuous. And what's more, gold-digging. Why else would a young and beautiful girl make eyes at a forty year old man?

In any event, who knows what a twenty-year-old wants—is she flirting with him or simply chatting: *I think that ethnic motifs are very trendy. Totally New Age. You probably like Castaneda? Your generation always likes Castaneda.*

The lunch-hour rush was already over and they were the last customers in the café. *It's so glamorous here*, Dasha said, looking around. Nikita halfheartedly listened to her chattering, picking apart a bass on his plate and only occasionally glancing up at her. A bit on the heavy side, with sloping, round shoulders and large breasts peeking out from her décolletage. A ring in her left eyebrow—he thought that piercings had gone out of style, were left behind in the nineties.

And at that moment, her tongue clinked against the spoon. Dasha started laughing:

"A youthful whim. I got it in tenth grade."

For us, that would be ninth grade, Nikita calculated involuntarily. Since they go to school for eleven years now, not ten like in his time.

"I wanted to take it out, but I'm too lazy. It can stay."

For a second, she stuck out her tongue; the barbel caught the lamplight and burst into a silvery flame.

"And it doesn't get in the way when you kiss?"

"Let me show you," Dasha answered.

Nikita hesitated for just a second, wanted to pull back, but didn't have time: the young woman leaned over the table, clasped his neck with one hand and kissed him, parting his lips with her tongue.

And that's how it happened: the metallic taste of the first kiss, the warmth of a young body, a smile in the office lobby, a room in the hotel across the street.

As the saying goes, he was rich and successful and she was young and beautiful.

Reason enough to sleep together, although Nikita doesn't remember when he last cheated on Masha. Might have been five years ago. Or seven. Also completely by chance—it just happened.

I ask myself: why didn't Nikita stop after that kiss? He must have been curious—after all, he had never been with a girl fifteen years younger than him. Or maybe he wanted to know if a tongue piercing really did enhance fellatio: he'd heard that it a movie once.

(Of course, Nikita can't remember which movie, while I don't have to think twice—it was Rosanna Arquette in *Pulp Fiction*.)

And now they're hastily undressing, either out of passion or because they're both in a rush—Dasha has to get back to her agency and Nikita to his office. *I'll cum fast and we'll go our separate ways*, he thinks as he caresses Dasha's breasts, sucks on the ring in her left eyebrow, and belatedly thinks he should have bought a condom.

Now, Dasha leans toward her purse and fumbles for a Durex.

Yep, she's prudent. And diligent.

It really is interesting to do it with a younger woman. In our time, girls were completely different.

In the end, they wind up in the missionary position. Nikita on top, Dasha under him, her arms spread. Noisy breathing and the squeaking of the hotel bed.

Because the hotel bed has to squeak, right? I've never fucked in a hotel, I've only seen it in movies and read about it in books. However, I've fucked in places that Nikita can't even imagine.

So, loud breathing, squeaking—maybe faint moans. Nikita thinks: I wonder what time it is?—he can't manage to cum and even starts to get a bit annoyed, just like he did a few hours ago, at the office, when they were talking about aquariums. He thinks: maybe I should change positions? But at that moment, Dasha starts to shudder, throws her head back, and trembles lightly. Her eyes roll back, her mouth opens slightly and a wave passes through her entire body.

Shuddering, quivering, vibrating, rocking, light trembling, and spasms. Every pore of her body seeps with moisture: a small pool on her belly, rivulets flowing through folds, wrinkles and crevices, drops of sweat emerging on her skin. Dasha writhes under Nikita, and he can't tell if this feels good or not. Whereupon a powerful sound rises up from the depths of her body—hollow, subterranean, inhuman.

This is how a prehistoric beast roars in a Ray Bradbury story as it swims out for a rendezvous with a wailing lighthouse.

The sound grows, fills the hotel room, and spills out into the corridor, on the staircases, and into the lobby. Nikita thinks: How does she have enough breath?—and the next moment, everything ends abruptly, silence strikes his eardrums, Dasha's body contorts into the knot of her last spasm and Nikita grabs hold of the round shoulders sliding under his arms, ejaculating with a loud, masculine roar.

He rolls onto the other side of the bed and asks:

"Sorry, what did you say?"

"What did you hear?"

"When we were cumming, you screamed out *love*. Why'd you do that?"

He thinks he knows the answer. Young women, foolish young women can't orgasm without being in love. If you're fucking, you have to say "I love you." There was a time many years ago when he had girlfriends like that—it was before Masha, of course.

But Dasha says something else:

"I go into some kind of trance." She's lying on her back, turned slightly toward him, with her arms thrown behind her head. "Sometimes I scream out some word. It's a different one every time. Not always, but often. It's beyond my control, I don't even remember what I'm screaming. I've tried to request a word, but it doesn't work." Beads of sweat glisten in her armpits. "I usually warn people, but forgot today, I'm sorry if it freaked you out."

Dasha smiles.

A smile, plump arms, a turn of the head.

"No, no, it didn't freak me out," Nikita reassures her. "It's amusing to cum to the word love."

"Think of it as a sexual oracle," Dasha says. "Sometimes you can ask questions before we start. You don't even need to tell me what they are."

Nikita sits down. The bedsheet is so wet, you could wring it out, his shirt and pants strewn somewhere on the floor with Dasha's dress.

All of a sudden, his cell phone rings. Dasha stretches her arm out, takes the Nokia from the nightstand and passes it to Nikita, glancing at the screen out of the corner of her eye.

It says "Dad."

Nikita says: *Hello*, and his father immediately says: *You know, Sasha died.*

I picture it: his voice is dejected and trembling. I'd like to believe that he loved his brother. It's too bad he didn't speak to him for thirty years.

Dasha sits up and hooks her dress with her her toe. Nikita asks: *Which Sasha? The brother?* and his father replies: *Yes*, and each thinks of his own brother. Nikita's father thinks of Uncle Sasha and Nikita thinks of me, Sasha Moreukhov.

We'd seen each other only a handful of times—first as kids and then at Grandpa's and Grandma's funerals. Why did he think of me? Maybe it was the February twilight out the window, or maybe—the beads of sweat on Dasha's skin, the mounting guilt, the thought *It didn't turn out too badly, huh?* As if it was nothing out of the ordinary for him to pick up a young woman, take her to a hotel, and fuck her brains out, as if there wasn't a fifteen-year age gap, as if he didn't have a wife whom he supposedly loved.

There he is sitting on the edge of a hotel bed as if he's some eternally young, eternally drunk, reckless man, kind of like his own brother, me, Sasha Moreukhov, the artist alcoholic.

So it's not surprising at all that, when he hears his father's trembling voice say: *you know, Sasha died*, Nikita doesn't immediately think of his uncle Alexander Melnikov, age fifty-six, just as I can't immediately recall what film I was watching the day Uncle Sasha died.

4.

PARTING WORDS

If you only knew, Alexander Mikhailovich, how angry I was at you this past year. Everyone was long paying fifteen, twenty dollars, and you still paid me ten. I tried dropping various hints, started coming in only once every two weeks, but you still pretended you didn't understand. You know I can't just up and leave you, I remember—after the economic default in 1998, everyone dropped me, and you kept paying me ten dollars. Though I knew that you'd lost your job and were barely treading water.

Well, by your standards, of course.

But I genuinely respect the way you acted during the default. And also for the formal way we addressed each other since we first met. Do you remember how I came from Donetsk in ninety-six? Left Serezhenka with my parents, moved in with Irka in a rented room. We slept together on a fold-out couch; she worked as a nanny for some New Russians and I also wanted to be a nanny. I thought I'd be able to send a hundred dollars to my mother in Donetsk on a regular basis. It seemed like a lot of money. Serezhenka would have clothes and shoes and it would make things easier for my parents.

But you know, they didn't take me. They said it was my Ukrainian accent. They said I was only good for the Azeris, who wouldn't care because they didn't speak a word of Russian.

Of course, I turned it down. I could have gone back home, but Irka introduced me to you. Ten dollars a day, once a week. Extra for washing the windows in the spring and fall. It wasn't much, but at least I could pay Irka for my share of the room.

I never said it, but at first, it was insulting for me to be a cleaning

THE ROUND-DANCE OF WATER

woman: after all, I am a daycare instructor, an educator, a specialist. On my way to meet you, I told myself: if I don't like him, I'll say no! But to tell you the truth, I liked you. An intelligent man in glasses, with a beard and mustache. Your hair was still black at the time, unlike now. You said hello so politely, said: "Come on, Oksana, I'll show you around the apartment."

You know, in those days, your apartment was much dirtier, of course. You think it was easy to wash dust off these corals and wipe the crab carapaces with a cloth? And you sat in this very armchair the whole time. By the way, I was flustered: as soon as I'd get up on the stepladder, my housecoat would fling open up to here. I was younger back then, with a solid build, pretty—maybe you remember?—very shy: what if you'd start harassing me?

But it's true that what didn't happen didn't happen. We just talked. About your travels to the Far East, the Pacific Ocean, the Valley of the Geysers. About how the hot water there gushes from the ground and there's no need for a boiler or a water heater. You showed me photos, beautiful ones.

As I remember, you were a geologist before perestroika, right, Alexander Mikhailovich?

Sometimes I think you brought me luck. Hardly a year went by before I was already making more money than Irka. Of course, I was working weekends and cleaning two apartments on Tuesdays and Thursdays, but at least I didn't have to travel far. But I still told everyone back home that I worked at a daycare.

I know I must have told you all this before. But would it be alright if I tell it to you again? Let me wring out the sponge and go over the shelves again.

Do you remember how I once asked you why you weren't married? After all, you're not old and you have money, and you replied that you have a love and are staying faithful to her.

When I heard this, I gained immediate respect for you. My husband went on a bender as soon as I left for Moscow. Although, even before, he drank so heavily that he was a complete good for nothing . . . except for giving me Serezhenka, which was good.

One time, I even asked you about this love of yours—what her name was, where she lived, why it didn't work out between the two of you. Do you remember what you said? *I'm an idiot, I ruined everything*, and that was all, never a word about it again. And I didn't ask anymore.

To tell you the truth, I was terribly angry at you this past year. After all, I was losing twenty dollars a month, if not forty. This morning, too, I was walking and thinking: I have to give notice, it's time. Cleaning isn't bread, people can live without it. If he doesn't have the money, he can do it himself.

Please forgive me for thinking that, okay?

At first, I was confused, I thought you must have gone away somewhere and that's why you weren't answering the door. I opened it with my key, came in and saw that the light was still on in the room, although it was already morning. I mean, you'd often forget to turn off the light, it drove me nuts, I would have preferred you save on electricity rather than pay me ten dollars.

I went to the bathroom right away, changed my clothes, took a bucket and rag, and only then came in the room.

And there you were, by the armchair, on the floor. I rushed over to you and took your hand, which was completely cold. I realized right away that it was all over, that nothing could be done.

I was terribly angry. I'd have to call the cops now, Alexander Mikhailovich, and what would I tell them? The cops would come, check my phony city registration papers and talk me into parting with some money—and it would all be your fault, by the way. I should have given notice a long time ago, ten dollars is no pay rate, let me tell you now. I wanted to do it for a long time, and now this

You let me down hard, real hard.

When I saw you and rushed over to you, I knocked over the bucket, there, look at the puddle in the middle of the room. And I was so uneager to call the police that I took the rag and started wiping it up. What else could I do? It's a habit. Nine years since I started cleaning your apartment. So much has happened—my Serezhenka grew up and enlisted in the army, my mom died, Irka got married, and I'm here practically every week. And I'm never coming back, by the way.

I mopped up all the water, wrung out the rag, went to the bathroom to get a sponge, and began to wipe the shelves with your corals and crabs and whatnot. This last time, I thought, I'll at least clean it properly.

What a shame, what a shame, I'll be honest with you, Alexander Mikhailovich. After all, you're only fifty-six, right? Only fifteen years older than me, by the way. You could have gone on living and living.

I think to myself: how'd you manage this? You must have been sitting and reading when, all of a sudden, you didn't feel well, right? Was it your heart? They say when you're having a heart attack, you feel shortness of breath and everything grows dark before your eyes. Is that true?

So why didn't you reach for the phone, huh? An intelligent, adult man, who knows everything but didn't have a phone close at hand. If you've got a bad heart, you should always have a phone nearby. An ambulance would have come, they would have resuscitated you, given you a shot.

You must have been in pain. You may have even screamed—I see that your mouth is still open. Why didn't your neighbors hear? Or is it because you didn't have the strength to scream?

Oh God, it's so awful. You're so smart, so handsome, had everything—how could it be that, at fifty-six, you were alone at night, in an empty apartment?

It's all because you didn't have a woman. A person shouldn't live alone, especially a man. If I were here, I would have called you an ambulance and dug up some nitroglycerine or something.

It's silly the way things turned out with your love. What do you mean, you ruined it? Couldn't she see how much you loved her?

It's even a shame that you never made a pass at me. Especially when I was young. Did you at least see how beautiful my legs were? Unlike now. Nine years have passed, after all.

Listen, I'm going to call the police now, I know I have to. Let me just fix your hair and close your mouth.

Of course, it doesn't work. I forgot about that. It's always like this with dead bodies. The jaw has to be tied with a handkerchief.

Too bad you can't see what a good job I did cleaning. Everything is spotless.

Forgive me for crying, Alexander Mikhailovich. I'll stop now.

I see that your hair hasn't gone completely gray yet. But the gray suits you, even when you're like this, dead.

What a disgusting word. Dead. I don't even want to say it.

Let me not call the police right away. Or else they'll come, take you away, and then we'll never see each other again. I better call one of your friends . . . or relatives or something.

Your address book is on the table, right? As usual? Let me go look for it now.

You had a brother, didn't you? You told me once. He had some common name. Kolya, Vanya . . . No, I don't remember.

Your handwriting is horrific, it's indecipherable, Alexander Mikhailovich. I can't understand a thing.

Ah, here. Vasiliy Melnikov—exactly, Vasya, not Vanya. I'll call him now and then I'll call the cops.

As soon as I stop crying.

I'll probably go back to Donetsk now. Serezhenka's all grown up and making a living. What's there for me to do in Moscow?

I'll call right this instant. Vasiliy Melnikov, that is, Vasiliy Mikhailovich.

Hello? Vasiliy Mikhailovich? This is Oksana, your brother's cleaning lady. You know, Vasiliy Mikhailovich, he died today.

Yes, I'll go ahead and say that. Let me calm down and call. And then call the police. And I won't go to the funeral—what would I do there? They'll laugh at me—the cleaning lady came to the funeral. What would I wear? I left all my nice dresses back in Donetsk.

You know, it's such a shame. I'll be honest with you: if you hadn't died, I would have even cleaned for free!

After this, we won't hear anything about Oksana from Donetsk. She never went to the funeral and no one ever saw her again. Only Vasiliy Melnikov heard her southern accent over the phone: "*This is Oksana, your brother's cleaning lady. You know, Vasiliy Mikhailovich, he died today,*" that's all.

The rest I had to invent myself.

Of course, it's silly, but I wanted there to be at least someone to cry over Alexander Mikhailovich Melnikov.

Let it be an unknown woman—let her cry with a pure heart, free of grudges and guilt.

They say that an unmourned corpse portends trouble.

5.

ALTERNATIVE WAKE

You want me to tell you about myself? Instead, let me tell you the story of four people, two brothers and two sisters, cousins and half-siblings, as well as that of our families, because that's our collective story—our families thus intermingled to bring us into the world.

There are four of us: me, Sasha Moreukhov, my brother, Nikita, and my cousin by blood—or my half-sister—Anya, if Uncle Sasha was in fact my father. And the fourth is Anya's cousin Rimma. Grandma Djamilya wanted the girls to be friends, but no friendship coalesced—after all, they're ten years apart, but still: from the same generation, same point in time, same city. There she is, Rimma Takhtagonova, who knows nothing about the death of Alexander Melnikov and probably knows nothing about me or Nikita, but I'll try not to forget her.

And, if I do, you'll remind me, okay?

Black figures powdered with snow, the black trough of a freshly dug grave, white flakes flying from the sky . . .

The funeral Oksana never ended up attending.

Khovansky Cemetery. February 7, 2005.

There's Moreukhov standing with his hands in the pockets of his torn jacket, shivering from the wind, pulling down his knit cap. A bit off to the side—Anya in a black, Chinese down jacket holding Tatyana Takhtagonova, her mother, by the elbow. Not too far off, in the same positions—Nikita and his father, Vasiliy Melnikov, the brother of the deceased.

A sculptural composition, Moreukhov thinks. They look as if they're made out of marble, standing there under the snow. Two male figures and two female ones. Symbolizing grief. Or maybe, not grief, but shame, remorse, and guilt.

We have short memories. We can barely remember our own lives.

We wouldn't have enough room for the lives of other people.

For us, a hundred years is mind-bogglingly long.

It's impossible to remember—you can only imagine that, on February 7, 1905, it was also snowing.

An old man stands by a windmill dam, leaning on a staff, gazing at the graying, snowy sky. The water is bound by ice that conceals dark moisture, slumbering crayfish, mute fish and rotten snags . . . The old man is silent—or perhaps, muttering something under his breath, as if he's speaking to the one under the ice, on the pond floor.

A little boy lies in his cradle, lace, ribbons . . . A father's intelligent face leans over him. *Mishenka, son*, the father says. The glass of his pince-nez twinkles.

Nikita, Moreukhov, and Elvira will call this boy *Grandpa Misha*.

We see them as if through a veil of snow, hardly distinguishing faces or figures: a multitude of people, the parents of Grandpa Makar, Grandpa Grisha, Grandma Nastya, Grandma Olya, Grandma Djamilya . . . scattered throughout the towns and villages of the Russian Empire, they know nothing about each other, the future, or the grandchildren and great-grandchildren who will bring them together.

There won't be an empire, there won't be a Russia, and later—no Soviet Union. At present, on February 7, 2005, we, their descendants, will gather at a cemetery, and snow will fall just the way it did a hundred years ago—except it will be slightly russet from the soot and ash of the freeway, the stanch smell of the Moscow Ring Road, where the cars go around in a circle like water molecules in a school textbook: water, vapor, rain, and snow; sublimation, evaporation, condensation, and freezing. The eternal water cycle, the windmill, the wheel of births and deaths, funerals and christenings.

Let us raise our eyes to the sky: white flakes swirl out of the white emptiness like at the end of Edgar Allan Poe's novel. Let's imagine these flakes are the embodiment of the dead man's gaze, the gaze from heaven. Let Alexander Melnikov see the coffin swaying over the snow-covered black hole. Let him take one last look at the people he lived with his entire life: there's his daughter holding onto the woman he divorced, there's his nephew embracing the man who betrayed him. There's the woman he once loved hurrying down the path. She says:

"I'm late."

The mascara on her face is smeared, obviously. In a snowfall like this. At a funeral like this.

Moreukhov puts his hands on her shoulders—the composition is now complete. Two men. Two women. A man and a woman.

Children and parents.

Don't look at us, Uncle Sasha: soon, you will meet God and the angels. That's me, Alexander Moreukhov, trying to see things through your eyes. You believed in the afterlife—in the seventies, it was fashionable to believe in it, so you did. Let it happen for you, angels in heaven, a kindly God on a snowy cloud, eternal celestial bliss. You taught me a lot, but you couldn't pass on this faith. Though, of course, I consider myself Eastern Orthodox.

I look into the falling snow and imagine I can make out the snow-white feathers of angel wings, but then think that Uncle Sasha isn't looking at us from heaven, but from a coffin, a wooden box that, for the last time, swings over a frozen black hole

To the eyes of the deceased, the coffin lid is transparent. Through it, he can see the snow flying down, the sky swaying in time with the gravediggers' movements as they lower the coffin into the earth. Along with the white, weightless flakes, he can see the dark, frozen dirt flying in his face. He hears a thud and now everything is pitch-black, night has fallen, the last night, the night of the dead dead, from which you can't rise up, can't pull your hand out of the ground with a greeting gesture—the salute of all the zombies of the world—can't break through the lid like Uma Thurman in *Kill Bill, Vol. 2*, can't see the winter sun.

I picture my father, Uncle Sasha, in the coffin; the gravediggers level the earth and my mother begins to sob, clutching my arm. I never did ask who my real father was. Does it matter? You can choose your own father—especially when the man you're bound to by your patronymic never said a word to you your whole life.

There he is, Vasiliy Melnikov, standing arm-in-arm with Nikita, my brother. A cousin or a half-brother—depending on whom I choose to be my father.

Nikita is wearing a nice overcoat. I don't know what that style is called. A bourgeois coat. If I still believed in the Revolution, I would have added Nikita's name to the execution lists. But for a while now, I've stopped believing in the Revolution—the Red, the Black, and the Orange.

Sometimes, I like to imagine how Nikita lives. I know he's got some sort of business. He breeds something. Pet fish, I think.

We leave the cemetery having hardly said a word to each other. As a matter of fact, you're supposed to express condolences to the family of the deceased at a funeral. But which of us was close to him? My mother, whom he loved at one time (his whole life, I believe)? The wife who divorced him when I was born? The daughter she took away from him?

Yes, I was his closest family member! They should come up to me, shake my hand, look me in the eyes, rattle something off, consumed by guilt, crushed by my suffering, my loneliness! And they're crowding around Tanya, his ex-wife, a woman he never loved! They're expressing condolences to Elvira, who even gave up her name and became Anya!

I gave up my last name, but that's a whole different story.

My mom pulls me by the hand. Is it possible she also wants to express her condolences to them? No, thank God. We walk in silence down the snowy path to the exit. I should probably say something, but I don't know what.

Anya catches up to us by the gates.

"Sasha," she says, "aren't you coming to the wake? I know Dad loved you."

I don't say anything. She knows that Dad really did love me—more than her. Knows and envies me even today.

"No," I say, "I'll have an alternative wake."

I turn and walk away. Anya is probably following me with her eyes. The snow cinematically covers my footsteps.

I put my mother in a taxi and shuffle off to the Metro. Maybe I should have gone with her? No, I'd rather be alone right now. Maybe Mom would like some solitude too.

I stand in front of the Metro and count the money Dimon gave me. Yes, I economized a bit on the flowers. They steal them from the cemetery anyway, what difference does it make to the dead?

And presently, Moreukhov gets a two-liter bottle of Ochakovo gin and tonic at a stall by the Metro. He drinks it in big gulps and his throat is seized by spasms. A taxi goes by—Elvira and Aunt Tanya, Uncle Sasha's colleagues, his friends, the crowd, the extras. Nikita is sitting behind the wheel of his Toyota, his father beside him asking for a ride home. Nikita drives through the snow in silence, recalling the trembling voice in the receiver: *You know, Sasha died.—The brother?—Yes.* And each of them thinks of his own brother.

They drive through the snow without saying a word, as if they're afraid to break the silence of guilt and shame, a belated echo of the silence that has kept the brothers apart for so many years. They're silent, and Nikita imagines Moreukhov alone by the stall, having his alternative wake.

Taxi. Elvira and Aunt Tanya. Meaning, Anya and her mom. They must both be crying. It's normal to cry on the way back from a funeral. Or maybe, they're still unable to cry, they're discussing wakes, groceries, and purchases. Or maybe, they're simply silent.

The taxi is driving through the wet Moscow snow. The driver's listening to a song about Lyalya, who was ruined, although she was a gentle girl. *No amount of vodka can stop my going insane from the pain.* Indeed.

All of Moscow is listening to hip-hop now—or imitation hip-hop.

Yes. Groceries, purchases, salads, living paycheck to paycheck, two brothers, one final expenditure. Here's Anya and Tanya, a story in pictures, look: it's a wake, they crowd into Tanya's kitchen, they sit on the couch, the chairs, and the floor, like this, well, you get it, rewind, now fast forward, and back in the cab.

Anya gazes out the window, squeezes her mom's hand, and thinks about how Mom always told her: *Your father never loved me.* And I never loved him either. And we've only seen each other three or four times. Ten years ago, I called him out of curiosity and we met up and talked. And before that, he didn't visit me once in twenty years. What kind of a father is that?

He used to say: my ex-wife didn't let us see each other. If he wanted to see me, he could have!

They're silent. Wet snow out the window. It's possible that the black earth on my father's grave isn't visible anymore.

Anya takes her mom's hand.

"Listen, I wanted to ask you . . ."

"What?" her mom answers.

And really, what? Anya holds her breath just as her grandma the sniper did before taking a shot, and asks the first thing that comes to mind:

"Did you love Dad a lot?"

She feels her mom's palm grow tense in her hand. Tanya turns toward the window and says:

"Yes."

This *yes* slips into my throat like a lump of ice. Because that's the big question and the big answer. Did you love him a lot? Yes. I loved him a lot too. And today, on February 7, 2005, as I stand in a snowbank five steps away from a Metro stall in an unfamiliar part of town, where you can't find *over thirty proof aqua vitaer*, I attack a second bottle of gin and tonic, already not thinking about where I'll get the money for the third, how I'll get home, or if I'll get home at all. The snow is coming down hard. My father passed away two days ago.

Yes, I tell myself and throw the empty plastic bottle in the snowbank like a grenade under an enemy tank. Elvira and her mom must already be home and the wake must have already started. In two or three hours, the guests will go home and Tanya will finally begin to cry; I don't need to wait that long. I'm crying right now, under a falling snow that hides my masculine tears.

My wake will be long.

PART ONE
TWO BROTHERS

(1960s—1980s)

Only brothers know that love and hate are sisters.
Sergei Blacksmith

Vasiliy (Vasya) Melnikov
Born 1945, Nikita's father

Alexander (Sasha) Melnikov
Born 1949, Vasiliy's brother, Anya-Elvira's father

Yelena (Lyolya) Borisova
Born 1950, Moreukhov's mother

Svetlana (Sveta) Melnikova
Neé Tikhomirova, born 1945
Vasiliy Melnikov's wife, Nikita's mother

Makar and Nastya Tikhomirov
Svetlana's parents, Nikita's grandmother and grandfather

Tatyana (Tanya) Takhtagonova
Born 1954, Alexander Melnikov's wife (1970-1975),
Anya-Elvira's mother

6.

REGULAR RIFFRAFF OUT OF
THE OUTSKIRTS OF MOSCOW

How did this happen? How did it turn out like this? How did I get here? Holding an empty bottle, as if I were throwing myself under a tank with a grenade in hand. Up to my knees in dirty Moscow snow, under the gusts of an icy February wind, wearing a tattered jacket, at almost thirty years old, without teeth, without a hat, with a face beaten to a pulp. How did I get here?

I was a little boy, my mom loved me, my grandpa loved me, my dad . . . I didn't know him.

I was a young artist, the critics loved me, girls gave it to me "just like that," I had friends, fame awaited me.

And now I'm a vagrant, a snow-covered drunkard, an alkie, a lush— and I drop down to the ground when I see the headlights of a car: what if it's the cops?

I'm roadkill.

My father died.

My father died and I got so drunk I can't figure out where to go. Where am I? Where is my home?

Where is home in general?

Ten years ago, everything was different. Reviews in the *Art Journal*, exhibits in cool, second-tier galleries, the looming promise of the Venice Biennale and Kassel *documenta*, and, afterward, television, the Ministry of Culture, my own studio, fame, honor, and solo exhibits.

As Don Corleone would say: an offer you can't refuse.

And if Sasha Moreukhov were truly offered all this—the biennale, the Ministry of Culture, solo exhibits, all that jazz, *all that shit*—he would have agreed. Because, after all, he dreamed of fame. Of money and women.

And then Moreukhov got scared. The system was breathing down his neck and its foul, sated belch whiffed of complimentary exhibit-opening grub; it tickled his throat with the bubbly kisses of Italian sparkling wine and laughed in English, exposing its straight, white, un-Russian-like teeth.

Sonya Shpilman, Moreukhov's then-love, was spending her last summer in Moscow before departing to her "historical homeland," Israel, which meant that they got busy spending the whole summer together. Miss the exhibit a few times. Stage drunken debauchery at the opening. In the end, declare to everyone you're working on a new long-term project called *I'm Regular Riffraff Out of the Outskirts of Moscow*.

Of course, the right way to say it was "from the outskirts of Moscow," but bad grammar was already coming into vogue.

The project turned out to be long-term indeed. You could even say it was successful.

More than successful.

As Malcolm McLaren used to say, failure is the best success.

Malcolm McLaren, the ideological father of punk rock, creator of the Sex Pistols.

God save the Queen!

Save the Queen—and save me, your prodigal son in the dirty Moscow snow, in the headlights of the approaching car.

Two thugs. In their warm police uniforms.

"Your papers."

I put my trembling hand in my inner pocket. Here's my Moscow passport, bitches. Better than a residence permit. Booya!

They leaf through it, check my face against the photo. Well yes, his teeth were in place then, so what? The thing with teeth is, here today, gone tomorrow. A natural loss, wear and tear.

In the fragmented light of the flashing siren—a sign with a street name. I certainly ventured out far. Where is this Mansurovsky Lane? In the very center, on the Golden Mile.

Regular people don't live in places like this.

Good thing I at least know where I am.

"Let's go to the precinct."

And so it begins. They'll rough me up, want to take my money—haha, except they can't because I haven't got any!—okay, then they'll just rough me up for fun, like Mr. Blond in *Reservoir Dogs*—"It's amusing. To me." Then—Dimon, Tiger Darkovich, an IV, withdrawal, sobriety.

Hell no.

"Guys," I say, my speech slurred, "why the precinct? I'm going home, it's not too far from here."

Not too far! Haha! I hope that, now that I know where I am, my "not too far" sounds convincing.

"Let's go, let's go," and they grab me by the elbow.

For a moment, there's a flash, as if we're being illuminated by a strobe light: right hook, tear the club out of his hands, hit the second one between the eyes. And run.

Well, yes. Seventies films, the video stores of my childhood, my forgotten abode.

I don't know how to fight like that.

"Let's go, let's go."

"Guys," I say, "listen. I'm drunk, I'll admit. But here's the thing: my father died. The funeral was yesterday. My father, do you understand?"

"Oh yeah," they say. "Of course. Everyone's father died, yeah, right."

"Listen, no, really. I was living with my mother and she said our father left us. And that, supposedly, he was just my uncle Sasha . . . well, he'd come over to visit, I went to his house too, he was a geologist, interesting to spend time with. Only later did it dawn on me, when I saw the photo of him with my mom at the maternity clinic. And me, wrapped up with a bow. Do you understand? That's no uncle, that's a dad. He hid it for some reason, probably because of his wife. Although he divorced her anyway, can you imagine? But he really loved Mom, I always sensed it. Kids sense those kinds of things, right? And now he's dead, do you understand? He's dead and they buried him. Yesterday. And they didn't even invite me to the wake, as if I'm not his son. How did this happen?"

As I talk, they drag me to the car, but all of a sudden, the one on the left stops and says to the other one: "Wait a second, Kolya," and we stand still in the middle of the snowbank—the two cops and me, crucified between them.

And at that moment, it's as if time stops and I can't feel the cold, I can only taste the words on my lips: *How did this happen, huh?* A silent mother, a beloved Uncle Sasha, an unknown Uncle Vasya, how did all this happen?

My brother Nikita has by now probably returned home from work
to his wife and is lying in their marital bed, holding Masha's hand, also
thinking: how did this happen? Dad, Mom, Uncle Sasha—and that
woman, what's her name, Lyolya?—whom he saw for the first time today.
What happened back then, thirty years ago?

7.

CATCH-75

Sveta is sitting by a dark window, swallowing tears. The yellow circle cast by the streetlamp, the lonely figures of passersby. How many times she waited for Vasya to appear—she won't ever do it again. Even if he does in fact stay. How could he stay? After all, he doesn't love her anymore. He loves someone else. A young and beautiful someone. They say she writes poetry. They say her parents work for the government in Leningrad.

Sveta swallows her tears. Everything's in the past—the opaque sheets of samizdat paper, conversations about Russia's future, the smell of children's diapers, the basin of boiling water on the stove, the cloth diapers on the kitchen clothesline, little Nikita's nighttime cries, everything's in the past. You can't live with a man who doesn't love you anymore. Better to be alone.

But Sveta is not alone. She has little Nikita, her son. And presently, she walks up to the crib, fixes the blanket, and . . .

No, not like this, it's all wrong. How do I know what she's thinking, how it all happened the year he turned seven? Let's try again, without false psychological logic, without melodrama, without names, with the old, logical style of the 1970s.

For instance, let's start this way: she, too, had a family . . .

She, too, had a family. Had a Husband. Her Husband was a fighter for truth and justice. In the locked drawer of his writing desk, her Husband kept typewritten sheets of paper containing the truth. Every evening, in the kitchen, her Husband blew the whistle on local authorities' misdeeds over the telephone, muffling his voice with a pillow. We live in a country of lies, said her Husband, our whole life is pervaded by lies. Just today, at the Institute, the Supervisor said about a colleague: "He's so talentless, we should give him a bonus." And they gave it to him. And no one objected. Because we live in a country where only a handful of people are brave enough to speak the truth. And her Husband muffled the phone even more, fearing the Authorities.

It was strange for her to hear him talk this way. Her Father and Mother had escaped collectivization as children, wandered the country for many years, obtained false documents using various truths and untruths, and had children at thirty-something—almost in old age, by village standards. Nevertheless, they indicated on all their forms that they came from impoverished families. They joined the party. They spoke at meetings. They almost learned to believe what they said. They lived a life built on lies. They couldn't even confess the truth to their own pillows at night. Because all the pillows they trusted were left in their parents' collectivized homes, and life had since childhood taught Mother and Father not to trust anyone they didn't know.

Lies were all they had left.

If Mother and Father listened to my Husband, she thought, they would have gone and reported themselves to the NKVD a long time ago.

But she never told her Husband this because she loved him. And he so enjoyed exposing false television reports in the evening that she didn't want to upset him. Furthermore, it was rumored in progressive circles that the open denunciation of lies would be allowed any day now, which meant that you would no longer need to muffle your voice with a pillow. When she told her Father, he said it was a sure sign they would start locking you up just for having a phone and a pillow in the same room. When he heard this, her Husband laughed a great deal and said that his father-in-law was a pessimist and paranoid. He was forgetting what colossal changes had taken place in the country in the past twenty years, and was therefore always expecting the worst. On the contrary, her Father said: because I remember what colossal changes had taken place in the country, I am always expecting the worst. That's reasonable, her Husband said, if it wasn't for the Khrushchev Thaw, the worst would have happened a long time ago and there would be nothing to expect. The worst did happen a long time ago, her Father said, you just didn't notice.

As always, her Father was right: the worst did happen a long time ago, but she hadn't noticed. Her Husband spent whole days at work, saying he was working on his dissertation, and now and again even traveled to the Institute on Sunday. We see so little of each other, she said, and he replied: that's because I love you and our Son and want to earn more money so you can live in dignity.

One evening, after putting her Son to bed, she sat by the window waiting for her Husband to appear under the streetlight that illuminated the path from the Metro to their high rise. We hardly ever see each other because he loves me so much, she explained to herself—and all of a sudden, she realized that she had already encountered this logic somewhere. The people's welfare is growing, which is why there are fewer and fewer goods in the stores. He's so talentless, we have to give him a bonus.

Then she began to find long blonde hairs in her Husband's things. Then she began to recognize the scent of another's perfume. Then she called the wife of a Friend with whom her Husband worked late, and found out that the Friend came home at seven every evening.

You said you loved me, she asked, how could you?

I told you the truth, her Husband said, I really did love you.

She looked at him and felt completely powerless before the world she was forced to live in. Father and Mother had lived a life built on lies, but they never lied to each other because they came from a different, older world. Where black was black and white was white. Where, if a man loved a woman, he wanted to be with her.

As for herself and her Husband, they were born into a different world. And the Authorities weren't to blame. The Authorities were nonsense, she thought. Father and Mother had them wrapped around their finger their whole lives. As for our generation, we're our own worst enemies. We and our loved ones.

Let's get a divorce, she said. I trusted you and you lied to me.

No, her Husband said, you're the one who lied to me. I trusted you, didn't hide from you, but you spied on me.

I would prefer to be alone, she said. It won't be easier. But it would be more honest.

But you love me, right? her Husband said.

No, she shook her head, not anymore.

So much the better, her Husband said. Since you don't love me anymore, nothing can prevent us from living under the same roof. Besides, I've already left that woman. And decided not to defend my dissertation.

That doesn't mean anything, she said. I can never trust you again. I'll never feel at ease by your side. It's as if the pillow you muffled the phone with has suddenly turned out to be a top secret tape recorder. It's better to throw out a pillow like that—and it's certainly better not to sleep with it in the same bed.

Let's stay together, at least for our Son's sake, her Husband said.

Let's, she said, because, all of a sudden, she realized how hard it would be to exchange their two-room apartment for separate homes.

Their Son grew up and, in due time, read the typewritten pages hidden in his father's desk; in due time, left his parents' home and got married. Nikita respected his father and loved his mother, but, for some reason, whenever he tried to imagine how his parents never ended up divorcing in 1975, the inflated paradoxes and absurd syllogisms of that period always came to mind. If a reprieve was being promised, it meant that everyone would get locked up. The higher the level of people's welfare, the fewer goods in the stores. We hardly ever see each other because I love you so much.. You're the one who lied to me: I trusted you and you spied on me. If you don't love me anymore, then nothing can prevent us from living under the same roof. Let's stay together at least for our son's sake.

Nikita and Masha didn't have children.

8.

THERE WON'T BE A THURSDAY

In the twilight of the winter morning, Nikita lay with Masha for a long time, trying to fall back asleep. Then he got up and went to the kitchen to make breakfast.

Masha likes to sleep in. She likes to have breakfast together. Nikita needs to get to the office by ten. Eleven at the latest. If he gets there later, everything will go topsy turvy and the day will be as good as lost, it will go to the dogs. So he explains to Masha.

They're having breakfast together. She's wearing a nightshirt Nikita gave her two years ago. At present, the nightshirt hangs off her shoulders like from a hanger. He's naked from the waist up, wearing only his jeans.

"Come home earlier," Masha says, "I'm bored without you."

Nikita nods and looks at his watch. Nine O-five.

"I think I've put on weight," Masha says, "I need to weigh myself."

All women want to lose weight. Masha dreams of gaining some. She thinks that her stomach is too flat and her breasts practically nonexistent.

Dasha has large breasts, full hips. Of course, she wants to lose weight.

Nikita passes another piece of toast across the table to his wife, Masha puts a slice of cheese on it and sips her coffee. Nine fourteen. If I take the car, I won't make it, Nikita thinks. What kind of a city is it if it's faster to take the Metro than the car? Maybe I should call and say I'm going to be late. No, I'll take the Metro, it'll be faster.

"You're not listening to me at all," Masha says.

Nine twenty-three.

"I'm off," Nikita says.

Toss on a shirt, a sweater, a winter overcoat. Damn, I hate taking the Metro in an overcoat. I can't wear a down jacket either—I have a business meeting tonight. Jeans and a sweater—that's democratic. The right people will see that the jeans and sweater are expensive—not from the clothing market, after all. And a down jacket is not appropriate, no matter how nice it is.

Nine twenty-eight.

"You're not listening to me at all," Masha repeats.

Nikita looks at her as if he is seeing his wife for the first time this morning.

"I'm late," he says. "I'm sorry."

He kisses her on the cheek and leaves.

On the way to the Metro, he dials Dasha's number:

"I'm sorry I'm late. There's traffic jams all over Moscow, all this snow."

He can't say he lingered over breakfast with his wife. And forget the Metro—he's a sugar daddy, he should be driving a car.

Nikita doesn't like driving. But every day he tells himself: "I'll leave the house earlier, I won't take the Metro. It's disgusting, the smell is nauseating, I get home all sweaty. Yes, of course, the traffic jams, the long drive—but I know that's not the real reason. Kostya has been telling me for a while: If you don't like sitting behind a wheel, hire a chauffeur, it's not that expensive, and you won't have to bother with parking. After all, you make good money, what's the problem?

No, Nikita thinks, somehow, I don't see myself in a car with a chauffeur. Chauffeurs are for serious men, ones featured in glossy magazines, ones who get interviewed by business publications. A chauffeur suits Kostya. Kostya is an Actual Successful Person, his mother probably didn't explain to him a hundred times that *money is the root of all evil, we're just fine without it, we have enough as it is.*

That's why I take the Metro: I feel like a human being, not a glossy personality from the business pages.

Dasha lives with her parents on the other end of town. Nikita called her again from the Metro to confirm the address, for some reason.

He's a bit on edge. Impromptu hotel sex, fair enough—but dragging himself to the end of the world, lying to Masha, lying to the guys, playing hooky for half the workday, is an entirely different story.

What a thing to say, "play hooky," Nikita scoffs, who's going to hold me responsible? Now that I'm head supervisor, the big honcho, the owner!

But still—Nikita's on edge. Why did Dasha call him two days ago?

Asked him how the funeral went—well yeah, he told her his uncle died, so what? They don't have the kind of relationship where she can ask him questions like that. Nikita replied: *Fine*. What was he supposed to say?

Dasha asked:

"And what are you doing the day after tomorrow?"

Nikita stammered, wanted to grumble "working, what else?" but instead said:

"Nothing, actually. I'm completely free the first half of the day."

He doesn't know why he said this. He should have coldly brushed her off, he wouldn't have to drag himself to the end of the world, wouldn't have to trudge in the wet February snow, roving among identical sixteen-story buildings, hesitating to ask passersby where complex 104, building 3 is.

Dasha opens the door. Dasha is wearing a barely closed, oriental dressing gown, the matte whiteness of her body extending from her neck to her carelessly tied broad belt.

Nikita takes off his coat, Dasha hands him a hanger. Just like ten days ago in the office lobby, they end up very close to each other.

The hanger falls on the floor with a dull thud and the coat slips out of Nikita's fingers.

Second coffee of the morning. In Dasha's tiny kitchen—in Dasha's parents' kitchen, to be exact. Five years ago, Nikita had one like it. Now, he's upgraded his refrigerator, bought a new microwave, then Masha put up new wallpaper, and it's a completely different story.

An incense stick smolders. At the edge of the table lies a pile of tattered paperbacks. Yoga, horoscopes, secrets of the mandala, what's his name . . . Paulo Coelho.

"I'm sure you'd like it," Dasha says, "he's my favorite writer! You can borrow it if you want."

She's sitting completely nude, drops of moisture glistening on her breasts. Nikita is naked from the waist up, in nothing but his jeans. His watch shows eleven twenty-five.

"Why do you shave your head?" Nikita asks.

"In solidarity with the NBP, the National Bolshevik Party," Dasha answers.

Kindergarten.

Who did I get involved with? Nikita thinks. She's still a kid.

Silly goose.

"NBP leader Limonov breathed magic into politics," Dasha says and Nikita nods, looking at her breasts. They are gently swaying in time to Dasha's words.

Sure, a breath of magic. A young woman's breath by his very ear. A weak moan, then again: her eyes roll back, her body grows tense, waves course through it, moisture seeps out her pores and then, like the last time, a guttural sound fills the bedroom, the apartment, and the building, and Nikita doesn't even have time to think that Dasha's neighbors must be having a blast listening to them! Because, this time, they climax together, gripping each other, and when Nikita resurfaces, he hears Dasha cry out: *Bend*.

Well yeah, she explained it: it's like that for her every time. Last time it was *love*, this time it's *bend*.

Nikita goes into the hallway, picks up his coat and takes his cell phone out of his pocket. So it is, three unanswered calls, all from Masha. And a text message: "Call me, I'm worried."

The Nokia erupts into trills right in his hands.

Masha.

"I'm sorry, I have a meeting," Nikita says. "I'll call you later."

Dasha giggles barely audibly in the kitchen.

Little bitch, Nikita thinks, suddenly incensed. Why did I come here? Twelve thirty-nine.

"I'm going to go," Nikita says.

"Of course," Dasha answers, "you have work."

Dasha has pulled on a T-shirt which, for some reason, makes her breasts appear even bigger.

Dasha smiles and, for a second, silver flashes between her teeth.

One fifteen, the office. *Hello. Hello. How are you? Terrible traffic, what a snowfall.* They're all on a first-name basis with each other, young people, slightly older than Dasha. Nikita likes them: Natasha, Victor, Zoya, his *team*. They trust him, maybe even love him. Or respect him, or simply tolerate him—who knows? A different generation and, moreover, his subordinates. His staff.

Nikita finds his employees on the internet—mostly on aquarium forums. Currently, they number fifteen and include saleswoman Zoya and managers Victor and Natasha. Of course, they're mostly young aquarists trying to make extra money. For five hundred a month, they call on clients, clean tanks, wash decorations, check on fish, and change the batteries in automatic feeders.

One fifty-five. Quick briefing. A big corporate client has demanded a copy of the articles of incorporation. Why does he need the articles of incorporation if he's buying only two—even if they are the most *exclusive* and expensive—aquariums? As a matter of fact, we never do this, but, for you, I'll send a courier and he'll bring everything directly.

Everything's great, Nikita tells himself, business is going well. I have a marvelous team. I'm full of energy. The day has been a success.

He's not angry anymore. He thinks: it's been so long since I've really fucked! I've even forgotten how great it is!

And then a call from Dasha. As if she's read his mind. Of course, he shouldn't have picked up the phone, but he couldn't help himself.

"Hello," says her dull, hurried voice, "I have to tell you something important."

Not now, Nikita thinks. Don't tell me anything.

"I'll call you back," he answers, "I have a meeting."

Oh yeah, he already promised to call Masha. He dials her number: "Something urgent?"

"No, I just wanted to tell you I love you."

Extraordinary.

"I love you too, baby."

Three unanswered calls to tell me that she loves me. Incredible.

He decides he won't even return Dasha's call—he's on a time crunch as it is, not a minute free. After all, morning sex can bury any business.

Perhaps, the hell with the business?

Nikita smiles.

Looks like I won't have time for lunch. Good thing I bought myself a forty-ruble shawarma on the way out of the Metro and ate it on the go, with everyone staring: a respectable-looking man in an overcoat gobbling down food from a plastic bag like a vagrant. And in any case, whenever I buy a shawarma by the office, I think to myself: the vendors are already starting to recognize me, they nod and say hello. They must think: that poor office rat, *that office plankton, worn out by management.* And I'm my own boss, I've worn myself out. I've got no strength left whatsoever, and where would I get it from? A man who isn't young or particularly healthy and is exhausted by life. The other day, as I was walking through the underpass, I was overcome by such misery that I could have sat down right there, leaned against the tile wall, and started to beg. Give me just a bit of strength, kind people. I would have sat down, the police would have picked me up, found twenty-two thousand US dollars in my bag, and what would I have told them? Forgive me, kind people, I just cashed in two contracts? Yes, we would have an interesting conversation, given my shady accounting and all.

But that was two weeks ago. Uncle Sasha was still alive. And there was no Dasha in living memory.

Now, everything will probably be different, Nikita thinks. It's not a big deal that I'm missing lunch. At least I'll have a *glamorous* dinner.

Glamorous—that's Dasha's word. Apparently, it means "fancy." *Major*, as we would have said fifteen years ago.

So, a glamorous dinner. Well, I'll have to catch a cab—it's not too impressive to take the Metro to Café Pushkin.

Nikita fastens his seatbelt—it's an old habit from the days when he was trying to make some extra money as a cab driver—and his cell phone rings. The driver's digital clock shows six fifty-two.

Dasha's dull voice:

"Hello. You promised to call me back."

"I was busy."

He purposely adopts an icy, almost grumpy tone. After all, he needs to show this young girl he's a busy person, no use calling him. He's got things to do, a business. A wife, in the end.

And he's received fifteen missed calls in one day, all from her.

"It's very important," Dasha says. "Come to my place right now."

"I can't, I have a meeting."

He should try to seem a bit more irritated, not give himself away, not let her sense that he is getting more and more aroused with her every word.

"It's very important, I'm serious."

Should he cancel the meeting?

No, he has to pull himself together. They're having casual sex, it's not even an affair.

Who does she think she is?

"I can't talk, sorry. I'll call you later."

Dial tone.

Something has been off since this very morning. Since the moment he awoke in the winter twilight, since Masha's body turned over sluggishly by his side. Something's off.

Seven twenty-eight. Café Pushkin coat-check. Twelve more missed calls on the screen.

Maybe he should call her back?

"Dasha, let me explain. When I say that I'm busy . . ."

"I'm so happy you called me back! Are you coming?"

"Dasha, I told you, no."

"I just don't want to do it on the phone."

I don't want to do it on the phone either, I want to do it in person, I want to do it with you, again and again, over and over—he catches his breath, after all, he's an adult man, that's what they should love him for. He says coldly:

"How about I come on Thursday? You can tell me then."

And suddenly, a piercing cry, practically a shriek:

"Thursday's too late! Come, I'm begging you!"

Hysterical woman.

"Dasha, I have a meeting, then, I'm going home, what is it?"

Maybe that's what it is? Maybe she simply wants him as much as he wants her?

No, that doesn't happen. Why would a young, beautiful woman need a forty-year-old, balding man?

Well, understandably, for many reasons. Money, gifts, a rented apartment. No doubt it's not much fun to live with you parents, on the edge of the world, right by the Moscow Ring Road.

"Come now, please. Please. It's really important."

"Tell me on the phone."

"You won't believe me."

Suddenly, a treacherous thought comes in a silver flash: *maybe she's pregnant?* No, it can't be, she took out a condom herself. Took it out herself? And what if? . . .

"I'll believe you. Tell me."

Dasha laughs, a strange, nervous sound:

"Tonight, everything will come to an end."

"What do you mean?" Nikita asks and sees Vladimir, who waves at him as he walks down the stairs.

"Everything will come to an end, everything. Not *bend*, but *end*. The end of the world, get it?"

"Uh-huh, I get it," he says, marveling at the absurdity of the situation: Pushkin Café coat check, his partner hurrying to say hello and a crazy girl pretending to be Maria Devi Christos or whatever that false prophet's name was.

How did he get involved with someone so young?

"No, really, I know we have to see each other, I'm scared, you understand, I don't want to be alone, I don't want to be with anyone else, come to me, don't bring anything, you see, there won't be anything tomorrow, I'm scared, I'm scared, I'm begging you, trust me, I know it, I've never done this before, I'm not lying, I know, don't come Thursday, there won't be a Thursday and there won't be a Wednesday, either . . ."

She's out of breath, talking a mile a minute. Is she crying?

Hysterical woman. Juvenile idiot and drama queen. Or worse yet—a drug addict. Predictions, incense, horoscopes, yoga, and . . . what is it called? Holotropic breathwork.

You can't expect anything good from a girl whose favorite writer is Paulo Coelho.

"I'll call you back," he says and extends his hand to Vladimir.

They're discussing a new project—a Moscow restaurant chain. Aquariums, suggests Nikita, should be the centerpiece of the décor. A focal point, so to speak.

"The ethnic motif," he says, "will vary in every restaurant. Rather than rely on outsize decor, we'll place an aquarium by every table and, at its bottom, the ruins of temples and cities. I can make exact replicas of genuine ruins; no one else does this. Plus, texts under table glass, historical references, so people have something to read while they wait for their order. I'll build the aquariums at my own expense—to be honest, I'm more interested in servicing them."

Yeah, yeah, yeah, at his own expense. Who knows how much that is except for Nikita?

Vladimir is listening like he's supposed to. He's listening attentively. This may be the first proper moment of the whole day. Must be because Nikita has turned off his ringer.

Eight fifty-five. Another fifty-four unanswered calls. The first twenty-eight—from Dasha, the last twenty-four too. Two in between from Masha.

Over the course of the day, Nikita didn't think of Masha once, if you don't count their afternoon conversation. What can you do: seven years of marriage.

"Yes, dear," he says, "I'm on my way."

"I'm at Olya's house. Can you come pick me up?"

Olya lives right by the office. Nikita sometimes picks up Masha on his way home.

He likes it when Masha goes to someone's house. Or to the shops. Or to the movies. Or when she leaves the house in general. Because, at times, Nikita thinks that, as soon as he closes the door, Masha turns stock-still, as if they've turned off her battery. She freezes in the deep antique arm-chair, curling into a ball, looking out in the darkness.

Unpleasant. A very depressing picture.

"I'm at Café Pushkin," Nikita says, "you should take a cab."

"Alright. Then I'll stay here a bit longer."

Maybe he should drive over to Dasha's now? Then again, no. He has to keep his distance. He has to show her he's an adult man with his own life, family, and business. Half-a-hundred calls, you could go insane!

The taste of cheap silver in his mouth, damp shoulders sliding under his fingers, a ring in her left brow, a weak moan, intense trembling, a roar breaking through . . .

I don't want to be alone, I don't want to be with anyone else, come to me.

I probably also don't want to be with anyone else.

But I won't go. Not today and not on Thursday. She said it herself: there won't be a Thursday.

So there won't be one. It's time to bring this story to an end.

Two more missed calls.

Twelve forty-three. Masha comes out of the bathroom, Nikita is lying in bed, leafing through a photography book with sights of India.

"How was your day?" she asks.

"I'm totally beat," Nikita replies, "I'm so tired, I don't have any energy left."

They go to sleep. Before he drifts off, Nikita remembers Dasha the way she was in the morning—not yet fully awake, warm, sweet, redolent of sleep and bed. No, he can do it just one last time. As a good-bye, before he gets hooked. She mentioned Thursday, right?

It's even charming: I don't want to be alone, I don't want to be with anyone else, come, come.

The end of the world indeed.

As he falls asleep, Nikita stretches his hand out and squeezes Masha's palm.

If everything does in fact come to an end tonight, Masha should know that he's by her side.

9.

FLIMSY REFUGE

Nikita falls asleep holding my hand.

He's got a beautiful wrist. Strong fingers, smooth, oval nails, protruding sinews. Light hairs that are barely perceptible to the eye but coarse to the touch.

He sleeps holding my hand, whereas I can't fall asleep at all.

I'm scared to go to sleep. It's like you've entered cold water, slowly immersing yourself and diving in headfirst, not knowing what you'll see on the sea floor.

That Crimean summer, I went diving alone. Nikita watched from the shore. Only later did he admit he was afraid of swimming.

I wasn't afraid of anything. I was twenty-nine years old. I had never been as beautiful as I was that summer.

And I never would be again.

Time has wrung me out like washed laundry, tossed me in the dryer like a crumpled rag. At one point, I thought that time does not spare anyone, but now I know this is not the case.

Time changes everyone, but a receding hairline, a leisurely manner, and a bulky frame suit a man. In any case, they suit Nikita. I've stopped caring about everyone else a long time ago.

His hands have barely changed. Except, seven years ago, a new engagement ring appeared next to an old one, his grandfather's, which Nikita never takes off.

My skin grows duller and dryer every year, lines cover it like a fine fishermen's net, the years past thrashing in it like caught fish. My hair falls

54

out, and, in the morning, I look at the pillow, trying to resist counting the strands.

One time, I couldn't restrain myself. Now I know: two hundred and fifty-three hairs, almost a handful. I'm scared of going bald. I'm scared that, in a few years, my breasts will vanish, my stomach will stick to my spinal cord, and my eyes will sink in. Sometimes I remind myself of the living dead.

Nine years ago, I wasn't scared of anything. Now I can't go to sleep, I'm so scared.

Meanwhile, Nikita has learned to scuba dive. I don't think he's scared of anything now. *Let's swap, eyes closed*, as we used to say in daycare.

I didn't want to go to daycare. I thought my mom wouldn't pick me up one day and leave me there forever. Only later, I learned where this fear came from: it was an echo of my infancy, the first few months of my life, which were spent in an orphanage.

Mom told me so herself: *You see, sometimes children are born to the wrong parents. And those parents can give them to a special place where their real parents can find them. Like we found you.*

I was six years old, I didn't know where children came from. I must have been thinking of a stork who could mix up packages or a store where you could buy a child after waiting in a long line—and where they could sell you the wrong one by mistake.

When I was ten, my dad explained to me: *ancient Hindus believed in the rebirth of souls. I believe you're the child mom couldn't have.*

I knew that children were taken out of a woman's belly, but didn't quite understand: how was it possible she couldn't give birth?

By then, I'd stopped believing in the stork and didn't believe in the store either, but I instantly believed in the rebirth of souls. And continue to do so. I believe that a soul can travel throughout and across time and from one body to another, even passing through multiple bodies in the same century, by some miracle not crossing paths with its previous (or subsequent) vessels. the same soul travels from one body to another, regardless of historical period, and can be reborn multiple times in the same century, by some miracle not meeting itself in its previous (subsequent?) guise.

I believe in that. Or, rather, I know it. Which is why I lie awake, squeezing Nikita's hand. I'm scared to go to sleep.

In the semitransparent, viscous space between reality and dreams, my past lives return and penetrate me like tentacles, filling me to the brim.

Men, women, children.

There's no longer room for me inside.

I curl up in a ball, trying to push the past out of myself—it was mine, it wasn't mine, maybe it didn't exist at all.

No wonder I'm losing weight: I probably think that, when I wither away completely, the phantoms will leave me to find themselves another vessel.

But maybe I'll get used to them. After all, these are my past lives. I already recognize them: an old woman spins before a mirror, a man gazes at the river, a young woman clasps her hands around her pregnant belly, a man puts a handgun to his temple, a soldier pulls the pin out of a grenade, a naked man makes breakfast, a girl looks out at the Black Sea, a man gets down on his knees before his male lover.

They scream, laugh, cry, moan, sigh . . . Sometimes I want to fling my arms open to them, hug them and say: come on in, here I am, your flimsy refuge, your future, your reincarnation, your rebirth. Don't cry, everything has turned out just fine, look at me, I'm much happier than you: I'm doing great, a loving husband, a home, a car, a life of plenty. I wasn't beaten at interrogations, my friends weren't killed, my flesh wasn't eaten away by radiation, I didn't have to wait for my own arrest. I don't have to think about money, don't have to think about surviving, don't have to think about where I'll sleep tomorrow or what I'll eat. As a matter of fact, I don't remember the last time I was hungry.

But ethereal phantoms drift before me, tremble in the depths of a dream, billow in the murky corners of the big apartment. They've already lived their lives, it's too late for them, their wishes never materialized, they didn't get their fill of the bitter water of earthly being, the bitter bread of posthumous exile. They are insatiable.

They're eating me from the inside out. My life is nourishment for the ones I once was. They sink their teeth into my flesh and, every month, blood flows out, proving that the feast goes on, the phantoms aren't sated yet, they are still miserable.

Every month, in accordance with the phases of the moon, plus or minus one day, I receive the exact same letter.

It says: *once again, you are not with child.*

10.

REINCARNATION. NINA

As we fall asleep, we hold each other's hand. Kolya, my Kolya-Nikolay. I'd like to sleep with my face turned to you, but this gets more and more difficult each month. It's probably safe to say that the three of us are sleeping together. Only two more months and our bunny will be born. I wonder if it'll be a boy or a girl? The old women in the village were always able to guess—by your gait, the shape of your belly, and other signs.

It's been close to five years now and I still can't get used to the fact that my Beryozovka doesn't exist anymore. Although old Georgich's great-nephew wrote last month that they're planning to build a State Farm in its place. I don't even know . . . it must be a good thing. The cows will moo again, the chickens will run around as if there'd never been a war. But you look at it and think: how can people go on living there after something so horrible happened?

I told Kolya and he says: and the fact that we live in a dead soldier's apartment is fine by you? That's how it's supposed to be. New fighters come and take the place of dead ones.

Only there weren't any fighters in Beryozovka. All we had were the two partisans who that idiot Lushka was hiding.

Nina looks out at the street—two-story wooden houses and a one-legged man sitting on a bench, chatting with two women. The sounds of a gramophone drift in from a neighbor's window.

This is Moscow, the capital of the Union of Soviet Socialist Republics, the first government of workers and peasants in the world. The godforsaken outskirts of Sokolniki.

Nina pats her round belly and tries to convince the boy or girl to wait a bit longer, stop kicking, lie still. The doctor said she could talk to him already. Or is it a her?

Nina is waiting for her husband. She sits at home for whole days at a time, afraid to go out. Even in the daytime, she may get attacked, robbed, or simply stripped in the street. She may get stabbed, may get shot. So many thugs around.

Kolya says it all started after the war. Moscow was different before. Now that people have been taught to kill, they won't stop.

Nina doesn't know how to kill. She only knows how to not die, how to hide.

She hid in the woods for two months, surviving on berries and sometimes digging out potatoes from Beryozovka's torched vegetable plots. At the sound of an engine, she'd drop to the ground and lie motionless.

Before, Nina used to love wandering in the woods. Her mom laughed, calling her "my little forest girl."

Mom was burned alive, along with the entire village. Nina survived—that morning, she had gone to pick mushrooms and, when the butchers came, she buried herself in the woods and didn't come out until it was over.

Until everyone was dead.

Kolya says he wouldn't have lasted a day in the woods. I'm scared of wolves, he says. He must be joking—he's not scared of anything.

Nina is scared for him.

She's scared they will stab Kolya to death to steal his pistol.

She's scared Kolya will stop someone to check their papers and they will start shooting.

She's scared Kolya will go off to storm a den of criminals and get killed in a shootout.

She's scared Kolya will walk into a building and there will be an ambush waiting for him.

Nina says: "Take care of yourself, for God's sake. At least, wait till our baby is born!"

And Kolya replies: "I gave an oath. If I don't stop them, they'll go on killing. The other day, a whole family was stabbed to death in the Maryina Roshcha district. Even the little baby. They took off with twenty-five thousand rubles."

This was an enormous sum of money. Kolya only made five hundred fifty. How much did you have to work to make that much?

"How old was the baby?" Nina asks.

"It was tiny, still in a bassinet," Kolya answers. "They killed it so that it wouldn't scream."

Why is he telling her this? Nina wants Kolya to tell her again how, when the baby's born, he'll take leave and stop going to work every day. No, Kolya doesn't want to talk about taking leave; he tells Nina: hang on, we'll put everyone behind bars and then we'll have a good, happy life!

Nina doesn't believe him. She remembers how people used to say: we'll drive the Krauts out and then we'll have a good, happy life! Where is this happiness now? Every day, she sends her husband off to work as if he's leaving for the front!

In any case, it's her own fault: she knew whom she married. From the very start. But still, Kolya was so handsome in his new uniform, blue with red piping. A service cap with a light-blue visor. Boots. She fell in love with him as soon as she saw him at the dance. Later, Kolya confessed that he joined the police force because of the uniform, they were distributing them for free and he had nothing to wear.

The service cap also had a star with a soldier holding a tilted rifle at its center. Nina liked him too.

At the time, Nina had just arrived in Moscow and the city simply terrified her. She made her way down the sides of the streets while the locals spat on the ground and swaggered past her. You could spot them right away: eight-angle peaked cap, box-calf boots, white muffler tied around their throat.

Later, Kolya said: "Those are the tough guys." Meaning, the criminals.

"So how come they walk around the streets just like that, without anyone arresting them?" Nina asked.

"Well, a person can't be arrested for wearing an eight-peaked cap," Kolya laughed. "But don't worry, they won't be walking around much longer. It's just too bad that capital punishment was abolished. That's alright, we'll deal with them ourselves, if we have to," he said and winked at her.

Capital punishment meant execution. By firing squad. It was abolished a year ago. Kolya says it was because there was no one to chop wood in Siberia.

Nina thinks: what kind of world will the child will be born into? Good thing the war's over. But still: must we live our whole lives in the city? No woods, no real river. Of course, we can go to the Central Park of Culture and Leisure—you can dive off the pier there, swim. Only Nina feels a bit awkward. After all, she swims like a villager, and in Moscow, people no doubt swim in a special style.

Nina sits at home and waits for her husband. She sits there, waits, and worries, anxious and afraid. She can't read properly, they don't have a gramophone, not even a wireless radio post—it's an old building. I don't know if they had televisions back then, but Nina and Kolya surely didn't.

I also sit at home, also wait for Nikita, also worry about him, although why should I worry? Nikita has a peaceful sort of business and drives carefully. But I still worry.

I'd like to say I don't know how worried I'd be in Nina's place, but I can't: I am she and she is me, meaning that I once sat like this waiting for my husband to come home from work, bored and looking out the window, stroking my pregnant belly, afraid to go out on the street.

How strange it is to feel others' lives inside me! Fragments of others' thoughts and extraneous pieces of information suddenly surface in my memory. Which berries are edible. The best places to collect mushrooms. How to climb a tree and settle in to sleep so that you don't fall out at night.

And sometimes, a ditty will get stuck in my head and play hour after hour. I can even make out the words:

> My father the von-Baron is fucking his beauty
> and I, like a son of a bitch, fuck my own aunt
> Every day, everywhere,
> From midnight till morning,
> From evening till evening
> And again till dawn.

> My father the von-Baron fucks only the rich ones
> and I, like a son of a bitch, fuck
> the lopsided, cross-eyed, and hunchbacked ones
> Every day, everywhere,
> From midnight till morning,
> From evening till evening
> And again till dawn.

I know the boys were singing this song when Nina crossed the courtyard and heard it. Now, it sounds in my head. *Every day, everywhere, from midnight till morning*—I don't know if it made Nina laugh, frightened her, or upset her. It gives me the blues. *Every day, everywhere*—meaning, in this life and in the previous ones, around the clock, night and day, I sit in the armchair, on the chair, on the stool—and wait for my beloved to come home. Afraid that something will happen to him.

When I—Nina—pat my big pregnant belly. When I—Masha—paint my toenails over and over, although I'm not going anywhere. I find it soothing.

Kolya comes home and tells me how they took down Kazentsov's whole gang in a shootout on the train. They were all packed into the children's car and the conductor spotted them and called the right place. Turned out the gang was in the middle of a carjacking. They'd ask a driver to take them outside city limits, then, kill him. Now, they were the ones getting killed—well, at least, two of them were.

Kolya says there are too many weapons in Moscow. Trophy weapons brought back from the war, snatched from police officers, stolen from the Hammer and Sickle plant, where old weapons are returned for smelting.

Kolya explained that a police officer's gun was attached to a special red cord so that it couldn't get snatched. The cord went up one side of his uniform, wound around his neck and went down the other, and was attached to a special loop on the pistol handle. Kolya explained it and even showed it to me, but I still don't get it: I'd prefer it if they just had their pistols stolen. As things stand, if a tough guy wants to take Kolya's pistol, he'll have to kill him.

I'm very scared for Kolya. Ever since I got pregnant, I've gotten even more scared.

At first, I was so happy! I pictured a little baby growing inside me, went to a doctor once a month—the doctor told me when the eyes would develop, when the hands would. It's just too bad that it will be born in Moscow and not in a village. How can you call this a life? Why did I come here? I must have known that I would meet Kolya here. There's not much else that's good about Moscow.

Good thing I wasn't accepted to vocational school. Then I'd have to study, and before you know it, the baby will come along and Kolya will change his mind. And the three of us will go away from here, wherever the road takes us.

I've lived here for about a year now and I still don't understand why people come here. As I was waiting to see the doctor, I met a woman who is near-term like me but older, goes by the name of Marfa, also from a village, but has been living in Moscow for a while, since before the war.

She was kind and consoled me, told me it's not scary to give birth. She said it was scary to live and even scarier to die. Then I said to her: I know, my entire village died. And she stroked my head, said, poor girl! and, for a minute, I felt that my mom was with me. Even though, of course, it is a sin to say so, I will never have another mom. I'm a mom myself now. I've got only two months to go.

In the waiting room, the women told each other frightful things: that, supposedly, you could pay to get rid of the baby. If you didn't want to have one. In Beryozovka, too, they said that girls drank various herbal infusions to the same end. I was small, but I knew what they were saying. Well, I knew what an herbal infusion was. And here, they were telling us how to find a clandestine doctor who, for fifteen hundred rubles would, you know . . . do all that.

Fifteen hundred rubles! What kind of money is that! It's scary to think what kind of a person would have it! Every month, I try to figure out how the two of us can live on five hundred fifty. We barely get by. And now that we're having a baby, we'll have to feed it, too.

I hope my bunny will be born soon. If it's a boy, let him look like Kolya. And if it's girl, let her take after my mom. Let her have these eyebrows and these ears, too.

Let her take after my mom. After all, I don't even have a photo of her, nothing. It all burned up.

Mom would be happy for me right now. She must have been happy for me as she was dying. She knew I escaped.

Kolya laughs at me, but I still know that there's a God out there somewhere. And my mom is beside him on a cloud, looking down at me, seeing that I'll be giving birth to my bunny, my boy, my girl, to take her place, the place of Dad, the place of Aunt Katya and Uncle Slava, the place of lame Mitrich and old Anfisa. The place of our entire village.

Hurry up and be born soon, little bunny. I mean, come out at term, but make it so that I don't have to wait very long. I'm a bit scared to give birth. Here, we have to go to the hospital, and we don't know anyone working there. What if they make a mistake? It's terrifying.

The other day I was walking down the street and I saw a girl playing hopscotch. With a blue skirt and a ribbon in her braid. I looked at her and I thought: if I have a girl, she'll be hopping just like this in ten years or so. And I felt so happy, I can't describe it.

There she is, sitting day after day, the young woman Nina from forty-eight, getting heavier and heavier, heavy like my heart. Because every day, everywhere, from midnight till morning, it's the same story and I know what will happen next.

Two weeks before she's due, Nina will put her jacket potatoes on the stove and suddenly remember that she's out of salt.

She'll go over to see Aunt Vera, her neighbor.

She will knock, but no one will answer, she will push open the door, yell: Aunt Vera!, go in, and they'll hit her with a clothes iron, aiming for her head, but she'll leap aside in time, then, hear someone whisper: Finish this bitch off!, she'll shield her unborn baby with her hands and start screaming, but not loud enough. Only when the second attacker hits her in the belly, she will start screaming so loud that everyone in the building, the courtyard, and even the street will hear it—and he'll race over the neighboring roofs, Sokolniki Park, the quays of the Moskva River, the attractions of the Central Park of Culture and Leisure, the cobblestones of the Red Square, the step-pyramid of Lenin's Mausoleum, the Kremlin stars, the empty foundation pit on the site of the detonated Church, the wooden houses of postwar Moscow, the criminal hideouts and dens, the police precincts, the prisons and forced-labor camps, the Metro station ticketing areas, the movie theaters and cultural centers, the whole of postwar Russia, the wretched Victorious City, the youths without fathers, the women without husbands, the men without arms, legs, a conscience, fear, families, memory and love.

While Nina falls down on the bloodstained floor, screaming and screaming . . .

One more blow and she would have been silenced forever. The burglars killed Aunt Vera and could have killed Nina, too. They could have cracked her skull, slit her throat, or bludgeoned her with any object in reach, but they ran away.

They would be caught in two days. It is possible that one of them would be shot dead at the time of arrest.

And Kolya ran down the street clutching the tiny body, the umbilical cord dangling from it like another piece of red piping and his whole beautiful uniform covered in blood. Kolya ran and cursed and cried and didn't make it in time.

It was a boy.

Two years later, they left Moscow. They were given a house by the State Farm built on the site of the incinerated Beryozovka: a good man always came in handy in a village. So they lived there the rest of their lives. Kolya was trained to drive a tractor and Nina worked as a milkmaid, a chicken farmer, a cashier at the general store . . . what didn't she do? At one point, she even worked as a caregiver at a daycare. But not for long.

They never had children of their own. Kolya died in 1985 and Nina a year later.

Sometimes, I see her as an old woman. With her hands folded on her knees, she sits on a stool by the window, while outside, high-school girls giggle with boys on a bench. Music drifts out of an open-top car.

Nina has no one to wait for, nothing to fear. Her life is over.

Only in her head, she hears, like a broken record: *every day, everywhere, from midnight till morning, from evening to evening and again till dawn,* like a delusion, an incantation, a promise that everything will repeat itself, that everything is yet to come.

11.

WET SNOW

As she comes out of the train car, a slight, drunk man tries to grab her by the sleeve: *Hey, squinty eyes, where are you going?* Anya dodges him out of habit and tosses a "leave me alone, moron!" over her shoulder, hopping to the platform.

Then, more of the usual: escalator, station hall, wet snow flying in her face.

That same snow is currently flying at my snout, that same snow is making squishy noises under my feet, that same snow, snow that feels so sweet to fall into when you no longer have strength left, when you think to yourself: I'm never getting home, I'm going to die here, in the street.

How well I know that snow!

How well Anya knows it! How well she knows the Metro's passageways.

Two winters at an outdoor clothing market, six months behind a stand in an underground passage!

You don't forget that kind of thing.

It's only now, after three years at IKEA, that she's qualified personnel. A saleswoman slash consultant. Official paperwork, health insurance, and all the rest.

Snow and rain—just her regular daily commute.

Stability. Just like Putin promised five years ago.

Turns out I've built a career, Anya smiles.

But above all, let's hope it doesn't all come crashing down again like in ninety-eight. Let's hope it bypasses us.

A good job, an inexpensive apartment, only three hundred a month. Five minutes away from the Metro, trees in the courtyard, she can take

Gosha out for a walk. The daycare is nearby. Although the neighbors in the next apartment over are alcoholics and the woman downstairs is a nutcase. If anything, she calls the police. Supposedly, someone is always raising hell at Anya's.

One word: nuts.

But none of that matters.

And Anya smiles under the wet snow, tramples the melted sludge, ten more minutes and she'll pick up Gosha from the daycare and go home. There, they'll watch cartoons and read a book. Pure bliss.

Anya has changed apartments five times in four years. In the first, the landlady unexpectedly passed away, the heirs couldn't come to an agreement, went to court, and she was forced to leave. The owner of the second kept hitting on her, but didn't even promise to lower the rent. In the third, after a peaceful six months, her rent was suddenly doubled.

In the fourth, Anya dreamed of rain one night and this woke her up.

It was winter and −8 degrees Fahrenheit outside, but as she lay in the dark, Anya could still hear the drumming of a spring shower. The Great Flood, the windows of heaven. She got up, looked out the window (where snow was silently falling), fixed Gosha's blanket (his small bare foot was sticking out with his toes tucked under, his heel looking pink in near darkness) and went to the bathroom. Flicked the switch on, opened the door—and gasped.

Everything was drowning in a milky fog, the curling whiteness burst out into the corridor, and she barely distinguished the stream of scalding water coming from the ceiling. She stood there until a serpentine trickle of hot water inched over the threshold and up to her feet, barely giving her time to leap aside.

She grabbed Gosha, ran over to the neighbors', called the emergency workers, and then the landlord. Turned out that a pipe burst upstairs—good thing there was no one in the bathroom when it happened.

Since then, once in a while, she'll dream she is standing in a room and water is streaming down from the ceiling—only, for some reason, it's not hot, but cold, like the endless autumn rains of those clothing markets from her past.

Anya's cell phone rings. It's incredibly awkward to be walking and talking at the same time, especially with all this wet yuckiness falling out of the sky. She looks at the Caller ID: Andrey.

She curses and takes the call:

"Hello, dear."

"Hello."

"Listen, I was thinking: what should we see Friday night? I'm looking at the events guide, it says . . ."

Anya grinds her teeth and grips her handbag more firmly. Wet snow flies in her face while Andrey's voice is already paraphrasing a second review.

They met in the summer, right at the shoe store, the same way she met Vika—where else could she meet people? For years, she struck up most of her friendships at her workplaces. With her shift switchers and shift partners, the salesgirls from the neighboring tents, the vendors from the rows of vegetable stands. The ones she celebrated birthdays with, who still recognized her and chose the reddest tomatoes and sweetest cherries for her.

Her own girls never cheated her, they could be counted on. The men—of course not, as her mom always said.

Oh yes, the men. Truck drivers, chauffeurs, security guards. At one time, criminals, our mafia protection. And, of course, the bosses and their lackeys, who came to collect their share in beat-up and, less frequently, new foreign cars.

They were all simple guys, no quirks. Sometimes they wanted the warmth of a human body, taut flesh under their agitated hand, a few kisses and an exuberant finale—and Anya, too, didn't need anything from them except a firm embrace, strong arms, measured movements, and a desperate swim to a convulsive, synchronous orgasm.

Last week, Zinka asked if Anya knew how to fake the aforesaid orgasm. She just shrugged her shoulders: she never needed to, it always happened on its own. And if it didn't, she wouldn't fake it—like she cared!

What's more, her men didn't seem too worried about it—well, the ones Anya had in the past, before Andrey.

After all, they were simple guys and didn't read men's magazines, it wouldn't enter their minds to study the events guide before going to the movies, let alone repeat what they read to their girlfriend as she walked under wet snow, pressing a cheap cellphone to her ear.

"Anyway, it says it's good, a touching melodrama. A chick flick. Want to see it?"

Anya likes neither chick flicks nor chick lit. And if she reads anything, it's Bushkov and Koretsky: tough, manly reading, shootouts, brutal sex, decisive men. Simple guys, no quirks.

In the mornings, when she does her exercises, Anya imagines that she's a superhero, Mr. Shot-at, Prodded, Sliced-and-Diced. Twenty-five minutes, like clockwork. Twenty-five minutes stolen from the sweetest morning slumber, from her sleepy son, who's been taught to dress himself and to exercise with his mom.

"Sounds good," she says.

Andrey's probably sitting in traffic. The interior of his car is warm and the wet snow swirls outside his window. He's got one hand on the steering wheel and the other on his cell phone.

Whereas Anya's purse keeps slipping off her shoulder while wet snow flies in her face—so uncomfortable.

"Kisses, dear," Andrey says.

"Right back at ya," Anya answers with relief, hiding the cellphone in her pocket and wiping her face with her palm. She remembers how, whenever Andrey kisses her, he slobbers all over her. She's called him out on it a few times and he seems to have stopped, but sometimes he forgets and does it again.

A while back, in the summer, he came in to buy shoes. Anya smiled her IKEA smile and he immediately smiled back, read the name on her badge, and called her Anechka. He chose good shoes, the Clarks, then asked what Anya was doing after work. Anya smiled a different kind of smile, said she was busy, and tomorrow as well, but on Friday, yes, she was free, starting from 8 P.M., when the shopping center closed.

"I'll come then," Andrey said, and Anya thought, the fuck he will, all he'll do is tell his friends he picked up a shopgirl.

But, holy shit, he came.

Anya recalls their first date and smiles. They went to the movies and she was sure Andrey would try to kiss her right away, but he sat still for an hour-and-a-half and only took her hand sometime toward the middle. She nestled her hand more comfortably in his and was bored stiff until the film ended. Later on, when they went to her house, everything was charming, too, even poignant.

Well yeah, Andrey is actually kind of charming. Only a bit oafish and awkward.

Two weeks ago, as she was leafing through her mom's old photo album from school, Anya suddenly realized who he reminded her of.

When Anya was in third grade, her mom and grandma made Anya a Little Mermaid costume for the New Year's Day matinee: they painted gauze with Brilliant Green, turned it into a green wig and pinned paper seashells and starfish to a long, pale-blue dress. They couldn't figure out the tail, so Anya was the Little Mermaid who sprouted legs. Of course, Andersen's heroine would have had to be mute all night, but Anya declared that she was the Little Mermaid from the other fairy tale, where she was allowed to speak, which is why it ended happily.

The other girls dressed up as snowflakes or little animals and the boys as pilots, pirates, or musketeers. They dashed around the fir tree laughing and shrieking. Lonely and proud, Anya, who was still called Elya at school, stood to the side in her unusual garb, which was, of course, the most beautiful. Ten minutes later, she got sick of being proud, but didn't feel comfortable running around in her long dress; she was busily pondering her course of action when the only boy whose costume was almost as good as hers walked up to her.

He was wearing a round motorcycle helmet and a suit of cardboard armor. In his hands was a genuine metallic trident.

"Who are you?" Anya asked.

"I'm Oleg," the boy answered from under his helmet, "from 3B. And you're Elya, we were in daycare together, remember?"

"Yes, I remember," Anya said impatiently. "I mean, what's your costume?"

"I'm a scuba diver," Oleg replied.

"Wicked," Anya smiled, "and I'm the Little Mermaid. Only I don't have a tail, or else we could go swimming together."

"And I'm a scuba diver who climbed on shore," Oleg said and took off his helmet. "Can't see anything in it anyway without my glasses."

He procured his glasses from the depths of his cardboard scuba-diving armor.

"Your costume is beautiful," he said.

Anya no longer remembers what they did at the carnival—most likely they talked, participated in a round-dance, or played some game. At the end of the big day, Oleg won the prize for best costume and Anya took second place; she wasn't at all saddened by this, the more so because the first-place prize was an illustrated book she already read, while the second was a set of colored pencils.

In the evening, her mom said:

"I don't understand why they gave first place to that cosmonaut."

"He's a scuba diver," Anya said, "I know him. It's Oleg from daycare, we're friends."

"Of course, he's a scuba diver," her mom chuckled, "he's a four-eyes. Do you know that rhyme? 'If you have four eyes, you look like you scuba dive.'"

Anya laughed, but felt somewhat uneasy. However, she did remember the rhyme and even repeated it to Oleg after winter break. He got mad and looked so silly that Anya called him a scuba diver a few more times. In return, he called her a tailless mermaid, and now it was Anya's turn to get mad. By the end of January, there was nothing left of their carnival memories. For a while, they continued to say hello during the breaks between classes, but when Oleg told her in May that he was transferring to another school, Anya didn't even ask for his phone number or offer to stay in touch.

I wonder what happened to him, Anya thinks. Some four-eyes don't fare too badly—look at Mark Borisovich, he keeps asking me to coffee, keeps hinting that he'd like to get to know me better. Zinka is already saying that if I keep resisting him, I could be laid off.

I'm not resisting at all, Anya thinks, I just don't feel like having coffee with him. He should say directly: "Can you stay after work and stop by the supply closet? I've got a thirty minute job for you." Instead, it's drinking coffee, listening to music, getting to know each other better. Yuck.

In the past, things were simpler: "Hey, squinty eyes, where are you going? Hang on a bit. Grab a glass, we'll pour you some too."

Simple guys without any quirks, not like these days.

How are you supposed to build a career after that?

12.

THANK GOD OUR YOUTH IS OVER

". . . And also, we swam inside an iceberg. It had passages like grottoes. Because the ice layers are different, they elute, meaning they dissolve differently. And we swam inside those caves. You know how in *Star Wars*, Han Solo flies into an asteroid—that's exactly how it felt. He doesn't fly into it? He's swallowed by a fish? Not a fish, but a worm, like in *Dune*? So I mixed them up. Oh yeah, Jonah was swallowed by a fish, and in a totally different film. The fish? Yes, there are fish in Antarctica too. But ugly ones. Not like in the Red Sea. And they can't swallow you. But then, but then—that's right, I wanted to tell you, there are killer seals in Antarctica! No, no, not like the cannibal tigers, not because they've been wounded and want revenge. They're simply carnivorous seals. Very dangerous. They're called killer seals. I met one . . . I mean, I was swimming and he was swimming, and we met. Eye to eye. No, I didn't shit my pants. A man who has stared three times into the muzzle of a gun won't shit his pants because of a killer seal. But it was a truly intense experience. You know, they say your whole life flashes before your eyes in times like that. So I saw a whole life in literally a single moment: eternal cold, snow, ice, raw fish, some abominable female mates . . . of course, this was the seal's life, not mine. I laughed so hard afterward: can you imagine what the seal saw? He must have learned a lot of things about Russian business. In any case, he swam away very quickly. I think he was horrified."

Nikita can empathize with this seal. Kostya, Nikita's friend from university, looks about thirty, if you don't pay attention to the starkly white, as if bleached, hair on his head.

It's not true that you can go gray overnight, Kostya says. In three years—easy.

Especially if those three years are at the end of the twentieth-century in Russia and, in the twenty-first, you emerge with a house in a gated suburban community, a driver, a security guard, housekeepers, two nannies for three kids, and a four-bedroom apartment on Ostozhenka Street. Not counting a small restaurant and a modest office. That office is a total madhouse—long legged secretaries and people speaking Chinese. Nikita doesn't have the slightest clue what they all do. Don't worry, old man, Kostya says to him, the bottom line is we don't deal drugs or weapons. Thank heaven for that, of course.

Six months ago, Kostya showed up at Nikita's office drunk and demanded vodka. This was an anomaly: in the past ten years, Kostya had cultivated a taste for expensive wines and Nikita completely forgot how they used to get wasted back in the dorm. But that day Kostya had been at some *really fucking complicated talks*, the complexity of which lay in the fact that he had had to drink the whole time. By the second hour, Kostya remembered that he used to like vodka, and, in another two hours, he brought the talks to a brilliant finale and wished to continue drinking in a more informal, friendly atmosphere. And Nikita's office was so close! *My dear Mikhail Valeryanovich, you must remember . . . we drove there last month . . . Nikita's my best friend in the whole world . . . he's the one who breeds fish*, and, for two hours now, Nikita has been trying to catch up to Kostya, while Kostya has been telling him about scuba diving, appearing to get more sober with every shot.

". . . I was going through my records—I wanted to have them digitized—and I found our university photos. We were so skinny, you wouldn't believe it! Skin and bones, that summer in Silver Pinewood, remember how we picked up two girls and then didn't know where to take them? I kept trying to drag mine into the bushes and you . . . did you fuck yours or not, do you remember? You know, the one with the big ass and a mustache, must have been Armenian or Jewish. Her tits weren't bad though. Nowadays, she's probably gotten bigger, given birth to a couple of kids . . . yes, you always liked the round-assed ones, I remember. Who else? The one you carried on with when they sent us to Moskovskiy State Farm to dig potatoes, when you tried to borrow a condom from me and I didn't give it to you because it was my last. Thank God she didn't get pregnant or I would have been mortified. You would have had to marry a village girl, haha. I didn't get to use my condom. That bitch Lyuska didn't put out in the end. By the way, have you ever tried, you know, taking stock, counting them, writing them all down? Me neither, and that's a shame. These days, I can't remember them all, especially the ones from later on. When I was young, I kept track of every single one. At boring lectures, I would always recall how many and when. I found it really invigorating. Oh, remember the TA from the fourth-year lab section? That girl was on fire, right?"

The lab assistant was named Nina. Nikita never thought about her, but, suddenly, he could picture her just as she was. Red haired, freckled, stout and, by their standards, old. Meaning, she was twenty-five and they were fourth-year students, or about twenty, twenty-one. One time, Nina came to the Saturday discothèque at their dorm and showed them how it was done. She was pulling up her skirt, spinning like a top, impersonating the popular singer Madonna and pulling any guy she wanted to dance with out of the crowd like she was some kind of hurricane. She probably went back to someone's room that night, but that didn't matter because, all year afterward, the guys from their year followed her around, trying to ask her out or fondle her in the lab corner. Nikita recalled his impression of her: a cool, adult woman, but now that he was almost fifteen years older, he realized that there was nothing particularly cool about her, only loneliness, desire for happiness, and the call of the flesh.

". . . dear God, do you remember the sort of ugly women we used to plow? I think that if a crocodile from the Nile put out . . . no, even a killer seal, yes . . . we would have, ahem, accommodated them, too. After all, all women looked beautiful to us then, remember, Nikita? That one, from group six, with pimples covering half her face—she was ugly, right? And as soon as Valerka started the rumor that she was easy, everyone flocked straight to her. She couldn't even understand why she was suddenly so popular. That son of a bitch Valerka decided to prank us. But she put out for me anyway. And you, too? Wow, I didn't know we were brothers, so to speak."

That's right, memory is selective. I can't remember the pimples. Her breasts were round with brown nipples. She covered them with her hands in a funny way when she undressed. And one nipple stuck out between her fingers, like it was peeking out. For some reason, I remember her panties—beige, synthetic, very *Sovok* style . . . anyway, back in those days, we didn't know the word *Sovok*, it appeared later when the Soviet Union became *Sovok*, but, as it turned out, not for long. Her name was Zhenya and, at the time, I thought that she was *passionate in bed*; now that I think of it, I'd say she was simply diligent. Astonished by the popularity that had befallen her and completely unable to say no from said astonishment. Then she got pregnant and married quick. I remember it was the first time I went to the wedding of a girl I'd slept with—and I was thinking that, if I hadn't had a condom, it would have been me standing there in a stuffy suit, listening to various phrases about the social unit. I remember I got drunk at that wedding and hit on the groom's sister; she even called me later, but I was taking my finals and missed my chance: when I called her back, it was clear she didn't want to talk. I was upset for a while afterward that someone got to it before I did. It's true, Kostya's right, that's what it was, it seemed like every woman was a revelation. Something new, something incomparable to anything else. They were all different in bed, yes. They moaned and moved differently, smelled differently, tasted differently, well, the ones who let you lick them . . . many of them were still shy—these days, it seems like things are a lot more straightforward. And to think this was all happening for the first time: just sex, and for her to kiss me there, and to let me kiss her there; how badly I wanted a blowjob back then—I can't believe it, I don't even like them that much now.

". . . too bad, too bad that you don't fly out to scuba dive with us. First of all, it's a good crowd, they may be useful to you, and they're great guys in general, no airs, democratic, treat me as an equal. No, no, they'll treat you as an equal too, to them, you and I are—one and the same. Less than ten million means we're poor. Alright, I'm joking, there are all kinds of people in the group, I'm just busting your balls. So, I was saying, the crowd. And the places are cool. Madagascar, Chile, Antarctica—when else could you go to Antarctica? What do you mean, you don't like scuba diving? You said you went diving once. Oh, you went in Turkey, nothing to see there, the scuba diving is shit, you could have at least flown to Egypt."

It was Masha who convinced me to dive. We had been together six years by then and took a beach vacation every summer. She would swim beyond the horizon, and I would try not to stray too far from shore. A few meters and back. As soon as I sensed the depth beneath me, I began to panic. I don't know what scared me so much. I remember, one evening, we were sitting in some lousy Turkish restaurant on a dusty street beyond the hotel gates. We were picking a lobster apart—*where else would we find a cheap lobster?*—and Masha said: you need to dive and it will all pass. You'll just realize that it's not scary underwater and start swimming. You have to face your fear in order to conquer it. I don't know where she got that from. I don't know why I agreed. Maybe it was because I was ashamed: my wife was cleaving the waters and I was scared to leave the shore. The next day I dove. That is to say, the instructor grabbed me by the shoulders and literally pulled me into the water because I was kicking and screaming until the end. I can't say I liked it. I have no recollection of what happened underwater. But a day later, I jumped from the yacht into the translucent azure waters of the Mediterranean and started to swim. Masha was standing aboard the yacht and waving to me, and I felt that my fear was gone. Before our flight back, I threw a coin in the sea and said to myself: *so I may return to the place where my fear left me.* Yep, that was my last childhood fear. I don't think I've been afraid of anything since.

"... you know, I think I'm sobering up. Let's go for a walk, get more vodka or pick up girls. Fuck, you won't believe how long it's been since I picked up girls on the street. I used to think: I'll have a cool car, drive up suavely to them and say: "Girl, let me give you a ride!" and as soon as I got a cool car I said, why the fuck do I need to pick them up on the street, I have so many willing candidates, I can chew them up and spit them out with my ass. Not literally, though, I'm not some sort of homo."

We went out onto the street. It was still light out and the asphalt sparkled after the rain; the driver was napping in Kostya's Audi A8 and the leaves of the solitary tree by the building entrance rustled in the wind. Maybe it was the vodka or maybe it was the memories, but I grew sad. Nina, Zhenya, Kostya's Lyuska, the young woman from Moskovskiy State Farm, the young women who led me on or gave me some, whatever happened to them? We're all pushing forty, they probably have children, husbands, maybe they, too, occasionally wet their whistles with a girlfriend and reminisce: remember how those two guys hit on us in Silver Pinewood? One was tall and gawky and kept grabbing at your chest, while mine kept trying to put his arm around me and rambled about something lyrical, what an idiot. Why didn't I fuck him? I'd have something to remember now—and they have a little to drink and giggle, momentarily turning into those silly girls you could pick up at the beach, with whom everything was joyful, carefree, funny, silly, and meaningless—and, that, nevertheless, felt new every time, it gave me butterflies every time. She can't remember why she didn't want to sleep with me back then? And who'll remember why I used to think that was so important?

At the store, Kostya thoroughly picked the saleslady's brain about their best vodka. Even in this wine section, which reeked of beer and vomit, Kostya behaved as if he were ordering à la carte someplace like Nostalgie. The saleslady looked like she was about to melt: after handing him a

bottle of Stolichnaya, she said, "Actually, boys, I get off in a half hour."
Kostya grinned from ear to ear and said: "Gotcha. We have a half hour
to determine if one bottle will be enough for the two of us."

". . . what did you think? I think she's just your type. Did you see the
size of her ass? I asked her to grab a bottle from the upper shelf on purpose, wanted to make your day. No, she's definitely not my type. I like
them younger and thinner, you know—I introduced you to Natasha and
Katya too. Which Katya? The one I rented an apartment for by my office
so I could fuck her on my lunch break. By the way, did I tell you? Two
months ago, she fucked off to Paris to film a commercial. Yes, I'm free
now, I don't have anyone except Ksenia. No worries, that's even better,
it's summer now, there's students running around the streets, we'll pick
up someone. More importantly, have you noticed? The issue of where to
fuck has been completely taken off the agenda. We put them in the car,
drive to the city center, find a hotel for two hundred bucks a night max,
and we're on! By the way, you have condoms, right? Let's go buy some
at the kiosk, it'll be awkward to get them in front of the chicks later."

Suddenly, we felt so giddy, it was as if the past eighteen years never
happened. Young, drunk, vodka in hand, now we'll just find some condoms and it's on! If I don't catch up, I'll warm up—as the rooster chasing
the hen thinks in that old joke. I'll have something to remember tomorrow. And in the next eighteen years too. Dear God, what will become of
me in eighteen years, I thought drunkenly and even tried to get some point
across to Kostya. Eighteen! Eighteen years ago, I was exactly eighteen, or
close to that. Which means that I have to divine what will happen to me
in the thirty-six years from then. I'll be seventy-two—it's mind-boggling.
But it's possible: both my grandfathers lived till eighty and, God willing,
I will too. "Eighteen years," I yelled out, "eighteen years!"

Eighteen years ago, all women were young, all women were desirable—and they didn't put out for me, no, they didn't put out. Eighteen
years ago, I thought I had it bad. Everything's terrible, I thought at my
eighteen years. And everything was excellent, everything was excellent,
Kostya, do you remember how excellent it was, we were eighteen and,
ahead of us, there was another eighteen, and, in the course of those years,
a lot, lot more happened than we could have even predicted! And there
were so many girls, we've already lost score, if we've ever kept it. We can't
remember everyone we slept with and kissed. We mix up names and faces,
blondes and brunettes, is this the onset of Alzheimer's, or not yet? We
haven't forgotten what's most important—that everything was excellent,

that we were only eighteen. Everything was happening for the first time, every position, except, maybe, missionary, was tried out for the first time. And missionary, too, was tried out for the first time at some point, of course, you're right, Kostya! You know, I remember them now, I remember all of them, give me the bottle, I'll take a swig and bring it all back, how fun it was and how sad, the kinds of fingers, bras, and panties they had, the goosebumps on their skin, the scent of Soviet perfume, do you remember? They were all so sweet, right? Not a single one was redundant, and as for the ones who put out for us, let's find them and say thank you to them. As for the ones who didn't, well, they can go to hell, who needs such boring girls? What would we do with them if they put out for us, the ones who didn't, right?

I roared with laughter and grabbed Kostya's sleeve, and he dragged me after him as if he had a set itinerary he couldn't stray from. And boom!—we're sitting at the table of a sidewalk café with the bottle stashed under it and two young women across from us. *No way, are you really eighteen? That's great, we've been talking about this all day!*

To be honest, I have zero recollection of what Kostya prattled about. To be completely honest, I don't remember what these girls looked like. The ones from when I was eighteen—as soon as I remembered them—I still can't forget. And these two—I think one was a bottle blonde and I'm blanking on the rest. Every so often, they laughed, Kostya laughed too, and I played the wing man, like in the old days.

I think that, in the end, they agreed to go with us. "Somewhere in the city center," Kostya promised. "I'm going to call a car." They started giggling, I remember one of them said: "Is it a good car? If not, I'm not going!" and they both laughed; Kostya took out his cell phone, said: "Mikhail Valeryanovich, can you find us, we're at a café not too far away," and the girls began to snicker again, I remember that laugh very well. We poured the vodka into our coffee cups under the table, clinked them, drank in honor of "eighteen, because it's a marvelous age for love," and they burst out laughing again; I remember that laugh and how it stopped short when Kostya's driver drove up, practically to our table, and affectedly flung open the door: "Konstantin Vladimirovich, where are we off to?"

The girls instantly stopped laughing, moved away from us, and huddled together. And I was struck by the moment of silence that followed their laughter. I immediately sobered up. We looked at each other across the table, and I realized that, to them, we were those same killer seals and they could see our whole lives in our eyes. Merry drinking binges and hangovers, infidelities and love, the first money we made, our first gray hairs, our first instances of morning erectile dysfunction, my endless jobs, Kostya's endless talks, all the vodka we drank, all our late friends, all our murdered friends, our wives, Kostya's kids, his model mistresses, his criminal business partners, his scuba-diving friends, *ten million and up*, Madagascar, Chile, Antarctica, the killer seal—eighteen times two times two, seventy-two years between the both of us.

I looked at Kostya too. A broad, gray-haired, serious man who was beginning to put on weight. He was smiling, but his smile was no longer deceptive: he was far from eighteen and had lived long enough to lose his lightheartedness and youthful zeal, no matter how much he tried to convince himself and the rest of us of the opposite. *So, are we going?* he asked—menacingly, I thought.

"We probably have to get going," the blonde one said, and the second girl nodded frantically, and, oh yes! I just remembered! Her eyes grew round with either astonishment or fear.

"Where to?" Kostya said. "Come with us. What are you, scared? We're not scary at all."

He reached out his hand and the girls started moving toward the car as if they were hypnotized, but at that moment, I said: "Forget it, let them go if they're not interested. To be honest, what the hell do we need them for?" And Kostya burst out laughing again: "Yes, really, what the hell for?" The girls also smiled and slinked back, looking at me obsequiously, while Kostya picked the bottle off the ground, put it on the table—"That's the tip!"—and plopped down next to the driver.

"You see, Kostya," I said, grabbing the back of the front seat, "it's a good thing our youth is over. It was great, but also foolish and miserable. We wanted such silly things—and those things were exactly what we didn't have. All young women were desirable. And it seemed that any one of them was worth the effort. Any one of them could have been mine if I found the right approach. Remember we used to think that? And now we really can—drink some vodka, pull up in a car, say 'get in!' and that's it. But we don't need this anymore, it's not interesting to either one of us. I love my Masha and you love your Ksenia, we've already found what we were looking for. Thank God our youth is over. Remember? It was such an anxious time."

I said: "I can't imagine what I'd do with the young ones. They don't understand anything. I think it would even be boring to fuck them, now that we know that sex without love is boring. We've had our share of fucking around and we've stopped, and that's sad, I know, but really, I don't need anything from them. After all, why did we let them go? Not because they were scared, we just realized we'd sober up and have to deal with them later, answer questions, show off, or the opposite—say nothing, listen to their confessions, take slips of paper with phone numbers, lie that we'd call them and lie that we had a nice time with them. Eighteen years ago, we believed that was all worth the trouble. To touch one more breast, kiss one more pair of lips, spread legs, hear moans, shudder together or separately—opportunities you couldn't miss. It was always just a little bit of love, but still love. And we were right, you couldn't miss out on love. Today, we don't need anything from them, we can no longer love them for their breasts, their legs, their kisses. We've done our share of loving, there's hardly enough love left in us. I hope to God there'll be enough for our wives, let alone girls from a café."

I was saying this or something along those lines, and felt as if I were saying goodbye to my youth forever. I shook Kostya by the shoulder and repeated: *We don't need anything from anyone, we have everything*, and then I realized Kostya was out cold, sniffling lightly in his sleep. I remembered how he used to fall asleep like this in the kitchen during our rowdy student parties.

Outside, it began to rain. I leaned back against the leather seat and this time, said to myself: *Thank God our youth is over. I can relax and not think about sex, not abandon myself to erotic fantasies, not imagine nipples, breasts, and hips, not count the days until my next encounter. I can live in peace.*

I really believed this, honest to God.

And six months later, I met Dasha.

13.

BUSINESS IS A GUNSHOT

The story of Anya's family is simple: Grandma Djamilya was born in 1924, to Great-grandfather Moussa and Great-grandmother Gulnara. In 1954, Djamilya gave birth to Anya's mom, whom she gave the Russian name Tatyana and the patronymic Olegovna. That's all that remains of Anya's second granddad—that and a family legend Grandma Djamilya used to tell and that I'll tell you, too, when the time comes.

Djamilya gave birth to her second daughter eight years later. She named her Gulnara in honor of her mother, and wanted to draw a line through the space for a patronymic, but then wrote in "Yuryevna." When they asked, she joked it was in honor of Yury Gagarin. And Gulya really was born around nine months after the first flight into space.

In 1971, Anya's mother married Sasha Melnikov; they divorced in 1975. Anya Elvira was born in 1972, ten years before her cousin Rimma.

No one knows who Rimma's father was. Which kept with the family tradition, so to speak.

Rimma lives on her own and almost never comes to family functions. I haven't seen her once, it's hard for me to imagine how she lives. Moreover, she works at an office, and I've never set foot in one.

I believe Nikita can handle this challenge better than me. He must have such Rimmas working in his office. Let him be the one who imagines Rimma, his half-sister's cousin . . .

Rimma wakes up easily. She doesn't like to be late. She thinks Sazonov is just waiting for her to slip up so he can rub it in her nose and put her in her place.

She won't give him the satisfaction.

High heels, knee-length skirt, beige jacket, bleach-blonde hair. Stiff upper lip. Tiny gold earrings in her ears.

She walks across the office, unlocks the door with her own key, and sits behind her desk in the reception area. She is Vladimir Sazonov's personal assistant.

Job description:

- Ensure the completion of the supervisor's assignments,
- Ensure document distribution, prepare meeting minutes,
- Provide documents and informational support to the supervisor,
- Schedule meetings and presentations,
- Plan business trips (order tickets, book hotels, prepare documents needed to obtain a visa).

Sex with superiors not included.

When she found the job, she called her mom for the first time in two months. Her mom said: *He's going to try to get you into bed.* Rimma answered: *Just let him try. I have everything under control.*

Sazonov didn't try.

A stocky, forty-five-year-old man. Expensive, eternally wrinkled suits, good shoes, a BMW with a driver. He brought to mind a bureaucrat from the old films and a former athlete forced to find another occupation.

Rimma even liked him.

He walked past her to his office, nodding to her and half-smiling, perused documents, received clients, and took orders—behaved like a boss—but still visibly trembled when they called him from *upstairs*.

What can you do—it was a big corporation. Exactly what Rimma was looking for.

Medical insurance, employee benefits, taxed salary, occupational record.

And, more importantly, the awareness of the power coming from the massive building in the heart of Moscow.

The awareness of her affiliation with that power.

High heels, knee-length skirt, beige jacket, bleach-blonde hair.

In the morning, Rimma looked at herself in the mirror for a long time. She imagined herself a kind of fair-haired beast, a covert sadist, like Ilsa, She Wolf of the SS in the film. She got into character.

No relaxing all day. No breaking character. No losing control.

Control was everything.

Her grandmother was a sniper. Business is a gunshot, a casual acquaintance once said to her in The Real McCoy bar.

In the evening, Rimma returns to her rented apartment, hangs up her skirt and blazer in the closet, pulls on a T-shirt and jeans, turns on the DVD player, and sits down on the couch.

She can relax, she can allow herself to feel like a little girl. Or at least try to.

Little girls watch cartoons. Rimma puts on a DVD with a new anime film, munches on trail mix as she drinks her fruit-and-nut tea, and watches little Japanese schoolgirls in short skirts and knee-high socks—who look just like her—shoot with both hands, soar under clouds, crawl down walls like flies, and plunge underwater, into the kingdoms of water creatures with saucers on their heads, into the multi-armed embraces of underwater monsters with octopus tentacles and catfish feelers.

And the creatures all look at Rimma with Sazonov's eyes, with that familiar, lascivious gaze, the same one I have when I note Dasha's every movement: the undressing gaze of a forty-year-old man lusting after young flesh.

14.

1984. THE BOY WITHOUT A FOIL

"Uncle Sasha, it's too bad there are no more duels, right? There can be some jerk out there, and you can't do anything about it."

"Sometimes the jerks won the duels," objected Uncle Sasha.

"I don't believe it."

"What about Dantès?"

Little Sasha clammed up, ashamed.

"Actually, you're right, Sasha," Uncle Sasha said, "it's too bad there are no more duels."

Uncle Sasha has a thick mustache like Mikhail Boyarsky in the made-for-TV movie about the musketeers. He laughs with gusto as the teapot boils on the stove. Little Sasha likes going to his uncle's. He likes that they have the same name. He likes his uncle's place, where there are hardly any books, but exquisite stones, dried starfish, and a large map of the Soviet Union with bright stars drawn everyplace that Uncle Sasha has traveled.

Little Sasha lived with his mom in a one-room apartment in a newly built high-rise in southwest Moscow. A forest extended beyond his windows, and beyond it, a ravine. When he strolled with his grandmother in the fall, Sasha liked to imagine that the ravine was a plain, and up there, in the hills, hid the pale-faced hunters, while he was Ulzana, the courageous Apache chief from the East German film he watched last summer while staying at a dacha in Kratovo, running to see all three screenings. They showed plenty of cool films, not only about Indians, but also about the musketeers, the Count of Monte Cristo, vengeance and law, a motor-cycle-riding vigilante, the mysteries of Paris, and the white sun of the desert. Even now, Sasha remembered the salty taste of the tears he cried when Vereshchagin's widow ran down the surf to the sounds of the song he used to sing—the taste of those tears and the taste of the ten-kopeck ticket that turned into papier-mâché in his mouth toward the end of the screening. Sasha imagined it was bubblegum, which so many of his classmates talked about and he'd never tried.

Uncle Sasha lived on the other end of town, on Kolomenskaya Street, but, a few times a month, on weekends, Mom gave Sasha permission to go see him, and he took a long ride on the Metro: first, to Marx Boulevard, then, transfer to Sverdlov Square—and not through the concourse, as the sign indicated, but by going up the escalator next to the third train car—then, it was right there. You couldn't miss Kolomenskaya because the train would emerge from the underground, riding over the Moskva River almost the same way it did before Leninsky Mountains.

The Palace of the Young Pioneers is at Leninsky Mountains. They say there's a fencing club where they learn to fight with foils like d'Artagnan. Maybe there's a fencing teacher like in the movie *Legacy of the Republic*: brave, valiant, honest. When I'm older, Sasha thinks, I'll definitely sign up for it.

At Uncle Sasha's place, he feels nice and calm and happy. Uncle Sasha has an interesting life—instead of going to work every day, he takes off on faraway expeditions a few times a year.

"Uncle Sasha, tell me something else about your travels."

"My travels? Did I tell you about the Far East? About the geysers?"

"Is that where you can boil an egg in the water? Yep, you told me."

"What about the time we almost froze to death in a blizzard?"

"Yeah. Then they found you half-dead but quite pleased with your-selves the next morning."

"Exactly." Uncle Sasha was silent for a bit. "Then I've practically told you everything already."

"And will I go there when I grow up?"

"Of course you'll go." And Uncle Sasha's voice is filled with such assur-ance that little Sasha thinks there is nothing easier for an adult than to zip off to the Far East, to the Valley of the Geysers.

Many years ago, in another apartment, in another city with the same name, in a country which was still to be the Russian Empire for a few more years, another man said those same words to his son. *Of course you'll go.* The map lay before them on the table.

India. Kashmir. The Himalayas.
Tibet. Shambala. Atlantis.
Remember, Misha, you will go to India.
Boys remember such promises for life.

"Let me tell you about the dark lake instead," Uncle Sasha says.

"The lake?"

"Yes. My mother told me about it, your grandmother. About a dark lake in a deep forest. A river flows into it and a lone water mill stands on its bank. Day and night, the mill wheel creaks, while in the dark water, the snags rot, the fish swim, and there lives a water creature."

"A water creature?" Sasha looks at him disappointedly from under his eyebrows. "So it's a fairy tale? I'm not a little boy anymore, I don't believe in fairy tales."

"What fairy tale? I'm telling you: it's a real water creature. You believe in the musketeers, but you don't believe in the water creature?"

"Uncle Sasha," the boy was offended, "the water creature is for little kids. Like in the cartoon where he sings, *I'm a water creature, I'm a water creature, no one wants to be my friend.*"

"It's a different water creature," Uncle Sasha said seriously, "you can't not be friends with him. He'll flood the dam and knock down the mill. You know the saying: 'The mill is powered by the water and will perish by the water'? You have to give gifts to this sort of water creature, you have to appease it. Pay it off. Remember, I sang you a song when you were little?"

"No," the boy shook his head.

Uncle Sasha bent down to his ear and began to sing softly:

The water creature'll come and carry off the rooster,
The second time he comes, he'll take away the cat,
The third time that he comes, he'll take the little brat!

As he sang the last words, he firmly grabbed Sasha. The little boy laughed and fought him off.

"When you were younger, you were a bit scared of this song, your mom would scold me."

"I don't think this song is scary at all."

"It's just that you grew up," Uncle Sasha laughed. "The water creature is frightful. You have to keep your ear to the ground with him. Which explains why our miller is a bit of a sorcerer."

"Uncle Sasha! There's no such thing as a sorcerer!"

"Like you'd know!" Uncle Sasha lit up a Belomor cigarette. "I haven't seen water creatures, but I've met sorcerers. In Siberia. They're known as shamans."

"Wow! Like in *The Sannikov Land*? Like the Indians have?"

And little Sasha remembered a shaman dancing in a scary mask, bubbles rising up to the middle of a lake and a raft with a dead deer spinning to beautiful music before it vanished underwater. This meant that the water spirits accepted the offering. Sasha watched *The Sannikov Land* seven times and always froze at this part in sweet horror.

Uncle Sasha said he'd been to the Valley of the Geysers, where they filmed *The Sannikov Land*. Maybe that's where he met the shaman?

When I grow up, little Sasha thinks, I will also travel. I will swim across the seas, swim all the way to America, and see real Indians. Then, I'll help them, and we'll throw out all the white Americans. And I'll be like the White Chief in Thomas Mayne Reid's book. And I'll also meet real shamans. They wear animal masks and horns on their heads and they dance to music around hot lakes. And I'll stay and live with them, I won't live in Moscow, I'll just take Mom, Grandma, and Uncle Sasha along.

"I haven't seen the dark lake," Uncle Sasha smiled, "but my mom did. As a little girl. The village sorcerer lived there. They said he was her father."

"So they didn't live together either? Grandma's mom and dad?"

"Seems like it," Uncle Sasha grew embarrassed, then, tousled the boy's messy, uncut mane and asked: "Do you want tea with biscuits?"

"Yes," little Sasha said, then, asked, "Is it true my father is your brother?"

"It is true," Uncle Sasha said, and his face became inscrutable. It wasn't clear if he was angry at the boy, for asking the question, or at someone else.

"So why haven't I ever seen him?"

Uncle Sasha fell silent. The bluish smoke from his cigarette drifted up to the ceiling.

"What does your mom say?"

"She doesn't say anything," the boy admitted. "And Grandma says my dad is a bad person."

"You see, Sasha, you'll grow up and understand how complicated everything in life is. There's no such thing as simply a bad person or a good person . . ."

"And Milady from *The Three Musketeers*?"

"What about Milady?"

"She's a bad person, right?"

All your life, you wait to grow up. You'll grow up and you'll go to school. You'll grow up and you'll go to the Palace of the Young Pioneers. You'll grow up and you'll go to bed late. You'll grow up and you'll understand.

Everything will happen. Almost everything. When Sasha grows up, he'll understand. About the bad and the good, the good, the bad, and the ugly, about the dark water with rotten snags, hollowed-out logs, and tree stumps at its bottom, the empty apartment with no books, the bluish smoke of the cigarette, and what it means not to have to go to work every day. He'll understand it—and forget it all, and, when he goes to visit the man he called Uncle Sasha his entire life, he won't know what to talk to him about, what to ask him. He'll forget it all and won't end up telling him how much he loved him as a boy, how much he looked forward to those weekend trips to Kolomenskaya Street, the maps on the wall, the tea in the cup with the broken handle. And there won't be any Indians or distant wanderings or the club at the Palace of the Young Pioneers or the foil in his hand—only snow from the sky, lumps of earth on a coffin lid, Mom holding him by the sleeve, the anticipation of the first swig, and an unfamiliar old man standing next to Nikita—so unfamiliar, in fact, that there's no longer sense in asking myself if he's good or bad.

"Uncle Sasha, I was thinking," said the boy, "that it would be better if you were my dad, right? We have the same last name anyway."

"Well, in a way, I am your dad," Uncle Sasha laughed uneasily, "all the more so because we have the same last name. Let's even think of it that way. Only don't tell anyone, it can be our secret."

And little Sasha was so happy that they shared a secret, that they were sitting next to each other, that Uncle Sasha held his hand, that the teapot was making whooshing sounds in the kitchen, that the evening was quiet, and the moon was laughing in the window of the five-story building.

15.

RIGHT TO VIOLENCE

The moon is laughing alright. It is roaring with laughter in the Moscow February snow, teasing me.

I don't know where I am. I don't know what day it is.

How many days can you stay afloat without money?

How many years can you live without money? Without money and fame.

Moreukhov lasted a decade. He traded his Moscow fame for the fame of an authentic underground artist. Rare exhibits in the Troparyovo forest. *Country style*. Rabin, Rukhin, Glezer, and other non-conformists, fucking Sixtiers. In the splendid, new, post-Soviet world, Moreukhov stood for the author, the bulldozer, and the police: he tore canvases when he was drunk and took swings at his fans. This only bolstered his fame, but scared off his audience: in the last five years, his renown existed on its own, unsupported by anything: no exhibits, no new works, no mentions in the press or, it's funny to say, the internet.

With that kind of fame, he didn't need money. He could always borrow from Dimon or Vitalik or, worst-case scenario, sell off some of the books, sketchbooks, or unnecessary things lying around the apartment.

He who has nothing to lose has nothing to be afraid of.

By the way, women love fearless men. And if the women love you, why would you need any money?

Moreukhov is standing in the half-dark February twilight, watching from a distance the brightly lit windows of Crossroads supermarket, shivering and quietly giggling. Not even giggling, but letting out a whistle through gritted teeth.

It seems that he has reached his good old southwest, but then made a wrong turn—and now he's in parts unknown again, on the curb of a parking lot, far away from the lights of the shop windows.

He's not sure where to go next.

It would be good to pick up some tail, Moreukhov thinks, crash with her, fuck her, and squeeze cab fare out of her. Call a car, give the address, and go home.

Moreukhov thinks that, if he gets home, everything will be alright. He'll be able to stop. This time, he'll escape the murky, near-bottom water, the slippery hands, the grasping pincers.

Where is my home? Moreukhov asks himself. Where is my past? Mom and Dad's love, the mystery of Grandpa's death, the mystery of my family's fate. I have to go, I have to get back, I have to get home.

But where is my home, where is my reason?

If I survive this time, Moreukhov tells himself, I will get to the bottom of everything, I will remember everything, I will find everything out. I will question my mom, I will meet with Nikita, talk to his—my?—father.

If only I can get home.

He doesn't have any money, doesn't know where he is, doesn't know where to go.

Against the light of the store window—a black silhouette. A young woman is taking grocery bags out of a cart and placing them in her trunk. Go up to her, smile, offer help. Don't mention money, just ask her to go for a walk, invite yourself over.

She'll definitely say yes.

A young, beautiful, wealthy blonde in a short shearling coat and tall boots will definitely go for a walk with a ragged, shivering alcoholic with a shiner under one eye.

A gift from the cops, who left him in a snowbank for dead.

He moved them to pity alright. He would have been home by now. But I really made my point to them, huh? They were simply stunned.

Turns out I do know how to talk to people, I must know some secret.

There is no secret. It's just that I was the right degree of inebriated. The degree where the whole world lies down at your feet, spreads with a February glaze ice, splashes with slush puddles, is as green as grass and rustles with yellowish-red leaves. In moments like this, it's as if everything is laid out for you. Every bluish shadow on the snow, every ray of sunshine on a gloomy day, every long-limbed beauty you meet on your way.

In moments like this, God admires me, Moreukhov would say.

In moments like this, he couldn't understand how people could live in this city sober.

To be honest, he couldn't get it at all.

At first, the intoxication gave Moreukhov an extraordinary lightheart-edness. A rare girl could resist; but then, a wave of *over-thirty-proof aqua vitae* rolled over him and swept everything away, even his memory. Only fragments remained.

And now, as he gazes at the female silhouette backlit by the store window, Moreukhov suddenly remembers his last, oh-so-recent bender.

The young woman had an automobile's name, Lada. She, too, wore a short, shearling coat and tall black boots, a foot fetishist's dream.

Moreukhov was indifferent to women's footwear—although, of course, he loved high heels because they were *stylish and feminine*.

He met her at the box office of the Horizon movie theater, where, for some reason, he was trying to get into *Constantine*, the cautionary tale of a man who smoked so much he almost wound up in hell before his time.

Lada bought two tickets for the last row. When she reached into her pocketbook for money, Moreukhov thought that, if he could get a good price for that pocketbook, he could probably live on it for a month.

On the tickets, the backseats were listed as "loveseats." The educated Moreukhov thought not of love, but of H. P. Lovecraft—not unfitting when going to see *Constantine*—but didn't say anything. At times, he felt embarrassed of his erudition: he was afraid of crushing his conversation partner.

While Keanu Reeves battled demons, Moreukhov explored Lada's leg between her boot and the hem of her skirt. Then he moved on to her tanga briefs—very convenient—and at first, Lada whispered *not now*, but then she apparently came, yes, she most likely did, because they went to her house and Moreukhov became familiar with all the details of her anatomy, including her appendicitis scar and not-particularly-prominent breasts.

Moreukhov was indifferent to large breasts. My cock is so big, he'd say modestly, that it's alright for a lady's breasts to be small.

And then—that scum, that fucking bitch, I couldn't even grab her hair, so I had to punch her in the face.

Were he sober, Moreukhov would have never raised his hand against a woman.

Then again, he can't even remember Lada when he's sober.

But now, in the February twilight, in the weak glow of the store windows, Moreukhov clearly sees, as in a movie: there he is, swaying in the middle of the room as Lada sobs in the corner and his right hand aches from the blow.

"It's all your fault!" he says.

Of course, he would have lasted a few more days on gin and tonic. On days like this, he could be sweet and witty, inventive and tender. He was only starting to get the shakes, he could still hold up, when he discovered a hidden bar in Lada's living room. He thought it was just a writing cabinet, searched for the key for a while. Wanted to take out some money is all, go to the local Kopeyka store one more time for a gin and tonic.

And it turned out to be a bar. If only Lada hadn't locked it, Moreukhov wouldn't have tried to break into it, wouldn't have opened the little door with a kitchen knife and a screwdriver, wouldn't have found a bottle of Red Label whiskey.

Now, why would a nice girl keep a bottle of Red Label whiskey? If you can call Lada a nice girl, ha!

Obviously, when she came home from work, the bottle was already empty and Moreukhov was standing in the middle of the room, beating out a rhythm on the polished tabletop and rapping:

"Tam-tadadam, I'm drunk as a ham, all 'cause of baby mamas and their dramas and a hundred grams. Hey, don't look, hey, come in, honey, sugar, suck my dick."

This was a poetic creation, how could she not understand? And Lada began to scream from the threshold: *Why the fuck did you break into my cabinet?* Sometimes, Moreukhov just hated it when young women cursed, hated being asked stupid questions, hated being misrepresented.

"I didn't break into it—I opened it!" he answered and gave her a big, gap-toothed smile.

It was then that Lada made a mistake. Of course, he didn't warn her, but she could have guessed that she shouldn't have used the word *drunk*.

And then, Moreukhov hit her—she hadn't even managed to take off her shearling coat when she fell back into a corner, legs splayed, and began to whimper.

Bitch. It's her own fault. I'm out of here! He opened Lada's purse, took out her wallet, pulled out twenty or so crumpled bills, put a few in his pocket, and threw the rest on the floor so she'd shut up and stop shouting *don't touch my money!* There it is, your precious money, go and pick it up if you want.

He slammed the door behind him. That's it. I'm never coming back.

Bitch. What can I say.

An artist has the right to violence, Moreukhov told himself, plodding under the wet snow to Kopeyka. Violence is the essence of art. The Surrealists dreamed of exploding bombs, some Kazakh butchered a ram at the Moscow Art Manege art fair ten years ago and he, Moreukhov, might put on a show called *The Punishment of the Shrew*. In public. In an exhibition space. He just needed to find the right curator.

Yes, when the Ochakovsky beer and gin and tonic period passed, Moreukhov's charm faded before their eyes—even now, his tremors were getting stronger and it probably wasn't the right time to pick up rich blondes, wasn't worth it to step out into the light, he had to retreat to the shadows before someone noticed him, swept him into a corner, knocked out the remainder of his teeth, broke his fingers, and crippled him for fun and laughs.

As soon as he thought this, he heard the screeching of brakes and was blinded by a bright light. The door was flung open and a bulky figure tumbled out:

"Watch it, drunk! Why are you getting under my wheels? Get the hell out." A sharp blow, a shove to the chest, Moreukhov flies off to the side and hisses through his teeth: *Faggot!*

Why did he say that? The second blow knocks him off his feet and a boot tip strikes him in the ribs. He has to pull himself together, cover his head, get his arms out of the way.

After all, he is an artist, he needs his arms to work!

"Who are you talking to?" Followed by a sharp pain. "You say that to me?"

Yes, you, Moreukhov thinks, faggot. You don't even know how to beat someone up.

Moreukhov has been beaten many times. He's been beaten by cops and street thugs, angry drivers, drunken mafia bros, and store security guards.

The cops were the worst. State servants. People who sold their conscience for a paycheck. Ready to beat and rob just so their kids and wives could wear nice clothes and they could always have money for a hair of the dog.

Moreukhov hopes it was the cops who knocked out his front tooth. Street thugs were too socioeconomically close to him. Like him, they were enemies of the system, not its servants.

On the other hand, who can figure out the system today—where does it end?

Just before he loses consciousness, Moreukhov thinks: "Looks like I won't be getting home after all . . ." or something else, something desperate and hopeless.

16.

LITTLE HARPOON

For some reason, Anya remembered: *Look at that funny-looking girl, her little face is totally flat*—it must have been the first time that she had her feelings hurt. You think my face is flat? I have a face, not a little face! A normal face, like Mom and Grandma. I should take some sand in a shovel and throw it at that awful woman and her crybaby, straight into their eyes, so they know what it's like, so they squint their eyes! Then they'll have something to cry about. Look at him fall, scrape his knee, and burst into tears. Calls himself a boy! Anya's a girl, but she doesn't cry for no reason.

That was a long time ago and the image is still fresh in her mind.

It's not surprising that she remembered it. A courtyard like Grandma Djamilya's, only with more trees. Good trees, especially in the spring and fall.

Thirty years have gone by and the playgrounds are still the same. Sandbox, swings, and slide. Now and again, they'll renovate them: install some metallic stairs, set up carved wooden figures, paint the swings a bright color, pour a new heap of sand.

The same children in the new sand, the same parents on the benches around them. Just like thirty years ago. Dads reading the paper, moms chatting with each other or sitting in silence and staring wearily into space, as if they don't notice their children. But only until the first argument, the first screams and tears. Then, it's the same thing all over again:

Don't cry, look at the kitty running, look at the birdie flying by, look at the funny looking girl.

Don't cry, men don't cry, how many times have I told you?

Stop fighting, boy! What do you mean he started it?

Give him the toy car, he can choke on it.

You have to let girls go first, you know that.

Did you hear what I said? Drop it!

How many times do I need to tell you: don't be greedy!

Boy, give me back the shovel, it's not yours!

Lady, look after your own kid!

Don't get involved with those boys, what did I say!

Let him learn to stand up for himself, or else he'll be . . . like his father his entire life!

Come here, sweetheart, come to Mom!

I'm asking you, where is the rake? Go look for it, I won't buy you a new one!

Sand in the summer, snow in the winter. Snow cakes, snow forts, snowballs, shrieks, screams, crying. Frozen feet like you're at the outdoor clothing market again. Whether you want to or not, you start dancing in place, start looking at who's wearing what. Usually—at their footwear. This woman's jacket is very plain, but her boots must have cost ten thousand. And the little girl is wearing a waterproof snowsuit. They must be rich. They must own their apartment rather than rent it. They own a car, probably a foreign make.

If Anya was a housewife with a husband or worked from home like her friend Vika, she would have known who in her building drove what car and who simply went on foot. But she is only there on weekends. She doesn't envy cars, but a good pair of boots, a waterproof snowsuit, your own apartment—sure, a little bit.

How many times do I have to tell you: don't you be jealous! No, I won't buy you the same toy pistol as Serezha's. We don't have the money.

Mama Tanya didn't have money. Mama Tanya worked at a large ministry. Grandma Djamilya was proud of her and bragged: "Not like me, who spent her whole life at a plant or a construction site. My daughter works at a ministry! Where it's clean!" The ministry was quite big but her post was low-level, so Mom never had any money and, as she'd fall asleep, Anya would often hear Grandma trying to convince Mom to borrow at least ten rubles from her *till her next paycheck*. "I can't pay you back anyway," Mom would say, and Grandma would reply: "What do I need it for? I'll die and you and Gulya will get everything anyway."

Anya thinks: this must be when I came to believe that working in a clean space meant you had no money. So I'm standing behind a counter for the umpteenth year. And I won't be seeing ten thousand-ruble boots in my lifetime.

No big deal, she tells herself, we'll make it somehow. We'll break through. Resurface.

Break through—she got that from her mom. At five years old, little Elvira saw her mother cry for the first time when the Trade Union Committee called and said they couldn't offer her a spot in the Mother and Child pension. Mama Tanya dropped the receiver, pinched her lips, clenched her fists, and sat at the table in silence, hoping that her daughter wouldn't see the two tears creeping down her tense cheekbones. Then she exhaled and said: *Well, no big deal. We'll break through*, and started calling some girlfriends of hers; those calls materialized into a wonderful dacha where they spent a whole month and which was much better than that Mother and Child pension, where they got in the following year anyway.

So what's become of this suburban pension where exhausted, single mothers lived with their children and the rare family went at the expense of the Trade Union Committee? There, they showed filmstrips about a baby mammoth's search for his mother, about heather honey and about the Famous Duckling Tim. There, the children participated in sack runs, ran relay races, did gymnastics—and-a-one, and-a-two, and now squats— and the parents watched with endearment. In the evenings, a couple from the Hammer and Sickle plant fought in hushed tones in the room next door and later on, their bed squeaked for a while, keeping the then-young Tatyana awake, making her remember that which would never happen again. She'd envy her boisterous girlfriends, who would drop off their children with the activity leaders and set off in search of adventures, almost always fruitless because all the men here were with their wives and children, if you didn't count the pretty-boy athletic instructor. Slender and fit, wearing an imported tracksuit, he would stroll the alleys of the former country estate keeping an eye out for someone to invite for a cup of tea, a glass of port and a single night of hasty—what if the child wakes up?—lovemaking. In his dreams, he must have felt like a land-owner overseeing his feudal harem and, perhaps, would picture how, in a few years, yet another mother would say to him, pointing to her child: *Remind you of anyone?*

Yes, it was so much better at Aunt Shura's dacha—and Anya forever remembered the *we'll break through*, the pinched lips, and the two tears on her mother's cheeks.

So we'll break through came from her mom and *resurface* was Anya's idea. At present, she longer remembered where she got it from—a book? A cartoon? Definitely not the swimming pool she'd gone to since first grade.

She started going there by chance: for some reason, her school didn't have an after school program for first-graders and her mom decided to send her to a club so she wouldn't hang around at home all day. The only place that was nearby and didn't require her having to cross the street was the pool. And that's how, at the age of seven, Anya swallowed chlorinated water for the first time, gritted her teeth, and swam.

She was a swimmer for nine years. It became clear a while ago that she wouldn't go on to swim professionally, but she still liked how the water parted before her body, how it streamed down her face with her every inhale, how her arm cut the water, barely making a splash. Sometimes, Anya thought that she wasn't human, but a creature born to live in the water, similar to a fish, a dolphin, or an exquisite crocodile. Or maybe, not even a creature, but a submarine, a torpedo, a harpoon being shot at a target. A small harpoon in a blue-rubber swim-cap, with gritted teeth and a cheap bathing suit covering her flat chest.

Anya clearly remembers the first time a man kissed her breasts. Vadik was a student at the college of physical education and noticed Anya at the meets: the coach picked her because she begged him and Dasha Skorbina got sick at the last minute, opening up her spot. Mom let her go, though reluctantly, deciding that the girl was fifteen already and should be able to do what she wants. *Better sports than the discothèque*, in my opinion, she told Aunt Shura on the phone the night before Anya left.

Anya remembers those kisses—inept, as she now understands—and the male hands that tried to unzip her tight jeans—a hand-me-down from Aunt Gulya, who'd put on weight. Anya no longer remembers where he got the key to the locker room that night or what he said to get her in there. It was nice and a little strange for her. "Is this what they make movies and write books about?" she thought, guiding a stranger's hands away from the stubborn button on her fit, flat stomach, and holding up her tank top with her chin.

Their hands would meet again and again on this button, and it began to resemble some game; who knows how it would have ended if the lights hadn't come on and the guard hadn't turned up, followed by the coach.

"What, are your hormones raging?" the coach screamed at Vadik. "You want me to go to jail? She's a minor, you don't have enough girls your own age, you moron?"

In the morning, Anya was sent home, which, was, of course, unfair, but understandable: she had no prospects for professional sports and Vadik's mom worked at the Professional Sports Union—the reason he was considered a rising star.

Anya never went back to the pool and buried a grudge in her soul—not against the coach or Vadik, but against the anxiety that, for some reason, prevented her from pulling down her tank top, leaping up, kneeing him between the legs, and running out of the locker room.

Mom is right, fifteen-year-old Anya thought, it's better that I don't get involved with boys. What a funny-looking girl, her little face is totally flat, don't cry, little one.

And now, she herself says: "Don't cry, little one" and wipes Gosha's tears. Should she tell him "boys don't cry"? Then again, no, it's always the boys who are bawling. I better wipe the tears, lean down even lower so no one can hear me and say right in his ear, which is still covered in fuzz from his hat: "Don't cry, little one! *The Takhtagonovs don't cry.*"

Of course, that's not true. They cry, you bet they cry. I cried when I lost my first important swim meet. I cried standing in the shower so no one could see my tears, and no one did. The tears ran down my cheeks and I repeated: *We'll break through, we'll resurface*—and I still repeat it. So I broke through, I resurfaced: I didn't die of hunger, I didn't become a prostitute, I gave birth to a child, and make decent money.

And the fact that my feet are freezing in cheap boots—well, I can jump up and down.

And-a-one, and-a-two, and now squats.

17.

ONCE, WE WERE YOUNG

A young blonde with curled locks, a short shearling coat, the hem of a jean skirt, cheap boots, and wool stockings. A young man in a ski cap, an earring in his ear, a puffy jacket, jeans wet up to his knees, and boots stained with salt.

That right there, Nikita says to himself, is what happens to your clothes when you walk around on foot in February in Moscow.

The curly-haired blonde and the young man in the jacket kiss between the display shelves at Crossroads supermarket, thinking no one can see them. The girl stands up on her tiptoes and the boy leans over her . . . no, not leans over, but, rather, shelters her the way snow shelters the freezing trees.

In the cart next to them is a lone bottle of cheap champagne.

That first day, Nikita remembers, we ordered champagne at the villa Ksenia. Without any hors d'oeuvres, I think. Exactly, without the hors d'oeuvres: two glasses standing alone on the table, bubbles slowly rising up. *Look, someone's breathing down there*, Masha joked, and I was suddenly frightened.

At the time, I didn't yet know I would be working with aquariums. I'd definitely see my share of bubbles.

What do people who eat at restaurants buy at the store? Toilet paper, toothpaste, mineral water so they don't have to bother with a filter, bread for morning toast, a jar of jam. No wonder our refrigerator is empty.

There was a time when Masha loved to cook. There is still a shelf of cookbooks in the kitchen. Indian cuisine, Chinese, Hungarian, Spanish, *DIY Sushi, 100 Fish Recipes* and so on.

Why would people who eat at restaurants need cookbooks?

There was a time when Masha returned from the store with full shopping bags. Eggs, cheese, meat, fish, butter, grains, four kinds of pasta . . . if we had the money.

Because, every so often, we didn't.

What job didn't I try! I even went door-to-door selling various crap like cheap mixers; I remember I spent a whole winter working as an unlicensed cab driver. I didn't make a whole lot of money—just enough to get by, as they say. Then there was an accident, a truck ran a red light and smashed the back door on the right and half of the passenger compartment—good thing that I had no passengers and was wearing a seatbelt. The traffic police wrote down the license plate numbers and drafted an accident report. It turned out the truck driver had been drunk; I wasn't guilty and they were supposed to cover my repairs. Masha and I were already figuring out what kind of car we could buy with that money when it turned out the guy's truck was registered in the name of a sham firm with no director or legal address, nothing. So there was no one we could get money from, and I wasn't insured because no one insured anything in the nineties.

I was so upset that I came home, went to the kitchen and sat there, on the brink of tears. Masha came up to me and asked what happened, and I just waved her off. Then she squatted beside me and put her head on my knees. I stroked her head as if she was a little girl. And thought that, ultimately, she has no one to count on but me. That she believes in me and is counting on me. Turns out I don't have a choice and have to find a way out.

I remember it well: it was evening already, out the window the sky was shrouded in dusk; we sat in the kitchen and I stroked Masha's head and felt relieved. After all, things were good: I had my apartment and my beloved wife next to me and we'd manage somehow. To this day, I think that if Masha hadn't placed her head on my knees that time, I wouldn't have been successful at anything. Not then, not later, not at my business, not at making money, nothing.

As for the business, it all happened on its own: three years ago, an acquaintance asked if I knew any aquarium specialists—the water had grown moldy in his office's fish tank and they needed someone to change it, wash the tank, and save the fish. If I had a normal job at the time, I would have said: *Look it up online* and that would be the end of it, but I said to him: *Well, let me do it, I had fish at home as a kid.* It turned out that they didn't have one aquarium, but ten, because it was a big office; then I offered to replace everything the pet store put on the bottom of the tank and someone asked if it was possible to, for instance, recreate the ruins of an Indian temple; and I said: Easy! I found designers, gave a hundred bucks to an expert from the Institute of Asian and African Countries, and things took off.

Now I have a staff of fifteen, an office, clients, a business. Now I know that, if it weren't for Masha, none of this would have happened.

I freeze in front of the dairy section. Multicolored, festive jars and cartons. Five years ago, when I'd make some money, I'd go to the store and buy Dannon yogurt for Masha. It was slightly more expensive, but she said it tasted much better.

Things were so simple! We thought that if we had a bit more money everything would work out. There was a time when an extra hundred dollars was a cause for celebration. Being able to go to a restaurant together was a great joy.

Once, we were young.

Now our fridge is empty—supposedly because we don't eat at home.

I wonder what Masha eats when she doesn't leave home for days. I'm not surprised she's lost so much weight.

She sits alone in our big apartment with the dusky sky out the window; I'm not at home. I'm at work, or worse, at Dasha's.

In any case, I don't go to Dasha's often. I could count the number of times on my hand. Four times, exactly. I remember it clearly.

Maybe a little too clearly—right down to the very last detail.

How in the world did I get involved?

Masha can't not be aware, not suspect something. That's why she's sad, that's why she sits there alone.

It's sad to think about it. Sad and shameful.

I want to buy her something tasty. Where are those Dannon yogurts she used to love so much? Oh, there they are. Two of each kind.

Also, a jar of caviar.

Things were so simple when we didn't have money. A container of yogurt and everyone was happy.

Mom is right: money is the root of all evil.

In the line for the cash register, the blonde girl and the boy in the puffy jacket end up in front of me. She's carefully wheeling the cart, as if it's a baby carriage. The boy leans down and kisses her on the temple. She turns around, raises her head and presses her lips to his.

I'll never kiss this way again. You can only kiss this way when you're young. Only when you think that it's all happening for the first time, when you believe that nothing but trifles stand between you and happiness—your own apartment, your own space, a bit of money.

I can't make out like this with Masha: you can only kiss a happy person this way.

I can't make out like this with Dasha: sugar daddies don't kiss young women in public. It looks ridiculous—there's snow on the roof, but fire in the furnace.

At the cash register, the boy takes a pack of condoms and puts it on the counter next to the champagne.

At his age, I was too embarrassed to buy condoms and, in any case, they didn't sell them at the supermarket.

I must still be a bit embarrassed. Masha and I don't use condoms, and I think that everyone would be on to me: look at that man buying condoms, he's planning to fuck his young lover.

It's possible that, in thirty years, I'll be buying condoms with pride: look, I can still get it up.

If I still can get it up, of course.

Nikita takes a pack of Durex condoms off the shelf and twirls it around in his hands. He thinks they're the ones Dasha likes. He should buy them and bring them along next time.

The rectangular package lands right next to the yogurts.

Durex and Dannon. Dasha and Masha, lover and wife.

So I've become a real businessman, Nikita thinks, as good as Kostya. Good thing I don't rent an apartment for Dasha, I bring my paycheck home like a decent man.

The cashier prints out a receipt, the boy empties the change from his jacket pockets for some time, then, the girl fumbles in her purse and takes out her last bill from her wallet. The boy shoves the condoms into his pocket, grabs the bottle by the neck with one hand and wraps the other one around the blonde's waist. They walk toward the exit and pause at the door.

Outside, there is wet February snow, a chilly wind, and cars splashing mud around.

They kiss one last time and the boy half-opens the door and lets the girl walk ahead of him.

Nikita watches them walk away, then, takes the pack of Durex condoms out of the cart and puts it back on the shelf.

Masha's sitting in her favorite armchair. Without even turning the light on. She doesn't even get up when Nikita opens the door.

"Look what I brought!" Nikita calls out.

He places all eight yogurt containers on a tray, puts a teaspoon on it, gets down before Masha on the carpet and tucks his face in her knees.

Masha smiles with the corners of her lips.

"Thank you," she says and kisses Nikita on the temple, just like that boy kissed his girlfriend.

"I forgot which one you like," Nikita says, "so I bought all of them."

"Darling," Masha replies, slightly irritated, "you forgot that I don't eat this."

"But you used to like it."

"Dannon hasn't been great for a while," Masha barely perceptibly shrugs her shoulders.

The things we once loved haven't been great for a while, Nikita thinks. And our love too, I suppose. We probably just didn't know how to love properly.

"Maybe some caviar?" he offers.

"I'm just not hungry," Masha replies.

What can you do? Really!

18.

CHILDREN'S TALES

If time is as malleable as clay, if the soul dashes back and forth in eternal travels, then why is it that I can't see the future? Why am I always being shown the past, Masha thinks, why doesn't my personal home theater, the flimsy barrier between dreams and reality, show what will happen to me?

I probably know what will happen anyway. Many fairy tales start like this: *There once lived an old man and an old woman and they didn't have any children.*

The old man and the old woman from the fairy tales must be forty to forty-five years old, the age where there isn't any hope left. Only a miracle can help here: God will appear, will insert a second "r" in your name, and produce a chosen people from your loins. A pea will roll into a crevice between the floorboards, a piece of pinewood will come to life, a Snow Maiden will start to speak, a chopped-off finger will turn into a boy, a girl will be born from a flower. A cuckoo bird will lay forty chicken eggs, a turnip will turn into a baby in an oven and, in the worst-case scenario, a log will turn into a boy, although you don't even need an old woman for that.

So, there once lived an old man and an old woman and they were both forty years old.

How old were my adoptive parents when they took me from the orphanage? It's much better to take a child from an orphanage than to adopt a log or a turnip. But Masha wants to have her own and only her own child. Because she thinks that adopted kids always leave.

Masha was twenty-four when her parents decided to immigrate. They were given papers for the whole family, took forever to pack the books among which Masha passed her childhood, put her school report cards and photos in a separate box, hired a shipping container, and took everything with them.

The empty apartment seemed enormous. They were in the middle of supper at the solitary kitchen table when Masha told them she wasn't going anywhere.

Why did she have to go? She was twenty-four, she wasn't a child, she was her own woman, got a degree in foreign languages two years ago, found a job as an editor at some scientific journal, just got a raise, planned to rent an apartment in the fall and, in any event, she'd never said she intended to go with them. She was merely helping them pack, that's all.

This was all true, but Masha left out the main reason.

There are moments when you realize that your life belongs to you alone. And only you can decide how to live it.

To realize this, Nikita needed his own business, Elvira needed a son and Moreukhov—a gin and tonic and aqua vitae. For Masha, it was enough to belatedly lose her virginity, have her first orgasm with a man, and have her period delayed by three weeks.

It was easier for her to say *I'm not going anywhere with you* than admit that she was pregnant, that the child's father was married and ten years her senior, and that he didn't have the slightest thought of divorcing.

An office romance of sorts. Not too many boys at the Department of Foreign Languages.

She said that she was merely helping them pack and her father immediately started yelling: "You've gone crazy, how can you stay here, you have no right!" and that "you have no right!" particularly irked Masha, so she snapped back something along the lines of: "Who do you think you are to tell me what to do, you're not even my parents!" slammed the door, and ran off to spend the night at Olya's.

She would have never been able to leave if everything remained exactly the same at the apartment. But the home she was leaving was a disemboweled corpse of the home she'd spent her childhood in, and was being thrown open to all the winds: thus, Masha was carried away by a magical tornado like Dorothy.

During the month she lived at Olya's, Mom and Dad didn't call her once. Yes, it was unfortunate she told them "you're not even my parents!" that time, but she wasn't planning on calling them first, she was nauseous as it was, threw up every meal, why, why hadn't she used protection?

Mom called her first. She said it was a miracle they'd found tickets, they were leaving in two days. I'll stop by tomorrow, Masha said, but in the middle of the night she was rushed to the hospital with a hemorrhage, and once she'd been discharged, no one replied at their number anymore.

She had become an orphan again.

Of course, later on, Masha wrote to them, apologized, even visited them in America once. But still, they had parted on bad terms that time.

Masha thinks: this must be why everything turned out this way.

The gynecologist at the hospital said it was unlikely she would ever have children. She didn't think about it much at the time, at the age of twenty-four. She didn't think about it when she turned thirty, either, when she moved in with Nikita. Three years ago, she suddenly realized that she wanted a child.

Carve a rod from pinewood, build a Snow Maiden, wrap a chopped-off finger in a piece of cloth, plant a seed that grows into a flower. Gather forty hen's eggs from the whole village and have a cuckoo sit on them. Place a turnip in the oven, close the door, and in the morning, take out a little girl.

Finally, pray to the Virgin Mary.

Only Masha didn't know how to pray—in her childhood, she'd been told more about the reincarnation of souls than God.

No, Masha won't build herself a Snow Maiden, a Thumbelina won't sprout from a flower, a Turnip Girl won't come out of the oven.

Only Masha pictures herself walking down the square and pushing a baby carriage while the passersby ask: Is it a boy or a girl?

And Masha replies: *A girl*.

People ask: *Why does your daughter have such gray cheeks?*

And Masha says: *She hasn't been bathed in a while*.

People ask: *Why does she have such fluffy paws and whiskers like her dad?*

Masha says: *She hasn't shaved in a while*, and the next thing you know, the baby carriage flips over and a striped, whiskered kitten jumps out with its diaper trailing behind, and runs to the nearest tree with a heart-wrenching meow.

And everyone can see that it's Masha, Masha Melnikova, the stupid girl, the poor woman, forty years old, childless, she should probably tell her husband, she should probably see a doctor, such a good couple, it's true when they say *Los Ricos También Lloran*.

Hell no, Masha tells herself, suddenly furious, this won't happen! I can't be frightened with children's tales, I'll read them to my child one day and tell him: *Look at that silly girl, she put a kitten in a baby carriage!* My child will laugh and Nikita and I will be happy again.

19.

REINCARNATION. MAKSIM

As she falls asleep, she holds his hand. Many girls like doing this: Maksim has strong arms, the strong wrists of a professional typist, fingers trained by daily exercise: qwertyuiop, asdfghjkl, zxcvbnm. The girls like it.

In the morning, he wakes her with a kiss and makes breakfast. Breakfast is supposed to be simple: a grapefruit, two eggs, and two thin slices of lightly toasted whole-grain bread. Grapefruit is hard to find, which is why he is only serving eggs and bread today. It may seem banal, but it's actually Bragg's diet, a miracle of fasting, the breakfast of a naturopathic practitioner.

Maksim used to like exquisite, elaborate, dishes. To this day, *The Book of Tasty and Healthy Food*, *The Cuisine of the Soviet Republics*, *Hungarian Cuisine*, *Polish Cuisine*, and, slightly off to one side—a neatly-bound, typewritten copy of *Jewish Cuisine*—stand on his shelves.

He walks around the apartment in the nude. He finds it funny that, in the morning, young women try to pull something on as soon as possible and lower their eyes bashfully when he gets up from the table, that they are embarrassed of their own naked bodies.

Today's guest simply threw on a button-down and is sitting with her legs crossed, blowing a blonde strand of hair away off her forehead. No embarrassment. Atta girl.

Maksim has a hairy chest, hair down to his shoulders and a thick beard. In a beard like that, gray hair resembles silver thread. Maksim likes this. He plans to age handsomely.

Maksim likes women. He isn't biased when it comes to the female body. The fat and the thin, the svelte and the full-bodied, blondes and brunettes, Lolitas who have barely reached legal age, and women on the verge of menopause have all spent time on the folding bed in his one room apartment in Chertanovo. They are all neatly inscribed in catalog cards, stowed in the rear drawer of his writing desk, numbered and entered in his planner.

A planner is a convenient thing. You never miss a birthday or a day you can call and say: don't you remember, tomorrow is our anniversary.

Numbers are better than names. The numbers are different, but the names are the same: every second girl is named Lena or Sveta. Of course, they do what they can to distinguish themselves, but still, there are only one or two variants: Sveta, Svetik, Veta, Lana. Here are some more: Lena, Alyona, Lyolya.

Today's Lyolya was Lyolya number two. In the general list—number thirty-four.

Maksim wishes to bring his number of girlfriends up to one hundred and eight—a holy number in Buddhism. That is his mission.

Maksim is a missionary by nature. An enlightener. A teacher and a guru. An apostle of an assortment of new religions.

In the 1960s, he typed up the poems of Tsvetaeva, Mandelstam, and Akhmatova and recorded reels of the Beatles and Okudzhava. He wrote his own songs, played the guitar, and wasn't too bad of a singer. One of his songs gained national prominence when a famous bard sang it at a concert. Being an honorable man, he announced its real author's name before he began—*This song was written by my friend, the poet and beautiful human being Maksim Rozhkov*—but the recording, which was later disseminated in hundreds of copies, skipped in that very exact spot and you couldn't make out any words besides poet and beautiful human being.

Admittedly, Maksim didn't get too upset. He quickly lost interest in songwriting and couldn't remember now what he had written—*Something about a forest . . . or the mountains . . . I think there was a bonfire and love. An ordinary song.*

All the more so because the seventies rolled around and Maksim discovered Meister Eckhart, Rudolf Steiner, and Helena Blavatskaya, as well as yoga, tantra, the kama sutra, and the Chinese treatises on love.

"The most important thing in the Chinese art of love," Maksim says as he brews his tea, "is to conserve your Chi. Which means that the man mustn't ejaculate. You might have noticed that I use a special technique for this. After we're done with breakfast, I'll show it to you again and you can teach it to other men."

Number thirty-four blows some blonde hair strands away and says: "I like it when a man . . . umm . . . ejaculates inside me."

Maksim is surprised. Women rarely interrupt him. As a rule, they hang on his every word, no matter the subject: sexual technique, seventeenth-century lute music, Fellini's latest film, or the search for Shambhala.

Maksim is almost never quiet. Instead of spewing sperm, he emits fountains of words.

"It's just the call of nature," he says. "You like sperm because you have the instinct for continuing the race. But you must conquer this instinct. Child-bearing is unnecessary. People have children out of ignorance, thinking children are a continuation of their lives. Nonsense! Our lives will continue after death anyway because we'll be reborn in other bodies. Buddha taught this as early as three thousand years ago: our next life will be determined by our karma.

And what will determine the lives of our children? asks number thirty-four.

"Their own karma," Maksim explains. "The combined total of their good and bad actions in a chain of preceding births."

"So children don't inherit anything from their parents?" Number thirty-four purses her lips and wrinkles her forehead.

"Nothing," Maksim says adamantly.

Then why do I look like my mom?

He doesn't know what to say to that and thus, replies:

"It's merely external resemblance."

A year later, Maksim takes out the catalog card and reads the small print: "No. 34, Lyolya, Yelena Borisova. Blonde. Blue eyes. Breast size average. Asked me to retype her poems. Poems are bad. When she came to pick them up, she stayed the night. November 12, 1973. Paid for the retyping. Temperamental in bed, but talks too much." The last three words are underlined twice. A phone number is jotted down below.

Maksim believes in techniques. Sexual, scientific, technological, communicative. He always says practically the same exact words: "You know, tomorrow is our anniversary, you are aware of that, right? I thought about you all year and decided to call." Then again, if he really likes a girl, he may call her in a month or even a week. It's sad to let them go forever, but it takes up too much time and energy to keep up old ties. Over the past year, the list had only gone up by seven. In any event, Maksim intends to work tirelessly till a great old age.

And so Lyolya is sitting in his kitchen again, still tan from the summer, in a knit sweater, brown pants, and platform shoes. On the table there's a cabbage salad, liver, and bread.

For some reason Maksim thinks that her breasts have gone up a size—he'll have to correct that on the card. And underline "talks too much" one more time. So much that he's not even attracted to her.

"You know, I also thought about us all year. I mean, about what you said to me. That children and reincarnation are the two paths to the after-life. I think that it must be one and the same: the mother's and father's karma create the child's karma. Like Michurin says. Cross breeding. Also, the child has its own karma that it gets from its previous life. And these three karmas dictate everything that happens to us. Only there are in fact more than three. Because there are also grandmothers, grandfathers, and their moms and dads . . . it's an endless chain of sorts. I even wrote a poem—would you like me to read it?"

And, without waiting for his answer, she launches into it: *Unborn daughter, I turn to you . . .*

Maksim waits patiently for her to finish and then says:

"Can I congratulate you?"

For the first time, he sees number thirty-four's face turn red.

"How did you guess?" she says.

"I'm sorry," Maksim replies, "it's a secret."

It is in fact a secret: it's not the first time he's noted that, as soon as a woman gets pregnant, he completely stops being attracted to her. He must be dismayed that he wasn't able to properly explain Chi energy and the absurdity of child-bearing to her.

Number thirty-four nods, bites her lower lip, clenches her fist, and keeps quiet.

"You see," Maksim begins, "child-bearing, of course, only magni-fies the biomass and creates new living creatures doomed to suffer and develop attachments, but since you've decided on this foolishness, it is my responsibility to recommend Doctor Spock's book on childcare. You must have heard about it already, but just to be on the safe side, I'll para-phrase the main ideas for you . . ."

All of a sudden, Maksim sees number thirty-four's lips begin to trem-ble and her blue eyes well up with tears.

"Hold me," she says, "I'm scared. I'm completely alone."

And then Maksim drops his talk about Dr. Spock and the biomass, hugs Lyolya by the shoulders, pats her sun-bleached hair, and finds himself telling her that everything will be fine, that her child will be born healthy and grow up happy. "It doesn't matter that you're alone now, it's not for long, after all, you're a very beautiful woman, talented, smart, write beautiful poetry, everything will work out, I swear." And, as he says this, Maksim truly believes that happiness is possible and you just have to wait a bit longer, read a few more intelligent books, learn a pair of new techniques, and explain everything to people so that they finally understand, and then, children won't be born destined for suffering, but for happiness, pure and serene happiness.

It crosses his mind that tears, too, contain Chi and he must learn to control them—it crosses his mind and he cries anyway.

He never ran into Lyolya again. Two years later, he was baptized by the name of Pyotr and married a woman he met in church at Easter.

If he had continued his list, she would have been known as number fifty-one.

But Pyotr no longer kept lists, called promiscuity one of the most terrible sins, believed that procreation was the sole justification for sex, and dreamed of having twelve children in honor of the apostles. In any case, he couldn't get anywhere near this number—which was a good deal more modest than one hundred and eight—because the doctors found he was infertile.

He was deeply upset by this, but in the end, found comfort in the words of Brazilian novelist Machado de Assis: "The balance is in my favor: I did not have children and did not bequeath to anyone the dross of my earthly being."

If you don't count the legacy of his misery, almost nothing remained after Maksim. After he was baptized, he either destroyed or gave away his enormous library of esoteric and samizdat literature. The same fate befell his collection of reels with one of a kind recordings of classic Russian bards.

Only the song written by Maksim and sung by the famous bard had outlived its author. To this day, homely girls and childish, bespectacled boys sing it in their parents' kitchens and on the fields of commercialized gatherings, in cozy campfire smoke.

20.

YOU DESERVE BETTER

"Anechka, why do you keep calling me Mark Borisovich? Just call me Marik, like my friends do."

He's one to talk—Marik! The man is forty-five years old, he's gone gray at the temples, his gut doesn't fit under his belt, yet he's still Marik!

"But, honestly, Mark Borisovich, it makes me uncomfortable. After all, you're the boss," Anya smiles flirtatiously.

"Okay, then just call me Mark. And we may as well use the informal 'you.' Let's drink to our brotherhood, as they say!"

Mark was drinking a cognac and ordered a Bailey's for Anya, sweet and thick. Andrey also treated her to it once, but Anya didn't like it.

They drank and kissed. The kiss turned out to be slobbery, just as Anya expected.

She washed it down with a sickly-sweet coffee.

"You know, Anya, you deserve better. What kind of a job is this for a young and beautiful woman—a shopgirl at a store? Not really romantic."

Suddenly, Anya cringed more violently than she had from the kiss. When she and her dad finally met—it must have been their third or fourth meeting—he began to lecture her about life: "It's too bad you became a shopgirl, nothing romantic about that profession." Meanwhile, he was working at some small private company—what a romantic place!

At the time, Anya was so angry she said: "Listen, I've lived without you for twenty years and I'll go on living without you! I only wanted to get a look at you. And now I have and that's that!"

Mom was right to send him packing—he was a royal asshole, though one shouldn't speak ill of the dead.

"Tell me, do you, for example, like to dance?"

"Dance?" Anya echoed him. "No, not really, Mark Borisovich. I like to swim."

"We agreed that you'd call me Mark—just Mark."

"I beg your pardon, sir . . . I mean, sorry, Mark."

"That's right," he laughed contentedly.

I wonder why he's beating about the bush? Anya warned him that she had to leave by nine. She lied that she had to let her mom off the hook, when, actually, she was going to the movies with Andrey. They usually went at seven, but he called and said that he was held up at work.

So she had two hours to kill. Zinka said: "Right on time, Mark is starting to get grumpy. No wonder he made me rearrange the shoe display twice on Monday, I busted my ass."

"I've been wanting to ask you: what is your ethnic background?" he asked, then grew embarrassed and added: "Don't think that . . . I'm an internationalist, as they say . . . it's just that your face is so unusual."

Anya once knew an internationalist soldier who came back shell-shocked from Afghanistan. His face was also unusual.

"Yes, I'm Tatar, Mark Bo . . . I mean, just Mark. And I'm just Tatar. It's pretty obvious from my last name."

She wondered if he'd ask her "Is it true that Tatar women's, um, you know, runs sideways?" Almost everyone asked. The first time, Anya was offended and muttered, "We have the same thing as everyone else," then, she'd just laugh and add, "That's Chinese women. It would make it very uncomfortable for us Tatar women to ride on horseback."

No, he didn't ask, only squinted at his gold watch and said:

"I always liked Asian girls. They're very passionate . . . and sex with them is very special. You get it, right?"

Anya nodded her head and moved the empty cup away.

"So, should we go? I have to run soon."

They went down to the warehouse, where it all happened. It took no more than ten minutes, whereas they had sat in the café for an hour. She'd have to run to make it to the movies.

In a word: Marik.

Now she knew for sure that he wasn't a Mark, he wasn't a Mark Borisovich—he was a Marik.

Slimy, fat, forty-year-old Marik.

She still got to the movie theater before Andrey: the Friday night traffic jams were such that you couldn't get anywhere by car quickly. She bought the tickets so he wouldn't think she had no money. She got there first, so she bought them. Now she was standing, leaning against a column, glancing at her watch, and starting to lose patience: after all, he could have left his car and taken the Metro. If she knew that she would have to wait, she would have grabbed a book, and now, all she could do was contemplate the crowd by the box office.

Anya thought she'd already seen these people somewhere: either at another movie theater or a café or at a restaurant she had gone to with Andrey. Everywhere she went with Andrey, she would see the exact same people: ones who smiled either smugly or nervously, talked loudly on their cell phones and, from time to time, fiddled with their car keys.

Anya first noticed these kinds of people two years ago, at IKEA. They came in the evenings, right after their day at the office, but more often on weekends. Alone and in couples, they bought linen, furniture, dishware, office chairs, children's toys, photo frames, CD cases, floor lamps, chandeliers, light fixtures, and fir trees for the New Year's holiday, which—completely unheard of!—they were allowed to return afterward.

Every month, their numbers grew, as if somewhere in Moscow a factory began to produce office employees, or maybe, they simply found out about IKEA after everyone else and flocked there to make up for lost time.

Before them, the customers were different, simpler. Unassuming, timid men came to the store on weekends with their families, their children. They ate lunch at the café, played computer games in the children's room, and examined toys, furniture, and bed sheets. They bought some stuff for, say, a hundred fifty rubles, took the receipt, and said a heartfelt thank you to Anya.

Businessmen from outside of Moscow loaded up full carts and tried to negotiate "a minor wholesale deal." Then they must have taken it to their provinces and sold it at their stores.

Fussy, noisy people flocked to the store opening, shoving each other, and ran to the section with slightly defective discounted goods. The cashiers secretly called this section the synagogue, though Anya didn't consider why.

There were also those who tried to tip her. Anya didn't accept tips (they warned her: if you take so much as a penny, we'll fire you), but still, this only reinforced her impression that she was working at a circus or a restaurant rather than a store.

This must be why she quit her job in the end. Also, her cheekbones were tired from smiling all the time.

On the other hand, she has to drink coffee with Marik now. Honestly, she was so stupid.

Although her salary is a bit higher and her title more respectable. A good job and, in any case—ten minutes at the warehouse with Marik is better than eight hours at the cash register with gritted teeth.

"Excuse me, young lady, are you waiting for someone?" came from a not-too-tall young man in a beanie and a Chinese jacket from the clothing market.

"Yes," Anya nods.

"Not me, by any chance?"

"No."

"Well, I'm sorry. I was thinking: you're alone, I'm alone . . . we could go to the movies, and, while we're at it, get to know each other."

Anya doesn't answer, but the young man doesn't let up:

"I heard it's a really cool movie. I like movies with special effects. I like all kinds of movies. I even like romance films. Do you like movies?"

Anya shakes her head. She likes two or three old films she watched about ten or fifteen years ago at the homes of those rare acquaintances who had enough money for a VCR. Of course, she has her own DVD player now—she can play cartoons for Gosha—but there was a time when this was a real luxury. She's remembered a handful of films from those days, mostly about female assassins and hitmen from secret services.

"What, you really don't like them?" the guy marvels. "Then why are you waiting? Maybe we should get out of here? We can, uh, go to the skating rink. Or go for a walk."

"Sure," Anya says, "let's go for a walk. Have you seen what the weather's like?"

"Yes," he sighs. "Well, maybe we can go over to someone's house, if you don't want to go ice-skating."

A skating rink is the last thing I need, Anya thinks irritably. She'd gladly go to the pool. One time, she even calculated that a two-person membership would cost all of four hundred dollars a month; on Saturdays, she would go there with Andrey and, on weekdays, she would occasionally stop by before work. However, she's not sure how she would do it: her commute is forty minutes, plus she has to drop Gosha off at daycare. But Anya knows that, if she had a membership, she would find the time.

These days, she rarely swims—in the summer, she sometimes gets out to the reservoir, but can't really swim there. She has to watch Gosha all the time—he hasn't learned to swim yet, but is drawn to the water. So it always ends in frustration instead of swimming.

The pool is a completely different story. Anya imagines herself parting the water like she did twenty years ago, moving in time with the wave, inhale—exhale, inhale—exhale, her arm entering almost without making splashes, the little streams down her face, the familiar smell of chlorine, a twenty-five-meter lane end to end, one stroke after another, like she is participating in meets again, covering a distance, like she must get there first.

As soon as Anya thinks about this, she starts to get angry at Andrey, although she has no reason to do so. She never mentioned the pool to him.

Thank God she hasn't been raised to depend on men.

No wonder her mom refused child support in her day—it was better to have no money than to take money from a man who *behaved with her that way.* Which way, Anya still doesn't know: she never even thought to ask.

"Maybe we can go to a club?" the guy continues. "Do you like dancing?"

"I don't," Anya says and looks at her watch irritably. The movie has already started, but there are still five minutes of previews.

"Hey, listen," the guy says, "maybe you should forget about him."

"Who?"

"The guy that you're waiting for. I don't think he appreciates you enough. You deserve better. Beautiful girls shouldn't wait for a long time, right? He's not worth it, I swear."

Seriously, Anya thinks, maybe I should give up and go to the movies with this guy? I'm standing here like an idiot.

"No, think about it, what normal guy would behave like this with a young woman? I think you should teach him a lesson so he won't be late next time, right?"

Anya laughs.

"You have a wonderful laugh," the guy says, "it must be a treat to tell you jokes."

He's not bad, Anya thinks, funny, not boring. Maybe I really should go to the movies with him and tell Andrey to get lost? We dated for six months, enough.

"My name's Anya," she says. "What's yours?"

"I'm Kirill," the guy answers. "Listen, I wanted to ask: what is your ethnic background?"

"I'm Tatar," Anya says, "why?"

Anya always says that, although she's only a quarter Tatar and doesn't speak a word of it. But still, she doesn't feel Russian. Add to that her broad cheekbones, narrow eyes, small breasts . . .

"No reason in particular. Your face is so . . . unusual. I like faces like that."

"I like my face too," Anya answers, and at that moment, Andrey finally shows up, apologizing as he's walking and railing against the Moscow traffic and its crowded roads.

"Thank you for the tickets," Andrey says, "let me pay you back."

"Forget it," Anya answers.

Don't count on men—they'll deceive you anyway. That's what Anya's mom said, and before that, her mom, the legendary sniper Djamilya Takhtagonova.

"Bye, Kirill," Anya says, looking over her shoulder. "Maybe we'll see each other again."

"Sure thing," Kirill answers. "If anything, come back, maybe I'll still be here."

What a nice life he has, Anya thinks. He can loiter half the day picking up women. And I have daycare—work—daycare five days a week. Well, at least I'll sleep in tomorrow.

21.

ZOMBIE GOES HOME

Sometimes I get so tired over the course of the day that I find it hard to drive. Sometimes I fall asleep right on the Metro—and then I dream of my brother Sasha coming home after a two week drinking binge.

Maybe a trusting young woman picked him up by Crossroads, maybe some kind people gave him money *for medicine* or maybe he found a wallet in the snow, but Moreukhov has magically overcome the barrier between the low-alcohol-content prelude and deepwater vodka diving. As usual, he is awaited by water devils, knotty branches, and near-bottom spirits, and plunges deeper and deeper, hoping to make it home before the drowned clutch him in their slimy embraces, before their pincers tear his flesh apart and the dark water fills his lungs. He hopes to make it home before he reaches bottom.

Vodka is fuel. I have energy while it burns inside of me, while it incinerates me. When this fire goes out, I stop being human. I'm a zombie, a living corpse, a creation of George Romero and Lucio Fulci. My hands are shaking, saliva drips from my mouth, an unsteady walk, a blurred gaze.

I should probably start eating other people, but thus far, I've ostensibly gotten along without it.

When I'm home, I enjoy being a zombie. The body of a zombie is devoid of a soul, it's totally free. This freedom is tempting—I'm so tempted to divine what will happen to my body in a minute, but it doesn't work. My body can fall, can trip for no reason, crash into a table, a sideboard, a closet. Miss the toilet seat. Sit down in the middle of the street. Lie down. Turn stock still. Vibrate convulsively. Vomit a mixture of three-day-old food and what I just had to drink.

The same body that walks around in circles with no effort, all on its own. An autonomous body of absolute freedom. A body of ecstasy and destruction.

I am not the zombie of horror and *giallo* films, I don't attack passersby, don't devour other people's flesh.

I only feed on my own.

An autonomous body really is autonomous: if you don't count alcohol, it subsists on its inner resources. It consumes itself, and the more it eats, the more autonomous it becomes.

(This is more or less what Moreukhov thinks and more or less how he explains it to Dimon—only more haltingly, convolutedly, and verbosely. Why would an alcoholic speak properly? And zombies aren't known for their eloquence either.)

I come out of my bender completely ill, Moreukhov explains. My liver is wrecked, my heart's out of whack, my pancreas is about to fail, and my nerves are, obviously, fucked. My body's destroyed.

I haven't hit thirty and I'm a walking ruin, a living corpse.

This is fitting. Turning into a zombie is the highest form of asceticism.

Think about it: if one beautiful day, corpses really do come out of their graves as Romero and Fulci prophesized, who will be the oldest zombies on earth?

The answer: the ones whose bodies haven't decomposed over all these centuries. The holders of incorruptible powers. The saints and the ascetics.

Turning into a zombie is an honest game. It's my body, who can prohibit me from exchanging it for ecstasy and autonomy?

It's an honorable exchange.

There is nothing sweeter than such an exchange, although, if you're viewing it from the outside, there is also probably nothing scarier.

It's good to be a living corpse in your own apartment. Chilly Moscow in February is not the best place for a zombie. In any case, Moreukhov can no longer feel the cold. He has chills and can hardly stand on his feet, but gets closer to home with every step.

This road has never been so long before.

Yeah, it's been a really long wake.

He's already starting to recognize his surroundings. If he had a bit of vodka, he'd be home in ten minutes. OK, forget the vodka—just a glug of beer, a small drop.

Moreukhov walks on with his last bit of strength. He thinks his old ottoman will keep him from plunging into the dark water.

I'll reach home, he tells himself, reach the places where there are no swollen corpses, where happy people sit on riverbanks and ships sail with vacationers, where music plays and jasmine never stops blooming.

Like in Venichka's Petushki village, haha!

Only I'm not Venichka, who am I kidding. Another time, another hero. I wouldn't have dared to walk into a commuter train, talk to a Sphinx, and stage a revolution.

Although I don't fritter my energy away on angels—I talk directly to God.

I know that angels lie.

Any film noir can tell us that story.

He thinks she really does look like an angel. A strange angel with Asian eyes who looks like Maggie Cheung. She came up to him on the street and asked: do you want a drink? Then took his hand, sat him down on a bench and handed him a bottle of Tuborg beer. A guardian angel, no less.

Although why would an Eastern Orthodox person have an Asian guardian angel? Perhaps, Moreukhov thinks, I am dying and this is my pre-death delirium.

With a brisk movement of the hand, she unscrews the cork. Yes, of course, pre-death delirium—beer is not vodka, you can't unscrew the top. Or maybe it's a kind of vodka? Tuborg vodka? Let's try it, no, still beer, and now, one more gulp and one more.

Moreukhov knows from experience that he's got five minutes and then he'll be overcome by another wave, pulled in, dragged away. He's got five minutes, but it seems as if he's got his entire life ahead of him.

And he says something funny and engrossing while the young woman smiles, smiles a bit sadly. He really must look a bit strange, this thin, middle-aged man in a tattered jacket with a knocked-out front tooth and a swollen face. He waves the empty bottle around and recounts how he participated in exhibits ten years ago, says that his father died and his mother worked as an editor all her life, but in fact she's a poet, a real poet, straight up, let me read you a poem, my favorite, and at that moment, he pipes down, he can't remember it, and the young woman leans over and kisses him on the mouth. He reeks of sweat, urine, booze, rotten teeth, and unwashed clothes. She kisses him, then says: *I'll see you*, and walks away.

Moreukhov gets up, takes two steps forward, stops, and begins to vomit.

Sometimes he thinks that, if he vomits for a while, he can cleanse himself, can vomit his entire life.

Vomit his hope for fame, his desire to be famous, his faith in the word, Vera, Galya, Nadya, Lyuba, Sonya, port wine on the sewer hatch, canned beer, vodka drunk straight from the bottle.

Vomit the graying, thirty-year-old man with bad teeth, the twenty-five-year-old with bags under his eyes, the twenty-year-old with hope for the future, vomit the teenager squeezing his penis like a pistol handle (pull the trigger a few times and shoot out a milky stream), unborn children, unfulfilled love, vomit the boy without a foil, the crooked fetus, his father's seed and his mother's cell, the fusion and engulfment.

Vomit, forget, self-cleanse.

Moreukhov takes another step and falls to his knees in the slush.

Lord, he prays, hear me, Lord. Here I stand before You, I am all Yours, in this rotten Moscow snowbank, drunk, ill, and old. Give me strength, Lord, hear me, oh Lord, if You have placed me here on my knees, then Your will be done, and therefore, You can hear me here, in the din of the Moscow street, among the roar of car engines and the hubbub of human voices. Lord, I think I am dying right now, but I want You to know: I am grateful to You for the rustle of angel wings, for the frosty air, for the first swig, for the blue sky, for the black branches, for all the women I've had, for movies and music, for Dimon and Vitalik, for the life I've lived, and the death I await. Take me away from here, Lord, if You don't want to teach me how to live in this world! Fucking stop all this now!

Look at him on his knees in the snowbank, shaking, summoning death when he has no plans to die at all.

22.

BREAKFAST LATER

"I apologize," Masha said, "I don't have a present for you. I didn't know what to get. And it's so silly to buy it with your money."

They were lying face-to-face in bed, covered by a single blanket as usual. Masha curled into a ball and one emaciated hand squeezed Nikita's shoulder. Under the blanket, you could make out her nose, her eyes, and her disheveled hair.

"That's fine," Nikita said, "the most important thing is that you're with me."

"Listen," Masha said, "if you want, we can figure something out. We can stop by Mega or some other place, buy you a really nice button-down . . ."

"My love," Nikita said, "you're absolutely right. Why do I need another shirt—and, on top of that, on my own birthday? Let's think of something we can do without having to leave the house."

"Let's," Masha says. "I can make you breakfast if you want. Usually you make it for me, but it's my turn today."

"No," Nikita says, "let's have breakfast later. I want a blowjob."

Blowjobs were a very special family topic. When he was young, Nikita was completely indifferent to oral sex, but eight years ago, his Crimean romance with Masha almost started with a blowjob—practically on the first night. Nikita was very impressed. But a few years later, Masha suddenly didn't like oral sex and didn't want to put anything in her mouth besides food. "How come?" Nikita was offended, "You liked it just fine before, but not now that we're living together? If you'd never blown me, it would be different,, but you did, and I remember it perfectly. You were good at it too." Masha replied with an impervious *I stopped liking it*. After conversations such as this one, they would stay angry at each other for a while.

At present, Nikita thinks it's a great idea. After all, what's a blowjob? Not pleasure, of course—what pleasure? No, it's a way for a woman to tell a man she's ready to do something nice for him without expecting anything in return. For instance, an orgasm of her own or any pleasure in general. In that respect, a blowjob as a gift is a fantastic idea. It would make me happy and Masha would have something to give me. As a matter of fact, the only gifts spouses should give each other are sexual ones. Something no one would agree to more than once a year. This rule must be extended to coworkers and parents in some way, but he's not sure how.

Nikita is no longer happy he suggested this gift to Masha. He is lying on his back and a disheveled head is moving back and forth somewhere on his crotch. No pleasure whatsoever and, moreover, Masha is beginning to get tired and lose momentum, and it's still a long way to climax. Nikita closes his eyes, puts his hands on Masha's temples, helps her find the right pace and thrusts his hips, but it all comes to nothing.

Remember how you used to fuck in Crimea, he tries to motivate himself, shouldn't you have any memories left after eight years together that could help you cum? After all, when we met, Masha was completely different. Beautiful, young, energetic, up for anything—if I said let's go swimming; we went swimming, if we were off to climb a mountain, we climbed a mountain; and when it was time to fuck, we fucked. What a marvelous woman I had, what happened to her? I'm a good husband, after all. I've only cheated a few times, that's practically nothing. Two weeks ago, I dumped Dasha. When I felt that jolt in my heart standing at the yogurt shelf at the store, it wiped out any feelings I had for her. I called her myself, told her: *It would be better if we didn't see each other anymore*, and blocked her number. And I haven't called her since, so there!

But now that I think of it, it was so great to fuck her! He remembers how the sweat ran down her skin in rivulets, how it gathered on her stomach in a puddle, how the drops sparkled on her short hair . . . and then came a sound, deep, hollow, guttural, like that, yes, like that! and, at that moment, Nikita abruptly and unexpectedly cums, gripping Masha's hair. In his mouth, he feels the half forgotten silver taste of Dasha's kisses.

"Thank you," he says, and Masha jumps up and runs to the bathroom, vomiting on the threshold. Nikita says, "Listen, I'm sorry," while Masha doubles over with her spine protruding and a trickle coming out of her mouth. "I really do feel *embarrassed*," Nikita says, and then Masha straightens up and screams:

"What do you mean, *embarrassed*?"

After all, he's well aware that she hates putting various filth in her mouth, but he deliberately forced her to do it because he obviously doesn't want to fuck her like a normal woman, where she should be fucked, but she's not offended, no, who would want to fuck her if the woman can't even get pregnant, she's not a woman anymore, of course, not even a human being, the only thing that's left of her is her mouth, good thing it's not her ass, but it seems like that will be her gift to him for New Year's, *yes, dear, for New Year's, we'll have anal sex, did I guess right?* and Masha stands there holding on to the doorpost, crying and screaming:

"No, I get it, if a woman can't get pregnant, then who needs her cunt?"

Here we go, Nikita thinks. Why the fuck did I need this blowjob? It turns out Masha's still upset she couldn't get pregnant, I'll have to talk to her about it later, when she calms down. Somehow, I lost track of this.

Yes, I definitely made a scene on my birthday, you can say that again.

But Masha is no longer screaming, she settles down on the floor and begins to howl softly on a single note, and Nikita hears the howl rising up from her very depths, those same depths where the guttural sounds of Dasha's orgasm slumber. He runs up to Masha with just enough time to think: *Who lives in Dasha's body? Who lives in my wife's body?*—and at that moment, he finally lifts her up, carries her to the shower, turns on the warm water and begins to wash her tenderly; and when she stops crying, he leans over and kisses her on her lips, which are redolent of despair, sperm, and vomit.

23.

IT'S ENOUGH FOR US

Everyone knows that children shouldn't die before their parents. Vasiliy Mikhailovich Melnikov told himself that younger brothers shouldn't die before older ones.

When Sasha was a boy, I fought for him in our building's courtyard. When I married Sveta, he was my witness. When Nikita was born, he gave us a canvas tent so we could go backpacking as a family. *With the little one.*

When he died, I stood at the cemetery and snow fell into the black trough of the grave. We stood motionless in three groups: Nikita and I, Sasha's wife and his daughter, and Lyolya and my son.

Lyolya-Lyolya, she looked so much older that I hardly recognized her. How I loved her once! And her Sasha's so thin—is he ill? He doesn't seem to resemble me at all, I wouldn't have recognized him on the street. And I've only seen him a few times—I purposely went up to the school to get a look at him. Didn't get to see much—he was too far away. At the time, I thought that he resembled me, now I'm not so sure.

I always thought that I'd have time to fix everything. Call my younger son, make up with my younger brother. But the only time that remains is a handful of frozen earth on a coffin in the place of words of reconciliation, in the place of regrets.

Younger brothers shouldn't die before older ones.

When he was leaving for the army, I didn't come to see him off. When he married Tanya, I didn't go to their wedding. When Elya was born, I congratulated him over the phone.

Yes, nowadays, it's even hard to imagine what those years were like.

Tests, test sites, arguments until morning, samizdat, poems, songs, my dissertation, the Institute, Lyolya. The five of us—Nikita, Sveta, Sveta's parents and I—lived in a two-room apartment, the ten of us from our group argued in the kitchen, Lyolya and I wandered around the autumn city, calling our friends from payphones to see who could loan us an empty apartment and kissing in Neskuchny Garden.

We were busy all the time, no chance of being bored, so there was no time for Sasha. And, to tell the truth, it was awkward for me.

But I was truly happy for him when he married Tanya! If it weren't for my work trip, I would no doubt have been a witness at their wedding. And when Elya was born, you could say I had a lot of work, the more so because this was always true, but in fact, it was simply because Lyolya had come back from Crimea, all tan and beautiful . . . I didn't get anything done for a whole month. Afterward, I congratulated Sasha, of course. I even brought him some gift, don't remember what.

That's how it worked out: when his daughter was born, I was with my mistress, and when my mistress had a son, Sasha picked them up from the hospital.

After that, Tanya left him. Since then, the two of us haven't spoken.

And now, we'll never speak. Unless I join him *there*, after death. "He became religious back in the seventies," father told me. I was dumb, kept arguing, called religion obscurantism and defended science.

I dedicated my whole life to science—and what of it? Did it help me speak with my younger brother? Did it promise us another meeting and eternal life?

Scientists don't know how to speak with the dead, and they don't teach this in church either. Dad told me that he attended a spiritualistic séance once, when he was little. Saucer, round table, everyone holding hands, the most important thing was not to break the circle . . . it was like young pioneers around a bonfire. I think they summoned the spirit of Napoleon—but why? What can Napoleon tell me, what can I tell him?

But I would talk to Sasha.

Then again, why would I speak with the dead, I don't even know how to speak with the living.

At this very moment, Sveta and I are sitting in the kitchen—Nikita came over. The three of us are drinking tea and seem to be talking, but about all the wrong things—politics, the news. Ukraine, Yushchenko, Yanukovych, Timoshenko, Putin. Free speech, not like thirty years ago, when I used to cover my phone with a pillow in this very kitchen. The kitchen looks about the same, except we bought a microwave and Nikita recently gave us a new fridge.

Nikita is wealthy now, an entrepreneur and a businessman. I didn't defend my dissertation and really hoped that at least my son wouldn't drop the ball, but it looks like it's not meant to be. There are no dissertations in business, I know that.

Sveta says our boy has gotten old. Bags under his eyes, a double chin, probably works a lot. She doesn't understand why. The two of us live on three hundred dollars a month and it's enough for us, but Nikita and Masha spend enormous amounts of money. That's understandable, they're still young, go to restaurants, go on vacation, have a car—but still, they could live on a thousand a month, maybe three. One time, he said: "I made ten thousand last month." Sveta asked: "In rubles?" Ten thousand dollars, what would you do with that kind of money? And, above all, they don't save anything, they spend it all, fritter it all away.

To tell the truth, I'd like to have grandchildren. Masha will be turning forty soon and they still don't have kids. Sveta once asked: "Are you planning to?" and Nikita got angry and started yelling: *Mom, when we're ready, you'll be the first to know, don't ask me stupid questions, I beg you!*

And that's why we talk about politics, what can I do? Don't ask about children, don't talk about money. Maybe I should offer him some vodka? Then the conversation might flow better. Because we're sitting here as if we're not family.

How's everything? Good. And you? Us too. End of story. If we each drank fifty grams, maybe we'd start talking.

Or else it'll turn out like with Sasha: you'll want to talk and have no one to talk to.

Nikita is looking at his parents and thinking: why are we sitting here like strangers? Maybe I should tell them something? But they won't find it interesting. I could tell them that I got a new order, twenty-five aquariums to start, more if things go well. So what? Dad will say: *Great job, son!* Mom will think: *Why do you need so much money?* End of conversation. I'm proud of what I do! Dad didn't defend his dissertation and I built a successful business! That means I'm a good son and a worthy heir. Too bad I can't make them see that.

I can't talk about work, and what can I say about Masha? They'll start asking if we're thinking about having kids—well, we obsessed about it for two whole years. Went to doctors, went to clinics—lots of time, lots of money, and zero results. Masha doesn't bring it up anymore—thankfully,

I suppose. Though I never told them about it either—Masha asked me not to and it's a sensitive topic.

It turns out that all our topics are sensitive. I can't ask about Uncle Sasha either: how can brothers not speak to each other for thirty years? I better not ask about my brother either: if it weren't for Uncle Sasha, I would have been totally in the dark about him, Dad never even mentioned him to me. I asked mom once and she shrugged her shoulders and answered: "I've never met him and neither has Vasya."

And there you have it: you can't ask your parents about anything, can't tell them anything. I should have asked Uncle Sasha, but it's too late now.

So they sit in silence, each with his own questions, and maybe not, maybe they're telling jokes, discussing politics, watching the comedian Yevgeny Petrosyan, maybe they're even discussing Uncle Sasha, saying may he rest in peace, or the opposite, they don't think of him or me at all and could care less that, at the other end of Moscow, I'm lying beaten in the wet snow, crying with self-pity, asking over and over . . . Why do they all need so much money? Why does Nikita need so much money? What does he mean, "it's enough for us"? How much money is enough for me to live on? How much would be enough if I didn't drink? Does Nikita look like his father? Do I look like mine? And finally, who is my father—Vasiliy Mikhailovich or Uncle Sasha? And what happened to them all thirty something years ago?

24.

1971. ACCORDING TO
LONG-TERM FORECASTS

Only in my dreams does a plane ticket seem like the holy grail. The
South and West are not for me—they're for resort guests with scads of
money. My lands are the North and the East; not the cities, but the taiga,
tundra, and sea. Big cities are all the same. There's a central avenue with
Stalinist architecture and new neighborhoods like our Cheremushki. On
the buildings are slogans and appeals like *The Party's Plans are the People's
Plans, Glory to the Communist Party of the Soviet Union!* and *Store Your
Money at the Savings Bank.*

No, guys, I have to go to the North and the East—for work, not
travel. Two years after I left the army, I was always on some expedition or
other. This summer, I stayed in Moscow against my better judgment—
and now my heart is calling "Go North! Go North!" like the three sisters
cry "To Moscow! To Moscow!" in Chekhov's play.

There's nothing for me to do in Moscow. This city has become
deserted for me.

You'll ask: how is it deserted? Don't six million Soviet citizens—honest
drudges, workers, scientists, and students—live in this city? Of course,
it's has its flaws, its money-grubbers and opportunists, bureaucrats of
every stripe—but aren't there so many good people in our nation's capital?

So many. If I had more time, I'd make a list, fifty last names in
alphabetical order, but I'm not in the mood today and can't remember
everyone.

However, I remember in great detail how I brought Lyolya over to introduce her to Vasya. She was wearing a short skirt, her small round knees stuck out and her legs looked touching in her stilettos—everyone turned around to gape at her when we walked down the street. And Vasya—what about Vasya? Rumpled pants and a sweaty plaid shirt. What can you do? July, the heat . . .

Sveta was staying at the dacha with Nikita, and Vasya was leading a bachelor's life in his own, empty apartment. I called him up and said: "Listen, old man, can I come over with this chick? She writes poetry." He instantly caught my drift and said: "By all means, Sasha."

Really, how were Lyolya and I supposed to do it with my parents around?

Lyolya and I do what? There's no word for it. There's a dirty verb, a medical term, but no word for it. Love each other? From kindergarten, we're taught to love Mom, Dad, the Communist Party, the Soviet people, and the Motherland. Vasya was around when people were supposed to love Stalin more than anyone else.

So what Lyolya and I have isn't love.

How can you find a word for when she looks at you, flicks a blonde strand of hair off her forehead, and laughs softly, and you think: this is it, I'm a goner. It's like something explodes in my chest every time, I swear.

Vasya produced a reel-to-reel tape recorder, got out his reels and fiddled with them in the corner for a while; then, the voices of Vysotsky, Okudzhava, and Klyachkin began to sing and we began drinking vodka and having a really good time, Vasya made jokes, Lyolya laughed and I was delighted—after all, this was my older brother and the young woman I loved, possibly my future bride, possibly the mother of my future children, according to long-term forecasts!

It must have been the last time I was that happy.

We were drinking vodka and Lyolya drank with us and laughed, then Vasya put on a tape with music from that French film with Jean-Louis Trintignant and Anouk Aimée, and they started dancing right there in the kitchen, and I found it so beautiful and so cool that my brother was dancing with my girlfriend, and I drank more vodka, then we wandered around Moscow and got some more at a restaurant, Lyolya read us her poetry and I was really loving it. Then, back at Vasya's, it was like I was sucked into a whirlpool; I said: "Guys, I'll be right back" and passed out.

You have to understand: it's impossible to work in the North and not be able to hold your vodka. I've got many nights like this on my conscience—battle-seasoned men would get knocked off their feet, and I simply kept drinking. It was crazy. And this time, I really blew it. I don't even know how it happened.

We're taught not to believe in God or the devil, only in science and technology. Of course, that's the right thing to do. Unprecedented progress has been made in science and technology. That's fantastic. And while I haven't graduated from universities like Vasya, I can personally attest to this progress. But still, I think there's a higher power of some kind that helps people. Supports them. Scientists just haven't discovered it yet, but they will. Our ancestors called it having a guardian angel.

That evening, my guardian angel deserted me.

Because when I woke up the next morning, I was more nauseous than I'd ever been. I lay fully clothed on a folding bed in Vasya's kitchen, my head splitting; and it became abundantly clear that, instead of having a night of love, I'd gotten abominably drunk, and it'd be better if Lyolya didn't see me like this.

I got up with difficulty, drank some water from the faucet, opened the empty fridge, took my shirt off, went in the bathroom, washed and dried myself from the waist up, made happy noises, decided not to wake Vasya and went in the foyer. And when I bent down to tie my canvas sneakers, I saw Lyolya's shoes.

They lay in the corridor as if they, too, were on their way somewhere, but, like me, hadn't managed it and fell. They lay there defenselessly— the left one on the left, the right one on the right—two meters apart. The right one on the threshold to Vasya's room, by the half-open door.

Guys, I even thought: where would she sleep in there? That's how stupid I was, I can't put it otherwise—and then I went to the door and peeked in.

Lyolya looked very beautiful. Even in her sleep, with her makeup smudged. She was lying on her back with her left arm hanging off the bed and Vasya's head on her breast—that's how they had fallen asleep, they didn't even bother to cover themselves. Her right arm embraced his shoulders.

That's how it all ended.

Lyolya called me afterward, but I hung up on her. First, I wanted to punch Vasya in the face—he was older, but I was always the stronger one. I'd lifted weights in the army and was really jacked, unlike him, a physicist-lyricist. I even turned up at his Institute's front desk, asked the guard to call him and tell him to come down and waited. I straight up imagined he'd come downstairs and I'd catch him with a right hook and knock him out. Then I saw him running toward me in his rumpled trousers and sweaty plaid shirt, with a big grin across his face, and thought: what am I going to do? After all, this is my brother, we've been together our whole lives, what was I thinking when I said I wanted to punch him?

So I say to him: "How could you?"

And he replies: "Old man, it just kind of happened."

I say to him: "But you have Sveta, Vasya, what are you doing?"

And he replies: "You're being bourgeois, old man, and you know it."

And I tell him: "But I love her!"

And he replies: "But she loves me."

And all of a sudden, I grew quiet, as if he'd broken through my trademark right hook. I didn't even call him a liar because I realized it must be true. My Lyolya wasn't the type of girl to fall drunkenly into bed with a man.

My Lyolya.

As soon as I wrote "my Lyolya," my heart skipped a beat. Guys, I can't do this anymore, enough! I'll go to the North, I'll go to the East, I just can't! And meanwhile, my mother asks:

"Why haven't I seen your Lyolya in a while, Sashenka?" What am I supposed to say to her?

I say: "We broke up."

"Oh," Mom says, "that's too bad. She was such a nice girl."

And I became afraid for myself. I physically felt myself falling to pieces. My nerves were like the strings of a broken instrument, lying there separately. I waited for the other shoe to drop so I could start screaming, calling a kind adult for help. I don't have the strength anymore to get through this life. It's time to throw in the towel.

This must be the typical intellectual soul-searching and grandstanding. Instead of wandering the streets of Moscow, I should go home, turn on the television and watch the *KVN* improv comedy contest, *The Thirteen Chairs Tavern* and *The Blue Glow* variety shows, *Kinopanorama, On the Country's Fields* or *Sports* with my parents. All of it free, all of it in our living room, watch and relax.

Instead, I waited in line at the tobacco kiosk and bought a pack of *Primas*, waited in line at the newspaper stand and bought a copy of the *Komsomol Pravda*, then saw a young woman, practically a girl, walking back from the grocery store, carrying a heavy bag—it looked like she had first stopped by the produce store for potatoes, then gone to the grocery store for two cartons of milk. Lovely girl, not Russian, looked

Vietnamese—maybe she really was from Vietnam. These days, we get a lot of Vietnamese people coming here on vacation, for their studies, and to prepare themselves for continued combat with the American aggressor.

So I lit up my *Prima* like it was a *Gauloise* and said to her: "Young lady, can I help you with your bag?" And she smiled and replied to me without an accent: "Oh, thank you, of course."

So that's how they met, Mom and Dad. And ten months later, I came into the world.

25.

A FROG IN CHLORINATED WATER

Something swims out of the tenuous twilight, the alcoholic oblivion, some shapes, contours, silhouettes . . . A tiny kitchen, narrow, but neat. A plastic-covered table, a teapot on the stove, jars of seasonings, a fridge with rounded corners . . . Two young women sit across from each other holding teacups with wisps of steam rising from them.

One has an Asian face with broad cheekbones and narrow eyes . . . my guardian angel of late with a bottle of Tuborg? No, why did I think that, of course not. It's Anya, also known as Elvira, my half-sister.

This is her kitchen and her friend Vika is sitting across from her; Gosha is sleeping in the bedroom while the young women drink tea.

I try to picture Vika: tall, red-haired, big-breasted, with delicate fingers covered in silver rings. She's five, maybe ten years older than Anya—Anya never asked.

They met six months ago, also at the store, like she met Andrey. Vika was buying shoes and, a few days later, came by to thank her and offered to give her a ride to the Metro. It turned out that they were practically neighbors, so they picked up Gosha from daycare together and went up to Anya's place.

And what's most surprising is that they did all this while completely sober.

Later on, Anya would ask her: "Do you make friends with all the shop-girls?" and every time, Vika would give her a different but always cryptic reply: "I knew it would be the right thing to do," "It seemed like I had to do this," and even "Our meeting is part of some great and important story."

Obfuscation must be a professional skill. Because Vika's a sorceress, a practicing Wiccan. She even changed her name from Marina to Vika, the same way that Anya refused to be Elvira.

So they're sitting in the kitchen, drinking tea, and Anya is talking about her life, her talks with Zinka, going to the movies with Andrey, and coffee with Marik, and Vika says:

"I could never sleep with my boss to keep my job. For me, sex is a sacred act, I can't do it with just anyone."

"Sex is just sex," Anya answers. "Sometimes, it's nice, sometimes, not really. It's like drinking vodka. Depends on who you're with. But what can I do? I can't quit. And I doubt things would be better at a new job."

"You're very strong," Vika says pensively.

"Not at all," Anya replies, "I'm just a swimmer. I've been swimming back up to the surface my whole life."

"Women always swim back up to the surface," Vika says. "We women are related to the ocean."

"No," Anya shakes her head, "I'm not in an ocean, I'm in a dirty puddle. Best-case scenario—an uncleaned, chlorinated pool. You know, the kind that's so dirty that, every time you inhale, someone else's hair gets in your mouth. That seems to be the ocean I was given."

"You know the fairy tale about the frog that whipped milk into sour cream?"

Anya nods her head and Vika says:

"I think you're that kind of frog."

Anya wants to say that the milk she was given is too low-fat: she can't drown in it, but can't whip sour cream out of it either. It's not milk at all, just a dirty puddle with chlorinated water and other people's hair. Anya wants to tell Vika this, but instead she says: "More tea?" and Vika understands everything, takes the cup, sips from it, and tells her that, not too long ago, she went to a special seminar on the Moscow Metro.

"I thought you practiced mysticism," Anya marvels, "why do you need the Metro?"

"The Moscow Metro," Vika explains, "is a mystical thing. As a matter of fact, the Paris, London, and New York metros don't have circular lines. And the circle is the most ancient sacred symbol. Hence all the village round-dances, the round table at a spiritualistic séance, or young pioneers around a bonfire. It's no coincidence that the main taboo in all these practices is to break the circle."

"So what does the Metro have to do with it?"

"It's a loop line," Vika says. "Twelve stations, like the number of zodiac signs. The zodiac also moves in a circle—after Pisces, it's Aries again, and so on."

"But they're saying they're adding another station to the loop," Anya says. "Then what's going to happen to your zodiac?"

"It's a special sign, the Serpent Bearer," Vika replies. "Let me explain it to you."

She takes out a pen and a notepad from her purse (real leather, Anya doesn't even want to guess how much it costs) and draws some lines, symbols, and numbers.

"Too many numbers for me," Anya smiles.

She's just not that interested in hearing about the Metro, zodiac signs and astrology. She's friends with Vika, but thinks her job is bullshit.

Though you can earn a lot more money doing bullshit than standing at a cash register. But it seems that you need a calling for it.

"It's a male myth that women are bad with numbers," Vika replies. "Our lives are governed by numbers. Nine months of pregnancy, a twenty-eight-day menstrual cycle. Our lives are subject to numbers and pain. Menstrual cramps, pain during defloration, during childbirth."

"My life," Anya answers, "is subject to other numbers. Three hundred for the apartment. Two hundred fifty for food. Fifty to a hundred for everything else. That's the arithmetic. I don't recall any de-flo-ration pain. And my periods are relatively painless."

Anya's numbers will hardly impress Vika: she must make that much in a week, if not in three days. Anya knows that, at one time, in the nineties, Vika even ran her own company—a consulting business, she says. It all crashed in ninety-eight, and all she had left were her old connections. By all appearances, they've lasted Vika till present day.

Vika practiced magic: she received clients at home, predicted the future, and clarified the past.

She muddied the waters, read fortunes over coffee grounds, and collected money for it.

It must be a strange job to talk to strangers, find something interesting in all of them, and use that "interesting" as the basis for the blueprint of her predictions.

Finding people interesting isn't for Anya. She could handle the women, but men are all the same to her on the whole.

And Anya doesn't believe in magic and sorcery.

"Tell me," she says, "can you change the future rather than predict it?"

"It just so happens that predicting means changing," Vika answers. "The ancients said: 'forewarned is forearmed.'"

"Well, no," Anya shrugs her shoulders, "I often know what's going to happen ahead of time. When I quit my job at IKEA, I realized that I'd have to sleep with someone at work again, but I still quit, and now we have . . . Marik."

Now, every time she utters his name, it repulses her, as if she's picking up a slug.

"Maybe if you realized something else, there would be no Marik. He would still be Mark Borisovich, without any coffee and all the rest."

"I don't believe that," Anya shakes her head. "Tell me instead: can you make him disappear?"

"Why?" Vika says. "Someone else will appear in his place. You said it yourself, the men in your life are completely interchangeable. If there isn't a Marik, there'll be someone else in his place."

"Maybe he won't be as gross," Anya sighs. "You know I'm actually pretty easygoing about this. If you have to sleep with the boss, then you have to. You take out Marik and we'll see about the next one."

"Listen," Vika says seriously, "I don't like to meddle in my friends' business. I'm not very good at interfering for little things—magical influences always lead to big changes."

"Even I know which ones," Anya snorts, "they'll fire me."

"No, they won't fire you," Vika answers, "the story here is not about jobs, it's about men. Tell me: in your lineage, how many generations of girls grew up without a father?"

"Well, you know about me, as for my mom, she didn't know her father at all. All she has left of him is the patronymic "Olegovna," grandma practically never told us anything about him. And my great-grandpa . . . I think he died young, in the early nineteen-thirties. Why?"

"So I can understand," Vika answers.

She sits in silence and gazes thoughtfully at the steam drifting over the cooling tea. In the next room, Gosha is sighing noisily in his sleep, and Anya's heart clenches.

She's certain that she has the best son in the world. Two years ago, he even managed to remove the IKEA plug from the electrical outlet in thirty minutes. And he's the loudest in his daycare center: Anya can hear the familiar voice from the front steps.

In the end, she got lucky with her son.

"You know," Vika says suddenly, "it says so in books: a maid will beget a maid, the second will beget a third, and the boy born of the third will become a sorcerer when he comes of age. That's about your Gosha."

Anya nods and looks at Vika as if she's Gosha and just said something very silly.

"Vika," she says, smiling, "did you at least understand what you said? Any boy's mother was begotten by another mother, and that mother by a third. You're saying that all men are sorcerers. Before, you said that all women were witches."

Vika sighs:

"A maid is an unmarried woman."

"Well, my mother had a husband," Anya answers and, at that moment, the doorbell rings.

As it happens, it's thirty minutes to midnight, who could it be? They say it's the police, open up!

There you go, Anya thinks, once again, the old hag called the cops, what can I do? If they wake up Gosha, I'll kill the bitch!

She clicks the lock open and sees two young cops on the threshold with machine guns, wearing full combat gear.

"Can I help you?" Anya says.

"We received a complaint," says the scrawny, fair-haired one. "You're, like, making noise."

"And are we being loud?" Anya asks. "I suppose you can hear us from the street? Even hear us over that car alarm, right?"

"Miss," says the second one, attractive, broad-shouldered, and dark-haired. "We can't do anything about the car alarm. What are we going to do, tow the car? But we received a complaint about you and we have to respond. Please show us your papers for the apartment."

Of course, Anya doesn't have any papers, she never signed a lease with the landlady, but thankfully, she does have her Moscow registration.

"You can't do anything about the car alarm, but you can do something about me?" Anya is getting more and more wound up. "Well, we'll see about that! If you woke up my kid, that's it!"

Anya still hasn't had the chance to figure out what "it" means when Vika comes out smiling and says in her throaty voice:

"Hello, boys."

The cops immediately nod their heads and smile self-consciously.

"Now, boys, you go downstairs, ring the doorbell for apartment fifteen, and explain the legal consequences for a false alarm. After that, go back to your precinct and write up a report about ignoring further complaints from apartment fifteen. A mentally ill woman lives there, she does in fact hear noises, but these noises are not from here on earth. And one more thing," Vika nods to the dark-haired guy: "You should be a little more careful with your girlfriend, else you'll be rocking a baby in a year or so."

"How do you know?" the cop asks confusedly.

Vika smiles:

"What's the difference—I just know."

When the cops' footsteps fade away, Anya sits down on the floor right there, in the entrance hall, and begins to laugh:

"Wow, look at you! And you gave it to him straight about the girlfriend! Now he'll wear two condoms. What if he didn't have a girlfriend? What then?"

"Well," Vika answers, "how could he not have one when he does? Seriously, don't make me laugh."

The women return to the kitchen. Gosha is still snuffling in his little bed.

"Fuck Marik," Anya says. "You should get rid of this old hag for me."

"You know," Vika laughs in response, "I think you're quite capable of doing it yourself. You just have to really want it."

"I can only shoot her down," Anya answers, "too bad I have nothing to shoot her with. Or else: bang bang!—and no more old witch."

"She's not an old witch," Vika takes offense. "An ordinary schizophrenic, nothing special."

"Of course she's not a witch," Anya sneers, "to be born a witch, a man needs to beget a man, the second man needs to beget a third, and then, it's the girl who was begotten by the third!" Anya raises her index finger tellingly.

"It's all a joke to you," Vika smiles. "That's not actually how you become a witch. There are a few ways. First, you can be born into the right family, a family of sorcerers."

"The ones begotten by three maids?"

"That's not important. But it's not enough to be born. A sorcerer must pass on his power to you before he dies."

"What if he doesn't want to?"

"A sorcerer wants to give away his power," Vika says. "If he doesn't part with it before his death, he suffers terribly. And if his children don't accept his power, they'll be cursed. Both they and their children, until this power enters someone else again."

"If I believed in all this," Anya says, "I would be worried for Gosha's children. And what's the other way?"

"The other way is traditional. Initiation. Terrible trials. Internal enlightenment."

"Oh," Anya laughs, "then I'm ready. I've had enough terrible trials in my life. You try standing for two winters at the outdoor clothing market."

Vika laughs. A gold pendant bounces on her chest: a sun inside a zodiac circle that is redder than Vika's hair.

26.

THE FOGGED-UP GLASS OF THE TOYOTA

Nikita often asks himself: why do people like fish? Must be because they're silent. Always silent. They keep secrets. They're more trustworthy than Midas's reeds. More trustworthy than the pit—a tree hollow? a hole in the wall?—into which Tony Leung whispers his secrets at the end of *In the Mood for Love*. You can trust fish with any secret.

An invaluable quality in business, I believe. Well, as far as I can judge, of course. Mind you, I'm no business expert.

But right now, I'm picturing Nikita in a dim room. It must be a part of his office. Shouldn't there be a place in his office for storing aquariums with fish? Either the clients haven't picked them up or a decoration isn't ready or they're work samples . . . Anyway, I don't know why he would need fish in the office, but there he is standing among the aquariums, talking to the fish. Quite literally like St. Francis. But birds can chirp, whereas fish are, thankfully, mute.

They simply wiggle their fins and open their mouths. The bubbles rise up and make a rustling sound. Very soft. Nikita, too, is speaking very softly, with his forehead pressed against a tank of guppies.

They're very simple little fish, easy to keep, multicolored. Very popular with aquarists who are just starting out.

"How could this happen, huh?" Nikita asks his fish.

I deliberately chose a crowded place, the affordable Asia Café with a red-and-white yin and yang symbol on the awning, waitresses in kimonos, and as many people as fish in a teeming aquarium. With some effort we found an empty table, sat down, and asked for the menu. Dasha sat down and clammed up. I thought she'd immediately start asking me where I'd vanished, why I didn't pick up the phone, and what happened—but she said "Hello" and fell silent. She sat there leafing through the menu and looking around. I also stayed silent and stared at her.

In my childhood, I used to love sitting in front of an aquarium like this. Guppies were my first fish. Easy to keep, multicolored. They swam to-and-fro in schools, like gaggles of girls in spring dresses. In any case, I wasn't thinking about girls back then. I thought I had a living kaleidoscope in my aquarium. I really liked it.

The girls in Asia Café also travel in schools. In colorful spring dresses. After all, it's the first spring day—if you look out the window, you can see yellow and orange spots on the pavement. And the girls arrive in groups of three or four, sit down at the tables, and talk about all sorts of things in hushed voices. I think that Dasha would probably rather be here with her girlfriends than a balding man she barely knows, who either vanishes for a month or calls her out of the blue wanting to meet up right away. Because he has a very important and time-sensitive question for her.

Dasha is wearing a white tank top with spaghetti straps and a long, colorful skirt. She hasn't shaved her head in a while: her hair sticks out like the spines of a sea urchin.

Sea urchins are cultivated in saltwater aquariums. Some species are predators, which is why you should avoid placing unknown sea urchins in an aquarium with sea anemones and corals. Sea urchins live in large groups and reproduce through broadcast spawning. The eggs and sperm are mixed in the water and the fertilized eggs are spread across great distances in thin layers of plankton, where they turn into larvae.

Dasha orders sushi and kaisō sarada, a Japanese seaweed salad.

"They say that the Japanese have low-calorie food," she says, "and I'm trying to lose weight right now. I gain weight every winter and then try to lose it in the spring. To look better in the summer."

She smiles at Nikita and he also orders a kaisō sarada, although he's not planning to lose weight at all.

Not all kinds of seaweed are edible to fish. An experienced aquarist can select a seaweed that will grow in harmony with all the other inhabitants of the aquarium.

Nikita can't identify what kind of seaweed the kaisō sarada is made from.

"And how are things with you?" Dasha asks.

She looks at Nikita with a slight curiosity, as if they've just met, or, the opposite, are seeing each other after many long years apart and are having trouble remembering each other.

"Things are going fine," Nikita answers. "My business is growing, more clients than I can handle. In general, while oil prices are higher than fifty dollars a barrel, everyone will be fine."

"Great," Dasha answers, "I just got fired three weeks ago. They said that I'm late a lot."

"So what are you going to do now?"

She shrugs her fleshy shoulders:

"I don't know. I'll find another job. Or live like this."

"What about money?" Nikita asks.

"What about money?" Dasha answers. "The world is not without kind people. You just need to change your consciousness so the money finds its way to you, and then you won't have to work. I believe that we're all fabulous enough to live for ourselves rather than our jobs. I mean, for the sake of our own spiritual development. Like Buddhist monks."

Among the numerous species of goldfish, there are a few bright-orange varieties that bring to mind the robes of Buddhist monks. Like Buddhism, goldfish came to us from the East: they're all varieties of Asian carp.

At his office, Nikita watches the goldfish dance in the aquarium and thinks that Dasha should always shave her head and not only in support of the National Bolshevik Party.

"At one time, I didn't work for a whole year," Dasha continues, "I rented an apartment with Lerka. Well, Lerka rented the apartment and I just lived there so she wouldn't get bored by herself. Lerka has rich parents, they rented a whole palace for her."

"So why'd you move out?"

"We got into a fight. Well, Lerka got into a fight with me. Because of a guy. Although the fuck did I need that Stas . . ." Dasha grows pensive, "or was it Valera? I can't even remember his name. And he fucked badly."

Many fish species are known for being polygamous, and this is not only characteristic of males, but also of females. For instance, female representatives of many Malawian fish species will spawn a few eggs with one male, wait for him to fertilize them, then, collect the eggs in their mouths and continue the breeding process with another male. In turn, the males are constantly fertilizing the eggs of all the females that appear in their territory. Unlike monogamous fish, the males and females of polygamous species have varied coloring, and this variety increases during the mating season.

Is nature trying to tell us that polygamy is more aesthetically pleasing than monogamy?

"Jealousy is just another attachment," Dasha concludes. "A truly wise person will not be jealous."

If you place two male fish from the genus *Ancistrus* in a small aquarium together, they will fight and one of them may die from the trauma, malnourishment, and constant stress. This is why you should place the *Ancistrus* in a spacious aquarium with multiple hideouts—ceramic pipes, flowerpot halves and so on. Each male will occupy the hideout that most appeals to it, leaving it only to eat, and returning quickly in case of danger or if a rival appears. They're very fond of various wooden snags, which they polish to brilliance over time.

Nikita pictures this Stas or Valera . . . probably the same age as Dasha . . . young, attractive and strong like her. Or maybe the opposite: ludicrous, stupid, with juvenile acne? Nikita wonders if Dasha came the same way as she did with him. How was it with other men? Should he ask? Since Nikita isn't planning to sleep with her anymore, they're going to be just friends. Although what sort of friendship could there be with such a big age difference?

"What do you mean, 'was it the same as with me?'" Dasha marvels. "It's different with everyone, obviously. What's the point of fucking different people if it's always going to be the same? I even say a different word every time—I've never repeated myself, I would have noticed."

The waitress comes back with the sushi and salad. She has a flat Asian face and is dressed as a Japanese woman, though in reality she's either Buryat, Kazakh, or even Tatar. Many fish disguise themselves as stronger and more powerful species. The difference is that, with people, you never know who will come out on top in, say, five hundred years. Could the Mongols from the era of Genghis Khan have imagined that the savage eastern islanders would conquer the world with the aid of rice, fish, and consumer electronics—much more effectively than they themselves did with horses and archery?

They bring the check. Nikita pays and Dasha smiles and says:

"Thank you for the marvelous dinner."

They walk to the exit. If we're friends, Nikita thinks, would it be awkward if I offered to loan her some money? If she's broke at the moment?

They come out to the street. Dasha is shivering—while they were having dinner, the temperature dropped drastically. Her breath comes out in clouds.

"Do you have your car with you?" she asks, turning to him.

Nikita nods.

"Can you give me a lift to Sadovaya Street? I'll catch a cab from there."

Some fish travel by latching on to representatives of their own or another species. The best known are suckerfish, which are capable of traveling great distances by attaching themselves to large fish by means of their front dorsal fin.

An hour ago, there were no open parking spots on the street and Nikita parked in a neighboring courtyard. Now his Toyota is shoehorned between two snow-covered Zhiguli, its anthracite sides glistening as if it were a velvety-black molly among colorless guppies. Dasha squeezes into the passenger side with difficulty. When she sits down, she furrows her brows (a small ring in her left one) and begins to rub her stained tank top.

"Do you have any water?" she asks and Nikita hands her a bottle of mineral water. Dasha takes a big gulp and spits some out on her chest. Nikita remembers: that's what his mother used to do when she ironed, prior to the arrival of steam irons with spray nozzles.

Dasha assiduously rubs her tank top and, eventually, Nikita can't take it anymore:

"Let me help you with that."

And that's how it happened, yes.

Fish from the genus *Poecilia* are peaceable and active. The female is usually bigger than the male. It's preferable to put a cover on an aquarium containing *Poecilia* because the females can easily leap out of the water.

What leaps out of Dasha? An underwater monster? A deepwater fish? Another woman, who lives in the watery abyss like a mermaid or an undine?

Dasha traces her finger along the fogged-up glass of the Toyota. Nikita thinks: for the first time in my life, I am inside an aquarium and not outside one. And we're like two fish in here.

"What is that?" he asks.

"Yin and yang," Dasha answers, "the masculine and the feminine. Like you and I right now. I understood it the second you invited me to Asia Café."

An hour l ater, Nikita is standing before an aquarium at his office. So what happened, huh? he asks.

The fish are silent. They're always silent, that's why they're fish. But

I can picture the Macropodus, also known as the paradise fish, leap out of the aquarium and say:

"What happened? Nothing special. It's just that, in your ninth year of marriage, you got yourself a young lover. It happens. Homo sapiens males are not known to be monogamous."

"But I love Masha," Nikita says. "Forget monogamy, what about love?"

The paradise fish splashes around and goes back underwater, this time without saying a word, the way it's supposed to.

27.

HOW CAN YOU NOT BELIEVE IN LOVE?

It's known as a flashback. My drug addict friends explained it to me: if you take LSD or whatever, after some time, the memories of the trip can return out of nowhere and seem more real than reality. This had never happened to Moreukhov before with alcohol, but this morning, he suddenly and distinctly remembered.

It's raining. Moreukhov is standing with two young women, taking cover under the same umbrella, passing a bottle to each other. This is all accompanied by the sound of raindrops bouncing off the taut fabric. Judging by the clarity and vividness of this sound, it's the third or fourth day of Moreukhov's bender.

Moreukhov doesn't know the young women's names. The taller one is wearing a khaki men's jacket and a short skirt, and has a chemical perm. The second one barely comes up to Moreukhov's shoulder and her little coat is unfastened—probably to emphasize her boobs. Chubby women often have big breasts—I almost said teats, although of course it's vulgar to say that, but it's not for nothing that the chubby one has a kind of calvish gaze, not to say a heifer's. She has these big, vacant eyes that are, moreover, made up with cheap mascara already running down her cheeks. Yeah, you can't cover three people with one umbrella.

And Moreukhov hands them the umbrella: "Hold it, girls," jumps out in the rain, throws his head back, and takes two big, hearty swigs from the bottle. All of a sudden, it dawns on him: *What am I doing here?* In any case, maybe there was no *what am I doing here* at the time, just a false memory, an aberration; never trust flashbacks. Maybe, at the time, Moreukhov was standing under the rain with his face turned toward the gloomy skies, shaking himself off like a dog that had just come out of the water, standing there and not thinking about anything in particular, in his sodden jacket and tattered sneakers, with cold raindrops on his unshaven cheeks . . . and at that moment, the chubby one asked: *What about love? Do you believe in love?* and Moreukhov tore himself away from the bottle and said:

"Yes, of course. How can you not? Love exists, it gives meaning to our lives, without it, we'd be no one and nothing. It's always at first sight, even if you don't know it at first sight."

So Moreukhov's talking, the two girlies are listening—huddled together under the dome of the umbrella, passing the bottle to each other—and he notices that they look alike: wet hair, overly bright lipstick, overly flushed faces, overly hoarse voices. Actually, their voices may be just right, who knows how long they've been drinking and if it's their first, second, or fifth bottle? Who knows if they've met here, just now, by the store, both already drunk, or if one had gone over to the other's place, say, for her birthday, for a modest girls' gathering of two, to drink tea, talk about love, and watch some movie, and drink wine—and then they found another one . . . What do you mean, *found?* Where was it before? Well, that's not important, so one more bottle and then they ran out to the kiosk for a third and finished that one on their way back, before they even got to the building entrance, at which point Moreukhov showed up: *Hey girls, are you drinking wine? Maybe we should drink vodka?* And what do you know, there's just enough money for vodka, so the girls are standing, practically hugging under the same umbrella, listening to a drunk stranger talk about love at first sight—and there you have it, they had a nice conversation as originally planned.

"And what about infidelity?" asks the taller one. "What do you think, is it possible to cheat on someone you love?" Moreukhov extends his hand for the bottle, takes a swig, then another, wipes his wet forehead, and answers:

"No, absolutely not, if you love someone, you can't cheat on them. Even if you're fucking someone else, it's impossible to cheat. Because the thing about love is, either it's there or it's not. And as long as it's there, infidelity is impossible. But when it's not there, how could it be infidelity?"

And that's likely when Moreukhov thinks: *What am I doing here?* And at that moment, he remembers Dubosarsky's performance-art piece of about five years ago.

This was the story, in a nutshell: Soros or some other charitable fund decided to bring Moscow artists to the Russian countryside. They put them on a steamship and sent them down the Volga. The artists stopped in every town and performed before the public. At the time, Moreukhov was still invited to such things, but no longer made it to them because, just before the exhibit opening, or, in this case, before boarding the boat, he happened to go on a bender. So he never sailed down the Volga, but someone told him about Dubosarsky's performance-art piece in one of the towns.

There was a monument of two soldiers' heads. Dubosarsky draped the pedestals with some orange rags and, in the middle, built a platform with a hole in it. He stuck his head inside to make it look like there were three heads. And all the residents could come up and ask him questions. And they did come up and formed a long line. Furthermore Dubosarsky gave his replies in all seriousness, without derision, which was unexpected for that kind of artist.

So, today, Moreukhov's also functioning as a talking head. All he's missing is an orange Buddhist vestment, and to be honest, the audience is a bit of a letdown: two half drunk skanks, the shorter one's face scrunched up with anguish as if she's about vomit, and the thinner one still gazing at Moreukhov with enchantment, asking: "You're a man, tell us, what do men need from women?" Moreukhov's mouth is opening to tell her candidly, like Dubosarsky, that all of us need love when, suddenly, he is repulsed. Seriously, he thinks, why am I showing off like some kind of contemporary artist? Why am I spewing high-minded words for show under the influence of two thousand grams on an empty stomach? Do I not care at all who I preach to, who I bullshit? Two sluts, young alcoholics, red-lipped harlots? Eternal love? What am I babbling about, even if I believe in all this, still, what is this drivel? Who am I telling this to, yeah, right, St. Francis, everything for sale, landscape after battle, ashes and diamonds, a disgrace and a shame. At least watch who your drinking buddies are! Go ahead and talk to them about art, about Wong-fucking-Kar-wai, ask them some question, ask them: *What am I doing here?* Have yourself a nice talk while they finish your vodka!

He snatches the bottle from the curly-haired one, takes one last, hasty swig from it, and throws it against the asphalt; the glass shatters, his arms are contorted by spasms and he opens his mouth to scream: "We need your pussy, whores, what did you think? Eternal love? Bitch, hike up your skirt and show me your hole, and you, fatass, get on your knees, open your little mouth, and suck me off," and Moreukhov is already unzipping his pants when the shorter one leans forward as if she really is planning to get on her knees, but abruptly staggers and vomits right into the gutter. The water instantly carries away the remains of her undigested lunch like the debris of a shipwreck.

Well, I got my blowjob, Moreukhov thinks as he swings and aims his fist at her face, hitting her in the ear and yelling: *Happy birthday, bitch!*

28.

1975. MOSCOW RAINBOW

A dusty evening, a Moscow summer, 1971. The hospital courtyard and two figures: right away, we see an enormous belly like a balloon, hidden under her dress like a flower bud, like . . . no, not like this. Let's try it another way:

THE ENDLESS EVENING OF A DUSTY
MOSCOW SUMMER WAS FADING

when Alexander Mikhailovich Melnikov carefully led a silvery angel with a large belly across a wide hospital courtyard. My little girl, he thought, holding Lyolya Borisova by her pointy elbow, my little angel, I knew I'd take you to the maternity clinic, pregnant, flushed, wilted, but still just as splendid, swollen breasts, veins protruding on your legs, a blonde ponytail, a shaved crevice between your legs, a burrow I won't ever climb into again.

Lyolya walked slowly and carefully, focused on the kicking inside of her, oblivious to the deepening blueness and the last glint of sunset lighting up a distant corner of Moscow sky. As she walked, she wanted fluttering poetic verses to form in her head, but as luck would have it, none came to her.

For a heroine *of a novel about the late sixties–early seventies*, Lyolya was atypical. Of course, she was bohemian, wrote poetry and so forth, but she didn't cry when the tanks entered Prague, didn't sleep with all the great Moscow jazz musicians, sculptors, doctors, and writers, and no one could have suspected her of being an informant because she had no one to inform on and no motive to. That's why, to be true to the era, we'll place her in the same maternity ward as Milka Plescheyeva, Lenka Belousova, Anka Borschaminer, and any other beauties of the late sixties generation, who, we imagine, suddenly all decided it was time to produce offspring, time to bless their lecherous men—their little goats skipping from bed to bed—with progeny, it was time, my friend, it was time. Oh, the beauties of an ending era, the little prostitutes, the little students, the little informants!

And as we sigh in search of a genre, Alexander Mikhailovich Melnikov gazes at the lit-up window of the maternity clinic and, also sighing, walks away into the thickening dusk.

Night was falling, night was falling . . .

NIGHT WAS FALLING

on the Moscow courtyard, on the dusty trunks of linden trees, falling to the sounds of domino players' cries at the table, to the sounds of the television blaring from the open window, falling on Tanya Melnikova, who carefully opened the squeaky entrance door. The car crawled out of the alleyway, hissing inaudibly. A step, then another one. Ring the doorbell and the monumental figure of Djamilya Takhtagonova appears on the threshold.

"My little daughter," she says.

Tanya Melnikova falls on her mother's breast with a tear-stained face and, right away, three-year-old Elvira also begins to cry, not understanding where they've arrived so late, why her mother's hauling a heavy suitcase and pulling her by the hand, and why she is, at present, sobbing on her grandmother's breast.

Retired Lieutenant-Colonel of the Ministry of Government Security Vasiliy Shantsov is riveted to his peephole. Yes, of course, how could we do without the KGB bastards, the old butchers? So we didn't. Doesn't matter if there's no reason for him to be here, plot-wise, there he is, standing by the peephole and mumbling: "Ah, so your husband left you. Shouldn't have gotten so high-and-mighty. 'My mother's a war hero, a sniper.' We know these snipers, the Tatars, the Chechens, they're all the same. Let's make sure she wasn't from Crimea, let's see who the old hag was shooting at."

And the young Tatar girl is very pretty, Shantsov thinks. Look at her shoulders shudder. Sends the blood rushing straight to my big vein.

IT HAD ALL BECOME INTOLERABLE

To stand in silence for a few minutes. To preserve at least a shred of human dignity. Not glance at the brief note on the table, the emptied shelves in the closet. I picked up the receiver and dialed my mother-in-law's number.

"Hello," Tanya answered in a congested voice.

"Tanya, it's me."

She dropped the receiver. In the empty apartment, the dial echoed like an ambulance siren.

I went to my parents' bedroom—my father and mother were in Sochi—rummaged in the cupboard, and took out a bottle of Stolichnaya. I found myself scrutinizing the label, looking at the familiar Central Russian landscape, the heart of Russia, the essence of aqua vitae, looked inside, then shook it, took a swig, and instantly felt my youth returning, objects coming to life, the anticipation of love, and wild, rhythmic dreams,

MYSTERIOUS LIKE JUVENILE MASTURBATION

Tatyana, Tanechka, my little Tatar,
the screeching of a tram
in the clicking of heels
weak flares over wires
where I was thrown out with a parachute
into the European night, my love for you
I remember you'd lift up your blouse
lower your stocking, bare your leg
this is how I prepared my escape
to the place where I'd driven my cattle
night after night, here, on the folding bed
and what happened earlier would recede
I'd forget about Lyolya and Vasya
and remember only Elya and you

Where are you, my kindred, my distant and tender, tenebrous, boundless, eyes sleepless and slanted, itty-bitty titties, nipples like kernels

wait, wait, stop: you just buried this man, he may not have been a very good father to you, but don't make him sound like an idiot and a hack. Drop your inept stylizations and shitty plagiarism, your inappropriate parody. It's shameful to write this way about the dead.

Let's make things simple:

Where are you, my kindred, my distant and tender?
Tanya, Tanechka, why did you leave me?

Fuck poetry. Drop the attempt to picture the distant 1975 and realize that people don't change, that the tears are still wet, the vodka still bitter, and the love—boundless. Forget everything your mom said to you, try to see your father weeping in an empty apartment, remembering that summer day, the banal "Young lady, can I help you with your bag?" The slanted eyes, the Tatar cheekbones, the first night of love, Mendelssohn's March, your first scream when he returned from an expedition and Tanya—your mom—was waiting by the window, how he hugged her and felt her small breasts under her housecoat and, eventually, all thoughts of Lyolya and his traitor brother receded, how was it possible that he himself didn't realize that this woman was his wife and he loved only her? This girl was his daughter, he was responsible for her.

Why, Sasha Melnikov asks himself, why did I go with Lyolya to the maternity clinic, if I'd known, I would have never, not in a million years, even if I'd loved her at one point, so what if Vasya abandoned her when she was pregnant, so what, so what.

Tanya, Tanechka, why did you leave me?

WITH THAT BITCH,

Mom, he went to the maternity clinic with that bitch, that skank, that lowlife, his brother's lay, his ex-girlfriend, the blonde whore, fucking Brigitte Bardot. The whole nine months, he went to her place, Mom, and I don't care if he didn't fuck her, I would have preferred it if he did when it came down to it, because this saintly Tolstoyevsky humanism bullshit, these intelligentsia tears, this lovey-dovey stuff, Mom, and when she called him, ow, I'm having contractions, and he rushed over to the other end of town in the middle of the night, I packed up my things, Mom, and here I am, and I'm not going back.

. . . and out the window lies the Moscow night, which once beckoned to us with adventures, escapades, restaurant lights, and Tverskaya Street, headlights, muffled moans, his tongue in my mouth, his fingers between my legs . . .

My grandmother Djamilya is already asleep, I—a scared three-year-old—am asleep, and only my mom, a twenty-one-year-old, still a young girl, lies on the folding bed in the kitchen and, over and over, slides three fingers inside herself, biting her lower lip, closing her eyes, picturing my dad and promising *it's the last time, I'll never think about him again*, and when her body contorts with tremors, she can't contain herself and screams.

At that moment, I wake up and start crying and my mother comes to me with tears in her eyes.

29.

A SINGULAR HOWL

As always, he found it impossible to remember those first few days after he emerged from a bender. Afterward, through a thick layer of water, he would glimpse some people in white lab coats, a glint of sun on the IV, a dead television screen and Dimon's anxious expression. Moreukhov wrinkled his face in anguish, squeezed his eyelids shut, and tried to figure out how many days he had been unconscious this time.

They were already in the month of March—holy shit! He made it through another winter.

He was always afraid of dying in winter.

For some reason, he always remembered that his mother's sister, Polina, died in the blockade of Leningrad when she was a little girl. They never spoke about it at home and Moreukhov learned about it by accident when he was around ten.

So he's glad that winter is over. He is lying under the IV with his eyes shut, picturing his brother Nikita coming home.

There he is, strolling from the garage down a springtime street, walking into the building, going up in the elevator. A lucky day, a good contract, stopped by Dasha's, *had an office meeting*—what else is it that businessmen do at the office? Oh yeah, made a bit of money. Five thousand greenbacks. A little "something."

So Nikita comes home and thinks: *And now I'm going tell Masha how amazing I'm doing*, but Masha isn't home, she's not even in her favorite armchair. Successful, strong men don't know how to return to an empty apartment. They need an audience for their strength. For a weak person like me, it's enough to have a sky overhead. I emerge from my place in full view of everyone. That's why I live alone, and Nikita's not used to being alone, he's out of his comfort zone.

He takes off his clothes, sniffs his sweaty armpits—businessmen sweat too, right?—and heads to the bathroom. He's probably ashamed of his own body and dislikes the smell of sweat. Whereas for me, this is normal and I like the smell of sweat, I like the way my apartment smells: a mixture of beer gone sour, an unwashed male body, rotten food, accumulating trash, and dried semen on the bottom of the bathtub. The scent of life. This is why I don't like to bathe.

In fact, Nikita doesn't like to bathe either. He's still as irritated by the sensation of water on his skin as when he was a child. But of course, he can't permit himself not to wash and so, goes into the bathroom, where a miracle happens. He doesn't turn on the shower, and instead sits down on the floor. Just the way he is, naked, on the tiled floor—right on the expensive Spanish tile with his bare, ordinary ass overgrown with fair, bristly hairs. He sits down and sits there, then starts to sway back and forth, covering his face with his hands, not knowing what hit him.

But I know. It's the moment of truth. He is finally alone—without his business, his office, his wife, his lover, or his clothes. At present, nothing can protect him from his fear.

What is he afraid of? A tax audit? Sudden illness? Falling oil prices? Inevitable death? Water in the bathtub? He doesn't know, he's even afraid to ask himself this question and so begins to howl. A forty-year-old, naked man clutching his head with his hands and howling in an empty apartment—not like a wolf at the moon or an animal caught in a snare or a woman who's lost her child, no, in a completely different way.

This is a singular howl that God has invented specifically for successful men who have come face to face with their fears.

And if I appeared miraculously at his side, I would have hugged him and said: *We're brothers, you and I are the same. Let's howl together!* I would have howled with him, my fear and his fear. We would have sat together and spoken without words.

It's too bad that there are no miracles, and if I were to suddenly appear I would only see a self-confident, strong, and successful man.

A man who's so afraid of his own fear that he can neither cry nor howl.

"To be honest, I'm still a bit afraid," Nikita says. "You know, that Masha will find out."

"You have a smart broad," Kostya answers. "Even if she does find out, she'll pretend that she didn't. Like Ksenia. You think she didn't suspect about Natasha, Katya, or Sonia? She probably did. But she kept quiet. Seriously, you can't get divorced over little things like that. A man has a few lays on the side—that's well and good. Instead, tell me about your Dasha, after all, it's the first time that you genuinely broke your fast, I'm curious, how did she get you?"

Nikita is poking with his chopsticks at unfathomable Japanese food on a square plate. This is no Asia Café. Half the names on the menu are completely incomprehensible. Kostya says it's Japanese fusion.

"Well, I don't even know," Nikita beats around the bush, "must be because she's young. Beautiful. Fucks well. What did you expect to hear?"

"Some details," Kostya gets animated, "what kind of tits does she have? Does she have legs growing out of her ears . . . or does she do something crazy in bed that we've never seen before? I had a gymnast once, she could do a split with a dick inside her!"

"And what did it feel like?"

"Well, nothing special," Kostya admits, "but it's cool to look at. You know I like them with long legs."

Nikita tries to remember Kostya's lovers. Yes, they were all invariably model types—tall, long-legged, with small breasts and painted doll faces.

"You won't like Dasha," he says with conviction.

"Old man," Kostya exclaims, pouring sake into their glasses, "you know me! To me, a friend's wife is a holy cow! Meaning, a heifer! Even if she's not the wife, but the mistress."

"What mistress?" Nikita answers, "we just fuck sometimes, that's all."

"Do you give her money?"

"No, of course not, what's wrong with you?" Nikita marvels. "What do you think she is, a prostitute?"

"I think that she's a twenty-year-old woman sleeping with an old goat. And if you enjoy sleeping with her, you should try to compensate for the age gap in some way."

"She doesn't need anything," Nikita objects uncertainly.

"What do you mean—doesn't need?" Kostya replies. "Where does she live? Alone? With her mother? In Vykhino? I'll be damned if she doesn't need anything! You're such a swine! You'll have to rent an apartment for her in any event, not downtown, of course, but still, somewhere where normal people live. I always rent my girls a place close to the office—it's convenient and not too expensive. If you get stuck in traffic, your wife can never tell if you're on your way to the office or to fuck."

Nikita pushes an emptied plate away with a sigh. Immediately, a waiter comes out of nowhere, the plate vanishes, and a new jug of sake appears in its place.

"Do you give her gifts? Do you take her shopping?" Kostya continues. "Honestly, you're scaring me. Say all you want that I'm paranoid, but if a young woman sleeps with guys like us, doesn't take money, doesn't get gifts and lives with her mother like a minor, something is off! Either she wants to break up you and Masha and have you marry her, or worse."

"What do you mean?" Nikita is confused.

"What do I mean, what do I mean. Worse means that she wants to take away your business. Take all your money. Or set you up and take someone else's money. Do you know how many cases of this there've been? Especially with the young, beautiful, and selfless ones!"

"Well, you can't really take away my business," Nikita shrugs his shoulders.

"Yeah, yeah," Kostya scoffs, "That's what Khodorkovsky thought. And where's his business now?"

"My business is like that Elusive Joe from the joke," Nikita replies, "nobody needs it. Why would important people want to bother with aquariums for fifteen thousand a month?"

"Stop it with the fifteen," Kostya says, "you can make a good twenty, if not twenty-five. Anyway, they could be gunning for me instead of you."

"You think?" this rattles Nikita. For the last three years, all his financial payments have been made through Kostya's companies. So it may be worth investigating where Nikita's cash comes from . . . "Could they be gunning for you?"

"Of course," Kostya smiles. "My profits definitely exceed fifteen thousand. And I have to work with all kinds of people."

"With criminals?" Nikita asks.

"There are no criminals, old man," Kostya says condescendingly. "They all switched over to government payroll a long time ago. Do you know how many security agencies we have? And who do you think works there?"

You can never tell if he's joking or being serious.

Four jugs of sake later, Nikita finally ventures:

"Listen, old man," he says, "I want to ask you to do this one thing. Come to the bathroom with me."

Kostya comically raises his brows:

"Nikita, you're a big boy, you should know this by now: there's nothing to be afraid of in the restroom."

"Go to hell!" Nikita laughs. "I need you to look at something."

"Male striptease? Are you expanding your business? Aquariums for gay clubs?"

They both laugh and Nikita thinks: that's actually a good idea, aquariums for gay clubs. The best ideas really do come this way, by accident, when you're just chatting.

"No, not a striptease. Can you just check if I have scratches on my back or not? Dasha really went nuts today."

He says this with pride. See, you're not the only one, I can turn a young woman on too. And can also earn decent money! I just can't see if my back has been scratched up or not without a mirror.

In the minimalist, silvery-black restroom, Nikita pulls his sweater over his head and takes off his shirt. Kostya smokes, leaning against the wall.

"If it's serious," he says, "you should rent an apartment for the chick so she won't fuck around. Or else she'll want some young dick, catch something, and then you'll need treatment, Masha too. When you rent an apartment for them, it's like you're marking your territory. Other guys won't go in there. What if you've bugged the place or something?"

"Jealousy," Nikita says, "is another name for attachment. That's what Buddha taught. Instead of lecturing me, just look at my back."

"No scratches," Kostya says. "And you'll thank me for the lessons when the going gets tough. God forbid, of course, knock on wood."

Nikita buttons up his shirt before the mirror and Kostya says to him from behind a cloud of tobacco smoke:

"So she likes to scratch, your Dasha? It means she's passionate."

"You don't know the half of it," Nikita answers. "Do you know how she cums? It's like fireworks! I've never seen anything like it. I never thought that I could . . . that I could do that to a woman! She's completely different when she cums, you know? As if she's not a twenty something, but a thousand, two thousand years old! Like she's an ancient, deepwater goddess, a *woman from the deep end*. I tell you, in moments like that, I even think I'm an Indian fakir, you know, the guy who coaxes the cobra out of a basket. He plays the pipe and is afraid to stop."

"Sure," Kostya says, "the flute. Made of jasper or whatnot? I knew a long time ago that you were capable of incredible things. Not only dick-wise, obviously."

"Oh stop," Nikita waves him off.

"Honestly! To start from nothing in 2002, with no seed capital, not even experience, it's in the realm of science fiction. And to get as big as you are! Believe me, in a year or two, you'll have a driver, a security guard, and new chicks to keep you cumming like fireworks! Bottom line is, old man, I'm proud of you."

"You know," Nikita answers, putting on his sweater, "it turned out to be easy. I just realized at one point that everyone is given exactly as much as they can take. You tell yourself: I'm responsible for this and that, and then you go do it. And everything's under control, you can handle everything. If I had realized that a decade earlier, I'd probably have a very different life right now."

"Yes, old man," Kostya says and, with a flick of his fingers, sends his cigarette into the sink, "if that's so, then I'm not only proud of you, I even envy you."

"Why?"

"You've been in business for just a few years, but you say you can manage everything. I've been doing this for fifteen years and I always think it's a miracle I'm still alive. This could all end at any moment." He looks at the astonished Nikita and adds: "Have I told you this before?"

You can never tell if he's joking or being serious.

At home, Nikita tells Masha about Kostya, talks nonstop, takes off his jeans, and pulls his shirt over his head. Can you imagine, he told me that he's always afraid! All these years! I would have never thought! and suddenly, he notices that Masha is looking closely at his shoulder. Nikita turns toward the mirror—sure enough, it's a hickey. Where the hell was Kostya looking? If Masha asks, I'll say I bumped it.

But Masha doesn't ask: she continues to sit still in her armchair and stare at a single spot—the same one where Nikita's shoulder just was.

Maybe she didn't notice?

30.

A BLACK SKIRT AND A BOW ON HER NECK

At one time, Mama Tanya was the most beautiful woman in the world. In the morning, Anya, whom her grandmother named Elvira, loved to watch her mom sit before a small mirror, painting her lips, lining her brows, and passing a special little brush through her eyelashes, making them even longer.

Anya knew that Mom worked at a ministry, that it was an important job and that Mom had to look good. Which meant that she, Anya, had to sit still, not poke her under the arm, and watch quietly.

She thought that a job at a ministry was the most important job in the world. Before she turned six, Anya was certain that her mom was a minister. Who else worked at a ministry? So she thought, until they asked at daycare: and now, children, tell us what your parents' jobs are, and the disgusting, fair-haired Mishka made fun of her: a minister, ha, a minister would drive a Volga, does Elya have a Volga? She doesn't even have a Zaporozhzhetz! She wanted to run over to him and punch him in the eye, but little Oleg, whom Elya (future Anya) never noticed before, made it to him first and hit Mishka on the head with a toy block with the letter L.

Mishka started bawling and the teacher put Oleg in the corner—and Elya, like a nice girl, went to him and said thank you, adding for good measure that if she were the one who socked Mishka, he would have been taken away by an ambulance! But that's not what she remembered: it was how bad she felt when they were laughing at her, as if they were laughing at her mom.

Admittedly, her mom also laughed that evening, stroked her head, called her Anechka, kissed her, and said that, of course, she had an important job, but not as important as a minister's: she was a secretary and made sure all the papers were in order. Anya was a bit disappointed, but when her mom sat down before the mirror again the next morning, she calmed down—a minister or a secretary, what difference did it make? Her mom was still the most beautiful.

Almost thirty years have passed since then. The ministry changed names a few times, and then mom's boss offered her a job in his cousin's firm. The firm received orders from the ministry and, as Tatyana understood, did the same thing as the department where she worked for twenty years. Her former boss became a client, her salary was paid on time and was even higher than at the ministry, but in two years the firm folded unexpectedly and when she called her old number, the straight-talking young woman who had taken her job said that there had been a change in top brass and no one ever lets anyone get their old job back.

A couple of times, Tatyana tried to get a job as a secretary at some firm or other before they explicitly told her: we realize you have extensive experience . . . But it's a bit too extensive. In the end, Tatyana took a job as a cleaning woman at the nearest store. They didn't pay much, as she told Aunt Shura, but still, she couldn't scrounge off her daughter. *It's enough for just me.*

Anya tried to find her mom a job as a cashier at another store owned by the same people as the shoe store. The salary wasn't much higher and Tatyana said that she preferred to make five thousand rubles less and not have to commute to the other end of town as well as stand behind a cash register. Any work is honorable, she said, and I think that being a cleaning woman is no worse than being a cashier. Besides, I have savings.

For some reason, what upset Anya the most was that her mom might stop doing her makeup before the mirror. After all the years they'd lived apart, she still imagined that Mom's morning started with a mirror and makeup, just as Anya's started with a shower and exercise.

She got upset, and then realized that mom would keep doing her makeup as usual. Even if a cleaning woman didn't need to wear makeup. She did it for herself, not for others.

Just like Anya tried to stay in shape all these years—for herself, not for men.

And now, when she takes a cold shower every morning, Anya imagines that, at that exact moment, her mom is sitting before the mirror, the same one as thirty years ago, painting her lips, lining her brows and passing a little brush through her eyelashes.

Just like now, Saturday, her mom is done up as usual, only what's with this strange outfit: a black skirt, a black jacket, and some stupid bow on her neck?

In any case, Anya doesn't say anything and, at present, Gosha takes the toys Grandma keeps for him to the bedroom. Anya and Mom sit in the kitchen, drink tea, and snack on the zephyr cookies Anya brought. Wet snow is falling out the window and, suddenly, Tatyana starts telling her about how, years ago, she met Anya's dad, Sasha Melnikov, how they lived together for a few years and how she left him.

"So you thought he had a kid on the side?" Anya asks.

"He didn't have a child," her mom replies irritably. "It was Vasya's, his brother's child. But Sasha ran around with her like it was his."

"So you left him because he took care of his brother's lover?" Anya still doesn't understand. What a silly story. Her father behaved like a normal man—showy acts of heroism, zero responsibility. Mom said it herself—you can't expect anything else from men.

"Yes," Tatyana replies, "you can say that. But Sasha never loved me. He only loved that Lyolya, that dumb Russian blonde. I was just an exotic distraction to him. I turned up on an unlucky day and got knocked up the second time around like an idiot. They didn't teach us to use protection back then, not like nowadays."

And she fixes her neatly set hair, which is as black as when she was younger, although she probably dyes it now.

"Don't look at me that way," Anya says, "my kid was planned. And quite a success. He's even got good genes: his father almost never drank, so there!"

The planned success is loitering in the bedroom. Judging by the sounds, he's managed to make a pistol out of a teddy bear or a spinning top.

Grandma Tanya stirs her tea and repeats wistfully:

"Sasha never loved me."

"Did you love him?" Anya asks, as if forgetting that she already asked this question after the funeral.

"And I loved him. That's the thing. If I hadn't loved him, I wouldn't have gotten a divorce."

So that's what it is. Wicked paradoxes don't lose their power: since you don't love me anymore, nothing can prevent us from living together—is that how it went?

"Mom warned me: don't fall in love! Sleep with him, have a child, marry him if you're an imbecile, but don't fall in love. And I fell in love as soon as I saw him. At first sight. He just asked if he could help me with my bag and that was it. He could have taken me instead of the bag and carried me anywhere. Thirty seconds and it was all over. My mom told me my entire life: if you fall in love, consider it done. You'll lose control over the situation."

What if I don't need control? Anya thinks. Vika says that women must know how to surrender to the flow of events. Only then will the water carry them out on the right bank. Of course, Vika says it, but I don't remember if I've ever fallen in love with somebody the way mom tells it. So they could pick me up and carry me to any old place. Thank God that's never happened. But I wonder why?

And, all of a sudden, she thinks: it's because she has no sexual hang-ups. Truth be told, she pretty much doesn't care who she fucks: she can always cum, regardless of who the man is. Of course, occasionally, she'll get someone completely useless like Marik, but that's just bad luck. But, generally, a man's a man and sex is sex—it's a great thing that doesn't leave room in Anya's life for miracles or love.

It seems like that's how it is in their family: either sex or love. Mom had love, but never really had sex. She got pregnant the second time around, lived with my father for four years at most, and after that, she had no one. For some reason, Anya is certain of this, although, of course, she never asked: Mom couldn't stand conversations about sex, the very word irritated her. It's all promiscuity, she said.

Anya tries not to think about it—she loves her mom too much to imagine what that's like: thirty years without a man. As for herself, when Gosha was little and she had almost no energy for anything, she would get in touch with one of her old acquaintances at least once every few months—those same truck drivers, chauffeurs, and security guards—so that it wouldn't grow over with spiderwebs, as the girls said. These meetings were infrequent and hasty, so Andrey is Anya's first regular lover in three-and-a-half years since Gosha's dad.

Anya tries not to think about her mom, but the thought catches her off guard at the most inopportune moments, like when Mom admonishes her for not having taught Gosha to show his age on his fingers. Or right now, when Mom has gotten to talking about love.

Presently, they're drinking tea in silence.

An old, tidy kitchen that somewhat resembles my parents' kitchen. A plastic-covered table, two women sitting at it. Slanted eyes, broad cheekbones. It seems like the Russian blood has dissolved fully in their veins. If you look for it, you will find a photo of Grandma Djamilya in her service shirt, with a Red Star medal. A spitting image of her daughter and granddaughter.

Or maybe it's because all Tatar women look the same to me?

When she is already by the front door, Anya can't restrain herself from asking:

"Mom, why are you dressed like this, all in black? Are you in mourning?"

Tatyana looks at her daughter point-blank, almost without blinking. Then she says hollowly:

"I'm telling you, I really loved him."

And then, presumably, Anya cautiously closes the door and walks to the elevator, while at that moment, I park my Toyota close to my building, once more imagine their conversation, and think: does a woman really need to maintain control? For a man, maintaining control is a sexual technique, a way to hold off ejaculating for a long time so you can satisfy your partner. The rest is secondary: business, politics, friendship. Control means that you don't ejaculate for a long time. Of course, with age, the problem resolves itself.

Except that, a few days ago, I came in ninety seconds like a teenager in love.

If you fall in love, consider it gone, Djamilya Takhtagonova used to say. That's why she lived her entire life alone and had two daughters by two different men. And both her daughters, Tatyana and Gulya, live alone. And both her granddaughters, too—Anya-Elvira and her cousin Rimma, whom Anya rarely sees, most often at birthdays and wakes.

31.

A REAL GIRL

Anya's aunt, Rimma's mom, is named Gulya Takhtagonova. She and Rimma had a falling out when Rimma dropped out of university.

A month before, Rimma had rented her first apartment—four hundred and fifty dollars, downright cheap for the city center—and her mom asked: aren't you afraid? Rimma didn't understand what she was supposed to be afraid of. If she lost her job, she'd move out of the apartment, that's all.

She didn't want to lose her job. There, in the big office filled with strange people, she discovered a world she wanted to live in. A world of familiarity and superficial contacts, a world without sincerity, feelings, or depth. A two-dimensional world. Like in the movies.

She wouldn't be able to take her finals and work at the same time, so she immediately collected all her documents from the university and left.

To get into the university, she had met with tutors thrice a week through all of tenth and eleventh grade. "Have you lost your mind?" her mom said. In response, Rimma hung up the phone.

Of course, they made up. But Rimma still preferred to talk to her mother over the phone. She rarely saw her other relatives and spoke to them politely when she did, giving them a perfunctory smile and saying she was happy to see everyone.

Rimma left that first job herself—it had no prospects. The new job was even closer to her apartment. She could walk there and not have to take the stifling Metro or wait in traffic.

Rimma didn't like Moscow. That is, she thought she liked it, but her Moscow was her office, her apartment, and a dozen cafés, restaurants, and clubs; in the summer—the boulevards, Neskuchny Garden, Hermitage Garden, and Aquarium Garden. The real Moscow—the Moscow Metro, the new high-rises, the dirty stairwells—Rimma didn't like.

When she stumbled into that Moscow, Rimma tried not to linger there and, back at *her place*, forgot about it entirely, expunging it from her consciousness as decisively as she had dropped out of university two years earlier.

Her life was clearly defined, contoured, and devoid of any undertones—like an anime cartoon or a comic book.

Rimma had a small collection of manga comics, about fifty DIVX discs, and a dozen DVDs. In any case, she eschewed otaku fan gatherings: she was irritated by girls who liked to dress up as little animals, had multicolored hair, and wore stockings and plaid miniskirts. She found the amateurish groups that spoke atrocious Japanese to be laughable: puppyish exuberance, adolescent passions, a freak parade.

The most important thing about anime is that it's two-dimensional, that it lacks depth.

The spaceships from *Cowboy Bebop*, the mutating mafiosi from *Gungrave* and the fighting vampires from *Hellsing* were devoid of depth. Even when they moved, they didn't change. They seemed to be frozen while, in the background, an invisible person wheeled in a starry sky, provincial cafés, and London edifices. There was always a gap between the heroes and the background, and this gap gave them freedom, disembodied them, and made them weightless.

She can't explain this to Mom, can't explain this to anyone, not even to herself. Rimma doesn't even try to explain and simply smiles amiably when asked about it and says: I like anime, it's nothing like Hollywood.

A perfectly acceptable explanation for a normal person.

Of course, Moreukhov would have tried to argue and name ten really good Hollywood films off the top of his head, *without counting the classics!* He may have even given examples of Hollywood's influence on anime: for instance, the first six episodes of *Gungrave*—specifically, episodes two through five . . . Anyway, that's if he had seen *Gungrave*. One way or other, Moreukhov would have found something to say and, in general, it would have been nice to hang out and watch it together.

In any event, even Moreukhov has trouble picturing them together. Only in the movies do little girls spend time with men over thirty who are missing a front tooth and have problems with alcohol and violence.

Such a pair would have looked terrific in a semi-pornographic anime about killer girls like *Kate* or *Assassin Beauties*. Rimma likes shows like that. Looking at gangly teenagers dressed in miniskirts and stockings, with disproportionately large breasts, handguns, samurai swords, bazookas, flamethrowers and laser guns makes her genuinely feel like a girl.

Ever since she was a child, Rimma wanted to be a boy—boys fought better and were faster, meaner, and more athletic. When she found out she would get her period and they wouldn't, she told her mom that the world was unfair.

Her mom started telling her that she, too, got her period—that it wasn't so scary—and Rimma wondered why she was telling her this. After all, she didn't say *the world is unfair because women menstruate*—she knew it had to happen, she wasn't an idiot, she understood.

She simply meant that the world was unfair because she, Rimma, had to menstruate.

All the more so because she didn't plan to have children, which is why she would have easily renounced the delicately designed and fussy female reproductive system.

OK, I don't feel like a girl, she thought, and I don't think I would make a great boy either. But it seems somewhat unfair not to be a girl or a boy and, on top of that, stress out for five days a month about having the right pads in your purse and not leaking onto your clothing.

Rimma didn't feel like a girl, but she obviously acted like one—especially at work. She dressed like a girl, smiled like a girl, read women's magazines, wore makeup and perfume, and once, in order to feel like a *real girl*, she even bought a self-tanner, or an auto-bronzer, as it said on the label. But she knew this wasn't it—tan or not, dressed this way or that, she still didn't look like the girls from the commercials, the customers in the trendy clothing stores, or the soap opera heroines.

But she sure as hell resembled the Japanese anime girls—teary-eyed, with a finger on the trigger.

Every day, she went to the office, smiled at Sazonov, dreamed of building a career, of making not nine hundred, but a thousand five hundred, then—two thousand, and if not, she'd go work for another company or the next department. By age thirty she'd be a good manager, take out a mortgage, and buy an apartment, and by forty, she would head her own department in base metals or the oil sector and everything would be great for her, until the oil ran out or global oil prices fell.

This was a convincing plan that was in line with the recommendations in *Company* magazine and on the *e-xecutive website*. Rimma was absolutely certain that it would happen just so.

But every time she tried to picture herself as that successful, forty-year-old woman, a department head with an apartment-car-dacha, nothing happened. She would still see Sazonov, only shorter and thinner, not in a suit, but in expensive shoes, designer jeans, and a blazer from a boutique.

Apparently, that's who she would become at forty.

32.

NINETY SECONDS

You know, Dimon, when I'm drunk, my erections are great. It's just too bad I cum so quickly in that state. Although that has its own charms—you shoot your load and go straight to sleep. I always thought that a young woman would be capable of entertaining herself. Her hands haven't fallen off, right?

If there were an erotic rapid-firing championship, I'd have a great chance of winning it. But you know, I just thought of something: my brother could beat my record.

Just imagine, there he is in his Toyota, trying to calm down, his hands still trembling. He doesn't even turn on the music. He's catching his breath. Fifteen minutes ago, he set a personal record: he came in ninety seconds. Like a schoolboy.

He thinks: I wish I could tell this to Kostya, he would appreciate it. But Kostya has jetted off to Madagascar or wherever, and Nikita obviously won't think of calling me. Because I'm an alkie, a lush, the black sheep must leave the flock, why would he hang with me!

So Nikita sits alone, sits there and thinks back on how it all happened.

A month ago, in the restroom of a *glamorous* Japanese restaurant, a fitting image came to mind. He told Kostya "she's some kind of woman from the deep end" and it stuck and split in two. She is Dasha, twenty-two years old, a ring in her eyebrow, a barbell in her tongue, Paolo Coelho on her bookshelf. And she is also the woman from the deep end, Dasha's deepwater essence that appears only on the threshold of a deep orgasm. Waves, quivering, vibrating, the guttural howl and bountiful moisture— these are the consorts of the woman from the deep end, Dasha's ancient incarnation, which Nikita was able to reach with the help of his *Jasper*

171

flute. He asked himself: does this woman slumber in the innermost depths of every maiden, every virtuous woman and skank, every plain Jane and beauty? Were Nikita younger, he could spend a lifetime looking for the answer—but all he could do at this point was thank his lucky stars for the marvelous gift Dasha had given him.

Of course, Nikita knows that the "woman from the deep end" is just a metaphor, an image of Dasha's unexpectedly blossoming sexuality. So today, for the first time, he has found traces of this metaphor in Dasha's daily life, in her routine bodily practices.

(I think I got carried away here, Moreukhov says. How would Nikita know such big words? I've almost forgotten them myself, I only remembered because I dragged the back issues of Moscow Art Magazine *to the bathroom. The paper's not that soft, but it's snazzy. So anyway, it doesn't matter what words Nikita uses to tell the story. What matters is the plot: my half-brother has ended up in the situation he did as a result of his work on a research paper entitled "where's my beloved's body and has she got anything else?")*

A week ago, Dasha's mom found her a job at an old university friend's office. As a secretary or an office manager—in short, a minimum-wage job with a single requirement: to be there between ten and seven. Minus sixty minutes for lunch, but not a minute longer.

In other words, goodbye to morning visits in the apartment in Vykhino. And poor Nikita had gotten so used to them over the past three weeks!

It turned out it was a lot more complicated to meet in the evenings: a business meeting would get pushed back or Masha would call or Dasha herself had important things to do—anyway, our lovers hadn't seen each other for a week, and today, Nikita deliberately decided to pick up Dasha during the day. He must have been hoping to find a hotel close to her office where they could spend an hour together without any lunch.

Obviously, nothing came of this: Dasha didn't know any hotels close by, only an excellent restaurant she'd been meaning to go to for a while. And of course, she wanted to eat because she was in a rush that morning and hadn't had breakfast.

So Nikita took her to lunch, what else could he do?

The restaurant really was excellent—at least judging by the prices. Nikita didn't even expect to find such an expensive a menu outside of the Golden Mile and the Boulevard Ring. Thankfully, there weren't many people there: you could say they were alone in the room, if you didn't count the waiters and a couple of baldish men in expensive, rumpled suits drinking vodka at the bar at two in the afternoon.

Admirable people, by the way. I like guys like that.

Of course, Nikita didn't even notice the men because Dasha went to work in a tight black dress.

"We have a dress code," she grumbled. "Cover your chest, cover your knees, your arms above the elbow too. So I have to wear this old junk, I wore it in school. It was *goth*. You can tell I was about seven kilos thinner back then."

The dress was in fact quite fitted to Dasha's body. As an artist—or a former artist—I have to tell you that a tight black dress on a young woman prone to excess weight produces a stunning visual effect. As we know, black is slimming and a tight dress accentuates all the nuances of a figure.

For greater emphasis, let's picture that Dasha didn't wear undergarments. At least not with the tight goth dress worn for the sake of the dress code.

Well, yes, you can see her nipples sticking out, that's a given. But that's nothing. The main thing is that all the folds are accentuated and magnified. The sides, the hips, the stomach—in this outfit, the flesh of Nikita's beloved becomes even shapelier than if Dasha were completely naked.

And of course, the breasts. The fabric is as taut as the skin on a ripe fruit. I can't figure out which one—a plum, a peach? They're not black enough. The only thing close is an eggplant, but it's a vegetable. And completely unerotic.

In other words, all in all, it was an indecent sight, like public masturbation.

(*As I say this, I, of course, picture the performance artist Alexander Brener, while Nikita pictures some chick. We're obviously talking about a chick and not Brener because I'm attempting to describe how Nikita saw Dasha.*)

So they're sitting across from each other. Dasha's every movement echoes throughout her body with a subtle quiver of the flesh and the tight black dress only magnifies it. And somewhere between his bread and his appetizer, Nikita recognizes this quivering, after which he completely loses interest in food, drink, and conversation.

For the first time, he sees the woman from the deep end winking at him in broad daylight. Bringing a spoon to her mouth, straightening her napkin, sitting more comfortably, leaning forward, looking around, raising her head—every gesture seems familiar, reminds him of the pre-orgasmic quiver of the flesh beyond Dasha's power, outside her control.

Now it's clear to Nikita: Dasha's body doesn't belong to her, it's the domain of the woman from the deep end.

I think that Moses must have felt something similar when the burning bush began to talk to him in God's voice. Yes, today, in the restaurant, Nikita experienced a combination of elation and horror so unbearable that he preferred to reduce it to banal desire.

And now, as he sits in his car, he repeats to himself: "I wanted to fuck her so badly, I almost lost my mind."

Of course, that's not exactly the case. You and I, Dimon, we're educated guys, we know that this whole story isn't about "fucking," it's about the Real, the Imagined, and the Symbolic. Everything you were afraid to ask Lacan, you can ask Žižek.[1]

As for Nikita, he's never read such highbrow books. He had no time, he had more important things to do.

But you can't accuse him of lack of self-control. He waits patiently for Dasha to finish eating and only then leans over the table and says:

"Dasha, I can't do this anymore. Let's get out of here now or else I'll have to fuck you where you're sitting."

Dasha smiles, shifts her shoulders (this gesture also means a lot to Nikita) and whispers:

"You should have told me earlier, you've been sitting there completely out of it. Don't worry—we'll find someplace."

They look for someplace for, say, seven minutes—believe me, Dimon, for Nikita, this is a very long seven minutes. Perhaps we should even add them to the ninety seconds that my brother spent specifically on coitus.

To be honest, I don't want to fabricate where Nikita is fucking his lover. In the car or in the restroom, maybe, in the building entrance. Of course, I would have liked them to do it in a junkyard, but that's highly improbable.

So anyway, Nikita zips up his trousers with a trembling hand, Dasha fixes her dress (I wouldn't say it's completely wet, but it's still excessively moist), looks at her watch and says:

"Okay, darling, I gotta run, my break is ending."

And now Nikita can't contain himself.

"Listen," he says, "fuck that job. Let me rent you an apartment and give you some money . . . While you look for something more suitable . . ."

Nikita says all this as his hands are still fiddling with the condom he's taken off; he stares at it as if he's talking to his drying semen and not to Dasha, who looks at him with . . . what? Gratitude? Gloating eyes? Triumph? Astonishment?

---

[1] Reference to *Everything You Always Wanted to Know About Lacan . . . But Were Afraid to Ask Hitchcock*, edited by Slavoj Žižek.

Nikita doesn't know, he can't tear his eyes away from his own fingers, which are crumpling and stretching the pink rubber cylinder.

So he sits in the car and repeats to himself: this isn't love, this isn't desire, this isn't lust—it's a delusion.

And Nikita has one remaining hope: sometimes, delusions dissolve.

What's key here, summarizes Moreukhov, are the words "delusion" and "woman from the deep end." Actually, these are my words because I'm the one responsible for the underwater spirits and hazy magical visions in our family. Because I'm so enjoying making up this story about Nikita, Dasha, and the "woman from the deep end." I probably see potential here for a film noir with a femme fatale and a gullible, goodhearted moron.

It's just not clear how well Nikita's suited for this role—doesn't matter, let's wait and see. In any case, we can always turn this story into a porno. Or a comic book.

Dimon, as a comic book fan to a former artist, tell me: is there such a thing as intellectual pornographic comic books? Let's make some, huh? We'll publish them anonymously and make a killing!

33.

NOT AIDS AND NOT CANCER

It's hard to admit to yourself that your closest friend is an alcoholic. The star of our graduating class, the man who jokingly gave himself the pseudonym The Most Talented Artist of Our Generation™ and nearly organized an eponymous exhibition at some warehouse. The youngest participant of all the notable artistic projects of the mid-nineties. Loverboy, drinking buddy, eminent party animal, one of the guys, socialite, personality featured in *Moscow Art Magazine* and the tabloid *Moskovskiy Komsomolets*, and simply Sashka Borisov, well, he made up the last name Moreukhov afterward, who the hell knows why, there was some story behind it—it was supposedly in honor of a famous underwater commando, a war hero. Who doesn't know Sashka, remember how we got wasted with you guys—Vitalik was there too—got wasted and marched down the street singing "*Everything is going according to plan*?" Who doesn't remember Sashka, whatever happened to him, I haven't heard anything about him in a while, did he really hit the bottle? Didn't he go crazy? Is he not on coke? Just the bottle? And is he done for? Has it been long since you've seen him? What about Antabuse capsules? Has he seen an addiction specialist? Someone told me about an old woman, an old man, a turnip, a cat, a mouse, a granddaughter, a dog. They pull and pull and can't pull him out, they throw up their hands, the hell with him, let him do it by himself, what do we care, we've got our own lives and he's got his, in the end, it's not a disease, and if it is a disease, it's not AIDS and not cancer, in this case, it's his fault, let him figure it out. I just saw him last week, I think he got an Antabuse implant, he was totally normal, only missing a front tooth, how awful, and he used to be a good-looking guy, remember, all the girls had a crush on him, he didn't let a single one get past him, well, he's lost a ton of weight, he's gaunt, but he seemed sober, he seemed normal, only he was talking nonsense, so I said I had to run—I had no energy to listen to that baloney.

Dimon knows it's always like that when he first comes out of a bender. His head's not working, his nerves are a wreck, so the most important thing is not to let him go anywhere, to sit with him, talk to him, talk to him, that is to say, listen, because he won't let you get a word in edgewise, ranting, ranting about something, telling you how things were *over there*.

"Can you imagine, Dimon, she looked just like Maggie Cheung from *In the Mood for Love*, so beautiful, I even thought I was seeing things, we sat on a bench together, drank a bit, then she went her way and I went home—because, by then, I was thinking: this is it, I'll die in a snowbank ten steps away from the store, can you imagine? Yeah, I also wondered why there would be a Chinese woman, especially Maggie Cheung. If she came to Moscow, they would have written about it in all the papers—after all, she's a star. Plus, Maggie doesn't speak Russian, but this woman and I had a conversation about something, I don't remember what, I don't remember anything, well, besides the usual, you know, fish, forest snags, dark water, those arms reaching for me, I don't want to remember."

If your closest friend is an alcoholic, you never turn off your phone at night because he could call you. From the precinct. From Vykhino, from Medvedkovo, from Kuzminki, from the other end of town, himself not knowing where, slurring his speech, beaten, dying, harping on about water, fish, asphyxiation—and you go to him, drag him to his apartment in Troparyovo, where the door is locked only when the owner's sober, clean up the vomit, change his clothes, shove him under the shower, call Tiger Darkovich, IV, saline drip, and as much water as possible.

"Of course, I'm a lush and an alkie, why are you stressing yourself out, why do you need me, huh? Is it because you're gay? Admit it! Alright, alright, I'm joking. I know we're friends, everything's cool, I'll rewire myself this time around, get the pill, stop drinking for good. You see, I always think I can do what normal people do: have a beer, a gin and tonic, an Ochakovo screwdriver. Remember how we used to drink with Sonya Shpilman, the mother of my unborn children? And everything was fine. When I start I always think: just don't drink vodka and everything will be fine. And later, later, I don't remember how it happens. I remember I extorted some money from the cops, but then, some thug kicked my ass and afterward, I bought vodka, and after that, I only remember this bench and Maggie Cheung. You know, she was so beautiful that I thought it was death coming for me. After all, I have the right to a beautiful death, I've earned it, right? Do you happen to know what we talked about?"

Maybe I am gay, huh? Yeah right, I have a wife and a daughter and I never liked men. Although my wife and I are divorced and, as for men, could I be lying to myself? How many times I promised myself not to get involved with Moreukhov—let him swim out of his dark water as he wishes. But, see, I still can't do it, once again, I'm sitting here, in this disgusting, vomit stained apartment, holding his hand and listening to his hungover raving about Maggie Cheung, who saved him from the snowbank. *What the fuck am I doing here?*

"I think it's the last time. It's all because Uncle Sasha died. I told you, I was convinced my whole life that he was my real father."

"I still don't understand—why?" Dimon asks.

"It's some shady story, I still don't know all the details. He had a brother, Vasiliy, who supposedly had an affair with my mom. And I was supposedly the result of that affair. Meanwhile, it turns out that Uncle Sasha knew my mom practically his whole life. He'd have me over on weekends, take me to see films with Gojko Mitic, then Sergio Leone films during pere-stroika. He was married at one point, but got divorced a long time ago, and he's never seen his daughter, that same Anya-Elvira. He never really even spoke to me about her. I think that everything is mixed up: I should have been Alexander Alexandrovich and Anya—Elvira Vasilyevna. There's also Nikita, the so-called legitimate son of my so-called legitimate father, Vasiliy. Another reason to consider Uncle Sasha my father: because, if Nikita were my brother, even my half-brother, he'd be the one sitting here and not you."

I know why I'm the one sitting here, Dimon thinks. Because for me personally, Sashka truly was the most talented artist of our generation. Without the capital letters and the trademark symbol, without the jokes and the banter. And now, Sashka's a degraded lush. It's like we divvied it up among ourselves: he gets the benders and the withdrawal symptoms and I get the career and the money. And it seems somewhat unfair—as if everything I have is thanks to him, thanks to Moreukhov. As if I am guilty before him.

On the other hand, no. It's just that the two of us are now a symbol of our generation. Two artists, one a drunkard and the other—a maga-zine art director. Those who come after us won't even despise us. They'll simply forget about us.

That's why I come here, because I still hope to see Moreukhov rise like a phoenix from the ashes, emerge like the underwater city of Kitezh, young and magnificent, rise up from the vomit and urine—and if that happens, then everything will be alright for our generation, we can forget all those years, start over, do something real and tell ourselves: I'm young and I have my entire life ahead of me.

"As for comic books," Dimon tells him, "I have my own big project. It's a whole family saga. It's completely based on old Soviet legends, songs and so on. For instance, I made up a storyline about a family of bombers. The great-grandpa blows up the Cathedral of Christ the Savior; then, in 1956, the grandpa blows up a monument to Stalin at a gulag, like in Galich's song, the dad . . . well, the dad works at an institution, some lab for hydrides and oxidizing agents, and the son is first a criminal, then a chauffeur. Oh yeah, there's also a scene where the boys go swimming in the Moskva pool, well, they're cutting class. And one of them sees the dome of the Cathedral underwater. Like the city of Kitezh, right? Then, at the very end, the chauffeur is driving the Patriarch or whoever to work, drops him off, and goes to park his car in an underground garage. And as soon as he gets down there, he is engulfed by the waves of the Moskva pool."

Dimon and Moreukhov are drinking tea in front of the television. Moreukhov has almost recovered from his alcoholic winter marathon. He is showing Dimon yet another Hong Kong film, occasionally grabbing his hand and saying: *This next part is genius!*

Dimon is watching without interest.

"Okay, do your comic book," Moreukhov says, "I know you can. For real, you've done everything you've set your mind to. You'll make money, loan it to me, and I'll spend it on booze."

"Listen," Dimon says, "as soon as you quit drinking, you'll have as much money as you want. You're a genuinely talented artist, far more talented than me. How many times did I get you projects? You did a fine job if you didn't start drinking."

"Fuck it all," Moreukhov says. "You know that I decided to stop being an artist. Being an artist is ridiculous. It's the same thing as talking about a revolution in earnest. And in general, how can you be an artist today? Everything is controled by curators. Grants are handed out by people who don't understand anything about art. There are no more quality standards. No one needs real art. What, should I go exhibit at Marat Guelman's gallery? I would throw up on the threshold, even if I was sober."

"Oh stop," Dimon says. "Marat is totally fine, he's sane."

"And the scariest part," Moreukhov continues, "is that no one will understand why I threw up. They'll think it's a conceptual gesture. They'll say: well, Brener took a shit and Moreukhov's puking. And I'll have to trademark it. For instance, put up street ads with vomit on them, like it's a type of graffiti. My relationship to consumer society, the refuse of civilization and human waste, blah blah blah. And if I don't exhibit and just vomit on the street, even better. Then the cops can play the roles of curators and critics."

"You can also vomit on icons," Dimon says, "à la Ter-Oganyan."

"You're a tool," Moreukhov says. "First of all, I'm Eastern Orthodox. Second of all, why would I vomit on icons? Even when I vomit on the street, it's still my discourse with God. An offering. A sacrifice, so to speak. Especially if I vomit out my bile. Here I am, Lord, completely before Thee, in full view of Thee!"

"The AES+F art group also did photos themed around vomit," Dimon remembers.

"Yes, they definitely did. At that show where Fridkes took all of our photos. I remember, I was walking past his thing-a-ma-jig, that long photo glued together from pieces depicting art critics, artists, and curators—the whole in-crowd lined up against the wall of his studio—so I was walking and thinking: damn, we're all so alike. And that's when I realized that it's shameful to be an artist. You can paint pictures to give to a chick or your friends on their birthday. But you shouldn't lie to yourself: it's not art, it's bullshit. Because art is over. And in general, it's shameful to be an artist and it's respectable to be a rock star."

"It's shameful to be an alcoholic," Dimon replies.

"It's hard to be an alcoholic," Moreukhov says, "it's physically hard. Do you know how shitty I feel when I binge-drink? Everything hurts inside, I'm nauseous. Meanwhile, I know that I have to stop, that it will get worse for me if I keep going. But the body remembers that there was a time when I drank and it made me feel better. So I drink again, knowing it's going to be a total disaster."

"You need treatment," Dimon says.

"Yeah, yeah," Moreukhov says, "sure!"

Why is everything so shitty? Moreukhov thinks. How come nothing happened, not the fame, not the money, not the family? I wanted it so badly. It can't be my fault. It's my father, my fake father, the one I never knew, and my real father, who, like Uma Thurman in *Kill Bill*, is looking through a thick layer of frozen earth, it's my mother, who never ended up getting married—they're the ones who taught me to fear my luck, they're the ones who taught me to never be happy, they're the ones who vaccinated me against happiness.

34.

1974. THE QUICK GOODBYE

Moscow rolled further and further on, hammered colossal cement pipes into ancient clay, covered the foundation pits, poured asphalt over them, destroyed without a trace, heaped tower upon high rise tower; in the mornings, the Metro stations and platforms were disastrously crowded and, every year, this crowd grew even thicker; every time she returned home to Moscow, either from Leningrad or from vacation, Lyolya marveled: "Where did all these people come from? Out-of-towners? The kids all grew up?"

We keep envisioning, keep building, keep molding whatever we've read and heard about, still hoping to resurrect, restore, think through, declare love to those who are no longer here, even if they are in fact alive, like Yelena Borisova, Lyolya, Moreukhov's mother—but even if they are alive, they've changed for good. And we keep remembering: 1974, the Brezhnev stagnation, thick journals, personal dramas, private life, seventies intelligentsia, the pseudo-educated, being charmed by the little church on Kalininsky Prospect, lines to see Tutankhamen, books you could only get in exchange for the kilograms of paper you recycled, icons brought from villages and Marina Tsvetaeva retyped on the typewriter.

Lyolya also wrote poetry, also thought *my turn will come*, even though she's already twenty-four, a mature adult poet, and recognition must be around the corner. Too bad her mother doesn't care for it, although she's a philologist, she should understand; instead, she wrote her from Leningrad asking how long it would be before she got married—what could Lyolya say to that? Married to whom, Vasya? He has a wife and a child. They've been seeing each other for a few years now, and at first, it seemed like a casual thing, a summer fling while his wife and child were away at the dacha; and it was so sweet to stroll around nocturnal, illuminated Moscow with him, to feel his hand on her hip and then, finally, to be alone with him in a stuffy room. Somehow, Lyolya quickly forgot about Sasha, who had first brought her to this apartment—she called him once and he dropped the receiver, it was just as well, she wasn't too keen on calling him anyway, who did he think he was to reproach her? She was a free, young woman, a creative individual, a poet who needed emotions for inspiration.

Still, there was an unpleasant, dismal scent to her romance with Vasya —maybe because he had a wife and son and, now and again, when it was winter and they were having lunch at a restaurant, Vasya would turn his head in embarrassment and a raw, unusual expression would appear on his face. And the more Lyolya looked at Vasya, the more her pity—her pity and vague joy—rose up in her along with a sense of superiority: she had that mysterious something that was necessary for happiness. Because she was happy and could share her happiness with others.

That summer, she returned from Crimea and immediately called him at work because she knew that she looked outrageously beautiful, that she'd tanned herself to a crisp, that her blonde hair was bleached the color of straw, that her delicate German lipstick gave her lips a moist, fresh, girlish sheen, while her eyes shone bright blue in her dark face. Later, when they lay together in one of Vasya's friends' apartments during a holiday (they always met in apartments like this) and his arm was milky-white against her tanned body, as always, she pitied him, stroked his pale, sunless shoulders, told him something about her mother, her father, her father's impending retirement—perhaps he'd be transferred to Moscow, his friends had lobbied for his transfer to the capital when he was approaching retirement. It recently occurred to her that she had never spoken to Vasya about her parents, so she started telling him about the way her dad used to shave his head in the morning, all covered in white foam, playfully dabbing her nose with it, making her laugh; and how her mom read Pushkin's fairy tales to her in the evening—she must have been the one who instilled a passion for poetry in Lyolya, she had just written a new poem in Crimea, did he want to hear it? But Vasya suddenly grew embarrassed, began to dress quickly, fuss around, then, at the Metro stop, gave her a wet peck on the cheek and disappeared into the crowd—pale, ridiculous-looking, and never going on vacation that summer.

A month went by and all things Crimean faded, or maybe, it was just that Moscow had closed in on her with its autumn chills, rain, haste, work, and running around the stores in search of rubber-soled shoes for rainy weather. It was only when she learned what happened to her that it hit her: Vasya hadn't called her once since that evening and, at first, she got angry and decided: it's just as well, I won't tell him, I'll ask the girls at work who I should see about it and it'll all be over. But in another two weeks, when he still hadn't called, she dialed his work number herself and had barely gotten a word in when she heard: *It would be best if we broke up*, asked him *Why?* And the answer was so ridiculous, so silly, she could hardly believe it, and burst out laughing, and continued to laugh as the dial tone hummed in her ear; then she sat down and cried, because of the foul weather, the cold, the slush, the Moscow autumn, her unbought shoes, and yet-unborn child—all this had closed in on her at simultaneously and she no longer knew what to do with it.

Lyolya came out on the street, stood in line for no particular reason, and left before reaching the counter, thinking: how is it possible, how could he leave me when I'm having his baby? Then she realized: he doesn't know yet and, when he finds out, everything will change, because, now she was on equal terms with his wife. And she grew so enamored of that idea that she didn't even stop to think that she had hitherto never intended to live with Vasya; she still thought she had her entire life ahead of her and this was just another adventure, a bit out of pity and a bit out of habit.

It's easy to imagine the seventies, even if I hardly remember this decade. The romanticism of those years is in our blood, a romanticism redolent of bitter cynicism, the taste of vodka drunk straight from the bottle, the memory of the Bulldozer Exhibition, the legacy of the underground, the despondency of the stagnation era. It's easy to imagine my mother, who wrote poetry, swallowed tears, dropped coins in a payphone slot—it's only impossible to imagine myself, who either existed or didn't. A single cell, then two, four, eight . . .

Lyolya called Vasya a few more times at work, but they wouldn't call him to the phone. She thought about it for another week and decided that she needed to tell him before she got an abortion, and called him again, and only then thought of dialing Sasha, whom, it seemed, she hadn't seen in ages. Lyolya knew that he was perpetually off on some expeditions, traveling, a wife, a child—it must have been a girl—but, luckily, he was the one who picked up the phone and she spilled her guts to him, told him right away about the baby, Vasya, the quick goodbye. She waited, but Vasya still didn't call her back; instead, Sasha came and brought her flowers, said he'd help her if she needed anything, thankfully, he had the money, the North, the East, *the zeros in his savings book scattering*—so he said. Lyolya shook her head, she didn't need the money, but now it was too awkward to say she was planning to get an abortion and, afterward, it really was too late, thirteen weeks, no one would do it, and that's how I came into the world, into the concrete-and-asphalt Moscow, the city of bus stops, slush, dust, lines at the State Department Store, certificates from the Housing Maintenance Office, the city of pity and love.

35.

THE WHISKERED FACES OF FISH

My sister Anya would never let a man rent an apartment for her. That's why she moves every year, that's why she tries to tread softly and not provoke her psychopathic neighbor, that's why she lives with her child on her small salary.

Dasha is twirling a bundle of keys in her hands. For the first time in her life, she's got keys to an apartment where she'll live all by herself. No parents, no Lerka, no one. Of course, it's a rental apartment—that's alright, Nikita said that the owners are looking to rent long-term.

And that's her birthday present. Twenty-three years old—an adult, at last.

"And if I don't like it, can I renovate it?" she asks Nikita. "Redo the wallpaper, hang a different set of curtains, draw something on the wall? Will the owners object?"

"No," Nikita smiles, "they said: do whatever you want, just leave a double deposit."

"You know," Dasha says, "I think I've dreamed of living like this since I was twelve. Of being my own mistress. Not having to depend on anyone. You can't imagine how happy I am! Thank you, thank you so much!"

She kisses Nikita on the lips and he whispers as he catches his breath:

"I have another little surprise for you, I hope you'll like it."

"Of course, I'll like it," Dasha replies and clutches the apartment keys even tighter in her hand: her talisman, powerful amulet, fabulous magic wand.

An aquarium stands between them. Eighty liters. Two lazy catfish are turning from side to side. Between them is a spinning mill wheel—it's made of plastic, but appears wooden. Snags lie on the bottom, hollow tree stumps. The stumps are ceramic, but also look real. Through the thick layer of water, Dasha sees Nikita's face: the face of a middle-aged man. Bags under his eyes, a double chin, some ridiculous graying scruff. The catfish swim between them, wiggling their whiskers. Through the double pane glass, Nikita himself looks like a fish. He half-opens his mouth and blows her a kiss, but appears to be silently exhaling an air bubble. Dasha's hand glides across the aquarium glass, reaching for him, and finds his Nikita's palm. Their interwoven fingers are like the artificial snags on the bottom, like the whiskered faces of fish.

Darling, Dasha mouths and, on her end of the underwater landscape, Nikita sees massive, quivering earrings that resemble exotic underwater decorations.

Happy birthday, he repeats.

They're alone in an empty, shadowy room. The aquarium is elevated and, as they extend their hands to each other, Nikita and Dasha circle the glass cube almost without a sound, as if they are carrying out a sacred rite, as if they are doing a round-dance.

How, on Dasha's birthday, we baked a round loaf. Yay tall and yay wide .

There was a children's film where the underwater dwellers sang ". . . baked a pie from clay." Yes, a film about a bogatyr who went down to the seafloor to liberate Marya the Craftswoman.

Every man must go down to the seafloor at least once in his life to bring back his beloved.

Or down to the deep end. Where there are snags, rotten stumps, cray-fish with pincers, and burbots with whiskers—where the sunlight can't reach.

That's what love is—a dark deep end.

You dive in headfirst, as into a deep end.

Every woman is a river. You enter her to surrender to the flow. Hair like seaweed, breasts like waves. Then you are carried out on a bank and you lie together embracing, as you once did with Masha on the Simeiz rocks.

That summer, they ran out of money and Masha came up with a plan: she put on a flowery skirt, tied a handkerchief around her head, grabbed a deck of cards, and went to the seafront to impersonate a Tzigane woman and read vacationers' fortunes. That evening, they had a feast: they bought wine and kebab right at the seafront. Only Masha had grown a bit sad. Nikita asked: *What's the matter?* And she said that, by the second or third person, she realized that she could in fact see these people's pasts and futures.

Could she see her own future, the lonely armchair in their empty apartment? Could she see Nikita's future, the aquarium cube in the middle of this room, the face of an unknown young woman through the thick layer of greenish water?

Every woman is a river, but for Nikita, Dasha turned out to be a deep end.

This must be why Nikita bought her the aquarium. It's the best present he could give her.

He had known immediately what the aquarium should look like. A dark lake somewhere in the thick of a forest. Snags, stumps, an abandoned windmill, catfish or burbots.

Well yeah, a deep end.

Victor shrugged his shoulders, but finished it in a week and didn't ask too many questions—who knows what personal clients the boss could have? And now, on Dasha's birthday, they are doing a round-dance around a cubic lake set up in the middle of a midsized Moscow room.

Round loaf, round loaf, choose whoever it is you love.

Dark snags, rotten stumps, whiskered faces. And there he is on the bottom with no strength to get up. Branches cling to his clothes, dark water fills his lungs. It's hard to breathe, it's impossible to breathe, yet again, all the oxygen he has left surfaces to his lips as foam. For some reason, you always remember when it's too late, when you can't stop, when the thirty ruble *aqua vitae* doesn't bring you peace, when the quiet deep end starts to pull you down to the bottom, to the stumps, snags, burbots and catfish. The fish will drink your brain, destroy your body, fill your lungs with a dark, near-bottom moisture—and this time, you won't be able to dive out, you simply won't have the strength, no one will reach a hand out to pull you up to the surface. No one.

Did you say flashback? Now there's a flashback.

Snags that grip my ankles like fingers. I try not to look down, I've already remembered it all, I know what I'll see. Dear Lord, Moreukhov starts to pray, give me strength. Not the strength to survive, not the strength to change what I can change—simply any kind of strength. He falls in the dirty February snow, wheezing faintly, foam on his lips, that's it, it's the end, I've come to the end of my suffering, I don't want to die. Dark waters close in over his head, fish feelers tickle his face, scaly bodies slide down his skin and, only on the edge of his consciousness, a female face flickers—slanted eyes, broad cheekbones, half-open lips . . . Maggie Cheung, no way, why would she be here!

And Nikita pulls Dasha closer to him, kisses her, takes off his sweater and unbuckles his belt. Dasha breaks free, giggling, and they race around the aquarium for the last time—*I'll admit that I love all, but Nikita most of all*—fall on the bed, mess around, laugh, moan, as if it's Nikita who's just turned twenty-three and has his entire life ahead of him. His lips taste of silver happiness and he kisses Dasha again and again until he runs out of air, his breathing's disrupted, his head spins and his embrace weakens.

The whiskered faces of fish watch through the thick layer of water, the seaweed quivers somewhere in the depths of the forest lake, and the snags darken . . .

36.

ZOO-ALCOHOLOGY

The best way to start a conversation about zoo-alcohology is by analyzing the well-known expression *drunk as a pig*. An uninformed individual might think that pigs drink a lot, hence the comparison.

I don't think that's at all the case. If pigs do in fact drink, then far less so than the likes of us.

Drunk as a pig is just one of the stages of drunkenness, not the first, but not the last either.

Human likeness is lost gradually. To completely lose it, you need persistence and determination. Darwin didn't labor in vain when he invented evolution—it's not easy to regress!

Of course, at first, man drinks like a *monkey*. At this stage, he is merry, playful, and prone to sexual escapades. He jumps from branch to branch, swinging his tail, so to speak, and is still quite capable of communicating with *Homo sapiens*.

World literature is rife with stories of some primate or other being passed off as a human in order to mislead high society. Likewise, a drunk-as-a-monkey has every chance of being passed off as sober. At worst, slightly tipsy.

To be sure, a monkey is unmasked by its smell. A monkey smells of sweat and dirty fur; at this stage, an alcoholic smells of socks worn for a week, dirty underwear, and a long-unwashed cloak of body hair.

It's at the monkey stage that Moreukhov meets women. That's understandable: a monkey is a very sexy creature. And still sufficiently resembles a human being.

You could say that sex with a monkey is not quite zoophilia. Only a regrettable mistake.

Zoophilia starts at the next stage—*drunk as a dog.*

Once again, don't get the idea that dogs drink. It's just that a dog can in some way consider itself man's best friend—until it becomes rabid, that is.

Just like an alcoholic, who, at the dog stage, is by turns friendly and aggressive.

At this stage, the smell of sweat and dirt is often compounded by that of urine. Less commonly—vomit.

If a male dog or bitch could talk, then, after producing a puddle on the rug, they'd accuse their owners of not walking them on time. The dog-alcoholic uses the same strategy: a combination of tail-wagging, accusations, barking, and attempts to bite.

His bark is still reminiscent of human speech and, if you've got a somewhat active imagination, you can even decipher what he is saying.

He's usually either complaining about life and begging for help or railing against everyone around him, accusing them of his troubles.

Two of these modes of behavior can subsequently be described as "whining" and "fibbing." The second term is particularly fitting: there is usually not a grain of truth in an alcoholic's accusations.

Some still hazard getting involved with an alcoholic at the dog's stage, but we wouldn't recommend it: you might get what's coming to you.

Young women especially take chances.

Here, I could make a witty comment about a nun and a Saint Bernard, but I think that a woman willing to go to bed with a dog-man deserves only our sympathy.

Like all living creatures, anyway.

Aum maṇi padme hūṃ.

After the *dog's* stage, finally comes the *pig's* stage.

As we know from zoology, dogs know how to *serve*, although they can stand on two paws for only a very short time.

You don't usually see a pig standing on its hind legs unless you're at the circus. Thus, at the pig's stage, an alcoholic is no longer capable of walking normally, preferring short sprints or, best of all, crawling on all fours.

A known peculiarity of the pig is that it's anatomically incapable of looking at the sky.

This is a metaphor for the fact that, at this stage, an alcoholic's upper chakras are tightly blocked—even if, at previous stages, he managed to have so-called transcendental experiences.

Well, you get it: standing on his knees in the snow, talking to God and so on.

But if you're drunk as a pig, forget about God.

Lie on your mattress and choke on your own vomit.

Yes, at this stage, the smell of puke is intensified.

As we know from history, pigs are extremely dangerous and rapacious animals.

In the Middle Ages, many pigs were put on trial for devouring unattended children.

At the pig stage, an alcoholic is capable of causing serious harm to his loved ones—especially those who are helpless and dependent on him. For example, children.

We should note that animal trials played an important role in the Middle Ages. In antiquity, a state of inebriation could sometimes serve to alleviate guilt (for example, the intoxication of maenads or Bacchae was considered sacred). Medieval jurisprudence was unequivocal: even if you were drunk as a pig, you had to answer for it.

Some will say that, at this stage, an alcoholic no longer responds to words and it's therefore of no use to threaten him with laws, penalties, and prison.

I object: pigs are among the most intelligent of animals. At the pig stage, an alcoholic is even more sensible than at the dog.

What's more, a pig's silence only serves as additional proof of its intelligence; generally, at this stage, no one listens to an alcoholic anyway. So it's better to simply snort. Ultimately, it's more pleasant.

Try it for yourselves: bark and snort. Doesn't the snort stir up something warm in the very depths of your being?

In any case, we digress.

Speaking of the intelligence of pigs, we just wanted to emphasize that, at this stage, an alcoholic is still receptive to simple messages: if you touch my child, I'll break your finger, if you steal the money, I'll report you to the cops. You just have to make sure that the threats are viable. Don't say: call me a bitch one more time and I'll kill you!—no pig will believe such a threat.

Pigs know that they get fattened up for a long time just to be slaughtered.

It's no coincidence that the pig stage is the best-known. An alcoholic's further progression depends in large part on his family history, medical background, and individual habits.

However, we can briefly summarize our acquired experience by saying that, at the next stage, an alcoholic ceases to be associated with terrestrial animals.

In some cases, he is delayed at the *wood louse* stage and, in others, he descends to the *annelid* or *barnacle* stage.

Rare and rather curious specimens prefer the stage of *snakes* and *lizards*—unsubstantiated data show that such individuals are often encountered among those born in the year of the Dragon.

All varieties of this stage are characterized by a refusal of endothermy—that is, a maximum adaptability to their environment.

For example, an alcoholic falls asleep easily in the cold because that's precisely what most reptiles do.

This stage is typically less time-consuming than the triad of monkey dog pig.

At this stage, the drunkard already hears the sound of crashing waves and strives to get to a marine environment as quickly as possible.

The allure of seawater to alcoholics is widely known: no doubt, everyone is familiar with the Russian word *alconauts*, derived from the Argonauts, the mythical Greek heroes who traveled across three seas to Colchis in search of the Golden Fleece.

The Golden Fleece is traditionally considered a symbol of sacred knowledge, but we should recall the tragic end met by all the heroes of this Greek epic.

Even though their leader, Jason, was promised a kingdom, he ended up a vagrant who roamed Greece, rejected by all.

In our time, too, such a fate is typical of the alconauts.

Another common expression is *no sea is too deep for the drunk*. When explaining his benders, Moreukhov was particularly fond of saying that he still had many seas to cross.

Then again, it would be erroneous to believe that an alcoholic wades across a sea: no, he moves along the sea floor, sometimes plunging to such depths that we have trouble finding an appropriate fish or mollusk to name this stage after.

Hence, we'll call it the *oceanic stage*.

The predominant fantasy harbored at this stage—becoming an *ocean wave*—is, as we know, unrealistic.

The best that an alcoholic can hope for is to lose his sight and hearing. The likelihood of the former is particularly great in the event of consuming low-quality alcohol.

The state of a man who is fully immersed in water and has switched off all his external sensory organs has often been described in professional literature.

Let's recall John Lilly's numerous experiments with an isothermic bathtub.

Academic science considers such experiments to be quite risky, and the fate of alcoholics who've subjected themselves to them confirms this.

A singular feature of such states is that the subject experiences intense emotional turmoil often accompanied by hallucinations and visions that are, essentially, a projection of his inner world and a visualization of his childhood and birth traumas.

As we know, Moreukhov is haunted by visions of an underwater kingdom and images of sprites and drowned bodies.

No doubt, expert psychotherapeutic or analytical work will help uncover the roots of these visions, explain their importance to the client, and help him positively integrate the acquired experience.

Unfortunately, alcoholics are generally incapable of maintaining a long-term relationship with a psychotherapist.

Let's return to the oceanic stage. Curiously enough, the upper chakras that closed at the pig stage sometimes reopen at this stage: like the participants of Lilly's experiments, surviving alconauts report having a transcendental and, usually, non-verbalized experience.

This experience is analogous to the Golden Fleece, the knowledge of the alluring and enchanting which, for the most part, does nothing to make your daily life easier.

In modern zoo-alcohology, it is the determination to re-experience these *states of altered consciousness* over and over that explains the reoccurrence of benders.

It should be noted that literature and film in particular abound in horror stories about people who have degenerated to the state of Neanderthals and Pithecanthropi as a result of experiments such as Lilly's.

Academic science doesn't confirm such tales, but they are quite fitting as metaphor: the oceanic stage of alcoholism is almost always characterized by an irreversible degeneration of personality.

Even if you can restore sight and sound, the internal changes—particularly in the volitional and moral and ethical sense—are too drastic.

The succession of stages referenced in this paper is known in zoo-alcohology as "the Lamarck-Mandelshtam mobile ladder" in honor of the scientists who first described the sequence of these transformations.

It is known as mobile because a portion of the steps may be skipped by alcoholics—some may go directly from the pig to the oceanic stage.

The last and lowest rung is especially important in the theory of the *mobile ladder*.

An experienced alcoholic arranges his life so that, at the last stage, some voluntary rescuer or addiction specialist always waits for him with all the necessary tools to smoothly bring the diver's body back up to the surface.

It's the certainty that a rescuer awaits them at that last rung of the ladder that allows the alconauts to set off on risky journeys.

In conclusion, we wish to add that, on the basis of our theories, our clinic has developed progressive methods for treating alcoholism. Thanks to contemporary foreign techniques and our own innovations, we were able to significantly reduce the percentage of relapses. We are proud to inform you that, instead of the widely advertised success rate of eighty percent, we guarantee our clients an eighty-five percent success rate.

We accept both cash and non-cash payments.

You can contact our admissions department at the number indicated in this brochure.

If anyone wants to laugh, go ahead and laugh.

If anyone thinks there's a certain heroism or selflessness in *backward evolution*, please speak to the alconauts' relatives or try cleaning their apartment post-bender.

Man's transformation into animal is a sad sight, doubly so when you knew the protagonist well at the human stage. If you're a woman, imagine you gave birth to a piglet or a wood louse. If you're a man, imagine that you went to bed with a pig or a foul-smelling monkey. If you have a vivid olfactory imagination, imagine a cocktail of sweat, cheap beer, urine, and vomit. Generally, the smell of unwashed socks in such a potpourri is almost indiscernible.

We often hear about how an alcoholic only harms themselves. As in, no one is forcing the *alconaut's* loved ones to save him. It's alright—he won't die. And if he does die—well, so will the rest of us, nothing we can do about it.

Let's conduct a cognitive experiment. Think of the ones you love. Remember everything you hold dear. Find a visual image for each of these memories—a photo or a portrait. Now, imagine that all of these images were spread out on the floors of cages with monkeys, dogs or pigs. The animals defecated and urinated on pictures dear to your heart. They copulated, covering the pictures with their secretions. They chewed them when they were hungry and tore them to pieces—playfully or out of spite.

Take another look at these pictures. Imagine that the aforesaid happened not with pictures, but with your memories. Now your memories are putrid. They're torn, incoherent, chewed up and crumpled. You cannot look at them without disgust, anger, or tears.

Such is the fate of memories held by the friends and relatives of alcoholics. Unfortunately, nothing can prevent this type of loss—you can cut off all communication, not come to their rescue, ultimately, even outlive an alcoholic, but nothing will restore your memories to their original state. From now until forever, your past will reek of age-old sweat, vomit, and urine.

37.

YELLOWISH-RED LEAVES

So Nikita comes out of his building dressed for spring weather in a blazer from a boutique, English shoes, and brand-name jeans, walks to the parking lot and gets in his car. What do we have today? Oh yeah, breakfast with the suppliers. A small studio that takes orders to craft ruins.

People have no imagination, Nikita thinks. They keep decorating the bottoms of aquariums with ship wreckage, corals, replicas of the Coliseum, Roman columns, and Greek amphoras. As if history ended two thousand years ago! I can offer you a State Emblem of the Soviet Union split in half, the ruins of the fourth power-generating unit of the Chernobyl nuclear power plant, a plaque of Stalin shot down from a wall, the exploded remains of Russian churches, a bell thrown off a bell tower, and a silver ruble with Tsar Nicholas II on it, covered with a green spiderweb.

A brief retelling of a hundred years of history.

For the very wealthy, I can make an exclusive series of personalized ruins. Daycare center, mother's home, school, and cement dancefloor—everything our memories couldn't preserve in full. Everything of which mere fragments, mere ruins remain.

I remember my mother's frame frozen by the window. I remember the World War II trophy watch on Grandpa Misha's wrist, Grandma Marfa with her hands folded over her apron. I remember Grandma Nastya's village parlance, which the fifty years she lived in Moscow couldn't erase. I remember Grandpa Makar's gray beard and the gruff voice that used to scare me so, certain phrases, arguments with Dad. For some reason, I recalled: "This is not a children's film and children laugh at it. It's a horror film—you, of all people, have to understand!"

Recently, I asked my father what movie they were arguing about—I didn't think he would remember, but he immediately said: *Welcome, or No Trespassing.*

"But it's a comedy," I mused. Father replied: "My father-in-law said it was a film about a man who had been deeply frightened all his life."

At present, I think I can recall Grandpa's frame: his arms outstretched like wings, his frightful, booming voice: *Why can't you understand, it's for life!*

Alas, these are mere ruins, barely perceptible through the thick layer of water.

Our past lies on the bottom of a large aquarium while we all sit on a bank, casting fishing lines with hooks, pulling so hard, we can't pull them out. Only from time to time do we get lucky and a priceless fragment flashes in the sun—either glass or a diamond.

After work, I drove to Dasha's. We made love and afterward, I lay gazing at her. Dasha was sitting on the edge of the bed with her side to me, facing the window. Outside, the streetlamps came on. She spoke about the Age of Aquarius and the New Age, explaining yet again: "At the time, I decided that if I called you exactly fifty-four times, the end of the world wouldn't come. Because fifty-four is half of one hundred and eight." I smiled faintly and Dasha said in a wounded voice: "Why are you smiling? It worked!"

I listened to her, but paid more attention to the way her left breast quivered in time with her body's movements. The drops of sweat on it weren't dry yet and I, too, felt wrung out and watched dully, without my usual arousal.

Her right breast wasn't in my line of sight and I thought that if I shifted over a bit, I'd be able to see the crookedly hanging mirror and the reflection in it. As we know, a reflection reverses sides so that the right arm becomes the left and vice versa. The same had to be true for breasts: the right one would become the left. I wondered if it was possible to see two left breasts at the same time—the reflected one and the real one.

I should mention that it wasn't lust, but curiosity that compelled me to crawl to the edge of the bed—my impulse being more childish and innocent than refined and voyeuristic. In any event, I peered into the mirror without Dasha noticing.

I must have chosen the wrong corner because, in the ghostly light of the streetlamps, I saw only the reflection of Dasha's legs or rather, her knees and hips. I probably should have raised my eyes a bit, but at that moment, the fishing line grew taut, the water was overrun with ripples, and a little memory flickered, one that had scarcely faded over the past twenty years.

I'm seventeen, it's early fall, September or October, the last warm days before a long winter. On Saturday after class, the guys and I decided to go to the movies. I don't remember what film it was—a few years later, a tidal wave of foreign films obliterated all my old film memories. The four of us planned to go together, but at the last moment, we were joined by two girls. I don't remember who the second one was, but the first one was named Nika Golubeva.

I'd been in love with her since that spring. We strolled demurely under the blossoming apple trees of the Moscow squares, I carried her schoolbag and spoke intelligently about "Star Wars"—the space-based missile defense system recently launched by Reagan against the Soviets. During these strolls, Nika stayed silent and I mostly saw her in profile—slightly upturned nose, thick brows, and a dark lock of hair that kept breaking out from under her hat.

Who chooses a person's first love? At seventeen, you're charmed by any female profile, the outline of a breast under a school smock, the soupçon of nakedness, the touch of a female hand to your elbow, even the sudden gust of wind that sets the hair on your female classmates' uncovered heads aflutter. At present, I can't remember what led to my and Nika's springtime strolls—I only recall that, in her silent profile, I would detect wonder at my knowledge, scathing remarks, an ecstatic declaration of love, and a categorical refusal. In other words, while Nika was silent I was free to imagine whatever I wanted and my aspirations didn't advance that spring beyond the realm of fantasy.

We didn't see each other that summer: Nika went away to the seaside while I was at some health resort with my parents, where a precocious fifteen-year-old from Kiev taught me how to kiss. Her name was Veronika: at present, the similarity of the names seems a bit excessive.

Nevertheless, my erotic summer experiences changed nothing about my relationship with Nika: she still seemed mysterious and otherworldly to me. In September, she sat in the row next to mine so that I'd continually glimpse the familiar profile in class. To me, it was the embodiment of ethereal beauty: as my teachers droned on and on, I stared at the slightly swollen lips, but the thought of kisses hadn't visited me yet.

The girls bought tickets separately and sat in another row. I don't remember the film, but I can clearly see Nika in the illuminated lobby of the movie theater. She'd managed to run home and change out of her school uniform into a light dress—too summery for autumn, even a warm one. A draft momentarily raised the hem and I didn't know if I should stare greedily or look away.

We walked to a nearby square with two benches that were half-buried under yellowish-red leaves. Someone took out a bottle of wine; the girls declined it, but didn't leave. We sat down and I ended up across from Nika.

In the autumn dusk, her dress seemed almost weightless, as otherworldly as I wished to see Nika. I think it was white with red polka dots, in keeping with the maple leaves under our feet.

We opened the bottle. I think it made two rounds. I don't remember what we talked about: we must have been discussing the film, reminiscing about the summer or wondering who would get into which university.

It grew darker and my classmates turned into blurry silhouettes. Nowadays, I see the same blurry contours when I try to recall a forgotten face or figure: when we look back, it's as if we see everything through a thick layer of water. Like that autumn evening.

The streetlamps came on and it was unexpectedly light. Nika sat there squirming from the cold, gripping her shoulders with her hands. Her legs were tucked under her. A light wind disheveled her hair and not one, but a whole three locks raced around her right temple. Nika felt my gaze on her, raised her eyes, smiled faintly, and fixed her skirt.

Today, I would have seen this gesture as flirtatious, but at the time, I thought it simple and artless. As she lowered her arm, I caught sight of a blue vein pulsating on her wrist; then, Nika wrapped her arms around her shoulders again and I again lowered my gaze to her legs—and, as if for the first time, saw her right knee, which was just barely covered by the white-red hem.

Unlike the gallants of yore, I had seen Nika's knees and even hips numerous times—after all, we had gym together. But I'd never seen them so close, so I stared, unable to tear my eyes away.

Today, I would have said it was the most ordinary young girl's knee. In shape, it hardly differed from the other knees I've seen over the past twenty years. Pale, almost untanned, covered in tiny goosebumps—probably also because of the cold.

What's more, there was a bruise on it. An ordinary bruise, the kind I'd seen a hundred times on boys. I'd scrape my skin like this when I would fall off my childhood bicycle or climb a tree. The bruise was the size of a three-kopeck coin, slightly asymmetrical. The color faintly echoed the red dots on the dress and the leaves under our feet: more pale-crimson than pink.

I must have thought she scraped her knee like a boy. That she was made of the same flesh and blood as us. That she could also bleed and experience pain, which meant that she could also feel down, scared and alone. She also couldn't fall sleep at night and lay there staring at the ceiling or a dimly lit corner of the window; she could also be sad, afraid, suffer. Could also die.

It must have all happened in an instant—or maybe, I stared at the bruise for about ten minutes. It was like time was switched off—and that's when I made a simple and impossible gesture: I reached out my hand.

My fingers touched Nika's skin. I managed to touch the bruise, to pass my fingertips lightly over it; then, Nika pushed my hand aside and pulled down her hem.

The pale-crimson spot disappeared, but that didn't matter anymore. I saw Nika with new eyes: a slightly-flushed-from-embarrassment, freezing girl who bit her lower lip anxiously as the wind continued to dishevel her hair. I thought I saw the blue vein still pulsating on her wrist.

My fingertips still remember that touch, that small cut, that bruise, remember Nika's skin, the flimsy barrier concealing her flesh from the world, the flesh of another which was the same as mine.

In that brief moment of contact, no obstacle stood between us: the ephemeral, weightless phantom of first love vanished and an ordinary girl sat across from me. She was just like me—alive, vulnerable, and defenseless.

A few millimeters of flesh separated her from the rest of the world—flesh that was velvety, tender and exciting, fragile and flawed. For the first time, I wanted to kiss Nika—not on the lips, no!—I wanted to shower her with kisses the way a mother swaddles her child; I wanted to tell every cell on her skin: I know how hard it is to be the barrier between a human being and the world.

For a moment, I saw Nika's body in all its plenitude and perfection—her dress fell away like a shroud, a superfluous husk. As I sat on a bench in the autumn park, I watched her lungs open and collapse under her ribs, her breasts quiver in time with these movements, and her blood run down the most delicate vessels to turn her cheeks red, the vein on her wrist blue, and the bruise—pale crimson. Never before had I experienced such tenderness, sadness, and pity—and, in the next twenty years, would never again.

I can't say I've never thought back to that autumn evening. Of course I've thought back to it, but it was like I was reading about it in a book, like it was happening to someone else. Just like I remember the conclusions of romantic novels, I remember our story's predictable and moderately happy ending: the first kiss, consuming caresses, stupid fights, and the final goodbye. It doesn't even matter if Nika was my first—the moment my fingers touched her knee was more vivid and special than any sexual revelation.

I confess I'll be turning forty soon, I've known many women, caressed their bodies, both beautiful and flawed, penetrated their moist crevices, touched them with my tongue and fingers, held them tightly in my arms and covered them with kisses; the human body has long ceased to be a mystery to me. Yes, the most intriguing and beautiful women are made of the same fabric as us, but this can only astonish you once in your lifetime. Of course, the memory of the astonishment stays, even if it fades away with the years.

Or so I thought until that evening a few days ago, when I saw a bruise on Dasha's knee the exact shape and color as the one I reached for in a St. Thomas-like fashion twenty years earlier.

This time, I didn't budge. There was a time when a small bruise allowed me to see a young woman instead of an otherworldly fantasy and opened up the possibility for tenderness and touch, carnal love and sensual intimacy. From the very beginning, Dasha's body was a source of pleasure for me, a body that I had to caress and touch, investigate, study and penetrate, in which I had to provoke arousal, palpitation and trembling, which I played like the flute that Rosencrantz and Guildenstern weren't able to play, from which I elicited sighs, moans, and screams so, in the end, I'd learn to summon the underwater goddess, the woman from the deep end.

Twenty years ago, I wasn't up for such a challenge, but I've had sufficient practice since then.

For a moment, the reflection in the mirror of a spot on her left knee turned me into a teenager, and another's body once again became an exciting mystery for me and not a problem to be solved, artistically or technically. A body has a life of its own: the lungs open and collapse, the blood pulses, and the color flows to your face. In an instant, I forgot everything I've learned over the years: the G-spot, the clitoral orgasm, erogenous zones.

There are times when the years we've lived through evaporate. For a moment, I was once again a seventeen-year-old, once again gripped by tenderness, pity and sadness, rapture and fascination—the taste of which I had almost forgotten.

A moment that was immediately followed by sadness. Twenty years ago, I thought that this rapturous tenderness, this tremulous pity would stay with me forever. Now I know how ephemeral it all is.

I suddenly wanted to be young, innocent, and ignorant again, charmed by fragile beauty, eternally seventeen, sitting in an overgrown park among yellowish-red leaves, watching the vein pulsate, the locks of hair flutter and the frozen lips quiver; I wanted to inhale the musty autumn smell as I lightly touched the knee of a girl as young as me.

I wanted to return and forget that, very soon, this moment would fall like a warm pebble to the bottom of an aquarium. Twenty years would go by, another young woman would be reflected in the crooked mirror and only then would everything return. Perhaps for the last time.

38.

EVERYONE LIKES MY POETRY

At one time, everyone called her Lenochka; in the upper grades, she started calling herself Lyolya. When her young colleagues call her Yelena Grigoryevna, she always gets upset. Why use a name and a patronymic? She's only fifty-five. Of course, that's no longer young, but who needs that youth? She read somewhere that truly sensual women reach their prime after fifty—as their system prepares for menopause, the body goes through one last, decisive growth spurt and reaches true sexual maturity.

Everyone in the world knows this, but in Russia, they don't understand it. Last year, she went on vacation to Turkey and young men hounded her at every turn. They asked her out for coffee, offered to show her the country, offered to take her to a leather or a jewelry shop. What's so surprising about that? She looks great, dresses on trend, has good taste, style—experience, at long last.

So let her be Lyolya, none of that Yelena Grigoryevna business.

Lyolya had almost forgotten how, thirty years ago, she would roll her first name patronymic-last-name around on her tongue for hours as if it were an icicle. *Yelena Grigoryevna Borisova. Yelena Borisova. Yelena Grigoryevna.* She pictured those words on a book cover. A modest black-and-white photograph, above it—*Yelena Borisova*, below—the title, then, the subheading: poems. She always came up with a new title: *Morning, Morning Album, Kilometers, Miles, Work, Labor, Soul, Snowdrop, Swan Stance*—good, laconic titles reminiscent of her favorite books. And in twenty or thirty years, she thought that her books would also appear in hardcover, with prefaces from contemporaries referring to her as Yelena Grigoryevna and Yelena Grigoryevna Borisova. And the titles would be different: *Selected and New Poetry, Selected Poems, Poems, The Portable Yelena Borisova.*

Not a single real collection of hers was published. But Sasha did gift her a typewritten volume of her work on her thirtieth birthday. The title page said: *Moscow, 1980, Sashizdat, 5 copies.* He'd typed it up himself, made a cover out of thick paper, and written in marker: *Yelena Borisova. Selected Poems.* Lyolya was touched—and at the same time, displeased: she would have selected a different set of poems, corrected and omitted some things. But still, it turned out he'd been collecting her poems all these years. You could say he was a fan. It was only too bad that he wasn't so much a fan of her work as simply a fan. A smitten Pierrot, touching and useless.

Deep down, she never truly liked Sasha. Even during the few months of their romance in distant 1971, when she was in her third year of university and he was back from the army for two years and took turns working in geological field parties and as an odd jobman, among other things. He told funny stories about the North—it was like you were reading *Territory* by Oleg Kuvayev or *Oranges from Morocco* by Vasiliy Aksyonov—but was awkward and inept at everything else. Lyolya even suspected that she was his first, but of course she never asked, knowing that boys were ashamed of that kind of thing and always pretended to be experienced lovers. What a hoot.

And now it's too late to ask.

As a matter of fact, Lyolya only stayed with him for so long that year because she liked the way he listened to her poems. He always had the same enraptured expression on his face as the people filmed at the Polytechnic Institute and Mayakovsky Square readings. She'd forget they were sitting on a park bench or the couch in his mother's living room or in her dorm room and imagine she was standing before a crowd of excited listeners, her words penetrating deep into their hearts, tears running down their cheeks.

"That's so cool, Lyolya," Sasha would say, "you're a real poet!"

At twenty years old, she had no doubt that she was a real poet. No wonder everyone liked her poetry: her mom, her friends at the dormitory and the young men she read it to between dances or in the foyer of a second-run movie theater, where she liked to go watch old black-and-white Italian films. Everyone liked her poetry, but only Sasha had that enraptured look.

At twenty, Lyolya was certain that she would become famous and this was all only the beginning. She thought that she had the talent and that all she lacked were new experiences, impressions, emotions, and loves. More than anything, she feared having a boring life—one like everyone else's. She cut lectures, strolled through Moscow, and kissed in squares, regardless of what month it was, always inventing a new love affair for herself: first, it was a professor from the Department of Ancient Philosophy, then, a famous actor, then, a musician from a semi underground rock group who could play The Beatles' music just like them, and now a young geologist, just like in the Aksyonov and Gladilin books she liked since grade school. But a great love still eluded her, and it seemed like this was the only thing preventing her from becoming a truly important poet. If Lyolya believed in God, she would have asked Him for this love, but instead of God, she believed in "they will offer you everything and give you everything" from *The Master and Margarita*—so she received everything in accordance with her faith, was given everything in spades without even having to ask.

Vasya was five years older than her, tall, and handsome. Furthermore—a physicist, a nuclear scientist, like in the film *Nine Days in One Year*—nuclear test sites, trials, secret experiments. As soon as she saw him, she realized right away that Sasha was just the tip-off, the dress rehearsal. They really did resemble each other—after all, they were brothers—but only in the way that a real poet's poems resemble those of his imitators. Even before she felt Vasya's hand on her waist as they danced, Lyolya knew: there he is, the man of her life, the one she must belong to, the one who will make her heart burn with love, her body tremble with passion, and her poems be enshrined in literature forever.

In the morning, she wrote: *"The one" is like an atom, like nuclear fission. "The" is the electron, "one" is the force. You gave it to me. You were with me all night, by chance* . . . Oh wow, I forgot the fourth line. I think it was very good.

Lyolya takes the aforementioned *Sashizdat* book off the shelf, leafs through it . . . No, of course, the poem isn't there, she probably didn't even read it to Sasha, everything ended so awkwardly that night: Sasha got drunk and she instantly hopped into bed with his brother.

But how great it was to be with him!

Lyolya leafs through the yellowed pages. *Unborn daughter, I turn to you* . . . It's a funny story—for some reason, she was certain it would be a girl. She was mistaken. If you think about it, she was frequently mistaken. For some reason, she thought that suffering steeled the soul, that an unhappy love made your poetry even more powerful. But when Vasya left her—in a way that was so stupid, so humiliating!—she had absolutely no desire to write and could only cry and remember how great it was to be with him. A few times, she sought consolation from her former lovers, but it always ended up being stupid, meaningless, and shameful . . . In the end, she went back to her parents in St. Petersburg, got into an argument with them the first evening, slammed the door, and went to live with Aunt Lida.

They strolled in the Summer Garden, which had already been abandoned for the winter, and Aunt Lida told her about the romantic canon. It was extraordinary: Aunt Lida was a chemist, but only spoke to Lyolya about literature. That autumn, she explained to her that romantic love was just a byproduct of the emergence, during the Renaissance, of the modern concept of the individual—meaning, a separate entity that didn't belong to a family or a lineage and wasn't a church parishioner or a guild artisan. Man asked himself: *What is the reason for all this? Why am I who I am, why am I living this particular life?* And it turned out that love was the answer, love was what separated human beings from the community to which they belonged all through the Middle Ages. This is the origin of the romantic canon, *Romeo and Juliet*, early Pushkin, Victor Hugo, and even Gustave Flaubert.

Lyolya clearly remembers Aunt Lida in her hat, trudging heavily with a cane in hand. At almost seventy, she was still full of vigor, and the pregnant Lyolya could barely keep up with her. Her loud, shrill voice echoed in the empty park:

"Clinging to the romantic canon is as silly as believing in the phlogiston theory or Ptolemy's system. For its time, it was an enormous step forward, yes. But that time is long gone. Lenochka, this is why, when confronted with reality, all romantic dreams turn out to be such shit. Because they've aged in the moral sense. People have withdrawn so far into themselves that they've hit the limit, and the time has come for them to once again find their communities."

Lyolya had never heard her parents' peers say the word "shit," and this both ruffled her and cheered her up.

"Is love shit too?" she asked.

"Romantic love, Lenochka, is phenomenal shit," her aunt answered, then added: "in any case, I can't say what the shittiest in this rotten bunch is: fascination with death, the charms of solitude, power over others, otherworldly passion, unrequited love . . . I'm turning seventy soon, I've seen it all."

"And what about creativity?" Lyolya asked.

"Creativity is also shit. Go ahead and read the German Romantics, who invented all these mad artists and crazy poets. It's no accident that it all ended with Baudelaire, who wrote about waste and shit as a subject rather than a metaphor."

"Baudelaire is a wonderful poet," Lyolya said with confidence, "Tsvetaeva translated him!"

"Tsvetaeva!" her aunt scoffed. "Can you at least imagine what this Tsvetaeva was like in real life? A querulous, hysterical broad who slept with everyone, men and women . . . ugh! Creativity is shit, I tell you."

"If I understand you correctly," Lyolya took umbrage, "then everything in the world is shit. What's left?"

"Nothing," Aunt Lida sighed, "there's nothing left. Simply living."

"And simply living isn't shit?" Lyolya said defiantly.

"No," Aunt Lida said. "That's the only thing that's not shit. Family, children, work. An ordinary life. Like everyone else's."

"So why didn't you . . ." Lyolya started and checked herself. In reality, Aunt Lida never had a family or children, maybe never even had a man. At present, she was about to turn seventy, an old woman, whereas Lyolya was young and had her entire life ahead of her, she wasn't going to argue with her and try to prove a point. And Lida simply envied her—envied her youthful body, her talent, her love, and her future child.

They returned home that day in silence, but a sudden calm came over Lyolya. She stopped dreaming of Vasya—it was as if someone flipped a switch in her brain so it could focus on her unborn baby. A month later, she returned to Moscow, saying that she didn't want to give birth in St. Petersburg. Her father gave her money and a Moscow colleague of his helped her find an apartment, where she lived alone for a year before her father received his own apartment in the Sokol district and relocated from St. Petersburg. That is to say, at first, she lived alone and then, with little Sasha.

Was it difficult? Of course. Lyolya wanted to be a poet, not a mother, she dreamed of spending nights writing poetry and was forced to wash diapers and daub her cracked, swollen nipples with Brilliant Green. Yes, her breasts were much better suited for tender, loving kisses than a greedy infant's mouth. She never went to the store without the pram, slept erratically, and got drowsy as soon as she opened a book, so what talk of poetry could there be?

Of course, from time to time, Sasha appeared, the older Sasha. He took her to the maternity clinic, brought her flowers, and visited her on breaks between expeditions. Vasya never even called. She, too, never called him, she'd be damned if she did, she had her pride. His parents—Sasha-senior's parents and Sasha-junior's grandma and grandpa—would invite her over, offer to help with their grandson. She'd go—*in my opinion, the child needs to have relatives!*—but would never, ever run into Vasya. She would only see his framed pictures on the walls. The last time she visited was before Grandpa Mikhail's death in 1991. By then, Vasya's photo hadn't changed in five years, which meant that, not long ago, at the cemetery, was the first time she'd seen him in twenty or thirty years.

He'd aged, yes. But his son—not their son, but the other son, Nikita—looked like the Vasya she'd known at one time. She cried that day at the cemetery, not knowing if it was because Sasha was dead or because Vasya had turned into an old man and Nikita into Vasya, which signified that so many years had gone by, a whole generation, and now, new girls dreamt of poetry books, sensed that they would become famous, and wheeled their babies around in prams, angry that love was eluding them or tearful that their love had gone.

Maybe my aunt was right? Lyolya thinks. Maybe love, poetry and proud solitude aren't worth anything after all? Maybe what's more important is a baby's cry at night, its snuffling at your breast, its tiny fists with clenched fingers, its head covered with fresh fuzz . . . seeing a vein trembling under delicate skin, life pulsating before the little brook is overgrown, while your son is still open to the universe, open to universal love, can't tell people apart, doesn't choose women for himself, isn't torn between a wife and a lover, doesn't reject, doesn't abandon, accepts everything the world gives him—the warmth of a mother's breast, a familiar voice, drops of milk on cracked nipples.

Maybe that's what was real? Most essential, most vital, more valuable than the unwritten poems, the unpublished books, the love that never was?

No, she couldn't live that way. Others probably could, but she couldn't. Above all, she was an as-yet unrecognized poet, unknown to anyone and unappreciated by anyone except for the deceased Sasha. But Lyolya didn't want to be a mother because that was even more frightening.

Poetry is the answer to the question *what is the reason for all this?* Why did she move to Moscow, why did she change men, why did she leave Sasha, why did she give birth, why did she work as an editor all these years? So that there'd be poetry. This was a dignified answer.

Poetry will always be poetry. In thirty years, the infant will turn into a dirty lout who smells like a hobo, a drunken ruin, an old man who looks older than his own father.

If this is the sum total of Lyolya's life, she would have been better off dying at twenty-four, killing herself, throwing herself under a train, hanging herself with a noose, not living to old age and thus carrying on the tradition.

In any case, I have carried on the tradition, Lyolya thinks: none of the great female poets had any luck with their children.

39.

AFTERNOONS: XXII CENTURY.

The Institute toiled at the forefront of science. The range of its projects was unusually broad, but the Laboratory where Vasiliy Melnikov worked specialized in developing space satellite communication systems. Melnikov himself specialized in mathematical models and was thus rarely away from the suburban Moscow town housing this branch of the Institute. This time, he managed to convince the boss to let him to visit a test site where another satellite, in whose development his ideas played a large role, was supposed to be launched.

Melnikov stood at the test site's observational post next to Yura Kochin. A minute earlier, Kochin had said:

"Sometimes I think all we do here is shoot sparrows from a cannon. Can you imagine how much goddamned work and thought was put into this satellite—and to what end? So that another thousand reindeer herders can watch television. Meanwhile, almost a half billion people are going hungry on earth. If we weren't wasting all this energy and instead directed it at resolving genuinely important problems . . . heigh-ho!" and Kochin waved his hand.

"Now wait a minute, old boy," Melnikov said. "That's how snobs and utilitarians talk. Do you remember what FF used to say about this?"

"I never met him," Kochin grumbled.

Melnikov ended up at the Laboratory in the late 1960s and had the chance to work with the famous FF—Fyodor Fomich, who had carried out tests with Sergei Korolev and launched the first rockets. FF was a legend—although, instead of academic degrees, he held a military title, either First Lieutenant or Major. It was FF who instilled his outlook on life in Melnikov, and Melnikov carried it with him through all his years of work.

"Now then," Melnikov said instructively, "FF used to say that the ultimate meaning of our existence was to expend energy . . . Ideally so that we'd both find our existence interesting and be useful to others."

"So what?" Kochin growled.

"That's what we're doing here—expending energy. It's obviously interesting to us and useful to a thousand reindeer herders. We are collectively advancing science and the evolution of humanity."

Kochin was silent.

"Don't look so sour," Melnikov said with conviction, "time to get to work."

"I'm well aware," Kochin snarled. He always snarled when they mentioned FF and the other old-timers he had missed. He was one of the last to be hired at the Laboratory, and had the sound reputation of a "very, very talented young man." It wasn't clear what was preponderant in this phrase—the recognition of his talent or the reminder of his young age.

"Don't be sad," Melnikov said, "you're only twenty-five, you'll have enough time for everything."

Melnikov had just turned thirty and felt like a fossil.

The satellite was launched the next day. In the evening, rocket engineers, physicists, and mathematicians gathered around the great table to toast the successful launch. Their faces were all joyful and excited, and only Melnikov sat there quiet and pensive. At the other end of the table, Lyosha Zhukov, a rocket fuel specialist, told a new joke:

"One cyberneticist (laughter, indignant cries of programmers) invented a predictor, a machine that predicted the future—a sort of assembled, one-hundred-level unit. And to start with, he asked the predictor: 'What will I be doing in three hours?' The predictor hummed until morning and then informed him: 'You'll be sitting and waiting for my answer.'"

Everyone laughed merrily.

"On the basis of what principle would such a predictor work?" said Ivan Sidorchuk, a graduate of the mechanical mathematics department, a favorite of the Institute's female laboratory technicians and an international Master of Sports in swimming. "The probability distribution of events? Then that certainly is a great challenge, you may need more time than the next morning ."

"I'd like to know what awaits us in the future," said Kochin, red-faced.

"Communism," Zhukov barked, "don't you know? Communism awaits all of humanity, and oblivion awaits us individually. The ingratitude of our offspring is a commonplace thing."

"The descendants are forgetful because the ancestors aren't resentful," someone said.

Again, Melnikov recalled FF. One time, they were drinking in honor of Cosmonautics Day and, at the Laboratory's request, FF began to tell them about Korolev. By force of habit, he called the head design engineer the Beard. At the time, Melnikov was very drunk and didn't retain all the details, but there was something about descendants and ancestors, the living and dead. Something like the descendants' debt to their ancestors. FF calculated that you had to explore all of space to be able to repay this debt. Someone told FF that this was all idealism and superstition, and he began to laugh jovially: the Beard had once confessed to him that he believed in angels. Idealism was the principal fuel of the space program, FF said back then. Six months later, he died of cancer; and as Melnikov recalled this conversation, he felt a slight prick of conscience, as if there was a debt he couldn't repay.

"In a way, the ancestors are always richer than their descendants," Zhukov said. "Their dreams are richer. The ancestors dream of what is mere routine for descendants. Our dream is to reach for the stars! We're ready to give up everything for this dream. And our descendants will fly to the stars the same way we fly to see to our mothers on summer vacation."

"Poor them," someone burst into laughter.

"Dear Lyosha," said Sidorchuk, "I'd really like to meet with our descendants. I have a few questions for them, primarily on the subject of unified field theory."

Everyone took another drink. Sidorchuk grunted and continued:

"We're so lucky that radionuclides can be derived from alcohol. Imagine if we had to drink this much milk after every launch!" Gradually, the gathering split up into groups. A few enormous guys—two aspiring Masters of Sports and a couple of athletes with official grades—were planning an outing to the mountains the weekend before they returned to Moscow. Zhukov, who wasn't seated too far from Melnikov, was discussing yet another version of the famous 1957 catastrophe at the Mayak chemical plant in the Urals:

"There was no nuclear explosion, these are all tall tales. There was a thermal explosion, but you can bet your life things got tossed around.

Some smart-ass with epaulets ordered them to pack the waste barrels tighter, prompting a spontaneous warm-up; and then everything exploded. There's a river there, the Techa . . . In any case, I'd advise against bathing in it."

The very, very talented and young Kochin talked about how a schoolmate of his traveled to America with his diplomat parents and saw the futuristic film *2001: A Space Odyssey*. It wasn't the first time Melnikov had heard this story and each time, he wondered what a black monolith—which sometimes appeared on Earth and sometimes on Jupiter, in the past and in the future—had to do with their work. Was it a rocket? Baloney.

Melnikov had another drink. Everything turned out so ludicrous—he had genuinely looked forward to going to the Test Site, and now he was on edge. Perhaps because, before the launch yesterday, he called his father, who said that, two days ago, Lyolya gave birth to a boy and named him Sasha. Sasha could have told him himself, but it had now been six months since they last talked. Stupid, stupid, stupid, Melnikov scolded himself. He needed to go back to Moscow, call his brother, finally reconcile!

His affair with Lyolya had lasted three years—and, to tell the truth, he never loved anyone as much as he loved that girl. A clever girl, a wonderful, incredible person. If only it were possible to live out two different futures, he thought, one with Sveta and the other with Lyolya. Alright, both futures with different probabilities, but simultaneously. Because, in the past three years, Melnikov felt ashamed, ashamed and suffocated—also because no one tried to understand him or offer any kind of support. Even the guys from the Laboratory said it would be better if Melnikov devoted more time to his dissertation. It's too bad FF died—maybe he of all people would have understood what was happening. The meaning of existence was to expend energy and, for three years, Melnikov didn't spare himself. Just as an atom releases energy during nuclear fission, Melnikov spent his energy by being torn between Lyolya and Sveta. He found it interesting, like FF said he would. However, it was questionable whether the energy spent was useful to anyone at all.

The hardest part was when his father found out about Lyolya. No need to guess how—no doubt Sasha spilled the beans. Mikhail Konstantinovich came to see Melnikov at work and called him down to the lobby. They went out onto the street and sat down on a bench. Melnikov thought his father would rebuke him for the infidelity and talk about his son and his debt to the family, but Mikhail Konstantinovich said:

"You, Vasya, probably want to tell me that times have changed and morals are different from what they used to be?"

Melnikov nodded yes, that was exactly what he wanted to say. He wanted to explain that personal freedom began with sexual freedom—he read that sentence in an article in the Institute's newsletter that criticized the latest bourgeois theories—but his father didn't let him answer.

"You're still young," he said, "you think that things were always the way they were in your school years here? And that only your generation was able to assert its right to sleep with someone without getting a stamp in its passport?" (Melnikov nodded again.) "That's total nonsense, is what it is. I'm seventy years old, I was around for the Russian Empire, the revolution, the New Economic Policy . . . Trust me, in my youth, everyone talked of nothing but free love, the Sexual Question, and the theory of a glass of water."

"A glass of water—what's that?" Melnikov squeaked. He felt like he was being shaken by the scruff, like a kitten. Ow, ow, ow, I'm so ashamed.

"It's a theory that says that a man and a woman sleeping together is akin to them drinking a glass of water. It's a thirst that must be quenched. It was a fashionable theory in the 1920s."

"I didn't know that," Melnikov said.

"You don't know anything at all," his father barked. "Knowledge isn't being accumulated, only lost. There's no such thing as your scientific progress, only degeneration. My father, your grandfather, knew so much more than I do that, compared to him, you and I are both dunces and illiterates. He was a man of the Silver Age, met Andrey Bely, Blok, was friends with the Symbolists! Nowadays we're allowed to talk about it, thank God. Your grandchildren will study them in school, and I spoke to them as you're speaking to me now! We're children compared to them, little children!"

Melnikov sat there with his head hung low. Suddenly he had a headache and frowned with anguish. Why was his father telling him all this? Alright, we weren't the first ones to figure out that we could have sex if we were in love, and not just in a marriage. What a discovery! This is not physics, it's not important who proved it first. It doesn't change anything. We still have our right—our right to happiness.

"What do you think," said his father, "why did I live my entire life with your mother and never once cheated on her? Do you think I never wanted to? Or do you think I never had the opportunity?"

"I don't know," Melnikov shrugged his shoulders. "I haven't really thought about it, Dad. You probably never met another woman who . . ."

"There can't be *another woman*," his father interrupted him. "That's what I'm talking about. You can't tear yourself in two. The most important thing is oneness. Nuclear fission! Ha! The fission of a human being, that's what it is! And the ensuing chain reaction is worse than the one that takes place in your bomb. There is no happiness in fission, son. Happiness exists only in oneness. One woman. One family. One country. Remember that!"

"Alright," Melnikov said softly, although he wasn't entirely sure he understood.

"And now you decide. It's your life, you have to live it." His father got up and set off huffily for the train stop. After a few steps, he stopped and grumbled over his shoulder: "Just don't tell your mother, no reason for her to know about this."

At present, Melnikov thought his dad was right. If Melnikov hadn't spent three years on this exhausting romance, he would have already defended his dissertation. Instead of solving his personal problems, he should have been solving scientific ones. As their algebra professor used to say: "If you reduced all your life's problems to polynomials, they'd be resolved. At least, approximately . . . At any rate, you can't beget children from polynomials."

Melnikov poured himself more grain alcohol, drank it, and abruptly stood up. The sounds of excited voices carried to him: "I see you've been completely stupefied—do you not understand what we're telling you? I believe we were discussing the questions that will arise in a decade, when the time comes for piloted flights to other planets."

Melnikov exited into the night. The salt steppe lay before him, voiceless and vast, like the starry heavens overhead. We'll send a man to the stars from here, Melnikov thought excitedly. In ten, maybe fifteen years. If worse comes to worst, at the beginning of the next century. Perhaps, if I participate in developing such a flight, I'll be forgiven all my debts? My debts to Lyolya, to Sveta, to my brother, to my children, to my father and mother, to the grandfather I've never met? I would like to fly off in this rocket myself, Melnikov thinks drunkenly, and return in two hundred years, sometime in the twenty-second century, when humanity has already found all the answers and reached the oneness my father talked about—and, in the process, has lost neither love nor freedom. Perhaps what they write about in textbooks is true: everything evolves through a spiral. Through hunger, the spilling of blood, war, and senseless injustice, we'll arrive at a free society of immeasurable material and spiritual wealth. That very Golden Age of our great grandparents. We will return—and when we do so, a new branch of the spiral will sprout, one that, if you think about it, will make your head spin. A wholly and utterly different branch, completely unlike the one we had gone through. And a totally new contradiction will propel us along this new branch: one between the infinite mysteries of nature and the finiteness of our possibilities at any given moment. This augurs a most interesting life for us for millions of centuries. And the fact that we launched another satellite today has brought it closer to us, right?

Melnikov remembered how the bright, man-made star launched by Kochin, Zhukov, and Sidorchuk, and readied by FF and Korolev, vanished into the sky, remembered it and threw his head back, trying to discern the pulsating satellite among the uniformly flashing dots. He whispered: we did all this in Thy name—and froze in astonishment, not comprehending what he said or whom he was talking to.

They returned to Moscow in late evening and, as they left the airport, it started to rain. The motorway became slippery and the driver—slight and dark-eyed—decelerated. He was driving a heavy-duty vehicle and singing softly, hardly moving his lips. Some old unfamiliar song. It was unusually dark and uncomfortable, the blaze of city lights wasn't visible yet, and Melnikov thought that the car must have been crossing the steppe again. Up ahead, the beams of the headlights danced across the uneven asphalt. There was no oncoming traffic.

The car carried Melnikov into the future, toward his ungrateful descendants, disappointed hopes, unfulfilled fantasies, and unrealized utopias. And that future contained neither a piloted flight to Mars, nor a conquest of distant stars, nor a scientific renaissance. Computers became cheaper, smaller, and faster; the entire cosmos could fit in them. And in that future, only aficionados of blockbuster films and computer games could get excited about flights to faraway worlds.

His hopes weren't fulfilled: no one needed the stars. Melnikov never understood why that was.

40.

THE WATER OF AN INSIPID DEATH

Outside, it is raining. The drops are falling, falling on the ground, pounding on the puddles, flowing into streams and rivers, seas and oceans. Fresh water pours from the sky, replenishing the fresh water of lakes and ponds, the salt water of bays and harbors.

Deep down—corals and sunken ships, fish and mollusks, seaweed, bottle fragments.

Milk bottles, beer bottles, vodka bottles, bottles where water was poured, bottles containing notes that no one would be able to read now: the ink dissolved.

Water obscures everything.

A sunken ship lies at the bottom of the sea.

An iceberg dissolves and sinks into the ocean.

An airplane fallen from the sky, the *Mir* space station, fragments of the *Challenger* space shuttle, the *Kursk* submarine—the ocean obscures them all.

The ocean is where we once came from. Run your tongue between a women's legs and you will taste salt. That's the ocean sending us its regards, telling us that sex is training before the immersion, before the greatest and last journey. Come to me, lower yourself, I will part before you, take you in like the Red Sea took the Pharaoh. You will see things that you've never seen before. You don't need instructors and scuba gear—you will swim freely among the seaweed, multicolored fish will slip between your fingers like fine sand, jellyfish will open over your heads like umbrellas, and octopus tentacles will seize, embrace, and squeeze you tighter than the most passionate lover. If you've never been to the seafloor, you haven't known what real love is, the last and greatest love.

The ocean is where all the rivers will flow. The ocean will soothe everyone. The salt will heal the wounds. It will cover us with its waves like with a damp, ever quivering blanket.

Are you seasick? Come down to the seafloor, no seasickness here.

Do you want love? Open your lungs, throw your breast open to me and my salty love will flow into you.

Are you afraid? Dive in deeper, you'll see—there's no fear here.

Ocean water is the water of eternity.

To emerge from it and return to it.

Fresh water in the faucets of our homes, in bottles and pots. When we're boys, we build fishponds and, when we get older—dams. The river water turns turbines, lights up as electricity in our homes, stands in a glass on our tables.

Ordinary, domestic water. We consider it life-giving water. About two-thirds of our bodies.

Look into the water, Brave Little Raccoon, who sits in the river? In the ocean, it's the oceanic tsar and the mermaids, in the ocean, it's the sunken ships and Poseidon's trident. Whereas in the river it's just you, Brave Little Raccoon, just your reflection. Clench your fist, make a face—or, better yet, smile, because your life is like a river, your time is like a river. If you swim for a while, you will find your peace at last in the salty ocean water. So, while you're still surrounded by the river, swim.

Swim, don't stop, swim. Be wary of turbulent rapids, don't drown in the riverside shoal, don't be captivated by the beauty of waterfalls. And most importantly, don't trust the deep end, the dark deep end, the quiet deep end—you know yourself who dwells there. Special kinds of imps, river sprites, water creatures, swamp witches, drowned bodies twined with seaweed. Catfish and burbots, crayfish and pikes, rotten snags, jutting sticks, long-submerged tree stumps.

These are all traps for those who have lost their way.

The children run into the izba screaming: *Daddy! Daddy! Come—there is a Deadman caught inside our net!*[2] The children sat on the bank for a while and their wait has paid off. Who was it swimming by in the river that the children have caught in their nets, swaddled like an infant? Not children, no—little imps, fishers of foolhardy people.

That's why you shouldn't stop, you should keep swimming, swimming

---

[2] Reference to Alexander Pushkin's poem *The Drowned Corpse*, which includes this line.

farther on. Everyone who looked back, who wished to take a break, get some R&R, settled down a bit too early, considered the journey over— river water awaits them all. The water of an insipid death, a manmade, domestic death. A commonplace death that is not followed by eternity, only a mill wheel that endlessly rotates by the pond, turned by water creatures and the drowned; and everyone who never made it to the ocean will also keep spinning in it like hamsters in an underwater exercise wheel.

This is our story, the story of those of us who haven't yet drunk enough water from the dark lake, enough putrid water from abandoned mill ponds. We still have plenty of drinking to do, plenty of going down to the bottom and resurfacing, paddling, awkwardly waving our arms around, yelling: "Hey there, on the riverbank!" and swimming on, tasting the water until salt forms on our lips.

PART TWO
BANG BANG
(ATLANTIS)

(1940s—1950s)

*The past seeps into the present
like blood—and turns into the future.*

Isaac Adamson

*Lord, watch us sink to the bottom—
Teach us to breathe underwater.*

Boris Grebenschikov

Grigoriy Borisov
Born 1905, father of Yelena (Lyolya) Borisova, Moreukhov's
grandfather

Polina Borisova
Born 1932, older daughter of Grigoriy Borisov

Djamilya Takhtagonova
Born 1924, mother of Tatyana (Tanya) and Gulnara (Gulya)
Takhtagonova
Grandmother of Anya (Elvira) and Rimma

Oleg
Born 1904 (?), father of Tatyana Takhtagonova, Elvira's grandfather

Mikhail Melnikov
Born 1905, father of Vasiliy and Alexander Melnikov
Grandfather of Nikita, Moreukhov, and Elvira

Konstantin Nikolayevich
Born 1865, father of Mikhail Melnikov
Grandfather of Vasiliy and Sasha Melnikov
Great-grandfather of Nikita, Moreukhov, and Elvira

41.

1913. THE CONTINENT UNDER THREAT

A fireplace festooned with rococo flourishes opened its black jowl, which had been obscured by a fine, ornate lattice as if with a muzzle; the porcelain clock that stood on it wasn't ticking. Father placed his fingers under the neckline of his vest, drummed a finger against this neckline and said:

"Atlantis! Atlanteans, the fourth race. We're used to a map of the two Americas, but we've forgotten that, before, there was no America, only the continent of Atlantis. The fourth race, which existed before humankind, before the Aryan race, before you and I! The great ancients knew"— he regulped some air—"what our scientists could never dream of."

Misha began to shiver, leapt up, and clenched his little fist with delight:

"What did they know? Will you tell me?"

"Shh!" Father brought his finger to his lips and trotted toward the door, closing it and retreating to the oak closet, whose little doors with carved edges opened, revealing goatskinned, leathered, and dustily-grayed tomes of Blavatskaya, Steiner, and Böhme. French, English, Latin, Hebrew, and Arabic. Books end to end.

He hooked his fingers into one of them and pulled it out.

The table was enormous—more like a throne than a table; the lamplight rounded over it. And, in the center of the yellowish circle, the book's pages puffened.

"Can you read it?" And Father pointed his finger at the cover.

Misha sniffled his little nose, wrinkled his little forehead, licked his little finger and traced out along the golden horizon of the page's edge:

"A—T as in toy—L as in lemon—A . . . Atlas?"

Atlantis?

Amid the splatter of eyelashes, his eyes opened wide.

Father snapped the clasp and flung it open—and Misha froze with his little mouth agape:

"Maps!"

The pages rustled parchment-yellow, the sea turquoised, the mountains red-bricked and the plains emerald-puddled.

Yes, maps!

"Look!" and the finger screeched down the ocher paper, "look over here! Here is India and here are the Himalayas!"

A little head stretched from a thin neck and the eyes opened still wider:

"And that?"

"That is the city of Shambhala, a sanctuary of the Ancients, a vault of mysteries."

"Is that where Atlanteans live? The fourth race?"

Father exhaled, scratched his cheek, and ruffled his whiskers.

"They all died, a long time ago. They were punished. For their perdition, their snorting and plunging and—how should I put it?"—he stopped to think for a second—"yes, the collapse and depravity, the black magic and—the continent was lowered underwater, abandoned in aphonic darkness. Consumed by water, as during the Flood."

Misha flinched:

"Like the city of Kitezh?"

His cheek moistened. His face was palish-porcelaining.

"No!" Father crossed his fingers. "Kitezh was hidden, Atlantis was flooded. Can you see the difference?"

And Misha nodded.

Father grew quiet; he fixed his gaze on the embers in the fireplace and began to think. His hand reached out and tousled Misha's mane.

"Or, perhaps, Atlantis was *hidden?* Who knows? Perhaps, you'll be the one to find out?"

And a laugh line flashed under his whiskers; his eyes flickered; his lips grinned.

Misha's little finger rustled the page, his little knees dug into the armchair:

"Where, Papa?"

"Right here, remember. Here is India,"—a flash on the map—"remember: here it is."

And he shook his shoulder as he reached out his hand.

"There, look," he curved his hand, calling Misha's attention, "do you see the ring on my finger?"

Misha had seen it more than once; now he was snub-nosed with wonder, heaven knows what next?

"Have a look," he unringed his finger, clinking the band on the table, "you can't take it directly from my hands, remember." Then he signaled with his head: *Go ahead.*

Misha's hands sweatened and his fingers moistened. The ring glided through them. He palmed and examined it:

"What language are the letters in?"

"In Sanskrit, an *Indian* language."

"Have you been to India, Papa?"

His fingers were crestfallen, crossing and uncrossing. Misha thought he saw his lips quiver under his whiskers:

"No. I didn't have the time. You will."

The ring goldened in his sweaty little palm, his lifeline chiromanced.

"When I die, it will be yours. And you will go to India!"

And he wiped his sweat away.

At night, he dreamed—or rather, *nightmared.*

The city was peopled like a great human anthill, dresses calicoed in the streets, workshops visor-capped, open carriages horsened; houses turned stone-still, doors brass-plated with their handles; wooden gray-coffee- and-coffee-brown houses variegated the streets while alleys crookened with the flowers' lively cries; and over it all, churches golden-domed while, further out, little houses stood, compressed, in twos and threes, pierced by chimneys, with the distant ribbon of Sparrow Hills forest like a carved enclosure.

Such was the continent of Atlantis.

It thunder-dawned, then—rumbled in the dim twinkling of distant lightning—the cross thrashing of driving rain, the splashes and screams like a kasha, it poured and played up, the night lavendered, the glass tinkled, the thunder burbled—and the flame biled and blanched!

With his hands fistened, his mouth agapened, his teeth bared and tears drip-dripping from his eyes, *he began to scream.*

Glafira gave him water, Mama palmed his forehead and, in the morning, the doctor white-coated around him. Touching his forehead with his finger and sadly sighing, he signaled that science was powerless here.

Misha *hehed* with a wink: science was powerless, but only the Great Ancients knew.

The doctor peered into the cannula, where the temperature mercuried: "The boy's simply frightened."

That fright manifested throughout his whole life.

The thunder of events grew louder and the sword of war hung over them. Soon the mother will weep over her son, who will perish in the Mazursky swamps; soon damsels will pinch surgical lint; the student will march with a rifle; and then a wave will rush over them! and 1913 will be further away than India, than Atlantis, while death will be closer than tomorrow. And just as a deck is shuffled—pick a card, any card—there was the Spanish flu and starvation, the Cheka and the Bolsheviks or, simply, thieves and criminals. Everyone will die his own death: mother—from the Spanish flu, father—from a heart attack.

But Misha slipped away from his fate, then, became nameless and left for parts unknown, taking his non-objectivity with him. And only the ring as a souvenir.

You will go to India!

He remembered.

42.

DOESN'T NEED A BODY AT ALL

How does it all begin? You meet a young woman while on vacation in Simeiz, beautiful, slightly unstable, but what young woman isn't unstable when she's not even thirty and it's summer in Crimea? You watch her swimming, her strong arms splitting the water, then, coming out wet and happy. And now you've struck up a romance, under the starry sky, you do something to her body and she does something to yours, the crickets are chirping, the waves are rolling, it's understandable—vacation, summer, Crimea. Then you return to Moscow, continue to see each other, everything is surprisingly tender, surprisingly poignant, although the young woman is still unhinged, phone calls at two in the morning and so forth. One day, she suddenly says to you in bed: let's do it without a condom, if I get pregnant, you don't have to marry me, I swear. It's the mid-nineties, everyone thinks that only drug addicts and gay men have AIDS, well, also prostitutes, which is why no one is particularly careful—at most, they'll ask a young woman if she's healthy. Or if she's able to do it that day. And if the young woman herself says: let's do it this way, it doesn't seem smart to refuse—what's more, you've known each other for a few months already, it's obvious she doesn't sleep around, doesn't shoot drugs. So a half hour later, they're lying next to each other, the semen slowly leaks out on the bedsheet, Masha doesn't feel like getting up and washing and tells him she doesn't think she can have children at all, she had some sort of botched surgery, the doctors warned her, although, technically, she wants to, of course, so she doesn't really use protection—if she gets pregnant, it will be a miracle, if not, then not. So, of course, it turns out that she doesn't this time around, nor the second, nor the third, then, six months pass—it all sort of happens on its own—and they're already living together, it's the mid-nineties, it's cheaper to rent an apartment together than to rent separately, sometimes, he has a job, sometimes—she does, and they're always short on money, by the summer of ninety-eight, it all levels out somehow, but then, the crisis hits, the collapse, and then, another economic boom, Putin, stability, fifty dollars a barrel.

Sometime after the crisis, when there was scarcely a boom on the horizon, Nikita offered her twice: maybe we should go see a doctor, find out about having kids? Masha replied that she didn't want to have children at all, or that she wanted them, but not right now, or that she simply had no time to go to the doctor and the conversation didn't go anywhere. Nikita told himself: alright, we've still got time, let's not rush, she should feel ready.

And indeed, about three years ago, when Nikita was just setting up his first aquariums, Masha said: alright, it's time to look into this seriously—at least, let's decide for ourselves, if yes, then yes, if no, then no, and they go to one clinic, then another. Everywhere, there are light-filled corridors, green lab coats, polite doctors, *payment to the cashier, please*—and zero results. Nikita learns the acronyms ART[3], ZIFT[4], GIFT[5], IVF and ICSI[6] and the words endometriosis, Decapeptil, and Menopur.

Then Nikita stops looking at the pictures in the brochures displayed at the fertility clinics and tries to familiarize himself with the texts, catching phrases like *your inability to conceive takes a toll on your self-esteem or you're angry that your infertility is preventing you from living your life or sex has become a dull chore for you*—at least the words are all comprehensible here. He reads it and thinks: thank God this isn't us!

Six months later, Masha said for the first time: *It must be because I don't deserve a child* and Nikita was surprised rather than frightened—she's an adult woman, what does she mean, she deserves, she doesn't deserve, it's medicine and nothing more, but then it started like the brochures predicted: *if we hadn't used protection in Crimea, if we'd started seeing doctors five years earlier, if I had a good diet, if you weren't so tired all the time* . . . Nikita quit being surprised, refreshed his memory of the advice for husbands and followed it as best as he could. If it helped, then only temporarily. Eventually, Masha stopped talking about getting pregnant. Nikita decided: she dropped the idea, that's just as well, if she wants to

---

[3] Assistive Reproductive Technology

[4] Zygote intrafallopian transfer

[5] Gamete intrafallopian transfer

[6] Intracytoplasmic sperm injection

try again we haven't gone through all the methods yet, we can afford it, thankfully. Just then, his business took off and Nikita forgot about it, somehow, put it on the back burner.

Presently, he thinks: I saw everything, I just wasn't paying attention! She sits at home for days at a time—well, Masha never liked to go out in the winter. She stays in the armchair around the clock—it's a comfortable armchair, her favorite, an antique, she found it herself at a consignment shop. She's lost ten kilos—alright, I love her like this too! She hardly ever talks—that's because I'm not home a lot. She's in a bad mood—she must be bored. We should spend more time together, it's just that I have a lot of work, plus, Dasha for the last two months.

Then one April morning, Nikita sees Masha climb out of the bathtub and takes fright. It seems as if, if she loses a bit more weight, Masha will evaporate—there's so little left of her body. She had always been on the leaner side, but, presently, her thin arms and legs no longer looked poignant. Nikita was reminded of a scarecrow with straw legs on the verge of breaking.

Nikita took fright, but didn't show it; he picked up Masha and carried her to the bedroom. As he ran his lips down her body, he examined how much weight she had lost. Indeed, her ribs jutted out and her breasts had almost vanished. This was not the right time for questions—they were clearly about to have sex—but when Nikita moved on to more serious foreplay, Masha stopped him: *I don't want to right now.*

Alright then, so they went to the kitchen to have breakfast and Nikita casually asked Masha how many kilos she'd lost, whistled and offered to take her to the doctor. The next day, he got her an appointment with a trendy nutritionist who ordered about seven hundred dollars' worth of tests and, based on the results, told her to eat more and see a psychotherapist.

During the two weeks that Masha was getting tests and listening to expensive banalities about a proper diet, Nikita spent almost all his free time with her. He went over to Dasha's twice, which wore him out even more. By the end of the second week, he once again offered that they make love, once again heard *not right now*, thought back and realized that they hadn't had sex all year. If you didn't count the ill-fated birthday, of course.

And even though Nikita didn't really feel like fucking anyone besides Dasha right now, he panicked. He called Kostya and asked:

"Old man, listen, what should I do? What do guys do when they have a young lover and their wife is depressed?"

"They buy their wife diamonds," Kostya said.

"Masha's not interested," Nikita sighed.

"Well, then take her away somewhere. As soon as I get a new lover, I always take my wife to Paris—museums, shopping, boat rides on the Seine, and, in general . . . Ksenia really likes it, she feels young over there."

So they traveled to Paris to hurry spring along. For some reason, spring was always delayed in Moscow—in the last few years, it even snowed in May—whereas here, it was warm, there was neither snow nor ice and the chestnut trees would soon be in bloom. Masha didn't like winter, so, perhaps, she'd feel better in Paris?

It's hard for Moreukhov to picture Paris, it's a jumble of different years, the New Wave creeps onto the New New Wave and his memory retains only hats, cloaks, the Eiffel Tower and the street where the American girl sold the *International Herald Tribune*.

It's hard for Moreukhov to picture Paris and it's hard for Nikita to picture himself there. When he was young, he dreamed about it like everyone else: chestnut trees in bloom, an accordion playing, Parisian women in short skirts, Paul Mauriat, *pardon, Madame. Oh là là.* And then he forgot about it somehow, all his acquaintances had traveled there at least once, the wealthier ones first, then all the rest, only Nikita couldn't get out, not even in the last two years, when he didn't have money problems.

To be sure, Paris was nothing like what Nikita envisioned. And it didn't resemble Moreukhov's favorite films with Alain Delon and Jean-Paul Belmondo either. If you didn't live there, it was just another city. Nikita and Masha wandered the streets he'd read so much about, sat in street cafés and reminisced about *how it all began*, Crimea and their first years together; repeated old jokes—Masha even laughed—went to the Louvre and Musée d'Orsay, took boat rides on the Seine, walked into a passageway, climbed up the Notre-Dame and the Eiffel Tower, watched couples kiss on the quays of the Seine, even kissed a few times themselves—and Nikita practically didn't fantasize about kissing Dasha just like this here; Masha was quite pleased and he, too, was very happy for the first time in a while.

In any case, it is also hard for Moreukhov to picture Nikita in Paris. But he can clearly see Masha, as if on a movie screen: she is standing in a *luxurious hotel room* in front of a large mirror. The gilded frame turns her reflection into the image of a painting—either a Toulouse-Lautrec or a Munch, but definitely not a Renoir. Masha looks in the mirror, touches her nipple, smiles sadly, then, heads to the bathroom, which is locked: Nikita is sitting on the toilet fully dressed, reading Dasha's texts.

A text is just letters. When Dasha writes "I miss you" or "buy me the latest Comme des Garçons," Nikita doesn't even remember the woman from the deep end, the wild sex, the passion, the haze. Only a young woman writing her rich friend in Paris, asking him to buy her perfume and also this, that, and the other thing, seven texts in total. And the rich friend is promenading his wife around Paris because it's the right thing to do—the young girls have their youth, let the wife have the joys of family trips, the Eiffel Tower, the Louvre, Palais-Royal, the Grands Boulevards, the boats on the Seine.

Kostya's idea really was excellent, Nikita tells himself, Masha really does seem to feel better. Smart man, what can I say.

And now I am almost like him. Business, mistress, trips with wife to Paris. Just like the big boys—Nikita smiles and types out on the cumbersome keypad: "I miss you too."

He comes out of the bathroom, sticks his cell phone in his hotel robe pocket, barely looks at the nude Masha, and lies down in bed. Such a comfortable bed, soft.

It's so great that you can just up and go to Paris. Pay the money and you're there. That's what true freedom is.

I used to think that if a person didn't have anything, he was free. When he had nothing to lose, he had nothing to be afraid of. *It's enough for us*, as my mom says.

I used to think this way fifteen years ago, when Kostya was already plugging away at his business and I still wanted *not to be afraid of anything*. Now I know that people who have "nothing to lose" are more afraid than I am. More than anything else in the world, they're afraid of their own fear. They willingly give up everything just so they won't have to be afraid, just to convince themselves they have nothing to lose.

And I do have something to lose. My wife, my mistress, my beloved job, even the money I've made, at the end of the day! Could I lose all this? Yes. If I lose the money, I'll make new money. Dasha will find a wealthier guy and I will also find someone else. And if God forbid something happens to Masha, it would still be a great thing that we were together, took a trip to Paris, for instance.

It would be shameful to let her go earlier so that I wouldn't have to be afraid of losing her.

I'm such a great guy, Nikita thinks. I've handled everything, everything is going well for me. I still have many, many years ahead of me, so much that is beautiful and unexplored: young women it's nice to sleep with, beautiful cities it's nice to take your wife to, young women's orgasms, old and tested jokes, Moscow rental apartments, European hotel rooms, breasts under my palm, Masha's hand in my hand, tourist crowds, camera flashes, museum corridors, paintings known from reproductions on the walls, in the galleries—marble statues of nude beauties stretching to infinity, every one of them like the promise of a new young body, new kisses, and new caresses as interminable as the echoing museum corridors.

Nikita is lying in bed and smiling, and the next moment, Masha comes out of the bathroom, sits beside him and says: You know, I realized what the problem is. If a woman can't have children, maybe she doesn't need a body at all.

43.

REINCARNATION. LYUBOCHKA

A great empty apartment, a withered female frame in an armchair, shadows billowing in the corners, lives that have been lived, voices that have fallen silent. She cannot remember the faces or the dates, it's all out of focus, must be the dusk or her age. Only from time to time, it's like somebody sharpens the picture, like the frames of old movies, unchanged, timeless, the colors unfaded, no scratches running across the screen— only the film keeps breaking and the scenes are so short, only a minute or two in length . . .

A tall man holds a little girl's hand. A small step, then another small step. Come on, Lyubochka, he says, come on, my beauty.

Gloomy winter morning, Lyubochka is dancing at a school festival. A ribbon in her braid, a blue skirt, the girls are all watching. She's playing a grasshopper in a school play, and wretched cigarette paper wings quiver behind her back. As she runs off stage, she catches her reflection in the dark glass of the window, behind which lie darkness, snow, post-war Moscow, and *the winter is nearby*. Lyubochka smiles—she smiles at the auditorium, at Sasha, who's dressed like an ant with a shovel, at her grandmother in the back row, at the portrait of Stalin hanging over the stage and at Anna Ivanovna, who involuntarily smiles back.

Lyubochka is the school darling, everyone knows her.

Moscow in the springtime. Lyubochka skips on the squares drawn on the asphalt. Out of the corner of her eye, she spies a stout woman dressed in village style. The latter looks at her for some time, then sighs and walks away with a heavy gait.

The sun is shining, the lavender's in bloom, Lyubochka kicks the flat stone and hops over to the next square.

The dark corridor of the communal apartment. Drunken snoring, Uncle Valera's blue-gray face, the stench of booze and male sweat. Lyubochka presses against the wall and tries to slip past, but a dirty hand overgrown with black hairs, like something out of *Crocodile* magazine, still reaches out and manages to pinch her. Lyubochka screams, *thump thump thump*, go either her heels or her heart, she slams the door and tries not to burst into tears.

She throws her schoolbag in the corner, pulls off her school apron and dress and stands before the wardrobe mirror, a ribbon in her braid, a frozen froglet, small breasts—a blooming bruise under the nipple of her right breast. Lyubochka sticks out her breast, comes closer to the mirror and looks at the small spot that reddens before her eyes as she holds back tears. All of a sudden, she freezes and sees a reflection of the photo of a man in military uniform, which hangs on the opposite wall.

She was nine when she last saw her dad, which was after three years of him coming to her in the form of letters folded into triangles and the line "kiss our little girl for me." Were he here now, Uncle Valera wouldn't dare pinch her, wouldn't grab with his hands, wouldn't stink of booze . . . But her dad was only here for one day and never came back, and Lyubochka only remembered how, upon seeing her for the first time in three years, he smiled and said: What a beauty you have become!

She looks in the mirror. A beauty? Yes, everyone says so. She takes her hands off her breast and spins before the mirror, like at the school festival six months ago.

"What are you going to be—a physicist or a ballerina"?

Lyubochka knows this quarrelsome, outraged voice all too well. It's obviously not a question, no one is interested in the answer. Grandma's just getting started. Afterward, she'll start to preach: it's all because the girl had grown up without a mother, what kind of a mother is that? Pshaw! And eventually she'll start to remember Yurochka, who didn't die at the front so his daughter could dance all night long, and would start crying; and Lyubochka would have to run to the bathroom, bring some water, and promise to change her ways.

Lyubochka knows this by heart, as if these are frames from a film she goes to see every day for a week because Vitka's dad works at the recreation center and they get in for free. She knows it by heart, but Lyubochka's sick of this film, and surprises herself by saying:

"I want to be an academic's wife and never see you again!" slams the door and goes off click-clacking her heels down the corridor of the communal apartment.

She didn't resemble a romantic heroine of the fifties: she wasn't an athlete, a good student, or a Girl with an Oar. Too-skinny legs, too-large breasts. She knew this and, in moments when women usually ask *Do you love me*, she'd smile proudly and say, "I'm beautiful, right?" And that question didn't require an answer, just like Grandma's question from long ago: what could you say in those circumstances?

When Lyubochka wasn't around, the young men could argue: perhaps it was actually Zinochka Sinytsina (an athletic blonde) from year 3 or the romantic, good student Natasha Shapitko from year 1, daughter of either a poet or an academic. Although Lyubochka wasn't too bad either, only too thin.

In a country that had just recovered from many long years of starvation, anorexic women wouldn't be fashionable anytime soon.

The guys argued—but only until Gerard Philippe, Fanfan the Tulip, Frenchman, dreamboat, hero of sweet female fantasies, hopped onto Moscow's cylindrical billboards. He was standing on the roof, peering at Adeline's décolletage, and smirking: *what a view!*—and *that view* was created to moisten the bedsheets of overcrowded Moscow dorms rooms, of all the dorm rooms inthe Soviet Union. For a few months, the ethereal shadow from the movie screen eclipsed her classmates, who were so accessible, so boring and banal compared to Adeline.

Only Lyubochka's classmates were in luck. Because Lyubochka, who looked nothing like the sculpted beauties of the Central Park of Culture and Leisure or the All-Union Agricultural Exhibition, turned out to be a doppelgänger of Adeline, Gina Lollobrigida.

Of course, it wasn't a perfect resemblance—but it was enough for the guys to forget about Zinochka Sinitsyna and Natasha Shapitko and, for Lyubochka, about her summer classes.

Lyubochka cried all night. Everything turned out so silly! She was certain—any guy would have been glad that his pregnant girlfriend didn't drag him to the civil registry office and instead got rid of the child like a civilized person—it wasn't for nothing that abortion had been legal for a year already!

Lyubochka explained to Kolya that it was too soon for them to have children, that she wanted to try to apply to university again, cried and kissed, but to no avail. Kolya kept repeating: "You don't want children from me because I'm not handsome enough for you!" and then Lyubochka flew into a rage and said that she didn't want to ever have children, that children ruined a woman's figure, that if Kolya needed a child, then Kolya should give birth to one himself and she would do just fine without them. Because Kolya would be a great scientist in the future and she, Lyubochka, had nothing except her beauty, and she didn't understand why she needed this wailing bundle. Didn't Kolya know all this would make her breasts sag—*Don't you like my breasts?*—and make stretch marks appear on her belly—*Don't you like my belly?* And she better not talk about what happened to a woman's private parts after childbirth because, if you tell me you don't like what I have *down there*, I'll leave you, thank God there are plenty willing, Pasha from the neighboring branch asked me out to the movies . . ." and that's when they definitively fell out, Kolya slammed the door and Lyubochka cried all night, and, in the morning, she looked in the mirror and decided that she wouldn't cry anymore because tears caused wrinkles.

And once more, Fanfan proclaims: *What a view!* and Lyubochka hears a child cry, what is this foolishness, who brought a child to the movies, they won't understand a thing and won't let the others watch. She turns around and shushes a woman with a two-year-old girl on her lap. "If you gave birth, stay home!" Lyubochka hisses, but the woman doesn't leave, she sits there until the end. And all this time, Lyubochka puts up with it, tries not to get distracted, although, for a long time, she's known this film *about her* by heart. And only when the lights come on and the audience members get up from their seats, Lyubochka turns around again: the woman has a round, flat face, like an Uzbek.

"Crooked-belly hick," Lyubochka says loudly, "Take your kids back to your mountain village!"

The woman doesn't reply, only lowers her eyes and says to her daughter: "Tanya, let's go."

Lyubochka is ashamed, even wants to apologize, because, really—a poor woman, not pretty and with a child.

Moscow doesn't believe in tears, doesn't believe in rain, snow, heat, or severe cold. It believes only in its green courtyards, humming trolley lines, seven high-rises on seven hills, the Kremlin's stars at night; it believes only in what's here to stay. It believes in fate because, whether you believe in it or not—your fate will happen, it's like Grandma's question that you shouldn't answer, even if your answer accidentally hits the mark.

In 1959, Lyubochka married an academic. He was thirty years her senior, so you could say they *made an exchange*: youth for fame, beauty for a Volga, a large apartment, and a dacha in Kratovo.

As is often the case, her husband loved her madly, although, until his death, he was upset that the doctors had forbidden his beautiful wife to have children: taught by bitter experience, Lyubochka lied that, *owing to a few particularities of the female anatomy,* she couldn't carry a child to term and, moreover, a pregnancy would be fatal to her. This was her only lie throughout their whole, long life together: despite the rumors, Lyubochka never cheated on her husband, although there was never a shortage of musicians, poets, athletes, and young scientists at their apartment on Frunze Quay. They dedicated poems to the lady of the house, invited her to the scientific district of Dubna and the Dombay mountain settlement and attempted to kiss her in the corridor.

No one could believe she truly loved her husband.

A large mirror in a gilded frame. Lyubochka lifts up her sagging breasts with her hands, smooths out the folds cutting across her stomach and contemplates her now-ample hips. She's still beautiful in a mature, fading kind of way—and, as usual, she spins before the mirror like those years never happened. Then she opens the wardrobe and takes a long time to pick out a dress.

Today she's turning forty, and all of Moscow is coming to visit them.

(Masha curls into a ball in the armchair. Why does Lyubochka come to her time and again? Maybe this is her armchair? Masha bought it three years ago at a consignment shop—her heirs probably sold it. In any case, what heirs could Lyubochka have? Maybe her husband's relatives?

Lyubochka never had any heirs. Masha is her heir, the sole guardian of faded pictures, the owner of a lacquered box with childhood secrets, a clair-voyant of lives past.)

A great empty apartment, a female frame in an armchair, shadows billowing in the corners, lives that have been lived, voices that have fallen silent. No one calls her Lyubochka anymore. It's Lyubov Yuryevna. She bites her nails, watches television, flips through the channels: the news, Mexican soaps, criminal chronicles, ballroom dancing—ah! Then she presses the button again and freezes: *What a view,* Fanfan says, Adeline says something back, and Lyubochka thinks: Lollobrigida hasn't aged a day.

She's watching television. She's getting sleepy—must be the dusk or her age. She doesn't remember the plot anymore, and the scenes are so short, it's as if the film keeps breaking. Lollobrigida dancing on the school stage, Lollobrigida examining her bruise, running away from home, asking: "I'm beautiful, right?," crying through the night, snapping at the young woman with a child . . .

What an enormous crowd scene, Lyubochka thinks, so many cameos, so many extras. What happened to them? The alcoholic neighbor is most likely long dead, and I buried grandma myself in sixty-five. What happened later to Zinochka Sinitsyna, Natasha Shapitko, the unknown woman at the movie theater? To all the musicians, poets, and athletes I last saw ten years ago at my husband's funeral?

Lyubochka gets up and shuffles to the bedroom. A one-hundred-candle electric chandelier bursts into light. The mirror has been covered since that day. Lyubochka pulls the dusty curtain aside. An elderly woman stands before the mirror. *I'm beautiful, right?* she says, and then, slowly and very carefully, turns twice around her own axis.

44.

TEA, NATURALLY

When I drink, God admires me, Moreukhov thinks. When I'm sober, I don't understand how you can live in this city. Spring arrives only around Easter, and before that, it's the underground Metro, dustings of snow, slush and drizzle. Filth. Right now, I'm traveling to the other end of town to see my mother—sober, for a change. She'll be so glad. I'll tell her I quit. Then again, she probably won't believe me.

So Moreukhov's sitting in his mother's kitchen, drinking tea, naturally—in the last three years, his mom hasn't kept any alcohol around, she's scared that her son will go on a bender. So Moreukhov's drinking tea, wondering about the best way to ask about Uncle Sasha. At fifty-five, Lyolya's blue eyes have faded, her skin is covered with ghastly spots and the doctors have forbidden her to travel to the South, just to be safe—but she flew to Turkey last summer anyway, after all, she dreamt of going abroad all these years.

An editor's salary isn't very big, Mom even hinted to Moreukhov that it would be a good idea for them to move in together, let out the other apartment. Moreukhov refused: he was too old to live with his mother.

They have two apartments: Grandpa's, where Yelena Grigoryevna lives, and the co-op in Troparyovo, which was purchased back in the seventies. After Grandpa died, Grandma Olya moved to the Sokol district and, after she died—Mom did. She says she could never take a liking to this neighborhood, that she missed the Troparyovo forest. She probably wants to visit, but how can he ask her over? A loving son wouldn't ask his mother to an apartment like Moreukhov's: chaos and decay, a scary sight.

And here in the Sokol district it's nice and clean, just like when Grandma Olya was alive ten, no, eleven years ago already.

Suddenly, Moreukhov realizes: this is the apartment his mom will die in. First, his grandma died here, then, it'll be his mom's turn. Must be scary to know this is your last abode, that they'll carry your coffin out this door.

Moreukhov hopes to die sooner. He loves his mother too much to bury her.

"You know, Sasha," Yelena Grirogryevna says, "I was talking to one of my friends, her uncle also, you know, drank. Looks like he was cured. There's a doctor . . ."

"Mom," Moreukhov sighs, "did I tell you that I wanted treatment?"

And it's like that every time. She always suggests herbalists, homeopaths, psychotherapists, addiction specialists, healers and psychiatrists, finds miracle drugs, support groups, Alcoholics Anonymous, and insanely expensive rehab centers they can't afford anyway. She tells Moreukhov about them and he winces, saying: "I'm doing good, I'm dealing with it perfectly fine on my own. You can say I've *already* dealt with it. I haven't drank in two weeks, I plan to beat my last record."

Sometimes Mom slips books to Moreukhov. She started out with medical brochures about the damage wreaked by alcoholism (liver—kidneys—heart), then switched over to more conceptual works. Moreukhov was tickled: the conceptual works usually placed part of the blame on the alcoholic's relatives. At any rate, that was Moreukhov's takeaway. Interesting, he thought, is Mom giving me all this to read on purpose? Is she, like, apologizing?

Anyhow, most of the books turned out to be boring, except for the last one: *Shame, Guilt, and Alcoholism*, which provided him with considerable amusement.

"You see," Moreukhov explained to Dimon, "the idea is that alcoholism comes from shame and guilt—and that part's pretty cool to read. I never thought about the difference between the two before, but now I know. It turns out that shame is when you think you're shit. A monstrous, good-for-nothing shit. And guilt is when you think you did something shitty. You did it and now you'll get what's coming to you."

"Can you give any examples?"

"Of course," Moreukhov replies. "Say, I submit a work to an exhibition and they don't take it. It makes me feel like shit, feel like I'm not an artist. And, like, ashamed. Especially if everyone knows about it. Now the opposite: I submit a work to an exhibition and they take it. My feelings are different. Like, I made some bullshit—betrayed my principles for some reason, sent my work to these morons and, on top of it, they liked it . . . A sense of guilt forms inside me. It's particularly shitty if I know none of the guys will invite me over or drink vodka with me anymore."

Dimon nods.

"And now, your attention please! Where would my shame or guilt come from if I don't submit *any* of my work? How can I be rejected if I'm not even angling for it? How can I make something bad if I do only good—which is to say, drink and watch movies? In short, I'm absolutely convinced that I have neither shame nor guilt. Which means I'm not an alcoholic."

"So why do you drink?"

"For pleasure!" Moreukhov answered and lied, of course: in reality, he drank out of fear.

At one time, Nikita wished to get rid of his terrible fear of depths and dove in wearing full scuba gear. Whenever Moreukhov gets drunk, he sets off toward slippery arms, rotten tree stumps, fins, pincers, barbels, and bubbles coming out of his mouth. He sets off and hopes that he won't see them. What if they vanish—then he'd be able to live in peace, even quit drinking.

Why do I drink? Moreukhov explains to himself. I'm a nervous, sensitive human being. I have monsters swimming inside me, decomposing drowned bodies—and I have to live here like nothing's wrong? I can't, I worry. I tie myself up in knots—what if they surface on their own, what if they run amok? That's why I have to visit them once in a while, to check on them.

In any case, Moreukhov doesn't tell his mom about his underwater meetings.

"You know," he says, "I always suspected that Uncle Sasha was my real father. Can you tell me the truth now?"

"I've always told you the truth," Mom answers. "Vasya's your father. Sasha's only your uncle. We dated a long time before you were born."

She tells him about how she and the young, bearded and happy Sasha went over to Vasya's, drank and partied all night and, in the morning, she and Vasya put the drunk Sasha to sleep on the folding bed and began to kiss right away. After that, it was the usual: friends' apartments, since there weren't any hotels, I've lived in a dorm, can't do much there.

"Why did he leave you?" Moreukhov asks. "Was he frightened by your pregnancy?"

"He knew nothing about it," Yelena Grigoryevna replies, and again remembers that day, the stupid line she waited in for fifteen minutes, until she practically reached the counter, before she left; remembers the autumn slush and feeling so hurt that tears welled up in her eyes.

"Why did he leave you?" Moreukhov repeats.

"He said it was because of Father."

"His father?"

"No, mine. Your grandfather."

Mom gets up and fills the tea kettle with her back to Moreukhov.

"And what's wrong with my grandfather?"

The water's running, and Yelena Grigoryevna leans over the sink in silence. Moreukhov looks at his mother. He wants to repeat himself, but realizes that Mom heard him.

"Nothing's wrong," she answers. "Remember: your grandfather was a good person. The rest is of no importance whatsoever."

45.

1982. A NON-WAR SECRET.

The plastic figurines of Red Cavalrymen. A slanting ray of sunlight on the veranda table. Grandpa is shaving his head over the water basin.

"Grandpa, did you fight in the Civil War?" Sasha asks.

"Not for very long, I was young. But my father fought in it, your great-grandpa. In World War I and the Civil War. He died a hero in Crimea battling the White Bandits."

"Great-grandpa was a Red Cavalrymen?"

"Something like it," grandpa replied, wiping his shiny scalp with a towel and carefully putting away the dangerous razor.

In Moscow, Grandpa lives in a separate apartment, and they're only together at the dacha. When grandpa comes to the table, everyone sits quietly—Mom, Grandma and Sasha. Grandpa eats thoughtfully, with concentration, leaning his shaved head all the way down to the plate. After dinner, he goes to his room behind the plywood partition. From there, you can hear the radio wailing and a foreign voice speaking Russian.

Somehow, Sasha knows that it's American radio. Enemy radio.

"Mom, why is Grandpa listening to that?" Sasha asks.

"He needs it for his job," Mom answers evasively, and Sasha wonders: what job if Grandpa's retired?

Americans are imperialists, like Germans; they want to start a war again. Sasha knows a lot about war: they tell them about it at daycare. In the fall, he will start school, where portraits of Young Pioneer heroes who died fighting the fascists hang on the classroom walls.

"Mom," he asks, "did my dad die in the war too?"

He knows from children's books that many dads didn't return from the war. Sasha doesn't have a dad—and he imagines that his dad died, too, and that his portrait, which somewhat resembles Sasha, is hanging in one of the classrooms.

"Don't be silly," his mom replies irritably. "He wasn't even born when the war was on."

"I see," Sasha nods without entirely believing her.

In the evening, while grandpa listens to the radio, Sasha studies books about heroes for a long time. If his dad fought in the war and died, what would he have been? A tank crewman? A pilot? Better yet, a submarine man.

The book about submarine men is the most beautiful. Long, metallic submarines swim among seaweed, the captain stands on the bridge, and the Soviet flag waves in the air.

Sasha knows them by name: Captain Marinesco, Captain Morukhov, Captain Matiyasevich.

Could one of them be his father? A perished, top-secret submarine man. Or maybe his father is alive? Travels the distant seas, doesn't return to the Motherland for long stretches of time, has a picture of Mom and Sasha as a baby in his cabin, since he hasn't been home in a while. The submarine's underwater location is a great secret, a war secret or maybe, a non war secret, since there is no war on now.

Americans tried to find the boat with their satellites, but couldn't. As soon as they'd find it, they'd blast it all over the radio that there was a Soviet submarine in such and such a sea. Bomb it, sink it, torpedo it. That's why Grandpa listens to the radio every evening: what if they say something about Sasha's dad? Maybe Grandpa will be able to warn him.

In the evenings, Sasha sneaks over to the partition to Grandpa's room, sits on the floor, and pretends to be reading a book or playing with his toy soldiers, when, in fact, he is listening to an unpleasant male voice with a foreign accent. What if Grandpa falls asleep? Sasha thinks. He is old and weak. He will fall asleep and miss an important message.

Sasha listens closely, but the radio doesn't say anything about submarines. Instead, day after day, they talk about the concentration camps where Communists were tortured and killed. The audibility is poor, but Sasha understands almost everything: at the daycare, they've already told him that the fascists wanted to kill all the Communists.

"Grandpa, are you a Communist?" He asks.

"Of course, Sasha, as you would expect," Grandpa answers.

"My dad was a Communist too," Sasha says. Grandpa silently pats the boy on the head.

And now evening falls, a most ordinary evening. Sasha is playing on the floor with his plastic horsemen, singing *snip-snap, snip-snap, carry off the stiff*, the radio booms across the thin plywood partition, a mosquito buzzes over his ear, Mom's dishes rattle on the veranda, the neighbors' children's cries drift in from the street—and suddenly, there's a thud, like something has fallen or a cannon was discharged.

"Mom!" Sasha screams and dashes toward his mother, but she runs right past him, throws open the door to Grandpa's room, and screams. The frightened Sasha runs after her and immediately sees Grandpa's glistening scalp and a dark puddle on the floor. Then he notices that Grandpa has fallen off his chair and is lying motionless, his hand tucked awkwardly under him. And only then Sasha sees the handgun—a real handgun, like in the movies.

Mom is no longer screaming, only quietly sobbing.

And the jammed radio broadcast sounds like wailing over the deceased.

46.

EVERYTHING UNDER CONTROL

His hands are trembling, his shirt is wet with sweat, his heart palpitates like a fish out of water.

All of the Atrium looms over him like a giant aquarium. People swim by as if in slow motion.

He's gasping for air.

And the morning started off so well! It was his first day back at the office after the trip to Paris, he spoke with everyone and breathed a sigh of relief—everything was fine. Technology is a glorious thing—you can be thousands of kilometers away and have everything under control: text messages, email, roaming.

Then Victor came in and began to drop hints: "The company's growing, we have new employees joining us, we have to start building a different kind of relationship with them if we want them to stay."

"What do you mean by different?" Nikita asked.

"We have to build team spirit," Victor replied, "we could have a team-building session."

Oh yeah, Nikita even knows what team-building is, he read about it in a magazine. It's when employees do something together that's not work-related. For example, play paintball. He nodded and said:

"Yes, great idea, let's talk about it later."

"And another thing," Victor continued, "we need to phase out the under-the-table salaries. The guys are saying they want normal paychecks so they can get loans at the bank and so forth. It's not the nineties anymore, it's time to start building a civilized business."

Nikita sighed. Kostya once drew for him on a napkin roughly how much it would cost him to report even a portion of his business earnings.

"That's expensive, Victor," Nikita said. "But alright, I'll think about it and see what I can do."

His mood was spoiled, but not that much. Overall, everything was going fine at work, he could call Dasha and disappear for a few hours.

Nikita missed her so much.

"Let me come over," Nikita said.

"Oh, today's not going to work," Dasha grew flustered. "Lerka's staying with me for a couple days. Remember I told you we used to rent an apartment together? Well, she got into a blowout with her father, moved out of the apartment, rented another one, and will move in there over the weekend, they just haven't finished renovating. I'm so embarrassed, I'm sorry, but I also couldn't turn her down, you understand."

"It's fine," Nikita answered, "I just want to see you."

"Me too! I've missed you!" And she offered: "Let's go to the movies. At the Atrium. It's a short drive, it's a multiplex, lots of movies to pick from."

Nikita pictured a half-empty theater, a matinee, his hand gliding down Dasha's moist skin . . . doesn't matter what film.

"Yes, let's pick one," he agreed.

On the way, he even thought: I understand that Dasha and I are an odd-looking couple. A young, beautiful woman and a bald, forty-year-old man. I don't care. I still think that, *when I'm with her, God admires me.*

To Nikita, the Atrium is a multi-tiered aquarium, the patrons swim by like fish, the glass elevators only reinforce the resemblance.

For me, it's a pigsty, a snake pit, a bedbug-infested hole. A slave market, a moveable whorehouse, a meat-processing plant.

Of course, I've only been here once during my endless alcoholic wanderings. I think I wanted to see the Kursk Railway Station, but ended up right by the Kremlin. Because, obviously, the Kremlin is also a pigsty and meat-processing plant.

A place where everything's for sale.

Tall boots, short skirts, slutty lacy lingerie. Pinstripe suits, matching ties, leather shoes, suede jackets, Swiss watches, Italian trousers, elite bullshit, exclusive fuckery.

They sell sushi, hamburgers, pizza, pasta, hotdogs, samplings of every national cuisine imaginable, fast food from the entire planet, self-service, restaurants with waitstaff, *next, please,* tip included.

They sell tickets for movies that no one will even bother to watch—they'll directly reach under their neighbor's skirt like Nikita, feel her up, finger her, slide along the moist folds.

They sell girls who would be up for anything with a sugar daddy as long as they could check out these shops—boots, skirts, panties, watches, keychains—just so Daddy pays for the purchases, the shopping, the car, the apartment, the sex, the young body, the fifteen minutes of a sweaty romp.

A pigsty.

A consumer's paradise.

In the afterlife, all consumers will turn into pigs. Spits as sharp as stilettoed boots will pierce them all the way through. A fire as intense as an old, slobbery lecher will lick their flesh. Fat that's as rank as a fast-food hamburger will drip on the broiler.

And we, the alcoholics, the hobos, the artists, will turn their smoking carcasses, tossing in their jackets and ties, trousers and short skirts and slutty, lacy bedazzled lingerie into the fire.

Burn, burn brighter!

The Atrium is a prototype of the hell that awaits its consumers.

It's hell because it offers everything except love.

Or maybe it does?

There's my brother Nikita Melnikov sitting at a small table. He's already on his fifth cup of coffee and is dialing the same number, hearing over and over: "The number you have dialed is not available right now, please hang up and try again ."

He is calling Dasha.

He has waited for forty minutes already.

He doesn't understand what's happening.

He is scared.

I'd like to tell him: Nikita, come to your senses. Is this how a sugar daddy is supposed to behave, a successful businessman waiting for his young mistress at the Atrium shopping center, a temple of our consu-whorish century? Remember how, in Paris, you pictured an endless row of young and beautiful women waiting for you? Look around. Choose whomever you like as if from a window display. Any one of them will go to the movies with you, any one of them will get in bed with you.

That's what Kostya would have done in your place.

Nikita orders another cup of coffee, drinks it, burns his mouth, and presses his cell phone to his ear. "The number you have dialed is not available right now."

Something must have happened to Dasha, he thinks. Maybe she had a car accident? Maybe she wasn't feeling well? Maybe she got attacked right in her building entrance? Beaten, raped, her cell phone stolen?

No, that's ridiculous. Her battery must have died or her train must have gotten stuck in the tunnel. Nothing serious.

But still, before his eyes—colliding cars, mangled bodies, smoking flesh. The very hell that awaits us all.

Have you been picturing the dark movie theater for a while, your hand on Dasha's hip? Have you been telling yourself for a while: technology is a glorious thing, everything's under control?

So where's your technology now?

It's not available. Not available right now.

For forty-five minutes already.

The waitress brings another coffee and looks suspiciously at Nikita: when did this one manage to get drunk, he seemed sober when he came in. His hands are shaking, his hair is stringy with sweat, his lips have turned pale. She thinks: maybe he's a drug addict?

Well yeah, a drug addict who didn't get his fix. It's been delayed by forty-five minutes.

A covey of young women chatters at the next table. Nikita closes his eyes: he can't stand the sight of other girls right now, he doesn't want to see anyone except Dasha.

She's not available. Right now? Forever? What if she threw out her phone? Decided to break up with him?

Alright, how much longer can I sit here? Nikita tells himself. She's not coming, stop lying to yourself. Get up and leave.

He gets up from the small table and walks unsteadily past the display windows. Tall boots, short skirts, pinstripe suits, matching ties.

The number you have dialed is not available right now.

He puts his cell phone in his pocket and suddenly, sees Dasha walking toward him with an unknown tall brunette (tall boots, short skirt). They're eating ice cream and chatting, and don't see him.

"Dasha," he calls out to her, "Dasha!"

"Oh, hey! Nikita, this is Lerka, Lerka—Nikita. Why didn't you call? We've been walking around for thirty minutes already."

"I couldn't get through," Nikita says.

Dasha reaches in her purse and takes out her cell phone:

"Shit, my battery died. And I was wondering where you vanished to."

"Well, I gotta run," Lerka says.

"Goodbye," Nikita nods.

"Later," Dasha says and, taking Nikita by the hand, asks: "So, are we off to the movies?"

Movies? Dark theater, hand slipping down her hip, hot breath, the spasms of young flesh under strong fingers.

"No," Nikita answers, "let's have a coffee instead and you can tell me what you were up to without me. I missed you."

They'll sit there and drink coffee, Dasha will tell him about Lerka and her parents, about her mom, about her plans to re-enroll at the university, about Haruki Murakami and Paulo Coelho, about Wicca and supporting the National Bolshevik Party. Nikita will listen to her voice and repeat to himself that there's nothing special about Dasha, a young, sexy piece of ass, an ordinary girl like all the others, like her Lerka, like the young women at the next table—ordinary Atrium patrons, buyers of lingerie, makeup, and footwear. Nothing special, it's just that I have gotten myself a lover like Kostya, like the other guys. Nothing special.

The waitress will bring coffee, look at them askance—and in her eyes, Nikita will momentarily catch a frozen reflection of himself from a half-hour ago: a forty-year old man in an expensive suit, stringy hair, hands trembling, lips pale . . .

Nothing special, he repeats to himself, everything's fine, everything's under control.

In the evening, he'll come home and tell Masha: *What a stressful day, I can't be away from work for that long.*

47.

AS THEY SAY IN A JOHN WOO FILM

Let's try this anyway. *What are little boys made of?* Frogs and snails and puppy-dogs' tails, something along those lines. No, that's not how it goes.

Boys are made of weapons. Of "Made in China" pistols, battery-operated machine guns, samurai katanas, Cossack sabers, grappling hooks, Russian swords, plastic shields, knightly helmets, semi-automatic guns/machine guns, helicopters, planes, tanks, toy soldiers, and action figures.

Ah, so many new toys out now! I only had Soviet toy soldiers, a red sword, and shield, and a horse figurine of the same color. That's it. I can only envy Gosha: a real arsenal. And not too expensive, by the way. Anya can afford it. She likes it when Gosha dashes around the apartment with a sword in one hand and a boarding axe in the other. Waves it all over the place till the splinters fly from the owner's furniture.

What a strike! The weapon is made of plastic. But if it were real—watch out! The old witch from the third floor wouldn't fare too well.

Too bad he's not my son. I wanted a son, but all the girls who got pregnant from me had abortions. Beginning with Sonya Shpilman.

If I had a son, I would play toy soldiers with him and, when he got older, we would watch Hong Kong thrillers and old American westerns together. I would raise a marksman, a real warrior. Like in The Magnificent Seven: "Friends—none. Enemies—none. Alive."

In any case, it's a good thing I don't have a son. What would I pass on to him? The dross of my earthly being? "No hat, no teeth. No whole teeth." A beautiful legacy, what can I say!

Andrey winces at the sight of the arsenal and says: "I think the boy is growing up too aggressive."

"He's just right," Anya replies. "We Tatars are a warrior people. And my grandmother was a sniper."

Exactly—Grandmother was a sniper and all that's left of Grandfather is Mom's patronymic and the family legend about how Oleg and Djamilya once met. That's basically it.

And in general, the men in Anya's family didn't have much luck.

In any case, Andrey knows nothing of this. But I wonder what he'd do if he found out.

I don't like Andrey. I picture him as a kind of fop, a fat cat in an expensive suit with a stack of bills in his pocket, always wearing a tie. I'm just like everyone else, I work at an office.

Sometimes I meet them on the street. They get out of used, foreign cars like every one of them is Boris Berezovsky in his heyday. One time, I came up to one getting out of a Volkswagen and honestly asked him for some money for a pick-me-up. Mind you, I didn't lie and say I needed money for medicine. Of course, the term pick-me-up is also inaccurate. It presumes that the process of drinking has been interrupted, the person feels sick and will only feel better once they've had something to drink. For me, drinking is a continuous process and there can be no talk of "feeling better." You have to drink without stopping and when you do stop, it will be a clusterfuck, not a hangover. It's a rather complicated theory that I didn't feel like explaining to that middle manager.

So I asked for money for a pick-me-up and the fat cat shooed me away with disgust and said: "Get a job."

I'm confident that he doesn't personally work, only manages.

I'd never be able to explain the difference between my work and his to a guy like that. So I didn't bother, I just vomited all over his windshield.

It turns out that Andrey also has a Volkswagen—maybe that's why I find him so irritating. Pushy, overly sentimental, and impenetrably serious. He probably thinks it his duty to entertain a woman—at a café, on the street, in bed.

I think that Anya isn't too thrilled about this either—after all, she's an independent woman.

So they lie in bed together and Andrey, that satisfied fat cat, is looking at the toy weapons in the kiddy corner, mumbling: The boy is growing up too aggressive. He knows what will happen when the boy grows up. He'll fuck Andrey up. If Anya doesn't dump him first, of course.

Alright. I can't manage to picture little Gosha at all, only his plastic weaponry. Let's have a look at Anya and Andrey fucking then. For a man who hasn't seen a real-life pussy in a month, there is no more interesting fantasy.

Andrey makes love seriously. Thoroughly. Carefully. He knows what a woman needs. Five minutes of kissing, then, her breasts, then—oral stimulation, and only afterward, it's full steam ahead. No imagination.

I only really fuck when I'm drunk. That is to say, when I start bingeing. At that moment, I must be exquisite—too bad I don't remember any of it afterward. But I think it's nothing like the boring, regimented sex Andrey has.

Anya doesn't seem too thrilled about it either. He's no Marik, of course, but still—she's had better. Sure, men are interchangeable, but if you date someone for so long, you start to evaluate them.

My cousin must be a very passionate woman. A distant relation, alright. But she's Asian, like my Maggie Cheung.

I wonder if my love for Asian women comes from Uncle Sasha (ah, so sad to part with the thought that he's my real father)? Or is it simply because the future belongs to them and we're trying to preserve our genes?

I'm pretty obvious: I like Hong Kong cinema, that says it all. Like everyone else, I started with John Woo, then moved on to Ringo Lam, Tsui Hark, and Johnnie To. And naturally, Wong Kar-wai.

I think that, if someone doesn't like Hong Kong cinema, they should go to the theater or the library instead. Because that person won't get film anyway.

Anya must also like Hong Kong cinema. Although I'm not sure where she'd see it, but that's not the point. Most likely, Anya's favorite film is Luc Besson's *Nikita*. Yes, yes, at times, she imagines she's a special agent. A real handgun in her purse and a sniper rifle under the cash register. After work, she comes out on the roof, lies down, assembles the rifle, aims her laser, holds her breath, and pulls the trigger.

Bang!

Ten years ago, in Hong Kong, they made a brilliant remake of *Nikita*—only don't talk to me about the Canadian TV version!—so, a brilliant Hong Kong remake called *Black Cat*. With Jade Leung instead of Anne Parillaud.

It's funny. *Black Cat* sounds like the name of the gang from the TV show *The Meeting Place Cannot Be Changed*. With Vladimir Vysotsky in the lead role.

In Hong Kong cinema, both men and women shoot well.

So Andrey takes a shower while my cousin Anya-Elvira picks up

Gosha's plastic pistol off the floor and weighs it in her hand. So easy to pick up, so hard to put down, as they say in a John Woo flick.

Then she puts it down with the muzzle aimed straight at the floor, straight at the neighbor's ceiling.

"Bang! Bang!" she mouths silently.

Bang! Bang!

48.

1953. ALL PASSION FOR LIFE

Bang, bang!

Missed it. Lost the knack. After all, it had been years since I'd held a rifle.

But I've seen enough of them in other people's hands.

Oleg aimed again—bang!—and the black figurine of a fat man in a top hat smoking a cigar tipped over. Oleg put down the twenty-two, went off to the side, and began to smoke.

At any rate, how would I know what my grandpa was doing that day? Why did I assume he enjoyed shooting at a shooting gallery? Maybe he was preoccupied with something else. After all, all day long, women women women poured onto the graveled and asphalt paths—athletes, fitness enthusiasts, students, workers, mothers with strollers. In untouched and touched dresses, indistinguishable in the evenings and thus, three times more attractive. Slipping past him, every one of them was a story onto herself: the life she'd lived, her possible (or impossible) acquaintance with Oleg.

How do you turn your body into stone?

Bang, bang, bang! A diminutive young woman put down a rifle and smiled victoriously.

"You're a good shot," Oleg said.

"Thank you," she answered.

She had a round face, broad cheekbones, narrow eyes. Probably a Kazakh, Oleg thought. On second thought, no, a Tatar.

In the last five years, he'd learned to distinguish the Russian ethnic groups.

Of course, it's much easier to picture young Grandma than Grandpa. At least I had seen pictures of her, which is a good start. Plus, I was always told: you, Elvira, are a copy of your grandmother. So be it. Broad cheekbones, narrow eyes, small breasts under . . . under what? What did our grandmothers wear in the fifties? Let her be wearing a golden-gray skirt and a georgette crêpe blouse that day. Let them walk side by side, and let the present once again give way to the past.

They walk side by side. The trees of the square have emerged black and clear. And look at the grass on the lawn!—luscious, long-forgotten.

Thus returned all passion for life.

They walked up to a cart and bought ice cream in small paper cups. One ruble fifty. Oleg gave one to the young woman and took the other one himself.

He hadn't tasted ice cream in five years. Before, it was a ball between two round wafers. That's how he pictured it all these years. In any case, they had other things on their minds besides ice cream *back there*.

(Where did I get the memory of the ice cream ball? Oh yeah, the TV show *The Meeting Place Cannot Be Changed*—in the first episode, a guy is walking and eating an ice cream ball sandwiched between two wafers.)

Oleg was tall, stooped, thin, and unkind. Djamilya spotted him as soon as she walked up to the shooting gallery. He was standing off to the side and smoking, clenching the cigarette stub in his palm like he was shielding it from the wind. His eyes were hungry.

They talked about swimming, the Indian film *Awaara*, and how much Moscow had changed. Oleg took drags on his hand-rolled cigarette until the last, tried to look cheerful and chatted with her, but was thinking serious thoughts. His heart was breaking from pity for someone: either himself, who, for five years, had dreamed of strolling the street like this with a young woman, or for the young woman herself given everything he would never tell her, everything she would never learn.

It was close to evening when they reached her building entrance, where it was darker, and they kissed. He pressed her against the wall, fondled her breasts, and tried to unbutton her blouse. Then he asked tersely and bitterly:

"Tell me, where'd you learn to shoot like that? They don't teach that in the Soviet Labor and Defense Readiness Certification Program."

Dhamilya was languid, didn't want to lie and besides, it was too late. She replied:

"That's where I learned how to do it. Then, at the front. I was a sniper."

He sneered:

"A sniper, ha, a comrade from the front. Then why are you acting like a prude?"

She lost her temper and wanted to break away from him, but suddenly said:

"I'm not acting like anything. I can't do it in an entrance hall . . ."

They hurried up the old stairs to the attic.

Here, I can allow myself not to describe anything. Look away, so to speak, content myself with a beautiful interlude. Simply say that there was everything: passion, power, moments when the building could have been bombed and they wouldn't have noticed, and those serene, weary moments when she sat down and asked:

"Where'd you come to Moscow from?"

Oleg chuckled wryly:

"Where I came from doesn't exist anymore."

And he reached again for her small breasts.

None of this is for us to understand or imagine. What did they talk about? Did Oleg say a word about the places he'd spent the last five years in? Did Djamilya tell him about the front, her first love, Major Voronin, the betrayal and eternal separation? What brought them to that attic? Grief? Despair? Their zeal to claim that for which all hope had seemed lost? A chance to settle scores with fate for the camp internment and postwar loneliness?

Words were superfluous here.

They never saw each other again. For some reason, I don't think my grandpa lived past the winter of fifty-three—he must have died in some fight or other or got hit by a nighttime police patrol bullet. After Beria's amnesty, they say there were so many ex-cons in Moscow that the police preferred not to arrest suspects and instead shot them on the spot.

For some reason, I picture him staggering, running down the street for what seems like an eternity, panting and clinging to the walls, then, falling; let him have a moment to recall that sunny summer day, the Tatar sniper, the footpaths in the square, the small paper cup, the green grass, his first kiss in five years, then, a flash—bang! bang!—a bright light, and a belated realization that this didn't happen here on earth, this didn't happen in the flesh, this was a dream and now he is dying, covered by a snowstorm, by the *vapors of an icy fog*, in the place where the ninety-nine are crying and one is laughing.

I don't know what he did time for. I know it wasn't for political reasons, they didn't let out political prisoners in fifty-three. I'd like to believe
that he wasn't a street thug either. Most likely, an ordinary man who had
lost his way in a vast empire in the mid-twentieth century. Maybe he had
killed someone when he was drunk.

Mom doesn't say anything to me about it and I never had the chance
to ask Grandma. Maybe Rimma knows?

49.

NO FRIENDS, NO ENEMIES

Rimma doesn't know. Rimma doesn't talk to her relatives. And she doesn't have female friends either.

Who would she be friends with? With someone her age, Dasha, for instance? I try to picture them together: Rimma stops by after work in her blouse-and-skirt-down-to-her-knees dress-code outfit—and Dasha, with her head shaved in solidarity with the National Bolshevik Party, redolent of the incense in her apartment and donning chunky silver earrings, a ring in her left eyebrow, and a tongue piercing. They could watch an anime together. Dasha would say something about magic and the New Age. Rimma would look at her like she's an idiot. Or like she's a little girl who lives at the expense of a wealthy man. Sells her beauty. Does she love him? No way, she's lying to herself, what kind of love could there be!

Love is something a woman can't afford. Love makes a woman weak. I think that's what Mom used to say, but Rimma believes that love doesn't exist, that it only exists in the movies. It's the love of an anime girl for an anime boy. Or the love between two girls (then it's called Yuri). Or between two boys (that's called Yaoi). They can love each other because they're both flat and drawn. Flesh-and-blood people don't love.

No, I don't think they'll be friends, the picture isn't coming together.

Perhaps Rimma could be friends with Anya-Elvira? After all, they're sisters, they have the same grandmother. But Rimma doesn't love her family. She thinks they're always trying to collect some debt from her. She's never taken anything from them. She's gotten used to never taking anything from anyone. That's why she rents an apartment for an insane amount of money, by Elvira's standards. It's unlikely that they could discuss the residential real estate market together. Rimma lives in the city center, while Elvira—on the city outskirts. Rimma rarely goes into stores, does her shopping quickly, and doesn't notice the cashiers. Elvira stands behind the register all day, contemplating the customers.

No, it's no accident that the two cousins aren't friends. They have nothing to talk about.

Who else could Rimma be friends with? The blonde girl from Crossroads supermarket? The secretary from the next department?

No, Rimma doesn't know how to be friends. She tried having friends in daycare, was once friends with a classmate for a whole six months, but spent the other ten-and-a-half school years and her one year at university completely alone.

She doesn't get why she should have friends. The girls said: so we could bare our souls to each other. In the morning, Rimma stands before the mirror getting ready to face Sazonov, imagining that she's the office bitch, and the reflection is completely flat. Like the cartoon protagonists on-screen. Where does the soul hide between these two dimensions? What is there to lay bare? She doesn't get it.

Rimma doesn't have any friends, but she has plenty of acquaintances. She has over three hundred contacts in her cell phone. About six hundred in her email contact list. Rimma maintains her social life, does everything as expected. If she's invited to a party, she always brings a gift. If it's time to wish someone a happy birthday, she gets a reminder on her phone or ICQ messenger. Rimma writes down the birthdays of all her acquaintances, even Sazonov's wife and children. She knows Sazonov likes it when people remember.

People appreciate it in general when you don't forget about them. That's why Rimma never has lunch alone, always goes with someone, tries to say something nice to them.

Rimma always tries to say something nice.

Always tries to talk.

She doesn't like silence. Silence is unstructured, chaotic, loaded. Silence is the equivalent of darkness. It's not the sleep of reason that produces nightmares, but silence.

Rimma fills the silence with conversation. Endless cyclical small talk, a collection of stock phrases, socially appropriate sayings, clichéd emotions.

Rimma doesn't know how else to talk. In conversation, she's just a knot in a social network, a translator of others' opinions, a transmitter of what she heard the day before. To her, a conversation is like a glossy magazine: every section is assigned a few pages and, as soon as one finishes, another begins. The topics of conversation also alternate—new releases, sports, movies, books, music, sex, fashion, sometimes politics, or the mysterious *life*.

In magazines, Rimma only looks at the ads. To her, photos and articles are mere vestiges of a tradition that fill the empty space between the advertising pages.

Magazines exist for advertising and conversations—for exchanging important information. To find out something *useful* to you, convince someone of something relevant, establish yourself in new territory.

Rimma knows there are no guarantees in advertising. People can look at a picture and end up not buying anything. The same goes for conversations. What can you do? You won't know until you try. So she has to ask questions, listen to her conversation partner and nod with understanding.

Today, at lunch, she sat with Inga, the secretary from the next department. They talked about their colleagues and then Inga asked if Rimma was sleeping with Sazonov.

"Are you sleeping with your boss?" Rimma asked instead of replying, and Inga launched into the story of her boss's passionate sex life. It turned out he just didn't have time for her, Inga—he was either at the bathhouse with his friends or at his mistress's, and his wife needed attention too.

"Of course, we tried a couple of times," Inga says, "but it was just for kicks, nothing serious."

Rimma efficiently finishes her business lunch and then asks:

"Have you met his mistress?"

"Of course," Inga says. "She drops by the office sometimes. You know, nothing special—head-to-toe silicone."

Inga harrumphs and Rimma smiles politely.

She doesn't want to sleep her way to the top. All the online resources and business publications teach you it's a losing strategy. In order to build a career, you need a social network, a work ethic, and a well-thought-out line of conduct.

In her childhood, she heard something else: careerists were cold and calculating people ready to betray and walk over dead bodies.

Rimma isn't scared of dead bodies, but she has no one to betray. She thinks you can only betray your friends. And only your friends can betray you.

Rimma wants to be perfect and lacking in details, nuances, and trivialities. Year after year, she gets rid of memories, sadness, fear, and hope, cuts them out as if she is making a paper doll out of herself.

She has no friends. No enemies.

Neither dead nor alive.

In a world reminiscent of anime, you can't afford to have even dead enemies: the dead keep rising. They're even more frightening than when they were alive.

Rimma doesn't have anyone.

"It was nice to have lunch together," she tells Inga.

"Sure," the latter replies, "we'll be friends now."

Rimma smiles and says: *Of course, we will.*

50.

PURE HAPPINESS, WHAT CAN I SAY

Vika says the most important thing about the Ring Line is that it has twelve stations, like the number of zodiac signs. That's all nonsense. The most important thing about the Ring Line is that you can always find a seat in the first and last train cars: people just getting off the escalator or coming out of the passage get into the third car at best, while the outermost cars remain virtually empty, even at rush hour.

So Anya is sitting in such a train car, the first or last one, reading a women's magazine she borrowed from Zinka: she finished Koretsky's crime novel on the way to work and needed to read something on the way back. In any case, Zinka's magazines are completely insufferable, Anya leafs through them almost without reading. How to become successful and build a career. The career is obviously at the office. They should write about how to become successful if you've been standing behind a cash register since you were eighteen! How to find Prince Charming and keep him. They should tell me why I need a Prince Charming in the first place; sometimes, I don't know what to do with Andrey. How to experience an orgasm simultaneously with your partner. I don't have problems with that either. Almost with everyone, almost always. Must be because you would get bored if you came early and be angry if it was all over before you could get off. A synchronized finish, like in the competitions. How many men have you had? That's also not interesting, to be honest. I've had as many as I've had, everything is in working order.

Anya lifts her eyes up from the magazine and examines the passengers sitting across from her, thinking that any one of them looks like someone she used to know. There's an overweight, flabby man of about fifty-five, suit, briefcase, glasses, looks like an aged, out-of-date Marik. Surprisingly, he even rubs his hands the same way.

Today, Zinka said they're transferring Marik to the company head-quarters to put him in charge of something. Turns out, he has also built a career. In his place, they promised to send a former branch manager from Mytishchi. No doubt, a belligerent woman, but at least I won't have to have coffee with her. Or, at least, our interaction will be limited to coffee.

I wonder if Vika will start saying that she removed Marik from me. This must be how she tricks her clients: "I can't promise anything, but I'll try." Then, if something happens—it was all her. And if nothing happens—well, she didn't promise anything. What an interesting job, creative. Beats selling shoes.

Anya turns her eyes to another passenger: bulky, round-headed. Somewhat looks like Nikolay, the security guard from the neighboring stand during her last stint at the outdoor clothing market. A tall, sturdy guy, just out of the army. She could never understand why he couldn't find a better job, but never asked.

He lived five minutes away from the market. With his mother in a small two-room apartment. His mother worked at the other end of town and he had the apartment to himself for about an hour a day. The sex was vigorous and efficient, without excessive tenderness. That was a good thing—adults have no need for tenderness.

Andrey was so embarrassed when I said: "Why beat around the bush? If we're in bed, let's fuck." It's funny to think back on it now.

I chose Nikolay myself, based on his exterior, like a male dog at a breed show. Good looking and not a drinker. I noticed him right away, we'd sometimes exchange a few words and, as soon as I was hired as a cashier at IKEA, I came by to supposedly have some vodka and get to know each other better. At IKEA, they promised me a taxed salary, a record in my workbook, and health insurance. Twenty-nine years old, it was about time, why put it off?

Of course, Nikolay never figured it out. When I got pregnant, I didn't say anything, there was no reason to. We fucked and that was that. Thankfully, a woman can do a great job raising a child without a father.

Mom raised me, right? I've seen my father only a handful of times, when I was already an adult. As soon as he brought up romanticism, I told him to fuck off. I said something along the lines of: "Dad! I didn't come to you for advice, I just came to have a look at you. I had a look and that's enough. You've lived without me for twenty years, so go on living that way."

Really, why did he say: Mom didn't let us see each other! If he wanted to, he would have come to see me. His mom, Grandma Marfa, saw enough of me, right?

It's too bad I don't remember how the three of us lived together when I was little. After all, it was three years. I'm curious: was he a caring father or not? Did he pick me and mom up from the maternity clinic like he later did Lyolya and little Sasha?

Mom picked me and Gosha up from the maternity clinic. I remember it well: Gosha was snuffling, wrapped in a plaid blanket, a tiny parcel. Long ago, I was the one covered with this blanket and this time, we wrapped Gosha in it. Maybe it remembers Mom too?

Next to the man who looks like Nikolay is a young couple holding hands and smiling. The young woman is wearing high heels, a knee-length skirt, and a beige jacket, and has bleach blonde hair and tiny gold earrings in her ears. The young man is wearing a pinstripe suit, a leather bag, and a large wristwatch that looks almost Swiss; they used to sell those at the market for forty bucks. Also a very familiar couple, two years ago, those kinds of couples swarmed IKEA—apparently, all of Moscow's clerks decided to marry each other at the same time.

The couples stood in line holding hands like children on a stroll, demonstrating their love to the entire shopping center as if that love couldn't exist without witnesses. Their faces exuded happiness, as on print ads. They even spoke breathily, unable to contain their delight with their love, with their life, and the fact that they were buying cooking pots and napkins together—not just anywhere, but at IKEA!

Anya looked at them with contempt. There she was, a young, free woman, mistress of her own destiny. She had the best child in the world. She didn't need to hold hands with anyone to feed and raise this child. She didn't need a family. Thankfully, she never had and never would have a family.

Anya scanned the barcodes, punched out the receipts, took the money, gave change, and smiled at the next person in line—and was glad she was a cashier and not a customer at this store. Nowadays, Anya says: I quit because it was disgusting to look at them. In any case, she would have easily forgotten about her disgust for the sake of Gosha's health insurance—but when she came home in the evening, her cheekbones hurt so much that the pain didn't let up till nighttime.

Anya quit and still didn't understand what happened—either she was too tired from smiling at all the customers or she was gritting her teeth too tightly every time another happy couple came up to the register.

Andrey said he noticed her even then. That he had a crush on her since he first saw her. That's why he approached her at the shoe store—he remembered her. Anya didn't believe him—if he remembered her, then why didn't he ask her outright: Excuse me, miss, didn't you use to work at IKEA?

In any event, Andrey found a way to introduce himself, right? So they've been meeting up once a week for almost a year now, Anya is even starting to get used to him, tells Vika: He's not too bad, just kind of boring. Vika asked her once: Are you planning to get married? Anya burst out laughing: To whom? I'd die of boredom if I had to spend every evening with Andrey. If it's only on the weekends, that's fine by me. Besides, what would I do with my son if I got married?

Plus, she's used to it being just her and Gosha. Right now, she'll come out of the Metro, pick up Gosha from daycare, they'll go home together, have dinner, and sit down to read a book by Samuil Marshak or Agniya Barto:

The girls know that,
At exactly two-thirty,
Papa's train
Will race past the station.

The taller sisters
Have lifted their brother:
Let him have a look
At the train cars racing by . . .

Anya will read the verses and think to herself: I would have never let Gosha stroll along the railroad embankment! Let Papa's train cars race on without us!

She will sit there, read the verses, be glad that Marik got a promotion, and recall her ride on the Metro, her men, her father, her mother, the customers at IKEA, Andrey and Vika; and Gosha will press against her side, peer into the book, and wait for her to turn the page.

A quiet family evening, pure happiness, what can I say.

So long as that bitch downstairs doesn't call the cops again.

51.

AUTONOMOUS TIME ZONES

In big cities, it is easy to slip out of time in your wanderings. You can even get lost.

The city center's streets are billboards for new films, the newest fashion trends, stylish young women, and luxurious windows displays. A prosperous city that has made it through all the perestroikas and economic crises, oil for who-the-hell-knows-how-many dollars a barrel, natural gas for Europe, base metals, what am I missing? Time races like a new automobile, like a foreign model that has just cleared customs with its sleek, glossy sides, and high-powered engine.

But as soon as you venture outside of the city center, time comes to a standstill. Sometimes, you wander into a co-op café and it's as if ten years never happened. Plastic palm trees, European-style remodeling, colorful liqueurs at the bar. Sometimes, you walk into a courtyard where not every piece of sidewalk is covered by parked cars and where a Girl with an Oar, a plaster trumpeter, or a Soviet Snow Maiden and her little brother, who signed up for the Young Pioneers, can be unearthed from the snow. Some places still have battle graffiti on the walls: *Boris, you're right!* And: *Bring Yeltsman's gang to justice!* In some places, you will encounter men in faded synthetic jackets emblazoned with 1980 Olympics insignia, and in some places, black-and-white snow is always falling and black prison trucks marked "BREAD" are always on the road.

These are autonomous time zones. If you know the itineraries, you can travel between the Moscow of the nineties, the eighties, the seventies . . . You can go all the way up to the start of the last century, break new ground on an abandoned islet of prerevolutionary parquet that has survived all the remodeling projects, and see the bricked over fireplaces, service stairs, and wooden rafters—perhaps for the last time.

As time comes to a standstill, it clings to objects, peels off their paint, covers them with rust and runs, crumbles the moldings of brick houses, sprinkles the floor with plaster, breaks the window glass, topples wooden fences, and breaks off either the trumpet or the oar. In these zones, we don't see the past—the seventies-eighties-nineties—but time itself. These zones are sanctuaries, time is poured into them like old wine into bottles. And all of Moscow is like one giant wine cellar.

The past doesn't live in these zones the same way it doesn't live in our memories—it fades as we forget details and mix up the words and dates; just a bit longer and we'll forget black and white television and a Moscow without traffic.

The people who lived here before us have died a long time ago. All we have left are movies, books, and photos, but they, too, show the work of time rather than a life that is no more. We can only guess, only invent, gather the pieces, roam around Moscow hoping a miracle will suddenly take place and we will plunge down such a portal in time, find ourselves in an autonomous time zone, and realize that the past really did exist.

Three years ago, Nikita ended up on such an islet. Seventies Moscow—an abandoned lot surrounded by a familiar shingle fence that usually concealed another *never-ending construction project* that little Nikita passed on his way to school. At present, the fence had been bleached by the sun, faded in the rain, slanted to the side, and, in places, lay on the ground. The lot was situated not far from a busy Moscow freeway, the roofs of the seventies high-rises had been overtaken by "elite residential neighborhoods" and it was hard to believe that no one had gotten their hands on this plot of land yet.

Next to the abandoned lot, Nikita saw a parking stand. A tilted gatehouse with a dog on a chain and, between the gatehouse and the fence, a small, square enclosure like a backyard that was separated from the street by two rows of barbed-wire fence. A gatehouse, a water basin, and a scarecrow, as if it were a village yard or a vegetable patch.

Something forced Nikita to fix his gaze on this yard. He pressed his forehead to the fence and scrutinized it. Gatehouse. Basin. Scarecrow.

That's it! Someone had put a brightly painted mask on the scarecrow and, even from his vantage point, he could tell that this was no child's handicraft, but an authentic, oriental mask like the ones used in Japanese Noh Theater. White face, narrow eyes, dabs of paint on the cheeks.

A bearded watchman—a representative of a dying breed of street-sweepers-and-watchmen—came out of the little house and approached Nikita:

"What are you staring at?"

"That mask is interesting," Nikita said.

The guard nodded, but didn't leave, as if he were expecting something to follow.

"Can I have a closer look at it?"

"You can't," the watchman shook his head. "The dog is mean, it doesn't allow strangers on its property."

"I was thinking that I'd like to buy it."

For the first time, the watchman smiled.

"It's not for sale," he said. "We need it ourselves."

"Why?"

"We need it." And the watchman walked away: the conversation was over.

The air around him thickened. Nikita thought that those ten square meters of Moscow ground had fallen out of a completely different time period—perhaps, one that was more ancient than this city.

Two steps away from a busy Moscow freeway, in the middle of a field, there stands an idol, a totem pole, a pagan god. His face impenetrable. Before him lie offerings. Chained dogs guard his peace. At night, sacrifices are made.

Compared to this field, the fence for the seventies never-ending construction project seemed brand-new.

As he scrutinized the idol, Nikita noticed another curious detail: there was a saucer on top of the totem's head. An ordinary, cracked saucer. Nikita even thought he could distinguish the General Nutrition logo on it.

He knocked on the gatehouse door and the bearded man came out on the stoop.

"I'd like to make an offering," Nikita said seriously.

The watchman didn't seem surprised. With a leisurely, somewhat habitual gesture, he stretched out an open palm and Nikita placed a hundred rubles in it.

"Anything else I should pass along?" the watchman asked.

Nikita shook his head.

When he told Dasha about this three years later, she asked:

"And what did you ask for?"

"I had to ask for something?" Nikita wondered.

"Of course. You should have at least prayed. Why else make an offering?"

"I was just fooling around," Nikita answered and suddenly realized: Dasha doesn't suspect he can just fool around. A serious, adult man, what sort of fun and shenanigans could there be? I mean, really, Nikita thought, when was the last time I fooled around? I've changed over the last three years. Masha's attempts to get pregnant, my business . . . No time for fun. Maybe that's what old age is like?

"And what were you thinking about when you gave him the money?"

"What do you think about when you give away money?" Nikita joked. "The fact that you have less money in your wallet than you did before."

He said it and remembered how, that very evening, he'd met a man who, a month later, asked him to clean the aquariums at his firm. And that's how his business had started.

"You know," he told Dasha, "let's drive over to the lot! I wouldn't be surprised if everything was the same as it was before."

"You're so silly," Dasha answered. "It's long gone. It only existed for a half-hour especially for you."

"And the General Nutrition saucer is the Holy Grail," Nikita said, thinking that, presently, he wouldn't have asked for money, but for his youthful insouciance back, that lightheartedness, everything that was once lost or maybe, simply hidden somewhere deep in one of his personal, autonomous time zones, those internal caches, private archives, hidden trunks, mystery boxes, silent, tranquil places where Nikita-the-infant, Nikita-the-boy, and Nikita-the-young-man slumber until the time comes.

52.

YOUNG AND BEAUTIFUL

The glide of the small brush down my nail soothes me. The nail is smooth and the strip of color lays down evenly. I can do it over and over: paint and remove. Like Penelope. And also as I wait for my husband.

So I sit and wait, Masha thinks, sit and wait, in the big apartment in the antique armchair. Although, essentially, I have nothing to wait for. My life has gone by. Everything that could have happened to me has already happened. All that is left is the afterword. And no matter how long it lasts, it is still an afterword, nothing more.

Once, I was a little girl, I grew up with a mother and father. I was lucky, I could have remained in the children's home, but no, they took me away, I survived, I was even happy sometimes. Well, a couple of times. Probably. Even though, at present, I can't remember when.

That's Mom and Dad. Grown-up books. Was I happy? Yes, I must have been. But what good to me is that *happy* which remains somewhere in the past? You can't take it with you, you can't lug it across thirty-something years, you won't carry it around in a bundle your whole life.

In the best-case scenario, you have the memories. But that's the best-case scenario. I barely have any left. I remember some trivial things—books, Dad explaining about the transmigration of souls, the way a ray of sunshine fell on the kitchen table. And the cup of tea on that table.

Perhaps those memories are in fact memories of happiness?

Mom and Dad. After all, I never knew a thing about their lives before me. They likely wanted children of their own and probably couldn't have them. Mom must have been upset. Mom knew how to get upset, that she did. Dad cheered her up. He must have been the one who suggested adopting a child from a children's home.

If I'm not able to have a child, I'd probably still not dare adopt from a children's home. I'd be afraid the child would leave me the same way I left my parents.

Although, to be honest, it was an accident. If I hadn't been taken away by ambulance that day, we would have said goodbye properly. I know of other children who stayed in Russia when their parents moved away. And nobody makes a big deal out of it.

Well, that's because they're their birth parents. Because their children didn't say to them: *Who are you to tell me what to do, you didn't even give birth to me!* The devil must have pulled my tongue.

Well, yeah, it was the devil who pulled it—the devil's collecting a debt from me.

Maybe if I told them I was pregnant, they would have found me a good doctor, everything would have gone fine, and I would have a child right now and be happy.

But it all turned out so stupid. My whole life turned to dust for no good reason.

And now, I look back and my whole life seems dispensable, somehow. Ridiculous. Arbitrary. It seems such that I don't even want to make it better. Let it stay the way it is.

I earned a degree in foreign languages and it turned out that this wasn't a profession, but a mere supplement to other studies. I translated for a few years and abandoned it. I worked here and there, but what's the point? I've made as much money my entire life as Nikita brings home every month now.

In any case, inflation must have also played a part. But still, it's all so ridiculous, so stupid, so arbitrary.

For example, I love Nikita—but if I met somebody else in Crimea, I would have fallen for that guy instead. And maybe that other guy would have sent me to the doctor a few years before I decided to go myself. And I would have a child.

I love Nikita—but does he love me? Does he cheat on me often? Will he leave me if I can't have a baby?

It seems like all this should worry me—but I just don't care.

I think it would be difficult to ruin my life. It's like a book: it doesn't really matter what they write in the afterword. Especially if everything has ended badly before the afterword.

I can take a piece of paper and write down a list of things that haven't happened in my life. Things that will never happen. And even this list would turn out rather silly. Various nonsense comes to mind: *I will never make love to a woman.* The question is: did I ever want to? Well, no. But Alisa tried to pick me up a long time ago and I turned her down. And now, no one will want me—neither a woman nor a man. Yes, it seems like I've got a lot to say on the subject of sex. But, for some reason, I want to write: *I will never want to have sex again.* I mean, I know it's probably not true. Anything can happen. But still—I can't imagine anyone would want to caress my body.

I was beautiful once, but now, yes, I can write it: *I will never be beautiful again.*

Wrinkled skin, diminished breasts, jutting cheekbones, ribs like those of a Holodomor victim.

Only my toenails are beautiful. Let me wipe them clean and paint them again.

What else? Oh yeah, I will never go to Paris at a young age. Or New York. And in general, I will never, at a young age, travel anyplace I haven't been to at a young age.

OK, now the short version: *I will never be young again. What I never had time to do—I never had time to do.*

See, I told you: even the list came out dumb and meaningless. It all boils down to one thing: *I will never be young and beautiful again.*

I will never travel to Paris or New York as a young and beautiful woman.

I will never be painted by artists as a young and beautiful woman.

I will never be a young and beautiful mother. Young and beautiful —never.

Never.

Never.

Many years ago, I thought: we'll make money and let's say, buy beautiful clothes, get an expensive car, and go somewhere. Then, you realize: OK, we're done here. You can buy whatever you want—but no matter what car you buy and what clothes you wear, the picture still won't come together. Because neither of us will ever be young and beautiful again.

And if you tell someone, they'll laugh at you. They'll say: *Los ricos también lloran.* The rich cry too. But that's the saddest part: getting what you wanted your whole life at a time you no longer need it.

Ridiculous. Stupid. Arbitrary . It's as if there is a small hole in me from which all my strength leaks out. I've got just enough left to sit right here, with my legs folded in the armchair, to either roll into a ball or to paint my nails over and over, listening to voices, seeing shadows, living out the lives of others over and over as if they were mine, and my own life—as if it were somebody else's, getting thinner every day, gradually turning into a shadow of myself, a phantom, a reminder of who I once was.

It's very cozy to sit here. It's as if these thoughts are lying on my knees. I cradle them, sort through them, stroke their hair. All these eternal *young and beautiful, stupid, ridiculous, arbitrary*, they're all lying on my knees like sleeping kittens, like stuffed animals, like my unborn children.

A woman must have a child. So it is written. And if she doesn't have children, she begets something else. So I beget emptiness and meaning-lessness, absurdity and despair, grief and hopelessness. I rock them on my knees, hand them to my loved ones. Would you like to hold it? Take it, I don't mind.

A woman named Mary couldn't have a child. The Virgin Mary gave birth to Jesus although she was a virgin. And I parted with my virginity back in the last century and still can't give birth to anything. Zero. Nihil. Emptiness.

Someone once told me: emptiness is the absence of Christ, the antichrist.

Maybe I didn't try hard enough? Maybe I should try one more time? One last time. Check into a hospital, do everything by the rules.

Maybe then it would work out.

I should tell Nikita tonight.

One more thing I forgot to add to the list: *Mom and Dad will never be at my wedding.*

53.

REINCARNATION. PAVEL

There is no one to hold my hand before I fall asleep. Pavel is roused by this phrase. What is this silliness?

Although there really is no one. What, Lyokha and Mikhas will hold his hand? That's preposterous.

There was something wrong with this phrase. It was as if he was complaining. As if it was essential that someone hold his hand before he fell asleep.

There are five other men sleeping in the crew's quarters, they, too, have no one to hold their hand. And, incidentally, they are not complaining. Though, back on shore, they have wives who, maybe, really do hold their hand before they fall asleep, but who would tell a thing like that?

Pavel comes out on deck and lights a hand-rolled cigarette. Not a single light on the left bank. No villages, no shepherd's fires, nothing. The Volga looks as boundless as the sea. In the anthracite sky—a slice of crescent moon.

This past year, more and more vacationers have traveled down the Volga, standing aboard in the daytime, watching the passing riverbanks and the calm waters. And everyone asks: where was it that they made a film here? Everyone's so joyful, so pleased. Simple Soviet folk, just like Pavel.

When you see so many people in your day-to-day life, you are constantly reminded of someone. For instance, yesterday, he saw a large man in a Red Army uniform with a gray mustache and rough peasant hands. For some reason, Pavel remembered his father, who, before leaving for the German War, tossed him and his sister in the air and caught them.

His sister was little then, she just laughed, but Pavel was eight years old already and kept yelling: *Higher, higher!* His older brothers stood on the porch in silence and only their mother wept, as if she knew that they were seeing their father for the last time.

The hand-rolled cigarette burns his fingers—look at him being all pensive, he didn't even notice he finished it. He throws the cigarette butt overboard and looks out in the darkness.

Of course, the passengers prefer the Volga by day: the vast expanse, peasant women in handkerchiefs washing laundry, a water carrier filling a barrel, a zeppelin flying in the sky, oncoming ships sailing by, music playing, young women laughing.

Yesterday, one of them came up to Pavel with a wreath on her head, emulating the actress Lyubov Orlova, and asked if it was a long way to Kuybyshev. Pavel answered her, and she said, "Thank you, comrade!" and returned to her cabin.

A beautiful girl. She looked like Lyuba, a student from Moscow who, a decade ago, was also sailing to Samara to see her parents. They fell in love. They'd stand together at night over the dark river—only they weren't taking it in, they were kissing. Since then, if anyone kisses in the movies or here, on the *Uritsky*, Pavel immediately thinks of Lyuba. Her eyes were intensely blue and sparks danced in them when she smiled.

They wanted to get married, but his mother wouldn't allow it—she said: *If you go to Moscow, who will I have here? Find yourself somebody else, a local girl!* Pavel didn't argue: who would argue with their mother? Besides, he promised Pyotr he'd take care of her.

So it didn't work out between Lyuba and him.

It's quiet at night, and in the daytime they play "The people's beauty, full-flowing like the sea!" on all the loudspeakers several times a day. It's a good song. But, for Pavel, there's no correlation between the song and the river. The song's a song. The river, too, is flowing now, its left bank hidden in the dark. In moments like this, it's as if nothing's changed. He's been sailing for fifteen years. He can probably count on both hands all the riverbanks.

Fifteen years. It's as if his whole life has passed here. Others have gone away, Misha went all the way to Moscow and works at a plant there, and Pavel is still here. Except that he's left the village for the town. His whole life on the Volga, like his father and grandfather. It's only nowadays that people travel from place to place all the time in search of something. In the olden days, you lived wherever you were born.

Of course, it would be better that he not tell this to anyone. Because things were bad before and they're good now. *In days past, our melancholy sang songs, and now—it's our joy that sings*. That's true. No one sings melancholic songs anymore. But still, his melancholy comes over him. Maybe it's because of the little girl he spoke with last night?

The little girl said straightaway that her name was Polina, not Polyasha, not Polya, not Polechka, only Polina, or else she'd get mad! Polina, the serious seven-year-old girl. In a little white dress, with a thick book in her hands. And a beautiful mother, who was also eternally carrying a book. *My dad had to work*, Polina explained. *He has a very important job*. And she raised her pinkie.

Pavel noticed that the passengers were endeared by the sight of Polina: what a serious girl. But Pavel didn't like serious children, his little sister was serious, and, with every new death, became even more serious and quiet, as if she knew that her turn was coming. And she had died quietly, too, Pavel didn't even know when. He simply took the wooden horse from his sister's hand and put it in his pocket. He didn't even start crying, just took a shovel and went off to dig a grave. At the time, many people ate cadavers, sometimes even their own children. They say that, in a neighboring village, a woman killed a girl, ate her and said: *She would have died anyway*. The entire neighboring village died out, at least some survived in Pavel's.

He doesn't like to remember this, but it came to mind.

Or how, a year ago, a factory head was sailing with his family. They were moving from Ukraine to a new home, and their nanny with them, also Ukrainian, a young girl by the name of Galinka. Pavel asked her why she was working as a nanny. She should have been studying or working at a factory. Or else she'd spend her entire life as a nanny. Galinka replied: "I can't, I owe it to them. They saved me from starvation five years ago. You probably don't know what real hunger is."

"I know," Pavel answered. "We starved in twenty-one."

"Oh dear," Galinka said, "they told us about it in school: it was because Denikin took away all the grain."

Pavel didn't say anything, but all his insides sank. In any case, what difference did it make now who took away the grain? Though, if Pyotr were still alive, he would have been offended by this.

Were Pavel five years younger, he would have made a pass at Galinka, married her, and had her live in his house, take care of his mother and raise his children. And now, who needed him? You could say he was old.

Pavel hears someone's cautious steps. He turns around: "Well, I never! Polina, what are you doing here?"

The little girl in the white dress is standing alone on the deck at night. Like a ghost.

"I can't sleep, Uncle Pasha. Dad tells me I need to get fresh air."

Pavel sighs and picks up the girl. "Let's stand together," he says.

"You, Uncle Pasha," Polina says, "must be a brave person."

"Why?" Pavel marvels, "I'm an ordinary Soviet person, like everyone else."

"You know, my mom told me about an ancient Greek philosopher," and Polina wrinkles her forehead, recalling a difficult name. "Ana-char-sis, there. He said that sailors were very brave people. Because they were only four fingers away from death. Four fingers," she explains, "was how thick shipboard was in Greece."

"Well," Pavel says, "look at the size of our ship, it's a motor ship, we don't have just one board, we have many. Four hundred fingers. No need to be scared."

"I'm not scared," Polina says seriously, "I know that if the ship sinks, we'll be saved. Like when the *SS Chelyuskin* sank."

They gaze at the river together.

"Uncle Pasha," Polina says, "you're strong. Almost like Dad. Do you know how strong my dad is? It's really something! One time he showed me an armored train. Have you ever seen an armored train?"

"I've seen one, Polina," Pavel replies and clams up.

He'd seen an armored train, seen a fire burst forth from its armored side, seen izbas burn down, heard the screams of the dying, the moans of the wounded, the orders of a firing squad, the spent rounds. His brother Pyotr had managed to hide Pavel in a haystack, said: *Take care of Mother!*, grabbed a rifle and run off somewhere. Toward the end, many people had rifles, but in the early days it was mostly pitchforks. That's what they called it—a "fork war."

Pavel thinks: I will die, some more years will go by and no one will know a thing about the fork war. Because they will never write about it in textbooks, and if they do, it will be two lines in the vein of "anti-Soviet peasant revolt." How was it anti-Soviet? It was only against the Communists and so they wouldn't take away the grain. They had slogans like *Down with the Communists and the Confiscation of Bread!*, *Long Live Free Trade!*, and *In Support of Christian and Muslim Faith!* because there were many Bashkirs and Tatars.

Polina's mom comes out on deck, tears the child out of Pavel's arms, carries her to the cabin and hisses something to her along the way—and suddenly Pavel is overcome with anger: she didn't even say thank you, just tore her away and carried her off like he was some sort of cannibal or was preparing to throw her daughter overboard like Stenka Razin in that song! City bitch! The husband is working somewhere, building socialism, and she's riding down the Volga! She's bothered that a veteran sailor is holding her daughter in his arms!—and he understands why he's angry at Polina's mother: he simply envies her.

Pavel looks out at the dark water and thinks: I, too, would have liked a daughter, I, too, would have liked a normal family. My father was a happy man: three sons and a daughter. My mother's right when she says he was lucky. He never did find out that Kolchak's men killed Nikola, the Bolsheviks killed Pyotr and Katerinka died of hunger. That there were no grandchildren to speak of.

They must have all died on purpose, Pavel thinks spitefully, died so they wouldn't have to learn what happened afterward. So I'd have to care for mother on my own all these years. No wife, no children, nothing. My whole life is just my mother and the river. My father and brothers have long gone to paradise, if there is a paradise, and Katerinka is definitely there—even if it doesn't exist, there should be one especially for her, although, nowadays, they say it's all fairy tales. And even if there isn't a paradise, so what: they're already dead, it's over. And I have to finish their work and mope around with our mother! Of course, I'm the youngest boy, I was small: I fought in neither the Civil War nor the German War. I was a few years off or I would have volunteered like Nikola, would have been a fallen hero by now as well. I was two years too young, two years— he recalls his recent conversation and thinks bitterly: four fingers away from death! It's all nonsense, who's afraid of death? Death is always one step away! But a life, a good, happy life, is also only a *vershok* away. If we hid the grain from the food requisition department back then, Katerinka wouldn't have died, Mother would have lived with her, and I would have married and had children. And even if she did die! I could have walked out the door ten years ago, married Lyuba, and later brought Mother to live in Moscow with me anyhow. I wouldn't have abandoned her.

And Pavel is so sad his life is all but over and nothing has happened to him, so sad, that he spits in the nighttime river, returns to his quarters, and falls asleep.

The spit falls in the dark water, dissolving in it, and the droplet of

Pavel's rancor flows into the river, where the catfish are swimming and the crayfish are crawling along the bottom, where the rotten remains of drunken boats lay silent, where the memories of those who are mute like fish and won't tell anyone about their lives slumber at the lowest of the Volga's deep ends—only the nighttime water, the black Volga, the empty riverbanks, and the slice of crescent moon in the anthracite sky.

In the morning, the sun is shining, the passengers stroll on deck smiling and laughing, the music is playing, people are waving to them from the piers, boats are dozing along the bank, water carriers fill the barrels—maybe even a zeppelin or airplane glides through the sky—the loudspeaker sings *"my dreams and wishes are coming true"*—and so it is, dreams and wishes are on the brink of coming true, happiness is so near, only a year or two away. Four fingers, no more.

Polina and her mom find Pavel and her mom says:

"I want to apologize. I woke up at night, my daughter was gone and I was so frightened! Thank you for looking after my girl!"

Pavel smiles and says: *Not at all, nonsense, you have a wonderful little girl*—and Polina just stands there pouting, as if to say, I'm not a little girl, I'm seven years old.

They walk away and Pavel looks at these happy people, thinking that if Pyotr were alive he would have liked it here. He always liked equipment, and nowadays, there were plants, factories, tractors in villages, brand-new motor ships sailing the Volga, beautiful music playing all day long . . . Turns out that the Communists made good on their promise, built a good life for the working class. Does that mean you fought and died in vain, Pyotr? Left a young wife, didn't get to really live, didn't watch any films, didn't listen to the radio—you were only twenty back then, now you're my younger brother and not the other way around.

And Pavel wished for there to be a paradise after all, for it to resemble the Volga on a summer day and for all the dead—his father, brothers, and little sister, all those who had died in the German War, who had starved to death in twenty-one, who had been shot by automatic rifles, cut up by sabers, stabbed with pitchforks, drowned, or hanged—to sail down a heavenly river on a heavenly motor ship, with their happy grandpas and great-grandpas standing along the banks, waving to them from the pier, filling water barrels, fussing around on boats—and for music to be playing everywhere and Lyubov Orlova to sing in her crown of daisies:

The people's beauty,
Full-flowing like the sea,
Free like the Motherland,
  Vast,
     Deep,
       Strong!

54.

BOAT, FLOOD, OLD MAN, BEASTS

"Mazai restaurant?" Nikita laughs. "Aquariums? What, with rabbits?"

"Well," Victor explains, "not just aquariums, but a whole water theme. A pool, a bridge, aquariums . . . a river motif."

Natasha laughs as well:

"Waiters dressed as rabbits, a boat-shaped bar, and so on?"

"That's none of our business," Victor replies. "They're asking us about aquariums and if we've got any ideas for a pool."

Morning brainstorming session, they're discussing a new client. Natasha is a petite, slim brunette who somewhat resembles Masha when she was younger. Victor, twenty-five, always dons a suit and tie. You can't call him Vitya, only Victor. A serious young man. Brought in a new commission today.

That's why I like my business, Nikita thinks—always something unexpected. Mazai restaurant, it's mind-boggling.

"What? We'll make an islet . . . how did the poem go? *Less than a sazhen of ground in width, less than an arshin in length.*

"And how much would that be in standard units of measurement?" Zoya, their wide mouthed, bleached-blonde saleswoman asks.

"Let's check online," Nikita says, "but it's obviously a bit smaller than our conference room. So a herd of rabbits could fit on it."

It's astonishing that so many years have gone by and I can still remember the poem about old man Mazai saving rabbits from the flooding river by heart. And why wouldn't I?

That day, Grandpa Mikhail came over and decided to check Nikita's homework. Nikita recited it from memory five times, from beginning to end, but kept tripping up somewhere. His father came home from work and said: "Stop it, Dad, why are you bothering the boy? Who knows what kind of nonsense they're being assigned these days. Check his math homework instead." Grandpa got really angry, forgot Nikita was listening, turned around and said:

"Vasya, you can't be so uneducated! Do you at least understand what your son is learning this poem in lieu of?"

"In lieu of math," Dad replied assuredly.

"You're an idiot with your math," Grandpa said. "You better not tell me you don't recognize the plot. A boat, a flood, an old man, beasts. Well, what is it?"

"Old Man Mazai and the Rabbits," Dad replied and began to laugh.

"Math!" Grandpa grew livid. "Physics! Your stupid science! You know everything and have forgotten what's most important! One more time: boats, rain, flood, ruin, salvation—what is it?"

"It's the myth of Noah!" Nikita began to yell. "I know, I read about it in a book called *Biblical Tales*!"

"There," Grandpa calmed down, "my grandson is my only hope. That's right, Nikita, Mazai is your Soviet Noah. Because in 1917, they abolished religion, but not entirely. They just replaced some stories with others so that fools wouldn't catch on. But of course, it's all the same: flood, boat, miraculous salvation. It's no accident that Mazai is an old man with a beard, which is how they draw God in children's books. It's a children's myth about the flood."

"Then why does he only save the rabbits?" asked Dad.

Grandpa only shrugged his shoulders.

As he sat in his room later that evening, Nikita overheard Mom and Dad watching the news. The weather segment predicted rain, Mom mentioned something about Heaven's Gates, and Dad recalled that it occurred to him and Grandpa Misha today that Mazai was a Soviet Noah.

"I didn't want to say it in front of the boy," Dad said, "but what's important is why they only save the rabbits and not two of every kind. It's a symbol of Soviet selection: evidently, only the most cowardly, thieving, and helpless will be saved. They twitch their ears and stay put. And that is what they instill in our children from childhood: sit there like a rabbit on an island and wait for salvation to come. And our whole lives, we sit there waiting to see who'll come for us: Mazai or Turgenev's Gerasim, salvation or drowning."

A film had started on television, but Dad wouldn't let up:

"The revolution is an endless flood. The entire Soviet regime is a flood. Valentin Rasputin's instincts were on the ball! His book *Farewell to Matyora* is precisely about that. All those sunken churches, the Church of the Intercession on the Nerl, et cetera—that's the old Russia, the one the Communists sank. Nowadays, it's a northern river bend, those stupid electric power plants. They're just causing floods—it's a well-known fact that nuclear power is cheaper and more reliable. But you can't trust convicts with nuclear power stations, only hydroelectric ones."

Mom told him to simmer down—her father, Grandpa Makar, built electric power plants in his day and always said that it was true about the workers' enthusiasm and so forth.

"I don't get your father," Dad said. "I think he still can't decide if he supports the Soviet regime or not. He can't forgive the Bolsheviks for collectivization, but always praises their construction projects. As if it isn't obvious that construction and collectivization are two links in the same chain."

"And what about science?" Mom asked. "You're a working physicist, isn't it the same thing?"

"I already explained it to you," Dad blew his top. "Science is something completely different. It's for the good of all humanity. Communism, capitalism—doesn't matter. We solve the fundamental problems of life and seek out alternative energy sources to avoid burning coal and oil. All of humanity needs physics, space flights, and astronomy. I often think of what would happen if my dad escaped in 1917. I'd be living in America, but would still, undoubtedly, be a classified rocket engineer—only I'd be flying to Nevada instead of Kazakhstan."

"But your father didn't leave, right?" Mom asked in a hushed voice. "With all his faith in the flood, he stayed, for some reason. Do you think your dad decided whether or not he supported the Soviet regime?"

Mom seemed to have gotten mad on account of Grandpa Makar, though Nikita didn't eavesdrop any further. But the story about the flood, the rabbits, and Noah was burned into his memory.

"I think this will be a very successful restaurant," he tells Victor. "We're all a bit like rabbits."

nd Natasha laugh and Nikita decides: let them think it's a fact, perestroika and the nineties were another Great Flood, we escaped. Now we're sitting here gathered in a herd, in a cheap office conference room in a cheap office building, on an island slightly bigger than Nekrasov's. We're the surviving rabbits, we were spared, we survived. We no longer await salvation, we're learning to swim, learning to dive, to go down to the bottom, be ready for a new flood. And the restaurant guests who are ready to shell out five hundred dollars for dinner for two have also learned to swim, have also resurfaced. They can afford to wait for a server rather than a savior.

As for me, thinks Moreukhov, I don't go to restaurants, the last time I saw a waiter was three years ago, and as for a Savior, my Savior is always by my side, always hears me, always takes care of me. Otherwise, how would have I resurfaced all these years, why would I only now invent this story about my brother, Grandpa Misha, and old man Mazai? If only in honor of my and Dimon's shared joke from our university days: a mega-project of a dozen rock operas based on the Russian classics. Although we only wrote one piece, to the music of Caiaphas's aria in *Jesus Christ Superstar*, where the chorus sings: "Must die, must die, this Jesus must, Jesus must, Jesus must die!"

Needless to say, our aria was called "Jesus Mazai."

55.

THE INCIDENT WITH YEVSEYKA

One time, the little boy Yevseyka—who was a very good person!—was sitting on the seashore and fishing. This is a very boring business if the fish are capricious and don't bite. Since the day was hot, Yevseyka began to doze off from the heat and—plop!—fell into the water.

Anya is reading a book to Gosha. For the fifth time today: a Maxim Gorky fairy tale that Gosha found at his grandmother's and which, for some reason, is a great hit with him. Anya thinks she must know the whole thing by heart already, but Gosha keeps asking: again, again!

When you keep repeating the same thing over and over, you fall into a strange stupor. Thoughts swim around in your head like fish in an aquarium and words float up like bubbles from a bubble machine.

The water lilies blossom and sway, the speedy shellfish flash like flies, a sea turtle trudges along with two small, green fish playing above its heavy shield like butterflies in the air, and now a hermit crab carries its shell over white stones.

Anya reads this and thinks of Andrey. When they were having breakfast on Saturday morning, he suddenly asked:

"Do you have vacation plans?"

Anya was even surprised: what vacation plans could she possibly have with her salary and a child to boot? Aunt Shura's dacha, where else? If the latter's own grandkids don't show up. Otherwise, the two of them will stay in the city. She shrugged—she didn't know yet.

"Maybe we can go to Turkey?" Andrey proposed.

"And what will I do with Gosha?"

And on whose dime? His? No, Anya never took money from men.

He sees that he's got a giant fish overhead covered in bluish-silver scales, with its eyes bulging out and its teeth bared, smiling amiably, as if it's already fried and lying on a dish in the middle of a table.

It's obviously not only about Gosha or the money. She can ask Mom to watch Gosha. But two weeks with Andrey! Even in Turkey. She would die of boredom.

Needless to say, she can't say to him: listen, darling, of course, you're a spectacular lover, I love spending time with you at the movies and all the rest, but under no circumstances will I be able to stand more than twenty-four hours with you.

And the crab wiggles its whiskers angrily and grumbles, stretching out its pincers:

"If I catch you, I'll cut off your tongue!"

So Anya didn't say anything to him—thankfully, the doorbell rang. Turned out the third floor neighbor had gone completely nuts—she called the police and, this time, in the middle of the day: *I heard a woman screaming, someone's getting murdered upstairs.* There had in fact been screams forty minutes ago. Over that time, they could have hacked the body into pieces and carried it out. And anyway, the witch must be aware that no one was being murdered and simply wants to exasperate Anya.

Anya tried to explain tactfully to the two young cops about the kind of screams there could be on a Saturday morning. The young cops acted like they didn't understand. In the end, Andrey barked: "We were fucking, why's that so hard to figure out?"

A sea cucumber that looks like a poorly drawn piglet climbs up his leg and hisses:

"I wish to get to you know better . . ."

A sea bubble trembles before his nose, pouting, snorting, and reproaching Yevseyka:

"Get a load of him! Not a crab, not a fish, not a mollusk, tsk tsk tsk!"

Thoughts swim around on their own, without coming into contact with each other, like fish, like clouds. They're not Anya's, they've got a life of their own, they're not even thoughts—simply fragmented pictures.

A sepia fish has swum by like a wet handkerchief, siphonophores flash everywhere like glass marbles, a shrimp tickles one ear, while the other is also being probed by a curious creature, and even small crayfish travel along his head—tangled up in his hair and tugging on it.

There's Anya walking on a sandy beach while Gosha runs ahead of her along the surf's edge, turning around and laughing. The waves splash at her feet, the sun drops behind the mountain and long shadows stretch out on the ground. A light breeze blows from the sea. Anya is slightly tipsy and follows the running Gosha with her eyes, smiling.

> *Fluttering her fins,*
> *Toothy and thin,*
> *Looking for her dinner,*
> *The pike circles the bream!*

There's Anya climbing on the roof of an adjacent building, opening a briefcase with a sniper's rifle in it. It takes only a few seconds to assemble. Lie down in a more comfortable position. Take the lid off the sight at the last moment. Aim it at the window. Catch the old viper in the crosshairs of the sight in her own kitchen. Hold your breath. Pull the trigger.

Done!

He sees that it's a beautiful day, the sun's playing on the water, the green water's splashing against the shore, roaring and singing. Yevseyka's fishing rod is floating in the sea, far away from shore, and he's sitting on the same rock he had fallen off of, completely dry by now!

"Yikes!" he says, smiling at the sun, "so I've surfaced!"

Anya closes the book. For a second, she thinks she can hear someone screaming downstairs.

A week ago, a hot water pipe under Anya's apartment's floor sprang a leak. The scalding hot water seeped between the slab joints and eroded the plaster; as a result, the size of the crack became critical. This led to a spontaneous expansion and bursting of the pipe, which caused a chunk of plaster to fall on the head of citizen M. P. Balakina, seventy-eight, resident of apartment No. 15 on the third floor. Following the blow to the head, Ms. Balakina lost consciousness and didn't regain it, going into a state of shock provoked by multiple burns from the water and dying.

56.

FAMILY ALBUM

I pulled the *District* newspaper out of the mailbox and read a brief description: the history of the Troparyovo neighborhood or, specifically, Troparyovo-Nikulino (Troparyovo was to the left of Vernadsky Boulevard and Nikulino to the right). It turns out it wasn't a part of Moscow until 1960. And before, it was a village like any other. Construction began in the seventies, when Grandpa bought a co-op here for Mom—ostensibly for Mom, but actually, for Mom and Grandma. Because Grandma preferred to live with us and not with Grandpa in his apartment in the Sokol district, where Mom lives now.

Which means that Grandpa had money for a co-op. And because of his job, was entitled to purchase an apartment in Moscow when he retired. And was a very good person. And Father didn't marry Mom precisely because of him. Though, at the time, Grandpa still lived in Leningrad and mom—in Moscow.

Interesting.

No doubt, the co-ops here weren't very cheap. In the seventies, it was increasingly scientists and party members who were given apartments here. And foreign diplomats—there was a whole little German town and a few buildings where foreigners lived.

I remember how, one time, Mom and I were standing in line for vegetables for about forty minutes when a black man walked in. Black bowler hat, umbrella with a silver clasp, a *fat cat*, as I would say today. And he started to explain in French that he was a diplomat and had the right to jump the line. The line told him in English that, if he was such a fancy diplomat, he should go to Beryozka. But he insisted: I don't understand

294

English, *je suis diplomatique*. And then, Mom stepped out and told him in fluent French what we all thought of him. I think he turned gray with rage and left. But as soon as we came out, he darted back in.

This was the only time in her life that mom's language studies proved useful to her.

But overall, pushy diplomats were the biggest hooligans in our neighborhood. Twenty years ago, this was what they called a cultured neighborhood. Which is why, today, you can meet the city's most unusual alcoholics here. For example, Asian women in fur coats treating various drunks like me to a beer.

Our only competition is the neighboring Konkovo. They've even got a catchphrase: *Fuck off, Rostov, we're in Konkovo!* And we are, obviously, in Troparyovo.

Next to my building is a two-story structure. There used to be a dry cleaner's there. Then, the dry-cleaner's shrank and some commercial group took over half the building. And now there's a gym and a Kopeyka discount grocery store. Last year, I tried to punch their security guard and almost got another tooth knocked out.

At one time, there was a handwritten sign in the second-floor window that said, "Happy Birthday!" Since every day is someone's birthday, every day, a person would walk down the street, see the sign, and feel happy that someone had remembered.

This was when, aside from official slogans, there was nothing hanging in the streets. Except for posters for Aeroflot, which were, essentially, still official slogans.

I sometimes drop by Kopeyka for groceries. I always buy alcohol at the little On the Clearing shop for some reason, although it's supposedly farther away. And it's got nothing to do with Kopeyka's security guard— it's not like I haven't been punched at the little shop before. When I'm sober, I don't always understand what I do when I'm drunk. My trips to On the Clearing are not the most inexplicable thing that happens.

So I come out of Kopeyka today and see my beautiful Maggie Cheung walking toward me. I guess I wasn't mistaken when I thought she lived

drunk, I would have easily struck up a conversation

her place, maybe even asked her to come to mine.

ne pillar and she says to me:

ners

at you? Hello," I say, "I haven't seen you in a while,

he replies. And is about to get on her way.

"Listen," I say, "what's your name? For some reason, I forgot."

And she replies: "Lena," and goes right in.

So I take out a Prima cigarette, lean against the brick wall and begin to smoke. About fifteen minutes later, I see her come back out.

"Lena," I say, "can I help you carry your bag? Walk you home, so to speak?"

"No need," she says, "I'm driving."

And she takes her car keys out of her pocket. She presses a button, something beeps to my left and she puts her grocery bags in the trunk and gets behind the wheel.

"I'll see you," she says. "Maybe I'll have something for you to do."

She smiles and leaves.

She has a good car, a foreign make.

Something to do? Very interesting.

I finish my Prima, grab my grocery bag, and head home.

By the way, she looks nothing like the alcoholics of Troparyovo. Her face is as bright as a button. Although they say Asians age differently. They, too, probably drink themselves to death.

If I were drunk today, it would be understandable. Crazier things have happened to me when I'm drunk. When I'm drunk, God admires me, as I've already said. But for the girl of my dreams to get out of her car just like that, in the middle of the day in the Moscow springtime, when I'm sober, say *hello* to me, then, and *I'll see you*, as if she knows that I'm not going anywhere, that I'll probably just keep standing here, propping up the wall, waiting until she has *something for me to do.*

Okay, I'll wait. For now, let's get back to Grandpa Grigoriy, who was a very good person, but one beautiful day, blew his brains out after listening for too long to the BBC.

What do I know about him? Actually, almost nothing. Mom and Grandma never really talked about him and we only have one photo of him left, which is displayed prominently in Mom's house.

Grandma didn't like to reminisce about the past in general. I learned almost by accident that she had another daughter before she had Mom—I found a box with old photos and asked: *Is that Mom when she was little?* And Grandma snapped: *No, that's my oldest, Polina. She died during the blockade.*

They didn't like photos in our home. I often think I'm retroactively trying to draw my personal family album. Only the end result isn't pe ple, but symbols of people: Dad, Mom and Uncle Sasha at the cr of a triangle. Grandpa Misha and Grandma Marfa drawn with very faint lines—it's just that they're depicted in a children's book style, in the State Children's Publishing House period of Kabakov and Pivovarov.

The person I really want to draw is Aunt Lida. Let her stand leaning on a cane in the kitchen of her lonely apartment on Vasilyevsky Island. Or better yet, be a statue in the alleys of the Summer Garden, where she liked to stroll.

She would lean on her cane and tread the paths of the Summer Garden, asking me about my studies, and later on, about my exhibits and paintings. She would frown with displeasure: she didn't approve of art in general.

I saw Aunt Lida, spoke to her—but still can't imagine what it means to have survived the blockade. In any event, I can't imagine what it means to have lived for ninety years, to have lived through the revolution, the Great Terror, war and starvation, to have outlived all your peers and to have never had a husband or children.

In all likelihood, I've learned everything I know about my family from Aunt Lida.

But what do I know really? I had a dad—and he left my mom. I had a Grandpa—and he shot himself. Only Grandma died a natural, peaceful death at the age of eighty-five, outliving her sister by six months.

If Aunt Lida were alive, she would have told me why my father left my mother and what Grandpa Grigoriy, who was a very good person, had to do with it. After all, at one time, she told me about little Polina, whom no one else ever talked about.

Yes, in the spring of 1941, Grandma brought her daughter to Leningrad to visit Lida, her older sister. Grandma herself was from Leningrad. Then, the war broke out, the blockade began, and they weren't able to leave in time. A great many people weren't able to leave in time, no one told them they had to run. The authorities must have feared mass panic.

They say that many, many children stayed in Leningrad. Little Polina also stayed—and died.

But Grandma survived. She was a strong, courageous woman—not only because she survived starvation and the death of her own child. Her real courage was in giving birth again, at the age of forty, in 1950.

And that's when Lenochka was born, Lyolya, Yelena Grigoryevna Borisova—my mother.

57.

1942. IN THE MORNING
YOU WAKE UP ALL VIGOROUS

I can't imagine what it means to survive the blockade. I can't imagine blockade life. Muscular dystrophy, food rations of 125 grams, lines, viciousness, stupor, corpses on the streets, ice-covered rails, trams stopped in their tracks, aerial bombings, ice-holes, hunger, hunger, hunger.

What do I know of hunger? Even when I had no money, I didn't starve. I quickly became a trendy artist, free hors d'oeuvres at exhibit openings and so forth. I know nothing of hunger. But thirst, hangovers, nausea that turns you inside out, the smell of your own bile that you vomited at your feet, headaches, shaking hands, frothy lips, and delirium—yes, I know about that. As for hunger—nothing. Except for a single poem:

> This is how hunger begins:
> in the morning, you wake up all vigorous,
> then, the weakness begins,
> then, the boredom begins,
> then, the loss of the force
> of quick thinking sets in,
> then, a calmness sets in,
> and then the horror begins.

They say it's Daniil Kharms. He died in a psychiatric hospital during the blockade. Of starvation, like little Polina.

Of course, he wrote these verses earlier—back in the thirties.

In the happy, prewar days.

A long, long time ago, in a scary, enchanted city, there lived a little girl. She lived with her mom and aunt and they were all very scared.

In the streets of this city stood buildings without walls so you could see all the rooms, even the bedrooms. But no one lived in these buildings.

The black sky over the city was crisscrossed with straight rays of white light. A white white snow fell on the city from this sky. In this sky soared enormous balloons that resembled flying behemoths.

From time to time, bombs fell from this sky.

One time, the little girl saw a piece of shrapnel hit a man right on the head, break through his cranium, and lodge in his brain. But the man didn't fall. No, he simply staggered from the horrible blow, took a handkerchief from his pocket, wiped his face, which was plastered with bloodied brains, and, turning to the girl, said:

"Don't worry, Polina: I've already been vaccinated. See—I have a pebble sticking out of my right eye. That was also an accident. I'm used to it by now. It's all the same to me!"

With these words, the man put on his hat and wandered away somewhere.

Strangely, neither Mom nor Aunt Lida saw this man with a pebble in his right eye, although they were standing right next to Polina.

Such was the enchanted city.

Also in this city, up on a high hill, stood a wooden shed, but the girl knew that the hill was magical. In the hill was hidden an indestructible cliff, and in the shed, a wondrous horseman awaited his hour. And when the time comes, the beams will fall away, the horse will stand on its hind legs, and the horseman will lift the spell from the scary city.

The people in this city lie down to sleep in the middle of the street. Then they were placed on stretchers in their sleep and taken away somewhere. Sometimes the little girl herself wanted to lie down and go to sleep in a snowbank, but her mom didn't let her and scolded her.

When the little girl slept, she had very strange dreams. Once, she dreamed of a man who was eating cutlets.

And he ate, ate, ate, ate, and ate, until he felt a deadly weight somewhere in his belly.

Whereupon he moved the insidious food aside and began to tremble and cry.

The gold watch in his pocket stopped ticking.

All of a sudden, his hair turned lighter and he could see clearer,

His ears fell to the floor like yellow leaves fall from a poplar in the fall

—and the little girl woke up.

In the enchanted city, there was no food at all.

In the enchanted city, cannibals wandered the desolate nighttime streets. Mom and Aunt Lida whispered about them when they thought the little girl was asleep. But Polina knew it anyway: cannibals steal little children and eat them. Because little children are very tasty.

Whereas other people eat stones. At night, they crawl out on the street and swallow cobblestones or building walls. That's why, in the morning, there were pits everywhere, and more and more buildings stood without walls.

But the girl didn't eat stones, she knew how dangerous this was. To make sure she didn't forget, she even made up the acronym "STIDE," which meant "stones inside dangerous." STIDE was easy to remember and she could think of it on the spot.

One time, the girl dreamed she spat into a cup of water and the water turned black right away. She squinted her eyes and looked intently into the cup. Her heart began to beat fast and, all of a sudden, something big and black rushed past her window. It was a dog that sat down like a crow on the roof of the building across the street. The girl looked in the cup again. The water was very black.

But just then the dog flew through the window, lay down by the girl's feet, and fell asleep.

There were no dogs in the enchanted city. There weren't any cats either. And hardly any birds, for that matter.

In her dreams, the little girl very much wanted to see birds and beasts: happy siskins, a bulldog and a dachshund, a tiger strolling in the street, four little mice sailing in a toy boat, and the cat that could fly on hot air balloons. But instead she dreamed that one man put an old, dead woman in a suitcase, while another, who was completely blind, snuck into a garbage dump where he was bitten by a rat.

Another time, the girl dreamed that she was wearing a wonderful, light-colored dress and a white ribbon in her golden hair, and that her dad tossed her up toward the ceiling, caught her, and said: *My little golden nugget!* And then her mom came in wearing a beautiful dress and high heels, they greeted their guests and everyone sat down at the table. And there were neither cannibals, nor men with pebbles in their eyes, nor people who fell asleep in the middle of the street, and little Polina lived in the most beautiful city in the world, in the happiest family in the world.

58.

I WORKED THERE, I'D KNOW

At first everything went like clockwork—they kissed a little, then Andrey took off her dress, yanked off his jeans and T-shirt, clung to her breasts for a few minutes, and used his lips to pave his way down her stomach to the hirsute triangle between her legs.

Anya didn't like foreplay that much in general, or in Andrey's execution in particular. But today, it was somehow completely boring and, as he used his tongue to trace out figure eights on her belly button, she completely forgot about him and was thinking some ordinary and not at all sexual thoughts: Should I or should I not go to Turkey? Where should I send Gosha for the summer? The new boss isn't too bad, although Zinka doesn't like her . . . Should I drop hints about my salary? I get the most sales, so shouldn't I be making more money? . . . My mother has aged so much over the winter . . . and what a horrible death befell that mad old woman.

The whole building discussed it—first, the blow to the head, then, the scalding water, she didn't stand a chance: a young person would have kicked the bucket, and Marya Petrovna was pushing eighty, she'd lived in the building since it was built, they said she was quite dynamic before, community-minded, fought for the playground, and convinced them to plant trees in the courtyard. In the past few years, her mind had gone, that's true, she didn't leave the house at all, claimed that someone wanted to kill her. In my opinion, the country's collapse did a number on her, you could say that Gorbachev and Yeltsin killed her. Yes, in the old days, they would have renovated on time. Oh, come on, what do you mean, on time? Everything is the same as it was before, only the building was new back then. Remember how it took them two years to seal the seams? Our ceiling was constantly leaking.

So that's who Gosha has to thank for the playground and I—for my favorite trees in the courtyard. Why did I do this to her? Okay, she did call the cops. An elderly, sick person, I could have gone down and spoken to her, explained it to her, in the end. The alcoholic neighbors were always fighting, they were the ones she should have reported to the police.

But no, she wasn't interested in the neighbors. I was the one who got under her skin. Maybe she didn't like the shape of my eyes. Or the fact that I'm young, have a child, am my own mistress, and have a man who comes over to boot, that I fuck in the mornings and scream like a hellcat.

Was I really screaming? Anya asks herself. I did my best to hold back. I scolded Gosha so he wouldn't run around the house and make noise. I was afraid to have people over in the evening—what if she called the cops again? If we were fucking at night, I was as quiet as a mouse—luckily, that's not too difficult with Andrey. I gritted my teeth, bit my lip, and you didn't hear a peep out of me.

Oh God, I'm so tired of all this! When the old crone was alive, I wasn't even aware how tired I was.

Doesn't matter—at this point, no one can order me around. From now on, I won't be a bother to anyone and no one can bother me, Marya Petrovna is far away, she won't hear me, the neighbors in the next apartment over are drunks, they couldn't care less. And the others are polite, they'll pretend they didn't hear anything.

Now I can.

And for a second, Anya returns to reality and realizes that Andrey is already moving inside her—wow, I really drifted off there, she thinks, then suddenly says: *I want to do it differently*, slips out from under the male body and gestures with her hands for him to lie down.

She doesn't know herself why she's using hand gestures. Only she feels like she's gritting her teeth, like she's at the register at IKEA or doing laps in a swimming pool. She can't speak.

Anya forgets about everything: Turkey, Gosha, summer, paycheck, Mom, scalding water, neighbor, playground. Anya thinks she's quickening the pace, hurrying with her last bit of strength; tremors seize her legs, the skin on her broad cheekbones tightens and it's as if her body is doing a final 100-meter race, as if this moment is her most important swim meet.

Why should she always reach the finish line in tandem? Like hell she will. No one will beat her today.

Anya's body is a speedy dolphin, a giant fish, a shark, a killer whale, a crocodile. Anya's body is a submarine, a flying torpedo, a harpoon that hits its target. Anya's body is narrow hips, flat stomach, small breasts. She flies unstoppably, irrepressibly to her target, faster and faster . . .

I wished for her death I'm not guilty of anything I did not kill her she fell herself fainted finished fell killed killed killed . . .

Anya is screaming—and her scream soars over the noisy Saturday courtyard, the hubbub of sandboxes, the squeaking of strollers, the screeching of swings, the rustling of new green leaves, the snail-shaped tin garages, the roofs of high-rises, the streets and squares, a whole city redolent of a Saturday hangover, gasoline fumes, and oil money.

The hollow, guttural sound of Dasha's orgasm rises up from within as Anya's scream explodes on the outside. Dasha's orgasm is the awakening of an unhurried ancient monster. Anya's scream is the supersonic shriek of a V-2 rocket, the whistle of a sniper's bullet, the rustle of the wings of the last angel, death in flight.

She opens her eyes and sweat streams down her face; her cheekbones hurt and her legs twitch from the receding tension.

I was the first to cum after all, Anya thinks with inexplicable satisfaction and looks down at Andrey. His eyes are closed, his hands are gripping her hips, and he's breathing hoarsely, trying his best to catch up to her.

He won't catch up to me, Anya thinks. I've already won. The swim meet is over.

And at that moment, Andrey orgasms, his face contorted, his nails scratch her skin and his penis jerks two or three times inside Anya's body before it subsides. For one brief moment, one microscopic moment after the orgasm, his face changes and she sees him as she's never seen him before: vulnerable, helpless, ridiculous, miserable, offended, and laughable.

If only your colleagues could see you, she thinks, then, leans in, kisses his half-open mouth, and freezes, her entire body pressed against him.

They lie motionless, then Andrey says something like: "Oh God, this has never happened to me before. How did you do it?"

What do you mean how, Anya thinks, how would I know?

And suddenly, she notices they're lying the wrong way. Awkwardly. She leans on Andrey's shoulders so her arms won't tremble, lifts herself up and sees . . .

What on earth? We're lying at the bottom, how did that happen?

"I think we broke your bed," Andrey says. "I think the front legs broke off."

Anya jumps up. So it is! Where will she get a new one? It didn't come with the apartment, it's her own—she bought it just three years ago.

Anya sits down on the floor—she can hardly stand anyway—and looks at the bed's pitifully splayed legs. Yes, if there's anything I know nothing about, it's fixing beds. What am I going to do now—prop it up with books? Old videocassettes? And what will I tell Gosha? Mom was jumping on the bed and it broke. If you jump on yours, it will break too.

If I say that, he will definitely jump on his bed.

Andrey's a real champ too, Anya thinks. Lying there as if nothing happened. Who broke the bed, me or him? Either way, it's my problem. Though he could have chilled out a bit with the thrashing around. And he scratched me all over, how am I supposed to travel to his Turkey and walk around in beachwear now?

Why am I mad at Andrey? Anya asks herself. As if I don't remember who started the race to the finish, who galloped like a madman.

Madwoman, I mean.

Of course, it was I, Elvira Alexandrovna Takhtagonova, thirty-three years old. And I'm angry because I had absolutely no plans to cum *like this* today, no plans to see anyone else cum, didn't want any races, any competitions, any victories or sprints toward the finish line. I just wanted the usual banal sex, no better or worse than every other Saturday.

It just happened. Of course, I can pretend it didn't, but I'll hardly be able to. At the very least because I have nowhere to sleep tonight.

"Do you know how to fix beds?" she asks.

"I don't," Andrey says nonchalantly. "Maybe, screw it? I mean, let's not fix it. We'll buy a new one and that will be the end of it."

"With whose money?" Anya asks spitefully and marvels at herself: she's never spoken to men about money before.

"Mine," Andrey says. "I was the one lying on the bed, so I'm the one who should pay. If it was you there, you'd have to pay. So let's get dressed, run overto IKEA, find a bed, and they'll deliver it tomorrow. And if we negotiate properly, they'll do it today."

Suddenly, Anya calms down.

"No," she says decisively, "we're not going to IKEA."

"Oh stop . . ." Andrey starts grumbling.

"Let's go somewhere else," Anya says. "The Three Whales, even. IKEA furniture is crap—I worked there, I'd know."

59.

FILM NOIR

Last night, I dreamed of Tony Leung. The one of two faces, between two moons.

That was my dream—either a dream or a poem. I understand why one of two faces. There are two Tony Leungs: Tony Leung Ka fai from the movie *The Lover* and Tony Leung Chiu wai from *Hard Boiled* and *In the Mood for Love*.

I was told that the original Chinese title for the latter is *Hua Yang De Nian Hua*, which more or less translates to "the years that were as beautiful as flowers." That's how the Chinese refer to the past, the good old days when the women were young and beautiful. In Russian, it would probably be "like smoke from white apple trees," after Yesenin.

In the Mood for Love is a film about a romance between two people who live next door to each other. Tony Leung and Maggie Cheung. They want to write a book together and end up falling in love. It's also a film about time because Tony Leung's character is actually remembering this story many years later. It's as if everything is covered with a patina, not because the images are unfocused, but the opposite—because they're shot in a clever slow-motion that lets you see every fold of a dress and crack in a wall. Brilliant film.

At our first meeting, the young eastern woman, Lena, appeared to me the spitting image of Maggie Cheung and I thought that we would share a beautiful love story together. She lived somewhere in the area, we'd catch glimpses of each other from afar at first, then start chatting about this and that, then decide to write a book together, then fall in love with each other, and, many years later, think back on it with tenderness, brushing away the

305

time from the paintings of our love just as an archaeologist brushes away sand from faded mosaics and wipes off the dust from ancient frescoes.

Last night, I dreamed of Chow Yun-fat. He smiled as he held a pistol.

I'd need to change it to "bat" to make it rhyme, but in my dream, Chow Yun-fat was holding a pistol the way he did in so many John Woo films. John Woo made Chow Yun-fat a star in the West and, eventually, the latter began doing Hollywood fluff. My only consolation is that he played the King of Siam in the movie *Anna and the King,* a role that was originated forty-something years earlier by Yul Brynner, the chief gunslinger from *The Magnificent Seven.* I think it would be cool if John Woo made a remake of *The Magnificent Seven.* And if Yun-fat wielded a pistol or two in it.

And held a match between his teeth.

The match between the teeth appeared for the first time in *A Better Tomorrow,* John Woo's debut thriller. For some reason, in Russian it's called *The Right to a Future.* When Quentin Tarantino first saw this film, he bought himself a cloak just like the one worn by Chow Yun fat's protagonist and walked around in it for a whole month, a match between his teeth the whole time.

After I watched *Leon the Professional* ten years ago, I, too, went around in round sunglasses for six months. The sunglasses broke a long time ago, but I grew fond of clenching a match between my teeth: it makes me feel like one of John Woo's protagonists.

In general, my life is like the movies. The most important thing is to guess the genre. And that's always easier to do when you're in the audience instead of on-screen.

For instance, here's a plot. An alcoholic artist meets a strange young woman. For a while, he's convinced that she's a vision or a guardian angel, but then, he sees her get out of a luxury vehicle. The young woman recognizes the artist and says she'll get in touch with him because she has something for him to do.

What is the genre, esteemed film lovers? Yes, you guessed it, the beloved genre of all film junkies: *le film noir.* Femme fatales, trusting marginalized men, money, corpses, and traitors. *Double Indemnity, The Lady from Shanghai, The Maltese Falcon.* In many ways, even *Basic Instinct,* although, of course, that's a neo-noir.

Beautiful, stylish black-and-white films. Ten years ago, they suddenly started showing them on television, but, for some reason, in color. At

state of wakefulness, I wouldn't put Amitabh Bachchan and Chow Yun-fat in the same sentence together.

As we all know, Bollywood films have wildly unrealistic plots. Some people like it, while I find it irritating. Plus, the characters keep breaking into song and dance, forgetting all about the plot and their better judgment. It's as if I were telling you about my life and suddenly began to speak in the rhythmic prose of Andrey Bely. Everyone would be astonished, but, in Bollywood films, this is considered normal.

In short, if I interpret this part of the dream as prophetic, then heaven knows what awaits me.

And I don't like the line about *another man's head on his shoulders*. It's either advising me not to lose my head or not to exchange heads with just anyone. What should I infer from this? Forget about movies and live my own life? Don't count on it.

Life can be boring. Movies are interesting by definition.

I was once told that, in order for a film to be interesting, it must have a sea monster. I believe that, in order for a film to be interesting, it must have an Asian beauty.

We can do perfectly well without a sea monster.

60.

REINCARNATION. ALYA CHERNOVA

That day, it had been very hot and sunny since morning.

Sixth-grader Alyosha Sokolov, sent by his parents to stay with his grandmother in Crimea, slipped away to the seaside bright and early. He left earlier than usual because he didn't like to swim at the city beach, which was filled with pasty vacationers. He had his own favorite cove, which Alya Chernova, the daughter of Lena, his grandmother's neighbor, had shown him. It was always deserted, and there was even a deep grotto you could hide treasures in.

To reach the cove, you had to walk for a long time down a narrow path between the rocks. Alyosha, however, took a shortcut through sea cliffs. Hopping from rock to rock and risking dislocating his ankle, he'd usually pretend he was an Indian in an Andean cordillera or a Soviet spy coming out on enemy shore in scuba gear. At present, after hiding his scuba gear in the cave, he had to find the transmitter, which had been left in the secret cove. before noon.

Exactly why before noon and what prevented the Soviet spy from coming out to the secret cove right away, Alyosha didn't know. He aimed to reach the cove before noon because he wasn't keen on climbing cliffs in the heat. It was much more pleasant to bathe in the greenish waters of the Black Sea, dive, and catch fish with his makeshift fishing rod.

There was no indication anything unusual would happen today.

Alyosha threw off his T-shirt and jeans and ran to the sea. A black shape appeared on the horizon—it was *The Spirited*, the on-duty destroyer guarding the Soviet Union's shores.

Alyosha swam for some time, then made his way to the cave with sweeping strokes. He crawled out on the bank, looked around, and saw that Alya had left him a message: three pieces of green glass forming a neat triangle. In their language, this signified: "Tomorrow I'm coming at three, I need to help mom." Of course Alya could have said this to Alyosha in person, but it was more interesting this way. Alyosha turned the triangle toward the sea (this signified: "saw it, read it, have nothing to add") and dove back in the water.

When he came up to the surface 30 seconds later, he thought his heart would leap out of his chest. Alyosha swam back to shore at full speed.

He needed to find Alya right away.

All morning long, Alya Chernova helped her mom around the house. They hung up the laundry to dry, then Alya washed the floors, and now they were on their way to the rural market.

Alya lived alone with her mom: her father, a submarine sailor, died fighting the German fascist aggressors. His photo, which showed him standing by the Sevastopol quay in a simple sailor's uniform, hung in Alya's mom's room, and Alya went in there often. She called this "talking to Papa," though she sat there quietly, without saying a word.

In his excitement, Alyoshka nearly knocked Alya's mom off her feet. He muttered "Excuse me, Aunt Lena, I'm here to see Alya," dashed to the astonished girl, and whispered something heatedly in her ear. Alya's blue eyes opened wide.

"You're lying," she said, "you're bluffing."

"You want me to swear?"

"Swear!" Alya said.

"May I never swim in the sea again if I'm lying!"

"'Swim in the sea,'" Alya teased, "I want a serious oath."

"Do you want me to swear on my mother's health?"

"No, give me your Young Pioneer's oath," Alya pouted her lips.

"I give you my Young Pioneer's oath," Alyosha rattled off. "Now you believe me?"

The kids ran the whole way without stopping. Aunt Lena didn't bother asking her daughter what Alyosha from next door had said—and that was a pity.

The children threw their clothes on the sand and rushed to the sea. In a few strokes, they reached the grotto.

"Here," Alyosha said with confidence.

They held their breath and dove in.

More than anything in the world, the boy was afraid they wouldn't see anything. Then Alya would think he was a liar and he would feel ashamed for the rest of the summer! However, his fears were unfounded.

In the murky, greenish waters of the Black Sea there shone a faint ruby light. It was coming from an elongated cylinder about fifty centimeters wide and ninety centimeters long. The glowing cylinder lay between two rocks at a depth of about two meters.

"Alyosha, what is it?" Alya asked when they crawled out on shore and caught their breath.

"I think it's a spy transmitter," Alyosha said. "I read about them in the *Young Pioneers' Pravda*."

"How did it get here?"

Only a girl could ask such a dumb question!

"There's a spy in town. He found this cove and hid the transmitter here. He comes here at night and sends secret intelligence to the enemy submarine."

"We have to report it to the police or border control! Let them lay an ambush and catch him!"

"No," Alyosha said, "that's not going to work. Think: we'll tell the police and they'll rush over here to check. I'm sure the spy has his own observation post. Why did he choose this cove? Because there's only one path that leads here! He'll find out that border control agents came here and that will be that. He'll never come back."

"So what do we do?" Alya said, confused.

"I know what we have to do," Alyosha said with assurance. "We'll catch him ourselves."

A decade or two will pass and these cliffs will teem with people. Bearded physicists with guitars and their loyal, short-haired girlfriends in plaid shirts; tents and songs till dawn. But, at this moment, on a June night in 1950, on the cliffs next to the town of S., there is nobody except two children, a boy and a girl. They are lying there without averting their eyes from the narrow path a few meters below.

They were old enough to remember the war beyond how it was portrayed in films and described in books—not just the war of ridiculous Krauts and heroic Soviet soldiers. They heard tales of robberies, criminals, and murders, and often came across underage thugs at school. They knew that thugs and criminals didn't only exist in the movies and that the good guys didn't always prevail. Sometimes the good guys were killed.

They knew about starvation. They knew about violence.

They knew about death.

But they were still children.

They loved adventure books and imagined themselves to be their heroes.

If they had lived in America, they'd be reading magazines like *Amazing Stories*, *Fantastic Adventures*, and *Astounding Science Fiction*. As Soviet children, they read *The Young Pioneers' Pravda* and the tattered books of Belyaev, Adamov, and Lagin, as well as, of course, Thomas Mayne Reid, Alexandre Dumas, and Jules Verne, which their parents loved in their time. Everything always ended well in those books.

They lay in silence, but, occasionally, shoved each other lightly as if to say: wake up.

"Are you sure he'll come today?" Alya asked in a hushed voice.

"I think he'll come today," Alyosha answered. "After all, he only hid it yesterday. If it were me, I would have definitely checked on it."

"He's not that dumb," Alya whispered, "why would he come an extra time? If he steals a military secret, he'll come."

"Ha!" Alyosha replied. "As if they'll let him steal a military secret. My dad said they guard military secrets with their lives!"

"What does your dad know?" Alya grumbled.

"Idiot!" Alyosha snapped. "He's the head engineer at a secret plant, he knows!"

"You're the idiot!" Alya took offense. "If you're so smart, then stay here by yourself, I'm going home."

She got up but at that moment Alyosha grabbed her hand and whispered:

"Quiet!"

In fact, while they were arguing, the children had completely forgotten why they were there. Meanwhile, someone had turned down the path.

It was a middle-aged woman—forty or forty-five. She was walking leisurely down the path, leaning on a wooden stick, every so often stopping to catch her breath. The path wasn't easy on her: the woman was pregnant.

While Alya and Alyosha were arguing about how the spy could possibly be a pregnant woman, if her belly was real or not, and if it was a woman at all, the nighttime traveler reached the beach. There she took off her shoes and sat down on a rock by the water. The rolling waves lightly brushed her swollen feet.

She didn't suspect she was being observed. Her tired feet ached, a baby turned over in her belly, and her thoughts flowed as of their own accord—ordinary thoughts, nothing secret: Grigoriy had nothing to worry about, it's so marvelous here, much better than in Leningrad . . . ouch, it's kicking hard! . . . I can't bear it in Leningrad right now . . . feel how warm the water is! . . . maybe we should move to Moscow? . . .

She sat there for a fairly long time. The children descended to the cove as quietly as they could. They hid among the rocks and were all eyes.

Above all Alya wanted to ask why, if the woman was a spy, she did not undress and retrieve the transmitter, but Alyosha would have likely said that Alya was an idiot and that the woman was waiting for a special time or some other nonsense. The thing is that, as soon as Alya saw the woman, she realized that she was no spy. Alya could not explain why, but all of a sudden, their idea struck her as stupid and childish. Catching spies alone at night on the sea cliffs? And what if there were real spies? They would have killed them and that would be the end of it. And how was Alyosha planning to catch them? Oh right, he merely wanted to remember their faces and then report them to border control. Remember their faces—as if! What could you see in this darkness? What an idiot!

Alya was getting bored and was thinking of an excuse to go home when, suddenly, the sea began to glow with a ruby light, the same light that was emitted by the transmitter. The light spread over the water and the children noticed a circle on the surface. It advanced toward the woman, who seemed oblivious to it. She sat on her rock and, with every second, the waves at her feet grew more vibrant. Alya had a good view of her face, which was slightly swollen, kind, and sad, and could clearly distinguish the wrinkles around her eyes, the horizontal furrow across her forehead, and her cracked lips and half-closed eyes. Her kerchief flew off her head and the sea wind tousled her fair hair. The cove was brightly lit, but just then, Alya noticed that the light wasn't coming from anywhere and didn't produce any distinct shadows. She turned her gaze to the cliffs towering above her: sun-bleached grass was bowing to the wind, tiny cracks lined the surface of rocks, and the shrub roots bit into the soil. It was the first time Alya had seen these cliffs in such detail, and she realized that something was happening to her and not to the cove. She looked at Alyosha and saw the same rapturous astonishment in his eyes. He squeezed her hand and, from that moment on, neither of them tore their eyes away from the ruby circle.

The ruby circle stopped by the woman's feet. The water at its center began to seethe, simmer, and bubble, then receded to the edges, and the children saw a mysterious creature emerge from the sea.

It reminded them of an octopus, though they couldn't count its tentacles. Its head was crowned by a ruby saucer, wherein faintly gleamed a small puddle. The drops of water on the creature's skin were also gleaming, as if it were lit up from within. Perhaps it was—Alya couldn't say for sure and only stared at it, riveted.

Just as she knew at first glance that the woman wasn't a spy, Alya understood that the creature wasn't threatening. A radiant joy spread all through her body. She could hear Alyosha's heart beating, the grass swaying in the wind, grains of sand creaking softly under the sea creature's body and the unknown woman breathing peacefully on the coastal rock.

The tentacles hugged the woman's calves. The octopus struggled to climb over the hem of her skirt and froze with its tentacles around her belly.

The octopus's skin turned every color of the rainbow; the colors flowed into each other and pulsated as if someone were blending paint or turning a kaleidoscope. The cove was beaming and the woman was still sitting there with her eyes closed; the word *blessing* floated into Alya's head, though she had no idea what it meant. *Dear God*, Alyosha suddenly said beside her, *Lord, it's so wonderful*, and Alya wasn't even surprised that a Soviet Young Pioneer spoke of God, how else would you say it, Lord, it's so wonderful, it's only too bad Mom isn't here, but there probably shouldn't be anyone else beside her, Alyosha, and that strange woman— it's only for them. Maybe her father, who's only presumed dead, sent her an iridescent octopus from a secret underwater base—a gift for her entire life, a reminder, a prediction, a portent.

It was as if the light piercing the cove formed a funnel (which seemed so close to Alya) and, when the funnel grew still, Alya saw an enormous metallic disc a few meters in diameter. It glowed with the same ruby light, and she heard a voice inside her: *The time has come!*—and it wasn't even the words, but their meaning that lit up inside her head. Alya stepped toward the flying saucer and came up against an invisible wall, through which she could see the ruby octopus slide down the woman's belly, make its way to the spaceship along the light strip, and disappear in the open hatch. Sand and dust flew into Alya's face; she closed her eyes, and, when she reopened them, the cove was just as it had been a few hours ago: submerged in darkness and lit only by the moon.

The woman stood up from the rock, fixed her dress, found her shoes in the sand, and began her walk back. Alya and Alyosha followed her with their eyes.

"Aliens?" the girl softly whispered.

Alyosha nodded.

They never played in that cove again, never spoke of that night. A few times, Alya thought she saw the woman again in the city market. In the daylight, her belly looked indecently large, though she tried to hide it under loose-fitting dresses.

In August, Alyosha returned to Moscow. That winter his grandmother passed away, and he didn't come back the next summer.

Alya grew to love visiting the rock that the woman had sat on. Sometimes she'd lie down, wrap her arms around it, and doze off in the warm surf.

She'd imagine that she sped off in the sky in a flying saucer and was now herself an iridescent octopus swimming in the greenish water of the cosmic aquarium.

After she finished school, she went away to Sevastopol, studied at teachers' college, then came back and taught Russian language and literature at the school until old age. The children loved her, although the principal always rebuked her classes for poor conduct. However, her students always came back to visit her years after graduation.

Alya married a local bookkeeper also named Alyosha. Their friends were sorry that they never had children, but still considered them a marvelous couple. But Alya never told him the story of what she'd seen at the cove. From time to time, she herself thought that she and her friend Alyosha simply dozed off on the warm sand and had a beautiful dream.

She had her share of joys and sorrows. Her mother died, she didn't have children of her own, and all those years, the depths of her soul were flooded by a steady light from somewhere and warmed by a 1950 summer dream: the moon in the sky, the warm cliffs, the ruby circle, the flying saucer, the tentacles wrapped around an enormous belly, a blessing, tranquility, and happiness.

61.

1941. THE GREAT GAME

Grandpa Misha told me the following story in late August 1991. He was eighty-six years old, lived alone, and took pride in the fact that he could take care of himself. The one-room apartment where we sat was indeed clean, but you could still detect the undefinable scent of old age in it.

We were discussing the 1991 collapse of the State Committee on the State of Emergency. I called what happened a bloodless revolution and looked to the future with an excitement that Grandpa didn't share.

"I've seen this before, Nikita," he said. "Not a great many people died in St. Petersburg on October 25; the real slaughter began later. This is all the eternal return. There's a law that everything comes back full circle. And I would have preferred if these circles were wider. I thought that I wouldn't live until the next spiraling off, but I was wrong. So as a person who has lived longer than was marked out for him, I can tell you that all your joy is in vain. Nothing good awaits you. Another Atlantis will sink, that is all."

I tried to argue with him, but Grandpa waved me off and began to bear a striking resemblance to Grandpa Makar, who died six months ago. For some reason, I remembered how, at one time, Grandpa Misha had talked to me about Mazai and Noah, while my father said that the revolution is a flood.

"Have you ever talked about this to Dad?" I asked.

"What's the use of talking to him," Grandpa replied irritably. "All he has in his head are scientific tables. Black and white, zero—one. Communists are bad and anti-Communists are good. Down with the Soviet regime, long live freedom."

"Grandpa," I said, "do you really like the Soviet regime? They took away everything you had, you told me so yourself."

"The Soviet regime took away everything I had then and gave me everything I have now. At the very least, I respect it for that."

Nowadays, I would have held my tongue, but at the time, I replied to him with youthful fervor:

"I don't think that's respect. That's fear. Like savages who fear foreign deities."

"What do you know about foreign deities?" Grandpa answered. "My father also accepted the Soviet regime, although, if anyone was an expert on ancient gods, he was. Ancient gods operate on a completely different scale, the Soviet regime is at their beck-and-call. I've been wanting to tell you a story for a while, I've hardly told this to anyone, but I'll tell you. After all, I'm going to die soon and want to tie up loose ends."

The order came completely out of the blue. Major Gogolidze collected our small troop and said that he'd received an order from headquarters to set off at dawn on a secret mission. They would explain the assignment to us later.

I'll skip ahead and say that I still don't know what the nature of our assignment was.

During this particular military campaign, the situation with our assignments was fairly muddled. A week ago, we knew that we were supposed to assist border patrol and be on alert for a potential invasion.

I remember Shevchuk and I were smoking in the cool evening air, watching the mountains darken in the twilight. Shevchuk said:

"Mikhayla, you're a grown man. Tell me, why on earth are we idling around here? Minsk was taken, Vitebsk was taken, Smolensk. Combat in Odessa, the Krauts are eager to get to Moscow . . . And we're waiting around for these camel jockeys like idiots." And he spat on the ground, which was cooling from the daytime heat.

I understood him well. On the one hand, what could I say? I hoped to God we would give the Persians a good fright—let them stay on the other side. Perhaps if we had placed more troops on the German border, Hitler wouldn't have broken through into the very heart of Russia in two months.

No one trained us to catch special operatives. However, we were accompanied by one Major Mahbub Ali, I don't know what his real name was. He spoke good Persian and even gave us five lessons. In any case, what can you learn in five lessons? Although I learned that there were a few soldiers among us who studied this language before. They must have been deliberately dispatched here.

One of them, Nikolay Biryukov, a student from Leningrad, was excited to be in such close proximity to a country whose language he'd studied for a few years now.

Five days earlier, after the morning formation, Lukyanenkov came running from headquarters, yelling:

"Brothers, we've entered Iran!"

At first, we didn't believe him—we entered where? We were right here, but it turned out that four army divisions had set off from the South Caucasus. Our ambassador in Tehran already presented his note, war had been officially declared and soon we would be going into battle—hooray!

Later, Major Gogolidze explained that Iran had long turned into a nest of German spies and special operatives and that the Shah himself supported Hitler in various ways. The Germans insisted to him that Persians were Aryans, too, and he believed it.

I remembered first hearing this word from my father twenty-eight years ago. Although Father said "arya" in the manner of Madame Blavatskaya, who used it to designate the fifth race currently dwelling on earth.

As I reminisced, Major Gogolidze told us that, while the Shah had promised to observe neutrality, presently, we had reason to suspect that he'd soon go over to the German side. Stalin requested thrice that the Shah forbid Germans to build military bases on Iranian territory, but the Shah continued to pursue a policy of rapprochement with Hitler. And so Great Britain and the USSR decided to bring their troops on Iranian territory.

Gogolidze said "We have reason to suppose" and was visibly nervous. He must have wanted to say: "At the moment, the Shah thinks Hitler will win the war," but even Gogolidze was scared to say a thing like that, even about the Shah.

This was August 23. For a few more days, we stood on our country's southern border awaiting orders. We knew that four of our army divisions (44th, 45th, 46th, and 47th) had crossed the border without any difficulty. They reported that many Iranian soldiers were surrendering and being taken prisoner. Our forces were advancing toward Tehran and we were waiting to be brought into action.

Unlike most of the soldiers, who were still very young, I wasn't at all eager to go into battle. As a boy, I had lived through the First World War and knew how much suffering it brought, although, to be sure, I didn't have the chance to see any real horrors. It was only later, during the Civil War, that I got an eyeful.

I never had the chance to kill anyone. And truth be told, I didn't want to.

But everyone was electrified. They were tired of waiting and thus the order to launch the offensive was greeted with cheers.

On August 27, our 53rd Non-Integrated Central Asian Division (*OSAA*) crossed the border and entered Iran. If you considered that our friends on the other side of the Caspian Sea were approaching Tehran, the outcome of the war was already clear. This could explain why we didn't encounter any real resistance. Neither did I see any of the German operatives they told us so much about. Although Gogolidze did relate to us that they'd found a garrison in the Rezaya settlement or rather, a small military town that the Germans had turned into a real arsenal—of course, with the cooperation of the Shah. These weapons were intended to be used against the Soviet Union.

Thus, on the morning of August 30, our small troop left the division encampment and headed south. A grueling mountain road lay ahead of us, so Gogolidze conducted a final drill before we started out:

"Go up the mountain with a calm, even step. Help a friend, they will also help you in your hour of need. When you hit a steep ascent or descent, help your horse and your mule. You are not allowed to beat the animal or spur it excessively. Save your bread and biscuits. Don't drink too much water, it only weighs you down. Lay down at the bivouac and keep your legs elevated, this is the best way to rest. Protect your gun and your automatic rifle from getting damaged."

Gogolidze spoke calmly, taking his time. There was excitement in the air, but the Major tried not to show it. He was a pleasure to look at. A tightened belt. Shoulders pulled back. Strong calves. Slightly clenched fists. The light-blue triangle of his undershirt emerging from an unbuttoned collar.

The first day, we walked along the ravine under a hot August sun. By all indications, we were headed south toward the heart of Iran. Besides the soldiers from our troop, there was the already-familiar Mahbub Ali. From his brief talk with Gogolidze, I gathered that only Mahbub Ali had received specific instructions.

It seemed that our troop was simply accompanying him.

Our troop made up a small caravan: twenty-two men, and horses and mules carrying munitions, food, and radio transmitters. One of the mules was loaded with a mysterious, long object covered by a tarpaulin. This was the cargo we were instructed to protect in every way.

We walked in a narrow chain, mostly through the mountain gorge, but sometimes down the mountain paths.

One evening, we came across a peasant. Mahbub Ali approached him and they spoke in Persian Farsi for a minute. Then, the peasant bowed and pointed south.

I asked Biryukov what they were talking about.

"The peasant asked who we were. Comrade Major replied that we're ambassadors. When he asked him who sent us, Comrade Major said: A Friend to all the World, he's one to be obeyed to the last flutter of his eyelashes."

I think he meant Stalin.

An unpleasant announcement awaited us at our bivouac: Gogolidze said we would not build a campfire so as not to reveal ourselves. The nights were cold and we sat wrapped in our cloaks. Gogolidze, who was no less worn out than the rest of us, asked us to hear out Major Mahbub Ali.

"Warriors!" Ali said with a faint eastern accent. "Everything that happened to you before was only preparation. The Great Game did not begin for you until today. I could have said nothing to you about it, but I will because there are circumstances in which I believe honesty to be a virtue. You must know that your mission is the main objective of the whole Iranian operation. The four armies to the west and your friends up north are only providing a cover for you. The outcome of the whole war with Germany depends on the success of the mission. The Great Game depends on it."

Shevchuk pressed a cigarette stub against the sole of his boot and asked:

"What is . . . the Great Game?"

Mahbub Ali looked at Shevchuk as if he were pondering whether he should answer. Then he uttered in sing-song:

"Where does the Great Game take place? Truly, it runs like a shuttle throughout all Hind, throughout all the world. Who participates in the Great Game? There is no one who doesn't participate in the Great Game— it's the best thing that can befall a man. When shall the Great Game end? When everyone is dead, no sooner."

We sat in quiet amazement. Mahbub Ali bowed with a smile like the peasant we met that day, and said to us gravely:

"In all seriousness, the Great Game is the name of the secret operation we're carrying out."

On the second day, we continued across the rocky, arid terrain between the two mountain ranges. On a narrow mountain path, one of the horses, a young steed, made an unfortunate turn and toppled into a chasm, taking two water bags with it.

Major Ali looked down and said:

"The place we're going will have water. It would be worse had it been the radio transmitter."

We unstrapped the radio from the mule and took turns carrying it. They must have thought a person was less likely to fall into a chasm.

By evening, we reached a small town situated in the valley. Before we went down to it, Gogolidze again asked us to listen to instructions from Major Ali:

"We are about to enter a village. You must not interact with the locals. However, you must also not be hostile. The people here are simple and far removed from politics. I don't believe they even know about Hitler and . . ." he stammered, "the Soviet Union. Respect the women—this is particularly important in the Great Game—for it is by means of women that all plans come to ruin and we lie out in the dawning with our throats cut."

Every time Mahbub Ali spoke of the Great Game, his voice changed. Needless to say, I seriously doubted this was just the name of our operation.

We passed through a street without meeting a soul. The residents had either left the village or were staying indoors. We didn't lift our eyes.

We spent yet another night in the mountains. I couldn't fall asleep because of the cold, so I got up and saw Mahbub Ali's motionless figure. He was contemplating the mountain peaks and the starry sky above them.

"I keep thinking," I spoke, "that these stones are more ancient than humanity."

"What do you mean by *humanity*?" replied Mahbub Ali. "Millions of years ago, humanity—or its monad, if you will—was itself a stone, then, a plant and only later, became an animal and a so-called human."

I looked at him with involuntary respect.

"You surprise me, Comrade Major," I said. "I didn't expect to meet an admirer of reactionary theosophical theories here."

Mahboub Ali shrugged:

"You don't think people like you and me have a greater chance of meeting here, somewhere in the heart of Asia than, for example, in Moscow?"

"It's possible," I conceded. In reality, in the past ten years, people who believed in Blavatskaya's five races usually met in Moscow, in the same prison cell.

"Why did you enlist in this war?" asked Makhboub Ali.

"Because I received a draft card," I answered.

"Would you have volunteered?" At present, his dark eyes were staring directly at me.

"Probably," I ventured cautiously. "Any Soviet citizen would do everything in his power to crush the Fascist vermin."

"Seriously," Mahbub Ali replied, "what kind of Soviet citizens could there be here, amid the mountains and deserts?"

I kept silent. Either he was an instigator or an idiot.

"Of course, I didn't mean to question your or anyone else's loyalty to the work of Lenin and Stalin," Mahbub Ali said more formally. "I meant something else. Lately, I often think about how almost no one among the millions of people participating in this war knows what it's for. Why it's happening."

"There's a war because Hitler has breached the agreement between Germany and the USSR," I answered, "and the Soviet people . . ."

"That's the answer to *why*." Mahbub Ali interrupted me. "And neither you nor I have the answer to *what for*."

"To use your words," I ventured cautiously, "war is a part of the Great Game. One can say it makes the Great Game more dynamic."

Again, Mahbub Ali peered at me closely.

"I'm glad I wasn't mistaken in you," he said, "but tomorrow, we must set out early."

The third day was no different from the day before. We didn't have much water left, but Gogolidze said according to Mahbub Ali it should suffice.

I was a bit concerned about his using the modal verb *should*. What did it mean, *should suffice*? I would have preferred to hear that there was definitely enough.

During the daytime, a soldier fainted from heat stroke. Mahbub Ali ordered us to load the soldier onto a mule and keep moving.

By evening, we descended into a vast valley. A half-hour later, Major Ali said he could already see our destination. He pointed his finger somewhere south, where a strip of green about an hour away from us could be seen, at a rivulet, or rather, a small stream surrounded by stunted trees.

Mahbub Ali squatted down and lowered his hands in the water. He stayed still for a while, and I was certain that his eyes were closed.

Major Gogolidze ordered us to dig a foxhole and set up camp. That day, we were allowed to build a fire. Shevchuk had to bring the radio transmitter to working order and get ahold of headquarters.

We were warming up by the fire when he returned.

"Two bits of news," he said somberly. "First, Iran has surrendered, and second, the Germans have surrounded Leningrad."

The outcome of the Iranian operation was obvious to us three days ago, and the bitterness of the second news considerably surpassed the joy of the first. We sat there dejected. Finally, Biryukov got up, grabbed a saddle and walked over to the horses.

"Where are you going?" I hollered at him.

"Home," he replied angrily, "to my mom and my sister. Iran can go to the devil, we have to defend our own country!"

"Sit down," I said calmly. "Are you planning to gallop to Leningrad on horseback? You'll be stopped by the first border patrol."

"I don't give a damn!" Biryukov responded and, at that moment, Mahbub Ali's tall figure emerged from the dark.

"Soldier Biryukov," he said in a steady voice, "put down the saddle and resume your current assignment, for which your Motherland has sent you here."

"Go to hell!" Biryukov said, but stopped in his tracks when he saw Mahbub Ali take out a revolver.

"Kolya," I warned him, but Biryukov was already putting the saddle on the ground.

Mahbub Ali pointed to the long bundle we'd safely delivered.

"Dig this in," he said, "somewhere on the opposite bank, not too far from the water."

Biryukov and I took the shovels and bundle and crossed the river in silence. Biryukov shivered from the icy water and I, too, was uncomfortable.

When we removed the tarpaulin, we discovered a wooden post and I thought that the people who sent us here must have been familiar with the local vegetation.

We dug in silence. It was dark out and we could barely distinguish our hands. I thought I could hear Biryukov sobbing.

A half-hour later, the post was in place.

We heard the splashing of water and Mahbub Ali approached us. With a few blows of a hammer, he fastened a plank to the post. Now the post resembled a low sepulchral cross.

"Soldiers," Mahbub Ali said, "I congratulate you on the successful completion of your mission."

A bright spot moved toward us: it was Major Gogolidze, who was lighting his path with a flaming branch.

"Comrade Major," he yelled out, "is that all?"

"Yes," replied Mahbub Ali, "now we wait."

Gogolidze stopped on the opposite bank. The branch burned so brightly that I could clearly see Biryukov's gloomy, dirt-smudged face, swollen eyes, and stubbornly pinched lips. Mahbub Ali's face was triumphant—if it weren't for his ironic gaze, I would have said that he looked fanatical.

Finally, I turned my eyes to the wooden structure. At this moment, in the light of the improvised torch, I was surprised that we didn't realize sooner that it was a border post.

On the crookedly-nailed plank, in neat Cyrillic and English letters, it said: USSR–India.

On the evening of September 2, on the other side of our marked post, a group of white men appeared, speaking to each other in English. Their negotiations with Mahbub Ali didn't last more than an hour, and then, they left. Mahbub Ali waited for them to depart, and then left the valley on horseback.

Two days later, Gogolidze received an order via radio transmitter to dig out the post and burn it. We carried it out and returned to our division encampment, where I remained until it was summarily disbanded.

I never saw Mahbub Ali again but already knew the answer to his *what for*.

Exactly two years of a World War had to pass so I could reach India like my father had promised me twenty-eight years ago.

My father never lied to me.

Of course, Grandpa Misha didn't share all the details with me. I made most of them up just now, and not very well, I'm afraid. It's hard to envision the Great Patriotic War with Central Asian scenery—I keep veering off into Rudyard Kipling, particularly since I've almost forgotten Grandpa's story. I remember only that the small troop crossed the then-border of Iran and Afghanistan, reached India, dug in a post, and, after briefly negotiating with the British, dug it back out and returned. I didn't even ask Grandpa when exactly this happened, believing the episode to be well known to historians.

I was mistaken: the experts I'd spoken to could only offer conjectures. They agreed that the raid took place during the Soviet-British invasion of Iran in August-September 1941. This must have been Stalin's way of pressuring the Allies either to open a second front or for some other political reasons I'm not aware of.

The Great Game, as Mahbub Ali would have said.

As far as I remember, Grandpa never talked to me about why his military commanders sent them to dig in (and then dig out) a border post. I think that something else mattered to him: in spite of the revolution, the Civil War, and the Great Terror, despite renouncing his last name and the Iron Curtain, he had still been to India.

Back then, in August 1991, I mostly wondered why Grandpa Misha was telling me this story. When he finished, he straightened his shoulders, heaved a sigh, and said:

"You see, Nikita, my father predicted my fate in 1913, almost thirty years ahead. My father never lied to me and I won't lie to you either. Remember: things will be difficult, much more difficult than you can imagine right now. Many will die. Still more will fall apart. But you, personally, will weather it. You'll be able to deal with it."

These words . . . I have never forgotten them. In the nineties, I thought to myself: Grandpa Misha told me that I would weather it, deal with it, wouldn't hit bottom, wouldn't become destitute, would be able to feed my family. Three years ago, when my business took off, I said to myself: yes, Grandpa was right, I'm thankful to him for predicting this.

But these past few months, I keep thinking: what if he had something else in mind? Not poverty, not destitution, not the search for work and money, but what's happening to me right now: Dasha, Masha, guilt, love, sex, helplessness? If so, let Grandpa be right again. I hope I can weather it and deal with it—whatever "it" means this time around.

62.

NOTHING WRONG WITH FANTASIES

"What do you mean, 'guilty?' In a karmic sense?" Vika is sitting with her legs folded under her. Right on the floor, in the middle of Anya's room. Over the very spot where a pipe burst a week ago. Vika's hair is radiating gold as if nothing happened.

Anya finds this calming.

"I don't know what I mean," Anya says. "It's just that, in that moment, I wished for her death with all my heart."

Vika's eyebrows creep up in feigned astonishment:

"So what? You're not a Christian, right?"

"I'm not a Christian," Anya says, "and most likely not a Buddhist. Definitely not a Muslim, despite my Tatar blood. I'm a simple Soviet girl. As they told us in daycare, cosmonauts flew off into space and didn't find God there."

"So what's the problem?" Vika asks. "Why can't you wish death upon your enemies? Your grandmother basically killed her enemies. She even got a medal for it, I think."

"Well, she was at war."

"What do you mean, 'at war'? She was killing strangers who hadn't done anything to her. Maybe they didn't manage to take a single shot, they were brought out to the eastern front and—bam! your grandmother."

Vika clasps her hands together and stretches like a big, satisfied, ginger cat.

"I'd still prefer to think it was a coincidence," Anya says.

"Well, that's your personal preference. You can consider it a coincidence."

"And in reality?" Anya sits down on the floor next to Vika, who takes her hands and looks her straight in the eyes.

"Let's try this," Vika says. "Relax and try to clear your mind. Answer the questions without thinking, tell me the first thing that comes to you."

Anya nods, although she doesn't really believe in any of Vika's mumbo jumbo. For some time, she looks her in the eyes, then a voice comes to her as if from afar: *How did you wish for it?* I imagined myself killing her. *Did you pray to the Great Mother for it? Did you put yourself in a trance? Build an altar?* I was reading Gosha a book *Which one?* A fairy tale *Which fairy tale?* A silly one. By Maxim Gorky. About a boy and fishes. *Did you read the story in your childhood?* Maybe. I don't remember. Gosha borrowed it from my mother. *Your mother?* Yes. Although Grandma Marfa had given it to me as a gift. I just remembered how much I used to like it in my childhood.

No, Anya thinks, that's baloney. I'm a simple Soviet girl, this shamanism isn't for me. It's for twenty or twenty-five-year-olds. To them, all this esotericism, all this paganism, Wicca, mysticism, magic, it's like breathing air. They were reading Paolo Coelho before they lost their virginity. They'll believe in anything: deadly children's tales, healing sorcerers, predictions of the future, visions of the past, even the fact that you can transport yourself to other countries through sheer force of mind, for example, to India, "Yes, it's really glamorous in Goa, just listen, Nikita, the Russians own the whole tattoo business there, isn't it cool? My friend's got a boyfriend there right now, they rented a house and bought a pig. They decided to teach it to look at the sky. Nikita, do you know that pigs can't look at the sky by themselves?"

"So where do they look?" Nikita asks. He's lying on Dasha's couch and she's sitting beside him with her legs crossed. A silver pendant is stuck to her damp bosom.

"They look at the ground," Dasha says with certainty. "They can't look up. But forget about the pig, it's just that everyone who goes to India immediately falls in love with it. It's the last country with any real magic left in it."

When he hears the word "magic," Nikita looks warily at the large aquarium. Two catfish are wiggling their whiskers and the water behind the dark glass is calm.

"Maybe you had a connection to India in your past life? If you ever go, you'll know it right away."

"In my past life," Nikita sits down, "I was a galley slave. And you were a beautiful Roman woman who occasionally summoned me for her pleasure."

"No, no, I'm positive that you've been to India before. Remember you showed me your ring?"

"This one?" Nikita asks. He's wearing two rings—his and Masha's engagement ring and his grandpa's old ring.

"Yes. There's something written on it in Sanskrit."

"Oh please," Nikita takes off the ring. "I think it's a sample of some kind. They made them at the start of the century. Meaning, the start of the last century. It's Grandpa's ring, it's very old, maybe a hundred years."

"I want to see."

Nikita sees the gold glittering between Dasha's fingers, looks at her fleshy arms, sloping shoulders, large breasts. He thinks: *Now there's a woman made to give birth to children!* and gets scared. For a second, a vision flashes before him: Masha's no longer around, she's doing well, it's just that she's vanished somewhere and now he's living with Dasha, they have a boy and a girl, they sit there across from each other just like this, only they're married and not having an affair, they go over to people's homes together, go on vacation together, make friends together. They're happy.

It's a split second, an instantaneous happiness, a momentary dream, and then Nikita tells himself: Masha will not vanish anywhere, Dasha and I will never live together, we're only lovers, I'm renting an apartment for Dasha, Dasha is sleeping with me.

That's all.

That's not true, Nikita tells himself, it hasn't been only sex for some time. Before, Dasha's every sigh was a reminder of her deepwater orgasms, but now I understand she's sighing because she's tired or upset or bored or simply wants to sleep. What does the woman from the deep end have to do with it? She's just a human being, Dasha, warts and all.

And I probably love her.

And Masha? What about Masha? I'm not planning to divorce her, no one said anything about divorce.

Right now, Nikita isn't really looking at Dasha, *warts and all*, and meanwhile, she has sat down across from him, crossed her legs, half-closed her eyes and begun in a guttural voice:

"I'm going into a trance, I'm going into a trance, I see a room, a man and a boy, before them a map. The man says: you must go here. The boy looks at the map . . . oh yes, it's a map of India . . ."

At that moment, Nikita finally bursts out laughing and Dasha jumps up and runs to make coffee. Nikita throws himself back on the couch, listens to the rattling of dishes and again imagines life with Dasha. At present, he tells himself: *there's nothing wrong with fantasies*, and the images come one after another. Nikita introduces Dasha to Kostya. Dasha greets Nikita after work. Nikita and Dasha in Paris. Dasha in ten years, matured and blooming with that special beauty of a thirty-something woman. Nikita in ten years: distinguished gray hair, a good car, an apartment in the city center. He comes home in the evening, yells: "Yoohoo, Dasha!," walks through the apartment, peeks in the rooms, and, finally, in the last one, sees: lights off, near darkness, a massive armchair in the center, and in it, Dasha curled into a ball, immobile and gaunt, almost like Masha, waiting for him.

The apartment doesn't have toys or children's things. Looks like, over the course of ten years, Dasha still wasn't able to give birth.

Turns out that an imagined life is just a version of the current one, Nikita thinks. Ten years from now, my new marriage will be nearly indistinguishable from my old. Was it worth it to dream about this?

Dasha returns with a silver tray in her hands, large breasts, sloping shoulders, damp skin and the scent of just having had sex and fresh coffee.

But how happy those ten years could be! Nikita thinks.

63.

THAT SAME OLD RESENTMENT

I often recall Grandma Djamilya. She died two years ago and even got to see Gosha. Every time we met in those last few years, she said it was a pity Rimma and I weren't really friends.

And why would we be friends? I'm a saleswoman, a single mother, all my thoughts are of how to make it to my next paycheck; she's an office worker, lives alone, has money. And she's ten years younger than me. But above all, Rimma has absolutely no desire to communicate with me or her mother. She doesn't want to be a part of the family.

But that's not important. There are still four of us: two boys and two girls; two office workers and two of Moscow's bottom-feeders; two unattached and two living with family: I have a son and Nikita a wife.

Rimma doesn't want to think about this. Of course, that's her business. But it makes me uneasy for our grandmother's sake.

Must be why I sometimes try to imagine how Rimma's doing, what she's up to right now.

Overall, there's nothing particularly personal about the work of a personal assistant. Ordering tickets, drafting a meeting schedule, phone calls, and so forth. But today Sazonov calls Rimma over and says:

"Listen, dear, I have a request for you. Confidential, as they say nowadays."

"Of course," Rimma replies. As in, how could it be otherwise, everything will be held in the strictest confidence.

"I have to deliver something . . ." Sazonov clams up, like he's hesitating. "I won't have time myself, and it must be done today. I'd send my driver, but he's new . . . and the item is expensive . . . if it goes missing, it will be very awkward for me."

"I'll deliver it," Rimma says, "just give me the address."

Sazonov writes down the address on a piece of paper and takes out a box with a pink bow from his upper desk drawer. The bow is almost bigger than the box. Sazonov holds it carefully, as if he doesn't want to let it out of his hands.

"The driver will take you," he says, "you're not going to take the Metro. But go up there alone and hand it straight to Angela. Tell her it's from me . . . I hope she'll figure it out anyway."

Rimma nods her head, says: *Just a minute* and soon after, reappears with a paper bag for the gift.

"That's good thinking," Sazonov says, "no need for the whole office to see it. And don't tell anyone, you understand."

"Of course," Rimma nods again, "everything will be held in the strictest confidence."

Angela lives in one of the Stalinist buildings once allocated to nuclear physicists whose grandchildren moved abroad in the nineties or settled on dachas, renting the apartments to foreigners and New Russians. The rents are astronomical: I found out when I was apartment-hunting. At least three thousand a month, and five or six if the place is furnished.

On the other hand, there are probably no drunken neighbors across the wall and old, newly-dead madwomen downstairs.

Rimma examines her face in the elevator mirror and fixes her hair. It's particularly important that she look good right now, though she doesn't herself know why

I'm wondering what this Angela looks like. She must be a model, tall, thin, big breasts. I'm curious to get a look at her.

An armored door, the number 24 in brass figures, a doorbell. A girlish voice on the other side: *Who is it?*

She answers slowly, in a reserved, dignified tone: "Vladimir Nikolayevich sent me."

"Are you alone?" asks the voice. "I can't see shit, it's so dark on the landing."

"Alone," Rimma responds, and the door swings open.

She can see why Angela asked: she was obviously getting dressed to go out and has only her bra and panties on.

Rimma hands her the small box and, as Angela unties the bow, discreetly scrutinizes the young woman. She is indeed tall with big breasts, but despite this, looks nothing like a cover girl. Maybe it's her figure: Sazonov's girlfriend is on the heavy side. A rounded belly, fleshy arms, a sumptuous derrière. A classic Arabian beauty, if it weren't for her bleached, platinum blonde hair.

"How lovely!" Angela says, closing the clasp. The bracelet from Sazonov sparkles in the dim light of the entrance hall. "We have to hold it up to the light, let's go in the living room. Don't take off your shoes, the cleaning woman will take care of it later."

In the living room, there are clothes scattered everywhere on the couch, on the armchair, even on the carpet. Angela steps right over her dresses, while Rimma carefully moves them aside with the tip of her shoe. She notices that it's a big apartment with parquet floors and antique bookshelves running down the corridor walls.

Then they stand by the window and Angela smokes and tells her today is her anniversary with Sazonov. "He's a good man," she says, "he rented an apartment for me, gives me gifts, no quirks in bed. Because, you know, there could be all kinds of things," and she winks at Rimma.

Rimma smiles back; she feels awkward in this large, opulent apartment, face to face with this mature and experienced woman.

Now there's someone who's never questioned if she's a boy or a girl, Rimma thinks.

"What about you, do you like working with him?" Angela asks. Her voice is deep and languid. When she doesn't receive an answer, she offers: "Do you want some coffee?"

They make a strange pair: the diminutive Rimma with a polished haircut, in a business suit and high heels, and the plump Angela in sequined, lacy lingerie, disheveled platinum blonde hair, and the blistering aura of voluptuous flesh. They have coffee and Sazonov's lover tells her how, as soon as she finished school two years ago, she came to conquer Moscow, wasted a year *with some douchebags*, and then met Vladimir.

Rimma is strangely perturbed when Angela's fingers brush her hand.

"Perhaps a liqueur?" Angela offers.

"No, thank you," Rimma says, "I should be going."

And thinks to herself: I wonder if her lips are silicone or also natural?

On her way down, Rimma looks in the elevator mirror again. She seems thin and unfeminine to herself. Suddenly she realizes: she'll never make enough money for a diamond bracelet, not in the office, not in bed, nowhere. She'll be a little girl for the rest of her life, then a little woman, and later on, a little old lady going to work, work until dark and build a career while the young and beautiful ones continue receiving expensive gifts and living in luxury apartments paid for by men. Rimma clenches her small fists. "Bitch," she says, barely audible, "scum, whore."

But that doesn't make her feel any better.

Rimma doesn't want to be a part of the family, but that doesn't mean anything. In the mirrored elevator of the Stalinist building, she becomes a curlicue of an intricate design, a finishing detail.

She resents Angela and doesn't know if it's the same resentment that swells in Moreukhov when he sees a car of a foreign make, the same resentment that colors my thoughts of how easy it is for her to make money and how hard it was for me to make a living ten years ago.

Rimma resents Angela with the eternal resentment harbored toward those who are wealthier, younger, and have a better life. The words "bitch," "scum," and "whore" are addressed to all the women who are living at their lovers' expense.

Including Dasha, about whose existence Rimma doesn't even know.

64.

DESCENT UNDERGROUND

I don't get it, Moreukhov thinks, how do people take the Metro sober? It's a total clusterfuck. It's hell on earth, I mean, underground. The turnstile is either Cerberus or Charon, stick a ticket in its toothy maw and walk on in, don't be scared. The escalator is an automated, underground waterfall that will carry you to the platform. Walk into a train car, get a load of the passengers . . . no, better that you don't look because the doors have already closed and you can't escape.

Across from me sits a woman of about thirty-five reading a book by Darya Dontsova. You can tell from her facial expression that she's carrying out deep spiritual work right now. Beside her is a guy a decade younger with a Stephen King volume. On the cover is yet another bogeyman. I respect Stephen King, especially *The Dark Tower* series, but still: c'mon, man! Buy me some booze and I'll tell you things that'll keep you up at night!

For instance. An artist-alcoholic who also suffers from hallucinations descends into the Metro with a killer hangover. The whole time, he's flinching, lurking around, and generally behaving suspiciously. Gradually, the reader begins to understand: he's got an idée fixe, a morbid fear of the flood. Atlantis, the city of Kitezh, and so on. He's scared that a vast sea will engulf Moscow. Not bad for a start, huh? It's going to be a short story, well no, not like Stephen King's.

So this artist arrives at Lenin—excuse me, Sparrow—Hills station, where a Metro bridge stretches over the Moskva River, when, suddenly someone screams on top of their lungs right next to him: "Look everyone, dolphins!"

I nearly shat my pants, I swear.

Look everyone, dolphins! Some man yelled and pointed out the window. Immediately, a group of schoolchildren flocked to him—either they believed him or appreciated the joke. Gosha, too, began to twist in his seat: "Where, where are the dolphins?"

"The gentleman was joking, sit still."

Gosha sits more comfortably and Anya goes back to her thoughts. She takes the Metro every day, so she doesn't think about it—right now, she's thinking about a Japanese film she watched last night. The film was called *Dark Waters*. It was about a single mother and her daughter. They lived together and the father tried to take the daughter away. But he didn't succeed, though another girl's phantom did manage to take the mother from the daughter. Some time ago, the dead girl drowned in the very building they lived in. And of course, now that she didn't have her own mother, she found herself someone else's. The phantom girl convinced the woman she wouldn't leave her daughter in peace unless the woman came with her, so the woman did.

Anya thinks: I wonder if Dad tried to take me away when Mom divorced him. Or does that only happen in Japan?

Anya thinks: it's too bad the woman gave up so easily! Who cares about a phantom? She could have just moved. I've moved a hundred times. And now that woman's daughter lives without her mother.

Anya thinks: I'd be curious to watch the same film, but about the dead characters instead. About the drowned little phantom girl. After all, she was very young when it all ended for her.

Sometimes Zinka says: *Gee, our lives sure didn't work out.* I think they worked out just fine. They didn't work out for those who lost at the very start. Those who died senseless deaths. Those who died very young. Who wanted to have a mom but didn't. Who wanted a child but couldn't have one. Who could only find peace in the ghostly world of Japanese cinema.

Seriously, though, why don't I take the Metro more often? Nikita thinks. I always drive. Of course, it's much nicer to drive—it doesn't stink of sweat, no one's shoving you—but even the Metro has its little joys. So many beautiful young women around! When I was poor and took the Metro every day, I hardly noticed them. And now I don't know where to look! For some reason I'm confident that, if I approached any one of them, we'd hit it off.

Across from me sits a blonde girl a bit younger than Dasha, very cute, only her makeup is horrid. But that may explain why it's bad—she's on the younger side. No big deal, she'll learn. The blonde girl sits there clearly watching me, smiling, looking away from time to time. So I'm dying here, my youth is over, my youth is over. This never happened to me when I was young. I smile back and she immediately beams at me, gets up, walks over and says: *Hello, Nikita Vasilyevich, do you remember me? I am Aleksey Leonovich's daughter, you've been to my dad's house.*

Yes, very awkward indeed.

It's okay that Mom couldn't get the time off, it's good, even, Anya thinks. I'll tell Andrey that I can't go to Turkey with him, I have no one to leave Gosha with. It's just as well, I don't know how I'd have put up with Andrey for two whole weeks.

It's sad I won't get to see the sea again. That's alright, I've lived many years without seeing it, what's a few more? Mom and Grandma never took beach vacations and I'll do without. Or did Grandma go away once? It's a pity I don't know and have no one to ask now. Grandma didn't talk much about her life and only grew fond of reminiscing in her last few years. I remember she told us about Oleg and the shooting gallery. And about going to a party on the day Gagarin flew into space. I must not have been paying attention and now I regret it. I should have asked for all the details: what was it like back then? I can picture what it would be like today, the people at a modern-day shooting gallery or a party. Or, the opposite, like in an old black-and-white movie, as if the world didn't have any color in it before I was born.

Anya thinks about her grandma. Anya thinks her family is like an illustration, a web, a hammock. In the knots—the children's births, the threads that connect them to their parents. And she lays Gosha down in this hammock as comfortably as she can so that he's cozy and safe.

Threads, ropes, torn ties. Anya, Rimma, Aunt Gulya, Grandma Djamilya, Grandma Marfa, Grandpa Misha. And somewhere on the side, the frayed ends: Grandpa Oleg, Dad, Uncle Vasya. Nikita. And I, Sasha Moreukhov.

Moreukhov comes out of the train: what is this miracle? In the middle of the platform, there's a column, like the monolith from *2001: A Space Odyssey.* A vertical pillar. What's it doing here? Oh there you go, two inscriptions: HELP and SOS. Which means you first need to ask a question and then you can ask for help.

Good thing there's a place in Moscow where you can ask for help now. Just walk up to the column, rest your forehead against it and repeat: *Help, help.*

No need to press a button as you do this.

Nikita's standing by the doors, looking in the dark glass that reflects a tired, middle-aged man in an expensive, but already rumpled suit. The lights flash across his face, the wheels rumble and he sighs: he's returning home from Dasha's place.

Dear Dasha, he thinks. Dear Dasha, I will never tell you this, but I probably love you.

No. I just love you. I love you very much. With one last, blissful, hopeless love. What started with sex, with a stream of sweat down your skin, the deep moaning, the deep-water orgasm, the woman from the deep end—it turned into love. I don't know how it happened. I never understood what love is and where it comes from. You probably don't either.

Maybe that's why we don't know what to do.

I come home, return to Masha—the lonely figure in the deep armchair, to ZIFT, GIFT, IVF, and ICSI, to melancholy, despair, and hopelessness. Somewhere out there in the enormous city, there's a girl I love whom I'll never tell this.

If I could write you a letter, I would write it and then burn it.

If I could find a tree hollow, I'd whisper into it about my love.

If I could find the words, I'd find them and forget about them again.

But words of love shouldn't have to be sought out and are impossible to forget: they're always simple. Dasha, I love you—that's all.

I love you and want to spend the rest of my life with you. I want you to be my wife, I want us to walk into a church together on a bright spring day so I can place a wedding band on your finger.

And that's when Nikita remembers: he left Grandpa's ring at Dasha's place.

65.

AROUND THE NEIGHBORHOOD

"Take a look," Moreukhov says and smiles his gap-toothed smile, "isn't this beautiful? You can see the flowers on the windowsill, the entire windowsill is in bloom! People water these flowers, take care of them. Doing so for years, can you imagine?"

The two of them are strolling past the nine-story Troparyovo buildings, peering in the windows. Moreukhov's talking and Lena's listening.

Today she's wearing a warm jacket and jeans that are too light-colored for the muddy Moscow spring. Two hours ago, Lena called Moreukhov on his building intercom. He told her his apartment number at their first drunken meeting. *Allegedly* told her.

The story's unfolding according to all the tenets of film noir. At this point, the femme fatale has to seduce me, he thinks. Well, we'll see.

"Take a look, they haven't changed the wallpaper in twenty years here. This wallpaper was fashionable in the eighties—do you remember? You won't find it anywhere these days!"

Moreukhov was working when Lena buzzed him: Dimon had sent him a project. Back in the day, after he ceased his activity as The Most Talented Artist of Our Generation™, Moreukhov immediately declared that he was ready to work as an illustrator or a designer.

"Well, yeah," he explained to Dimon, "I was opposed to hackwork before. But why? Because hackwork is disorienting: you start to confuse what you're creating for eternity and what you're doing for money. Where the art begins and the hackwork ends. As a result, your work turns into hackwork and your hackwork no longer satisfies your clients. But if you don't work at all, there's nothing shameful about hackwork. Work is work."

For a few years now, Dimon has worked as an art director for a famous, glossy magazine (possibly the same one Anya borrowed from Zinka) and has sometimes commissioned graphic art from Moreukhov. Graphic art was just coming into vogue. Moreukhov had his own style—nervous and sloppy, but unmistakable. And, in general, he wasn't a bad draftsman—especially now that he hadn't had a drink in two months.

"Sometimes I want to draw all this," Moreukhov says to Lena. "The benches by the entryways, the rusty garages, the snail-shaped garages from perestroika . . . it's all endangered wildlife, like in the Amazon rainforest. In five or six years, none of this will be here. It'll be wall to wall European style remodels and various statuary by Tsereteli."

He hadn't invited Lena up: as always, his apartment was a *bit messy*. When he came downstairs, he suggested that they *go for a stroll around the neighborhood.*

"I'll show you Troparyovo!" he said with panache.

"Is there anything to see here?" Lena wondered.

"You bet!" Moreukhov replied. "It's the best place in the world! I once read an Aksyonov novel where the protagonist supposedly finds God . . . like my father and many others did in the seventies. So he finds God and suddenly notices a divine harmony in the newly built high-rise building he lives in. I was always convinced this was about southeast Moscow, where they've managed to make remarkable arrangements of standard block buildings—towers, semi-circles, rectangles. And a forest and river close by."

It was true that, in the nineties, divine harmony had abandoned Troparyovo—all the open spaces were developed straightaway. As it turned out, divine harmony was an exclusively Soviet phenomenon.

So they stroll between the sprawling nine-story buildings, peering into the low, ground floor windows. Flowers on the windowsills, lace curtains. Now and again, an open curtain reveals an imitation crystal chandelier, the upper section of a particleboard wall and Czech bookshelves that go all the way up to the ceiling.

"You see," Moreukhov says, "almost nothing's changed. It's as if the Soviet regime didn't end fifteen years ago. No European-style remodeling, no Italian furniture, zero interior design. It's as if time has stopped in there. We used to find it shabby, but now we can see that it's beautiful!"

"Why?" Lena asks.

"You see, twenty years ago, people strove to imitate the West. And that included western design and western fashion. These reproductions were very inept and easy to mock—and when consumer products appeared in stores, all these imitations were swept away by a wave of Chinese mass-manufactured crap. But in reality, this attempt to recreate western design and western fashion was absolutely and inherently valuable. There was an astonishing discrepancy between the materials and the concept. A paradox. A visual demonstration that the material as such was imperfect. This is why a copy is better than the original: it simultaneously includes the idea of the original, the material of the copy, and the discrepancy between the two. And all of global philosophy is easily flushed down the drain of this discrepancy. Look: these people can live without even closing their curtains. They have nothing to be ashamed of, nothing to hide. They have a simple, ordinary life, as they should. But an IKEA chair in there and everything will go to the dogs, everything will be ruined."

"IKEA is very primitive, of course," Lena wrinkles her nose, "but I wouldn't want to live in that kind of apartment."

"Primitive is a very good word," Moreukhov echoes her. "Coziness is a primitive thing, life is inherently primitive. Objects shouldn't be beautiful, it'd be better if they were hideous, tasteless, repulsive. Only then would you want to breathe your soul into them, bring them to life. Think of Soviet cars—we always fixed them ourselves, without any body shops or repair shops. These cars were a part of our family. In my class, there were two boys who had cars: one had a humpbacked Zaporozhetz and the other—a Zhiguli. These boys loved their cars as much as kids usually love a cat or a puppy. It's nothing like that now!"

"I think that domestically made cars are unsafe," Lena says.

"I think that Russian life is unsafe," Moreukhov answers. "Look over there, that's what I'm talking about!"

Three men in dirty jackets and rumpled earflap hats are bent over an open hood. They're passing a flashlight over it and gesticulating excitedly.

"You see, they're making the car homier together, with their family or neighbors. The car cements their friendship. And if you send it to a body shop, what friendship would there be? It would just be a transaction."

"This neighborhood really does remind me of a village," Lena says and nods toward two elderly women sitting on a makeshift bench by a building entrance. "Have you lived here long?"

"Since I was born," Moreukhov replies and, after a short pause, asks: "And you?"

"Doesn't matter," Lena says, "I'm asking about you. You've lived here your whole life and don't want anything to change. For it to remain a museum of your childhood. That's kind of touching."

"Bah." Moreukhov doesn't want to be touching, he wants to be radical, paradoxical, unexpected. "I don't want it to be a museum. I want it to have a life of its own—one that's different from life in the next neighborhood or in the city center. Here, it's like the last fifteen years never happened. Elsewhere, things are different. It's a dynamic museum, a monument to itself, eternally changing and self-destroying."

Seems like Lena's not listening.

"Your whole life in one neighborhood," she says pensively.

"I hope I'll be here my whole life," Moreukhov replies and thinks to himself: how can you leave a neighborhood once you've spoken with God under its every bush?

Not too far from here, in the summer, he and Sonya Sphilman used to drink on the sewer hatch, which stuck out of the ground like a small, round table. The port wine was brought from Crimea and the beer was bought by the Metro stop.

When winter came, they'd warm up with vodka at the edge of the local forest.

In the spring, Sonja got an abortion and emigrated with her parents to Israel.

How can you leave a neighborhood where you drank so much?

"Did you really say you were an artist?" Lena asks.

"Kind of," Moreukhov replies. When he's sober, he's ashamed to be an artist. He would have preferred to have been a film director or a rock musician.

"Do you draw?"

"Yes, sometimes," Moreukhov nods, "when you came, I was just finishing up an illustration for a fashion magazine."

"Do you take commissions?"

"When I have the time," Moreulkhov says authoritatively. "Why?"

"I'd like to have my portrait drawn. Will you draw it?"

Wow, he thinks, what a beautiful plot twist! Film noir at its finest! I haven't done portraits in a long time.

"Absolutely," he says. "It's not really my specialty, but I like doing it. Especially if it's a portrait of a beautiful young woman."

Of course, Moreukhov doesn't explain why. He would have told Dimon: when you draw them, they fuck better.

"How much will it cost?" Lena asks, and Moreukhov looks up thoughtfully at the darkening evening sky.

"I think we can make a deal," he nods and, immediately changing the subject, points his finger somewhere in the distance: "Did you know that, in 1941, the Germans got all the way up to there? There's a sign on Lobachevsky Street. We can say we're behind the front lines now."

66.

REINCARNATION. BORIS

He took Boris's hand: *Don't tell anyone, don't do it.*

It sounded like a quote from a pre-war film. A spy film, most likely.

They picked up the stretchers and carried them away. In a few minutes, the medical train would depart for the east, its wheels rattling.

Boris has to go west.

Boris is going to Berlin. In the very center of the city, Hitler's hiding like a vicious spider. Boris once saw a poster showing Hitler pinned against the wall, impaled on a Soviet bayonet.

Boris wants to march all the way to Berlin so he can see it for himself.

His unit is stationed two kilometers from the train station. He walks down the road, the sun shines brightly, the grass is lush; it's the third summer of war and Berlin is still so far away.

Mikhail examines the German wristwatch, presses it to his ear, lovingly wipes the glass, and puts it back in his rucksack.

"It's nice, huh?" he says. "I'll come back a victor and wear a German watch everywhere. The Germans have a way with technology."

"You, Mikhal Konstantinych, are an educated man," Boris says. "I've been wanting to ask you for a while: in your opinion, is it possible to make a bomb so that, you know—BAM!—and the whole war is over?"

They're sitting in a bunker, with five or six other soldiers beside them. Everyone's preoccupied with their own business: one man's sleeping, another one is writing a letter, and a third is cleaning his automatic rifle.

"No, Borya," someone answers, "there's no such bomb."

It's the third year of war. Submarines are gliding in the seas and, above them, their targets—ships. Tanks, tanks, tanks are crawling all over the fields of Europe. Planes in the skies, among the clouds. Below them, their targets: buildings, factories, airfields. And people everywhere. In submarines, ships, and factories, in tanks, planes, buildings, and on airfields. Targets for no reason at all, easy prey, cannon fodder. The unarmed are accidental casualties, civilians, while the armed are soldiers. But both die.

When you're at war, it's important to know what you're ready to die for. Or maybe it's not important because you only die once, and when you do you die for all of it: for the living (so they can go on living), for the dead (to avenge them), for those who stayed home, for those who are by your side, *for your friends*; and, at the same time, so you can kill more Krauts and not get captured, crippled, or commit treason, so you never make it to old age (you or that of those you love), to get a monument so your children can be proud, so your grandchildren can remember you, so your mom will cry out all her tears, so Lyuska, Zinka, or Ninka will marry somebody else, and everything you didn't have time to do would forever be left undone, everything you did wrong will forever be irreparable, and the first postwar spring and the first postwar summer and autumn and winter will take place without you.

And that's everything you will die for, if you must.

That's why you should get cracking. Do what you haven't done yet; ask what you haven't asked yet. All the more so because of how many people are around, and all of them so different! Mikhal Konstatinych is an engineer, Pyotr is a factory worker from Leningrad, Nikolay is a land surveyor from Ufa, Yefim Vladimirovich is a teacher, Dmitry Polikarpovich is a collective farm worker like me, and, of course, our squadron captain, Comrade Startsev, is a military man, whereas secret agent Yegorov was sent by the government.

I need to ask him about Dzerzhinsky. Whether or not he knew him. And, I need to ask him about catching spies and infiltrators because that must be a very interesting job—catching saboteurs and other enemies of the people.

I also need to ask someone, Boris thinks, what life was like in the Tsarist era. I asked my parents, and they made it sound as if they didn't remember. They say life was the same, they plowed the earth—and that was that. But there were no tractors, no collective farms! And they reply: *but the earth was there. And the grain. What do you think, the earth was invented by the collective farms?* Mikhal Konstantinych is an educated man, he can tell me.

Boris is only twenty; he doesn't remember all that well what life was like in his village before the collective farm. But he does know that he owes the Soviet regime and Comrade Stalin for everything there is. Ever since the first day of the war, he was eager to go to the front on behalf of the Soviet regime and Comrade Stalin, but they didn't take him, saying: *You've still got growing up to do, there'll be work for you in the village.* What they said was true: as soon as the men all left for the front, he became the one in charge. They collected three harvests and survived three winters, and then Boris said: *Enough!*

He was scared that the war would end, everyone would return a combat veteran, and he'd have been the only benchwarmer. Moreover, Boris wanted to see the world because he hadn't really been outside of his village—well, maybe to the regional center, but that was still a village, just a bigger one. Although they had a movie theater, where, as a boy, Boris had watched many films: *Circus, Volga-Volga, Jolly Fellows* . . . From the films he had gathered that, somewhere in the Soviet land, people lived differently. First, they never went hungry. Second, their work was different from village work—it was easy. They could take a break and sing a song. It wasn't the same as working and singing—plenty of that going on in the village!—no, they abandoned their posts to sing. In his favorite film, *Volga-Volga*, almost everyone in town became an artist, and it was no big deal! His entire village would never get away with something like that!

When Boris grew up, he realized that that's what made the movies movies—nothing was like in real life. But still, he wanted to visit a big city and see what all the papers wrote about: the big modern factories, the electric power plants, the enormous stadiums, the beautiful parks, and the university, where boys not much older than Boris studied to be engineers, teachers, and agronomists.

And city girls must be so different, nothing like village girls. He needs to ask if city girls are stuck-up or, the opposite, would readily go on a haystack with a handsome fellow. Or is it like in the movies: kisses and nothing more?

He wants to ask, but doesn't know how.

They'll laugh at him for his stupid questions.

I better not. Maybe there'll be time for that later.

Everything went off the rails because of a stupid accident. We were supposed to dislodge the Germans from an altitude of 21 meters, which blocked access to the valley. The Germans, too, grasped its importance, and thus, concentrated men and equipment on this altitude and all access points to it. They had complete control over each access point, and it was decided that we would attack suddenly, by night.

At first, everything was going well. The infantry had just about set off for the marked positions, we surrounded the hillock—five more minutes, and we'd add a bit of fire—and then, in the name of the Motherland and Stalin! A nighttime battle is a terrible thing. Especially if you strike suddenly.

The hillock would have been ours by dawn.

I don't know who screwed things up, but, just before the attack, a light training plane appeared over the hill. German speech amplified by loudspeaker sounded from the sky. Those who *sprechened* it translated for us: *They're telling the Krauts we took Kharkov!* That's understandable, a propaganda flight. The most important thing was to demoralize the adversary. For greater effect, the pilot shone a spotlight over the hill and dropped a few aerial bombs as he flew away. This was really poor timing. The aerial bomb descended on a parachute, fully illuminating the surroundings so that, as we crawled to the hillock, we ended up right in the Fritz's palm. And he tore into us with all his artillery. A nighttime battle is a terrible thing. Especially if you're showered with both machine-gun fire and artillery fire while groping in the dark for shelter without any idea of what's going on—are we attacking or retreating?

Boris was lucky: when the unremitting hell began, Mikhal Konstantinych grabbed him by the shoulders and dragged him into a little swamp, a sort of shallow, naturally occurring trench. They pressed themselves to the ground and waited. The artillery would refocus any minute now and open fire along the hill: at least then the infantry would get a break and retreat. But, for the time being, Boris and Mikhal Konstantinych lay there waiting, nothing left for them to do besides listen to machine gun rounds slicing the air, explosions rocking the earth, the wounded moaning and the dying wheezing—and Boris was terrified and confused, although this was neither his first battle nor the first time he was under fire; everything had happened so suddenly today.

They didn't know that one of the fascist rounds had struck the artillery captain's trench. Everyone perished and the radio transmitter and telephone were destroyed, which explained why the artillerists didn't open fire—they were waiting for a signal, afraid to shoot their own.

Day was already breaking and the German cannonade didn't let up.

The remaining troops were saved by the morning fog: when the forest

drowned in milky whiteness, the fascist batteries fell silent and the surviving soldiers trailed back to the trenches.

Boris plodded behind Mikhal Konstantinych, occasionally losing
sight of him in the fog. In the morning light that filtered through the
white veil, the forest seemed unreal—not even magical, but like it was
sketched. Time and again, branches, trunks, wet bushes, and even other
combatants jumped out at them, just as unreal as the shroud itself. They
were almost out of the engagement zone, and the terror that had gripped
Boris at the very first sound of gunfire had disappeared; he was following
Mikhal Konstantinych with sufficient confidence, thinking that, one way
or another, he wouldn't get lost in this forest, where a villager could surely
give a city dweller a run for his money; and the fog—what of it, it's not
like his village didn't have fog; and then, either Boris picked up his pace
or an opening appeared in the fog, but he saw, with unreal clarity, how
Mikhal Konstantinych stuck a knife in the back of the soldier walking
in front of him. It was so unexpected that Boris let out a scream, but the
fog swallowed his voice—and then Boris froze, hoping that the killer
wouldn't turn around.

He didn't turn around. He calmly stepped over the body and continued walking.

Boris rushed over to the body, turned it onto its back and glanced at
the face: *Oh God, it's Yegorov, our secret agent! Mikhal Konstantinych must
be a spy and Yegorov caught on, so he killed him and . . .* but Boris didn't
have time to finish his thought. Once again, the German cannons began
to howl and he began to run for dear life, this time, managing to hide in a
dug-out shelter or trench, and then—finally—our artillery went to work.

All day long, the killed and wounded lay almost at the front line of
the German defenses. They could only be collected the next night. The
wounded were sent to a field hospital and the dead, including secret
agent Yegorov, were buried in a communal grave; no one even noticed
that Yegorov didn't have a gunshot wound.

Boris suffered this entire time—what was he to do? In any film,
Mikhal Konstantinych would have definitely turned out to be a spy. He
had to report him so that they could arrest him before he killed anyone
else! But an inner voice told Boris that everything he was seeing was nothing like the movies; just that morning, Mikhal Konstantinych saved his
life, why would a spy do that? The two voices kept arguing all the way till
evening, when Boris decided that he had to find Mikhal Konstantinych.

Before he could confront him, Mikhal Konstantinych was wounded by shrapnel. He fell face down in the wet grass, but immediately came to and crawled over to the trenches. They sent him straight to a field hospital, and it was there that Boris found him the next day as they loaded the wounded on a train headed for the rear.

Now Boris is sitting beside the stretcher, telling Mikhal Konstantinych who made it out alive and who perished, saying rumor has it that, tonight, they'll storm that blasted hill again, but all the while thinking how easy it would now be to ask him about city girls, about the university, and anything else he wanted to ask him just the day before yesterday—anything would be easier than to ask: "Mikhal Konstantinych, why did you kill Yegorov?" And Boris tells him the latest news and crumples his garrison cap; the train is leaving in ten minutes and he must make up his mind, but Boris still can't do it and despises himself for his cowardice, and then Mikhal Konstantinych whispers: *Lean in.* Boris leans in and the wounded man mutters right into his ear: *I was told he was investigating me. If I hadn't killed him yesterday, he would have put me away tomorrow*, then takes Boris's hand and adds: *Don't tell anyone, don't do it*, and Boris thinks it sounds like a line from a pre-war film, a spy film, and feels relieved because, somehow, he immediately *believes* him and watches as they load the stretchers onto the train, then, walks along the road to his unit as the sun shines brightly, the grass is lush, and it's the third summer of war.

(Nikita's dad still has that trophy watch, Masha thinks. After he was wounded, his grandfather never returned to the front, he was demobilized. The doctors said: you've done your share of fighting, enough!—and that is how my father-in-law was born, in 1945, a few months after victory.)

That night, they took the hill after all: the artillery hit right on time, the storm-troopers and armor-clad infantry broke in first, and the regular infantry followed them, with Boris among them screaming "For the Motherland! For Stalin! Hurrah!" ready to kill and ready to die; he didn't die this time around, nor the next, and this went on for a whole month, and then there was an attack, wave after wave—sometimes in the German trenches, sometimes in ours, and we were in the midst of retreating when a machine gun round struck both his legs—no one realized straightaway that he was left behind, someone turned to run back—either Pyotr from Leningrad or Nikolay from Ufa—but it was too late, you couldn't go back there.

Afterward Boris crawled into a trench and fired back until his ammunition ran out; then he took out a grenade and waited, and when the Krauts burst in, he pulled the pin and wanted to yell out "For the Motherland!" but never had the chance.

After the explosion, nothing remained of Boris—neither his boots, nor his party membership card, nor his lavaliere, nor his stripes, nor the letters from his beloved. Boris doesn't have a grave—there's no star, no sign, and no cross. They didn't find his body: it was scattered to the four corners of the world—North, South, East and West.

Up North, there is now a Stadium. Marathon runners run laps around it, soccer players chase after balls, athletes fling javelins. Beautiful young women sit on bleachers, laughing, clapping, and eating ice cream.

To the South is the University. Men and women are enrolled there, studying physics, chemistry and mathematics so that they can build better tractors and tanks and plow and defend the land better. And when the bell rings, they run down the main staircase arguing, laughing, and joking around. And if any of them are in love, they kiss.

To the East is the Factory. Laborers come up to the new machines, make parts and assemble Tractors to plow the land and tanks to defend it. They eat lunch in a clean, orderly canteen, where the first course is soup, the second is meat, and the third is compote.

To the West is the Electric Power Plant. The power lines hum, the turbines turn and the engineers walk around to make sure there's enough electricity for the remotest villages and settlements so, even at night, there is light everywhere giving people warmth and joy.

And on the spot where Boris died, there is a Park. Young, beautiful mothers come to the Park. The ones with young children have strollers, while the ones with older children guide them by the hand. The children play in the sandbox, slide down slides, and climb up and down ladders. When they grow up, they'll go to the Stadium, the University and the Factory and, afterward, the boys and girls will come here in pairs, with their arms around each other, to kiss in the most out of the way corner of the park. And when they grow old and gray, they'll come here to feed the pigeons and watch the children, lovebirds, and young mothers.

The Stadium is Boris's legs, the University is his head, the Factory his right hand, and the Electric Power Plant his left.

The Park is Boris's heart.

And, as long as the Electric Power Plant is working, as long as people go to the Stadium and the Factory, the University and the Park, Boris's body won't fall apart, his love and strength will keep people safe.

The elderly say that the day will come when the Stadium will overgrow with grass, the University doors will close, the Factory machines will stop humming, the Electric Power Plant Lever will be lowered, and guards will be placed before the Park gates. At that moment, Boris's body will fall to pieces, the earth will split open, there will be an Explosion and Darkness will descend upon the world.

Nobody knows what will happen after that.

67.

THE FRIENDSHIPS OF MEN
AND THE FATES OF WOMEN

What is male friendship? It's when you meet rarely, but drink a lot. Or when you meet often, but speak honestly.

Kostya and I don't drink a lot. As a drinking buddy, Kostya isn't that much fun. Usually, he buys a bottle of Château-something-or-other for four hundred euros and asks for my opinion. Yes, Kostya, it really is a marvelous wine. No, I'm not kidding, marvelous.

Another feature of marvelous wines is that you have absolutely no interest in getting drunk on them.

It turns out that the last time we drank together was a year ago, when he told me about the iceberg and we picked up girls on the street. Usually, we don't drink, we talk.

What do men talk about? Mostly about work.

"Let me tell you what you need to do next," Kostya says. "By the end of the year, your revenue will reach about seven hundred thousand. By the end of next year, it will go up by one and a half times. What's your profit margin? That's what I thought. You can live pretty decently off of that. But it won't be enough to grow the company. But if you take out a loan in the same amount, you can hire decent salespeople, do a marketing campaign and become a recognizable brand. Why? Just so that, in three years, when you're sick of it all, you can sell the company."

"Right now, I find it all terribly interesting," I say. "I have zero desire to sell it. Can you imagine, I was contacted by some people from Kiev who asked me to open a branch there."

"So open one. Your company will sell even better if it has a branch. Because you always need to have an exit strategy in mind. In your case, it's obvious: build a successful company, then make your accounting somewhat more transparent than it is now, then sell it for, say, five million and invest in some sort of new business."

I thought I heard him wrong. I still can't get used to the idea that the five million could refer to me. In three years, sometime in the summer or autumn of 2008.

"You just need to do two things: find an investor and work for another three years."

"Would you want to be that investor?"

"I'll think about it."

What do men talk about? Mostly about women.

"Old man, remember you asked me what new experiences we could have with women when we're over thirty? I'll tell you: I flew off to scuba dive in the Philippines and the Filipina instructor gave me a blowjob right on the seafloor. What do you mean, not possible? Inhale—suck, inhale—suck. Mouthpiece—cock, mouthpiece—cock. Plus, the bubbles tickle the glans."

"Go fuck yourself!"

"You have to start diving. I have no one to go with. You've already done it once! Take Masha, I'll take Ksenia, we'll go to the Red Sea, or Cuba, if you want somewhere exotic."

I would have never gone diving if it weren't for Masha. *You have to face your fear in order to conquer it.* And when I began to swim normally for the first time, she stood on the barge, waving to me.

It's too bad I don't have any words of wisdom for her or a barge I could wave from. Under our feet—under the two of us, the three of us—is some kind of bottomless abyss. You can't dive in there, not even in scuba gear.

What do men talk about? Mostly about the meaning of life.

"I even envy you, old man. This is all new to you and I'm sick of it. I'd like to drop it all, but I don't know what else I'd do. Maybe buy a yacht and sail around the world, what do you think?"

"I don't think that's the issue, Kostya. I told you, my uncle died. And I thought a lot about, you know, my parents, my grandma and grandpa, about all those generations that came before us. They each had a purpose in life—a common one, not an individual one. For instance, our grandpas and grandmas believed they were building Communism."

"Well," Kostya says, "mine didn't believe that. My grandfather was a priest with all the expected consequences. Labor camp, deportation et cetera, et cetera."

"My grandfather wasn't a peasant-and-laborer either. Well, one of my grandfathers was a peasant, albeit a dispossessed one, which is even worse. But still, both my grandfathers believed that they were doing something important. Building electric power plants, digging the Metro, what else? Let's say they didn't believe in Communism, but in God or Russia. My father still believes in Science. In something greater, something they were ready to devote their whole lives to. A kind of power source, understand?

"Old man, power comes from God."

"Of course it comes from God. But tell me, how much of this power do you derive from God? You fuck girls, make money and you're still miserable. Because you can't derive any power from girls or money. For example, my father worked at the Institute, he was a scientist. Well, not a particularly great one—he didn't even defend his dissertation—but he was a part of the Great Soviet Science. Moreover, he kept samizdat literature at home and believed he was bringing the bright future closer. The bright future came—and it turned out we were left to fend for ourselves in it. Left to fend for ourselves and exist for ourselves. And all the power we have is our personal strength. When we run out of it, we'll hit rock bottom."

"Well," Kostya says, "there are two ways out. First, you can consider how you created fifteen jobs. In the US, this would be deemed an act of patriotism. In that sense, you are also working toward a brighter future and so on and so forth. Second, you're living for Masha and your future children. For your family. Again, like your grandpas and grandmas and mom and dad."

What do men talk about? About work, about women, about the meaning of life, about politics, sports, the economy, the Orange Revolution, base metals, other natural resources, and about what the Russian land stood, stands, and will continue to stand for, about their lives, about their friendship, about the friends that are no longer with them, about the time that has passed, and the time that remains. And very rarely—about the fear, the latent fear that is always with them.

They very rarely talk about that. Practically never.

Which is why I nod to Kostya instead of saying: *I'm not really sure about children*—because I'm trying not to think about it. Children would mean more medical bills, tests, hospitals, light-filled corridors, snowy alleys, colorful booklets, beautiful promises, zero results. Children would mean more of Masha in the armchair with the lights off, in the empty room, with empty eyes, an empty uterus, emptiness inside, emptiness outside, emptiness that spreads and surrounds us, filling our lungs until we can no longer breathe.

If you'd sent me to the doctor right after our wedding, maybe it would have all worked out, she said, and anyway, I have the feeling that you never wanted it: I deliberately didn't say anything for six months to see what you would do, and you didn't say a thing!

I replied that I didn't want to traumatize her—after all, it's her decision. Yes, I'd be happy to have children, but if we won't have any, then we won't. Or perhaps we can adopt.

Then she sat back in the armchair and fell silent.

I don't know what's worse—when she sits there like this or when she's explaining how everything is my fault.

Lately, I've developed a special voice, a soft, soothing one. I tell her: "You'll see, everything will be fine, it'll work out this time, we have plenty of time, you're not even forty, my grandma gave birth to my mom when she was over thirty, at what was then considered an advanced age, and everything was fine. And with modern medicine, if worse comes to worst, we'll go to America or Europe, we'll find the best doctors."

"What do you mean we'll go?" Masha says. "You have your business."

I reply: "*The hell with my business!*" Although I know she's right and I won't be going anywhere, but I keep talking and I think of my mother, who stayed with my father only because of me. I think of Sasha's mother, Anya's mother, Rimma's mother, who raised their children alone. I think of Grandma Nastya and her three children, whom she gave birth to in quick succession as soon as the war ended. I think of my sister Anya, of all the women in our family, their fates, and their children. I think of them and I see a kind of enormous net, a mycelium that gives a common meaning to their lives, of which men are deprived, a meaning Dasha hasn't even started to think about, that Masha can't seem to get. She doesn't need anything else besides this meaning.

This is a woman's fate. It's why, when they drink, men so rarely talk about children, and when they do talk about women, they talk about sex, underwater blowjobs, gymnastics in bed, merry adventures, and love conquests. Because when a woman comes face to face with her fate, there is nothing a man can do, no way he can help. Except sit down beside her in an empty, pitch-black room, squeeze her hand, and hope that she'll squeeze his back.

68.

TWO RUSSIAS

The first time Nikita came to this church was with Grandpa Makar. Not long before his death, Grandpa asked to be taken there. Nikita didn't know his grandpa was Eastern Orthodox and marveled: *Why, are you baptized?* Grandpa scowled from underneath his gray brows.

"What am I, a heathen? I was born in 1915. How could I not be baptized?"

"But you never went to church?"

"I went when I needed to," Grandpa snarled.

Grandpa Makar was seventy-five and walked with difficulty, continually stopping to catch his breath and leaning on a knotty stick with a metal tip. Nikita caught an unlicensed cab and sat Grandpa in the front, and the old man gave the driver excessively detailed directions.

They arrived at the Church of Ioann Predtechi on the Presna River. Nikita wanted to go in, but Grandpa checked him:

"No reason for you to go today. You'll go without me if you ever want to. I have to go alone. I would have gone with Nastya, but I won't go with you."

Nikita bought an *Ogoniok* magazine at a kiosk, sat down on a bench, and began to read a long article about the submerged Russian churches. He thought it was an unintentional metaphor: as if the churches sank to the bottom of their own volition, like the invisible city of Kitezh. Grandpa Makar—and probably many other religious people—also lived, not underground, but expressly underwater all those years. For a second, Nikita saw the bells ringing in the sunken churches and gray-haired men who resembled either Grandpa Makar or old man Mazai from the famous picture riding in boats. *With every minute the water was closing in on the poor animals*, Nikita remembered and turned the page. Next up was an article about the crimes ensuing from the cult of personality.

Forty minutes later, a massive figure appeared in the church doors, leaning on a stick.

"Thank you," Grandpa said, "I did everything I needed to. Let's sit for a minute and then we'll head home."

They sat. Grandpa looked at the copy of *Ogoniok* with aversion.

"Are they trying to expose the truth to the people again?"

Nikita started heatedly talking about restoring historical justice and painting an objective picture, about the memory of the victims and the butchers' crimes. Grandpa interrupted him:

"Nikita, listen to me. After all, I was around at the time. You have to understand that the more horrors they tell, the more exposés they churn out, the harder it will be to work out what really happened back then."

"And what really did happen?" Nikita asked defiantly. He had always been a bit afraid of Grandpa Makar. Grandpa was impossible to talk to—he was eternally disgruntled. He seemed to have an opinion about everything, but no intention of sharing it—it was no use asking him. However, he was not disposed to listen to the nonsense everyone else was spewing either. When Nikita would gather the courage to grill him, Grandpa would reply tersely and unintelligibly, as if trying to confuse him even more.

"It was people living back then, Nikita. They loved each other and sometimes, hated each other. When they loved each other, they wanted to be together. And when they hated someone, they wished for his death. Sometimes their wish came true and sometimes it didn't. That's all."

"That's all?" Nikita was exasperated. "But it's always been that way!"

"That's what I mean," said Grandpa Makar. "It's always been that way. Back in the day, they harped on about the Stakhanovites, the highly productive workers, and the large construction projects carried out by Komsomol members—and now it's about the cult of personality and crimes against humanity. Who were the udarniks? Some of them were criminals, of course. But some of them were hard workers who loved the Motherland and wanted to have a good life there. And that's why they worked. And built a lot. The Dnieper Hydro-Electric Power Station, the Magnitogorsk Iron and Steel Works. Your Grandpa Mikhail built a Metro! They made a technologically advanced country out of a backward one and then they flew off into space! That was all about love. Not only about love, of course. But all the good that came from it was because people had love in them."

"And the camps?"

"The camps! The crimes! The repressions!" Grandpa pushed the *Ogoniok* onto the ground. "It was merely some people killing others, or not killing them and sending them to camps. Out of envy, out of vengeance, out of fear—why else would people do a thing like that? It's just that, in the thirties, you could write a denunciation on your enemy, which was easier than shooting them. And believe me, as soon as you handed people weapons, they started using them."

"Grandpa, but nobody killed anybody during the stagnation era."

"Nikita, if you don't hand out weapons long enough, people will find a new way, or uncover an old one. This," and he jabbed the magazine with his stick, "is what's happening here."

"Well," Nikita said, "I don't believe they'll start putting people in jail again based on denunciations."

"Then they'll start shooting again," Grandpa said.

"And the Twentieth Congress of the Communist Party of the Soviet Union?" Nikita asked. "What did you say when the Twentieth Congress was taking place?"

"When the Twentieth Congress was taking place," Grandpa answered, "I kept quiet. What was I supposed to say? I'm explaining it to you because you're my grandson, and weren't around at the time. But they were around and didn't get it. So why should I talk to idiots? I can't change their minds. What about the Twentieth Congress? Did anything change in life afterward? Nothing!"

"But not everyone was an idiot," Nikita objected. "For example, I read something recently. Anna Akhmatova, you know, the poetess, I mean, the poet, well, at the time, she said that the two Russias would presently meet—the one that put people away and the one that had been put away."

"Nonsense." And Grandpa crossly stomped his foot in his slipshod boot. "Two Russias! What does she know, that 'poetess' of yours, that 'poet'! It's all one Russia—it was all the same people who, first, put people away and were then put away. There is no distinction whatsoever. The two Russias are something else. It's those who survived and those who didn't. And those who didn't . . . well, there were countless reasons for it! Collectivization, famine, criminals, war, at long last! What do repressions and that Khruschev with his congress have to do with it? All that matters is whether or not you survived. And those 'two Russias' will meet no sooner than a Trumpet will blare, which you don't believe in," and Grandpa nodded toward the church.

"Grandpa," Nikita said, "but, in the long run, everyone will die."

"In the long run," the old man mocked him. "But some will have managed to leave children behind and others won't. That's what it means to survive! Your race continues or ends with you. That's what matters."

It was a summer day. People hurried about their business; some went into the church, while others bought newspapers and magazines at the kiosk. The sun was shining, the grass was lush, cars drove by, and Nikita realized that today, his grandfather had taken stock of his life. He was fit and season'd for his passage. Nikita began to feel sorry for Grandpa, who had lived a difficult, peripatetic life and was about to die, and for himself, who'd never managed to fully understand this bad tempered old man with an affinity for paradoxes. Nikita wanted to hug him, but at that moment, Grandpa placed a heavy hand on his knee:

"Enough talk. Take me home."

At home, he poured Nikita some strong tea and spent two hours telling him about his pre-war life, when he and Nastya roamed around the entire country and couldn't even consider having children.

Shortly after Grandpa's death, Nikita was baptized in this very church. In the first few years, he tried to keep the fast and attend service and confession, but gradually, he lapsed; moreover, Masha wasn't christened, preferred to celebrate Christmas on December 24, and would forget entirely about Easter.

Today, he had gone in only because he had a meeting in a nearby building. He thought of Grandpa, walked up to the bench where they once sat, then went into the church shop.

Nikita lit a candle, recited *Our father who art in heaven* to himself twice, tried to remember another prayer, couldn't, and then began to pray with the words that came to mind.

"Dear Lord," Nikita prayed, "You can see that I'm a bad Christian, a bad husband. I'm probably a sinner, Lord. I should probably ask You to strengthen my faith. But I simply ask You to strengthen me, to give me strength. Because I'm really struggling, Lord, You know how much I'm struggling. I have my work, I have my family, I have Dasha. I'm lost, Lord, You can see that. Remember how You asked Your Father to let this cup pass from You? So I ask You to let it pass from me . . . not the cup, what cup, just whatever awaits me, let it await me in a somewhat different form, alright? I'm being incoherent, but You'll understand, right? I just want everyone to be happy, for me and Masha to have a child, for Masha to stop sitting like that in the armchair, for everything to go back to the way it was ten years ago, when it all began. Because everything was good, so why take that away? Give it back to me, please, give it back and leave it. Leave me my parents, leave them for a while longer, I'm a bad son, I know, but I love them, I'll have a hard time without them. Leave me my friends, there aren't many of them, so leave them, alright? And my job, I love my job, it's good, there is no sin in it, I think. You don't consider money to be a sin, right? So leave me all that. Also, I know it's dumb, but I'll still ask: please leave me Dasha, I know it's a sin, but I love her, and Masha and I weren't wed in church anyway, so you wouldn't care, do I understand correctly? Yes, leave me Dasha and also, leave me the yellowish-red leaves, my youth, the benches, dusk, the light of a streetlamp, everything that was good in my life, please leave it to me because, in the end, I'll have to give it back to You anyway, and I think it would be better if I gave it up all at once, alright? When I die, I mean. And as long as I'm alive, I want to be happy. That's no sin, I know. Do this for me, I beseech You."

What am I going on about? Nikita thinks. Why am I asking Him to leave everything as is? What, is my life so great that I don't want to change it? Am I really planning to live the way I do now, only long and happily, and die on the same day as Masha and Dasha, for better or worse? What I said is shameful and disgraceful!

Nikita left the church, got into his car, and only started it when Victor called; they began to discuss a client who was asking for some unthinkable discounts, yeah, they should have doubled their quote right away, it was always unpleasant to have to do that . . . And it was only fifteen minutes later that Nikita hung up the phone, stopped at a stoplight, closed his eyes and said: Lord, I am speaking to You, I am Your servant, Lord, and I have sinned. Your will be done and not mine, Lord, You show me the way and, if I don't see it, help me make the right choice.

69.

THE YEAR 1936.
THE TALE OF AN INDUBITABLE WIND

As conscientious members of the working class, Makar and Nastya were given a room in a dormitory. At the construction site, Makar was fed a nutritious black kasha, while back home, Nastya poured glasses of white milk that, sadly, didn't smell of live cattle.

In the evenings, a melancholy of some kind swelled in Makar's chest. With Nastya in his arms, he'd drift off into dreams in which he saw a lake, birds, and a forgotten village grove.

Nastya's mother was Makar's godmother. Having drawn the kulak's lot in life, they didn't join the collective farm, and collectivization, with the undisputed hand of activist Mikhail Yeropkin and other leading landless peasants, who aimed to thus liquidate the kulaks, threw them out into the cold of a wooden train car. The kulak class was peering through the cracks of the train car; these people wished to forever remember where they had been born.

The locomotive puffed with brisk bursts of steam. On its way uphill, a few versts away from the village, it got stuck to the rails and its wheel bands screeched to a halt. With all the sorrow of a working hand parted from his farm, Makar's father threw his weight against the train door. The chilly air of the eerie expanse rushed in from the opening—and their parents pushed Makar and Nastya out into the cold of the adult world; then, breathing heavily, the locomotive overcame the inertia of its bulky weight and pulled the train cars onward toward the closest railway connection.

A wind blew from distant, desolate places, covering up their footprints on the snow, showing them where to go, the better to get lost among the displaced masses. They slept in each other's embrace owing to the cold, and year after year, the melancholy of growing up seeped into their minds and bodies.

When they reached the age of consent, the municipal office issued papers for them under the surname Tikhomirov; first, the documents said they were brother and sister and, a few years later, they wrote a declaration of the loss of marriage certificate and had it stamped. Nastya came up with the last name—it was the name of the miller from the neighboring village who drank with her grandfather on carnival days. Clutching the certificate in hand, she suddenly burst into gushing, urgent tears.

Makar couldn't cry. His mind still recalled how his father kissed the pickets in the yard being collectivized, but his empty heart was closed to sadness and crying. He didn't suffer—he worked out of habit so as not to leave his intelligent hands idle.

The wind drove them through rows of unanimous masses from city to city, factory to factory, construction site to construction site. Everywhere they went, the working man toiled in silence, longing for a fulfilled life and the welfare of the proletariat.

Moscow turned out to be a city of scientific and technological miracles, a city of towers and formidable structures under construction. Everywhere, the ground was wracked with pits, people bustled about and unknown machines hammered stakes into the soil. Kasha-like cement dripped down the hutches; other construction events, too, took place before people's very eyes. It was obvious that a city was being built, but it wasn't clear for whom.

In Moscow, Makar settled on a construction site for a large building. One downcast evening of the city kind, he was walking through a square past a large hotel. As he cocked his head to the side, he noticed a familiar figure in the main entrance.

Clenching his cap in his hand, Makar walked forth with all the fury of his rigid consciousness. His thoughts reared in his head like bristles fighting their way through his skull.

I can always tell a foreigner from a fellow Soviet citizen. They, the bourgeois foreigners, have a very different expression set in their faces. Their faces are, how should I put it, stiffer and more condescending than ours.

This is a job requirement because many unconscientious citizens try to pass themselves off as foreigners and march right into the hotel. My job is to keep my eyes peeled and not allow just anybody in. Because it's one thing if it's a foreigner useful to our Soviet country or some deserving proletariat, and another thing if a citizen comes charging in like a horse. I'd give that kind his marching orders.

And brothers, I immediately noticed this citizen. An unassuming type clenching his cap in his fist.

Soon as I saw him, I immediately said to him:

"No use coming in, citizen, we don't have vacancies."

And he asks me:

"Comrade, who is the man who just walked to the elevator?" As in, look here, kind people, I have no interest in your rooms, I just wanted to ogle your guests out of curiosity.

Of course, I said to him politely:

"It's none of your damn business, citizen, who's walking to our elevators."

This vagrant acts as if he hasn't understood my polite address and keeps asking:

"Wasn't it Lyoshka Nagulny, my friend from the Civil War and collectivization fronts?"

My word, the man sure is a good liar!

Of course, I said to him politely:

"That's no friend of yours from the Civil War and collectivization fronts, that's Comrade Mikhail Yeropkin, a delegate from Bright Dawn State Farm to the convention of the highest-performing workers."

And he says:

"Oh, Mikhail Yeropkin, please excuse me, I was mistaken. People really do look alike! I would have never guessed," he says, "that it's Mikhail Yeropkin, he's the spitting image of Lyoshka Nagulny!"

The man must have made a mistake. Then I said to him:

"Get out of here, citizen, don't block the entrance. Because we have foreigners useful to the Soviet land walking around here and the highest-performing workers have come for the convention, to see Comrade Stalin in person. There's nothing for you to do here."

This citizen is crumpling his cap in his hand, repeating pensively:

"To see Comrade Stalin in person . . ."

He must have been jealous.

He twirled his cap in his hands and left. I even thought to myself: Let him go. I misjudged him. I thought he was some kind of hustler and he turned out to be a conscientious citizen with vision trouble from the Civil War, he mixes people up.

That's alright, he's allowed. And my job is to know all the guests by face so that they don't kick me out of my place of employment like some Shakhtinsky conspirator or saboteur.

As a platform-standing party member, I must, of course, report that, at this very moment, at the Metropol Hotel, by the very walls of the Kremlin, resides citizen Mikhail Yeropkin, who has come from Bright Dawn State Farm to the convention of the highest-performing workers from collective farms and other production centers. I know with full certainty that the aforementioned Mikhail Yeropkin has come to our Motherland's capital with a secret assignment from a group of saboteur kulaks TO KILL COMRADE STALIN! This is a terrible crime he plans to commit during the convention of the highest-performing workers, where COMRADE STALIN has to deliver a keynote address.

Citizen, or rather, Gentleman Mikhail Yeropkin, has long harbored saboteur plans toward the leaders of the Soviet Government and the Bolshevik Party. Over the course of many years, by means of lies and cunning, he's earned the trust of his neighborhood's leadership, supposedly heading up the construction of the collective farm. Meanwhile, all these years, he secretly received funds and instructions from other members of Trotsky's saboteur gang, which was active throughout the entire country.

Having observed C̶o̶m̶r̶. Citizen Yeropkin all these years, I long wished to report his true face, I mean, mug, and the counter-revolutionary discourses he had, on multiple occasions, led in my presence; however, I feared retribution from his collaborators. But now that COMRADE STALIN'S life is in danger, I can no longer conceal the truth.

Dear Cheka comrades! I beg you: stop the mad beast Citizen Yeropkin!

I am not signing this letter because I fear retribution from Trotskyite-saboteur degenerates.

At dawn, the factories hummed over the city. In the alleys a gray blur of fog, night and drizzle trailed, dissolving in the sunrise and indicating that the day would be gloomy, gray, and wet. The streets were desolate at this motionless hour. A great black automobile froze before the tall hotel doors without turning off its engine; the smell of gasoline mingled with the cold, damp, pre-dawn air.

At the far end of the square, a slight man unseen by anyone stood slumped against the wall, his strong, coarse hands crumpled his cap. Through the frost and foggy blur of the Moscow morning, he saw three men come out of the tall hotel doors. Two men in leather jackets and shiny boots were holding a third up by his elbows. He staggered as if he weren't yet fully awake, but spoke fervently to his companions about something.

The man by the wall waited for the noise of the automobile engine to die down, then, almost begrudgingly, put his cap on his head and walked away from there, toward the approaching day, the din of the hammers at plants and in forges, the chatter of factory looms, the whistling of loco-motives, the roar of automobiles and the tap dancing of tram bells, tele-phone bells, and doorbells, while the black car carried his enemy toward other sounds, toward the clank of the door bolt, the click-clacking of heels, the clicking of the tongue—I'm with an inmate!—the whack of a palm against an unshaven cheek—admit it, bastard!—toward a bright light shone in his face, the spit in his face, the blows to his face, a snap behind his back, a shot to his temple, and an anonymous grave—or toward the clatter of wheels, the crackle of frozen wood, the clanging of a pickaxe, the barking of dogs, the shouts of security guards, and an anonymous grave.

A yellow day rose over the city in the foggy blur. Makar was walking through the gray alleys, thinking he didn't know where his father and mother were buried, or Nastya's father and mother.

When he came in, she was bent over a washbasin. Drops streaked her ample bosom.

"Where were you?" she asked sleepily. "I was worried."

"Running some errands," Makar answered.

Then he embraced her, feeling his wife's warm body under his icy hands, kissed her on the neck, and walked over to the window, behind which the great machine of the city rumbled, meshing together the cog-wheels of people's lives; behind which men with briefcases and women in knee-length skirts and deceptively-clear stockings passed by, the occa-sional car drove past, the foggy blur enveloped buildings and people's fig-ures, and rain began to fall.. Early in the next century, Makar's grandson would walk these very streets, changed beyond recognition, through new fogs smelling of gasoline exhaust, the breath of fifteen million residents, American filter-cigarettes and thirty-ruble beer and vodka. He'd walk down them and think: it's unpleasant to know that your grandfather was an informer, even a noble informer, a Count of Monte Cristo of sorts;

we were always taught that informing is bad, though killing is also bad and everyone kills during a war, and sleeping with a young girl while your wife's still in the picture is bad, and he, Nikita, is sleeping with her, so how can he judge his grandfather, although, yes, it's still unpleasant, still unpleasant, he doesn't even want to think about it, why on earth did Grandpa Makar tell him this story back in the day—and the frosty haze will obscure his figure just the same and he'll shiver just as much till he sits down in the warm interior of the car that will carry him through the crammed streets of Moscow through which vehicles, crowds, human time, and the gray day course.

Without turning his head, Makar said:

"We have to leave Moscow. It's becoming too dangerous here. Too many people."

Outside, the cold wind scattered wisps of fog. Year after year, this wind drove Makar and Nastya all over the country. The wind of fear, agitation, and hatred; the wind of cautiousness, care, and foresight; the wind of a villager's smarts, survival skills, and care for one another. The wind drove them through dizzying triumphs, through the industrialization of the entire country, through the first five-year plans, the Stakhanovite movement, the great construction projects, the treacherous invasion, through the Not A Single Step Back, through The Motherland Is Calling, through For Motherland, For Stalin, through To Berlin! and through We Made It!—and it was only following Victory that they stopped running and, in the course of four years, Grandma Nastya gave Grandpa three children, two girls and a boy: Sveta, Marina and Andrey.

70.

BASIC HUMAN RESPECT

Maybe I should get an Antabuse capsule implant? Moreukhov thinks. Dimon has been trying to convince me for a while. Abstain a bit longer from drinking, draw Lena's portrait, get paid for it, fix up my apartment, and start living like a normal person. Buy myself a new fridge, fix the toilet so it stops leaking, throw out the broken furniture, get some new furniture at IKEA, and then the apartment will be shipshape.

It'll be so much to fuck it up when I start drinking again!

After all, a home should only have functional objects: a bed to sleep in, a TV, a VCR, a table, a kettle—and that's it. Or else I'll end up with, God forbid, suits and ties worth a couple of hundred bucks. And then I'll be sitting wistfully at a bar, wearing all this junk and thinking: what should I have to drink? Because, truth be told, I wouldn't even feel like drinking at that point . . .

Truth be told, he didn't even feel like drinking. Nikita's sitting at the bar of a provincial hotel, staring at a long row of bottles. He doesn't find them inspiring.

How did he get here? Obviously, he's here on business. What sort of business could an aquarium vendor have at a provincial hotel? To be honest, I have no idea. Maybe he decided to change suppliers? Or perhaps there's a well-known fishery nearby that will supply him directly with catfish? Doesn't matter. He's here, so he's here. On business and that's that.

So he's here on business, sitting completely disoriented at the bar and eyeing the bottles when he hears a little voice: *Excuse me, sir, do you have a cigarette for me?*

He turns around. Unmistakable: a provincial whore. Dressed like a whore, made up like a whore, behaves like a whore—she's a whore.

"I don't smoke," Nikita says, "and if you work here, you've got the wrong guy."

"I'm not working, I'm selling," Olga says, and leans down to his ear: "Sex."

"To be honest," Nikita says, "I have zero interest. I'd go to sleep, but I passed out on the plane for two hours and now I'm wide awake. Would you like to just sit for a bit?"

"Yes, let's do that," Olga agrees, "it's still early, it's not even 8 P.M. in Moscow, where you're from."

So the two of them sit together in the empty hotel bar and at first, they chitchat about this and that—time-zone changes, who's traveled where, local city sights—they chit-chat and, meanwhile, Nikita is rather openly studying her, not because he likes her, but just because he's curious how old she is and doesn't dare ask. Her lips are swollen, her eyes are big, and her nose is upturned. Her figure's just about average, it seems, no wonder she sat down first and then started talking. Her legs must be too short and her ass—too big. By model standards. She doesn't know that those are just the kind I like. Like Dasha.

As soon as he thinks of Dasha, his mood takes a dive. What could she be doing without me, he thinks. Maybe she went to a club, picked up a young guy, and now they're dancing? She can't dance with me, I'm no dancer. And definitely not at a club.

"I have a girlfriend, she looks like you," he tells Olga for some reason.

"And how is she in bed?" Olga livens up. "Care to compare us?"

"No," Nikita says and for some reason, he starts telling this strange woman about Dasha: she's almost twenty years younger than him, she could be his daughter, and sometimes, he doesn't understand a thing she says—the lexicon is completely different, the lexicon, meaning the words, but he is certain that Dasha really loves him—it's not the money, the money's got nothing to do with it, and it's not his status—*status is, you know* . . . I know, Olga says, and Nikita continues talking and tells her about Masha now, about how she couldn't get pregnant for many years and how much money they spent, all to no avail, and now she sits in the armchair, staring into the darkness, growing thinner and thinner, and he can't take it anymore. And then, they order a second bottle of vodka and Olga starts telling him about how, back in school, she got hooked on heroin, became a prostitute, then got pregnant and got clean for her child's sake, yes, got clean, although everyone says it's impossible, actually, no, it is possible, you just have to really want to, although she wasn't on it for that long, well, doesn't matter, many don't even try and she did, she got off heroine, and now she works here, at the hotel, and not out on the highway, it's so much better here—on the highway, the long-haul truck drivers amuse themselves by covering you in engine oil and down feathers and forcing you to run in front of the vehicle. And if the client isn't happy, they cut crosses on your breasts to, you know, damage the goods, while the pimps do it the other way around, on the hips, so it's less conspicuous, but now she works here, at the hotel, and that's immense *socioeconomic success*.

And when Nikita reaches for his wallet, Olga says: "Listen, give me some money, I can't work today because of you anyway," and Nikita gives her money, even more than she's asking, then heads back to his room, for some reason drunkenly slapping her ass in farewell, and thinks: Why did I get so drunk? What a woman, I wouldn't be able to endure all that, and neither would Dasha, not to mention Masha. That's what they're like, Russian women, stopping galloping horses and walking into burning izbas—and he feels basic human respect for Olga and is proud of the fact that he feels only basic human respect and not, say, pity, which is demeaning, or some sneaky Dostoyevskian desire to save her, and it goes without saying that he isn't the least bit attracted to her, which, given her profession, is a rather unfortunate sign.

Afterward, Nikita stands in the shower for a while, painfully sobering up. He dries himself off and looks at his watch: wow, he got drunk fast! He takes out his cell phone and dials Masha.

"Is that you?" Masha sobs into the phone.

"Yes," Nikita answers, "what happened?"

"Can you come home right now? Or at least tomorrow morning?"

Nikita starts to explain to her that tomorrow morning he has a business meeting, which is why he flew down here, because the flight is once a day, in the evening, but when the meeting is over, he'll head straight to the airport and be home in Moscow this time tomorrow. He says all this, but more to himself than to Masha. Masha has never acted like this before. Well, he gets it, they'll be trying again next week and Masha is nervous.

"What happened?" he repeats.

"I just miss you," Masha says, and he realizes that, no, there's something else, and holds a pause. Then, Masha admits: "I was also thinking, what if I get pregnant tonight when you're not here?"

Then Nikita stands by the window for a while, staring at the sparse lights of the provincial square. Maybe he should go down to the bar for another bottle? He takes out his cell phone again and calls Dasha.

He can barely hear her: he can't tell if there's loud music blaring or it's just background noise.

"Listen," Nikita says, "can you talk right now?"

"Of course," Dasha replies, "what happened?"

"I just miss you," Nikita replies, Dasha falls silent for a bit, the music blares and, in his head, Nikita watches a fast-forwarded porn film with Dasha in the lead role and a dozen extras of all genders and races.

"Hello," Dasha says, "what's wrong? I can't hear you very well!"

"That's alright," Nikita says, "everything is fine. I'll call you tomorrow."

He hangs up and thinks: what's wrong with me? I've never been jealous before. I must be hallucinating. So Dasha went to a club with her friends and is dancing or drinking, what's the big deal?

She never goes to a club with me, Nikita thinks sourly, and she's right not to. Because I haven't been to a club in a while. My partying at clubs ended at around the same time as my drinking binges at the dorm. Except that I never really went to clubs and now it's too late. You should go to clubs when you're young and handsome, and if I go in my present state—tired, old, and balding, it would be even worse than if I didn't go at all. I guess that I'm not meant to dance into the morning hours and pick up young women on the dance floor—all that's left for me are whores in provincial hotels and the TV in my room.

He lays down in bed and clicks the remote. He tries to find CNN—the hotel website boasted "satellite and cable television"—and ends up on a porno channel. A young woman with an enormous ass like Olga's and Dasha's is taking turns raptly sucking two cocks. A third one is inside her.

Why do they always show a bunch of men fucking one woman? I would have preferred two women and one man. He tries to picture himself in bed with Dasha and Masha. Or Dasha and Olga, or all three of them, and without finally figuring out if he finds these images gratifying or repulsive, he falls asleep. In his drunken dream, Nikita sees a vast, murky backwater, crayfish tangled up in the hair of drowned bodies, crab pincers, octopus tentacles, burbot whiskers, the mute mouths of fish and air bubbles . . . in a word, the most ordinary dream of a man with an aquarium business.

71.

NOT ENOUGH

"See how nice this is," Svetlana Makarovna says. "If it weren't for IKEA, you would never see your mother."

That's her joking. But in fact, she's mad at him. Nikita irritably shrugs from behind the wheel of his Toyota: he doesn't know what to say himself. Masha, Dasha, the business . . . no free time at all. But isn't it strange he doesn't have time to visit his own parents?

They bought some junk at IKEA—Nikita isn't sure why they needed to go to the one on Moscow Ring Road, but Mom says it's cheaper, more worthwhile.

That must be true. If you don't count his, Nikita's, time.

The people you love, Nikita thinks, are the time that you spend on them. When you're young, you believe you can love many people. But as you get closer to forty, you realize that you don't have time for everyone.

But Nikita knows that's not true. If he didn't have time, then why did he get himself a lover? He could have gone on living with Masha as he did before and had more time.

Yeah, about five hours more a week.

"Do you go to church?" Mom asks.

"I went not too long ago," Nikita answers, "why do you ask?"

"No reason, Vasya was asking the other day."

"Does he wants to explain to me that God doesn't exist?" Nikita sneers: he still remembers how his father told Grandpa Misha: *Don't be an obscurantist!*

"More like the opposite," Mom says. "And Nikita, while we're talking,

I also wanted to tell you. You should pay more attention to your father—you don't even know that he has thought a lot about God in the past three years! You know him: his whole life, he would laugh when your Grandpa Misha would bring up the great mysteries and mystical veils. And two years ago, when Yura Kochin died, you remember Yura?"—Nikita nods, although he hardly remembers him—"When Yura died, Vasya thought a lot . . . thought about different things. And one day, he comes to me with a popular science journal, you know, a review of physics, chemistry, history and literature, like *Science and Life*, you remember?" Nikita nods and says to her: "You know, Sveta, I read that water is a symbol of death. In every culture, wells, rivers, and deep-ends are all metaphors for death. Fairy tales talk about water to avoid directly talking about death. So I was thinking, what did Christ's walking on water mean? That he was more powerful than death? That he was stepping on it?"

"*Trampling it*," Nikita says. "Risen from the dead, trampling down death by death."

"Trampling," Mom agrees. "It's no coincidence that the ancient Roman symbol for Christ was a fish. Because Christ swims in death, He died and was reborn."

"That's beautiful," Nikita nods. "So what now, Dad wants to be baptized?"

"Well, he hasn't thought about it yet," Mom says, and Nikita wants to ask: what do you mean "yet"? When is he planning to think about it? And suddenly, he realizes that he, Nikita, will also be sixty-something one day and also think he has plenty of time. It's only now, at nearly forty, that he thinks life will be over at sixty.

"I heard a theory," Nikita says, "that water is the Holy Spirit. Because, well, in the beginning, the Holy Spirit flitted over the water and was reflected in it, which means that water is actually the reflection of the Holy Spirit."

"You know, I had an easier time with all this," Mom says. "My parents were Eastern Orthodox, they even baptized me in secret. Although I never went to church, I always remembered when Easter was, when Christmas was."

"But we never celebrated it," Nikita marvels.

"Well, at the time, Vasya thought it was all superstition."

Wow, Nikita thinks, I'm pushing forty, got baptized, and only now find out that my mother has been baptized since she was a child.

"Are the two of you coming over next week?" Mom asks after a pause.

"Sorry," Nikita says, "but I doubt it. Masha's checking into a hospital next week."

"Is it serious?" Mom asks.

"No, it's gynecology-related," Nikita replies, "she's only staying there for a day."

"I see," and Mom purses her lips. "At some point, you have to stop. I'm not saying it's a sin, but I think it's time you had kids."

At first, Nikita doesn't understand; then, he bursts out laughing:

"No, Mom, it's not at all what you think. Masha has never had an abortion. I mean, there are various modern methods . . . but I don't think any of my acquaintances have had abortions. Masha's going for a completely different reason, nothing critical, but definitely not an abortion."

Time is not the issue, Nikita thinks, it's just that I've arranged my life in such a way that none of the people I love can even have a normal conversation with me. I can't talk about Masha's problems, I can't talk about my affair with Dasha, I can talk about my business with some caution—but who would want to hear about it anyway? I should have married Kostya, I can talk to him about anything.

"I had one once," Mom says suddenly, "I had an abortion."

"Were you pregnant by Dad?"

"Of course. I've never had other men. And he had other women. And when I found out about his affair with what's her name . . . Lyolya, I was already pregnant. I didn't even tell him, just went ahead and got it. I took a day off work and that was that."

"How old were you?" he asks and Mom replies: *About thirty.* And Nikita thinks: younger than I am now! Oh yeah, I remember how, as a teenager, I was surprised that grownups had love affairs and heartaches too. And now I'm surprised that my father is interested in God and death at sixty years old. When else would he think about death other than in his old age?

"I never told anyone about this," Mom says, "but what difference does it make now? I was so disgusted back then—that Vasya had another woman, that he was lying to me, and that the doctors scraped my insides out . . . I couldn't forgive him for many years."

"Have you forgiven him now?

"Later, I thought: it seems kind of silly to live your entire life with someone you can't forgive for something that happened ten or fifteen years ago. You should either get a divorce or forget about it. So I forgot about it. Ultimately, I think we have a good relationship."

And in my childhood, Nikita thinks, I wanted a sibling. I probably still do, so I keep picturing Moreukhov or Anya-Elvira. Turns out that I could have had a little brother or a little sister if my dad hadn't stolen his own brother's girlfriend.

Nikita sighs and thinks with anguish: *Everything is wrong, everything is wrong, I have to arrange my life in a way that's different somehow, in a way that's better, more sincere, more honest.*

"I'll visit Dad," he says, "I promise."

"I know," Mom replies, slightly hurt, "but you never have time."

Fuck time, Nikita thinks, *time is not the issue: if only I had enough love*, and I think that's exactly how this conversation should end, because when any one of us—either me or Nikita or maybe even Anya-Elvira—when any one of us starts talking to our mother, all you can count on is love. Because, the whole time, you sense some sort of void, a gulf between you and her, and it makes no difference what you're *doing with your life*— drinking or making money.

Or is it a gulf between the mom you remember and the mom she's become, the gulf of time between Mom when she was young and her present self?

And I dare say we can all relate to this, Moreukhov thinks.

I think this is called: *there are times when we realize we are all one family.*

PART THREE
FAMILY VALUES

(1910s—1930s)

The real question children should ask is not 'what did you do with that time?' but 'what did that time do to you?'

Niall Ferguson

Olga Borisova
Born 1910, Grigoriy Borisov's wife
Lyolya's mother, Moreukhov's grandmother

Lidiya (Lida) Minskaya
Born 1905, Olga's sister and Moreukhov's great-aunt

Marfa Melnikova
Born 1914, Mikhail Melnikov's wife
Vasiliy and Sasha Melnikov's mother
Nikita's, Moreukhov's and Elvira's grandmother

Makar and Nastya Tikhomirov
Svetlana Melnikova's (Tikhomirova's) parents

Gulnara (Gulya) Takhtagonova
Born 1962, daughter of Djamilya Takhtagonova
Maternal half-sister of Tatyana (Tanya) Takhtagonova, Rimma's mother

72.

REINCARNATION: NIKOLAY

As I fall asleep, I hold Yan's hand, but even so—at night I dream of my lovers. Of men whom I've never been with. A boy from our Gymnasium, one year my junior, his wavy, flaxen hair sticking out from under his peaked Gymnasium cap; he was hit by an automobile right in front of my parents and governess. A Menshevik agitator with cracked eyeglasses, his thin voice breaking into a brief, shrill cry as the bullet blossoms into crimson rose petals on the breast of his jacket. A Red Army soldier in a dusty helmet leans silently over the dead body of a comrade captured by the White Cossacks, a five-pointed star carved into his back, powdered with salt and already more brown than red. A fifteen-year-old teenager screams through his tears: "Bastards, bastards!," his red hair drenched with sweat and clinging to his forehead, makes you want to run your hand over it. A stocky man, his temples just barely gray, looks back one last time before stepping onto that barge, the spark in his dark iris like a reflection of the light from the other bank.

As I fall asleep, I hold Yan's hand. His strong arm is overgrown with pale, tiny hairs, his nails are trimmed short, with funereal black edges. I kiss his fingers and imagine that the black, narrow strip is clotted blood, the curdled blood of those he ordered to be shot. I kiss his hand and think this is the hand of a man who separates life from death, who splits human lives in half, the hand of a man who is used to deciding for others whether they live or die.

My lips trail up his palm, glide along the veins of his forearm, and rise up to the curve of his elbow. When he clenches his fist, my lips grow as tense as a belt drive—and I can feel the blood flowing and the faint

thrusts as my lips continue their journey; and I kiss the armpits, the hair
infused with the odor of harsh military sweat—the sole islets of hair on
the body, if you don't count the thick copse by the base of the mighty
shaft that rises somewhere below. I forbid myself to think about this, I
glide my tongue down the bare chest, barely touching the nipples—and
at that moment, Yan's hand rests on my back and his nails begin to lightly
scratch my skin, always in the same spot, between the shoulder blades
and—even after who-knows-how-many reincarnations, I still freeze when
Nikita caresses my back like this—I freeze, then I tremble and my tongue
dashes down the narrow path between the rising ribs, traversing a raised
scar from a saber wound—"That bastard still managed to get me after I
gunned him down . . ."—and now I run my finger along the scar, imagining some White Army officer aiming his saber with the cold fury of
desperation, as my lips descend to the rose of the belly-button and Yan
places his palm on my temple, pushing me, guiding me, speeding up my
already irrepressible path. And then my hand tousles the fair hair—fair,
but darker than his moustache, darker than the locks that usually stick out
from under his peaked cap—and I draw spirals with my tongue, feeling
the great axis swell, rising higher and higher. And finally, I squeeze the
two spheres with my hand, open my mouth, and swallow the crimson
tip, inhaling the air with my quivering nostrils as if it's cocaine, moving
my head, feeling the heaviness of the palm on my temple, the firmness of
the member between my lips, the trembling of the testicles in my hand,
the quaking of a strong male body.

Over the course of my life, I discovered the taste of many male members. My tongue and palate have learned to discern teenage longing,
animal fear, vitriolic hatred, tremulous adoration, impatience, burning,
intense itching, haste, the pressure of unejaculated semen, the onslaught
of lust, and the convulsions of passion.

Yan tastes of gun grease and engine oil. Viscous and sticky, he makes
me shudder. I'm holding on to his testicles—so easy to pick up, so hard to
put down—and it feels like I have a gun barrel moving inside my mouth.
A large, almost toy-like gun barrel whose taste has become familiar to
many over the past few years. No, the enormous, heated barrel of an
artillery weapon, a component of a machine built for destruction, simply
awaiting your order and ready to fire a round.

I work faster and faster, my lips burn with a sweet pain—I press
against Yan with my entire body and from the depths of my heart, a
sacred word rises up, traverses my veins, flies up in my throat, opening my

mouth wider, bursting forth as a fierce, sorcerous command—Fire!—and at that moment, the thick stream of semen explodes in my head.

At a Scripture lesson at the Gymnasium, we were taught that the sperm die and give life to abundant fruit. Yan's semen is dead, stuck to my lips like a whitish plaque. The fruit it bears . . . it's beautiful, and tears stream down my cheeks. Then he takes his palm off my temple, sits up in bed, and brusquely pulls me closer. My sticky lips dig into his shoulder as his hand languidly grazes my back.

Then Yan begins to talk. He remembers the Civil War, the Kronstadt rebellion, the Antonov mutiny, counter-revolutionary plots. He tells me how his day went.

His day is filled with humdrum concerns. Making lists, dictating telegrams to Moscow, listening to reports, denunciations, interrogations, resolutions, decisions. These days, Yan hardly ever shoots anyone himself: "Let the others do some work," he says. When our liaison started, I asked him if he remembered how many people he'd killed, and he replied: "You don't count in battle, and when we were sinking barges, we certainly didn't count." Sometimes, I tell myself I am now weeping on the chest of a man who has killed countless people and my heart clangs like a hammer. I ask:

"Would you be capable of shooting me?"

"Of course," Yan grabs my shoulders, "of course I would be. I've shot men I've slept with before. They were traitors. I'm serving the Revolution and, as you know, Kolya, the Revolution does not forgive treason."

I don't ask him about the men he's slept with. I'm afraid that he doesn't remember them just as he doesn't remember the ones he has killed. I'm afraid of getting lost in a list that's as long as that of his executions.

I don't ask him if he has slept with women. The thought of it is unbearable: Yan with a woman, his mighty member plunging into musty, wet, human entrails. A woman's secretions are loathsome, like the rust that erodes the barrel of a weapon. I can't picture Yan's semen, the semen of death, flowing into a female womb, that nauseating source of new life.

I would have liked to forever grip Yan's member in my hand or squeeze it with my lips so that I could be certain that not a single drop of his semen would impregnate a woman. Small children are revolting, their cries a parody of the irrepressible cries of passion, their foul smelling diapers, prams, and bonnets a grim prophecy of the feebleness of old age, which I won't live to see.

One morning, I will see my member slumbering between my thighs like a weak worm. One evening, it will not be stirred at the sight of a nude male, it will stay shriveled and pathetic. That day, I will realize that old age has arrived. And I will ask Yan—because Yan will always be by my side, always be young—to add my name to the execution list and shoot me with his own hand, in memory of our love.

These days, Yan hardly ever participates in executions. "I'm saving bullets," he jokes. "But I do have one dream: to execute a countess. A real countess."

When he first told me this, I was frightened. I envisioned some sort of high society romance: Yan the little page boy, the countess he lusts after (or who lusts after him), the old count who reveals to him the secrets of same-sex love in the shadows of the conjugal bedroom, a female silhouette on the threshold, cries, hysterics, perhaps the police or a whipping at the stable, an oath to avenge himself, underground organizations, the Bolshevik Party, the revolution, war, the secret police, execution lists, my tears on his shoulder . . .

Yan put my mind to rest:

"You see," he said, "I've never seen a real countess. Only in films. I'd like to see how a countess behaves before she dies, how she dies, what color her blood is."

"Aristocrats have blue blood," I joked, but Yan didn't say anything back.

I saw his member grow tense again and, in a fit of jealousy, I squeezed it again, and Yan's nails dug into my back. Then, he opened my fingers and began to laugh:

"What, are you jealous? If you want, I can bring you along when we send her to Dukhonin at headquarters."

Since then, we spoke about it often. Yan's dream had become my dream. We would imagine all sorts of scenarios in which we'd find the countess: she would be a spy planted here by White émigrés in Paris; an aristocrat who had gone into hiding and waited out the revolution in some inconspicuous mansion; or one who was masquerading as a peasant or a student at a workers' school or a university. The day of the execution, she would be wearing a white lace dress and black laced-up, low-heeled ankle boots, holding a parasol in her hand. In our dreams, we would sometimes lead her down a brick corridor to the back wall and, at other times, out into the snowy Cheka courtyard (I know it hasn't been used for executions in a while, but in my dreams, for some reason I'd see her walking across this courtyard, stumbling in the snow); sometimes, we'd drive her out of town, to the shores of the Gulf of Finland. But even in my dreams

Yan didn't let me carry out the sentence myself—I only handed him the gun—and then, he'd squint his eyes and slowly cock the muzzle as the countess grew pale, opening and closing her parasol with trembling fingers or dropping it in the snow and shielding her face with her arms, on which she wore long, white, elbow-length gloves. And Yan would always say: *Good bye, countess!* The semen of death would erupt from the barrel, the white dress would turn red, soaked in blood—common, crimson blood, the same color as everyone else's whom Yan had executed.

His dreams didn't extend beyond that gunshot, but in mine, I'd get down on my knees before him, kiss the smoking muzzle of the revolver, and then carefully take another barrel in my mouth, loaded and ready to fire.

As I fall asleep, I hold Yan's hand and think: today, I felt as if Yan wasn't with me, as if he was thinking of something else, not even the Revolution—the austere virgin I've stopped envying a long time ago—but of another young man, perhaps a year or two my junior, a twenty-two-year-old Adonis with wavy, flaxen hair—and now, in my languor, I can see the three of us together; then, Yan goes off somewhere, my new lover kisses my lips, and at that moment, Yan's voice rouses me and I don't immediately understand what he says, but when I do, I squeeze his hand even tighter and finally awaken.

"I found her," Yan says, "I found the countess."

There was a joint meeting on combating gang violence that brought together the police, the Criminal Investigation Service, and the Joint State Political Directorate. When they finished, Yan went out in the street and saw a young woman. She stood leaning against the gate, nearly motionless, her whole figure permeated by a kind of bourgeois refinement, an old regime aristocracy. She seemed out of place here among the strong men in leather jackets. I should ask for her papers, Yan thought, but at that moment, an unknown Criminal Investigation Service operative ran up to the young woman, embraced her, and kissed her.

Yan walked off to the side so as not to attract attention and only then asked: *Who is that kissing that woman?* and heard a man's last name in reply.

Everything else was a mere formality. Yan made inquiries and found out who he was. A Civil War hero, a fighter against gang violence, a distinguished comrade. When it came to the girl, however, he had to do some digging. A university student—well then, Yan went to her department, checked her enrollment documents—everything was in order, she was a working woman, but her last name put him on guard. He went to the address where she lived with her mother and sister. *The revolutionary instinct did not deceive me,* he sneered. When he showed his mandate at the housing committee, they told him everything. She was a former aristocrat. She must have gone to work at the plant not too long ago to worm her way into the university. The janitor volunteered to show him where they had lived before—it turned outto be a private residence. And there, Yan couldn't believe his ears when he heard that they were *the wife and daughters of the late count.*

"I'll collect all the paperwork," he said, and I could feel his fingers tremble in my palm, "and file a report to Comrade Meyerson stating that, upon enrolling at the university, a representative of the exploitative classes had concealed her origins and, harboring criminal intentions, entered into a liaison with an employee of the worker-peasant militia. And that's a death sentence, believe me, Kolya—I know just how to write it."

I pressed my entire body against his, absorbing his trembling.

"Why didn't you say anything?" I whispered. "This is a gift for us."

"Yes," Yan said solemnly, "in time for the birthday of the Revolution."

The one-year anniversary wasn't until next week, but I understood that Yan was already counting the days to his *Good-bye, countess!* and that a crimson rose would blossom on a white dress.

He spoke of the Revolution's birthday as if the Revolution were a human being, a woman he was in love with. I loved that chivalry in him, that submissiveness, that sterility, the cold flame of an unearthly passion devouring him from the inside. To Yan, we were both lovers of the Revolution, and our intimacy was just an attempt to get closer to it so that, after the long years of war, we could replace the screams of those dying with cries of pleasure, and the leaden semen of the gun with the semen of our love drying on my lips.

In the morning, I watched Yan get dressed. He turned his back to me and I gazed at his buttocks, which were round and firm, at the scar between his shoulder blades, his broad shoulders . . . Tenderness, arousal, and shivers—I ran up and kissed his closely-cropped temple.

Yan smiled over his shoulder:

"Not now, Kolya, I have to go, and you ought to get going too."

Yes, I, too, went to work. It was a tedious post at a bureau—if I hadn't met Yan, my life would have been as bleak as the papers I shuffled. I despised my work, although Yan would say: *You, too, are serving the Revolution.*

I got dressed and wanted to go out with him, but Yan didn't wait for me.

"Are you hurrying off to see your countess?" I asked.

"Our countess," he smiled from the threshold.

I often think that these words were the greatest confession of love I received in my life, a beautiful epilogue to our romance, a final period to a series of nights redolent of semen and gun grease, the long nights that we split in half just as we split the Revolution, that stern Mother of God; just as we split the countess—the snow-white lamb doomed to be slaughtered in Her name.

In the evening, Yan didn't return. There were times he was held up till late, but he always informed me. After midnight, tormented by suspicion, jealousy, and fear, I ran across the entire city to the great Joint State Political Directorate building. I imagined an attempted arrest that met with resistance from counter-revolutionary conspirators, a senseless stray bullet, and bloody dew on a broad, hairless chest.

I asked the watchman if Yan was at his post and, in reply, heard: "Get lost, counter-revolutionary!"—an address rendered doubly frightening by the fact that it was uttered on the threshold of the JSPD. Perplexed, I wandered off and, when I turned the corner, heard an engine noise. The car stopped—a young man was sitting at the wheel. I recognized him— he'd dropped Yan off after a few nighttime operations.

"Are you Kolya?" he asked.

I nodded, hesitating to say: *Where is Yan?*—but he launched into a story without waiting for my question. Later, I thought that they, too, might have been lovers—there was sadness in the young man's voice and he told me the truth, which a JSPD employee was not supposed to tell a stranger unless, of course, nothing tied him to that stranger except for the nighttime street, the pre-dawn hour, and the dim light of streetlamps.

"We received an alert," he said, "it appears that Yan was previously associated with the Socialist-Revolutionaries and was currently preparing a terrorist act. A Criminal Investigation Service operative reported it—incidentally, during a police raid, some petty thief gave testimony in that regard."

"What is this nonsense?" I babbled. "Yan never associated with any thieves . . ."

"I don't know," the young man said, "as luck would have it, the thief was killed when he tried to escape. But the man from the Criminal

Investigation Service is such a distinguished comrade, a Civil War fighter, you can't not believe him. He spoke with Comrade Meyerson in his cabinet for two hours and Comrade Meyerson personally signed the arrest warrant."

In the labor camps, people sometimes recalled how they found out about their loved ones' arrests. They usually said: *we trusted it would all be sorted out and they would be freed.* When I heard this, I'd sneer ever so slightly. From that first night, I didn't harbor any illusions—I knew how this apparatus worked, I knew I would never see Yan again, I knew it was useless to go to Meyerson and tell him that the lover of said Criminal Investigation Service operative is a former countess and that he denounced Yan when he realized that Yan was on to her. Yes, I knew this was all useless. Useless and dangerous.

If there were roosters in Leningrad, they could have crowed thrice in a row that night. I renounced my love in an instant, said, "Well, Comrade Meyerson must know better," and, hunching over, walked toward the looming gray sunrise.

My love died even before the bullet entered Yan's closely cropped temple, at the very spot I kissed him for the last time. My love died—the one I loved couldn't sit in a chamber, couldn't answer the investigator's questions. He could only ask questions, only lock others up in chambers, affirming with his every gesture the great, life-giving force of a revolutionary death seething inside him like an inexhaustible fount, strengthening the roots of a mighty tree, filling with juices the sturdy trunk that swelled between my lips.

After Yan's disappearance, I was overcome with melancholy—as if the time had finally come for all the *post coitum tristia* our nights lacked. My dreams became bleak and desaturated, like sheets of a daily newspaper reporting on new achievements, new construction projects, and new enemies. I returned to my hopeless, lackluster existence, which became even more monochrome than before I met Yan. Even the youths and men didn't trouble me now—it was as if, in the depths of my soul, I found a secret inner courtyard where I put to death the very possibility of intimacy and love.

Once, toward morning, I dreamed of a young woman in white with a parasol in her hand and laced-up ankle boots. She was walking arm in arm with an unknown man in a leather jacket, and I had no doubt that this was the man who had murdered my love. I remembered the unbearable contrast between the white lace and the black leather jacket where their arms touched. The man seemed to have been about my age, with broad shoulders and a round head, shaved bald like many had in those years. He gazed at the young woman with tenderness, but as soon as he turned away, his eyes became two black circles, two endless tunnels, two rifle muzzles ready to be discharged.

I woke up and felt the forgotten taste of gun grease and engine oil on my lips. For the first time since Yan disappeared, I began to touch myself in solitude, rolling onto my back, closing my eyes, and grasping my stiffening member in my hand. I imagined Yan—his strong hands, his fingers overgrown with blond hairs, the scar on his back and the one on his belly, the thick veins on his forearms, his hairless chest, and the forgotten, harsh smell of military sweat—but the familiar features would fade and Yan's killer would imperiously peer through, as if Yan had turned into him, as if the killer was devouring him. And when the metamorphosis was complete, a thick stream gushed and fell with dead drops on my stomach.

The countess was a haze, a mirage, a Fata Morgana. A set trap, a temptation Yan couldn't overcome. The Revolution didn't forgive infidelity—its jealousy was far graver than my puerile kind. The promise of sacrificing this false lamb couldn't deceive it—in the secret order to which Yan and I belonged, there was no place for women—only Her. The passion that didn't belong to the Revolution could only be given to another man, as if to your reflection in the mirror, your double, your partner in the austere service to the cruel virgin.

I knew that, sooner or later, my turn would come. I'd pay for the dreams I shared with Yan, pay for our countess. I waited for many years and, when the time came, I signed the investigation protocol without reading it—but I didn't tell them anything about Yan, about our love, or about the sorcerous Fata Morgana who lured us into the perilous sea depths.

Sometimes I think that I haven't betrayed our love after all.

I expected them to execute me, but times had changed: the Revolution required slaves rather than sacrifices, and I was sent to a labor camp; I was sure I would die there. I could have died at this stage, in Siberia, at the colony, or after the second arrest, in the holding prisons in Dzhezkazgan and Vorkuta. Perhaps I didn't die because the death-infused semen that slid down my throat for so many nights had filled me with strength.

In 1956, I returned to Leningrad on the wave of Khrushchev's rehabilitations. I believe that Yan was rehabilitated too. I thought to myself: perhaps I could learn the name of the informant from the Criminal

Investigation Service, meet with him and gaze into his deep, dark eyes ... But I didn't look for him—what would I have done if I met him? In my dreams, I would sometimes kill him, sometimes make love to him, and often, at the critical moment, the countess's white phantom would come into the bedroom and watch us in silence while the mighty, round headed member went limp between my lips.

There was a time when I dreamed that a bullet—my lover's leaden semen—wouldn't give my flesh the chance to wither. I was twenty-four years old—and lived just as long after returning from Kazakhstan, although, again, I thought I would die soon. The memory of Yan, the memory of our love, the memory of the camp, the countess and her round-headed companion, of everything that happened over seventy-something years, wilted with time. I lived alone for almost my entire life—and in my old age, not even the phantoms of the past could disrupt my solitude.

I know I'll die this way. In solitude, in an empty apartment, in the summer of 1980, sixty-three years after the birth of the Revolution.

Death is a great deceiver, a haze, a Fata Morgana. There was a time when I dreamed of it, and over and over it would slip away. In the end, I gave up, grew weary, retreated.

And now it comes to me and I say to it: listen, I don't understand, why did I love you at all? In response, you press my old-man's fingers in your cold hand.

Is this what I fantasized about a half-century ago?

It's a pity you took so long that I'd almost forgotten how much I once loved you!

73.

DIDN'T WORK OUT

Nikita is dreaming that he's young and carefree again, maybe slightly intoxicated, sitting in a dark movie theater, barely glancing up at the screen, and is instead reaching his hand under his neighbor's skirt—in the dream, he can't tell if they know each other or not—in any case, his companion is willing, and now they are moving synchronously and in concert, and a few seconds before he cums, Nikita awakens, startled by an intense sense of shame.

Although, why shame? He had an erotic dream, could happen to anyone.

This is a Moreukhov-type dream, he thinks, as if I'm some kind of alcoholic, a freak with missing front teeth, mauling young women at a movie theater, can't even take them to a hotel—and that's when Nikita realizes it's a dream about him and Dasha, and it's not even the fact that they've had those kinds of movie dates, no. It's their whole affair that suddenly seems shameful to him.

Maybe it's because Masha checked into the hospital last night, said it's her *last attempt*, and he accompanied her, then almost drove over to Dasha's—thankfully, he restrained himself, went back home, and almost fell asleep by the television. He crawled into bed with his last bit of strength and in the morning, awoke from a *shameful* juvenile dream.

Fuck that—it was an ordinary dream. Take a shower and forget about it.

Nikita is sitting in the kitchen, sipping his coffee, and leafing through a book Dasha foisted on him a week ago, *The Egyptian Book of the Dead*. He didn't read it—but can at least leaf through it right now before he returns it. The two of them are having lunch today, he should call her and remind her about the ring, he keeps forgetting to pick it up. She should bring it with her.

Nikita is studying a picture: Osiris is judging a human soul. Before him are scales: in one cup—a heart, in the other—a small feather, and, next to it, a beast of some kind that looks like either a crocodile or a hippopotamus. The deceased, Nikita reads, must utter a so-called negative confession, a renouncement of all his possible sins, and if he lies, his heart will tip the scales and he'll be sent into the beast's maw. Ah, Nikita thinks, so it's neither a crocodile nor a hippopotamus, it's the Ammit monster, the devourer of souls.

So a *negative confession*, huh? Nikita skims the text: *I never caused harm to people. I never caused harm to beasts.* Yes, that's about right. I don't know about people, but I'm innocent before beasts. Even if you consider aquarium fish beasts. *I never raised my hand to the feeble.* No, I don't think I have. *I never committed an act that was vile to the gods.* I don't think so either, Nikita tells himself, and for some reason, remembers his dream. Well . . . hardly. *I never caused an illness.* No, I haven't, I haven't—and he thinks of Masha, who is in the hospital now, no, he's not to blame, whatever Masha says. *I was not a cause for tears.* Who among us hasn't caused tears? Of course I have. Masha cried, Mom must have too, I don't think Dasha has, but I'd like to say: "Unfortunately not." *I never killed. I never ordered to have anyone killed.* What a subtle distinction! No, I have never killed and have never ordered it, what's next? *I never brought anyone suffering.* Well, that's unlikely, every one of us has brought someone suffering, the ancient Egyptian hippopotamus would have eaten us all . . .

You know, Nikita thinks, the Egyptians were right: one sin is reason enough to be sent to Hell. I was a cause for tears and brought suffering—that means it's silly to brag that I never killed and never ordered to have anyone killed. Big deal! Our grandfathers killed in one war and our great-grandfathers in another. Grandpa Makar wrote a denunciation—that must be the *ordered to have killed*—and what? Who am I to give myself credit for never killing and never ordering to have someone killed?

It just didn't work out that way.

Nikita and Dasha are wrapping up lunch—they're drinking coffee and Dasha is smoking a hookah. The hookah is set up for both of them, but Nikita doesn't even touch the mouthpiece: he doesn't like hookah in general, and especially not in the middle of the workday.

Nikita is watching Dasha and thinking: with everything that's happening with Masha, he didn't even notice it was summer. Dasha is wearing a light tribal dress. Or rather, a pseudo tribal one: real tribal dresses don't have necklines cut like this. Reach out your hand, tug at the edge and one of the nipples is bound to pop out—both, if you're lucky. For a second, Nikita thinks he won't be able to contain himself and really does reach for her breasts.

Dasha fixes her dress with a careless gesture and throws Nikita a flirtatiously indignant look.

When they're together, Nikita likes to pretend that he's a young, boorish idiot—it's dead easy for him to put his hand down a woman's top, pinch her hip, or make out with her in front of everyone.

Dasha's hair is continuing its slow regrowth. She keeps patting the tender bristles on her temple, showing Nikita her smoothly shaven armpit. Nikita recalls the scent of sweat and the slight prickling on his tongue of hair that, no matter how much you shave it, always grows back. He thinks he can smell Dasha's deodorant. When they make love, Dasha peels this scent off last—after her dress, her lingerie, and her jewelry; it vanishes just before she orgasms, when her body ejaculates sweat, rivulets flow down her flesh, and a triumphant, guttural wailing swells somewhere deep inside her.

Nikita looks away. At the table next to them are three teenagers only slightly younger than Dasha. Two girls and a boy. Nikita doesn't understand teenagers at all, can't even tell if what they're wearing is trendy, expensive, or conventional. Are they friends or are they dating? He can't even tell if the girls would be considered beautiful or not. *They're like aliens to me*, thinks Nikita, *and Dasha, too, though I love her. My love has vanquished outer space, like at the end of Alexey Tolstoy's* Aelita.

The teenagers giggle as if they've read his mind. Maybe they really are laughing at him?

Dasha grips the mouthpiece with her lips; Nikita sees them strain and a warm wave immediately rises from his crotch straight to his heart.

"You know," he says, "I was thinking: when I was . . . twenty-something, if I saw a man with a young woman, I was certain that he'd bought her. In exchange for his money, his influence, doesn't matter. At the time, I wouldn't have believed you could selflessly love a forty-year-old man."

"I love you," Dasha says and inhales. Dasha's *I love you*s always sound poignantly careless, as if she's saying: *I love Balkan and Celtic music, I love you, I love Chinese food and sometimes Japanese, but not sushi.*

"But why? I'm bald, old, unhip, and unattractive. I'm not even very wealthy, to be honest."

Dasha takes the mouthpiece out of her full lips and exhales a wispy cloud. From under a veil of smoke redolent of an Arabic quarter, he hears:

"My mom taught me that only morons hassle young women with questions like that."

"I know," Nikita says. "But it'll be the the first time. And the last."

The little cloud dissolves in the air, Dasha raises her eyebrows, gently bites her lower lip, and sighs:

"Okay, fine. I don't take money from you, and I can pay rent on my own, split it with a girlfriend or someone. To be honest, it's not that expensive. I'll find a better job, in the end. And influence? What would I do with your influence? Work as an aquarium cleaner?" She brings the mouthpiece to her lips again and closes her eyes.

She's teasing me! Nikita thinks with spite and tenderness.

Dasha is still inhaling the hookah. She seems to be at a loss. Like, what if she says something dumb as a joke and Nikita gets all worked up? Is this necessary? Boy was her mom right on account of morons.

"I honestly don't know," Dasha says, concealed by a fog. "Sexwise, everything is fine, good, even. But—how do I put it so you won't get mad? It's just good. Nothing extraordinary. My mom also warned me about that—only idiots talk to men about this. I guess I'm having that kind of day—forgetting my mom's lessons."

"No big deal," Nikita replies, "if the sex is good, you can tell me. But if it's bad, you should either say nothing or lie."

He says it and freezes: what if Dasha had lied?

"The sex is good," Dasha nods, "but that's still not why. At first, I must have been flattered—a mature, wealthy man who could find himself a glamourous model, and he's fucking me? It's good for my self-esteem. But my self-esteem is pretty good anyway, so that's not the main reason."

"I see," Nikita says, and thinks: she doesn't know why and you're pestering her! What do you want to hear? Maybe you'll give her a clue? Help her pass the exam?

"Oh, I remember," Dasha perks up. "The first time, I was curious. I wondered how grown-up men fucked. Maybe they knew some secrets."

"I don't know any," Nikita says, and sweat seeps from his armpits: the completely unerotic, sticky, shameful sweat of fear and confusion. *I'm as nervous as a boy*, he thinks.

"Also, how should I put it?" Dasha continues. "I'll say what I'm thinking, but don't get mad, okay? Keep in mind I mean it in the best way possible!"

And she wags her finger as if trying to be playful, but Nikita looks at this finger in complete seriousness: dark, almost black nail polish, a few massive silver rings stacked so tightly they could neither be budged nor pulled off.

"Well, to put it simply, you're funny. Funny in a good way, with a sense of humor. You don't take yourself too seriously, don't get mad about little things. And funny because you genuinely don't know anything that everyone else knows. About the music that's in right now, about night-clubs, drugs, blogs or how to send an MMS. You haven't even read the books that everyone else has! I have to explain a million things to you— it's like I'm raising a younger brother: I lend you books, play music for you, just wait until I take you to a nightclub."

"So you like that I'm ignorant and uncultured!" Nikita says and knows this isn't the end, Dasha has a list as long as an Egyptian scroll—an inventory of Nikita's virtues that Kostya, Victor, Natasha, his mom and dad—and even Masha—would all find both odd and unnecessary—in a word, virtues that are useless to everyone except the girl sitting across from him. A ball of poplar fluff is caught in her stubbly hair; it reminds him of a hedgehog with an apple stuck to its spines. Her eyes are thickly lined— she wears so much mascara that her bed linen is perpetually covered in splotches, the surrealistic sketches of Dasha's dreams. And sometimes, the black-and-white graphics of passions, embraces, and convulsions.

Today, his arousal is mixed with trepidation about Masha's surgery and his talk with Dasha. What if she ruins everything right now? Even his arousal is bothering him, but today, every single one of Dasha's gestures brings a wave of memories. He wants to reach out and touch her, move closer to her, press against her, not give a damn about propriety—cap-ture, captivate, carry her off—wherever—to the car, to the restroom, to the nearest hotel . . . and there, to finally hear the deep, guttural sound he's missed so much. To hear it and keep moving as the sighs and moans pass through Dasha's body.

Or maybe Nikita is sorry he asked the question, and is even prepared to undress Dasha in the middle of the restaurant just to avoid hearing her main reason.

"You don't know anything," Dasha replies, "but you believe that every-thing I say is fucking cool. Even when you don't feel like looking into it, you still take my word that it's awesome. For instance, you don't say:

your Coelho is bullshit—I mean, I know you don't like Coelho, but you don't think he's bullshit."

To be honest, I do, Nikita thinks, but now, I definitely won't admit it. Grandpa was right when he said: hold your tongue and you'll pass for intelligent.

Nikita nods without taking his eyes off of Dasha's full lips, which again grip the mouthpiece of the hookah, sucking lightly on it. Then, Dasha slightly puffs up her cheeks, which are covered with a light, almost imperceptible fuzz, like the skin of a peach if you run your hand down them.

"You don't think Coelho's bullshit and when I tell you something, you listen. Adults rarely listen. My parents never do. My grandma listens, but I can't tell her everything. And with you, I can talk about anything— well, almost."

What does she mean—almost? In any case, I don't need an explanation: she can't talk to me about boys, about her peers, about sex with somebody else. And I'd rather she not talk to me about love either. I have to admit, I don't know the last thing about love.

"You listen," Dasha repeats and adds, smiling: "Or at least you pretend to."

No, Nikita thinks, I'm not pretending, I really am listening, but you don't know what I'm listening to. Because I'm not listening to the words, but to the intonation. The timbre of your voice. Its inflexions. I listen to—and watch—the quiver of your lips, the silver flash of your tongue, the change in the contours of your cheeks. I look at your hands, I notice the way the nail polish lays down on your fingernails. If you have a bruise, I watch it heal. I watch your fingers move: there's your thumb rubbing your index finger, there you are deep in thought with your fingers interlaced, and now, you're waving your hand in the air. And when you're naked—that's when I love talking to you the most—when you're naked, I observe the movements of your body. Every word is the work of your entire body. You fill your lungs with air, your breasts rise, your shoulders straighten, your belly swells . . . a moment goes by and, as you exhale, the word flies away, your breasts fall, slightly swaying, and your shoulders droop, your stomach flattens . . . Your parents will never look at you this way, you understand.

As soon as Nikita thinks *parents*, he remembers Masha. Will they listen to their own children, will they have someone to listen to if they stay together? Will they stay together at all if Masha doesn't get pregnant today? If she never gets pregnant?

"What am I, an improved version of your parents?" he says to Dasha.

"Don't be stupid, what do my parents have to do with it?" Dasha retorts and he can see her shoulders flinch, the folds of her dress come into motion and a quickly-fading wave run down the curve of her breasts—and in this quavering, Nikita reads her unsaid words: *Before you asked, it had never even occurred to me, but it could be true—only I don't like this truth at all, this gross, cheap Freudianism!*

Nikita thinks: It's funny, when I was a kid, I thought it would be great to learn to read minds. It turned out to be quite simple. I can't do it with everyone, but that's for the best. Otherwise, it's easy: you just have to love someone so much that their words and flesh become indistinguishable.

"I also realized," Dasha continues, "that you respect me. Unlike . . . the other, younger guys, the twentysomethings. Maybe all older men are like this, I don't know, or maybe it's just you—I've never been with any other . . . men your age."

When Dasha stammers, her gaze changes. For a second, it's as if her eyes lose focus, stop seeing Nikita, and stare out into space. He likes such moments—moments when she loses touch with reality. When Dasha orgasms, her entire body loses touch with reality and, in those few seconds, it exists entirely for itself, by itself—just like her eyes during an unexpected pause. Every one of Dasha's pauses is a tiny orgasm. Devoid of pleasure, localized in her eyes.

"Like, I'll date some boy," Dasha continues, and her cheeks grow slightly flushed (*she's embarrassed—only slightly—but embarrassed*, Nikita realizes), "anyway, that boy calls me at night, throws jealous fits, asks what I was doing while he was at his mom's, who I met up with when he was out getting drunk and wasn't answering his cell phone. Long story short, gross."

Dasha gesticulates as if she's stuck her finger in a dead jellyfish and is flicking its gelatinous body back into the sea. *When did she date this infantile jackass?* Nikita thinks.

"And another boy will do the opposite and disappear for a week, even though we had plans to call each other the next day! And it's not like he's busy—he's already passed his finals and isn't leaving for Crimea till next month—what is he busy with? On the other hand, you're a married man—I'm sorry I'm telling you this. You can't always call me. You can't always pick up the phone either, you have your family and all that. But this guy lives alone, doesn't have anything to do, doesn't answer his cell phone and then—hey!—like nothing happened, drop everything and come over, Dasha, I miss you."

Dasha's voice reverberates with the dull rumblings of irritation. Nikita lowers his eyes to the smoky vessel of the hookah pipe—he doesn't feel like looking at Dasha and seeing how jealous she is, so as not to recognize the distant echo of the tremors that shook her body when she was with these other men.

"I think that if a man acts this way, he doesn't respect the girl. You always ask: are you free? Can you talk? Can you meet up tomorrow morning? Can I come to your place at such-and-such a time? And you're renting an apartment for me just so you can come over whenever it's convenient for you. But you still ask."

Nikita raises his eyes: Dasha is smiling, he heard this smile and knows that, between her full lips, he'll see the glinting white of her teeth, slightly smeared with dark-red lipstick.

"I don't know," Nikita says, "I just ask to be polite. Doesn't everyone?"

And immediately remembers that no, of course not. At twenty-five he, too, behaved like Dasha's friends. That's funny, Nikita thinks, there they are, the advantages of middle age. It turns out young women put out for well-mannered men who know how to listen. That's all there is to it. If I had known earlier, I would have lived my life differently.

In any event, no: if I had lived my life differently, I probably wouldn't have learned to listen and respect.

He raises the hookah: behind the glass are murky clouds of smoke like a trapped genie.

Remove the stopper, set him free, make a wish—what do you want? You don't know yourself. To sleep with Dasha right this second? To continue observing for many years how her body, with its guttural moan, loses touch with reality? Or do you want everything to work out for Masha today, after all? For the two of you to have children, or for Masha to stop wanting children—but above all, for her to stop sitting in the dark, losing weight, and talking to phantoms? Or do you want your business to grow, your profits to rise—and let the money help fulfill your other desires? Or do you wish that moment when the red maple leaves and the barely-perceptible bruise on the young girl's skin briefly opened you to the beauty and vulnerability of the world had lasted forever? Do you wish for your youth to never end? To love old age when it comes? Or to see in every human being, in everybody, what you've uncovered in Dasha? Harmony and beauty, the possibility of loving, the need to be loved? Or, when the time comes, to come clean before Osiris and read out a long list and not have been a cause for tears, to not have brought anyone suffering, or have harmed anyone, or have removed any weight from the scales or added any? Or—the hell with the Egyptian list, you're Eastern Orthodox, after all! The Ten Commandments, how did they go: Thou shalt not make unto thee any graven image, Thou shalt not kill, Thou shalt not steal, Thou shalt not commit adultery . . . And to wish for all ten commandments to be easy to obey, without wanting to violate any of them.

In short, what you wish for is not to violate any commandments, not to divorce Masha, and to leave Dasha. It's unlikely that any genie will accept such a wish.

Then again, soldiers are allowed to kill in wartime—so maybe the genie will pray for your personal reprieve from the Seventh Commandment? Just for Dasha, not for any other girls? On the other hand, what could a Muslim genie obtain by entreaties from the Eastern Orthodox Christ? Let him entreat Allah—in that case, there isn't much to ask for, three wives would be overkill, two are enough. Perhaps you should suggest to both of your beloved to convert to Islam?

Nikita puts the hookah down on the table and says:

"Smoke on the water."

"Sure," Dasha replies. To her, this is an ordinary English phrase. In general, Dasha cares as little about Deep Purple—the music of the old farts—as Nikita does about the young people's Coelho.

Classic rock just never caught on with the younger generation, what can you do?

Nikita pays the bill and suddenly says:

"Listen, the fact that I love you, does it matter to you at all?"

For a second, Dasha freezes, passes her hand along the bristles on her head (the poplar fluff is gone, the scent of her deodorant is even sharper, and, once again, Nikita gets shivers down his spine), bites her lower lip like at the start of the conversation, and then, decisively tossing her head (setting her dress in motion, her breasts swaying in that low décolletage), replies:

"Well, it used to matter to me whether you loved me or not. Up until this winter. And then I realized that our affair is so non-committal—you love me a little bit, I love you a little bit . . . It's easier and even nicer that way. And more convenient. If we don't overdose by accident . . . You know it yourself: it's exhausting when somebody loves you intensely."

"Why?" Nikita asks.

Dasha shrugs:

"The way you looked at me today, I would have preferred that you'd gone ahead and fucked me. It was a typical love overdose. But usually, your love is just the right amount . . . although I'd be totally satisfied with a regular friendship. Benefits optional." And she smiles.

Nikita forces himself to smile back:

"It's too bad I keep failing at regular friendships," he says bitterly. "For now, at least."

"Don't worry about it. Maybe you'll get there," Dasha replies, still smiling. "With somebody else or maybe even with me. Worst-case scenario—in another lifetime. We're not doing too badly in this one, right?"

Or rather, not too terribly, Nikita thinks, and says suddenly:

"What if I asked you to move in with me?"

"You mean, you'd divorce your wife?" Dasha asks. "That's a bit too unexpected . . ."

Her face conveys astonishment and alarm, and Nikita quickly adds:

"I just asked out of curiosity." And Dasha smiles at him radiantly, the silver barbell flashing in her mouth, her hand patting Nikita's cheek.

Good thing Dasha can't read minds, read unspoken words, Nikita thinks. Too bad she can't and won't ever be able to. With me, anyway.

They share a brief, fleeting kiss, but as soon as Dasha pulls back her lips, four words surface in her mind: *it didn't work out.*

What does it mean—it didn't work out, she thinks when she is already outside, what *didn't work out?* A great lunch, good hookah, soulful conversation . . . and in general, Nikita is terribly sweet. I'll give him a Coelho book—he should at least read *The Alchemist*, it's a classic.

She goes down to the Metro, mulling over where she should go tonight, whom she should call, whom she should meet up with, since the weather's so fine, summer and sun, and not everyone's left town yet, she's standing on the platform, scrolling through the contacts list on her cell phone . . . and in her head, a haunting thought, the clicks of a metronome, the ticking of a clock, unwarranted, meaningless, and from out of nowhere: *it didn't work out, it didn't work out, it didn't work out.*

74.

BEYOND THE HORIZON

Anya was at the shoe store when Andrey called her and said: "Listen, since you have nowhere to send Gosha, what the hell, let's all three of us go!" She was just on her way to fetch another pair of sandals for a blonde customer with the proclivities of a first-class bitch and the looks of a second-rate model. Anya carried these boxes with her phone pressed to her ear, and when she heard: *What the hell, let's all three of us go*, the corners of her lips began to stretch outward on their own. And that's how Anya returned to the leggy customer: boxes in hand, neck tilted to the side, cell phone about to hit the floor—and a grin from ear to ear. The blonde looked at Anya with suspicion, then smiled back warily. Anya immediately tightened her lips: seriously, what am I smiling about? It could all be canceled ten times over. We might not get our visas or whatnot.

It wasn't canceled. And it turned out they didn't need visas, only vacation packages and plane tickets—all you had to do was pay. "How much are the packages?" Anya asked. Andrey replied either brusquely or self-consciously: "What difference does it make, I'm treating you both."

I'm used to paying for myself, I'll pay you back, Anya wanted to say, but said nothing. Why argue when she didn't have the money anyway? Or maybe she was touched by the "I'm treating you both."

Andrey asked for a hotel where *there weren't many Russians*, and there were in fact almost no Russians there, but there were Germans drunkenly belting out songs, Poles getting drunk right after breakfast, and teenagers from provincial France who behaved so audaciously that, by the end of the third day, Anya had forgotten about her Tatar roots and became a Russian patriot. Granted, Andrey said it was because she'd never stayed at a hotel with Russians before. Anya laughed—it was strange to hear herself talk like that, since she was so used to saying, "The whole world will belong to us Asians," and in Turkey, she was suddenly Russian.

On the whole, she became completely different: satisfied, calm, almost happy. You could even say almost wealthy—you had to pay for things at the hotel with a special plastic card. Of course, Anya still looked at the prices and chose whatever was cheapest, but when you had to sign receipts rather than dig into your wallet, it was easier to forget you didn't like it when men paid for you.

You only needed cash for souvenirs, which you could buy in the tourist shops that lined both sides of the dusty asphalt road that passed through their resort. In one of the shops, Anya met a Russian cashier and they chatted for close to ten minutes about the job, the pay, and whether people were more inclined to spend money at home or on vacation. Anya thought to herself: at this moment, I can't even imagine that there's a Moscow and a shoe store where I work forty-eight weeks out of the year.

Andrey didn't forget about his job: he spent an hour at the internet café every evening. This was called *I'm going to go check my email.*

"And what'll happen if you don't read this email of yours on vacation?" Anya asked. "Are they going to fire you?"

"Of course not," Andrey answered, "but we're launching a big project and I entrusted it to Grisha, who's not particularly familiar with it. I'm worried."

Andrey sat at the internet café for an hour and Anya took an hourlong swim in the sea. Of course, they spent practically all day by the sea—with the exception of those three hours when the sun was so hot that no sunscreen could save them, the three of them were usually splashing together by the shore.

But for an hour, Anya swam out on her own and swam the way she liked to.

The first time, she was scared: what if she had forgotten everything after so many years? But ten minutes in, she felt like she was fifteen again, her arm cutting the water, barely making a splash, the little streams running down her face the way they once did, her body cleaving the waves, inhale—exhale, inhale—exhale. Instead of chlorine, the air smelled of salt, seaweed, and sun-warmed skin. Inhale—exhale, inhale—exhale, in time with the waves, in time with the Mediterranean Sea, the new rhythm of thirty-year-old Anya. Inhale—exhale, inhale—exhale, she couldn't stop, she swam farther and farther out and; back on shore, Andrey could hardly distinguish the little black dot among dazzling blue specks.

"Can you see Mom?" Gosha asked.

"I don't think so," Andrey said, "but don't worry, she just swam out very far."

"Very far?" Gosha asked.

"Beyond the horizon."

Gosha asked what a horizon was, Andrey explained it, and then they tossed pebbles into the sea trying to reach the horizon; afterward, Anya's wet, black-haired head emerged over the waves, and you could see her arms go up and down—inhale—exhale, inhale—exhale; then, Anya herself came out on shore—wet, salty, and happy.

In the evening, the two of them sat on the balcony gazing at the southern stars, listening to the thumping of the nightclub, and drinking smuggled rakia—those cheap Turks didn't allow outside food and drink in the hotel. They even had to sign a paper stating that they acknowledged this rule. Anya was outraged and Andrey explained: that's how it worked in Turkey if the hotel wasn't all-inclusive. But the all-inclusive was too expensive for three, I didn't have enough money, he added, as if apologizing.

So they're drinking the rakia—abominable stuff, Dimon brought it over once many years ago, when he still wasn't afraid of drinking with me—they're drinking rakia and Andrey tells her that today, when Anya swam out, he dreamt up a tale: if a young woman swims *beyond the horizon*, she will turn into a mermaid. Instead of legs, she will grow a tail as scaly as a fish's. And in order to return to shore, she would have to find a sea witch or say, an underwater sorcerer—a mere technicality—to get her legs back.

"Did you tell Gosha that?" Anya was horrified.

"Are you kidding me? Of course not," Andrey said, "*he'd get scared.*"

He wouldn't get scared, Anya thinks, it'd be worse: he'd jump into the sea to save me. To battle sea monsters so they would give me back my legs.

Good thing I turned back before I reached the horizon, before I exchanged my legs for a mermaid's tail.

Her legs ache a bit, and Anya puts them across Andrey's knees. His hand slides slowly upward and she wags her finger:

"Don't even think about it! Gosha's sleeping in the bedroom and everyone at the hotel will see us on the balcony."

"The bathroom?" Andrey offers.

Anya replies . . . in any case, it doesn't matter what Anya replies. Hundreds of kilometers up north, a sober and cross Moreukhov is imagining this scene. Maybe I should draw a comic? he thinks. Or write a rap song? This is turning out to be crap anyway—how could Andrey, that office rat, make up a story about mermaids? It's the plot of *The Big Blue* in reverse—that only a woman who is ready to swim well beyond the horizon and doesn't have a child waiting onshore can become a mermaid. And Anya-Elvira has already missed her chance—if she'd gotten here four years ago, she would have been a splashing mermaid in the underwater kingdom right now. Corals in every color of the rainbow, jellyfish, seahorses, brisk, colorful fish. Let Kostya fill in the remaining details for my brother, he went diving, he knows.

I, for one, know that the underwater world is completely different. Rotten, slimy snags, crawfish pincers digging into your flesh, the bloated corpses of the drowned, and sneaky, clinging tentacles, H. P. Lovecraft's emanations of terror.

Maybe if my sister grew a tail, she would have met me down there, underwater, met me and saved me.

75.

1920. 7, OR NOT ABOUT LOVE.

It was the fourth year of the revolution and Grisha still hadn't seen a single dead body. Of course, this couldn't have gone on forever.

Grisha attached himself to the troop in late September 1920. He was hungry and counted on dying.

He was saved by Yuliy Brysov, a bald, hulking man from Bessarabia with large hands and an unforgettable gait.

Early in the next century, the trendy *Marquee* magazine would hail this gait heron-like.

There was always a freshly whittled toothpick sticking out of Brysov's mouth or, at the worst, a blade of grass.

Grisha remembered that toothpick quite well. It was the first thing he saw when Brysov leaned over him.

"Do you want to eat?" Brysov asked.

"Will you feed me?" Grisha asked.

Just after the revolution, his parents moved from Moscow to Vologda to live with a grandmother thrice removed. In 1918, this was where all the embassies had been transferred—as far as possible from the front line and the capitals.

Embassies meant bread and rations. Grisha's mother found a job as a typist and was able to feed the entire family.

In 1918, there was still bread in Vologda. In Petrograd, people fainted of hunger in the streets and, in Moscow, cannons bombarded Ostozhenka Street.

Six months later, the embassies began to leave Vologda.

Grisha's mother got herself a French passport—just in case. No one knew how she'd finagled it. His mother was a beautiful, black-haired woman. Grisha's father adored her.

In 1919, they returned to Moscow, where they learned that Grisha's grandfather, his mother's father, had been sentenced by the Revolutionary Tribunal and executed by firing squad.

Grandpa was a hereditary military officer, but retired from service before the war.

Early in 1920, Grisha's parents decided to break through to the White Russians in Crimea.

We've all seen the carnival ride with the large, spinning disc and a centrifugal force that flings people out to its edges. People laugh and try to hold hands with each other. They laugh because you're supposed to laugh at a carnival.

The Russian Revolution was like this disc, and it flung people to the edges of the former empire. Few of them laughed—most cried or cursed.

Grisha lost his family on a railway passage. The crowd almost trampled him to death, but he found his way out.

It's hard to keep holding hands like that.

Grisha never saw his parents again and never learned what happened to them. For some time, he harbored the hope that they'd escaped to Constantinople or Paris. But, after many years, he brought himself to believe that they were gunned down by the Bolsheviks.

This belief vindicated him.

Autumn 1920 found Grisha in Pryazovskaya Steppe. With teeth gritted, he headed on foot to Crimea.

He didn't wish to stay in Russia because he didn't believe in it. Russia seemed vast and meaningless to him. He couldn't fathom it.

It's hard for a fifteen-year-old boy to fathom a big country

Brysov fed Grisha a hearty soup and gave him a fatty chunk of pork. "Where's the pig from?" Grisha asked. "We confiscated it," Brysov answered.

Nobody knew what Brysov's military title was. It appeared he had proclaimed himself commander of the troop, and nobody objected to this.

These were the remains of a White Army landing party that touched down in Northern Tavria in the summer of 1920. Now they were in the midst of a forced march to Crimea.

It was rumored that they had to hurry because the Reds would capture the peninsula any day now, and then shoot or drown every White Army officer and soldier.

In the meantime, there was still about a month left before the storming of Perekop, so the only valid rumor was the one about the fate of the White Army.

In any case, General Wrangel's approach to executions didn't differ much from General Frunze's.

There were only six men in Brysov's troop, including himself.

"Do you know how to shoot?" Brysov asked. "No," Grisha replied, "but I can learn." "I'll teach you, if I have the time," Brysov promised.

After three days of marching on horseback down the deserted autumn steppe, Brysov's troop came to Kallaskoye Village. Brysov picked an empty barn, stationed a sentinel out front, and ordered everyone to go to sleep.

Early in the morning, three peasants approached the barn. They were dressed in patched-up clothes, but their eyes were serious and intent.

Without removing the toothpick from his teeth, Brysov got up to greet them. "Hello, fellows," he said.

The peasants whispered among themselves and asked: "Who is in charge here?" Brysov answered: "I am," and, for thirty minutes, the four men discussed something in hushed tones. Then the peasants left, and Brysov, pensively picking his teeth, said: "It will be as you decide."

The soldiers surrounded him. Brysov told them that, yesterday, some local gang dropped in and did a bit of looting, then tried to rape the elder's daughter. The oldest son had taken a pitchfork and run it through the rapist's throat just as the latter was pulling down his trousers.

The dead man was left lying there, trouserless and impaled.

The other bandits rode away and promised to return in two days, but, before they left, one of them had managed to empty his gun into the elder's son.

"And what about the rest of the peasants?" Pilsky asked. He was a large man with a broad chest and long arms. Grisha heard he had been a cavalryman during the war. He was the only one in the whole troop who carried a saber—everyone else carried firearms, mostly ones they'd confiscated or captured in the August clashes.

"The people are keeping quiet," Brysov answered. "Or, rather, the people have come to ask for our aid and protection."

"Who is this gang?" asked Fomin, a young officer with a delicately curled moustache. "The Reds, or, maybe, our men?"

"They don't know," Brysov said. "The bandits call themselves Wolves."

"Yuliy, you want us to get involved?" Fomin asked. "Why? Why should we protect these peasants? They're just like the ones who burned down our estates and raped our sisters. Rabble."

Brysov shrugged and spat the chewed-up toothpick onto the dusty ground. "Let everyone have his say," he said. "Anyone who so wishes can go talk to the people. Group meeting in an hour."

"Yuliy Borisovich," Grisha asked, "do you think we should stay?"

"I am an officer," Brysov said, "I gave an oath to the Tsar. And now there is neither a Tsar nor an oath, and everyone must decide for himself what to do. You, too, must decide if you're staying or going."

There were about twenty yards in the village, and the five soldiers took the whole hour to visit them, asking the owners questions and figuring their reward. Afterward, they met back at the barn.

"I spoke to these peasants," Pilsky said, "Fomin is right. I asked: 'who burned down the Manor House three versts away?' And they shake their beards and say: 'Surely it was the Bolsheviks, who else?'"

"Yes, yes," Fomin nodded, "we'll leave and they'll tell the next gang: these Whites have killed all your people, it's not our fault."

Belousov was the oldest in the troop, with a gray, leonine head of hair. He stood up and began to speak.

He knew that when a person speaks standing up, others listen to him differently.

"These peasants," Belousov said, "they've always lived here and will go on living here. The Whites will pass through, the Reds, and many others who don't have a designated color, and, what's more, they'll shoot, and they will all pass through—but Kallaskoye will remain. The peasants will always win. And these peasants or their children will go on living here under the Bolsheviks, under the All-Russian Constituent Assembly, and under Makhno. Because they've got nowhere else to go: it's their village, they were born here, and they will die here.

"And we'll go to Paris or Constantinople because Wrangel won't be able to hold down Crimea and we don't want to die.

And that's why we will leave and never lay eyes on Russia again. So we must do everything in our power for her in the next few weeks, before we board a steamship.

It's hard to do anything for Russia from Paris. The distance is too great.

The only thing we can do, then, is save these peasants.

Their lives are worth more than ours, and I consider it an honorable exchange."

Belousov finished and sat down, and a man in a leather jacket stood up.

Grisha never learned his name: everyone simply called him "the Mechanic."

A man's craft changes him.

A machine changes a man more than anything else.

As such, we should call people by the names of their professions.

For example, Belousov was a powderman.

The Mechanic got up and said: "I'm not concerned about peasants—peasants grow bread and I love cars.

"I'm not concerned about Russia because a car engine is assembled the same way in Paris and Constantinople as it is in St. Petersburg and Moscow.

"But one of the peasants had an Mk-V standing in an empty hen-house, and I've always wanted to see it in action."

The Mk-V is an English armored vehicle. It accelerates up to 8 kilometers an hour and has an armor of up to 16 millimeters in thickness.

It has a special tank engine known as Ricardo, and a Wilson planetary four-speed gearbox.

The Mechanic was eager to take the tank out for a spin, but didn't know there was no gasoline in the village, which rendered the vehicle useless.

In any case, there was also a Hotchkiss machine gun in the Mk-V. It even had a few belts.

Don't ask me what an armored vehicle was doing in Kallaskoye Village, or why the gang they planned to use it against hadn't taken it for themselves.

Perhaps the Wolves hadn't suspected there could be anything useful in the henhouse.

I'll go ahead and tell you that the peasants found another machine gun and a stockpile of explosives. In any case, after so many years of war, it was the least you could expect to find in a thriving village.

As the Mechanic spoke, another member of the troop, a man of about thirty with a military bearing, whispered with Brysov about something. The man's name was Orlovsky, and he was informally considered Brysov's second-in-command.

Orlovsky said: "I'm also staying," and sat down in his place.

Next, it was Fomin's turn. He twirled his moustache for a bit and said: "Gentlemen, you'll laugh at me, but I, too, am staying."

"Has your opinion of the peasants changed?" Pilsky asked.

"No, but my opinion of peasant women has. I saw the elder's daughter—the reason for the brouhaha—and she really is worth it.

"And, in my view, her brother vindicated this hellhole: it's commendable to die for a woman, like a real knight.

"Especially for a peasant."

"Let Brysov have his say now," Pilsky said.

He slapped his bootleg irritably with a freshly whittled switch.

"Alright," Brysov said. "I don't know what Pilsky will say or what Grigoriy will say, but there are four of us who are staying. And, as commander of the troop, I am staying with them.

"And if they weren't staying, I'd have stayed on anyway.

"Because I am an officer and I gave an oath to the Tsar and the Fatherland.

"And now there is neither a Tsar nor an oath, and my Fatherland has been taken away by the Bolsheviks.

"While you visited the yards, I thought to myself: what could a man die for today?

"And, more importantly, what could a man kill for?

"Because I don't like to kill, although I'm a career soldier.

"Murder is an excessive waste of human material. When you kill, you don't only kill one person, your enemy. You kill his unborn children, you kill all that could have happened in his life, including the future, in which you've already ceased being enemies. And you also destroy the lives of his wife and children. That's why I believe that, if you're going to kill, you have to know what you are doing it for.

"Because there is nothing left: no Tsar, no Russia, no oath."

Brysov fell silent and Grisha saw a fly crawl down his smoothly shaven head.

The fly must have thought itself a great traveler. It's just too bad that the fly won't meet any of its own kind on its way.

Before he attached himself to Brysov's troop, Grisha was just like this fly: he was crawling down a bare wall and there was no one around him he could trust.

Yuliy Brysov fed him and took him into his troop—and Grisha waited to hear what Brysov would say.

Grisha had never killed anyone.

All boys dream of killing—until they see their first dead body.

For a man and, especially, for a man who had lived in Russia during the revolution, the sight of a dead body was inevitable.

When the Whites were in Kherson, they would hang people from the streetlamps in the main streets.

They would hang them there and leave them hanging.

The children get out of school and gather around the streetlamp. They stand there.

And this—all over Russia.

Fifteen-year-old Grisha had never seen a dead body—and there were less than twenty-four hours left before this miraculous situation would change.

That's why he was listening to Brysov more attentively than the others.

"And I thought," Brysov said, "that if we don't have a Fatherland, a Tsar, or an oath, then what does each of us have left? His family.

"And there's noo shame in dying or killing for your family.

"You know, my parents died, my brother was shot by either the Reds or the Whites. I don't know myself.

"I don't have a family of my own: that's why I'll stay and kill for the families of these peasants."

Pilsky asked, without getting up from the bench: "But how will we fight? The Mechanic wants his tank, but do we have some kind of disposition?"

Brysov smiled: "We'll think of something."

"To tell you the truth, I intended to leave," Pilsky said, "but since the rest of you are staying, I will, too. Of course, I could have left and then repented tomorrow, and come back like some sort of a Khanzhonkov.

"So I will stay put. But on one condition: when you start to plan your disposition, please include a cavalry charge. For at least one horseman. I would like to wield my saber once more before I die."

Brysov nodded and glanced at Grisha. "Of course, I'm staying," the latter said. "Although I reckon I won't be very useful."

"No matter," Brysov said. "Who knows how it will go? All in all, there are seven of us and about thirty bandits. But we have the advantage of time and the fact that we know about them, but they don't know about us.

"I'll speak to the elder and then we'll discuss the disposition."

I think you'll recognize this plot. A small village, seven men, lily-livered peasants, and a bandits' raid.

You've probably even seen it in a movie—if not in the one, then in the other.

Before they go into battle, the soldiers have to talk about their dreams or some memory, so that the viewer doesn't get confused and instead feel sorry for the ones who get killed.

In this day and age, a halting phrase is more powerful than a saber attack.

Brevity is not only the sister of talent—it is its sole surviving relative.

I think that a brief synopsis of the next forty minutes of screen-time will do the trick.

And, since we're talking film, I'll tell you that Fomin reminded me of the Marquis from *Property of the Republic* and Belousov—the customs agent Vereshchagin from *White Sun of the Desert*.

I think this will be enough to help you keep them straight.

Pilsky told Grisha that he had a strange dream: he wanted to cleave a horseman in half with his saber. He'd been at war for many years, but never had the chance to do it. This would most likely be his last bat-tle—what battles could there be in Constantinople—and he wished to fulfill his dream.

Orlovsky said he knew for sure that a train was robbed two years ago not too far from here—fifteen versts away—as it transported a military coffer. Orlovsky was convinced that the money was hidden in the village. "Brysov knows this, and that's why he's getting involved. I told him that I wanted to be in on it," Orlovsky said. "I'm not inclined to be abroad and penniless in my old age."

By evening, the plan was ready. It combined the finest attributes of classic military dispositions and utilized all combat divisions, ambushes, and a broad range of technical innovations, making the best of the terrain.

The road bisected Kallaskoye and passed through a small square, at the center of which stood a wooden platform. On this platform, Brysov ordered them to build a gallows and hoist the corpse of yesterday's bandit. Inside the platform, they hid a few boxes of dynamite that they found in the village.

At the bottom of a ditch concealed by wooden boards lay a safety fuse that led to the cellar of the nearest house. Belousov would be waiting in that cellar.

When the dynamite exploded, all hell would break loose in the square.

For those few moments, it would be important to concentrate the adversary's manpower there.

Of course, some of the attackers would try to remove the corpse from the gallows, but that wasn't enough for Brysov.

After talking it over with the elder, he arranged for the peasants to harness the village horses to the Mk-V tank and place them in one of the outer yards. All they needed to do now was to open the gates and push down the tank.

Aided by gravity, the tank would roll down the hill and block the road through which the bandits entered the village, halting their retreat. They'd be forced to stay in the square, where the two roads began.

On one road, Brysov placed a mounted detachment of three men: Fomin, Pilsky, and Orlovsky. The second road climbed up to the bell tower, where Brysov set up a machine gun.

The plan was simple: when the bandits ride into the square, release the armored vehicle, creating a panic in their ranks, and forcing those who'd gone on further into the village to return.

At that moment, Belousov would light the safety fuse and, half-a-minute later, an enormous stockpile of dynamite would wipe out nearly all the bandits.

The explosion would serve as a signal for the horsemen to go down to the square and finish off whoever was still alive, rounding up the remaining bandits at the bell tower. The machine gun would take care of the rest.

The Mk-V, too, came with a machine gun, and the Mechanic couldn't wait to test it out.

At first Brysov wanted to take Grisha up to the bell tower with him, but then he changed his mind. Grisha was sent to the attic of the house facing the square. A cord was extended from the attic to the cellar—when it was time for the tank to go into action, Grisha was supposed to pull the cord to signal Belousov in the cellar.

"If everything goes smoothly," Brysov said, "we'll have a good chance of getting out of this without any casualties. Or hardly any."

Again: you've all seen this film—if not the one, then the other. Nothing ever goes smoothly and, of the seven men, only two or three usually survive, including the commander of the troop and the youngest soldier.

Just in case anyone has forgotten. Oh, I do love to talk cinema.

Tonight, Brysov will give Grisha his first shooting lesson.

A man's craft changes him.

A horse turns a man into a cavalryman.

A weapon makes him braver.

A weapon not only extends a man's reach, but also extends into him.

"If you want to learn how to shoot well," Brysov said, "you have to remember three rules.

"I do not aim with my hand; he who aims with his hand has forgotten the face of his father.

"I aim with my eye.

"I do not shoot with my hand; he who shoots with his hand has forgotten the face of his father. I shoot with my mind.

"I do not kill with my gun; he who kills with his gun has forgotten the face of his father.

"I kill with my heart."

Years later, Grisha will try to conjure his father's face, but recall Brysov's.

Around noon, the lookouts came running. In half an hour, the Wolves would be in Kallaskoye.

"Godspeed!" Brysov said, and the elder made the sign of the cross over him. Everyone assumed their positions.

Grisha was sitting at the attic window, watching the dead body swaying on a rope—the first dead body he had seen in his life.

As he gazed at the hanged man, Grisha felt nothing.

Possibly because the man was already dead when they arrived in the village.

By one in the afternoon, the first horsemen appeared. They burst onto the square on fiery steeds and froze when they saw the gallows.

These people were long used to the sight of a man dangling from a noose, as were almost all Ukrainian citizens after three years of civil war.

The bandits were shocked by the audacity of the peasants. They were expecting the elder to greet them by the village gates and offer profuse apologies, but the windows were shuttered and it was as if Kallaskoye had died out.

Almost every man in the village was crowded around the armored car, at the ready to send it down the hill.

Slowly, another three dozen horsemen and a machine-gun carrier rode onto the square. Grisha ran to the other window and looked out at the road: the Wolves' rear guard was approaching the village.

The Mechanic couldn't have known about this from his position in his yard. After waiting a little for the cavalrymen to pass, he signaled.

The gates were opened.

The behemoth of a tank rolled slowly downhill, then accelerated. The Mechanic sat inside and attempted to steer it. The Mk-V crashed into the fence of a corner house, just about blocking passage to the square.

As agreed, Grisha pulled the cord and rushed back to the window.

His involvement in the battle was over.

Thus far, everything was happening exactly as Brysov predicted. A stampede broke out. Some bandits tried immediately to get away from the armored vehicle and its machine gun, while the horsemen who had gone ahead had turned around and were riding back to the square.

At that moment, the Wolves' rear guard reached the village. Seven astonished horsemen reined in their horses when they reached the tank that obstructed the road.

Four minutes had passed. The safety fuse should have burned a long time ago, but still, no explosion came.

When he saw the rear guard, the Mechanic knew that his time had come. The Hotchkiss began to rap hollowly—the very first round mowed down five men. Those it had missed turned back their horses. Shooting in their wake, the Mechanic killed them, too.

As the Mechanic peppered the Wolves' rear guard with bullets, one of the bandits on horseback in the square rode up to the armored vehicle; from the attic window, Grisha saw a pillar of fire and smoke leap up over the vehicle, and the Wolves began to holler and shoot in the air.

Before it had ended up in a Kallaskoye henhouse, the Mk-V had already served in action: in one such battle, its manhole had been ripped off.

The bandit had tossed a hand grenade into the Mechanic's lap.

Grisha froze and watched the gray-haired Belousov walking briskly through the square. The Wolves didn't notice him right away, but then one horseman struck Belousov with a saber with all his might.

Not knowing what he was supposed to do now, Grisha rushed down the stairs.

Only later did he learn what had happened in the cellar.

A safety fuse is lit with a hand-rolled cigarette rather than a match. Belousov had leisurely lit his cigarette, then the fuse, and waited.

The allotted seconds passed, but no explosion came.

In all likelihood, someone's horse had knocked down the walls of the ditch through which the fuse ran.

Belousov then took out a stick of dynamite, attached a longer fuse to it, and came out into the yard and lit it. Then he tucked the stick in the inner pocket of his leather jacket.

It was twenty meters from the doors of the house to the wooden platform.

"They won't try to kill me right away," Belousov thought. "I'll make it. Above all, I mustn't fall."

At that moment, the hand grenade detonated—and Belousov entered the square.

The bandits saw the gray-haired, leather-jacketed man walking briskly toward the gallows. The bandits were riled up: they heard the machine gun rounds and knew that their rear guard was destroyed. One of the Wolves struck Belousov with a saber while riding at full speed.

The blade hacked off Belousov's ear and scraped off part of his scalp. The blow was so severe that it knocked Belousov off his feet.

The platform was still five meters away. Belousov began to crawl to the sounds of jeers and laughter. He managed to get the better of two meters and his last thought was: "Close enough. It should work."

It did.

The platform flew up into the air like a giant rocket. The blast shattered windows, and horses and men dropped to the ground—dead, shell-shocked, and wounded.

Grisha ran out into the square. Someone's bloodied arm lay on the ground.

When a human limb is torn off by an explosion, for some time, it's still alive and moving, like a headless frog attached to an electric generator.

The fingers on the hand were twitching.

Deafened by the blast, Grisha couldn't hear anything. Meanwhile, horses were neighing and people were wailing. A strange man ran up to him, then, collapsed on his knees and fell face first to the ground.

Shooting from two revolvers, Orlovsky galloped toward him with two horsemen at his sides.

Grisha stood on the threshold. "Why are you standing there, get out!" Pilsky screamed right in his ear, but Grisha wouldn't budge.

A horse thrashed on the ground. Its legs were broken. The horseman was still alive and continued to straddle the croup with his knees, his left leg crushed under the horse when it fell. He tried to pull it out of the saddle. The horse convulsed. Pinned to the ground, the horseman reached for his gun and shot the animal in the head. The horse spasmed and fell silent. The man climbed out with difficulty from under its carcass and opened fire, standing on one knee. Grisha couldn't see whom he was shooting at or if the bullets hit home.

Fomin swooped in on the shooter on horseback, firing from two revolvers like Orlovsky.

The man's gun dropped and he fell across his horse's carcass.

Hardly five minutes had passed since Grisha descended to the square. The fog had cleared and Grisha could hear again.

The square was strewn with the bodies of the killed and wounded. Grisha looked around for Belousov, but didn't see him.

Of Brysov's troop, Grisha had only seen Fomin. The latter had guided his horse toward the overturned machine-gun cart. The side of a face and a shoulder could be glimpsed under the overturned cart. The person was stirring—they were still alive.

Fomin drew his revolver and immediately lowered it, cursing.

"It's a dame!" he exclaimed, and leaned down to help the young woman.

In Ukraine, Grisha had heard much about female commissars, Makhnovist anarchists and gang leaders, such as the infamous *St. Petersburg étoile* Marusya. Grisha believed that these were all tall tales.

And now, a young woman was climbing out of the rubble before his very eyes. Her dress was torn, but you could tell by its cut and fabric that it was beautiful and, at one time, expensive.

"My lady," Fomin said, extending his hand, "what a pleasant surprise to meet such a beautiful young woman in the midst of this hell!"

The woman smiled. Her fair hair was clotted with blood, and you could barely make out her face beneath a layer of dust. Fomin, an inveterate womanizer, looked her over out of old habit. He died wearing that characteristic expression on his face—appraising and, simultaneously, gallant: the woman shot him, and Fomin hardly had time to be surprised.

The horse bolted and Fomin's body dangled from the saddle.

Grisha shrieked with fright and the woman turned toward him.

"And what are you doing here, you little bastard?" she asked, lifting herself up. The pistol smoked in her hand.

Grisha grew dumb. What was he supposed to say? Really, what was he doing here?

"Those bastards took everyone down, everyone!" cried the woman. "Well, you wait and see, you'll get what's coming to you."

In moments like this, time slows down. Grisha distinctly saw her pistol rise: any second now, the black circle of the muzzle would be level with his head. A shot rang out, Grisha yelled, but he didn't feel any pain, and then, he saw the woman tumble to the ground.

Grisha turned around and heard a faint voice: "Here . . . here . . . come here!" Orlovsky, who was covered in blood, lifted himself up on his elbow, clutching a smoking revolver.

Grisha ran to him.

"I'm dying," Orlovsky said, "but did Yuliy at least tell you what it is? A military coffer, right?"

"No," Grisha replied, "a Tsarist treasure trove. With gold coins, precious stones and jewelry. Honest to God, the seventh share is yours."

"That's good," Orlovsky smiled and closed his eyes.

The sporadic clattering of a machine gun could be heard coming from the bell tower. Grisha took the gun out of Orlovsky's limp hand, removed a handful of bullets from his pocket, and reloaded.

The remnants of the gang retreated along the road that led up to the bell tower. There, Brysov lay by a machine gun tripod, waiting for them to approach. He didn't have a lot of bullets and wanted to get a sure shot.

It's believed that, the later a machine gunner gives himself away, the better his chances.

Just under twenty horsemen emerged from the carnage in the village square. They raced straight to the bell tower down the only open road, pursued by Pilsky, who was waving his saber left and right.

When the last surviving Wolves ascended the knoll, Brysov opened fire. He counted at least eight horsemen who flew out of their seats onto the green grass.

At that moment, the machine gun jammed.

Brysov jerked around the jammed belt, trying to figure out if he should take it apart, and peeked out cautiously.

The survivors pranced on horseback around the bell tower. The moment Brysov stuck out his head, shots were fired—the Wolves' revolvers seemed to lack long-range capability, but Brysov didn't want to risk it.

When he had gone up the bell tower, Brysov had locked all the doors from inside; it was unlikely that the bandits would break in quickly.

In the bell tower, Brysov was safe.

But it was out of the question for him to go down.

Around twelve bandits remained below. If everything had gone well in the village, Orlovsky and his horsemen would turn up now, with

Belousov and the Mechanic to boot. But two or three of them would be quite enough to distract the bandits from entering the bell tower.

Time passed and no one came, and Brysov realized that his friends were dead. Soon, the bandits would work out that the village was at their disposal.

Brysov wasn't worried about himself: he had two loaded guns. Moreover, he could fix the machine gun within the hour. It would be utter suicide for the Wolves to storm the bell tower.

The bandits were still galloping around below. They must have hoped their wounded comrades would catch up by now.

In five, at most, ten minutes, they will realize that no one is pursuing them, thought Brysov, and then they will return to the village to take their revenge.

Which means that all of today's deaths will have been in vain.

Brysov grew pensive for a minute, then reloaded both his guns.

If he hadn't erred in his calculations and could hit his targets, he had a chance.

Grisha was afraid to mount a horse—he ran panting with a loaded revolver in each hand, repeating to himself: "A weapon not only extends a man's reach, but also extends into him."

Midway up the hill, he saw Pilsky. His horse was dead, and Pilsky lay with his head on its croup. When he heard Grisha's voice, he said: "Oh, the kid! You're alive? That's good."

"What happened to you?" Grisha asked.

"I'm dying," Pilsky answered, "three bullets to the stomach . . . almost point-blank . . . if I was in a good hospital, perhaps they could have done something, but not here. Who from our men has survived?"

"Brysov, most likely," Grisha answered and grew instantly scared that he wouldn't reach him in time. "I'm going to him . . . to help . . . if he needs me."

"You're doing the right thing, helping him," Pilsky said. "You just help me first, alright? Brysov will take care of himself. Take the revolver out of my saddle bag and I'll lie here for a bit."

The saddle bag had been flung to the side. Grisha took out the gun and passed it to Pilsky.

"Thank you," Pilsky murmured, "also . . . over there . . . a bay and its rider . . . will you have a look?"

"Have a look at what?" Grisha didn't hear him clearly.

"Have a look if I . . . hacked him in half?" Pilsky whispered, his voice weakening.

For a moment, Grisha stood motionless over the horse carcass and horseman.

"Well?" Pilsky said hoarsely.

"Hacked in half!" Grisha replied, and thought to himself: "I'm going to vomit right now."

"That's good," Pilsky said. "If Brysov is alive, tell him he's a bastard! If not, I'll tell him so myself."

"Of course," Grisha cried out, and it was then that the bells began to ring up on the hill and a shot sounded behind his back.

The surviving Wolves couldn't immediately tell what was happening. First, the bells began to ring, then, they fell silent.

After a few minutes, a bell cord flew from the top of the bell tower and a male figure began to slide down it. With his shaved head glistening in the sun, Brysov held the rope in his left hand and squeezed a gun in his right.

On his way down, Brysov fired off an entire cylinder. Five of the seven bullets hit their mark.

He threw the spent weapon on the ground, grabbed a second revolver from his belt and kept shooting.

If my favorite actor, Chow Yun-fat, was in Brysov's place, Moreukhov thinks, he wouldn't have had a seven-chamber revolver, but, say, a Beretta 93R with a twenty-round magazine—and then, without taking his signature toothpick out of his mouth, he would have shot all the Wolves. And if Chow died in the end, John Woo's white doves would have soared over the bell tower into the sky.

And, Moreukhov thinks, if this was in fact *The Magnificent Seven*, Brysov would have lived like he was supposed to.

And don't tell me this is real life and not the movies. We don't know what happened in real life eighty years ago, which means that we can only assume Yul Brysov got down on one knee and, without changing position, took down another seven bandits, then, rolled over on the ground, hoping to grab a revolver from one of the dead bandits.

As he ran up the hill, Grisha managed to see Brysov fire his last bullets at his target. Then the gunslinger rolled down the green grass and two bandits jumped out from behind the bell tower as if they had been waiting for him, and opened fire.

And, at that moment, Grisha forgot about his fear, his dead friends and the bodies torn in pieces and hacked in half, and screamed "Die! Die!," discharging an entire cylinder at the nearest bandit.

The latter dropped next to Brysov, and Grisha threw the spent revolver to the ground, shifted his remaining gun from his left to his right hand, and fired almost in unison with the last Wolf standing.

Something hot struck Grisha in the chest and he fell.

All around, the grass was covered with splatters of blood.

Blood remarkably red against the green.

How terrible to think there are people who died before you had a chance to say a tender word to them.

And these people died lonely.

When I was fifteen, I killed a man for the first time.

Two, to be exact.

It was me against two men, but I had the element of surprise on my side.

The first must not have even had the chance to realize who killed him.

The second wounded me before he died, and I spent a month lying in delirium on a cot in the village my six friends had given their lives to save.

When I recovered, I learned that the Reds had captured Crimea.

I had nowhere left to go.

I didn't sleep all night, and, in the morning, went to the village elder and asked him to give me a document stating that I, a Red Army soldier, had distinguished myself defending the Kallaskoye Village against bandits.

The elder asked for my first and last name.

"Grigoriy," I began, and stopped short. My parents had a good surname, beautiful and well-known. I thought that, in the country where I was destined to now live, it'd be better to have a more modest surname.

For the last time, without opening my lips, I repeated the surname that my ancestors had borne with honor for five centuries, and then spoke: "Let it be Brysov."

The elder must have not heard me properly. And that's how I became Grigoriy Borisov.

I took the revolvers of Yuliy Brysov, the White Officer who died for Ukrainian peasants in Kallaskoye Village, and, with these revolvers, set off across the entire country to Petrograd, where no one knew me. I'd never been to this city and it would not remind me of anything.

In the very first town on my way there, I walked into a barbershop and asked them to shave my head. Many people did this back then: they were afraid of getting lice.

A real head is one that's been scalped.

As I came out of the barbershop, I glanced in the mirror. A fly sat on my clean-shaven head and crawled slowly, like a traveler on a terrestrial globe.

In St. Petersburg, I took my document to the Joint State Political Directorate and said I wanted to continue combating gang violence.

Of course, I lied and said I was already sixteen.

Why did I go work for the Bolsheviks, when they destroyed my country and deprived me of a name and family?

I could say that I didn't go to work for the Bolsheviks—I went to fight criminals. The kind who killed Brysov and his friends. Of course, that's also true.

Brysov taught me that a man's craft changes him.

A horse changes a man into a cavalryman.

A weapon makes him braver.

A weapon not only extends a man's reach, but also extends into him.

On my first day of battle, I decided that I wanted to spend the rest of my life with a revolver in hand.

A thing that's easy to grasp and hard to let go of.

And I wanted to die that way, too—with a weapon in hand.

On the way out of Kallaskoye, I stopped by the cemetery. Six of my comrades lay there. A month and a half after their deaths, there were still fresh flowers on their graves.

I doubt that anyone looks after their graves now.

People have short memories.

As for me, I try not to forget what my adopted father Yuliy Brysov, an officer and a gunslinger, taught me:

And now there is neither a Tsar nor an oath, the Fatherland has been taken away by the Bolsheviks. What does each of us have left? His family.

And there's no shame in dying or killing for your family.

76.

THE PAST TENSE OF THE VERB

"I love old buildings," Lena says. "You can sense a living soul in them."

"You can breathe a living soul into anything, given the will," Moreukhov answers.

The attic studio is a mess. Its owner, Vitalik—an old pal of Moreukhov's—had switched to some form of computer art five years ago and was creating at his dacha. Presently, he gave his keys to Moreukhov and went away to the US for a month. Vitalik inherited the studio from his parents, famous Soviet artists who'd relocated to Germany a while ago.

Moreukhov clears a spot in the middle of the room—there, now bring the armchair over here, have Lena sit in it, and everything should be fine.

"It's too bad this is all being so barbarically destroyed," Lena continues. Right under the roof, she saw the numbers 1905 and can't get over it: wow, the building is a hundred years old!

"It's too bad," Moreukhov says and hoists the canvas stretcher on an easel. "Would you wanted the whole city center to be turned into a museum?"

"Why a museum?" Lena replies. "In Europe, every city has a normal, lively city center, but they don't demolish entire neighborhoods like we do. They preserve their traditions—a café may have stood in the same place for two hundred years! What's so bad about that?"

Moreukhov pensively grinds his paints. The last time he drew portraits was about twelve years ago, if you don't count various small sketches. They say you can't drink your talent away, but Moreukhov isn't so sure of that right now.

"Well, we're not in Europe," he says. "We no longer have cafés that have been around for two hundred years. We have a city where there's always something happening—revolution, industrialization, war, perestroika, Mayor Yury Luzhkov. It would be dishonest to pretend like we're Switzerland."

I'm trying to picture this and marveling: Moreukhov is speaking a bit too coherently for an alcoholic. In any case, we should consider that he hasn't had a drink since March and it is already summer.

Maybe he's not an alcoholic after all? Maybe he's just pretending? Feigning alcoholism the way others feign common illnesses. Goes on a bender two or three times a year and smells like a bum sometimes because—well, he just doesn't like to wash.

And he feigns it because, in fact, he's a bad artist and is scared everyone will figure it out.

Interesting take. Convincing.

So Lena sits down in the armchair and throws one leg over the other:

"Like that?"

"We'll decide in a moment," Moreukhov replies pensively. The clean canvas is as vast as the years during which he never touched a brush. "You like this building and meanwhile, it was taken away from its owners in the early twenties. Maybe they were executed. It's a stolen building. You and I don't know what sort of a soul it has. For instance, the nine-story buildings in Troparyovo have a soul. The people who first moved into them are still living there. Or their children and grandchildren. And the people this place was built for lived here for about fifteen years before it all began: communal apartments, alcoholics, squabbling. And arrests."

"Why necessarily alcoholics and squabbling?" Lena replies. "I saw a plaque downstairs that said some famous actors lived here."

"A memorial plaque," Moreukhov says, "is the best kind of historical monument. Especially one inscribed: 'On the site of this building was located . . .' The most important thing here is the past tense of the verb. Was. Before, there was a church or a pool, and now there's nothing or there's something completely different. Before, actors lived here and later on, alcoholics. As I said, we're not in Switzerland."

"So you won't feel too bad when they tear this building down?"

"When they tear it down—no, but when they build a business center for office degenerates—yes. But that's because I don't like degenerates. And because they won't think of putting up a plaque that says: 'On the site of this center, there was once a building built in 1905 by architect so-and so, but it was excluded from the list of historical monuments in exchange for a bribe.'"

Lena laughs:

"Are you going to do any drawing today?"

Looks like I'll have to, Moreukhov thinks, and I was planning to weasel my way out of it.

"Of course," he says. "Do you still want a realistic portrait? Not a stylized one or a post modernist pastiche?"

"An ordinary one," Lena replies. "A painted photograph."

She reaches into her purse and takes out an old Polaroid camera.

"I read somewhere," she says, "that it helps the artist if they take a few shots . . . so that you can draw me even when I'm not here. Will you take some pictures of me?"

What a great idea, Moreukhov thinks: I'll take pictures and then, if the portrait doesn't come out, I'll find a student to draw it for me.

"Let me show you how it works," Lena says, pointing and shooting. A little black square crawls out, humming, and gradually a disoriented smile, a gap in place of a tooth, and some jawline scruff emerge on it.

How horrid, Moreukhov thinks, now I know why I don't have a mirror at home. He studies the Polaroid for some time and pokes at its glossy surface.

"Let's begin," he says. "Sit down and relax. Imagine you're at the dentist."

And he smiles his gap-toothed smile.

77.

ESSENTIALLY, BANAL WORDS

Nikita is sitting in his office. On his desk is a photo of Masha, a mountain of papers, and a computer. He is very proud that he has his own office. Back in the day, obviously, he never had one, wherever he worked.

Nikita remembers all the places he's worked, all the jobs he's had. After graduating from university, he worked at a small company, washed windows at industrial plants, worked as a door-to-door salesman, and drove a cab on the side, until his car was totaled. Then, he almost became a concession-stand vendor, but got a job at some office—wholesale deliveries, a serious business—which shut down six months later. He worked in the sales departments of tens of those kinds of offices, dabbled in advertising—*you're creative, you'll make it*. The hell he did, by the way. And now he has his own business, his own office, fifteen employees, responsibility, all that jazz.

When members of his university graduating class hear he's got his own company, they say: *Oh yes, you're a New Russian now!* and laugh. Nikita laughs too: he's not going to explain to them that a small business brings in less money than what a good manager makes at a big company.

Three years ago, when he was only starting out, he thought his revenue would double every three months—at the very least, every year. But no, as soon as it leveled off last year, it just stayed the same. His profits are even falling because he has to give people raises. What kind of New Russian does that make him?

He couldn't explain it to his classmates, and when Masha recently provoked him: *You'll probably leave me, you're rich and successful, you need a different kind of wife, a young and beautiful one*, he got mad and yelled at her. He said, what do you mean I'm rich, I have a small business, I'm a mom-and-pop without any prospects. I got lucky by accident and tomorrow, a big player will come on the market and wipe me out.

I told her the truth, that's how it is. But I was yelling because I got ticked off about the *young and beautiful one*, which made me immediately think of Dasha. Although, at the time, I was only talking to Masha about business and money.

Everyone knows that money can't save you from death. It can't save you from fatigue, melancholy, disgust with your own body, or awkwardness at the thought that you—balding, with a protruding belly, bags under your eyes, and smelly armpits—yes, that's you—are with Dasha—young, beautiful, big breasted, and with a tongue piercing. And the certainty that she can tune in to cosmic energy currents.

And she really can, you've seen it, you can confirm.

Whereas you can only tune in to financial currents and, to be honest, are not that great at it—you're no match for Kostya.

So you've been sitting in your office for the last forty minutes mindlessly popping balloons in a stupid game you downloaded off the internet. Yesterday, you spent about three hours playing this game. Gearing up for retirement, eh?

Three balloons equals thirty points. Pop, pop, pop.

The phone rings—it's Kostya.

"Remember I told you that you have to find an investor?"

Of course, Nikita remembers. An investor, three years of work, five million.

"Well, I have one. He's quite interested. You have to meet with him."

A week ago, Nikita asked Kostya again:

"Are you sure you don't want to do it?"

"Nah," Kostya said, "I don't like doing business with friends or in areas I know nothing about. Pet fish aren't my thing."

"I don't do pet fish," Nikita said, "I do aquariums."

"What's the difference?"

So they have to meet. They'll meet, they'll talk. Kostya promised to help if anything. An investor, three years of work, five million. He only hopes it all works out for Masha. In the next few days, it'll be clear whether or not it did.

A row of five balloons, all at once. Pop. Fifty points.

Five million.

Pop.

Victor knocks on the door and peeks into the office.

Nikita, we have a situation, he says, *you should probably let Natasha go home.* Is she sick? *No, she came in and she looks awful, I think she's crying.*

Fucking hell! This is what three years of work gets you. You come to the office and your top employee is *crying*. OK, I'll go deal with it. And you go take a smoke break, Victor.

Natasha, a petite, lean brunette, is sitting at the corner desk, looking out the window. Her shoulders are trembling. It seems like Victor's right: she's crying.

He leads her into his office and sits her on the couch. Well, what happened?

Natasha takes a tissue from the desk, wipes her tears, and blows her nose.

"Nikita, tell me, why do married men take lovers?"

This is a question you have to ask the right person. At the right moment. Why the fuck do married men take young lovers who they then fall in love with, and don't know what to do about? Because they watched the film *Autumn Marathon* as children and are asking for trouble, that's why!

He starts mumbling: well, men seek variety, adventure, intense feelings. Should he say there are wives who don't like oral or, say, anal sex, and that sometimes men want it every which way? No, that would be completely tactless, he better not.

It's also because men get older, Nikita says. They're scared. And with a young lover—wait, where'd you get a *young* lover? Nobody asked you about *young* ones—with a lover, they feel as if they're young again for a spell.

And their wives get older too, Nikita thinks, grow overweight and repulsive. Or become so thin that you can see their bones through their skin. And a man looks at the woman he loved so much and thinks: this is what my death will look like.

"So why do they leave us?" Natasha asks.

Well, it's because they get tired of lying. Because they can get fed up with their lovers too. They want variety, adventure, intense feelings.

Natasha is sobbing.

Jesus Christ, Nikita thinks, why do we leave them? Sometimes, we leave them because we're in love. Because it's too complicated to fall in love with one woman and live with another one, that's why!

And then Natasha starts to tell her story, but Nikita hardly listens to her. Dear Lord, he silently prays, I don't want to lose Dasha! I don't want to get old again! To stay with Masha means to give up everything!

Everything that might still happen to me! Carefree joy, fun, and light-heartedness, my child walking along the surf, the yellowish-red leaves of my youth, the dim lamplights of the Moscow twilight, metaphysical revelations, the anticipation of happiness. Dear Lord, if You could again send me an effigy with a Holy Grail on its head, I would know what to ask for. Let it all work out by itself somehow, OK? Let me and Masha have a child and let me live with Dasha.

And all this time, Natasha is telling him where and when she met her lover, how they spent their time together, how much she loved him, how wonderful he was and what a great couple . . .

And Nikita realizes: yep, that's his job—you come into the office, there's a young woman weeping her eyes out, and you listen to the story of how she got dumped as you pray to God because you don't know how to sort out your own life without His help.

It looks like that's what you'll ultimately get your five million for.

Being a salaried manager is incomparably easier.

Nikita remembers a Sufi parable Dasha told him. There once lived a man in, say, Baghdad. An angel or a Green Dervish came to him in a dream—doesn't matter which one, some messenger—and bade him to drop everything and move to, say, Istanbul. And not to work as a shoe-maker, as he did in the past, but to become a carpenter, for instance. The man did just that, moved to Istanbul, worked as a carpenter, began to slowly move up in life, bought a new house—and at that moment, the angel said to him in a dream: now go to Teheran or, say, Medina, and take up, I don't know, fish farming. Or supply Turkish delight to the Shah's harem. Some bullshit, not particularly prestigious. And thus, the man spent about twenty years dashing around the entire Islamic world for no purpose at all, well, from our point of view, and apparently from his point of view as well. In the end, naturally, he ended up a saint. He worked miracles, healed by the laying on of hands and so forth.

Nikita places his hand on Natasha's shoulder and says: "Everything will be alright, in a few years, you'll realize that this was a beautiful adventure, a real love, like in the movies. Your memories will become faded and forgotten—and you'll be a bit sad, but still find it pleasant to reminisce about a time when you were so young (how old is she? I don't remember!), loved a married man, you made a beautiful couple, and then it all ended." Nikita says all these, essentially, banal words and Natasha stops sobbing, takes another tissue, blows her nose, and says: "Thank you, Nikita, I'll go work now."

And I think: So I've dealt with that. And I'll deal with all the rest too, what choice do I have?

I think that maybe I was also bidden to first work as a traveling salesman, then as a sales rep, then as a manager, and then to start my own business. Maybe an angel also came to me in dreams with specific instructions, my life plan for all these years. Came, but I didn't remember it? Maybe I'm already a saint, but don't know it? Maybe I'm unworthy of knowing?

Eight o'clock in the evening. Covered parking lot. In a far-off corner, a Toyota. In the car—a balding, forty-year-old man. He is swaying monotonously, as if he's praying.

That's me, Nikita Melnikov. If you come closer, you'll hear me howling.

This isn't the howl of a wolf, a trapped animal, or a woman who has lost her child. No, it's that singular howl predicted by Moreukhov, a howl that the Lord has invented specifically for successful men who have come face-to-face with their fear.

When I drove into the parking lot five minutes ago, Masha called and said: *It didn't work.*

I replied: *I'll be there soon*, but instead of parking and running home, I stayed in the car.

I'm scared.

I'm afraid that I won't be able to deal with it this time around.

78.

TEAMBUILDING

The same provincial town. The same hotel. The same bar. Late evening. Two people sitting at a corner table. A stocky man in an expensive suit and a young woman with dark hair. She's wearing formal shoes, a knee-length skirt, and a beige jacket. Rimma and Sazonov.

Of course, I don't know why they've come to this town. They must be here on business. It's a special sort of town, people come here for work, check into the hotel, and then go down to the bar. You could say I made this trip up one sleepless night at this same hotel, when I alternately dreamed of Dasha, Olga, and the porn star from television.

Rimma has just finished talking. They must have been discussing their meeting schedule for tomorrow. There's an empty shot glass in front of Sazonov and a full one in front of Rimma, and, between them, a bottle of Hennessy. Sazonov is contemplating Rimma's hands. Lightly-tanned skin, long fingers, crimson, flawlessly shaped nails.

Rimma lowers her eyes in silence. It's their first time alone in an informal setting, so to speak.

Very slowly, he covers her hand with his. Rimma sees his protruding sinews, his slightly swollen fingers, his wedding band. She remembers his wife and then, Angela.

At last, she lifts her eyes and says: "I have to tell you, Vladimir Nikolayevich, that it won't work out between us," but doesn't pull back her hand.

"Why?" Sazonov asks in a low voice.

"How can I put it," Rimma says more confidently this time, "I have very specific sexual preferences."

"Golden showers?" he asks with unfeigned curiosity and a hint of irony.

"No, no," Rimma frowns, "that's disgusting. I'm just not interested in men."

"Oh," Sazonov says with disappointment and removes his hand, "I thought it was something kinky."

"Though," Rimma shrugs, "barring that, I can say I find you quite attractive."

Sazonov pours the cognac in the shot glasses, drinks from his, and ponders the bar behind Rimma's back. A bored bartender, a long row of bottles, and a lone female in a miniskirt. Sazonov looks over at Rimma:

"If you find me attractive, then I have an idea. Would you like to try it?"

"What do you mean?" Rimma asks coolly.

"You'll understand in a moment," Sazonov replies and partly gets up, waving his hand. "Young lady, young lady," and his face melts into a smile, "yes, I'm talking to you. Would you like to join us? I see you're all alone at the bar. Just take a shot glass, I'll pour you some cognac, and we'll drink to your health. What's your name? Olga? Very good. You see, Olga, we have a professional proposition for you . . ."

I see them in a cheap, provincial luxury suite, frozen on the wide bed. Sazonov lies propped up on one elbow, drops of sweat glistening on his graying tufts of hair. He's breathing heavily, his eyes are open, his lips are clenched, and his jaw muscles stir beneath his gray stubble. Then he drops his head back onto the pillow and reaches his hand out to Rimma, who is sitting motionless at the foot of the bed. Rimma is smiling, her eyes half-closed, her dark-cherry nipples tense and appearing to pulsate in the morning twilight. She reaches out a thin hand with crimson nails—one of which is broken—to Sazonov.

Olga is lying between them, diagonally splitting the bed like a mythological sword, a crumpled towel, a broken toy with unscrewed hinges, a used condom. She's lying on her stomach and her body is limp, as if it dissolved in the twilight.

Large breasts, a round belly, a voluptuous behind. Hair bleached to the state of total whiteness.

Rimma opens her eyes. Her gaze meets Sazonov's over Olga's prostrate body. All three of them are still immobile.

The clock on the wall is ticking—an old Soviet model; the clock is ticking, the portable alarm clock is buzzing, and Olga is sobbing.

She gets up and slowly begins to dress. Drab, overwashed panties with faded lace trim, a short skirt, shoes on her bare feet, a jacket over her naked body. She picks up her stockings from the floor her top from the armchair, and stuffs them in her purse, continuing to sob.

"Take the money," Sazonov says.

Olga shudders, looks around, and freezes in fear.

"Get the wallet out of my purse," Rimma says, glancing at Sazonov, "take six thousand out of it. Put the wallet on the table and leave."

Olga nods, counts out the bills with trembling hands, and stands still for a second, as if not knowing where to put the money. Finally, she stuffs it in her crammed purse and walks out, trying not to look in the doorway mirror. The rapid click-clacking of heels resounds like she's running.

Rimma and Sazonov are still sitting motionless; then he gets up, his satyr legs crooked and hairy, his member slightly raised and his belly drooping. It's already light out.

Rimma is still smiling. She pulls her knees up to her breasts and, between her legs, Sazonov glimpses a pink crevice bordered by a whisper of dark hair.

In the course of the night, they hadn't touched each other once.

Sazonov puts on a silk shirt and, smiling crookedly, says:

"We can call that a team-building session."

79.

1928. INFLUENZA, OR DAYS AND NIGHTS ON VASILYEVSKY ISLAND AND OTHER LENINGRAD NEIGHBORHOODS

The staircases in the Public Library were as easy to climb as in a theater. The vaults of its ornate ceilings were as groined as in a monastery.

They say that the people who come here treat books as their equals, walk here with a quiet gait.

So, as if testing the waters, Olga steps tenderly on the dry parquet staircase—and, as always, the step replies to her with a creak.

Olga had just turned eighteen and was studying at the university. She wanted to be a philologist, hoping that the discipline would become her sanctuary and that, at the university, she would find people indifferent to the distasteful virulence of the day.

She was mistaken. The Department of Philology brimmed with excitement: in the lecture halls, they debated speech production and the subject of poetic form. In the corridors, they talked about the Left Front of the Arts, Mayakovsky, and Khlebnikov. Olga thought the students boorish know-nothings—with all her youthful passion, she refused futurists the right to be called poets. Olga believed that Russian literature had ended in the nineteenth century and that all that remained for her contemporaries was tomfoolery.

Having not found likeminded peers at the Department of Philology, Olga gave her love to the Public Library. She thought that the library would be capable of stopping time.

Here were books that sprouted from books and books that had been conceived of for the very first time.

People came here young and left old and gray.

This was the kind of life she wanted for herself.

Lida, Olga's older sister, was her opposite in every way. Olga wished to hide from time and Lida was afraid to fall behind. Olga looked into the past as if it were an algae-covered pond where even your reflection seemed shrouded by a patina, while Lida stretched toward the future, secretly hoping to gauge its fanciful trajectory. That was why she enrolled at the Leningrad Polytechnic Institute—and, unlike her sister, was perfectly happy.

Lida was studying chemistry and, in her dreams, would see organic molecules spinning in an endless Kekulé round-dance. Sometimes she would leap out of bed to jot down formulas on a yellow sheet of paper in the pale light of a Leningrad spring night.

Olga would shudder in her sleep, curl into a ball, and wrap herself tighter with her blanket. She loved her sister, but sometimes feared that Lida would end her days in an insane asylum.

"The entirety of the Soviet world is one big insane asylum," Lida answered.

She despised the Bolsheviks because they envisioned the future as a vague, voiceless backdrop on which you could sketch any utopian project, from a European revolution to a single universal language. To the Bolsheviks, the future was something like a red banner for holiday slogans, while Lida saw it as a source of colossal energies aimed toward the present and traveling down hitherto undiscovered power lines.

It was as if the Leningrad Polytechnic Institute of 1928 had been created for Lida. Little by little, the old-time professors exiled by the Bolsheviks returned; they still had a few years ahead of them until the next wave of arrests and deportations. It's possible that some of the old men were able to tap into those very same power lines between the past and the future, to get hold of the inauspicious schedule of Leningrad repressions for the next fifteen years, and develop a survival strategy summed up by the camp maxim "the sooner you get locked up, the sooner you'll get out."

This assumption may seem excessively brazen and even anti-scientific, but the old-time Polytechnic Institute professors were in fact behaving as if they wanted to be sentenced before the *ten years without the right to correspondence* came into vogue. They didn't yield to the new orthographic rules, didn't read Karl Marx, and despised the Civil War heroes sent to the Polytechnic Institute with a view to eradicate illiteracy.

They considered the Bolsheviks to be ignoramuses and ruffians.

At the Polytechnic Institute, there was a running joke about how Professor N., a frail, gray-haired old man, administered an exam to the illiterate, cocky, and intimidating sailor Baltfleet. In the middle of the exam, Professor N. suddenly asked him:

"Tell me, fellow, do you have a knife?"

"A knife?" the sailor grew nervous. "What knife?"

"Excuse me, but aren't you a Bolshevik?" the professor continued.

"Yes, I am a member of the All-Russian Communist Party."

"Well, if you are a Bolshevik, where's your knife? What do you mean, a Bolshevik without a knife?!"

The general atmosphere at the Department of Chemistry was in keeping with this joke; yesterday's peasants and demobilized soldiers mingled with students from among the city's *former residents*, who held their redemptive irony close at hand, as well as the traditional weapon of *giving someone the finger behind their back*.

It was to that nonconformist atmosphere that Lida and Grigoriy owed their acquaintance.

When Lida—tall, upright, and calm—would appear in the lecture hall with a pile of notebooks under her arm and her hair tied back with a revolutionary headscarf, no one could have suspected that she was an heiress of an ancient but impoverished clan harking back to the eighteenth century. In the meantime, as recently as ten years ago, the two sisters were living with their parents in their own small home. Thus, Lida, who at present shared a tiny room with Olga and her mother, had more than merely metaphysical reasons for disliking the new government.

Grigoriy wore army boots and a leather jacket, shaved his head bald, and looked more like a recently demobilized Red Army commander than a young Mayakovsky. Grigoriy was silent and self-reliant; he didn't have friends or acquaintances in the Department of Chemistry.

That day, he was late to the introductory lecture on thermodynamics and, after glancing around the lecture hall in confusion, headed toward the only open seat, which was next to Lida. Without saying a word, she moved her notebooks aside and continued to read her book.

The lecture on thermodynamics was as dull as dust.

For a minute, Grigoriy looked at Lida. Black-haired and big-eyed, she had the severe beauty of a woman who faced the prospect of surviving the Great Terror and the blockade, working for forty-something years at the same desk, retiring and, upon reaching ninety, greeting death with the indifferent calm of someone who had learned everything that interested them.

Grigoriy glanced over her shoulder and saw neat, even-metered columns of verse flowing down the page. Lida was reading poetry.

Grigoriy was amused by this. He made a serious face, leaned over to Lida and said soberly:

"I see you're reading poetry. I, too, am a poetry enthusiast. May I inquire what book this is?"

Of course, he was lying. He was indifferent to poetry, but, in his eight years of life under a fabricated last name, Borisov had proven to himself more than once that lying was the shortest and most reliable route to any objective.

Lida hesitated and then, with the nonchalance of someone who had nothing to hide, showed him the title page.

She lied with her gesture the same way Grigoriy had lied with his words. The poems were written by a poet who was gunned down a few years earlier for participating in an anti Bolshevik plot. There was nothing counter-revolutionary in his poems, but the Cheka might not have taken that into consideration. Cheka servicemen didn't know much about poetry.

Lida thought that the clean-shaven man in the leather jacket could very well be from the Cheka.

She wasn't far off the mark: Grigoriy had been sent to the Polytechnic Institute after seven years of intensive work at the Criminal Investigation Service. He was responsible for arresting two dozen dangerous criminals and liquidating a few gangs that inspired fear throughout Petrograd territory. That winter, Grigoriy was still combining his education with his operative work; then, he was planning to transfer to another division. He was fed up with running around the damp Leningrad backstreets, yelling, "Halt, halt!," shooting at shadows, and dodging others' bullets.

The Criminal Investigation Service was not interested in the poet Gumilyov, but Lida didn't know that. Of course, she could have slammed the poetry book shut and pretended she was listening to the lecturer, but doing so would have been both suspicious and rude. Thus, when she nonchalantly opened the title page, she was hoping her impertinent neighbor wouldn't recall his last name.

Grigoriy appreciated the elegance of her decision. He started laughing and quickly closed the book.

"Beautiful poet," he said, "but a crowded lecture like this one is hardly the best place to read him."

Lida smiled. They introduced themselves.

Here, the reader is entitled to suspect the author of making excessive use of a device known in literary theory as *narrative parallelism*. Seems like the story of Sasha Melnikov, who introduced Lyolya Borisova to his older brother at his own loss, was only a reproduction of the story of how Lyolya's parents met.

Unfortunately, this remains pure supposition/speculation because we know nothing about Grigoriy and Lida's relationship. It's possible that the young man courted the black-haired, fine-boned beauty. It's possible that Lida hopelessly dreamed about the tall, round headed Grigoriy, about his broad shoulders and strong arms. And, of course, the two young people could have been gripped by a mutual passion.

The episode with the Gumilyov volume took place in the winter. It was windy and the roofs were drab and thawing.

Grigoriy and Olga met in late spring, which means that our protagonists had at least three months together.

Aunt Lida loved to tell the story of how they met at the lecture on thermodynamics and, once, even showed me the poetry book to which I somewhat owe my existence. She gladly remembered that day in May when Grigoriy first saw my grandmother, his future wife. However, my aunt never once mentioned what happened in the preceding months.

In short, the facts neither confirm nor refute the aforementioned versions of the events. The reader is free to choose whichever they prefer, but we shall believe that the young people shared a mutual affinity that never managed to blossom into a romance and, instead, served as the foundation for a long-lasting familial friendship.

Rain is falling on desolate Leningrad fields.

Peter, Peter, why'd you build the Russian capital in this dying place?

So Grigoriy Borisov thinks on the tram as it rattles under his feet. Borisov is going to visit Lida because he hasn't seen her at the Polytechnic Institute for three days already. He thinks she might have fallen ill, caught a cold in the chilly Leningrad wind.

The tram drags itself along the boulevards and crawls onto the bridges, and the rails wail, intolerably so.

Grigoriy Borisov doesn't know he's riding toward the love of his life.

Olga hastily pinned back her fair hair in a bun before the small, cracked mirror. Lida had a fever, she hadn't been out of bed in three days, and Olga went to open the door herself.

Borisov was standing on the threshold. His wet jacket was as taut as reptilian skin around his body. A few raindrops remained immobile on his round, shaven head. Slowly and very seriously, he extended his hand and introduced himself:

"Grigoriy."

Olga blushed slightly and, in reply, extended her own hand, which was as thin as a Roman candle.

Borisov walks home with his head thrown back, examining the black sky and the shred of moon. It is dark. The trams have stopped running for the night.

Her name is Olga. Well, what about it? Nothing, really, he just remembered the name.

Olga was taciturn, fair-haired, and very pretty.

Walking down the Fifth tram line, he met a dog and sullenly contemplated it for a while. The dog was sitting in front of the gates—shaggy, disappointed, and hungry as dogs are. Borisov said hello to it and barked.

An inexplicable joy was suffocating him.

He wanted to clown around, laugh, provoke the passersby. But the night was deserted. As sleepless as an owl.

Borisov walked with a spring in his step and his jacket flung open, with the wind raising it on both sides like wings. He began to run down the wet pavement whooping, feeling younger with every step, casting off years of his life. Eleven years ago, he was a little boy from a wealthy family. Eight years ago, he obtained his own last name, a different one.

He is laughing for no reason. He is chatting without end. He gives away all his hand rolled cigarettes to the first person he meets, without exactly knowing why. Everybody's laughing at him and he's laughing too, not recognizing himself.

Finally, he figures out that it's time to go home, that the night is waning, that he's in love.

When he comes home, he can't sleep. Every sound is distinct, right down to his heartbeat.

The room folds up before his eyes with the din of a blacksmith's bellows. Borisov looks dully at his heavy hands. He doesn't know what to do with them. Now, he's not so sure himself he's in love. He collapses in bed and falls into a deep sleep.

He is feverish.

Aunt Lida never talked about how Grigoriy and Olga's romance began. I don't know where and when they first kissed, can't imagine the words they said to each other. I don't even know if Grigoriy told us his real life story—Grandma didn't want to talk about it. Aunt Lida said she always suspected the last name "Borisov" wasn't real—Grigoriy's father was probably a White Guardsman who had died in the Civil War. But Grigoriy never spoke to her about it and she never asked.

Borisov knew Olga's life story. To enroll at the Department of Philology, Olga went to work at the plant and wrote in her papers that she was a worker.

Her attempt to conceal her origin must have served as the grounds for her arrest. He told us about it with an unnatural calm, the mad calm of a man prepared to defend his woman.

How did Borisov find out about the impending arrest? The boundary between the Cheka and the Criminal Investigation Service must have not been so impervious at the time. Secrets weren't kept—they seeped out like blood through a bandage.

Olga never learned to what subtle, integral moves Borisov resorted back then. He told her everything when the danger passed.

"And the people . . . who wanted . . ." Olga had no idea how to ask.

"They are no longer here," Borisov replied seriously.

The answer was as flawless as a sphere, as round as his clean-shaven head. There was nothing left to say about it.

A month later, he brought the sisters new papers. And in another two, Grigoriy and Olga were married.

Borisov didn't return to the Polytechnic Institute in the second year: he was suddenly swamped with work.

80.

A REAL RESORT ROMANCE

Anya's walking down the sandy beach and the waves wash away her narrow footprints, Gosha runs slightly ahead of her along the edge of the surf, turns around and laughs. Seafoam twines around her feet, the sun sets behind the mountain, and long shadows lie down on the sand. It's warm and only a light breeze blows from the sea. Anya is buzzed and follows Gosha with her eyes as he runs, smiling.

Today is their last evening in Turkey. Tomorrow, they're taking a charter flight to Moscow.

And that's the end of my vacation, Anya thinks, my first normal vacation in God knows how many years. Maybe even my first real vacation. Abroad, at a hotel, with my son and my lover. At the seashore.

Anya went swimming every day. In the second week, she thought she not only re-experienced the joy of moving in and conversing with water, but also felt her old athletic skills return. She calculated the distance between two piers by sight and asked Andrey to time her—unfortunately, she'd still have plenty of training to do before she could get anywhere near her old records. And, at that point, Anya said she would simply swim without thinking of time, sports, and the years past. Just swim. Inhale—exhale, inhale—exhale. Leisurely, in time with the sea waves. Inhaling the smell of salt and seaweed, glancing back at the shore where the two male figures were standing—a big one and a little one.

Inhale—exhale, inhale—exhale. Day—night, day—night.

Thus, two weeks passed.

Today they woke up early. Gosha was sound asleep, with his fist placed behind his head and a water pistol clenched in his other hand. Andrey said: let's go to the beach, he won't be up before seven, we have a whole hour.

At first, they swam by the shore, clowned around, even kissed a little, trying not to get out of breath; then, they both froze when a thin, radiant sliver appeared over the horizon. Anya suddenly said: I'm sorry, I won't be long, gave him a peck on the cheek and swam down the golden path toward the sun of her last vacation day.

She is swimming in the splendor of the dawn, inhale—exhale, inhale—exhale, leisurely, but still, very fast. The sun is blinding her eyes, Anya shuts them tightly and swims in the golden darkness. Two weeks ago, she thought that her body remembered its youth, remembered its childhood, but each subsequent day brought back new memories. For some reason, at present, she had no interest in her mom's *we'll break through!* and her own *we'll resurface!* For some reason, the children who once laughed at her seem ludicrous and pathetic, and her mom's words about friends and lovers—silly and powerless. For some reason, she remembers a tall man lifting her up in his arms to the very sky . . . no, only the chandelier. Anya feels the touch of masculine hands and hears a booming voice while a beard tickles her cheek—it's both pleasant and a bit painful. She wrinkles her little nose—and at that moment, her mom's arms take her away.

And for many years, I wanted my father to return to us, Anya recalls. I pictured him and mom living together again. I was angry he didn't come. I didn't even know he came many times, wanted us all to move in together, to see me, at least, but Grandma would chase him away and mom would lock herself in her room and cry.

I didn't know any of this, but still wanted to have a father again. So when did I forget him? When did I believe Mom and Grandma, agree with them that, yes, he lied to us, he doesn't love Mom, he doesn't want to see me?

It must have been around the fifth grade, when I first began to participate in swim meets. I remember how nervous I was—and how much I wanted Dad to come watch me. So he'd sit on the bleachers and yell "Go, go!" or whatever it is parents yell at children's competitions. Now I realize that he didn't even know I went to the pool. But that one time, the whole while I was swimming, I was picturing Dad watching me. And when I lost and wept in the shower so no one could see my tears, I told myself: it's because Dad didn't come. And I decided not to wait for him anymore. To forget him.

So that's what I did. Even when we met, I didn't forgive him, didn't remember how I'd fly up to the ceiling, or the prickling of his beard. I forgot everything, as promised. And only remembered it now, when Dad is already gone. Five months, give or take a few days.

I parted ways with my father. When he was alive, I thought I didn't have a father. When he died, I remembered how much I loved him.

Vika could probably tell me where his soul is now, Anya thinks, and swims without opening her eyes, dissecting the sea at daybreak, inhale after inhale, splash after splash. Vika could tell me, but I know it myself: he's somewhere where he can see me. Watch me, Dad, watch me swim, where else would you look but at your own daughter? You're everywhere now and that means you can see everything: the stifling Moscow streets, the markets and shops I once worked at, the apartments I once rented, the men I once had, the pool lanes I swam in, my female competitors who lost to me and to whom I lost, the fine pebbles of the Turkish beach, Gosha in his little bed, Andrey on the shore. Look at my life, look across all these years, watch me swim in the radiance of the morning sun, I am swimming for you, in memory of all the meets you couldn't attend. Can you hear me, Dad? Can you see me?

I finally remembered you. I'm sorry I'm so late.

Anya wants to cry, and she probably is crying, although who can distinguish the salty water from her tears? The more so because her breathing is even, her strokes are confident, and the sun fills the sea with a sunrise gold, and, even if Anya is crying, Andrey can't see it. He's standing there without taking his eyes off the black dot of her hair, which flickers among the sunny specks, wanting this moment to last forever.

Like many years ago in the shower room, the water washes away Anya's tears—she opens her eyes and turns back to shore. I only hope Gosha doesn't wake up, she thinks, or else he'll see I'm not there, get scared, and cry. Quickly to shore—and even faster to the room, to check on him.

But when they open the door ten minutes later, Gosha is sound asleep. Only the water gun has fallen out of his small, unclenched fist.

And now, it's her last evening, Anya stands ankle-deep in the surf, peering through the seafoam at her red toenail polish, listening to the waves rolling in—even, calm, and steady. Gosha's voice mingles with the hum of the sea—he's throwing pebbles in the water, yelling something. Probably battling an invisible enemy as usual.

All her past misgivings seem laughable now. Only two weeks ago, she was worried about whether Gosha would get along with Andrey. In Moscow, they went to a café together once and almost had a falling out afterward. Andrey said: I think the boy is growing up too aggressive, and Anya answered: We Tatars are a militant people! Andrey said that Moscow is a civilized city and not some desert or wherever it is Tatars live, and Anya was offended: A civilized city? Care to try working as a cashier at a shopping center? They made up only in bed—and only because Anya didn't want to waste time: since she dropped off her kid at her mom's, she might as well fuck and finish the argument later.

To Andrey, Turkey must have borne a greater resemblance to the desert where Tatars lived. In any case, he was completely unconcerned about the boy's growing up too aggressive. Here, Andrey wasn't irritated by Gosha's desire to make a sword out of every stick and a grenade out of every stone. They played certain guys' games together and, when she returned from her swims, Anya would see them splashing by the very shore and hear delighted shrieking. Perhaps, even two shrieks: Andrey's and Gosha's.

But, most importantly, this time, Anya wasn't at all bored with Andrey. On the second day, he stopped trying to *entertain* her, and instead read his *Da Vinci Code*, played ball with Gosha, and swam. Even now, he is lying in his lounger a bit off to the side, gazing at the sea, at Anya, at Gosha running.

He's a good-looking man, Anya thinks, I glanced around the beach and there's no one who can hold a candle to him. Tight stomach, broad shoulders, muscles—well, all the regular muscles a man should have, not a gym rat's muscles. Beautiful hands, though you can't really see from here. And his eyes, dark and velvety. I like eyes like that. He's a perfectly fine guy, even Gosha likes him. I wonder why I thought he was only good for going to the movies with and fucking? Caring, tactful, not greedy. Has money, a car, a good job, a good apartment too, I suppose, though I've never set foot in it. Not to worry, when we get back to Moscow, we'll come over and see how he lives, maybe clean it up.

Oh dear, Anya thinks, be careful, girlfriend. It's fantastic that your vacation went well, throw a coin in the sea in farewell, come back next year, just don't get too comfortable. In Moscow, it will start all over again: Friday evening to Saturday afternoon—that's your time slot. Or else you'll accidentally fall in love—melt from all his attentiveness and lack of clinginess.

So I fell in love—so what? Anya replies to herself. I'm on vacation.

When was the last time I had a decent vacation? Why shouldn't I fall in love? This time, I had the real thing: a resort romance, walks in the moonlight, watching the sunrise together, we even fell asleep holding hands once . . . like those people at IKEA. Vacation. Tomorrow, we go back to Moscow, then we'll see what happens.

Anya stands there in her cheap bathing suit with the wind tousling her hair and the waves tossing up the foam at her feet—and millions of lone young women stand just like this at all of the world's resorts, on sea or ocean strands, in Turkey, Greece, Egypt, Spain, Thailand, Goa, Cuba, Crimea, and Sochi—in every place where, over and over, the saltwater rolls onto the sand, the fine pebbles, or the rocks. So they stand there as evening falls and the sun is about to set and smile faintly, stand there and think about their men and their children, about their lives, about love, their *relationships*, sex, money, their girlfriends and mothers, sometimes about marriage, sometimes about their fathers. Almost never about loneliness, old age, illness, or death.

Meanwhile Gosha runs back along the surf, dragging a rock the size of his head—wow, where did he find one that big?—dragging it with his last bit of strength and laughing. Anya looks at him, looks and thinks: dear God, how small he is compared to the sea!

And I look at all of them, look at all of us, look and mumble: my God, how small we are, how small we are against the backdrop of what is happening to us, against the backdrop of what has happened already, what you can't bring back, cannot fix. With our last bit of strength, we drag a rock along not knowing where we found it or who it's destined for, drag it and try to laugh—and we're engulfed by history that's as vast as the sea.

81.

GENEALOGY IS FATE

"My other trouble is terrible insomnia," Moreukhov says as he does a pencil sketch. "At first, Valerian root would help me, but then—nothing. I was told Corvalol worked wonders. I come out of a drinking binge, I can't sleep, I try Corvalol. Right away, I can sleep well and my mood improves. Then I notice that I'm using more and more Corvalol. Then I run out of money."

"Money for Corvalol?" Lena asks. She's sitting in an armchair in the middle of the studio, being disciplined about not moving. *Tell me about yourself, it's boring to sit here like this*, she said, so Moreukhov is telling her about the exhibits in the mid-nineties, the alcoholics in Troparyovo, the man who swore he saw a flying saucer in a secret hangar in Konkovo, and, in it, alien mummies who looked like octopuses with plates on their heads. *A saucer and plates, get it?* he laughs and continues drawing.

Lena asks: "So, in the beginning, it was champagne?" and he tells her about how delicious the first swig was and how easy the road to the granary those first few days.

Lena asks: "Then what?" and he tells her how the vodka is replaced by gin and tonic as inevitably as night replaces day.

Lena asks: "So, after two weeks, you'd get back to normal?" and he tells her that the most terrifying thing isn't the bender itself: it's coming off the bender.

So, Corvalol.

"All my money, all of it. I don't have much left toward the end of a binge, see. And that's when I start getting real withdrawal symptoms. Foam coming out the mouth, spasms, epileptic seizure. It turned out that Corvalol was banned all over Europe because it's a strong fucking narcotic."

At present, Moreukhov studies Lena without restraint. Maybe she does have a passing resemblance to Anita Mui, the Hong Kong singer and actress who starred in a half-dozen films about love and the martial arts, and who was Jackie Chan's girlfriend.

Moreukhov didn't like Jackie Chan that much—if you don't count his film *Drunken Master,* of course: *Money and power have no power over us / We only need one thing: wine / People gnaw at each other's throats like wolves / And only he who drinks shall never die.*

Anita Mui died in December 2003 and Zhang Yimou dedicated *House of Flying Daggers* to her—not his best film, to be honest.

She was only forty.

I wonder how old Lena is, Moreukhov thinks, but instead asks:

"Are you of Chinese heritage?"

"I won't tell you," Lena smiles, "I won't tell you anything about myself. Draw me as I am—without my biography, my last name, without knowing what my husband's job is."

"And what is your husband's job?"

"I won't tell you. Maybe I was kidding. Maybe he doesn't have a job. Maybe I don't even have a husband. You go ahead and draw."

And Moreukhov draws, draws and talks. It's been a long time since he talked so much sober. Probably as long as since he last painted in oils. Lena's sitting motionless, which makes it seem as if she's listening intently and responding.

"It's the first time I've met someone who likes the outskirts of Moscow. Everyone I know is trying to move to the city center or the suburbs."

"They must be wealthy people," Moreukhov scoffs. "And besides, they think a building from 1905 is amazing. You could say it's a prehistoric building."

"Why prehistoric?"

"For me, history started in 1917," Moreukhov replies in a tone that is half-serious and half-joking, "but that's not what I'm talking about. For me, the most important thing in a city are the islands of time standing still, the fragments of the past. There's practically none of this left in the center, but plenty of it on the outskirts. The past isn't that old on the outskirts, but that's actually a good thing: I remember it better."

"Right, so you don't remember 1905 either," Lena smiles.

"You can say I don't remember it at all," Moreukhov agrees, "but, in general, I believe in genetic memory. Does that ever happen to you—you're watching some old movie and suddenly think you were there? Although the movie is, say, from the prewar era, before we were even born."

"To tell the truth," Lena says, "I rarely watch old movies."

"I really like them," Moreukhov says. "What's the most important thing about them? It's not the plot, it's the spirit of the times. If the image hasn't been remastered, then that's even better. I like the past in general, I believe that every person is made up of his ancestors."

"I think so too," Lena says, "you have to know your ancestors. Your genealogy is your fate."

"They're not in your head, they're in your genes," Moreukhov explains, "when I was a child, I read a sci-fi story about a scientist who invented a time machine. It would send the person into an ancestor's body—and, if I remember correctly, he ended up in the body of a Neanderthal."

"Did he like it in there?" Lena giggles.

"I don't think so," Moreukhov answers, "I think he was just a bit lost. Who would enjoy finding out that there's a primitive, psychopathic killer inside you? Whereas I'm certain that you can reach your ancestors without a time machine, you just have to want it. And you don't need to invent anything to feel like a Neanderthal: there's a time-tested method. It costs thirty rubles. The author of that story must have not known about it."

So they keep talking, day after day, session after session.

Moreukhov tells her about the *non-military* secret and the dark puddle spreading around his grandpa's glistening bald head; how, in his childhood, he watched films about the Civil War—*Bumbarash, White Sun of the Desert, Legacy of the Republic*—how great was Mironov in that one? And in the end, when he's blindfolded in his white shirt and goes: *I don't shoot women!*

Lena listens in a way that makes Moreukhov think that one day, a miracle will happen: at the end of the session, Lena will get up, throw off her dress, come up to him, put her arms around him, and kiss him. And his whole life will turn around, will be brand new and beautiful.

What's more, he says to himself, it's in the film noir canon: the beauty must seduce me, how can you do without it? And he tells her about rotten underwater snags, dead arms, horned water creatures, black crayfish, the swollen bellies of drowned bodies, and their mold-green skin.

"Okay, corpses and water creatures," Lena says, "that's at the very the end. But what happened before that?"

And he tells her about Sonya Sphilman, whom he was in love with, and how Sonya aborted his child because who would want a child from an alcoholic, and how she fled to Israel for good, so there's no point in talking about her. Moreukhov tells her how, a few times, he asked God to finish him off and God didn't heed him once, tells her how easy it is to meet women when you're drunk but how impossible to maintain those relationships. He tells her about his drunken adventures, his chance girlfriends, and love in garbage dumps and vacant lots.

He tells her about his family, about his businessman brother, his sales-girl cousin, his mom and dad, the fact that his dad abandoned his preg-nant mom and she says it's because of his grandpa.

"The one who killed himself?" Lena asks, and Moreukhov isn't taken aback, he's used to the fact that she's listening to him closely. It's been years since young women have listened to him this way—possibly because he reaches under their skirts too soon.

Moreukhov tells her about Grandpa: they don't know anything about him, everyone who knew him is dead, the only one left is Mom, but she doesn't say anything either. At one time, Grandpa told him he'd fought in the Civil War, but it's likely that everyone fought back then.

"Have you looked him up on the internet?" Lena asks.

"I don't use the internet," Moreukhov says with an air of dignity.

A few years ago, Sonya Shpilman sent him her email address through mutual friends. Moreukhov ended up writing to her: his love was alive and carnal, redolent of summer grass, Crimean port wine, and lukewarm beer. There was nothing virtual about it and never would be.

"The internet is a toxic globalist invention," Moreukhov says.

"Can you tell me his name again?" Lena says, "I'll look it up. You have to know your ancestors."

"And who were your ancestors?" Moreukhov asks.

"I won't tell you," Lena smiles again.

And again, Moreukhov tells her about his mom and uncle Sasha, his father and Lyolya, Nikita, Anya-Elvira, and Rimma, tells her how he conjures them all up, imagines their lives, imagines them conjuring each other up, conjuring him up.

"But were you sober on February 4th?" Lena asks.

That's anybody's guess. That was only a week since the drinking binge. In theory, he was sober.

"Good. And how did you learn about your father's death?"

Yes, she looks like Maggie Cheung and Anita Mui. And when she gets up—Michelle Yeoh, but only a little bit. It turns out that the whole cast of *Heroic Trio* is here.

Heroic Trio is a violent fantasy film from Hong Kong, an adult fairy tale. Three superwomen against the forces of evil. The Russian title was *Executioners*.

This doesn't bode anything good for Moreukhov.

82.

LIKE INCEST

I've been to this bowling alley once, Andrey convinced me to go, said: you're a former athlete, you must like physical activity, let's go throw some balls—and we really did throw them. By the end of the third hour, I was hitting all the pins. Sharp eye, Grandma's sniper genes, a salesgirl's practiced legs, plus, twenty-five minutes of exercise every day.

Of course, it was harder for Nikita. He's got a sedentary job, never played sports, and went to the bowling alley for the very first time not on a date, like I did, but with a whole gaggle of employees. Victor, the one in the suit, I think, called this a teambuilding session.

And so, Nikita's sitting at the table, drinking some lemonade—he's driving, so he can't have alcohol—and his fifteen staff members are bowling and drinking beer.

"Nikita," says Zoya, a wide-mouthed bleached blonde, "why are you sitting there? Let's go, I'll show you how easy it is."

Nikita goes with her—what is he supposed to do, what kind of a teambuilding session is it without the boss? Zoya's wearing a short dress and high-heeled shoes and her chubby legs are covered with fishnet stockings. It's horribly vulgar, if you think about it. She's walking a bit ahead of him and swaying—it's either the beer or she's wagging her ass. In the office, Nikita almost never pays attention to this kind of stuff, but here, he is looking and involuntarily noting her movements.

"Look," Zoya says, "you stand like this, put it in your right hand, no, let me show you." She stands behind him and her breasts practically fall on his back.

Looks like she's trying to pick me up, Nikita thinks. Sex with an employee is the last thing I need.

Interesting, he thinks, there was a time when I was convinced that all bosses slept with their employees, especially if they were young and pretty. And in the span of three years, it never even crossed my mind. I wonder why.

So, fingers in the holes, take a few steps, and let it go. The ball crashes down and rolls into the gutter, flying away into the black chasm on that side of the lane. Not a single pin out of place.

"Let's try it one more time," Zoya says. "The first time is always hard."

Would it be hard for me to place my hand for the first time on her hip right now? Pretend that I'm trying to improve my throwing skills? And then—again for the first time—make a not-so-innocent gesture, then another and another, and later, offer her a ride home and fuck her right in the car, at her place, or even drive to a hotel? And afterward, constantly run into each other at the office and have a quickie at the end of the workday? Would that be hard for me?

Hard isn't the right word, I think, simply impossible.

Although Zoya is very cute and, apparently, completely unopposed to flirting with me, and I'm probably even a bit aroused by it—in any case, it must be because I haven't seen Dasha in a week.

In the next lane—Victor and Natasha. Would they be able to sleep together? Natasha's lover left her and Victor is a lonely young man. They'd make a good couple and it would probably be useful for work. They could sleep together and that would be their personal teambuilding session.

But it looks like they're just bowling together.

Meanwhile, my ball has knocked down three pins. Zoya emits a victory cry and encourages her capable student. I think about how nice it must be for Anya-Elvira to come here with her Andrey—they could cuddle openly, not like with Zoya. Anya would probably drink an exotic cocktail at the bar, Andrey would probably get a beer—if he was smart enough to leave his car at home.

I didn't think of it, but it doesn't matter. At least my grip is firmer and the next ball knocks down half the pins, ending up right in the middle of the formation. By now, Victor and Natasha have finished their round and are applauding my throw. They probably want me to do well.

I wonder if they understand what's happening to me. Do they care at all? Or do they just see me as the man who hands out their pay once a month—unfortunately, not in an envelope anymore, but legally, over the counter, like they wanted? Probably not. Because, to me, they're not just the people who ensure my company's revenue. I see them every day and have shared a moment of true intimacy with every single one of them. Whether it's explaining to Natasha about married men or reminiscing with Victor about how, as children, we used to keep red midges for fishing bait in the refrigerator under a moist rag. And here, at the bowling alley, I realize that these aren't just my coworkers, they're my close friends. Not all of them, of course, but at least these three: Victor, Natasha, and Zoya.

A team? I don't know.

Another one of my balls takes down the pins with a thud. I've turned out to be an able student, Zoya can be proud of me.

"Let's play for points now," I say, and we line up. They're making noises, laughing and reacting to every lucky throw with loud screams. Like children, I swear.

What a great word: children. I get it: it's as if they're my children. That's why it never crosses my mind to sleep with Zoya or Natasha—it would be like incest. It's enough that I sleep with Dasha, who is young enough to be my daughter.

Victor, Zoya, Natasha, and Dasha—that's a few too many children, isn't it? Let's throw in Masha—small, gaunt, longing to have a child of her own.

I think to myself: maybe that's why we don't have children of our own, because Masha is herself like a child to me.

Nikita's on his way home. Tonight's traffic jam doesn't seem so dreary to him. Maybe it's because I had a good time for the first time in six months? he thinks. Had a good time like a normal human being, didn't fuck my lover, didn't take my wife to doctors' appointments, didn't get drunk with Kostya—no, I went to a bowling alley with a bunch of young people and bowled. And everyone was happy, everyone enjoyed it, no one hurt anyone's feelings.

Joy and peace wash over his soul. He drives out of the bottleneck, where he was twenty eternal meters away from the traffic light. The oncoming lane is completely empty, but suddenly, a siren blares and a blue-and-white police car catches up to him from somewhere on the side.

It's always like this, Nikita thinks, as soon as I relax, it starts all over again! Good thing I didn't drink a single drop.

The usual dialogue—license and registration, insurance, you've crossed the double lane marker; Nikita is prepared to take out his wallet already, but at the last moment, he says:

"Listen, boss, there was nobody there. Nothing dangerous. And there was traffic in the other lane. I would have lost another ten minutes and instead, I helped unclog the gridlock. You can see that I'm sober, just tired and wanting to get home. Let's forget all this, alright?"

"Did an infraction take place?" the police officer asks and replies to himself: "It did. That means we'll draft a protocol and revoke your license."

"Why my license?" Nikita says.

"Going the wrong way," the officer explains.

Nikita doesn't care about the money, but his mood has been ruined. He gets into the police car, carries out the required ritual, pays them, and takes back his license. He drives home thinking, what would the guy have done if I said to him:

"Listen, man! No one will tell you this, but I will. You have a shitty job, nobody needs it. You're not catching criminals, you're collecting money. If I were drunk, you would've still let me go, right? You would've just taken more money from me first. And then I would've hit someone with my car, right? A woman or a child? Given you money and then hit someone.

"So I'm telling you: you have a shitty job, nobody needs you, everyone hates you. You come home in the evening with this trail of hatred and contempt dragging behind you. And you chose this for yourself. Don't tell me that you have to split the gains with your superiors—if you can't work in an honest way, then leave and find yourself another job. You'll respect yourself and people will thank you. Is that so bad? It's better than collecting bribes. And don't tell me that there's no such thing as a good, honest job: I found myself one and so did the guys who work with me—so why can't you?"

I wonder what he would have said to me, Nikita thinks. Would he have revoked my license for real? Thrown my bribe in my face? Cursed me out and left?

Or maybe, he would have sighed and said: You're lucky, man, your parents must have had an apartment in Moscow, you must've gotten an education or whatever, had a happy childhood. It's easy for you to make money. And I just want a normal life for my family. Want my wife to have a beautiful dress, my daughter to have a white bow on her head, a life of plenty, a happy childhood for my kid, like you once had.

And what would I have replied?

83.

REINCARNATION. ALEKSEY

Lika says I should go to the doctor, says that psychotherapy works miracles. Psychotherapy will teach me to have a different outlook on life, my present and past. You'll feel so much better, Lika says, you just need to make the effort.

Fifty dollars an hour—twice a week—for a few years. And you'll see diamonds in the sky, you'll be able to enjoy yourself, Lika says.

You'll understand that Mom and Dad still love you.

You'll understand that that they have long forgotten, long forgiven, long said goodbye to you.

You'll understand that you shouldn't stress out, you should relax, and then you'll be able to have a child.

You'll understand that, even if you don't end up having one, everything will be okay. You can be happy without a child.

You'll understand that everything is going well in your life.

Everything is fine.

You'll become happy.

Fifty dollars an hour, twice a week, for a few years. You'll have a completely different outlook on life.

Katya says I should go to yoga, says that yoga works miracles. Yoga will give me a completely different outlook on life, my present and past. You'll feel so much better, Katya says, you just need to make the effort.

Sixty dollars an hour, twice a week, for a few years. And you'll see diamonds in the sky, you'll be able to enjoy yourself, Katya says.

Olya says I should meditate, says that meditation works miracles. Meditation will teach me to have a completely different outlook on life, my present and past. You'll feel so much better, Olya says, you just need to make the effort.

Who the hell knows how much it costs?

Meditation is probably free.

Of course, the girls are right. I can have an entirely different perspective. I can come to terms with the fact that everything is going well in my life.

But all of them, what do I do about them? The young woman from the village, which was reduced to ashes, the little girl on the warm sand at night, the soldier who pulled the pin from the grenade, the sailor who is four fingers away from death, the withered old woman by the mirror and many, many others—what do I do about them? They already died, they're all dead, it's all over for them.

They won't get another perspective on life. They won't come to terms with the fact that everything is going well for them. I'm encircled by their souls—their gentle stirring, translucent shadows, and flat bodies. These people were unhappy. They were refused what they had come into this world for.

Everything ended with them.

Everything ended for them.

They will never be happy.

I won't either.

As she fell asleep, Irina took my hand. Her hand was small and clasping, like that of a small animal. For an hour now, I've been trying to disengage my hand from it. I'm sitting by the foot of the bed and fear I won't be able to leave till morning.

The moon is shining in the window and I have a good view of Irina's tranquil face. Her lips are partly open and her fair hair is strewn across the pillow. Were it a bit lighter, I would have seen the shadow cast on her cheek by her long lashes.

Three months ago, I noticed this shadow for the first time—it trembled on her velvet skin in the bright lights of Tverskaya Street's display windows. Irina's breath came out of her mouth in an invisible, damp cloud.

Irina bumped into me without recognizing me in the crowd and I saw her crying.

That's how I learned about the death of Apollo Andreyevich. Officially, Karelin was called the head of the Secretariat of the All-Russian Association of Anarchists, but an initiated few knew him as the founder of the Order of Light, the Moscow chapter of the Knights Templar.

Like the rest of us, he believed in eternal life, the Golden Ladder. For him, dying was merely climbing up another step.

I took Irina by the elbow and she simply sobbed. For those of us who remained, Karelin's departure was a misfortune and a loss—the steps of the Golden Ladder were steep and I didn't know if I could follow Apollo Andreyevich, or if my karma would irrepressibly drag me down to be born anew into the shackles of the flesh.

At *Bonjour*, we each ordered a cup of coffee and Irina began to talk about reviving the dead. *It's not resurrection, it's revival!* she repeated, pointing a delicate finger to the ceiling. *Our main debt is our debt to the dead.* I remarked that Nikolay Fyodorov's ideas seemed overly utopian to me, and the deceased Karelin, too, had pinned his hopes on less corporal paths. As I usually did at such times, I began to talk about Vladimir Solovyov, about the path indicated by his philosophy. When we parted, Irina asked me to accompany her to the funeral, saying that she didn't want to be alone on a day like this.

I never saw her cry again—and, all these months, cherished the memory of the tears. One small tear lingered on her cheek for a long time, like a matte, precious pearl.

Afterward, we began to meet often. We'd usually sit in one of the privately owned cafes permitted under the New Economic Policy; twice, Irina convinced me to go to the movie theater. Neither of the films were worth the time we expended: an insufferably crude melodrama of some kind and the contrivedly avant-garde *Aelita*. Aleksey Tolstoy's novel always seemed hopelessly vulgar to me: the retelling of the Atlantis myth alone was excruciatingly so. Furthermore, I thought that Aelita was prim and pretentious in the film. The director must have wanted to create an image of cosmic love but, instead, conceived an operatic femme fatale with a repulsive third breast.

It was an unseasonably chilly spring day. I vividly remember Irina's petite frame in a chinchilla coat and carrying a large, patent leather purse. As it grew hotter, she'd take turns flinging her coat open and lowering it past her shoulders. As usual, I was reminded of the defects of the flesh, which suffers from cold and heat and requires lodging and clothing.

"I read Tolstoy, too," Irina said. "After all, it was his idea that the

Atlanteans flew off to Mars, wasn't it? Blavatskaya says nothing on that account, right?"

Irina ended almost every phrase with a question, and our conversations often resulted in my nodding and repeating "yes," "indeed," and "I know." I was unsure if I should confide the intricate vagaries of my philosophical and magical views to my new acquaintance. Irina wasn't flustered by this—she was never at a loss for a subject of one of her monologues.

"I was always convinced that the Atlanteans lived on the ocean floor. Given their wisdom, it probably wasn't very difficult for them to relocate underwater with their continent, am I right? And that means they dwell somewhere on the ocean floor, wriggling their fins and tentacles, correct?"

"Why fins and tentacles?" I asked. "If they're so wise, they could retain their human appearance underwater."

"They never had a human appearance," Irina says. "Blavatskaya has written about this, remember? I think," Irina continued, "that the Atlanteans who flew off into space didn't resemble humans at all. Remember how the Martians, too, had tentacles in *War of the Worlds*? That's because the underwater and space creatures descended from those same Atlanteans. As above, so below, you see?"

And she burst into a clear, sonorous laughter. The sound flew from her lips and dissolved in the air, reminding me of golden marbles bouncing down stairs. Quite possibly the same ones that Apollo Andreyevich had already ascended.

. . . Again, I try to disengage my hand. Irina's slender fingers encircle my wrist like octopus tentacles. She sighs in her sleep, but doesn't unclench her hand.

Wherever Karelin is now, Moscow mourned him that spring. The city sprawled out like a body abandoned by its soul, like a house abandoned by its owners. Predictably, new residents appeared in the house not long after: Moscow spring life was hurried and feverish. Every so often, new circles, salons, and even brotherhoods were announced in great secret.

The city was being jolted as if someone was trying to galvanize a corpse.

One evening, we sat at a round table in a Moscow apartment that had hardly changed since those happy pre-war years. The candles burned and I recalled how, years earlier, in an apartment just like this, we strived not to break the circle while the medium summoned the spirit of Jakob Böhme.

Irina brought me to this apartment with the statement that people with an interest in Buddhism and eastern wisdom gathered here. Today's speaker—a short, black-haired man of Semitic appearance—explained his theory of the scientific transformation of Buddha's teachings.

He proposed to complement the idea of personal karma with that of family karma. Therefrom, he derived the possibility of two pathways to reincarnation—into a new body after one's death and into one's children in the course of one's life. We concurrently belong to two infinite systems, he explained. On the one hand, we're a link in a chain of rebirths and deaths and, on the other—a knot in our family history.

I'd long wondered if Buddhists believed that reincarnation was a sin to be avoided, and if this meant that child-bearing and the sexual instinct were sinful in general. I asked this, and the people at the table exchanged looks, holding back smiles. Irina smiled too. In the bright candlelight, her lips appeared almost black.

The host replied that it was a great advantage to be born into a human body. If there weren't any human children, everyone would be reborn an animal.

Disappointed, I didn't reply. It turned out that the beautiful and upright Buddhist system was designed to glorify carnal love and the repugnant act of physical childbirth.

Knowing that it was unlikely I'd return here, I asked about Shambhala —whether it was a real place or simply a metaphor signifying the highest state of spiritual development.

A heavy silence hung over the round table. It spread like a stifling cloud that drank in our breath. Everyone was still, and only Irina's bottomless eyes gazed at me across the table.

"That's a complicated question, in my opinion," the host said hesitantly. "And how do you know about Shambhala in the first place?"

I felt like a bumbling grammar-school boy, gangly and big-headed. My face turned crimson and, even as we returned home along Tverskaya Street later that night, I thought my cheeks were burning in the dark.

"Tell me, Irina," I asked, "was my question tactless?"

"It was out of place," she replied, "I can't explain it to you. If they wanted to, they would have told you themselves, right?"

The squeaking of Irina's patent-leather boots echoed in the nighttime silence as if they were in a rush to pry themselves away from the pavement and soar into the frigid skies.

"It was lovely to call on them," I said. "A pre-war Moscow building. I didn't think those still existed. It's as if those terrible twelve years never happened. I wonder how they escaped consolidation."

I'd long noticed that Irina avoided looking at her conversation partner. At the café, she twirled a little spoon in her hands and, in the street, she fiddled with her purse. At the very least, she gazed through half-lowered lashes. I found this mannerism touching and virtuous.

Of course, I don't think of it that way anymore.

That night, Irina looked directly into my eyes for the first time. We were standing by an illuminated display window, and that was how I discovered her eyes were azure-blue.

"These people escaped consolidation," Irina said, "because they work for an important government agency. Don't you understand?"

I wanted to ask if the government agency, too, had ties to Shambhala, but restrained myself.

. . . At the moment, Irina's blue eyes are closed. Perhaps I should simply tear my hand away and leave. She probably wouldn't even wake up. That's what I should do, I tell myself, but I don't budge.

When Irina sleeps, she looks like an angel, although I know she is merely a woman.

In late May, we saw each other almost daily, and these meetings helped me a lot. I was having a difficult time—I usually have trouble adjusting to the onset of summer. In those months, the planetary positions elicit an agitation in me that I can't express, a vague premonition. When I was younger, I waited for a miracle and a vision every year, but then my joyful anticipation was replaced by despair. Many a time I reread the poem "Three Encounters" and prayed that St. Sophia would come to me as she had to its author, Solovyov, in the British Museum and the Egyptian desert. I dreamed of seeing Her radiant smile and the celestial scintillation of purple cloth, of touching the Soul of the Worlds. I fasted, prayed to St. Sophia, the luminous daughter of dark chaos, and asked Her to consecrate me, but alas, my prayer went unheeded.

It was this despair that drove me to join esoteric circles and groups. All the while, I thought there were people close by who could open the Way to me, give me what my soul was pining for. I dreamed of seeing Sophia on the throne and experiencing the bliss that Solovyov had written about. Alas. Over the course of my life, I had encountered many truly wise people who possessed that knowledge, but none of them helped me—not even Apollo Andreyevich. My despair grew deeper every year.

In the end, it brought me to the brink of catastrophe.

Yes, my meetings with Irina helped me a lot. Even now, I can admit that, despite her feminine frivolity, she is educated and intelligent, including in the spiritual sense. We could talk for hours and her very voice seemed healing to me.

Presently, I observed that, in our arguments about the spirit and the flesh, we avoided the subject of sexual relations. The subject was unpleasant to me and Irina, as I now realize, never noticed the effect her sexual instinct had on her.

Yes, for all her etherealness, Irina is a very earthly creature. I never took an interest in the material world myself and never noticed her dresses and fur coats, her habit of going home in taxicabs, and her lazy promenades by the reflective shop windows of Petrovka Street.

Irina knew how to remain ephemeral and fragile in expensive ensembles that would seem vulgar on any other woman. It was if she was on the verge of soaring and, like a butterfly, abandoning the chrysalis of her attire. This flickering, incessant flight charmed me and I couldn't take my eyes off her.

I must myself have been at the mercy of a delusion and didn't see how vulgar it was to discuss eternal life before a window display of silk stockings.

Irina's interest in shops and privately owned cafes appeared excusable to me. Over the years of devastation, we had grown unaccustomed to shop windows. A few years earlier, I'd personally gone to see a Moscow Food Supply Division window that featured a drunken clerk who'd fallen asleep among a plethora of goods.

Of course, we visited the Second Moscow Art Theater and Yuriy Zavadsky's Theatrical Studio more often than we did women's lingerie shops.

At one such meeting, I saw Konstantin Nikolayevich. He was my university professor, I'd even been to his home a few times. Back then, in 1913, we discussed the Indian roots of Plato's philosophy. Konstantin Nikolayevich shared my opinion that Shambhala was indeed a fragment of Atlantis.

Over the span of fifteen years, he'd aged terribly. He was scarcely over sixty, but looked ancient. I asked him about his wife and son (unfortunately, I couldn't recall their names) and learned that his son lived with him and his wife had died of the Spanish Flu in 1919. The professor's voice faltered, but, alas, I could find no words of solace for him. I asked him if he was still interested in Atlantis and Shambhala.

"Atlantis," mumbled Konstantin Nikolayevich, "we didn't understand anything about Atlantis. We thought what mattered was the Atlanteans' great civilization. But now we know it's not the civilization that matters, it's the flood. We have the Bible for the flood, we don't need Plato or Blavatskaya."

"Why does the flood matter?" Irina asked. "Why do we need the flood?

"The flood can serve as evidence of Christ's mercy," he replied. "The Flood in the Old Testament and Plato's flood, which destroyed Atlantis, are the embodiments of God's anger. The Hebrew God is merciless, which is why the Flood destroyed all living things save those preserved in the ark. Since then, the sea serves as a solemn reminder of that punishment. Thus, millennia pass. And what happens when Jesus comes into our world? Even before He dies and is reborn, He works miracles. He heals the ill, feeds the hungry, and revives Lazarus. This is the expression of His mercy. And amid those miracles, the senseless walking on water. Why would Jesus walk on water? Even Moses could part the waves, why couldn't the son of God?"

By force of old professorial habit, Konstantin Nikolayevich held a pause, as if waiting for an answer. I turned my eyes to my companion: her lips were parted and her azure-blue eyes were wide.

"He walked on water because he wanted to say: My mercy overrides God's anger. I am eternal life and have come to atone for human sin. Those who have been engulfed by waves shall find salvation with Me and in Me." Konstantin Nikolayevich grew quiet and then added: "And that's welcome news for those of us who were around for this latest Flood. Jesus is more important than Atlantis, mercy is more powerful than anger."

"But Eternal Life isn't earthly life," Irina said. "What difference does it make to you if your wife is in paradise? After all, you're here on earth."

"I, my dear young lady, have been luckier than many," he replied. "I am already old and won't be here too long. So I am hoping for God's mercy. And you young people are left with earthly hopes. Including the hope that the Bolsheviks will be merciful. Unfortunately, you'll have to pay for it, and more than you think."

"Should I become a fellow traveler?" I asked. "I suppose that, because I translate at the People's Commissariat of Education, I am one. But in all other ways, I live as if the Bolsheviks didn't exist. And what are the Bolsheviks, really, against the backdrop of millennia?"

"Fellow travelers can't count on mercy," he answered. "Better you go to the factory right away and become just like them. Because, if the Bolsheviks are a scourge from God, we can only welcome it. I said the same thing to Misha: go to the factory, join the Komsomol, forget everything I've taught you."

"Correct," Irina said, "if there is a flood, you must grow out your tentacles. But I think you're being unjust to the Bolsheviks. There are sympathetic people among them. They're interested in occult knowledge and have a good grasp of it. All this talk of workers and peasants is for laymen. In fact, at this very moment, they're preparing to build a magical empire that stretches from Europe to India. You have to seek a magical meaning behind all of the Bolsheviks' initiatives! Acknowledge that, behind these new Huns, there are secret magi."

"And where do your secret magi happen to work, young lady?" Konstantin Nikolayevich asked. "At the Joint State Political Directorate?"

"Yes, there, too!" Irina replied, and I started to laugh to defuse the tension.

"I must admit that the old way of life is over," Konstantin Nikolayevich said. "Our grandchildren and great-grandchildren won't live the way we and our fathers did. Not only won't they seek occult knowledge, they won't even take their wives to Paris or their children to Biarritz like everyone once did."

Now it was Irina's turn to laugh. The sound didn't evoke the scattering of golden marbles for me, but, rather, a ringing of metallic bells.

Summer came. A few times, I invited Irina to come stay with friends of mine at a dacha, but she was detained in Moscow on business.

In the phantom moonlight, I see Irina's bedroom, which looks as if there's never been a war or devastation. What business could she have had in Moscow? What does Irina do in the first place? But this question is just an attempt to avoid another: what am I doing here? Why am I not leaving? Why didn't I leave directly after it all happened?

Unwittingly, I recall that other bedroom. I was seventeen—it's scary to think this took place a half-lifetime ago! Rays of sunlight streamed out of the crevices in the curtains. The woman I worshipped slipped off her peignoir and said: "You little fool, what are you standing there for? Come here."

That's how I saw what was obscured by clothing. Fatty folds of flesh on her hips. Large, quivering breasts. A belly overhanging the place where I was afraid to lower my gaze.

The woman I had worshipped was completely different. She didn't seem enormous to me and avoided superfluous physical contact—ethereal, eternally surrounded by the scent of floral perfume.

Now she's beside me with her breasts hanging down and her hand unfastening my trousers, and I'm struck by a harsh, nauseating odor.

"What, is it your first time?" she says. "That's alright, we'll sort that out right now," and she tugs at my member, which I'd tried to touch as little as possible. It's as if she wants to sever it—I scream, break free, and run away so as to never return to that house, never see her again . . .

A few years later, I'll realize that I'd been unjust. Every woman has a dual nature: Eternal Femininity can't fully vanquish the sexual instinct, can't vanquish the flesh. Vladimir Solovyov called it *woman's nature as such*, and hoped to attain harmony in the triune kingdom of androgyny, spiritual corporality, and the godliness of man.

Fifteen years ago, I read *The Meaning of Love*, and my soul briefly settled in a fleshly cocoon. I thought that I now knew the way.

The years had dissipated my dreams. *Spiritual corporality* turned out to be *dry water, cold fire*—an oxymoron, a phantom, a decoy. At the German front, on the streets of Moscow, in friends' apartments—there was no place where corporality was linked to spirituality. It always signified suffering, depravity, and cruelty.

I swore that I wouldn't allow any woman to lure me into this trap.

. . . Irina is sleeping, covered up to her very chin with a blanket. I can't see her body—and thank God for that!

What deceived me, lured me, forced me to forget my oath?

The beam of celestial blue between her eyelashes?

Slightly parted lips?

Slender, fragile fingers? The same ones that squeeze my wrist right now like an iron band?

Two weeks ago, I'd forgotten my oath. Irina appeared to me in a vision as my Bride and my Wife. I decided that her level of spiritual development was high enough to create a reliable barrier to the revolting manifestations of woman's nature.

For two weeks, I prayed in the hope that St. Sophia would give me a sign and, yesterday, in the June twilight of Pushkin Boulevard, I told Irina I loved her.

The words flew from my lips—and I, too, wanted to become a word, turn into the air, envelop Irina, allow her to inhale me, fill her lungs, and then leave her body with the exhale, merging with the ethereal vibrations of her soul, quivering on her dark lips.

I told her I loved her—and, with these words, surrendered myself to her. She took me like a patent-leather purse, tucked me under her arm, and placed me on the backseat of her Renault.

I also remember what followed, but hope that Jesus's mercy will send me oblivion.

It was horrible, repulsive, vile. And the worst part is that I didn't stop Irina, no, I became just like her. Now I know that *man's nature as such* is no better than woman's nature—it, too, is the embodiment of *animal nature*.

Coitus is revolting, if only because, at the peak of ecstasy, the man expels semen—a whitish, malodorous slime. And afterward, he feels apathy and shame.

So I sit in the dim bedroom and, suddenly, I begin to see clearly. Irina's hand on my wrist signifies the shackles of the flesh tethering my spirit. Nothing is easier than liberating myself—I just need to be more decisive. So I sit there in the dark, spineless and inert.

Only understanding brings liberation. No, I don't pull away, but a great peace descends upon me. This must be what the deep meditation of yogi is like. For a moment, the world ceases to exist: there is neither a bedroom, nor Irina, nor my body.

I discover the answers to all my questions. I realize that Irina and her Buddhist friends are collaborating with a special section of the Joint State Political Directorate on secret projects in the areas of hypnosis, neuro-energetics, and magic. Any day now, they're expecting Roerich's expedition, which was sent to Tibet in search of Shambhala, to return to Moscow.

They don't know yet that the expedition ended in failure: Shambhala still has not been found.

And it won't be found. In any case, not by the Cheka.

In the dim bedroom, shackled to Irina's body by her slender fingers, I can see the future.

I can see how, in five years, Irina's superior will sign an order for the arrest of her friends, the Moscow Knights Templar, Karelin's students.

I can see how, in another few years, her superior himself will be led to execution by firing squad. By that time, there'll be nothing left of all the various manifestations of esoteric, mystical Russia.

I can see Irina in new dresses, new furs, sitting on the leather seats of automobiles, and in the opulent interiors of government dachas.

I can see her husband and their vile, dirty romping in bed. I can see Irina's wide-open womb and a wrinkled red body covered in slime. I can hear her son's first cry.

I can see Irina's husband up on a podium—an elected official, a writer, a scientist?

I can see the wilting of Irina's flesh, wrinkles, folds of fat. I know that, in old age, she'll become practically deaf but, until her very death, will continue gazing through her eyelashes with those celestial blue eyes.

I can only see the flesh, I don't know what Irina's feeling, what she's thinking.

Does she love her husband? Is she happy? What is she dreaming about? Does she remember me?

I will not learn the answers to these questions. As for the flesh, I always said that the flesh is of no importance.

A moment—and then I'm back in the bedroom. Perhaps I fell asleep? In any case, what difference does it make—that dream felt so real.

Suddenly, I realize that I know Irina's future, the future of our friends and enemies. I just don't know what will happen to me. For some reason, I remember: *if you want to swim in the ocean, you must grow out your tentacles.*

Yes, I've seen that ocean—decades ahead. It has neither a beginning nor an end, and I don't want to turn into a fish, an octopus, or an H. G. Wells Martian who drinks human blood. I don't want to swim anywhere.

I know what to do . . . I gently but decisively disengage myself from the bracelet of another's fingers. No resistance.

Ridding myself of Irina's shackles turned out to be easy. I think the shackles of the flesh aren't much sturdier.

I walk to the writing desk in the adjoining room. If my dream was prophetic, I'll know which drawer to open . . .

The metal feels cold against my palm.

Yes, my body shall not lie in the holy ground.

So be it. As I said, the flesh is of no importance.

I know that I'm not committing a sin. Is it really suicide if a butterfly flies out of the chrysalis?

You don't need a body at all. Ridding yourself of one is akin to tossing out clothes that no longer fit you.

Now I will pull the trigger—and my soul will fly toward Eternal Life and climb another step of the Golden Ladder.

. . . And I hear thunder, see a bright flash, and then, I'm surrounded by an unfading azure light, and a beautiful Virgin appears before me in the golden blue, in the celestial gleam of purple, and looks at me with such familiar, fiery blue eyes.

And I ask:

"Is that you? Soul of the Worlds, the bright body of eternity, the sweetness of the ever present God, the image of unearthly beauty, tell me, is that you?"

She replies to me and Her voice sounds so familiar:

"Don't you know me? I was next to you this whole time, and you don't know me? Yes, it is I."

And I fall on my knees before Her; an ethereal, milky-white, virginal light descends upon me and I cry tears of happiness and repeat:

"So I wasn't mistaken—it was You all along. Why did You act this way with me, why all this filth, repulsive flesh, mucus, and sweat?"

She replies and Her voice booms with spring thunder:

"You understood nothing. You asked for an initiation and I gave you one. The initiation is always the most frightening experience a person can stand."

"So I passed?"

I hear Irina's vibrant, radiant laughter:

"No, you did not pass. You renounced your love, killed yourself, didn't leave a son or a daughter to the world. You lived an empty and fruitless life."

And I cry again, presently, from shame and repentance, cry and say:

"What a fool I was, my Mistress, what a fool. I have sinned, yes, I have sinned. Wrest me from your heart, for there's no forgiveness for me."

The milkiness envelops me in a pearly fog and a voice filled with immeasurable love replies:

"I forgive you."

"Thank you, thank you, Great Mistress. Tell me, how have I earned this forgiveness? Through my loyalty to You?"

"No, you weren't loyal to me. You renounced me, you didn't pass the initiation."

"Perhaps I earned it with my love for You?"

"No, not your love. You never could grow to love me."

"My Mistress, my heart is an open book to you. You can see my repentance is unfeigned. Perhaps this is what I've earned Your forgiveness with?"

"No. You can't earn forgiveness. I forgive you because my mercy is boundless."

If your mercy is boundless, Masha thinks, then why are we all so miserable? Why do we return, time after time, into the bodies of people here on earth? Why aren't we given peace?

The girl on the Crimean cliffs, the young woman from the incinerated village, the old woman before the mirror. A sailor sails down the Volga, a soldier pulls the pin from a grenade, an old man awaits his death, a man brings a revolver to his temple. And more and more new souls crowd behind them . . .

They are all me.

Dear God, how many of them there are! They didn't leave anyone—neither a son, nor a daughter, neither an heir, nor an heiress—there is no one left, no one and nothing, there isn't even anyone to remember them, spare a thought for them, speak a word about them to those who came afterward. No one can see or hear them.

Only me . . .

And Masha weeps, weeps for everyone who has vanished without a trace, weeps for Grandfather Makar's *second Russia*, weeps and repeats to herself: Only me, only me . . . and that means, I am their heir? That means, I have to carry all this, store their souls in my emaciated body, eternally bring them to term instead of my unconceived children?

I'm all alone, Masha tells herself, I never knew my birth parents, I chased away mom and dad, I don't have brothers or sisters, I'll never have children—how will I carry this burden alone? Am I really a medium? Did I summon the dead? No, they came to me on their own, penetrated me the way a rapist penetrates a woman who doesn't have the strength to resist.

It's just as well, make yourselves comfortable now that you're here, eat me, treat yourselves. Eat my Body, drink my Blood, they don't serve bread and wine here. Be my guests, but just so you know, this is only temporary. Because I won't be able to take any of this much longer.

I won't be able to bear this alone.

And I won't be able to call for help either.

I'll come to Nikita and say: I hear voices, there are other, dead people living inside of me. In response, he'll start to speak to me with compassion, patience, and positivity, the way they speak to small children, sick patients, or madmen.

I better not say anything to him. As long as he stays by my side, doesn't leave, holds my hand.

I better say: "Weren't we happy in Crimea nine years ago? I even read fortunes, pored over cards on the promenade, remember? Sometimes I think that must've been when it all started. Perhaps that's when I let all these lives into me, all the perished, dead, miserable, and infertile. I'll tell him: Remember everyone having fun, drinking wine, eating shish kebab? We were young and stupid. Strong and self-assured. Perhaps there is a little bit of that strength left on the bottom, perhaps it'll be enough to last us a lifetime, what do you think, Nikita?

Don't answer, you don't have to. After all, we don't know ourselves how much we can take. Don't answer me, alright? Just don't leave, please, don't leave.

I'll simply hold your hand—we will all simply hold your hand—and, perhaps, we'll swim up to the surface, perhaps, we will finally learn how to breathe underwater.

84.

TWO-THIRDS

The dark water of the deep end, the water of secrets and mysteries, underwater devils, water creatures and sea witches, catfish and crayfish, burbots and pikes, carnivorous fish, whiskered fish, deepwater fish, and river fish.

The rotten water of mill ponds, the water of timelessness, stagnation, and eternal return, of the drowned and the dead that turn the mill wheel kalpa after kalpa.

The blue ocean water, the Big Blue of sirens and mermaids, the salty abyss of the lure of death, romanticism, eternity, the tremor of anticipation, the doors of perception, *all that—that's rock-n-roll*, as we said in my youth.

The aqua vitae of vodka, the water of deception, Moreukhov's water, the water of unfulfilled promises, of a squandered life, of emptiness and dross, of the vomit, piss, and shit to which it all turned.

The smoky water of a hookah pipe, the water of hope, the water of return, sweetness, and passion, the water of oncoming old age, Nikita's last love.

The domestic water of an aquarium, the water of artificial ruins, plastic wreckage, feeders and flakes for pet fish, of the long and happy life of aquarium pets, the water of comfort and money.

Calm, reflective water, water that reflects the stars, water that turns people into silhouettes, flat water, Rimma's water.

Murky water, drops of semen falling in the bathtub, unborn children, wasted sperm, everything that *didn't work out*, that appeared to you in the murky water, the water of everything that never materialized.

The salty water of tears, Masha's unwept water, water in memory of those who are no longer here, in memory of those who never did get here, salty like the ocean, like the eternity that engulfs everyone and washes away the footsteps from the strand, the water of those who vanished without a trace, the water of all those inherited by Masha.

Dead, scalding hot water, Elvira's deadly water, which bursts pipes and burns with a fury, a hatred, and a palpable, earthly death.

We are a tribe of water merchants, water masters, and water slaves.

Two-thirds of our bodies, two-thirds of our lives.

For every one of us, every one of us.

85.

THE LAST STROKE

About ten years ago, Moreukhov recounts, foreigners liked to come to Moscow and contemplate the ruins of the great empire. Perhaps they still do—at the time, I was a trendy artist, a part of the Moscow exotica, and now I'm just regular riffraff out of the city's outskirts. That's why foreigners still don't know that, a few years ago, I found the best symbol of squandered Soviet Communism.

No, of course it's not the stockpile of monuments at the Central House of Artists on Krymsky Val, the Moscow State University building, or the Central Park of Culture and Leisure.

It's an out-of-service escalator at Lenin Hills.

The Soviet government had two great achievements—the Metro and outer space. Fittingly, one was aboveground and the other—below. It should be noted that only specially selected citizens flew to outer space, but for free. Meanwhile, everyone could ride the Metro, but for money. So neither outer space nor the Metro could serve as a communist symbol, which must be universal and free.

Whereas the escalator at Len-Hills completely fit the bill. It was open to everyone—Communists and non-party members alike, the drunk and the sober, the rich and the poor, and the ones with absolutely no money. You could say it brought together the Metro and outer space. Because any escalator is part of the Metro; however, this one didn't lead down, but up. Not underground, but to the sky, like a real *stairway to heaven*, and what's more, a moving one.

Plus, it was mainly built for children traveling to the Palace of the Pioneers—also a good symbol. When I was a child, I dreamed of signing up for the fencing club; too bad it didn't work out.

To be sure, both the Metro and outer space have been preserved in the new Russia, while the escalator at Lenin Hills has gone out of service. Lenin Hills itself has been renamed Sparrow Hills, so what talk of Communism could there be? All it's good for is filming the TV show *The Brigade*.

In short, for me, the escalator ruins are much cooler than the stockpile by the Central House of Artists. I suppose that the only thing better is the Moscow State University's ruins—but the MSU is still around, which is why the abandoned pavilion with its smashed glass windows is second to none.

Moreukhov looks at Lena—she is sitting motionless as usual. The work is nearing its end; another session or two and the portrait will be finished. It's coming out not too badly—thankfully, his hands remembered everything on their own. It's just that a film noir plot isn't shaping up—Lena ignores all his erotic innuendos. This could be why Moreukhov tells her the story about the escalator, although he's not being particularly truthful, changing some details as he goes along and turning a tale of drunken sex into a romantic parable about an artist and his model. Such hints can't go unnoticed, Moreukhov thinks.

Two years ago, I was courting a young woman, he continues. I won't tell you her real name, let's say it was Yulia. We dated for quite a while, but I still couldn't win her affection. And I realized that this escalator was my last trump card. Can you only imagine: sex on the ruins of a great idea! A rare young woman could resist.

Of course, Moreukhov is lying. First, he has no recollection whatsoever of the young woman's name. Second, he dragged Yulia (let it be Yulia) to the escalator fifteen minutes after they met on the observation deck. Obviously, they were both fairly drunk already, which Moreukhov also omits just to be on the safe side.

Needless to say, the interior of the abandoned building turned out to be outrageously dirty. The floor was scattered with glass fragments, rags, pieces of crumbling plaster, remnants of winter bonfires, and solidified shit. Yulia froze in place, afraid to slip, and Moreukhov dashed back and forth like a Bandar-log, yelling: "What, you've really never been here? It was freaking awesome here! Even during the Soviet Union, there were no cops around and the guys and I would dare each other to run down the up escalator!"

Yulia looks at him with apprehension. "Got any more beer?" she asks.

Moreukhov had bought beer with Yulia's last bit of money. The bottles are jangling in his backpack. He grabs one as if it were a samurai sword and smashes it against a column, breaking its neck.

"Hold this!" he says.

"Um, no thanks," Yulia replies, "are you, nuts? You couldn't open it normally? It's glass, I'll cut myself."

Moreukhov opens a second bottle and drinks from the broken neck himself. Then, he throws the empty bottle on the floor, wipes his lips and looks at his bloodied fingers: "Fuck!" He goes up to the wall and, with a few strokes, depicts a woman's parted lips over the peeling paint.

As he tells his story, Moreukhov removes some details and changes others: he doesn't mention the beer and draws with Yulia's lipstick instead of his own blood.

Afterward, he continues, I picked up a piece of coal and dashed off her portrait. I'm actually a master of the dash-off, I'm only taking my time with you. And when she came to appreciate my artistry, of course, she could no longer resist me.

Yulia does in fact have trouble standing. Whether it's the alcohol or Moreukhov's artistry, she really is up for anything. Or almost anything.

"Okay," she says and rummages in her purse, "but only if I have condoms left."

Moreukhov tries to yank up Yulia's tank top, she resists and mutters under her breath: "Damn, I think I'm out!"

"That's all right," Moreukhov says, "just give me a blowjob then."

"No, I don't want it like that," Yulia mumbles, struggling weakly.

Moreukhov practically forces her down to her knees; she drops her purse and a single Vanka Vstanka condom falls out, along with her menstrual pads and powder compact.

They fuck hastily and fussily, without any joy or excitement. Yulia rests her hands on the wall and looks her own portrait in the eyes. Moreukhov cums, she fixes her skirt, and picks up the change that fell out of her purse.

Standing with the condom in hand, Moreukhov critically studies his work. Something is missing. He dips his finger in the ejaculate and leaves an oily stain on the parted lips he'd drawn with his blood.

"We can say you really did give me a blowjob," he says, satisfied.

"You're a bastard," Yulia says. "Do you have any beer left?"

Moreukhov won't tell any of this to Lena. In his story, they will fuck for a long time and Yulia will climax only when it occurs to him to turn her face to the portrait.

And then, Moreukhov says, as she got dressed, I walked up to the wall and saw that something was missing. I realized that there was no love in this portrait. Only youthful bravado, only a *look what I can do!* And presently, after we'd loved each other, the portrait seemed incomplete, a quick sketch, a draft. I picked up a piece of coal off the floor and fixed the drawing, then, dipped my finger in my own semen and made the last stroke. And at that point, the portrait became good, and feeling, passion, pleasure, and suffering emerged on it. A parted mouth, disheveled hair, blurred facial features . . .

And drops of my semen running down her cheeks like matte tears.

86.

DONE PLAYING

It's not true that people can be divided into predators and victims. There are also natural born rescuers, and those are the worst kind.

Take Dimon, for example. He rescues Moreukhov after every bender and then seethes with anger: what have I done to deserve this cross, let his relatives save him!

If I ever met Dimon, I would tell him: you don't need to rescue anyone. A rescuer is a laughable, ludicrous figure.

Let me give you an example.

At one point, Kostya told me about a special diving exercise where one person plays dead while the other lifts him up to the surface. Rescues him, so to speak.

"Who do you think they train with this exercise?" Kostya asked.

I replied:

"The rescuer."

"Nope! This exercise isn't for rescuers. The point of it is to visualize yourself dead. It's a very important exercise if you're a recreational diver."

This is why I don't go diving. But consider this: the rescuer thinks it's important how he carries out the exercise, poorly or well. In reality, the better the rescuer rescues, the more the rescued feels like a dead person. And if the rescuer doesn't rise to the occasion, the dead person will come to life and swim up perfectly fine on his own. And the next time, he won't pair up with that rescuer, he'll demand another one.

Turns out that rescuers exist so some people could safely play dead. And the better Dimon saves him, the less Moreukhov is worried before embarking on his next binge. He's confident that he can safely play dead and still go on living, triumphantly rising from the dead. Doctors, IVs, heartfelt conversations . . . Just like Easter after Lent, God forgive me for the comparison.

Nikita thinks: I'll soon be a rescuer like that for Masha. The brochures advise you to find out as much as possible about infertility, support each other, tell your partner about your fears and feelings, and also come to terms with the fact that, every so often, periods of anxiety and depression may set in. To simply accept it.

What wonderful advice! *Simply accept it.* Only these are no longer *periods of anxiety and depression*. It's non-stop anxiety and depression—six months, a year, even three.

Once upon a time, I met a driven, energetic, joyful young woman. So why am I now married to a depressed, miserable woman as thin as a concentration camp prisoner? I tried to get Masha to see a psychologist—she said no. I spoke with doctors myself and they gave me a series of brochures entitled *If Your Partner Is Infertile*, which contained such lovely advice as to stay patient, sensitive, well-informed, and, needless to say, do everything together.

Unfortunately, it didn't say how long you were supposed to stay patient and sensitive.

Yesterday, Nikita was told about another option—a special treatment course in America, a new technique, a bit expensive, though, and they would need to live there. For a year.

And so Nikita's telling Masha about it—in a patient, sensitive, well-informed way—holding her hand and saying soulfully: "You see, everything will be alright, like I promised!" and Masha says: "You obviously wouldn't come with me and, once again, it won't work."

At first, he calmly asks Masha what the connection is between his coming along and everything working out for her—still patiently, but not particularly sensitively anymore.

And Masha replies: "It occurred to me that if you really wanted a baby with me, I would have gotten pregnant a long time ago."

Nikita wants to say something patient and sensitive, but can't think of anything in time—he stands there with his fists clenched and his eyes bulging out and, in his anger, screams without being aware of what he's actually saying.

He becomes conscious of it at either the phrase "you're out of your fucking mind" or the word "bitch":

". . . go find someone who would want a child with you! Go find someone else, bitch, and leave me be! Of course it's because I don't want to have a child with you badly enough. Of course everyone else *dreams* of having children with a woman who is always depressed and always blaming her husband. First, it's: *no, I won't go to a doctor, I don't want to have children!* Then, it's: *ah, if only I'd gone to the doctor sooner, I would have had children by now! Why didn't you make me, how could you not know that I wanted children?* Then, it's: *let's do this or let's try that* and again, *we should have come here six months ago, why didn't you take me?* and when nothing works, then, yes, of course, it's my fault again, once again, it's *why did I check into this clinic and that clinic? Why didn't you stop me, what were you doing?* Dammit, Masha, how long will this go on? Stop this for good or fuck off, for God's sake!"

He slams the door, runs out of the room, and wonders: *What's with me?* And answers himself: What's with me? Everything is great, it's just that I'm sick of it all. Masha, Dasha, the business, money, the fucking fish—everything. No, I get that she's depressed. And of course, everything's coming up roses for me, everything is just fucking great.

No, seriously, I'm sick of it all.

So Nikita's standing in the middle of the kitchen, clenching his fists and muttering curses under his breath and, with every second, feeling increasingly better, as if all his problems have vanished,, as if the dam has broken and the torrent swept it all away. And Nikita himself is no longer a husband, a lover, a second-rate businessman, no; he's not even a human being anymore, he's a waterfall, a mountain stream.

A stream doesn't ask for permission, doesn't calculate its own trajectory, it flows, dragging along rocks, destroying dams, and taking down bridges.

Moreukhov is an expert on such states.

He genuinely couldn't care less.

Nikita never thought it could feel so exhilarating.

Now I'll kick all your asses, he thinks. I won't rescue anyone anymore. Let them rescue me. And I'll drop the reins, let the horses gallop in the open field, into God's soul, hey, let my shoulder stir, let my arm swing, I'll kill everyone! And one! Hit Masha in the mug so the bitch stops sitting in the armchair in silence! And two! Hit Dasha's beautiful ass so she values my love and loves me more. What, Moreukhov can and I can't? Now I'll be the one raising hell and swearing, plundering and pillaging—and then I'll fall on the green grass, in the dirty snow, will lie there knowing that, somewhere in the city, there's a good person, a Rescuer who is looking for me and wants to rescue me. Hurry to me, Rescuer, I'm already sinking to the bottom, I already can't hold myself accountable for anything, I'm not worried about anyone, come on, Rescuer, lift me up to the surface, hurry up and save me!

That would be great.

Only there is no Rescuer for Nikita, God's plan doesn't provide for one. And then he returns to the room and says *patiently and sensitively,* like the booklet says:

"Masha, listen, forgive me, alright? I talked some garbage, let's forget about it please? After all, we love each other and that means everything will be fine."

And Masha replies:

"I don't really give a damn about love. What can love do for me? Enough, we're done playing."

And Nikita sits down beside her again and begins to *patiently and sensitively* explain that he can't leave the country, that he has a business, that of course he'll visit a few times a month, *fuck the jetlag, I love you, but I still can't leave for long, Kostya just found an investor, he says I'll need to work for three years . . .*

He's talking and, deep inside him, there's a little boy sitting in a wooden cage, sinking slowly underwater, struggling, calling for help, grabbing the bars—and no one comes to his rescue.

He's talking and suddenly, he notices Masha's eyes, which are inhumanly large and pitch black—two tunnels into emptiness. She looks at him with these eyes and says only one phrase, only six words. But even before she utters them, Nikita knows *what* she is going to say, knows that this isn't a metaphor or a figure of speech, it's how it is, he has long suspected it, just didn't believe it, didn't want to believe it, and now everything will finally be said out loud and he'll have to *simply accept it.*

Masha looks at him with eyes as dark as the deep end, looks at him and says: *Without you, I'll go insane.*

87.

1951–1952. LITTLE BROTHER

(a picture book)

Andryusha was born in the spring. The lavender was in bloom and Nastya was glad it was over—and had gone smoothly. A healthy child, and what's more, a boy. Makar will be proud. I remember how the doctors shook their heads: thirty-seven years old and she wants a child!

Giving birth! Big deal! Of all the things that could befall a woman, childbirth is the easiest. God created women for that very purpose. Whereas roaming around the entire country, changing cities and republics every six months—women aren't built for that. That's for the men, not for us.

I'd rather have a house of my own and stay put for at least a few years.

Andryusha's lying in a pale-blue, metallic bed. The two sisters are gazing at their brother. The youngest, Marina, is wearing a pink polka-dot dress, so short, you can see her white underwear. Four-year-old Sveta is wearing a black dress with a white collar, just like an adult. They lean over the walls of the crib, looking at their gloomy brother. Andryusha has yet to learn how to smile.

He has to learn how to smile and Marina and Sveta—how to rock a baby carriage, wake up from the baby's cries, chase mosquitoes away, shield their brother from the rain, comfort him when he's afraid, and take strolls together. And, on top of that, love him.

Nastya isn't worried about love: of course, they'll love him. How could it be otherwise?

Andrey sneezes and, already, the girls are jubilating:
"Look, mom, just like an adult!"

Bathing is a total production. She has to heat up water in the kitchen for a whole tub. Bring over the buckets, sponges, and soap. Lower Andrey into the water. Let him hold her finger so he doesn't get nervous.

Nastya stands in a beautiful white skirt, telling her daughters:
"See how happy he looks! Must be nicer here than in the baby carriage!"

Andrey only squints his eyes in response.

In the morning, they take the pram out to the park. The dew on the shrubs is blazing, the breeze is stirring up the leaves. Sveta is rocking the pram by the roots of a tall pine tree, kicking a red ball. The drapes over the baby carriage are rising like sails.

Sveta thinks: what if he understands everything already? Can hear what we're saying, see what we're doing, notices everything, and makes a mental note of it . . . he'll grow up and do the same. Follow our example.

Sveta remembers with concern all the trouble she and Marina have recently gotten into. Then, she leans over the pram and says huffily:
"When you grow up, don't even think of fighting!" And adds kindly: "Fighting is what we did yesterday, you understand?"

Summer has arrived. On a hot day, they take the pram out to a shady garden. It's cool there, she'd have gone herself to escape the indoor heat. She'll go out as soon as she finishes making lunch. In the meantime, she is slicing vegetables, watching out the window as Marina waves a branch in the air, leaps around the pram, and yells something. She'll wake Andryusha up, Nastya thinks, and he's just fallen asleep.

"Mama, Mama," Marina cries out, "I'm chasing the mosquitoes away from him! Tons and tons of them here, makes you want to run!"

Yes, there are tons of mosquitoes and Marina's alone. They're unequally matched. Nastya watches out the window as her daughter smacks the blanket with all her might. Then, Andrey's bawling drowns out Marina's victory cry.

And now he's awake! I knew it!

Nastya comes home from the store. Sveta and Marina race to her, yelling over each other:

"Mama, Mama, did you see it?"

"A thunderstorm!"

"I'll say! It grew so dark!"

"And then it got very windy!"

"I got sand in my eyes, there!"

"Me too! And all the doors in the house began to slam!"

"And then there was a bang!"

"And lightning in the sky!"

"I grabbed Andryusha—what if he got scared?"

"And I grabbed the blue blanket so it wouldn't get wet."

"And then it started!"

"We ran to his room!"

"If he got scared, we'd rock him!"

"But he didn't notice a thing."

"Can you imagine, Mama?"

"All he did was stare at his hand."

"Out the window, boom! I even got scared myself—well, a little bit."

"And Andryusha just lay there . . ."

"Looking happy!"

"Yep. Good thing you came home, Mama, we were waiting for you."

The thunderstorm didn't scare him, but, one day, a sparrow sat down in the window and Andryusha grew so frightened that he shut his eyes. He was dressed head-to-toe in pale-blue—even his hat and booties. He was already holding his own rattle, but grew so frightened of the bird that he began to cry and call out to his mama and sisters. Mama came running: "Who made you cry, son? It's just a sparrow. An itty-bitty sparry, and he's behind the window, too. Don't be scared, nothing to be scared of."

Mama hushes Andrey, repeating: *Don't be afraid, don't be afraid,* and thinks to herself: better he be afraid, he'll keep still, he'll be safer.

Andrey settles down and Nastya returns to the kitchen, thinking that she and Makar have long lost the ability to be scared: fear has become such an integral part of their lives that they hardly notice it.

Andrey has learned to sit. Nastya has laid out a few blankets on the grass by the porch, thrown down some pillows, and sat her son on them. She put a rattle in his hands. A yellow one with a brown bell.

The little boy shakes it and marvels at it: what's that sound? Where's it coming from?

Sveta and Marina squat over the garden beds. It's a small vegetable garden planted with carrots and peas, even ones you can't see behind the weeds. Nastya sent her daughters to pull weeds. Let them work for an hour—in a month, the carrots will grow and we'll make juice for Andryusha.

Today, for the first time since Andrey was born, Nastya's going to work. She and Makar work at the railroad—he is an engine driver and she is a railroad attendant.

She's wearing her dark service coat with epaulettes and a red service cap, and Andrey doesn't recognize her at all.

Sveta explains to her brother:

"This is mom's uniform. She's going on duty. She has a job."

Andrey studies her suspiciously, but as soon as Nastya starts talking, he recognizes her voice and reaches for her.

Nastya takes him in her arms—ah, so easy to pick up, so hard to put down.

Sveta and Marina are sitting in front of the radio. They've sat Andrey down between them.

"Let him listen too, it will do him good!"

On the radio, there are trumpeters, pioneers' songs, and a children's choir.

"Mama, Mama, if Andrey starts crying, can we turn up the radio?"

"Because the children's choir is louder than him, right?"

Sveta rolls the pram down the street. Look, she tells her brother, you're riding in your very own pram, fancy not just any old way!

Andrey's wearing a pale-blue jacket and a blue hat with a red pom-pom. He sits there and glances around. A pale-blue stroller descends from a hill and, in it—a girl. Andryusha reaches out for her, but her mom whisks her away.

For some time, Andryusha watches in her wake, and then he begins to bawl.

On the hillside, the girls have spread out a striped blanket, sat down on it, and are gazing out at the railroad.

First, there's a long-distance train, all covered in smoke, racing non-stop to parts unknown, cities they haven't yet visited.

Then a drawn-out whistle resounds over the plain and Sveta says:

"There! That's Papa's train."

She knows that, at two-thirty, Papa is supposed to pass their station.

Makar also knows that, at this time, his children will be standing on the hillside and his daughters will lift Andryusha up higher so he can see the green cars of the commuter train passing one by one. Makar looks out the window: the three figures on the hillside are almost indistinguishable.

But Makar knows they're there. He thinks he can see Marina waving her white handkerchief.

A minute later the embankment is far behind.

Twenty-five years will go by and the grown children will relocate to different cities.

And, in another fifteen, these cities will turn out to be in different countries .

While their parents were still alive, Marina and Andrey visited Sveta in Moscow once a year. Now they only call each other on their birthdays, International Women's Day, and New Year's. Everyone has a family and personal troubles, and what can you really discuss over the telephone?

Only, every so often, the elderly Sveta remembers a summer day, an embankment, a green commuter train, a striped bedspread, and herself and Marina lifting up Andrey with all their might: *Look! Look! It's Papa's train!*

88.

AND THE ARMOR BROKE

When Moreukhov was still a trendy artist, he drunkenly wandered into the Tretyakov Gallery. That day, the world was glorious. A soft-hearted snow fell over the city, eternity smelled of oil, and death was the motherland. As you can guess, the band Civil Defense was playing on his Walkman. Moreukhov stopped in front of Malevich's *Black Square* and, before he could remember Alexander Brener's Dutch performance piece, he was bowled over. Moreukhov discerned the subtlest shades of black and saw the uneven layers of paint, the perfection of the geometric figure, and a square-shaped, open door, behind which lay emptiness. As Yegor Letov of Civil Defense sang, *that means there was someone who nee-nee-needed him.*

For instance, a painting created just short of a century ago.

Moreukhov stood before Malevich's *Black Square* until closing time and walked out almost sober under the soft-hearted snow. He used to sober up easily when he was young.

Perhaps it was then that Moreukhov decided to cease being an artist: it was ridiculous to continue painting in the face of such absolute perfection.

You could only paint for money or as a favor to acquaintances. *To give to a chick on her birthday.* Moreukhov has been painting Lena for almost a month now, he's already told her his entire life story, studied every detail of her face, and still won't finish the job, stalling for time, no longer hoping for sex, but for some sort of miracle—he just doesn't know what kind.

He tells her about his friends and family and, sometimes, thinks it's not Lena answering him, but Anya-Elvira, or her mother, or his mother, or his grandmother, and—sometimes—Sonya Shpilman, the mother of his unborn children, or Masha, his brother Nikita's wife.

But in the end, Lena herself tells him: *That's it, enough!* She has to go away for about ten days and, when she returns, she'll pick up the portrait. Say, next Friday.

Moreukhov finished the job in three days and still had a week left for small fixes; today, he is sitting with Dimon under the Moscow poplar fluff, smoking Yava cigarettes, listening to Dimon's stories of working for glossy magazines and thinking: well, this story, too, is coming to an end.

"Want to see Letov at Luzhniki Palace of Sports tomorrow?" Dimon says. "I ordered a VIP ticket online. Remember how, in our second year, the three of us with Vitalik used to scream 'Everything Is Going According to Plan' at the top of our lungs? The other day, I bought Yegor's digital album, it's still a great listen, though the meaning has totally changed. Only Grandpa Lenin was a great leader, all the rest were such shit. Timely song. Revolutionary."

Moreukhov tramples his cigarette angrily in the white fluff. *Timely song*. They'll go out to protest in yet another Orange Revolution—a Pink, Baby Blue, or Violet one—singing *they fed my wife to the crowd*. If you want to start a revolution, you shouldn't work for glossy magazines. You have to live honestly, give up everything, own nothing, throw away your car, your MP3 player, your three-thousand *u.e.* Mac computer, throw out that shit and all your other possessions, turn your apartment into a dump, and then pretend to be a revolutionary. The realization of cowardice, the exhaustion of bravery, the geology of stupidity, the oncology of conformity.

"I'm not fucking going to see Letov at Luzhniki," he says, "that's the last thing I need. Listen to yourself: Letov at Luzhniki! In the VIP seats! You might as well as say the Kremlin Convention Palace!"

"Well, as you wish," Dimon says, clearly hurt, "I'm not forcing you."

"And what's that digital album thing you mentioned?" Moreukhov asks.

And that's how Moreukhov arranged a Civil Defense concert for himself. On Friday, he grabbed a bottle of Ochakovsky beer and Dimon's MP3 player, walked up to the little square next to Novodevichy Convent, verified the concert start time on his watch, and put the album on shuffle.

According to the *District* newspaper, Troparyovo once belonged to

Novodevichy Convent. Moreukhov's lying on his back, staring at the sky, and thinking: turns out that we live on monastery land. Troparyovo land, into which we'll all dive someday.

Poplar fluff tumbles out of the sky and a few bits of it fly into his open mouth. Moreukhov washes them down with beer, shifts in place to get more comfortable, and sings along: *And the answer to every question is "always alive!" aye!*

A kilometer away from Novodevichy, in the half-empty auditorium of Luzhniki Palace, successful non-conformists and young people from vocational-technical school also sing along: *A long, happy life for every one of us, every one of us!* Few of them understand the meaning of "long" or "happy," and every one of them has his own take on life.

Meanwhile Moreukhov empties the bottle and gets increasingly wasted with every swig. Is it possible that I really am a shitty artist? Maybe I'm a great writer of fiction, a genius storyteller? Lena was all ears!

The portrait is finished, he thinks, so be it, let it all be over, may I never see her again, *I don't give a shit about my face*, yes, no one gives a shit, neither Lena, nor Dima, nor Mom!

On stage, Letov is singing: *A shot shell struck the tank and the armor broke, the tiny fragments wounded me.* Unlike the audience at Luzhniki, Moreukhov used to know a different song—an old, authentic song: *Why didn't you burn down with the tank, you bastard?* But that song isn't on the MP3 player and Moreukhov can't sing along. He throws the empty bottle in the grass, rises to his full height, walks in the direction of Novodevichy, looks at the domes, and makes the sign of the cross. I rarely recall that I'm Eastern Orthodox, he thinks. But I do know how to talk to God. Especially after a bottle or two.

He is about to turn off the MP3 player when he hears in his headphones: *torturing my flesh with a touching little knife, torturing my flesh with a touching little knife*—and Moreukhov is bowled over, like many years ago at the Tretyakov Gallery. He's standing on the patriarchal stockpile of outdated notions, tired images, and polite words, standing under the monastery wall, a few steps away from the cemetery, mumbling: *Call things by their own names, sow the sensible, the kind and the eternal*—and doesn't know that, at this very moment at Luzhniki, Yegor is singing the same song and the crowd joins in, forgetting about the VIP seats, the ticket prices, their age, and conformism versus non-conformism. The young cops in the cordoned-off area take their cell phones out and film Letov dancing by the microphone, with his hair fluttering like it's

1989: *What does it mean to inherit the earth? Isn't that what we need?* And Moreukhov has a heartrending realization that the monastery land, the fenced-off cemetery, the green grass under his feet, the *stuff the grave with your body*, the Troparyovo parkland, and the boxy new high-rises—that all this is the true *Russian Field of Experiments*, experiments that don't end and should not end, that cannot end until the philosopher's stone begins to shine, yes, he thinks: *begins to shine*, until we stop being ourselves and become something else, something greater, am I right, Lord?, and *the soft-hearted snow is like frost*, the poplar fluff, the empty ears of grain, the black soot of incinerated villages, the down of cut-open pillows, the ash of crematoriums, and, over and over, the soft-hearted snow, nine months out of the year, over and over, tumbling splendidly on

on

on

89.

IN THREE GENERATIONS

Behind her stretches a long row of shoes, shoes, shoes. Then come the sandals. Flowery, beaded, gold, and sequined. Before they go on vacation, young women buy themselves new footwear—only later do they realize that it's more comfortable to walk down the beach in flip-flops or barefoot.

Anya smiles her IKEA smile at the customers, every so often glancing at herself in the mirror—tan, beautiful, well-rested.

She's also confused. For the first time in fifteen years, she doesn't know what to do about her man.

For fifteen years, everything was going great: she would meet up occasionally with someone, wham-bam-thank-you-ma'am, they'd grow tired of one other, and move on. For fifteen years, Anya knew exactly what she wanted: sometimes, it was to keep her job, usually, it was simply to fuck. Once, she wanted a child, and that went over smoothly too.

She wanted to move in with Andrey. A silly, ridiculous, meaningless desire that Anya, of course, could have easily ridden herself of. She could have, say, visited her mom, told her about her vacation, listened to what she'd have to say about Andrey, and returned home cured of any dumb wishes. She could have simply stopped picking up the phone, stopped calling him, and quickly taken up with someone else. There were many surefire ways, and Anya could have used any one or all of them if it wasn't for Andrey.

On their last night in Turkey, they put Gosha to sleep; it turned out that Andrey had hired a babysitter so he and Anya could go out one last time.

Andrey found a restaurant on the very outskirts of the village. A whiskered Turk poured them coffee and brought them slivovitz; for some reason, Andrey ordered lobster—*they have the cheapest lobster in the world!*—but how were you supposed to eat this cheap lobster? So, while Anya wrestled with the dead underwater creature, Andrey leaned over the table and said:

"Listen, why don't we move in together, huh? The three of us are good together. We'll get married, I'll adopt Gosha, and we'll live like a normal family. What do you think?"

Yes, what do I think?

I think I like that idea.

It scares me.

So I'm standing in the middle of the store, in the middle of the work-day, and can think of nothing else.

A young, fair-haired woman in cheap jeans comes up to me. She tries on sandals, asks about prices, and examines her feet in the mirror. Neat pedicure, tiny toes. Must also be getting ready to go to Turkey.

Of course, everything was marvelous in Turkey. And Andrey was marvelous. But the fact that they had a great time at the beach didn't mean they would be happy in the same apartment, right? And, anyway, in the past, Anya liked a completely different type of guy. Decisive. Energetic. Perhaps even mean. Anya had all kinds of lovers, but believed she was partial to that type.

It's likely that her grandfather, her mother's father, who vanished long before Anya was born, was like that—a reckless, ex-con who got out of jail during the amnesty, picked up a young sniper woman in the shooting gallery, fucked her in the attic, and dissolved in the night.

Or, maybe, Grandpa's got nothing to do with it, and it's all the fault of Anya's first love; he was a year older and wore a punk-rock mohawk, a swastika, and an anarchist pin. They loved each other the summer after she graduated high school; he'd been expelled from university in his first year and she was still deciding if she wanted to apply anywhere.

His name was Georgiy and, as she thought of him for the first time in years, Anya realized she named her son in honor of her first love.

He really was great, just got hooked on heroin and Anya immediately broke it off. She didn't even need her mother's advice.

And now she's frightened: what was she thinking when she picked out her baby's name? What body part was she thinking with?

On the whole, Anya can imagine what her mom thinks of Andrey.

She's well aware of what Gosha thinks of Andrey. Since being back from vacation, he's already asked five times when Uncle Andrey's coming over. Good thing he isn't asking if Uncle Andrey's going to live with them—that would make it sound like chick lit.

The young, fair-haired woman sighs, takes the cheaper sandals, tries them on, puts them back, and grabs the expensive pair again. Poor girl, Anya thinks, honey is sweet, but the bee stings. I can't afford those either. Although they're beautiful, what can I say?

Vika listened closely to Anya.

"So what does your mom say—'don't trust anyone,' right?"

"Well, not exactly. More like: don't trust men, don't take anything from them, don't ask for anything, and, most importantly, don't fall in love. That's what she taught me. And I'm grateful to her, look how many girls got hitched and whose husbands now drink or cheat on them left and right, or have abandoned them with children, with no income, or experience. Meanwhile I'm doing great, as you can tell."

"No," Vika says, "I can't tell."

Honestly, what am I scared of? Anya thinks. So we'll move in together. If we don't like it, we'll split up. After all, I've got an income, experience, a child—and not his, by the way, so at least there won't be a custody battle. What am I scared of? Vika also said: *don't fear anyone*. That's funny: Mom says *don't trust anyone*. Don't trust, don't fear, don't ask. Sounds like either a Tatu song or a gulag aphorism. Grandpa would have probably known which.

The fair-haired woman picks up the sandals, sighs again, and heads to the register. Anya taps the young woman on the elbow:

"Don't buy them now," she says in a hushed voice, "come by next week, we'll be having a sale. We've still got three pairs left and they're not exactly flying off the shelves. I know that they'll be twenty percent off."

The woman looks at her in amazement.

"Next week?" she repeats after Anya. "That's when I'll be on vacation, next week is too late. But thank you, anyway." She smiles and heads for the register, and Anya follows her with her eyes, wishing that, before they get back to Moscow, the man this woman loves will suggest: *Let's move in together. We're good together, right?*

And hopes that the woman won't agonize over what to reply.

Anya puts the box with the sandals in the bag and suddenly realizes:

I'm so lucky! In three generations, I'm the first woman in my family to get a real proposal. Not because I got pregnant, not because I turned up at the right time. But because he loves me.

90.

2003. FORTY-TWO YEARS AGO

Djamilya Musayevna had just put the kasha on the stove when the phone rang. In the first minute, she couldn't figure out if it was Tanya or Gulya—it's not that the girls' voices were alike, it's just that her hearing had become so poor lately that she couldn't tell if she was being asked "How did you sleep?" or "How are you?"

"Good," the eldest Takhtagonova said irritably.

She still couldn't understand what her daughter was asking. She hadn't sleep well, had heartburn all night, and had the bitter taste of bile in her mouth. It would have been more truthful to say *bad*, but then she'd have to explain why, and she wanted to finish the call as soon as possible and eat breakfast.

The girls still can't get used to the fact that she gets up later every year. Eleven in the morning and she's still hungry, sleepy, and in her nightgown.

"Rimmochka dropped out of university," her daughter says loudly. *Ah, so it's Gulya*, Djamilya Musayevna thinks, and asks:

"Why?"

Rimma finished two years of university; Djamilya's daughters always said the first two years were the hardest. Djamilya never had the opportunity to study—always something else going on. First, there was the war, then she went to work—at the plant and, afterward, the construction site. Everywhere, she'd meet young female engineers, yesterday's students. They didn't have a good grasp of how everything functioned, but Djamilya still envied them: they were lucky, they'd had five years of a happy student life, the kind she saw in the movies. That's why she tried so hard to have her daughters enrolled at a university, and her efforts were not in vain: neither Gulya nor Tanya ended up working at a construction site or a plant. One worked at a ministry and the other at a medical clinic. Ah, if it weren't for Yeltsin ten years ago, she could have been proud of them to this day.

Though who would she brag to? Verka died five years ago, and it's Lusya's second month at the hospital—they say she doesn't recognize anyone, not even her own children.

Djamilya Musayevna thinks Gulya said something about a broom. Such idiotic slang. She asks: *What broom?*

"She says she's got no money!" Gulya yells. "Mom, are you completely deaf? Go to a doctor, how many times do I tell you?"

"I'm not deaf," Djamilya is hurt, "you have to speak clearer. You always had problems with elocution."

"I never had problems," her daughter replies, "Gulya did."

Oh, so it's Tanya? Then why isn't Gulya telling me about Rimmochka? Did something happen to her?

"And how's Gulya?"

"Upset, of course," Tanya replies, "doesn't want to worry you. Don't tell her I called."

Then why did you call? Djamilya Musayevna wants to ask, but only says: "I won't."

"I wanted to ask you to talk to Rimmochka. She always listened to you. Perhaps she'll change her mind before it's too late."

"Alright," Djamilya replies, "she promised to stop by this week, I'll talk to her then."

Though it's the second month that Rimmochka has been promising to *stop by this week.* And Djamilya isn't eager to talk to her granddaughter about the university, especially not over the phone. But if you don't promise Tanya, she won't leave you be. Stubborn like her dad.

Djamilya Musayevna has long ceased to argue with her daughters—she agrees to everything: to go to the doctor, to go out of town someday in the summer, to talk to her granddaughter . . . they'll forget everything she has promised them anyway.

They've been like this since childhood—in one ear and out the other. Djamilya herself was no better when she was young.

While she was talking to Tanya, her kasha burned a bit. She scrapes the top layer off, puts it on a plate, and throws the pot in the sink. She thinks to herself: well, now my heartburn will definitely get the upper hand, and sits down to eat.

Djamilya always envied the young female engineers. And why shouldn't she have? At twenty-something, they knew and were capable of so much, while at their age Djamilya only knew how to kill. So as not to let her envy loose, she tried to look after the girls in various ways. She showed them how to save ten minutes and pop into town on their lunch break. She told them which safety techniques were precautions and which were essential. In short, she filled them in. In the first two months, the girls adored her, then they found their way around and barely nodded hello to her upon meeting. Of course, they were engineers and she was a regular worker, what friendship could there be? Besides, Djamilya was almost twice their age and had turned thirty-seven that spring, though she looked only thirty.

Yes, forty-two years ago, thirty-seven seemed old. But it turned out it wasn't even the middle of her life—what a scary thought.

That spring, Uncle Marat procured a pair of stilettos for her—*all the rage*, as they said. When she wore them, Djamilya felt seven years younger—probably because she was instantly ten centimeters taller.

If only she had shoes like that fifteen years earlier, when she used to agonize about her height! Maybe she would have gotten married, wouldn't have had to raise Tanya alone. At least they help her out at work—they sent her daughter south for the summer and put them on the list for an apartment at the Novye Cheryomushki station. They promised to give it to them by the end of the year. They'll be so happy!

Djamilya Musayevna puts the plate in the sink and thinks: *I'll wash it later, first, I'll have some tea.* She pours water from the kettle: *I'm so scatter-brained, I didn't turn on the stove, the water's cold.* She fiddles with the automatic lighter for a while and the blue halo of a small flame shoots up on her fifth try. She goes into the other room, turns on the TV, and sits down in her armchair.

That April, they sent students to the plant for practical training for the first time. No one wanted to take them on, and someone suggested Djamilya train them for community service. She tried to refuse it: "What training, I'm a single mother, I have to run straight to daycare to pick up my little girl!" but they reminded her about Novye Cheryomushki. She was obliged to take on the students and was even quite pleased about it afterward.

The girls turned out to be careful, considerate, and cheerful. She instantly got on with Galya Okuneva—perhaps because Galya was already twenty-five. She tried to enroll at the Architectural Institute twice and, in the third year, gave up and took her father's advice to study engineering. Galya told Djamilya in great confidence that she suspected her dad called the university provost to ask that they give her high marks on the entrance exams. Galya's dad was a government physicist, which she believed could open any door for her. *If he wanted it, I could have enrolled at the architecture school.* Whether her dad helped her or not, by the end of her fifth year, Galya was on track to graduate with honors—and this time, she certainly didn't need her dad's help.

Djamilya had barely known her own father; he died in the early thirties after working his whole life as a street sweeper in Moscow. Djamilya was terribly jealous of Galya—and mentored the young woman more than the others. Perhaps that's why Galya invited Djamilya over for a get-together Tuesday evening.

"Why Tuesday?" Djamilya asked. "Is it your birthday?"

"No, it's just that there'll be no one home: my dad is going away for work."

Needless to say, Galya and her dad had their own apartment. It was a special building for physicists working on classified projects, Galya explained. She wrote down the address on a piece of paper—Djamilya even noticed that the apartment number matched her birth year.

No worries, Djamilya thought, I'll move to Novye Cheryomushki and have my own apartment. I just need someone to watch Tanya tomorrow—I don't know who, but, for once in my life, I would really like to feel like a student. I'll wear my stilettos, the new dress I bought last summer—I can't keep going to the plant's recreation center all the time. Then I'll sit quietly in the corner and watch.

Djamilya Musayevna goes to the kitchen again. So it is—the whistle is lying on the floor and the kettle is shrouded with steam. Again, she didn't hear anything! Oh well, there's some water left, just enough for one cup. She throws a Lipton teabag in the boiling water.

Lusya volunteered to watch Tanya: Lusya was working the night shift the following day, and even agreed to take the girl to daycare in the morning if Djamilya brought her over that evening. Everyone was meeting at Galya's at eight, so Djamilya had plenty of time to make it to Lusya's and back.

Of course, she arrived late: first, Lusya critically eyed her new shoes, then she complained about work troubles for fifteen minutes. When Djamilya finally got to Galya's, it was almost nine, the music was blaring, and excited voices drifted from the living room.

Forty-two years have gone by, Djamilya Musayevna thinks, and I remember it like it was yesterday: a three-room apartment, parquet floors, armchairs with slip-covers, sparkling chandeliers, bookcases lining the corridor. In the living room, a round table, plates with salads, red wine, crystal wineglasses, and silver forks and knives.

Djamilya had only seen such luxury in the spring of forty-five. For a moment, she thought the doors would swing open and scowling, sooty soldiers would burst in, going through the drawers and cleaning out the closets.

Her only war trophy was a small watch, a parting gift from Major Voronin: the war was over and he was going back to his family. *You betrayed me*, Djamilya said to him at the time, her voice hushed with fury. It was then that Voronin took out the watch and said: *I'm tearing it from my heart.* She wanted to throw it in his face, but kept it. All these years. Presently, the watch fell an hour-and-a-quarter behind over the course of the day and the bracelet clasp was broken.

I'll die, Djamilya Musayevna thinks, and the girls will inherit my watch. They'll throw it out or give it away—for me, it's *a memory of love* and for them, it's a broken trinket. *A Memory of Love* would have made a great soap opera name. One hundred and fifty episodes, a slice of Brazilian life. Say, Voronin meets Tanya, begins to woo her, then sees the watch, recognizes it, and realizes that she's his daughter. Except that Tanya is not his daughter, but, in the show, she would have been.

Djamilya Musayevna smiles: she can still picture Voronin at thirty. At the time, he seemed practically old, but now I think he was quite young. This year, he's turning—let's see—eighty-five. He must be dead already. And if he isn't, he must be very old and deaf like me, or blind, or doesn't recognize anyone like Lusya. And his wife is an old woman too.

I wonder if he remembers me. After all, he, too, must remember me when I was young, twenty-one, with a wasp waist, raven-black hair, tiny, pert breasts . . . Only he remembers me like that and only I remember him when he was young. If we lived together and saw each other every day, we would have long forgotten, we'd only have photographs to remind us how we used to look.

It turns out that growing old apart is a good thing—keeps your memories intact.

I should give this watch to Rimmochka or Elya, tell the girls about Voronin. Or else they'll continue to think their grandma was a spinster her whole life, never loved anyone and got knocked up with her daughters.

And why shouldn't I have't gotten knocked up, if I left my love some-where at the front anyhow, in the land of blood and death.

Djamilya Musayevna goes to the restroom and sits down with a grunt. Why did I remember all this? It just upsets me. As soon as I thought: *and saw each other every day*, my heart stood still. Such silliness.

When everything has already happened, what difference does it make exactly what happened? Does it really matter what happened and what didn't?

Alright, enough about sad things. Instead, I should recall that evening at Galya Okuneva's.

Shurik is wearing silly glasses on his nose, he's all disheveled and ridicu-lous-looking. Galya's younger brother is studying to become a physicist at the university, which means he'll be like his father—work on classified projects and live in a private, lavish apartment. At the moment you can't really tell: he's scratching his hair with his hand, fixing his glasses, and talking nervously and loudly: *The future isn't physics, it's cybernetics!*

Djamilya understands: Shurik is the youngest, he wants some atten-tion. But they're already moving the table and starting to dance. Yes, yes, those very same *stilyagi* dances that are being inveighed against in the newspapers. Djamilya is used to a completely different style of dancing and is, thus, the only one to stay on the sofa and listen to Shurik.

"What is cybernetics?" she asks.

Shurik starts to explain, half-heartedly at first as he watches a tall, fair-haired student (Nina? Natasha?), but soon, he gets into it. A few minutes later, Djamilya is decidedly confused.

"Cybernetics is the science of intelligent machines. That much I understood," she says. "And what does information have to do with it? That's like the news."

Shurik sighs:

"Girl, you don't get it! Everything in the world is information! If I say something, my words are information. If you see or hear something, then your brain receives information. Even dancing is an information system. Information is transferred from an X-ray film to the needle of a record player, turns into soundwaves, and then, when it's in your ear, into electromagnetic signals that travel to the brain to be analyzed. Information about other people's movements is concurrently transmitted to the brain and, after analyzing it, the brain decides which instructions to send to the arms, legs, and . . ." Shurik stammers, "the other parts of the body. Got it?"

Djamilya nods her head, although all she understood was that, in his last phrase, he was referring to Nina (Natasha?), who bends her knees slightly as she gyrates her hips.

"I especially understand about the other parts of the body," she says, pointing to the young woman.

Shurik turns crimson. After all, he's still a child, Djamilya thinks, and Shurik begins to explain his theory of the two types of informational transfer available to humans: a familial one, through the genetic inheritance mechanism, and a symbolic one, through books, paintings, movies . . . well, through culture. Every one of us exists at the crossroads of these two informational streams—from our mom and dad and from the rest of humanity. Why do people write books? Why do they have children? Because they know that the most important thing is to transfer the code to posterity. The cultural and the genetic one.

"And this," Shurik says, "is the only immortality . . ."

He keeps pouring more wine in the crystal glasses. Djamilya almost never gets drunk on wine—she started out on spirits, her body is used to it—while Shurik got drunk in an hour. He's using increasingly obscure words, his sentences break off midway, and he swings his arms around with greater vigor, trying to dance on beat.

"Let's go dance," Djamilya says.

She's already worked out how the *stilyagi* dance. It's not so complicated if you're paying attention.

Shurik hesitates, and she lifts him from the sofa almost by force.

First, Djamilya tries to move carefully, letting her body test out the unfamiliar motions. But soon she is effortlessly making circles around the room, as if she has always known how to do this. What did Shurik say about waves? Presently, she feels one wave after another pass through her. She even closes her eyes to stay out of her body's way. I'm so happy, Djamilya thinks, it's been so long since I've felt so happy.

She thinks she can hear the trumpet playing right inside her head—guiding her and widening her circles. Her hair sticks to her forehead and a stream of sweat runs down her back; Djamilya shakes her head out and opens her eyes: only she and Natasha are dancing now. The others have retreated to make room for them.

It's turned into some sort of competition: a tall, curvy blonde against a lean brunette who's not so short thanks to Uncle Marat's stilettos.

The trumpet roars one last time and falls silent. The final roar reminds Djamilya of the way men scream when they ejaculate.

"You're a groovy dancer," says the blonde and reaches out her hand: "I'm Nina."

So it's Nina and not Natasha, Djamilya thinks, and one of the guys says: *Good style tonight*; then, the doorbell rings.

"Could it be the neighbors?" someone wonders, and Galya runs to open the door. In a moment, she returns, completely confounded.

"Guys, let's clean up quickly," she whispers. "My dad missed his flight."

Djamilya had pictured Galya's dad completely differently. She thought he was like a professor from the movies—a slight, bespectacled man with a thick briefcase. It turned out he was tall, trim, and even handsome, only his hair was all gray.

Flicking sweaty strands of hair away from her forehead, she greeted him and explained that she represented the trade-union committee and party committee of the plant where Galina underwent her practical training, and that their comrades instructed them to conduct an informal meeting to discuss the preliminary results of the training.

"To be honest, I owe you an apology," Djamilya continued to the sounds of excited whispering behind her back. "Our initial plan was to have the meeting at the recreation center, but when I found out Galina had her own apartment, I suggested that we meet here. I wanted to attract more young people and tell them about working-class life; unfortunately, there are very different kinds of gatherings at the recreation center, as you can understand: vodka, dancing, debauchery . . ."

It turned out that, with his return, Galina's dad had effectively jeopardized an important ideological meeting, but, of course, everyone was ready to leave so as not to interfere with his work for the benefit of the people.

Galya's father waved them off:

"What work—I'll take a shower and go to bed. But please, carry on, don't be shy. I'm going to lie down in my office. As long as Galina cleans up so it's all spick-and-span in the morning."

To walk around an empty apartment, avoid looking at the dirty dishes in the kitchen sink, shower at one o'clock in the afternoon, not hear the telephone ring when you're in the kitchen—and this, day in, day out. The second part of life is duller than the first—only the memories help kill the remaining time, show better films than anything on TV. Occasionally she can fast-forward her memory.

Everyone is seated at a round table, drinking tea from porcelain cups. The boys are jabbing each other, trying to be witty.

"They're like monkeys," the drunken Shurik whispers in her ear, "they'll read one book and then quote it for six months. So what if I read Ilf and Petrov before everyone else did?" And he puts one arm around her shoulder, reaching for her knee with the other.

Then Djamilya goes out for a smoke in the kitchen. Shurik follows her. The cigarette butt dies out in the kitchen sink with a hiss. They kiss. Djamilya stands on her tiptoes and Shurik doesn't know what to do with his hands. It's a big kitchen, spacious. Bigger than a communal apartment, and all for a single family.

Presently the young people are saying their goodbyes to Galya in the corridor. They rush off to the Metro, thinking Shurik is already asleep, and completely forgetting about Djamilya.

Shurik's kiss is awkward, inept, and wet. Djamilya is tired of standing on her tiptoes; she presses against Shurik and feels a hard lump against her belly. Shurik gets flustered and backs away.

Now a perplexed Shurik is sitting alone in the kitchen. He must be trying to figure out what went wrong, where the *data center failed*. He twirls a pack of *Belomor* cigarettes in his hand, takes one out, inhales for the first time in his life and coughs for a while, leaning over the sink.

There's Djamilya and Galya in the living room.

"We thought you'd left," Galya says. Of course she wants to say: *I'm sorry, we kind of forgot about you*, but hesitates. Instead, she offers: "You can stay the night. We'll go to the plant together in the morning."

Djamilya pictures herself traveling across the entire city at night and says yes. She puts all the dishes on a tray and walks unsteadily to the kitchen. A few seconds later, a crash is heard.

"It's your stilettos, Milochka, you still need to learn how to walk in them," Okunev says. "You know, the guys at the Institute calculated that the pressure produced by high heels is equivalent to that produced by an elephant's foot."

"I'm not an elephant, though," the intoxicated Djamilya takes offense.

They're sitting in the kitchen together. Roused by the sound of breaking dishes, Okunev Senior told his children to go to sleep and took out the first-aid kit and a bottle of laboratory ethyl alcohol—*to clean the wounds*.

They immediately drank a hundred grams—*to lower the stress*.

Her throat burned so much with memories that her eyes welled up with tears. This was how she used to sit with Voronin long ago: dug-out shelter, table, bottle of grain alcohol, and two glasses. She caught her breath and said hoarsely: *Let's do another.*

He began calling Djamilya "Mila" right away and, when they drank for the third time, Milochka.

"My Lyudmila was good at walking in high heels," Okunev says, "though we didn't have such high ones in my time."

Djamilya takes his hand:

"Galya said she died . . ."

"Breast cancer," Okunev replies. "For young women, it all happens very quickly. She had surgery, but it was too late. She had metastases and, in six months, she was gone."

During the war, Djamilya had seen many deaths, buried friends, and killed enemies. She got used to people dying from artillery fire, bombings, gunshot wounds, and stabbings. That night, she realized that those who'd escaped death at the front were destined to die of illness and old age. For a moment Djamilya saw Vera's and Lusya's futures, and her own.

They washed away all thoughts of death with another shot of alcohol and chatted about this and that. It was much nicer to spend time with Okunev Senior than with Shurik or Galya's friends. Must be a smaller age difference.

"How old are you?" she asks.

"It's scary to admit," he smiles, "sixty-five. And you?"

Djamilya asks him to guess, Okunev says: "twenty-seven," she laughs: "higher, higher!" and he doesn't believe her, so then Djamilya says: "I don't believe you, either, what do you mean, sixty-five? Forty, forty-two at the most." Okunev tousles his gray hair, flings his dressing gown open, and reveals his chest: "See, I have gray here, too, and wrinkles . . . I'm an old man, Mila!"

"No, look at the muscles you have," Djamilya says, pokes Okunev's chest and doesn't remove her hand, slowly guiding her palm along his skin and smoothing out the wrinkles; they both already know what will happen next. Looks like some information-carrying bytes have been transferred from the fingers to the chest or vice versa and, when Djamilya carefully removes her hand, Okunev says almost soberly: "Let me clean your wounds before we drink all the alcohol" and, this time, it's his turn to glide his palm along her skin, move it down her leg, higher and higher, probing under the hem of her dress, and not stopping there. Djamilya closes her eyes, the trumpet's hoarse groan sounds again in her ears, and small ripples run through her body.

They start to kiss and Djamilya says: "Let's go to your room. It's a bit awkward to kiss the father and son on the same night in the same place."

Djamilya pulls her dress over her head and takes off her bra and underwear. Okunev throws off his dressing gown. In the pre-dawn light, the wrinkles, gray hair, and sagging skin are quite visible. Djamilya lays down on the ottoman and closes her eyes. His lips pass over her body, reach the nipples, and freeze.

Djamilya hears sobs. Without opening her eyes, she places her hand on the tousled gray temple and caresses it tenderly.

"I'm sorry," Okunev says, "I . . . I don't know that I can. I haven't been with anyone in ten years, since Lyudmila died. I'm an old man."

"Let's just lie here together," Djamilya says.

"She died on this very couch," Okunev says, "I was with her. Lyudmila was a doctor and she described . . . everything that was happening to her . . . how her feet grew cold and then the cold climbed up to her knees and hips and rose up her belly. As if you were entering icy water. And when the water came up to her breasts, she died. And I began to cry, began to kiss her when she was already dead . . . until my lips came to the . . . where her breasts had been . . . there were only scars left . . . since then I haven't seen a woman's body . . . I'm sorry . . . I've already done my share of loving, the machinery is out of order," and Okunev lifts up his penis, which is limp among gray, curly hairs.

It's getting lighter outside. I have to wake up Galya and hurry to the plant, Djamilya thinks, but keeps lying there, drifting in and out of sleep.

Okunev is speaking and Djamilya hears some fragments as she falls asleep: Lyudmila's funeral, the space program, and then he practically screams:

"*We are all taking the place of the dead! Lying on their sofas, living in their apartments! Our cities are standing on top of bones! It's not enough to respect them, we must revive them, revive the dead!*" and Djamilya thinks: what a strange dream! She must force herself to wake up and hurry to the plant!

Meanwhile, Okunev continues in the same vein: "*It's not resurrection that the Christians believe in, it's revival, a scientific and material process!*" and, at that point, Djamilya drifts away on the waves of her strange dream and barely hears his mumbling:

"For that, we have all of outer space . . . the great Tsiolkovsky said: we must build rockets so, when the dead rise again, they can settle the Universe . . . we must fly into space . . . must make room for the dead, do you understand? . . . rockets, enormous rockets, aren't for dogs anymore, not for Belka and Strelka, a rocket in which a human will fly . . . I see it, I see it!"

Okunev pictures a fiery pillar, a burning column, a flaming tower going up to the very sky—and feels his virility returning to him.

Djamilya dreams of a field under an eternal gray rain and wanders down that field, now and then stumbling over mounds and hills, with Vera and Lusya walking not too far ahead and Tanya running somewhere behind. Djamilya is aware of all this, though she can't turn her head. And she walks along, looking straight at her girlfriends' backs when, suddenly, Vera falls and Djamilya and Lusya run up to her, slowly and laboriously, as befits a nightmare; then Lusya begins to founder and Djamilya catches her as she's about to hit the ground, gazes into her empty eyes, rhythmically jerks her by the shoulder and screams: "Lusya, wake up! Don't you recognize me? Get up and walk, can you hear me?" Screams and weeps because she can't hang on to Lusya's body.

Then, through her sobs, Djamilya hears a droning rise over the plain and grow louder with every minute. She throws her head up to the sky and hears the sound more clearly, it sounds like a wheeze, moan or wail coming from somewhere deep inside of her. It's Dizzy Gillespie's trumpet and, in her dreams, the sound is even louder and more beautiful. Lusya opens her eyes and sits, she's young again, like in forty-three, when they'd all just met, and the three of them stand there—Vera, Lusya, and Djamilya, young and beautiful. The trumpet plays louder, yesterday's waves convulse their bodies, the field stirs beneath their feet, every mound straightens its human back—and now Mom and Dad are standing next to her with their arms around each other, like in a wedding photo; Oleg comes up to her, smiling cockily, and new people rise one after another— Djamilya doesn't always remember where she met them during her life.

They surround her and, at that moment, Djamilya realizes that the trumpet voice is coming from her. Her body is one giant trumpet. Streams of air pierce it all the way through and the wind rushes into her loins and comes out of her open mouth with a moan. Djamilya arches her back, the sound intensifies, the bodies of the men and women standing beside her also begin to carry their tunes, and the sounds combine into one, like the blare of a thousand trumpets; for an infinite moment of happiness,

Djamilya merges with all these people, the trumpet lets out a final, piercing sound, and Djamilya feels Okunev's last tremor as she awakens.

"Wow," he breathes. "Thank you. I'm sorry that I . . . I was scared it wouldn't work again . . ."

"No worries," Djamilya says sleepily, "I liked it."

She kisses Okunev on the lips and then Galya bursts in, yelling, "Dad, we oversle–" and freezes.

Djamilya sits up and asks matter-of-factly: "What time is it?"

The massive clock on the writing desk shows 9:09 A.M. Okunev throws on his dressing gown, walks up to it, and adjusts the perpetual calendar box. Djamilya reads the date: April 12, 1961, Wednesday.

Until the day he died, Okunev was confident that, on that day, he had seen the launch of the *Vostok* spaceship with his inner eye. That vision was his reward for many years of work as a nuclear physicist; it gave Okunev strength for the last orgasm of his life. The sperm expelled in the loins of a chance partner was the sparks, the fireworks in honor of the impending revival of the dead, the semen of the new era—the era of the conquest of space.

In forty-something years, no one will be interested in outer space, but Okunev will never know. Nor will he know that his semen had ascended: nine months later, Gulnara Takhtagonova was born.

As she filled out the papers, Djamilya got stuck on the box for a patronymic: she had never asked for Okunev's first name that drunken night. She wrote "Yuryevna," most likely in honor of Yuri Gagarin.

That day, he spent exactly one hundred and eight minutes in outer space.

What delicate hooks linked everything that evening, what a multitude of informational chains was created, what a great many times the hundreds of signals were transferred, processed, and analyzed, and all so two people could ultimately exchange genetic information, merge databases, and create a unique information unit.

As Shurik prophetically said, the most important thing was to pass on the genetic code.

Some philosophers believe you can find hidden meanings behind any historic event. There are dozens of clever theories and exhausting monographs to help you uncover these meanings.

But the most heart-stirring, poignant thoughts can't be found in thick books: they emerge when the story of a human being and his family is woven into the fabric of the Great History.

A man says: Hitler attacked Russia so my father could keep his word. An old man thinks: a rocket flew to the stars so I could get an erection. A mother believes: Gagarin waved his hand so I could have a daughter. The birth of a little girl and the orgasm of an old man—what could be better?

Does a space flight really need to have any other meaning?

Galina Okuneva must have decided that Djamilya set her sights on their apartment, and even notified the party committee; the party organizer— on the whole a benevolent guy—had a good laugh about it, summoned Djamilya, and gave her an earful: "What, there aren't enough men for you at the plant?," then let her get back to work. They didn't even issue a reprimand.

At the plant, her pregnancy was counted as an additional child. They barely had time to process her revised application for an apartment. You could say she went directly there from the maternity clinic—and lived there for forty-something years. At first, she was proud—new housing development, city of the future, Novye Cheryomushki. She had no roommates and had her own kitchen, bath, and water closet, even if the latter were combined. Even later on, when people condescendingly nicknamed these buildings Khrushchev's slums, Djamilya continued to love her apartment.

They say they're going to demolish all the five-story buildings in Moscow. The residents will move to new buildings with improved layouts.

Djamilya Musayevna has absolutely no desire to move. It's easy to move when you're young; the elderly are hard to budge.

That's why she's hoping it will all work out somehow.

Old age makes your bones fragile and your bowels capricious.

Old age takes away your strength and desires, your sight and your hearing, takes away your life day in, day out.

It takes away almost everything, but, in exchange, it makes you fearless.

At present, you mustn't fear the future—there's hope that you'll die before it comes to pass.

Even death isn't so scary: you live your life day in, day out, lose your sight and hearing, and immerse yourself in it as if in a forest lake.

The cold touches her feet, knees, hips, and belly. At this moment, it rises up to her very breasts—and Djamilya Takhtagonova's heart stops beating.

In the cool, dark lake, stripped of jealousy, desires, and fears, immobile and calm, she waits for the trumpet to start playing again.

91.

POWERFUL STUFF, WE KNOW

Sex in Rimma's life never went anywhere. She'd read about it in books and watched it in hentai films. Ideal sex, immaculate, between equal partners.

Occasionally, she'd forget how this worked in real life and end up in bed with someone.

She'd strive to never see this person again.

She liked neither her own nor other people's bodies. A person can choose her clothing, makeup, and accessories, all of which belong to her. A naked body belongs to no one. It has a life of its own, which is of no interest to anyone. One does not know what to do with it. Press here, pull there, lick, bite, and marvel that, occasionally, these meaningless and chaotic gestures make a buried contact and produce feedback—a sigh, a sudden cry, a moan, trembling.

Bodies didn't belong to anyone, and neither did desire and arousal. They governed bodies, leaving no room for Rimma and rendering her incapable of comprehending why she was there. Sometimes, she imagines how two bodies—a male and a female one, a female and a female one—continue to move and rub against each other, an unwieldy mobile, a biological mechanism laboring in vain.

When it happened, the orgasm also didn't belong to her. A second of complete emptiness, a short and, simultaneously, infinite moment when time was switched off, followed by fatigue and a kind of melancholy supposedly characteristic of all living creatures at such times. Post-coitum, Rimma thought, more than ever, that she was a boy and not a girl: she didn't need physical affection, wanted to be alone, and, better yet, to go to sleep.

All that remained after sex were memories of the fatigue and sadness that occasionally overtook Rimma long before orgasm. To chase them away, she'd start calling the shots and giving out orders, pressing, jerking, pinching, and possessing another's body every which way, pretending that what they were doing was a reasonable activity under her full control.

Rimma strived not to see her partners again. Not just in bed—to simply never see them. Sometimes, this desire was mutual, sometimes not, and then she'd end up in the ridiculous and unpleasant position of being the object of another's passion.

This is why Rimma avoided sex—especially with people she knew.

It was unpleasant to see a strange body that did something with yours. And seeing a strange body that you did something with was also unpleasant. Wherever you met or whatever either of you were wearing.

That night, she and Sazonov never touched one another.

They had Olga's body for everything their own bodies desired.

Rimma knows how to talk about sex. Magazines teach this to girls born in 1982. Everything that's written about in magazines makes for a great topic of conversation. Feeling each other up, masturbation, oral sex, lesbian love, S&M, threesomes, jealousy, love, and contraception. Conversation partners and magazines provide topics and terms for conversations about sex, which is why Rimma will never say that sex is meaningless, partners are boring, and the human body is something to be ashamed of. A modern woman can't say things like that.

Rimma will never tell anyone about her most intense sexual experience. Only once was sex harmonious and sublime, almost perfect. She will never tell anyone about it, never work up the nerve to repeat the experience. The memory will remain unexpressed and a bit muddled and fragmented.

Not long before she left university, Rimma went to a party. High-heeled boots, striped knee-high socks, a mini-skirt, a white cotton GAP tank-top and bright-red, lacy bra straps. A classmate was celebrating his birthday, it was a large crowd and half of them were his grade-school chums, unknown to Rimma. They drank, then, smoked Moroccan hash, and Rimma smoked with everyone too, although she didn't think that weed did anything for her.

Brief flashbacks: a couple is kissing in the kitchen and a boy's hand hikes up his girlfriend's mini-skirt. A dusky living room, confused dancing. A scrunched-up conversation about finals. Then, Rimma walks into an empty room, but isn't quite sure why.

It's dark in there and only the rectangle of the monitor glows on the table. The chairs have been carried away to the next room; Rimma leans over the table and gropes for a mouse.

There's an unfamiliar game on the screen. Something in the vein of *Star Wars*, but more repetitive. A spaceship is dodging asteroids and shooting at approaching enemies.

The first asteroid catches Rimma off guard. She keeps having to start over and over. The rocks fly erratically, chaotically, from every direction. Rimma tries to shoot at them from a cannon, but the cannon seems to be reserved for enemies who will probably appear in the next level. She tries over and over, thinking: *I think it's impossible to get through this game*—and suddenly, starts smoothly bypassing asteroid after asteroid. At first, she thinks she's on a lucky streak, but no, she really is getting into the rhythm.

A new universe appears on the screen. The lumps begin to fly toward her in a more harmonious and balanced way. Chaos is replaced by a melody characterized by beauty and an inherent logic.

For some reason, the music that drifted in from the other room disappears; Rimma can't feel her presently-numb back, her tired legs, her sweaty palms, or her parched throat—the body she dislikes so much vanishes.

She is flying through space as if she is executing the intricate steps of an unknown dance, smoothly and effortlessly gliding past asteroids in the anthracite darkness of the monitor. She is almost perfect, weightless, light and rapid. Outer space embraces her shoulders, the melody lifts her up and carries her through the boulders that dance in the dark, swiftly, even swifter, if only the flight would never end!

Moroccan hash is powerful stuff, we know.

Or maybe it really is the call of outer space.

Rimma doesn't like her own body. She doesn't hear the creaking of the door, the footsteps, the breathing. Doesn't pick up the smell of alcohol, tobacco, sweat. Doesn't notice the lips on her shoulder, the hand under her skirt, the knee between her legs. A brief jolt of pain—don't pay attention to it, don't interrupt your flight, let your body deal with it.

Then—rhythmic thrusts, the beating of a cosmic rhythm. She sees every protrusion in the stone boulders, every cavern, every fold, every grain of sand, dazzling trajectories, a cosmic ballet, an ode to joy, like that, and again, like that, and now, a bit off to the side, bypass the asteroid, again and again, dear God, I only hope I don't fall out of rhythm, I only hope I don't stop.

The black cosmos, vast emptiness, infinity embodied. No asteroids, she has flown all the way through and fallen into nowhere—and from the depths of this "nowhere," a flashing dot flies toward her, turns into a sphere, blooms, and expands. It is as brilliant as snow, as vast as the sun, unthinkable, consuming, frightening . . . and at that moment, Rimma presses a button, the black phallus of the cannon spits out a flash of fire, pulsating over and over—and a deep scream that was buried inside her for so many years bursts forth, lacerates the air, burns, scorches, and explodes over Moscow.

Rimma collapses back into her own body, sinks to the floor, falls and hits her head on the keyboard, flinches, and maybe even weeps.

In stories such as this one, the man is merely an extra. Even if we suppose that he didn't leave right away, Rimma remembers nothing about him. She gets up, fixes her skirt, tries not to look at the monitor, walks to the bathroom on shaky legs, and tells no one about this—not then and not later. She practically never thinks back to that evening and wishes that sex could always be like this—not having to see the other person's face, know their name, or feel either of their bodies, and only watch two-dimensional shadows flying across the black cosmos of a screen in the build up to the explosion.

92.

IN ANTICIPATION OF THE LOOMING CURRENCY DEVALUATION

I believe there are rules in life, unbreakable rules that apply to everyone. Fifteen years of Russian business have taught me this. Those kick-ass fans of making their own rules—where are they now? In the best-case scenario—in Herzliya, Spain, and London.

In business, you have to play by the rules. In life, too.

You don't get it? Well, let me explain.

I'm an adult, well-off male, my fortune is held in various assets, and is valued at ten to twenty million. This means that I need to have an apartment in the center of Moscow, a house in the Moscow suburbs (additional house in Europe or the US optional), a chauffeured car, a security detail, a wife and children, and one or two lovers on rotation. These are the rules and you're better off not breaking them. All the parameters are clearly defined: a big apartment, an even bigger home, an expensive car, a wife who you've been with since your student years, well-educated children (possibly—abroad). Your lovers must look like models and not be too smart.

Why is it important to follow the rules? Unlike laws, rules weren't thought up by people—they emerged on their own. You can't bribe your way out of it, you have to pay for your infractions in full.

For example, if you don't have a wife, you have to waste all your energy on warding off the young skanks who want to make you their husband. If you don't have children, your wife worries, she has nothing to do, she falls into a depression and everything's ruined. If your children don't get a good education, they could fall in with a bad crowd, get hooked on drugs, ruin their lives, and yours too. If you only have one lover, you may develop a strong emotional attachment to her and as a result, God forbid, want to get a divorce. If, on the other hand, you don't have a lover, what will you do with your sexual energy? If you fuck your wife the way you fuck your lover, your wife will get mad—and she'll be right: marital relations are built on mutual respect, and "give me a quick blowjob while I wait for this fax from London" is completely uncalled for here.

And so on and so forth.

Oh yeah. Also, you must have an old friend with whom you don't have any business ties. Because, typically, you lose the old friends you go into business with—that's also a well-known scenario.

Anyway, more than anything else, I'm worried that I didn't explain this theory to Nikita two or three years ago, when he started his business. Knowing the rules would have saved him from making mistakes—unfortunately, I realized this too late.

When Nikita said he had taken a young lover, I was happy for him. First, one, then another—everything by the book. But months passed, he still had the same lover, and there was no additional one on the horizon. Then, Nikita introduced me to his Dasha and I knew that the jig was up.

I already said that lovers must be young, dumb beauties. Because if a young woman has a perfect body, a man treats her like an expensive accessory and joyfully, readily exchanges her for another when he's fed up with her or when she goes out of fashion. If a young woman isn't particularly beautiful, you start treating her like a human being—and then you're a stone's throw away from love, divorce, and other catastrophes.

Dasha turned out to be far from beautiful. A bit on the heavy side, chubby legs, overly broad shoulders. Her only advantage was her huge tits, which are pretty typical among heavy women. I remember joking that this wasn't even fire in the furnace, it was devil-knows-what in the furnace. Not out loud, of course—there's a separate rule about that: "Don't joke out loud about your friends' girlfriends." And when Nikita asked: *What do you think of her, Kostya?* I replied that she was unconventional, revealed him to be an original and idiosyncratic man who even found himself a lover that would make no one think that he, Nikita, was a New Russian in the throes of a midlife crisis.

He had a laugh and I realized that, a month later, he'd be crying drunken tears on my shoulder, telling me how much he loves his Dasha. Of course, that's exactly what happened.

Speaking of midlife crises, not too long ago, I figured out the real reason for them. I had been wondering why, at almost forty, I was tempted to break the rules, and rather than find myself a new lover, get rid of all the old ones and do entirely without them.

It is traditionally believed that, as men near forty or forty-five, they starting hitting on (and, if they're able to, banging) young chicks with double the zeal just to prove that they can still get it up and death is far away. By consuming others' youth, they supposedly extend their own. Maybe it works, but it should be evident to any reasonable man that the youthfulness of an unfamiliar woman's pussy can't rejuvenate your cock—pardon my French, as my foreign colleagues say.

I think there's a completely different reason for it.

See for yourselves: for twenty-five years of their lives, these successful, forty-year-old men told themselves and others that sex was very valuable. That if there was a chance to find out what was under a woman's dress, you had to take it. Every missed opportunity to have sex was an irrevocable loss. Being aroused was reason enough to drag the one who got you fired up into bed, even if the real culprit was alcohol or drugs. It also helped our self-esteem that girls put out for us. Erotic experiences were very important for our emotional life. Moreover, after a night of love, you felt a surge of energy. And so on and so forth; everyone articulates it differently depending on his talent and education level.

And so, around the age of forty, these splendid men—meaning all of us—suddenly realize it's not true. That sex isn't valuable. Love is valuable, power is valuable, even new experiences are valuable, but not sex. We're sick of sex. And when these suspicions visit you for the first time, you feel horribly disappointed. Does it mean that you've spent half your life on bullshit? It's such a letdown that you don't want to believe it. And you try to prove to yourself that you're wrong. No, you tell yourself, sex is a beautiful thing, it's just that the young women are all wrong or the relationships didn't work out or some other reason.

At that point, men start going on benders. They fuck minors. Spark passions. Plan orgies. Try to switch to boys, master BDSM, coprophagy, golden showers, and other, excuse me, filth.

And the result is the same: sex is not valuable, it's a trifle.

For example, money. It's obviously valuable. Because you can exchange it for a lot of things. For your health. For your children's education. For those same new experiences. For charity. Money was invented to be exchanged. But you can't exchange sex for anything. As the expression goes, exchanging a cock for a cock is a waste of time.

Some people exchange sex for money or money for sex. But I think that's blasphemy. Money and sex are not equal in value. You can't get a lot of money for sex and you won't get good sex for money.

At one time, a highly educated young woman explained to me that you can only exchange sex for death. This theory must be a turn-on when you're going through puberty, but it's not particularly inspiring as you start pushing forty—we know as it is that death is near.

This is the origin of the midlife crisis with its awful tawdriness, male histrionics, expensive cars, and trips at your own expense and on the company dime to distant islands with imported and local hoes. It's like a gambling addiction: you've already realized that it's impossible to win at the casino, but you feel bad you've spent all this money, can't stop, and keep placing new bets. When you should simply say "I'm out" and exit the game.

The same goes for sex. You should simply say "sex doesn't interest me anymore" and exit the game.

This doesn't mean you'll never fuck again, no. You still have love, your old friendships, plain human affection for certain creatures of the opposite sex—various beautiful, valuable things to which you can add sex like a spice to a well-cooked dish. But sex for sex's sake becomes as nauseating as a salad made of salt and pepper alone.

Of course, there are times when you can't restrain yourself and go back to your old ways, do it for old times' sake—and then the *post coitum tristia* overpowers you before you even initiate intercourse. If this happens to you a few years in a row, and with different women to boot, my advice is: don't lie to yourself that next time will be better. Stop messing around. Exit the game. Go home instead and ask your wife how her day went. If your wife is away, then call your parents and talk to them, at long last.

That too is valuable. Not because your parents are going to die soon—although that's a fact and it's better not to kid yourself on this point either—but because they're already at the place where you'll be in twenty years. They are already old and you are just getting familiar with this age. Talk to them, ask them casually—how are things over there, in old age?

I believe that old age is a great equalizer. Over the course of our lives, the things we value disappear one by one, and sex is far from the first to leave us. We just haven't noticed how the things we loved in our childhood and early adolescence have faded into oblivion—of course we haven't, we were so busy looking for sexual partners! Now we can look back and ask ourselves: do we want ice cream as much as we did in first grade? And is

The Three Musketeers still a book we should have on our shelves? Does it really matter what grade we got on our third semester finals? Does anyone still want to drink port wine with their friends on their building stairs? I think that, among successful, professional people, there won't be anyone particularly covetous of port wine, *The Three Musketeers*, and a full carton of ice cream. You can do it as a joke, to be sociable, or out of nostalgia. But you can't consider any of this valuable.

I believe that, in old age, this will happen to everything we've accumulated. As we get closer to ninety, power, money, and new experiences won't matter any more than *The Three Musketeers* or an extra blowjob.

When everything has already happened, what difference do the specifics make?

The thought of old age is a powerful one. If you're upset about something—a business deal fell through, an employee of yours quit, oil prices fell, or, the opposite, the price of silver skyrockets—imagine yourself in forty or fifty years and consider if this will still bother you. And while you're at it, re-examine your past—what about it doesn't work for you? You didn't tell your dead grandmother everything you wanted to? And even if you did, what would those words, your grandmother, and you yourself matter in fifty years? This doesn't mean you shouldn't say nice things to loved ones, but if you've never had the chance to do something, there's no point in beating yourself up about it. When you get to a certain age, it won't matter what happened in your life and what didn't. As we know, time erases all.

I have doubts only when it comes to love: if I'm anything like my father, then I'll love my wife, children, and friends—both living and dead—until I die.

This is how The Beatles' *All You Need Is Love* should be interpreted—love is enough to keep you alive. Because if love also ceases to be valuable, then there's nothing holding you here, you can die in peace. Why live if you have nothing valuable left?

To be sure, many die sooner, without losing all their baggage, so to speak. Of course, it would be nice to hold on to only love—I believe that there are people to love on the other side too. It would be silly to die convinced that money is valuable—it's obvious that, after you die, you will never see that money again, which is why your afterlife is bound to be rather anguished. Kind of like a youth without sex.

You want to come to death having rid yourself of everything that is valuable—and the rules I'm talking about are of great help here. If you do everything by the book, then, in old age, you and your beloved wife will be living together in a small house by the sea.

And if you break the rules, then you'll be sitting across from your friend in an expensive restaurant, spending an entire hour asking him whether you should leave your wife for your lover or stay with her. I find this question to be completely meaningless and a *total waste of time*, which is why, an hour later, I change the subject.

"You know," I say, "I've been thinking. There's no point for you to meet with the investor. Because your business isn't scalable after all. It was a small business two years ago and will still be that way in three years."

"Not at all," Nikita takes offense. "It's just that I've neglected it lately. There happens to be reasonable potential for growth. I have to hire some salespeople, develop a new marketing strategy, and expand into new markets."

"Totally," I say. "Hire yourself a director of operations, some salespeople, and a marketing manager. And you and I can, for instance, come up with something new."

"Me and you?" Nikita marvels. "But you always said you don't like doing business with friends."

"I don't," I concur, "but I have a project and need someone I can trust."

"What kind of project?" Nikita asks and I start to tell, draw, map out, describe entry and exit strategies, crunch numbers—*yes, it really is a lot of money, this isn't selling pet fish*—set dates, assign shares . . . Nikita's listening closely, he seems sold on it. He reaches for his pen, asks questions, makes suggestions: *What if we do this, this and that, would that be better? There'll be instant synergy!*—and I can see that he's very pleased that I'm proposing such a serious business, that I'm recognizing him as an equal, so to speak. Nikita is right on this point: if he comes along, he'll be on a completely different level and could take pride in that.

"But it'll take a lot of work," I say, "you'll have to put everything else aside. Or else we'll lose the project and the money."

"Yes, I got it," Nikita nods. "Twenty-four hours a day, seven days a week. Do I need to give you my answer straightaway?"

"No," I say, "think about it, of course. But not for long—two weeks, or better yet, one. Because if your answer is *no*, I'll have to look for someone else."

Of course, I doubt it will be *no*; after all, I've known him for twenty years. His entire life he's just fallen short of genuine success, and now he has a real opportunity, the kind he's always dreamed of. He won't turn it down, he won't be able to.

"Listen," Nikita says, "and what about my current business?"

"Do what you want," I reply. "If you want, you can sell it, if you want, you can give forty percent to your Victor and let him run the show."

"That's also an option," Nikita says and again begins to ask questions, verify details, and take notes. People who haven't yet made up their minds don't act this way. There's another rule that stipulates that, if you can give your partner the illusion of agency, do it. And as we recall, rules have to be followed.

What about the "Don't start a business with close friends" rule? There is such a rule, yes. But if I don't give Nikita a good jolt right now, he'll be lost with his Dashas and Mashas and do something stupid, you never know. And after all, I'm his closest friend. I mean, he's my closest and most beloved friend. Who will help him besides me?

And rules . . . what are rules? Rules can be broken. Of course, I'll have to pay for it . . . with something, someday—alright, I'll consider myself warned.

I just know that, when I get old, all the rules will lose their value, whereas love and friendship will remain.

You could say that, in anticipation of the looming currency devaluation, I've invested in more secure and long-term assets.

93.

SOMETHING WILL END

It was impossible for him to avoid a bender, and Moreukhov knew this. Of course, when he would open a gin and tonic, a beer, or a bottled screwdriver for the first time in a month, he thought he could easily stop, but after the first swig, he would quickly realize that this swig would be inevitably followed by trips to On the Clearing, memory lapses, and wet, scaly arms—it was only a matter of time. He couldn't avoid a bender, but he could fast-forward it. For that, he would need to switch over to vodka as soon as possible, drink lots of it, dive in deeper, so to speak—and, two days later, call Dimon or Tiger Darkovich so they could set up an IV and pump him up with water. Worst-case scenario, he could try to find his own way out—after resurfacing, he wouldn't go to On the Clearing and, instead, drink water. Ten, twenty, thirty liters of water a day are a good replacement for an IV. This way, he could reduce a drinking binge to three to five days and, a week later, start moving around and re-establishing contact with friends.

So that Friday, Moreukhov—pale, with sunken eyes and shaking hands—is waiting for Lena in Vitalik's studio. Good thing he managed to finish the portrait before the ill-fated concert—presently, he can't even hold a brush. Lena turned out . . . well, she turned out fine. A beautiful dame, small tits under her dress, a pensive face. An eastern mystery. The East is a delicate thing.

The only thing Moreukhov remembered from his bender was that, after downing another half-liter, he saw the name of the vodka: "Russian Paradise." I'd like to believe, Moreukhov thinks, that this label depicted yet another *Russian Field of Experiments*, à la Pshenichnaya vodka.

There it is, mainstream painting! Bottle labels!

I made it out pretty fast, Moreukhov thinks. What if I'm not an alcoholic after all? Maybe I'm just pretending to avoid painting.

Moreukhov knows something will end today. There will be a denouement to the film noir he made up. For example, instead of Lena, her husband—a criminal in a jeep—will come here and kill Moreukhov in a jealous rage. This will help Lena, say, cover up her real affair. Or she won't turn up at all—and for many long years, Moreukhov will conduct conversations with the portrait like a total madman.

However, Lena does turn up and says she likes the portrait—maybe only to be polite.

"It's a decent painting," Moreukhov nods his head in agreement, "to give to a chick on her birthday, yeah."

He takes the canvas off the stretcher, rolls it up, tells her where to go pick out a frame. Lena gives him the money and gets ready to leave.

The story is nearing its end and there is no foreseeable continuation. I'm going to miss her, realizes Moreukhov. It's been a while since I had such a good talk with anyone. The hell with the fact that there was no sex, maybe I never really even wanted to fuck her, it's just that sex is the most basic thing a man can do with a woman.

"Wait, don't leave," he says. "Tell me something about yourself now."

Lena looks at her silver watch, sits down in the armchair, and crosses her legs—for the last time, realizes Moreukhov—and he thinks his hands are shaking from nervousness and not because he's going through withdrawal.

"What can I tell you?" she says. "My name is Lena. I'm half-Korean, half-Ukrainian. My father and his family moved to the Soviet Union before the war, he met my mother and they got married. I enrolled at a university in Moscow, then got married. We don't have children. My husband is a businessman."

"Is he a wealthy man?" Moreukhov asks.

"No," Lena says, "he's well-off. Like your cousin. Small and medium-sized business, less than a million a year in revenue, what kind of wealth could there be?"

She's going to leave now, Moreukhov thinks. Forever.

"I thought there was some criminal intrigue," he says. "Like in the movies. For instance, your husband was a criminal or a government official or . . . I don't know."

Lena smiles her familiar smile:

"You know, Sasha," she says, calling Moreukhov by his first name for the first time, "you're thirty. It's time to live a real life. With a head on your shoulders. Movies are movies."

"Very well," Moreukhov says, "but still: why me?"

He knows the answer, he knew it from the very beginning. Lena is a guardian angel, even if she doesn't know it herself. Something important has happened to him in this attic, he still doesn't understand what, but he can feel it.

"Oh, right. My husband asked for my portrait. I don't know why. I hope he's not planning to hang it in his office. Long story short, I didn't want it done by one of those, you know, trendy artists. First of all, it's expensive, and second of all, I would have died of boredom with them."

I hope she wasn't bored with me, Moreukhov thinks, and Lena continues. She wanted there to be a story behind the portrait so she could tell her kids when she had them: *This artist was famous in his time, I knew him a little.* And she was weighing her options when she met the drunk Moreukhov, he told her about himself, they shared a beer, and then they ran into each other again at Kopeyka—awful store, by the way, I don't understand who would shop there!—it turned out this was a possibility and, most importantly, a hundred times cheaper than going to a society portrait artist. *It's always cheaper to buy from an alcoholic. An apartment or a portrait—makes no difference.*

"And your husband won't be jealous?" Moreukhov asks, but already understands that this is no film noir, it's a completely different film, a romantic story where nothing happens, almost like *In the Mood for Love.* It's no accident that Lena looks so much like Maggie Cheung.

"Jealous of you?" Lena repeats the question with a smile on her face and takes the Polaroid snapshot out of her purse: a disoriented smile, a missing tooth, and scruff on his chin. "I'll show him this and he'll settle down."

That's it. The portrait is painted, the money is paid, and now Lena will leave forever, and Moreukhov doesn't even have her phone number.

"Will we meet again?" he asks.

Lena smiles again:

"Stop imagining things. It's all over. If we do, it'll only be by chance. And it's better if we don't acknowledge each other. What if my husband really does get jealous?"

Moreukhov nods his head. Yes, it's all over, he tells himself. He can pretend that Lena has immigrated to Korea, her historical homeland, like Sonya Shpilman.

Lena is already standing in the doorway. Suddenly, she turns around, digs into her purse, and hands Moreukhov some sheets of paper:

"Almost forgot. As promised, here's what I found online. It doesn't say anything about your grandfather in official sources, but there are references to him in all these prison camp memoirs—he's virtually in *The Gulag Archipelago*."

Moreukhov twirls the paper in his hand.

What, it's that simple? he thinks with disappointment. I was hoping there would be some kind of mystery here, and everything is so banal.

"How much time did he do?" he asks Lena.

"Sasha, your grandfather didn't do any time. He put people away. Grigoriy Borisov was an investigator in Leningrad in the thirties, at the very height of the Great Terror."

94.

I'M AFRAID

Today, we won't fill out the form, alright? Today, we'll simply chat like old friends. I'm interested in only one question, and you, as loyal citizens, must answer it for me voluntarily. After this, we'll let you go. This won't take up too much of your time.

Now then, tell me about your fear.

Nikita: What if oil prices fall too quickly? An economic crisis will set in and I'll have to close my business. I won't earn as much as I was planning to, I don't have any savings, and don't know what I'll do.

Anya: What if I get sick? Seriously sick and can't work? What will happen to Gosha then?

Moreukhov: Everyone knows what I'm afraid of: snags, fish, the arms of corpses on the seafloor. I've talked about this a hundred times already, you could have remembered.

Rimma: I don't think I'm afraid of anything. I have everything under control.

What is this nonsense? Who do you take me for? I need normal answers, stop fooling around! About real fear, not this bullshit! Quickly, I said! Okay, let's begin.

Nikita: I'm afraid that I won't be able to deal with things, that I won't resolve things with Dasha and Masha after all. I'll stay the way I am, like shit in an ice hole.

Anya: I'm afraid that something will happen to Gosha. God forbid, something serious . . . He'll get sick, get into an accident . . . die.

Moreukhov: I'm afraid that I'll never again see the world as beautiful as I see it now. As beautiful as it is after my first swig.

Rimma: I'm afraid that I won't manage, that I won't be able to control everything.

That's better, but you've still got some work to do. Get it together, guys, you're doing great, but we're just getting started. One more try!

Nikita: I'm afraid that Masha won't ever get pregnant. I don't know how I'll be able to live then.

Anya: I'm afraid that Gosha will abandon me when he grows up and I'll have no one to love.

Moreukhov: What if the reason that I haven't done anything with my life isn't because I drank too much, but because I'm a talentless hack?

Rimma: I'm a weak little girl, why are you asking me what I'm afraid of? I'm afraid of people who are stronger than me. What if they cause me pain, hurt my feelings? I have nothing to defend myself with.

If you keep beating around the bush, we'll be stuck here till morning! Sit up straight and look over here. I said, look over here. Now start talking, or else we'll make the lamp even brighter.

Nikita: I'm afraid that Masha will go insane . . . I'm afraid she already has . . . I don't know what to do.

Anya: I'm afraid to love someone . . . Andrey . . . any other man. I'm afraid that he'll betray me.

Moreukhov: I'm afraid that the next time I dive, I won't find those snags, those fish, those monsters. I'm afraid that they'll disappear.

Rimma: I'm afraid of other people. I don't know what to do with them. I don't understand what to expect from them, what's in their heads.

Very good. And now, the dash to the finish line. The scariest thing in the world is Orwell's room 101. What's inside? Tell me, I'm listening.

Nikita: I'm afraid to be left alone with Masha. I'm afraid that her voices—the voices of those who didn't survive—will consume me. I'll become just like them. There'll be nothing left of me.

Anya: I'm afraid to be weak. The weak don't survive. I'm afraid that I won't survive.

Moreukhov: I'm afraid that everyone will realize I'm a piece of shit and turn their backs on me. My mother, my friends, women, God—everyone. Drowned corpses, water creatures, even crayfish.

Rimma: I don't know who I am. I don't know what I really want. I don't understand what goes on in my head. I'm afraid of myself.

Great job, guys! Turn off the light, enough! And now, listen to those who have been here before you—perhaps, you'll recognize their voices.

I'm afraid that my husband doesn't love me, I'm afraid that he won't come back, I'm afraid that he'll leave, I'm afraid that she'll be arrested, I'm afraid that I'll be arrested, I'm afraid, I'm afraid that they'll find out my real name, I'm afraid that my father lied to me, I'm afraid that I'll never see India, I'm afraid that I'll never be young and beautiful, I'm afraid it was all in vain, I'm afraid that we lost the war, I'm afraid that there's neither a heaven nor a hell, I'm afraid that I won't be beautiful anymore, I'm afraid that the world won't be saved, I'm afraid that everyone will find out who I was, I'm afraid that everyone will find out who I am, I'm afraid he was just a lowlife, I'm afraid that they'll find us, I'm afraid that my life ended too soon, I'm afraid that I died a long time ago.

I'm afraid that everything I loved won't last, that everything I loved will vanish without a trace, I'm afraid that I won't be able to do a thing about it, I'm afraid it was all in vain.

I'm afraid that all those who teach us how to save people, how to save the world, I'm afraid that they don't know the answer, that they are misguided or misguiding, I'm afraid that it's impossible to help anyone, to teach anyone, I'm afraid it was all in vain.

I'm afraid that I've become completely unattractive, that no one needs me, I'm afraid that I've done something wrong, I'm afraid that the winter from the fable about the grasshopper and the ant will come, I'm afraid it was all in vain.

I'm afraid that the Communists kept their word, but Pyotr was already dead, I'm afraid that there is no heaven and I'll never see my father, nor my brothers and sister, I'm afraid that my mother will die anyway and I've ruined my life for her sake, I'm afraid it was all in vain.

I'm afraid that none of this ever happened. Neither the octopus nor the flying saucer. It was a transmitter, Alyosha and I fell asleep on the rocks and had a dream. And those people killed us in our sleep. And I became a ghost because it's sad to die a little girl. And everything that's happened in my life—my husband, the school, my students—none of that was real, it was all in vain.

I'm afraid that the stadiums, factories, parks, electric power plants, and universities—I'm afraid that they'll never be built, I'm afraid we didn't manage to win, that we lost the war, I'm afraid it was all in vain.

I'm afraid that it was a lie, a delusion, not the spirit of the worlds, but a haze, I'm afraid it was all in vain.

And last of all, a fresh reprise, especially for you.
New recording, please.

I'm afraid (reprise):

oil prices will fall
nothing will be left of me
I'll have to close my business
I won't have any money
I'll get sick
I won't be able to deal
I won't resolve things
something will happen to him
he'll leave me
I won't manage
I'm defenseless
I'm a talentless hack
she's insane
and I won't be able to deal with things
everyone will turn their backs on me
it was all in vain

I'm a fraid of being weak
I'm afraid of being alone
not surviving
others
myself

I'm afraid it was all in vain

95.

1919. A TREAT

Once upon a time, there lived an old woman named Kondratyevna; in her youth, she had been observant and garrulous, and though her eyes grew weak as she got old, she became even more hawkeyed; though she had just one tooth sticking out of her mouth, the chattiest chatterbox couldn't out-mumble her. She had a daughter, Marya, who went out to the village outskirts for a stroll and became in the family way. When Marya began to swell, Kondratyevna asked her:

"Who was it that ruined you, daughter? A cruel person or a demon of some sort?"

Marya didn't reply and simply started to cry.

Then it came time for Marya to give birth; she had a girl and died in labor.

They called the girl Marfushka and she lived with Kondratyevna.

When Marfushka turned three, she wanted to go to the woods to pick mushrooms and berries, and her grandmother said to her:

"You can go wherever you please, just don't go to the dam that the mill stands on. There's a water creature there, he will drag you underwater."

Marfushka asked what this water creature looked like and Grandmother said:

"He is small and dark, looks like the devil, and has red whiskers, a long beard, and hair so wild you can't brush it with a comb."

When Marfushka turned five, she forgot Grandmother's warning and went to the dam. There was a mill on the dam, and in it lived a miller. He was old and gray, with long, unkempt hair, a tangled beard, and untrimmed nails. In the summer and winter, he wore a sheepskin half coat with a

527

waist-belt and leaned on a long shepherd staff as he walked. He didn't know anyone in the village and only went to church for the big holidays.

Now Marfushka went to the dam and the miller noticed her and called her over.

"What's your name, little girl?" he asked, "And who are your parents?" She replied:

"My name is Marfushka, I'm old Kondratyevna's granddaughter. My mother, Marya, has gone to God and I never knew my father."

The miller then said:

"Since you're here, little daughter, come in, I'll give you a treat."

Marfushka approached the house and saw a black rooster moseying around the yard. She'd never seen a rooster like that before and asked:

"Gramps, why do you need a black rooster?"

And he said to her:

"When the water devil comes for me, I'll give him the black rooster and he'll leave me alone."

Marfushka went into the house and saw a black cat warming up by the oven. She asked:

"Gramps, why do you have a black cat? Folks say that black cats serve Satan."

The miller got angry, thumped his staff against the floor and said:

"He doesn't serve anyone! The water devil will come to me, I'll give him the black cat, and he'll leave me in peace."

The miller took out various treats for Marfushka, whom he called his little daughter. Marfushka liked being at his house and began to visit him. One time, the miller said:

"I'm old and I live alone. When it's time to die, no one will bring me water, you're my only friend and helper. I ask only one thing of you, swear to me in the name of Christ you'll do what I ask."

Marfushka swore it to him.

And the miller said to her:

"If I die in a field—don't carry me into the izba, and if I die in the izba—let them carry me out not feet-first, but head-first, and stop by the river to cut the veins behind my knees."

Another time, he said:

"I'm old and I live alone. If I take ill, what will I do?"

Marfushka said to him:

"If you take ill, Gramps, send me a message."

The miller pondered it, pondered it awhile, and made a little wooden wheel on a stick. He gave it to Marfushka and said:

"Hide this little wheel somewhere safe, don't show it to Kondratyevna. If you see it start to spin on its own—that means I've taken ill. And if water starts pouring through it, that means I'm already dying."

That's what Marfushka did—she brought the little wheel home, hid it in the drying shed, and went to check every day to see whether it was spinning or if water spilled from it.

Marfushka turned six, and the time came to harvest the wheat. In the morning, Kondratyevna went into the field and took Marfushka along to help her. All day long, Marfushka walked around the field helping her grandmother. By evening, she was tired and returned home, and was getting ready to go to sleep when she remembered the little wheel. She ran to the drying shed and saw the little wheel spinning on its stick, as if it were being spun by some force.

Marfushka ran to the dam and went inside the mill, and the miller said to her:

"Thank you for coming, my little daughter. I waited a long time for you and thought I wouldn't see you again. It's not time for me to die yet, it's not time. Thank you, and here's a sweet treat for you. Run on home, little daughter, and don't forget about the little wheel."

Marfushka came out on the stoop and saw that the black rooster wasn't in the yard. So she asked:

"Gramps, where is your black rooster?"

And the miller said to her:

"The cat tore it to pieces."

Marfushka came home and her grandmother asked:

"Granddaughter, where did you go at this time of night?"

And Marfushka replied to her:

"I was playing hide-and-go-seek with the other children."

Grandmother didn't believe her, but said nothing.

A long or maybe a short time passed and, one day, Marfushka returned from the field, ran to the drying shed, and found the little wheel was spinning. She didn't say anything to her grandmother and ran to the mill. She saw that the miller had grown very thin and his eyes had sunken in. He said to Marfushka:

"Oh, little daughter, I felt very ill today and thought you wouldn't make it in time. But it's not time for me to die yet, it's not time."

He gave her another treat and again charged her to keep an eye on the little wheel. Marfushka asked him:

"Gramps, where is your black cat?"

And the miller said to her:

"He ran away to the forest."

Marfushka came home and her grandmother asked her:

"Granddaughter, where did you run off to at this time of night?"

"I was playing *gorodki*[7] with the other children."

Grandmother didn't say anything, but noticed her granddaughter went to the drying shed every evening. Marfushka lay down to sleep, and Kondratyevna went to the drying shed and found the little wheel.

She took it and brought it to a woodworker, and the woodworker made an identical one—you couldn't tell them apart. Kondratyevna placed this little wheel in the drying shed and threw the enchanted one outside the village gates.

Marfushka kept going to the drying shed, but the little wheel didn't turn or spin. One day she looked out over the village gates and noticed a curious wet patch in the grass.

The autumn was dry that year, and it hadn't rained at all. And so Marfushka wondered at it, then forgot about it, and went to play with her girlfriends.

The next day, she looked out and saw a puddle in place of the wet patch. Marfushka marveled at the puddle, but her grandmother called to her and she forgot about it.

On the third day, she saw that the puddle had grown so large you couldn't jump over it. This time, Marfushka went to inspect the puddle and found her little wheel at the bottom of it.

She realized what her grandmother had done, but said nothing and ran to the mill.

Marfushka came in and saw the miller lying on the threshold convulsing; he'd turned blue and his swollen tongue was sticking out of his mouth. He said to Marfushka:

"You see how ill I am, I can't lie on my bench, my chills are forcing me to the floor. For many days now, I've been at death's door and still can't die. What took you so long?"

Marfushka began to tell him, but the miller didn't let her finish and asked her:

---

[7] An ancient Russian folk game similar to bowling. The goal is to knock out groups of skittles arranged in various patterns by throwing a bat at them.

"Bring me some water, my little daughter!"

Marfushka scooped up some water with her dipper and brought it to the miller, but she was frightened by how dreadful he looked. She put the dipper on the floor and leaped aside. The miller said:

"I'm ill, my daughter, oh how ill. I'm dying. Come closer to me and I'll give you a farewell treat."

In his hour of death, he looked so dreadful that Marfushka was afraid to come closer to him.

Meanwhile, Kondratyevna noticed her granddaughter was gone, started fussing and running hither and thither, and the busybody neighbor said to her:

"Your Marfushka ran down to the river."

Kondratyevna took to her heels after Marfushka.

And the miller is shaking, his whole body is writhing, he's in pain, and doesn't want to die. He strikes his head against the threshold until it bleeds. Again, he asks Marfushka:

"Come closer to me, daughter, I have a treat for you, the likes of which you won't find anywhere else in the world."

Marfushka stands without moving a muscle, she's scared.

Kondratyevna runs down to the river, where she sees women washing laundry. They say to her:

"Your Marfushka ran to the mill."

And the miller begs Marfushka again:

"Didn't I love you, didn't I spoil you, didn't I give you sweet treats? Come closer to me, reach out your hand and I'll give you a treat as a keepsake, I have no one to give it to, only you, my blood daughter. Take it, and then I can die in peace."

Marfushka becomes curious and she asks:

"What kind of a treat is it?"

The miller says to her:

"It's an invisible treat, you can't smell it with your nose, you can't touch it with your hands, you can't see it with your eyes, you can't give it a name. Come closer to me, I'll reach out my hand and say: 'Here is your keepsake!' and you have to squeeze my hand, then it will be yours."

Marfushka came up to him, the miller extended an empty hand and said:

"Here is your keepsake!" At that moment, Kondratyevna burst into the yard and began to scream:

"Give that back to the one you got it from!"

The miller began to moan more miserably than before. He began to twist and writhe, his arms were contorted and blood started running from his mouth. He said:

"Too bad you didn't take it, Marfushka. Now, neither you nor your children nor grandchildren will have peace until they find me and take my treat."

Marfushka took fright and leaped back. Kondratyevna said to her:

"Run to the woodworker and ask him to get his axe and hurry over here."

Marfushka ran, and Kondratyevna says to the miller:

"Suffer, old sorcerer, suffer, this is your punishment for my Marya! You knocked her up and ruined her!"

The miller began to moan still more miserably and stuck out his tongue, which he'd bitten through. He can't say a word and really is dying.

Marfushka brought the woodworker, who climbed up on the roof and began to remove the horsehead. And as soon as it fell off, the miller died.

They left him in the izba overnight, and when they returned in the morning, there was no body—only wet, inhuman footsteps on the ground leading to the dam.

Marfushka and her grandmother went back to their lives, and a year later, mean people rode into the village and took all the grain and horses, and half the village died of hunger over the winter, including old Kondratyevna. Marfushka left for the city, but who knows if she made it there?

Ah, our sins are heavy.

96.

AS IF IT WERE MELDED TO IT

I used to be named Marina, now I'm Vika. I say it's in honor of Wicca, witchcraft. I'm a witch, that's my job.

I tell my old friends:

"Witch is simply a word. Many people won't ever turn to a psycho-therapist, won't ever do meditation or yoga: some will go to church and others will come to me. I have the most ordinary profession of a guru, no mysticism.

"A guru is someone who helps. A doctor, a priest, a therapist. People come to me for help. All types of people, and every one of them with a life of his own. What do you mean, what can I help them with? They don't know themselves, don't know their own lives. If nothing else, I try, try to help, try to tell their story together with them.

"Telling stories is a woman's business. Men compose epics and romances; women tell stories. And I'm telling my thousand and one tales as if I'm afraid that, as soon as I stop speaking, my head will be chopped off like Scheherazade's."

Old friends listen and nod, satisfied, and then, tell me about their jobs and families. Sometimes, I tell their stories together with them.

Because I lied. Being a witch is no ordinary guru's profession.

Being a witch means turning yourself over to the Great Mother. Turning yourself into an empty vessel that She fills. This is why I'm not the one telling all my stories—it's the Great Mother speaking through my lips. I don't know myself how the story will end.

Sometimes the stories I get from her are stories of people. Sometimes they're stories of objects. Or about a link between phenomena, a secret, deep connection that spans countries and decades. Sometimes they're about grandfathers and great grandfathers, the living and dead, women and men, heaven and earth, water and fire, posthumous suffering and rebirths, the unborn and the newborn.

I get that the Great Mother needs raconteuses. She loves me, but sometimes I think she's keeping me on the sidelines so she can play me at the right moment, the way a swindler pulls his ace from his sleeve.

And that's when I want to tell stories about myself.

For example, this one.

If you've worked as a professional witch for a decade, you've accumulated things: crystal balls, magic crystals, healing herbs, a whole wardrobe . . . objects have a way of finding you and then, you don't always have the strength to part with them when they outlive their usefulness.

The same goes for people. At some point, you start recognizing the girls that come to your lectures time and again, then you invite some of them to a closed seminar, have them over at your place, tell them all kinds of things, and now you've got a stable circle of admirers who hang on your every word and run to you with their troubles and joys like you're their favorite teacher in secondary school.

Every witch is something of a teacher, it comes with the territory.

Darya became one of "my girls" a few years ago. Young, not dumb, capable—she could have learned a lot if she wanted to. Unfortunately, Darya never delved too deeply into anything. I taught her Wicca, and, at another place, she studied sex magick, yoga, Tantric Buddhism, and who knows what else. I said "capable" because, from to time, she managed to pull off pretty complicated things.

There is an exercise where you articulate a problem, go into a trance, and state the solution. Everything will happen within the specified time frame.

Obviously, when they're in a trance, most people simply see the solution to the problem. To be honest, there's no sorcery at work—even psychotherapists can do this.

Anyway, while she was in her trance, Darya said she wanted to arrange her life as follows. She needed a middle-aged man with money who'd fall in love with her and rent her an apartment. He had to be interesting to talk to and he had to love Darya and not try to control her life (including her sex life). About fifteen years ago, in my youth, this was known as a "sponsor." Sometimes, long-legged blondes with model physiques or provincial beauties who'd come to conquer the capital would land those kinds of men.

Darya is not long-legged and definitely not a beauty. She is attractive at best, which is why the story she told herself seemed rather implausible. I even felt bad for her.

Three months later, Darya met a small-business owner of about forty and, before long, she was living in an apartment rented by him. He was interesting to talk to, madly in love with her, and didn't try to control her life (including her sex life).

Darya admitted that the result terrified her a bit. She thought she had created this man. One moment, he wasn't there—and then, poof, he appeared. And now I am responsible for him, she said.

They've been together for about six months now, and all manner of things have happened. First, Darya was a bit in love with him, then, she became disillusioned with him, then, she began to appreciate him, then, she grew weary of his love . . . in short, once again, the old rule had proven to be true: the more powerful the magical intervention, the greater the consequences and the magician's responsibility.

Half-a-year or so before all this happened, I myself made a new friend, a salesgirl from a shopping center. Her name was Elvira, but she'd renamed herself Anya. Must have been another thing I liked about her.

I've long gotten used to the fact that certain things just happen in my life. I don't even remember how Anya and I met or why I went to her place that first time. Anyway, we became friends—maybe this was also because we lived two buildings apart.

A month ago, I realized that Anya is Darya's sponsor's cousin.

I learned this by accident. Darya brought me her lover's family ring and said: Alright, tell me about him, you must know how to tell stories using objects. She said that, lately, she, Darya, has been thinking: Maybe I should marry him? Reliable, honest . . . and, as a matter of fact, she said, maybe I do love him. Maybe I should have his baby? It'll be a boy or a girl. Nikita isn't a greedy man, he'll give us money. And the wife—he can continue living with her if he wants to. Or move in with me, doesn't matter.

So, Darya says, can you look into him? Tell me about him, okay?

She produces the ring, which truly is old, and I take it in my hands and can feel that it used to belong to a woman. Meaning, it used to belong to a lot of different people, but once had an owner with such intense energy that it comes through even after decades. I try to tune into this energy and, at that moment, I literally collapse.

I rarely experience this with objects, and it's first time that I experience this so intensely. It's as if I go off the deep end and, when I resurface, I feel as if a whole hour has gone by, but Darya hasn't noticed a thing, she's barely managed to finish her sentence, that's how quickly it happens.

I catch my breath and ask: Who did you say your Nikita got this ring from—his mother or his father? She tells me: His grandfather. She thinks that his grandfather got it from his own father a long time ago, before the revolution.

I say, you're sure it's not from his mother?

Positive, replies Darya, do you know how much he's told me about his family? On his mother's side, he had Grandpa Makar and Grandma Nastya, and, on his father's side, Grandpa Mikhail and Grandma Marfa.

"And Grandma Marfa," I ask, just to make sure, "was she from a village?"

"I think so," Darya replies, "her name is rather folksy."

Of course, Marfa is a folksy—and rare—name. And I'd heard it somewhere not too long ago. Even both names: Mikhail and Marfa. What, I ask, is your sponsor's last name?

And when Darya says his last name—and I already know what she'll say—I take the ring and tell her: You know, there is something I need to check, I'll give it back to you later, I'm sorry.

After that, I was swamped with work for two weeks, then Anya went away on vacation, then something else came up—anyway, I didn't drop by her place until yesterday. I brought the ring in my purse and didn't say anything.

Anya has an interesting story. Three generations of women in her family raised children without husbands. Her grandmother had given birth to two daughters from men she had only met once; her mom divorced her husband when Anya was three. In her turn, Anya chose the father of her child *based on his exterior*, as she says. Either a security guard or a truck driver from the adjacent market-stand. For Anya, it wasn't an unequal match, but she didn't even tell the guy she was pregnant: she was like, thanks, but my child doesn't need a father.

She gave birth to a boy. A brash, energetic boy. Pretty challenging, if you take the time to observe him. He's about three now.

These days, Anya has a regular lover. They see each other once a week, but the three of them went on vacation together, and, on their last night, her lover proposed to her in a restaurant, by candlelight, the whole nine yards.

Now Anya doesn't know if she should say yes, although it seems like she's a bit in love with this guy. But still, how can she fathom living with a man? Grandma and Mom lived by themselves, but she's going to live with a guy? There's got to be some sort of a catch.

Anyway, we're sitting in Anya's place, her son, a young ruffian, is away at her mom's friend's dacha, and, just then, Anya utters an obviously pained phrase:

"Can you imagine," she says, "I'm the only one in my whole lineage who received a proper proposal."

I congratulate her, of course, and then, say:

"You keep forgetting that your lineage is far more extensive than just your mother and grandmother."

Anya says something about her cousin, who, needless to say, also comes from her mother's side, but I insist:

"You also had a father, even if you never really saw him. And there were also his parents, with whom your mother sometimes let you stay. What were their names?"

"Grandpa Mikhail and Grandma Marfa," Anya replies.

At that point, I take out the ring and tell Anya that it belonged to Grandma Marfa. And that she shouldn't ask me how it got into my hands. I believe, I say, that I received it specifically so you could come into contact with your father's ancestors. Because without your father's side, you are not complete, you won't be able to raise your son, or work out who you'd like to live with and how.

"And what do I do with this ring?" Anya asks.

"Let's try this," I say. "Sit over here, close your eyes, I'll place the ring on your palm and talk to you for a bit. Breathe deeply and evenly, and notice the images that appear in your consciousness."

Anya shrugs her shoulders and says:

"What nonsense. Well, if you want, we can try."

She sits down, closes her eyes; I place the ring on her palm, start bringing her into a trance—and, all of a sudden, she's gone.

there is no room there is no vika there is no moscow behind the window there is only a dark forest and a slanted house a mill pond a deep-end icy water and so I'm swimming and then I dive in deeper and deeper see a black rooster swim by a black cat swim by an old man swim toward me with a long gray unkempt scary beard with a long red mustache, horns on his head, and flippers on his feet swim toward me reach out his hand say: *My little granddaughter, how long I've waited for you! See what I look like now, and I used to be a human being! Let me go, I haven't got any strength left. Take what I don't need anymore. It will be a keepsake for you.* And at that moment I see him crying why did I think you couldn't see tears in the water? there they are the tears rolling down the old cheeks and I remember how many times I cried like this and say: alright, what is it you have? and he extends an empty hand to me and mumbles: *here, take it as a keepsake!* and I cover his hand with mine and feel something like a light electric shock and now I'm being borne up and I'm thinking I just hope I don't drop it and I squeeze it tighter and then I open my eyes unclench my fist and see a ring in my palm

"Your great-grandfather," I say, "was a miller. In Russian villages, millers are, to some extent, sorcerers—they associate with water creatures, know how to placate them, conquer them, even how to make servants of them. When he dies, any sorcerer must pass his power onto an heir. Naturally, the Christian Church has inculcated in us that we can't accept this power under any circumstances, whereas the ancients knew, of course, that you couldn't *not* accept such a power.

"Why? Because any gift is a sign from your fate. That's why you can't turn down gifts—especially family gifts. Turning them down means renouncing your fate, crossing yourself out of your family. And not only you—your children and grandchildren, too."

"That's all hogwash," Anya says to me. "Let's have some tea."

We're drinking tea as if nothing happened, and Anya's still expounding on whether she should try living with Andrey or not, and then, as I stand in the doorway and get ready to leave, I remember: *Where's the ring?* and Anya answers calmly:

"I have it, where else could it be? It's my ring, right?"

I see it on Anya's finger, as if it were melded to it. Anya gives me a very serious look and says:

"Grandpa gave it to me."

97.

A BRIEF BUT PASSIONATE ROMANCE

When Anton left me, it was horrible.

After all, I loved him madly. I thought he was the last love in my life. I'm forty-five, I'm no spring chicken, it's time I get used to the fact that a lot of things are happening in my life for the last time.

You know, Milka, whenever I leave a cool place, I throw a coin in the water—do you know that superstition?—so I can return there. I've done this every time. But then, I thought, enough: no matter how many coins I toss in, sooner or later, I won't return—I'll die or get too old. At some point, I'll probably stop tossing in the coins—I'll come to terms with the fact that I won't be back.

So, anyway, my entire life, I wanted to experience a mad and passionate love. Something was wrong every time, but I stubbornly asked for it again and again, as if I were tossing in a coin. And my romance with Anton was exactly one of those recurring romances. And so, at the very height of this madness, I suddenly realized this is it, it's the last time, I won't be tossing any coins in this water again. I won't have the strength for another such romance in this lifetime.

You've seen him, right? Wasn't he so handsome? Beyond words. Not just modelesque, but exactly my type—plump lips, but not too plump, strong profile, ears—did you get a good look at his ears? They're like two seashells, I swear! When he slept, I'd sit there and ogle them. If I were a guy, I would have fucked him right in his ears, that's how good they looked . . . Of course, I tried! He didn't like to be licked in general! And he's pretty conservative in bed, if you're wondering. Which is strange for a young guy. Well, he must be jaded, I've seen how girls always looked at him.

You know, it's ultimately very difficult to be involved with a guy six-teen years your junior. I was always afraid that people would stare at us on the street or at the restaurant . . . Of course, I gave him gifts. No, I didn't straight up offer him money, well, yeah, I didn't want to offend him. Alright, listen, I'm not talking about money.

All this lasted six months, and then one day, suddenly, Anton stops answering his landline, stops answering his cell phone, doesn't return my calls. At that point, I completely lost my mind, to be honest. On the sec-ond day, I race over to his apartment, ring the doorbell, he opens the door . . . you know, I can still remember him standing there half-naked, with a muscle right here . . . like a hill . . . yeah . . . anyway, he opens the door and says: "Why're you here? I'm having a party. How would I introduce you? As my mother's friend? Or a cleaning woman? A call girl for gerontophiliacs?"

He'd never brought up our age difference before, and suddenly, this! I'm, like, about to burst into tears in the middle of his doorway, and that asshole stands there, leaning against the wall, pouting his lips like, *don't cry, little baby!* Then a young woman comes out, you know, looking like she's just stepped out of *Cool Girl* magazine, a glamorous vocational student—and says: "Oh, Anton, I want a Filipina maid too!" And that bastard says: "Take her! She also knows how to fuck!"

He must have been drunk. Or coked out of his mind, who the hell knows.

I slammed the door and ran out on the street. I can't describe how I was feeling. It was as if someone had wiped their feet on me. No, it wasn't the age thing, I know that I don't look eighteen at my forty-five, but, you see, for six months, I was involved with someone who . . . no, what are you saying, what difference does it make if he only said it once, he was prob-ably thinking it the whole time, right? Well, whatever, it's all in the past.

I didn't even get in the car, I was shaking so hard. I decided that I needed a drink, it used to help me when I was younger. I went into some bar, ordered a drink—I don't remember what it was, might have been a martini or a margarita. And, pretty soon, a guy sat down next to me and we started drinking together, we even danced afterward, he groped me, and I—well, you understand—couldn't give a damn anymore, I was dead inside, it was as if my insides had been scorched by napalm.

Anyway, I have no idea what happened next, and, later on, I remem-ber going down on this guy right in his car. His car was small, cheap, and horribly uncomfortable, plus, I was feeling nauseous, I was piss drunk by then.

No, of course not! I've had years of practice, I managed. You can't drink away your artistry, as they say. Then the man says to me: "Thanks, honey! You sucked it real well!" and gives me a thousand rubles!

It's funny to me now, too. But you know what I did at the time? Punch him in the face? No. I said thank you and put the money in my handbag.

No, those kinds of men don't know anything about handbags, he didn't understand.

Anyway, I climbed out of the car completely wasted, miserable, a thousand rubles richer and my face covered in semen, pardon me, and kept on walking, because, to be honest, I didn't really know where I was. I came to a kiosk and picked up two bottles of Tuborg—it was really awkward to carry a handbag and two bottles of beer while in my fur coat. Two because I didn't want to drink alone. So I went looking, and in the end, I found him.

You know, only Anton could have crushed me so hard that I'd . . . How should I put it . . . there's a word for it: *drunk*. There are hobos, there are alcoholics, and then there are plain *drunks*. That's how he looked: an autumn jacket, obviously, no hat, half his teeth missing, shaky hands . . . and that's who I chose for my drinking buddy! I must have deliberately wanted someone on the ugly side so, God forbid, I wouldn't feel like having sex with him, I can't remember anymore.

So we drank the Tuborg and talked for about five minutes. He was spouting utter nonsense. But the way he was spouting. You could tell he was a man with a rich inner world. I believe that, in the span of five minutes, he managed to tell me I was an angel, then tell me which movie I was an angel from, then something else along those lines. To be honest, I couldn't understand shit, but it was the most pleasant conversation I'd had all day. This man was genuinely admiring me! Not so he could fuck me or humiliate me later on, or get beer or money out of me—no, he was doing it sincerely, from the bottom of his heart. I think that, if he had an ulterior motive, he would have probably expressed himself in simpler, clearer terms.

We talked and I decided it was time to go. I said "Bye!" to him, stood up, and started walking. No, I'm sorry, first, I kissed him—don't ask me why I did it, I was drunk!—and then, stood up and started walking. At first, he ran after me, then I heard him fall. So I turned around and saw him on his knees, begging me to come back! And the way he said it—I genuinely never heard anyone call to me that way. In the vein of: here I am, no one needs me, I'm unworthy of you, I'm on my knees before you and am so grateful you spoke with me . . . and, if you don't come back, I'll die.

Yes, I came back.

That's right, that's how it ended. We went up to his place—don't ask me *what state* it was in!—and I gave him some. Phew, it wasn't easy, plus, he could barely get it up.

I think that, if it weren't for Anton and the-thousand-rubles-in-ex-change-for-the-blowjob, this would have never happened. But I must have wanted to, like, completely lose respect for myself, you get it, right? And, to be honest, this guy isn't the worst thing that could have happened to me.

Why did I decide to keep the child? Well, I'm forty-five, it's like that coin toss—what if it's the last time? And I do want children—if I don't, then I won't understand why I lived, if nothing remains after me. I always believed that I must pass on what I've inherited from my ancestors, I can't take it with me into the ground.

No, I know who the father is. I tracked him down. I knew the apart-ment number, and it's not too hard to look someone up if you have their address. He's quite a character: he used to be a famous artist before he became an alcoholic. But he was pretty big in the mid-nineties. No, a contemporary artist, you know: happenings, performances, the works. In my opinion, his paintings are fairly average. I commissioned a portrait from him to learn a bit more about him. No, he didn't notice—I wore such baggy sweaters that . . . even now, my belly doesn't show that much.

No, he was sober. But, you know, it's as if he's drunk even when he's sober. I mean, he doesn't make any sense. It's like there's an aquarium inside his head with fish or all kinds of underwater reptiles swimming in it, and you're observing all this. It can be interesting to watch, it can be boring, but it's got absolutely nothing to do with you, it's always about him. Even if he's talking about you.

Why did I get in touch with him at all? For the child's sake. I believe a person should know his genealogy, genealogy is fate. I thought to myself: my boy or girl will grow up and ask: *Who was my father?* And I will say: Child, your father was a famous artist, we had a brief but passionate romance. Your father was a very talented man. In the mid-nineties, he was exhibited in the best art galleries in Moscow, but then he cut ties with the mainstream and dedicated himself to personal projects, what is known as *performance art*. He knew how to enjoy life: he loved wine and women, could talk for hours about movies—sometimes, quite obscure ones. I wouldn't call him a mystic in the full sense of the word, but he was no stranger to religious quests, mainly gnostic ones. In other words, he was a unique, extraordinary human being.

Unfortunately, real talent is often accompanied by a difficult temperament. This could be why your father and I decided to separate before we even learned about your coming into this world. I felt hurt and swore he'd never find out that he had a child . . .

In any case, you probably want to know what kind of family your father came from. Well, listen closely.

During the Khrushchev Thaw, his mother, a young Sixtier poet, had a brief but passionate romance with a physicist. Unfortunately, they decided to separate before she even knew she was pregnant. Little Sasha grew up in his mother's family: Sasha's grandmother was a renowned Leningrad philologist and his grandfather worked for a secret government agency . . .

98.

AS PLUTO, NOT ORPHEUS

Ay! And an empty bottle shatters against the asphalt. Sounds of music, a folk orchestra playing, merrymaking in Ancient Rus'.

Look at the gift you've given me today: music playing from the stand, like ten years ago. I'll drink to the memory of beers past, I'll drink to the memory of the nineties, when it was all just starting.

Troparyovo, I love your urban forests, I love the enormous, red-brick buildings standing along Vernadsky Boulevard like so many Bastilles, the green sixteen-story triplets lining the way to the metro, I love your shops, granaries, and stands, your liquid courage, your withered grass, your yellow snow.

Sonya Shpilman, the mother of my unborn child, I hope that, in your *historical homeland,* you reminisce about how we used to drink port wine and beer on the tall sewer hatch. Now, a music school stands on that spot, but they'll never hear the music that sounded for us.

You know, Sonya, everything has changed around here, I've also changed. I love this city, I won't leave it, but now I know that it doesn't matter where you live. All you have to do is drink and God will talk to you from every bush.

By now, I probably don't care that you left. I hope your beer will always be cold and your vodka tasty.

One more swig, then another. It's been a while since I drank this much.

What's bad about a short binge is you get back to normal too quickly. I'd say that's also the beauty of it.

Who says I fucked up my entire life? What does "fucked up" mean?

Does it mean it's all over and there's nothing left? Does it mean that nothing will happen to me anymore?

What does that mean, nothing left? And the drunken conversation with God, the multicolored shadows on the screen, the underwater leviathans awaiting me on the sea floor of my binge—what's that?

Before, I used to say that I didn't squander my life—I exchanged it for another one. And no one has the right to judge whether it was a good exchange.

But now I know that I didn't exchange it, I paid for it.

What does it mean to truly drink so, by age twenty-five, you look thirty and by thirty, you look forty, and not to make it to forty at all? It means that, every time, you go down underwater to a place where slimy hands cling to your flesh, a place with corpses and drowned bodies, with rotten branches, putrid stumps, forest snags, and the remains of floated timber, with all those who had gone down to the sea floor, under ice, into the dark. And they are all waiting for you, swelling in the dark water.

I thought that I had chosen gin and tonic, beer, cocktails, and vodka so as not to have to choose exhibit openings, biennales, fame, and money. I thought that, if I went down to the sea floor, I would hear underwater music unknown to the dwellers of the earth, unfamiliar to those who swim close to the surface.

I thought that you could only be free if you've lost everything.

Moscow, I wanted to be your last hobo, your last alkie who warms his frozen hands by your eternal fire. I wanted to descend into your hell as Pluto, not Orpheus, but every time, an unfathomable force pulled me out, like in that old film about the diver who almost sees mermaids, but forces himself to resurface.

What have I forgotten in this above-water world?

I thought it was my choice, and it turned out it had all been decided long before I was born. Inaudible voices called to me, invisible hands reached for me, grabbed me, pulled me—God forbid you ever see and hear what I did.

Fish fins? Burbots' whiskers? Slippery scales? No, no, quilted cotton jackets, haggard faces, shaved heads, thin arms. I can't tell if they froze or starved to death or had gone underwater while they were still alive. They reach for me, grab me, refuse to let me go, drag me down . . .

The people who my grandfather put away.

99.

1937. THE DESERTED HOUSE,
OR GOING UNDER

By now, it is light out. The Neva is piled high with dirty yellow snow.

Women stand along the quay. They are shrouded in kerchiefs, and almost every one of them wears felt boots and galoshes. They are stamping their feet and blowing on their hands. Every one of them looks as if she's waited for a train at a way station for hours on end. There are women in dressy overcoats and common women. Their faces are all greenish— perhaps they only seem that way in the morning mist?

These people stay here all night, sign in at eleven or twelve, check in every two hours, keep lists, hide in building entrances. Then, they stand in line at the little window for sometimes as long as three, four, or five hours, only to return closer to midnight, as if they were going to their jobs.

Borisov sees these people when he works the night shift. In the morning, when the streetlamps go out without a sound on Liteyny Bridge, Borisov walks home from the Great House and passes the line, the blinded red wall, walks past it as if he doesn't notice it.

Borisov knows that, in a month, any one of these women could turn up in his office. He tries not to look at their faces, lowers his eyes. But he still recognizes these women when he meets them in the streets and squares of Leningrad, recognizes them by the particular way they carry themselves, their eyes, and their posture. The same way a doctor spots someone at a dinner party or the theater and instantly makes a diagnosis, instantly recognizes one of "his" patients.

"Daddy, daddy!" yells out Polina. She is wearing a light-colored dress and has a white bow in her golden hair.

Borisov swoops his daughter into his arms, tosses her up to the ceiling and catches her:

"Ah, my golden nugget!"

Olga comes out of the bedroom, drowsy, wearing a simple housedress, her fair hair tumbling onto her shoulders.

"Hello," she says with hardly any expression.

Borisov sets his daughter down on the floor, walks up to his wife, hugs her, and kisses her on the cheek. Olga imperceptibly moves away:

"I told you a hundred times . . ."

"Yes, yes, one second, I'm sorry," and Borisov unbuttons his service jacket.

"You could have at least come in civilian clothes for my birthday," Olga says.

"If I could have, I would have," Borisov replies irritably and heads to the bathroom. "Wake me up in an hour-and-a-half, alright? I'll help you set the table."

Some hours later, Olga is receiving her birthday greetings in a pearl-gray silk dress. Her fair hair is set in a double wave and her tall, straight heels rap on the parquet. A smiling Borisov (circles under his eyes, tailor-made suit, a hint of eau de cologne) says hello to the guests. On the table— Georgian wine, iced champagne, chilled vodka. It isn't a milestone birthday, but the Borisovs like to have people over.

The guests gather slowly—they were expecting fifteen to twenty people, but only Sveta and Marina showed up with their husbands, along with a few colleagues from Pushkin House, and Lida, of course. They sit down at the table, Borisov pronounces the first toast in honor of Comrade Stalin and then, almost without pausing, dedicates one to the birthday girl; following a clinking of plates and a jingling of shot glasses, the dinner party breaks up into a few separate conversations. Borisov goes out for a smoke with Sasha, Sveta's husband.

They discuss the premiere of the opera *Battleship Potemkin* at the Kirov Theater and the films *Baltic Deputy* and *The Return of Maksim*; then, Borisov asks Sasha how things are going at the Institute. Borisov doesn't know himself why he asked: Sasha is either a physicist or a mathematician, and Borisov has only a vague notion of what he does.

"At the Institute?" Sasha repeats his question. "Ah yes, the Institute . . . I was just about to ask, perhaps you could point me in the right direction, Grisha. I have a colleague at the department, his name is Alik, a very talented mathematician, really, very talented. Anyway, there must have been a mistake because he was arrested last week. Of course, I understand that they'll sort it out and let him go because Alik is a wonderful young man, a Komsomol member who takes absolutely no interest in politics, but I wanted to ask: is it possible to speed things up somehow? So they'd let him go sooner?"

Tapping his fingers on the cigarette case, Borisov takes out a cigarette and lights it. He knows the *right* answer very well: *don't worry, if he's not guilty, they'll let him go soon,* but Sasha is Olga's friend's husband . . . so Borisov says, carefully choosing his words:

"You see, Sasha, this is a very difficult time for our country. You read the papers. I'll tell you that not everything makes it into the papers. In fact, the intrigues of the enemies of the people are far more nefarious. They've even managed to penetrate government agencies, can you imagine? That's why you can't vouch for or petition on anybody's behalf today. Just imagine, Trotskyite spies have drawn your friend into their network by means of deceit—and somebody comes to petition on his behalf. Already, that seems suspicious. After all, the Soviet people know that, if somebody's innocent, they'll be let go soon. So why did you go, or worse, send somebody else? That means you're not so certain of your friend's innocence, there is no smoke without fire, and it will call more attention to your friend and you along with him. Of course, if your Alik is not guilty, they will let him go, but . . . You get it?"

I think I've said everything right, Borisov thinks. If he's not an idiot, he'll understand and, if he is a subversive, he won't be able to scheme his way out. But, just to be on the safe side, he adds:

"We shouldn't interfere with the authorities' work."

Sasha smokes without looking at Borisov.

"That's too bad," he says after a pause, "I thought you'd help. Well, it doesn't matter, the guys and I are planning to write to the Academy of Sciences, maybe they have some leverage."

It's impossible to save them, Borisov thinks, no one will help them. They have faith in the Soviet government and they will all die. I just hope I won't be assigned his case.

Borisov knew that, sometimes, the arrested were assigned to investigators who had known them in their old life. At the NKVD, they loved to tell stories about how, when a detainee saw an acquaintance at an interrogation, he would rush over to him and say: "Kolya, I'm so glad it's you!" and, instead of replying, Kolya would spit in his old acquaintance's face or punch him in the gut: *I'm not Kolya, you Fascist rat!* Borisov suspected that such meetings were deliberately arranged to test the operatives.

On the other hand, it would even be safer if he were personally in charge of Sasha's friend's case: what if this idiot puts someone on Borisov's tail and that person decides to bolster the body of conspirators with a colleague from the NKVD?

How should I tell him that he mustn't mention me at the interrogation, Borisov thinks, regretting that he started this conversation in the first place, that Olga invited guests, and that there are people inside his home besides his wife and daughter.

Later that evening, Olga stands at the mirror braiding her hair for the night. Borisov stands by the dark window in only his underwear.

"I think it went well," he says.

Olga is silent, then coldly replies:

"I think it went abominably."

"What's wrong?" Borisov asks, shrinking inside.

"Enough," Olga says, and, suddenly, she erupts and begins to spout words, barely catching her breath, bending her long, beautiful fingers, dropping her hairpins, knocking down jars of her feminine products from the dressing table: "almost nobody came, Sveta and Sasha left looking completely distraught, the conversation dragged, and it's all your fault, my girlfriends are afraid of you, everyone I know is afraid, especially after Oksman's arrest, and what's more, all my girlfriends have husbands, and those husbands don't work at the NKVD and could thus be taken away at any moment, while you walk around looking all smug in a good suit, that's what they say to me, that I'm lucky because my husband can't be arrested like theirs."

Borisov stands there looking pale; it's unnerving for him to have a conversation with hardly any clothes on, he stands there like an idiot, wondering if he should put on his uniform trousers or go get his house pants from the back closet. He doesn't want to reply to Olya—in essence, he has nothing to say to her, and she says that, while everyone around them is in deep trouble, she is ashamed, yes, ashamed, that her family isn't under threat and, at that moment, Borisov can't help but hiss in a stranger's voice:

"What do you mean, not under threat? Do you understand what you just said? Where are all your school friends? In exile! In the camps! Who knows where! They emptied Leningrad of its *former* residents two years ago, and if it wasn't for me, you would have been arrested in '28!"

"Don't yell at me!" Olga yells in reply, "I remember everything, I didn't mean myself, I meant you!"

This would be a good time to hold his tongue, but Borisov hisses softly:

"You idiot! You think that no one in the NKVD can get arrested? Do you know how many people were politically repressed along with Yagoda? I could be arrested tonight, like your Sveta's husband!"

Borisov waits for Olya to say something scathing, but she suddenly slumps down in the chair and utters dejectedly:

"So that means it was all in vain? And we can't be certain of anything either? I was thinking that we at least had it okay," and that voice takes the wind out of Borisov, he stands in silence and the words boil up, collide in his chest: *No one can be certain of anything. Only the dead can smile, exulting in their peace. You hear so much about arrests not because I'm your husband, but because Leningrad is an appendage to its prisons, and thousands, legions of bewildered people make the same journey, the locomotive's whistles sing a farewell song in their honor, the bloody stars shine over them year after year while Russia writhes in agony—but I wasn't the one who started this, I wasn't the one who chose this. I chose you and Polya.* At that moment, Olga would burst into tears, throw her arms around Borisov and say, *I'm sorry, I understand how hard it is for you*; but Borisov says nothing, remains gloomily silent, and Olga starts to braid her hair again while he watches her long fingers, then, comes up to her, rests his head on her shoulder and awkwardly kisses her somewhere on the neck. She idly caresses his clean-shaven cheek, looks in the mirror, and says:

"I want a divorce. I can't do this anymore."

Afterward, as they lie embracing and catching their breath, Borisov passes his palm over Olya's cheek and wants to ask: "Were you crying?" but instead, kisses her swollen lips, convincing himself that it's all blown over, that they've reconciled, that Olya won't leave, it's just that everyone's on edge and saying stupid things, after all, they can't split up, they're a family—Olya, Polina, and he, Grisha. Borisov caresses his wife's slightly damp hip, whispers: "I was very happy with you just now, thank you," and she replies: "No, thank you," and they know this is a ritual, that, each time, it's anybody's guess if it was in fact good.

"Do you remember," Borisov says, "your dress with the ruffles? And the parasol? The summer we met?"

"Yes," Olga replies sadly, "it was an altered dress of my mom's, old, from before the revolution. Beautiful. No seamstress could make one like it now."

"We can try," Borisov replies and kisses Olga on the shoulder.

"We shouldn't," Olya says. "You see, we were together just now and I thought: what do little girls dream of? Of being princesses—beautiful dresses, a palace, balls, and, later, a prince, a future husband, children— say, a boy and a girl, and they don't think beyond that. And when I was a little girl, I dreamed of just that, and somehow it all came true, but, you know, it's like, instead of the old dress with the ruffles, I had some- thing sewn for a ludicrous price by a seamstress patronized by the wives of your NKVD colleagues. Understand that I love you and Polya," and Olya patted Borisov, "but there's something wrong with our family. Too many lies. It's like that dress: it seems like something I've always dreamed of, but is absurdly expensive and of poor quality. Sometimes I think it would be better if I were like Sveta or Marina, or had gone *over there* with everyone a long time ago. It would be more honest."

"Don't say that," Borisov replies, "we'll think of something. Maybe we'll leave this place, you know I don't like Leningrad."

"Where will we go?" Olya says, "I'm a philologist. What will I do for work? Teach literature in a village school?"

A minute ago, you were ready to go to Siberia, Borisov thinks, and runs his fingers through Olya's fair hair. Then they kiss again for a bit and talk again for a bit, and, just before the sun rises, Olya cries and Borisov consoles her—whereupon the streetlamps go out on Liteyny Bridge, the bundled up women standing in the main and service entrances look over lists while Borisov's colleagues beat their fathers, sons, and husbands, while the Black Marias return with their nighttime haul, and, back in their apartments, military men, party members, scientists, and writers finally fall asleep, pacified that the danger has bypassed them today, that no one came for them.

Olya and Borisov are sleeping with their arms around each other and he dreams of a granite quay over heavy black water—water and silence. He can see the silence, which curls up like smoke. Curls of silence—and some strangers prodding Olya toward the water with sticks as she holds little Polina in her arms. Also in silence. Closer and closer to the edge—and, at that moment, Olya's foot slips, she swings her arms, a scream is heard, and the dark water closes in over their daughter's head.

We should probably leave Leningrad after all, it's getting too dangerous here, Borisov thinks. When Yezhov follows in Yagoda's footsteps, we shouldn't be anywhere near this city. We should go somewhere in the republics, work on a construction project, and get a travel voucher from the party rather than go through a government channel. We'll live quietly and happily, Borisov thinks, but isn't too certain of that. Olya really does want a divorce. Yes, he can try to convince her, can stall for time, take her to Ukraine or someplace else—but each time they made love this year, he thought it was for the last time.

Perhaps he shouldn't have left the Criminal Investigation Service for the Cheka in '28? He got too frightened when he realized that the Cheka serviceman was collecting documents on Olya. He decided he would have more peace of mind if he himself worked at the Cheka. In the end, he swore to defend his family—but not a single other person. He didn't owe anything to the people brought to the inte. More and more often, these turned out to be people who, twenty years ago, deprived him of his childhood, set him adrift across the country with his father and mother, and then deprived him of his parents, too. When I joined the authorities, Borisov thinks, all the Soviet government's real enemies had already been eradicated. And I don't pity those who've served this government. Party members, Komsomol members, fellow travelers, experts, Mensheviks, and Socialist Revolutionaries—they *deserved* it.

Not an innocent soul among them, none! Everything they were accused of was true—these people genuinely were traitors. They betrayed the country where little Grisha lived, a country that hadn't existed for twenty years already.

It was so easy to hate them. He just had to remind himself that it was people like them who shot his parents dead somewhere in Ukraine.

And I'm no better, Borisov thinks, I, too, deserve the arrest, the interrogation, the transporter, the lamp in my face, five nights without sleep. Yes, I deserve it, but it's like being at war: you're killing those who haven't done anything to you and they're trying to kill you. All is fair. Above all, you mustn't think about the fact that, when you kill, you don't only kill one person, your enemy. You kill his unborn children, you kill all that could have happened in his life, including the future, in which you've already ceased being enemies. And you also destroy the lives of his wife and children.

Brisov had explained this to him seventeen years ago. But it was easy for Brisov—he died at war.

If I always thought about other people's unborn children and wives, I would have lost my mind a long time ago.

It'd be good if war broke out again—then, the enemies would have weapons too. Perhaps then I could die an honorable death—one that befits a man who comes from a long line of military officers.

I simply wanted to defend my family, wanted my wife to have a beautiful dress, my daughter to have a white bow on her head, a life of plenty, a happy childhood for my child, like I once had. And if Olga leaves, it's just as well. Sometimes you lose even those things you were able defend.

Too bad the late Brisov didn't warn me about that part seventeen years ago.

There he goes, Grigoriy Borisov, a clean-shaven, tall man in boots and a service jacket—my grandfather. I hardly know anything about him—not even his real last name. He walks down the quay past the famous line, the ships sail down the Neva, the prison dove coos from a distance, he walks without raising his eyes or committing the faces to memory. He walks and he doesn't yet know that they will, in fact, relocate to Ukraine, he'll manage some kind of construction project—a regular job, no interrogations, no arrests, no night shifts. But Grandma Olga will leave him anyway.

In the deserted house, Grandpa will repeat to himself: *I'll manage somehow, I'll forget everything, I'll learn how to live alone,* yet, every morning, he'll dial Olya's number to check if she's still there. If his former colleagues have dropped in on her yet.

And afterward? Afterward, it will be the summer of forty-one, Grandma will be visiting Aunt Lida, the blockade, hunger, Polina's death. And for him—the front, Ukraine, Warsaw, Berlin.

He's got no family left—his wife left him and his daughter died. In forty-five, Grandpa could have crossed over to the Allies, remembered his real last name, found his relatives—but he came back, though he didn't have anyone to defend anymore. He came back and still found Grandma, and they began to live together again after all.

Why? Perhaps because they still loved each other. Perhaps because Grandpa's love was so great, it was enough for both of them.

Or maybe, a little dead girl came to them like a phantom in a Japanese film, took their hands, and placed one palm on top of the other as a last, posthumous request.

In 1950, my mom, Lyolya, was born, and, in 1975, I was.

And afterward? Afterward, there was a quiet dacha community, BBC on the radio, the wailing of jammed radio stations, prison camp memoirs, and, suddenly: *My case was conducted by NKVD investigator Grigoriy Borisov*—and the details that Grandpa had almost forgotten.

He just wasn't able to say about himself: *Enemies—none. Alive.*

When you reach the end of your life, it's silly to try to explain that these people were Bolsheviks, that there wasn't an innocent soul among them. It's silly to say: I was simply defending my family. It's silly to try to justify yourself: I left the agencies later on, didn't I? Who would you explain it to, who would you justify yourself to?

A long time ago, when he was young and knew nothing of life, he dreamed of dying with a weapon in hand.

Only it had come true.

He wished to defend his family and his wife left him, his older daughter died, his younger daughter was thrown out by her lover, a boy who knew nothing of life. As he threw her out, he said in farewell: *I can't get involved with the daughter of a killer.*

It's likely that this boy's father never killed anyone.

It's likely that his father spent the entire war at a headquarters or the home front.

It's likely that, when he uttered *daughter of a killer*, the boy felt that he was committing an act of civic heroism.

And that's how my father disowned me. He disowned me in advance, before I was even born, without even taking a look at me.

It's not for nothing that I always hated these liberal bastards.

On the upside, I don't risk forgetting my father's face—I never knew it. Instead, I'l try not to forget the face of Grandpa Grisha, Grigoriy Borisov—the gunslinger, murderer, butcher, my grandfather.

100.

FROM UNDERNEATH THE DARK WATER

I can picture it: they're sitting and drinking, not like me—from the bottle, on the street—no, like intellectuals, with *zakuski*, from shot glasses, while having a conversation. My father and my half-brother. And my father says to Nikita: *I've been wanting to play you this one song for a while, I don't know why, it touched me somehow, though I don't especially like rock*—and he reaches his hand for a CD or even a cassette, while Nikita thinks: gosh, what a nice get-together, good thing I came. We'll listen to a song right now, and it will be beyond silly for me to ask: Dad, why did you leave that Yelena or whatever her name was, Lyolya, and stay with us? Like, he chose his family for his son's sake, and his son is asking about it.

I don't have any children, Nikita thinks, how would I choose?

Because, by now, he knows for sure that he'll have to choose, he can't go on like this, time has run out.

"There, listen," Vasiliy Mikhailovich pushes the button, and Nikita immediately recognizes the song: *how a solitary bargeman goes up and down the Volga*, it's Grebenschikov, wow! It's been years since he heard it.

He wants to say: *Dad, I know this song*, but he sees his father listening closely and seriously, and Nikita also listens and thinks of Dasha, with whom he's so dumbly in love, and Masha, who's curled up alone in her armchair, and he doesn't have any strength left, his arms fall to his sides, what can he do, if *I don't care, I am almost ready, ready to sing to you from underneath the dark water.*

And the bells are ringing from underneath the dark water,
Underneath the ancient wall, there's a dazzling yellowbird.

Absolve me of my sins with the first flap of your wings;
Absolve me of my sins—why aren't you saying anything?!

Absolve me, says Nikita, not knowing whom he's talking to, absolve me—
and all will be easy. And if I want children, Dasha will give me children.
It would be unfair if everything were interrupted, everything that I've
received from my grandfathers and great-grandfathers, the blood line,
the lifeline, came to a halt merely because the young woman I met in
Crimea eight years ago turned out to be infertile, right?

So Nikita sits there nodding in time to Grebenschikov, the song comes
to an end, and Vasiliy Mikhailovich says thoughtfully:

"And wherever I go, I keep knocking on doors, so dear God,
have mercy on me . . . It's a good song. Also, they said on TV that
Grebenschikov is a Buddhist."

"It's an old album," Nikita says. "I think he was Eastern Orthodox
at the time."

"I often think," Vasiliy Mikhailovich continues, "about my father,
your grandfather. The two of us never talked about God together, but he
came from a good family, a professor's family, he must have been baptized
and gone to church in his childhood. You know that his dad deliberately
sent him to the plant and then the workers' school so he'd have a worker-peasant's background. And Melnikov was my mother's last name—she
came from a village, while Grandpa Mikhail was a nobleman and registered under her last name. Well, you know what sort of a time it was."

They drink a bit, then, a bit more, and that's when Vasiliy Mikhailovich
says:

"You know, son, I've been wanting to talk to you for a while, just not
in front of Mom. I know that you still haven't forgiven me for that whole
story with Lyolya. Sasha blabbed it to you, I know. What can I say? It can
happen to any man, and it only happened once. I mean, only with one
woman. It was that sort of time—there was a sexual revolution going on
in the West and we, too, had . . . freedom. As for Lyolya, she was perfectly wonderful, so young, naive, wrote poetry. When I saw her at the
funeral, I didn't even recognize her. And I didn't just want to bang, as
your generation says, no, I really did love her. I didn't love her the way
that I love Mom, but I loved her. I loved her, but I stayed with Sveta.
And it wasn't even because of you."

"Because Lyolya's father was a former KGB man," Nikita says.

How does Nikita know this? Let's say Uncle Sasha told him. Or, a month ago, he went to see my mother and she told him for some reason. Or maybe it was Dasha with her magical instinct . . . no, not very likely . . . What does it matter how Nikita knows! Suppose that I called him up and said: *Hey, listen, it's your brother, Sasha. I have a request for you: can you go see our father and ask him a question?* And he says to me: *Hey man, how great that you called. I was just thinking of you the other day. Maybe we can meet up sometime and, I don't know, get coffee.* Of course, he wants to say *beer*, but at the last moment, he remembers: oh yeah, my brother is an alcoholic! But anyway, we supposedly decide to meet up, and Nikita goes off to our father, asks, and our father replies:

"I'm ashamed of it to this day. I did it because of Sveta. Of course, I should have told the truth. I suddenly realized that, no matter how much I loved Lyolya, I always knew I would be with Sveta for the rest of my life, I don't even know why I'd decided this. And I never cheated on your mother again. Never. Not on work trips, never. So you have to understand, it can happen to anyone, once." And he sighs, looks at Nikita and asks: "Why aren't you saying anything, son? Say something to me."

And it sounds like an echo of the song: *absolve me of my sins, why aren't you saying anything?* To which Nikita replies:

"I understand, Dad. Everything's fine, don't worry."

"After Sasha died, I gave Lyolya a call. She told me that, for half his life, our son was convinced that it was Sasha who was his father, not me. At first I was hurt, but then I thought: what did I expect? The only time I saw him was at the funeral this winter. What kind of a father am I to him, in the end? Do you think I should call him? Or is it too late already?"

"I don't know," Nikita replies.

For some reason, I imagine how, in the late seventies, my grandfathers met by chance at Uncle Sasha's place: Mikhail Konstantinovich Melnikov and Grigoriy Borisov, whose real last names I never did learn. They drank some vodka and Grandpa Grigoriy said: "The younger generation hasn't got a clue what kind of a time it was. And I had a family, tried to protect it, save it."

And Grandpa Misha said: "Yes, I understand, I spent my entire life on the run. Family's a very special thing . . . I took my wife's last name to hide my nobility ."

And Grandpa Grigoriy replied: "I had a similar story with my last name . . ."

And they recalled their fathers' last names and found out that their fathers knew each other, used to meet in, say, poetry or high-society salons, courted young women, and drank champagne; and now their children are drinking vodka together, and the longstanding fear, the lifelong fear, reconciles and reunites them. Such was the time they were fated to live in, each of them made his own choice—and they both chose family over honor, they both did everything so I could come into this world.

Like hell this would happen, Moreukhov thinks. Ha! You wanted a happy ending, a general reconciliation, a cohesive family history. As if it doesn't matter who put people away and who was on the run—as if they were all in on it together. Like hell they were! Drink some more beer and stop fucking around, don't you dare absolve others of their sins, you don't have the right! Only the dead have the right to forgive, you don't have the right to speak for them, speak for yourself, tell yourself: it's not my job to forgive, it's not my job to judge. I had two grandfathers and would have wanted them to hug it out and forget everything that separated them before they died. I don't actually know if it happened, and the picture I painted is quite implausible—my two grandfathers sitting and drinking—almost as implausible as if I called Nikita and he said: *Hey man, it's great you called. I was just thinking about you the other day,* and we'd meet up and have coffee because Nikita would be scared to treat me to a beer.

101.

EXACTLY MY CASE

So I'm standing in the kitchen, making an omelet, trying to figure out what she said to me. Good thing it's not hard to make an omelet, nothing to it, a conventional dish.

This is why I love omelets. I'm also a conventional person. A most ordinary man. Average, as they say.

I remember how, during perestroika, all the papers said that the Brezhnev era was the triumph of the average man, the mousy person. That must have been be the case—and what's the time period people wax nostalgic about? Stalin? Perestroika? No, Brezhnev and his average people.

Because average is reliable, simple, and without any quirks. Not a straight-A student and not a slacker.

I've always been like that.

School, university, a job, then another job, I tried one thing, then another thing, and then it turned out I'm a middle manager.

The pop group Leningrad has a song about that too.

I like it.

I like the song, I like the job, and the *middle* part.

Because below me are the losers and above me—the careerists. And I'm in between.

Of course, movies are made and books are written about heroes and losers because the plot has to be interesting. Like, what'll happen next? Whereas, in my life, what happens next is more or less the same thing as what happened at first. If you make a film about my life, it'll have no plot whatsoever. It'll be an art house film.

Men's magazines write about average people. At first glance, the articles seem to be about celebrities and various socialites, but, actually, the hero of *Men's Health* or *Maxim* is a guy like me. He's told how to exercise, how to tie his tie, how to pick up a woman, and how to pretend he knows a thing or two about wine. Who'll teach you that? A manager just like me. For example, would Johnny Depp give me advice on how to pick up a girl at a club quickly? All he has to do is walk up and say: *Hey! I'm Johnny Depp!* Yeah, great advice.

Again—who do people compare lives with? With the lives of their acquaintances, people just like them. Or whatever they see in the magazines. Because magazines are our number one acquaintances.

Yesterday, I cleaned my entire apartment. Why? I tried to make it look like in the magazines. Because that is exactly what a nice apartment should look like. "Nice" as determined by a magazine.

I cleaned the kitchen too. Now I'm standing in the middle of the clean kitchen, beating eggs in a bowl for an omelet, waiting for the frying pan to heat up. Because you have to pour an omelet over a heated pan, I know that.

Yesterday, I vacuumed the room and thought: Anya will come over and see how stylish, clean, and tastefully decorated my place is, and she'll like it. Because when a woman comes over for the first time, your apartment has to be shipshape. I can't remember if I read this somewhere or thought of it myself.

And, in general, almost everything I know about women, I've learned from magazines. I can't ask the guys, I never had a father, my mother raised me on her own. In other words, if I didn't know how to read, I would have stayed a virgin.

Anya is my girlfriend. We've dated for almost a year. To tell you the truth, it all started just for kicks—I went into a shoe store, the salesgirl looked cute, I said something to her, and she didn't send me packing, she played along. So I carried on in the same spirit.

This had never worked for me before—I happen to be shy—but, suddenly, it worked. Not a week went by before I was unhooking her bra.

Her breasts turned out to be small, but sensitive.

To be honest, I was pretty proud of myself—are you kidding? I picked up a girl at a store. Practically on the street!

At the time, I had my sights set on Natashka in the next department over, I was trying to impress her almost every night—except on weekends. Because, on weekends, Natashka would go to her parents' dacha. And my shopgirl would drop her child off at her mother's and would be free. I thought to myself: what a great situation! I always had someone to fuck on a Friday night! And by Monday, I'd go after Natashka with renewed zeal.

And when, by all appearances, Natashka was ready, we got swamped with work, and for a month I had no time for romance. When I recovered, I saw that I had missed my chance. While I was keeping my nose to the grindstone, that bastard Valerka hopped to it. In the beginning, they were cooing like doves, it was disgusting to watch.

I didn't even want to call Anya the shopgirl: we fucked for a bit and that's that. And anyway, picking up a shopgirl is nice, but dating a shopgirl is the pits. That's why, that Friday, I went to the club instead.

I came home at 3 A.M., drunk, lonely, and with a hard-on.

If I were Johnny Depp, the night would have gone differently. But things being what they were, the following Thursday, I called Anya and asked her to the movies. Anya didn't make a fuss and said: *Let's do it.*

And that's how we spent the whole winter: movies, café, bed. For some reason, we always spent the night at her place—the first time it just worked out that way, I was ostensibly walking a young woman home and then everything went like clockwork. I didn't complain—my place is usually a total mess.

What's more, I liked it at her place. It reminded me of my childhood, of the way my mother and I lived. A poor, but clean apartment. Tiny, just big enough for a mother and son. Exactly my case.

The magazines don't tell you what to do if your girlfriend already has a kid. In the scenarios, the young women are always childless. But it makes a big difference if she has a child.

A single woman doesn't know what to do with herself and waits to be entertained. Whereas my Anya was always busy: shopping, laundry, cleaning. Again, everything cost double for the two of them, so she had to make ends meet. In short, she had a lot to do and no use for my entertainment.

I didn't get that right away—maybe not until spring. But, as soon as I got it, things took a turn for the better. Rather than taking her to the movies, I took Anya to Auchan supermarket, helped her carry grocery bags. It had been a long time since I carried grocery bags—probably not since I was a boy. As I carried them from the car to the building entrance, I even remembered: winter, snow, me and Mom walking home along the snowbanks from the supermarket, cold, heavy bags, aching arms . . .

So every Saturday, I sit in Anya's kitchen; we fuck once a week and, every now and then, we go to the store, sometimes other places; but, in the back of my mind, I'm always thinking this is only temporary, before I find myself a girlfriend I can take to the club and have a good time with, or whatever. Don't think I'd be ashamed to go to a club with Anya—she's a beautiful girl with Tatar-Russian roots, comes from a mixed marriage—everyone knows that the most beautiful women are mixed. That's not why. I just don't get why we would go to a club. I don't like to dance and she doesn't seem to either. We don't have the same group of friends. Why waste time— it's better if we go home right away.

Because I really like it at Anya's place. It's cozy and everything's familiar there.

And suddenly, in the spring, I met this one woman, the type they idolize in the magazines. Blonde, big tits, long legs—basically, a model. She was sent to our office from St. Petersburg or wherever. Like, on a business trip.

I hit on her right away. We had lunch together, then we went to a café in the evening, then some club the guys recommended, and, finally, we took a cab to a hotel. We made out the whole way, but then she waved good-bye and ran upstairs. What the hell, I thought. And the guys tell me: all the girls are watching *Sex in the City* now, where they say you can't sleep with someone before the third date. So, onward, my man—two more nights and she's yours.

That's how it went. She arrived at the office on Tuesday and, by Thursday, we were already messing around in her hotel room.

I believe that a real man shouldn't reveal what a young woman does in bed. When guys say *she gave it to me this way and that, in this place and that place*, it makes me sick. In short, without giving too much away, we had a good fuck. And more than once. Then she says something along the lines of: "Darling, I'm sorry, I want to sleep, everything was wonderful, we'll see each other tomorrow, I've already called a cab." And I even thought: awesome! I was just trying to think of a polite excuse to bail.

So I'm heading home in a cab and, suddenly, a melancholy comes over me. And it's not even that it sucked—everything was first-rate, I swear—it just comes over me for no reason. I'm sitting and watching the lights flash out the window, and I almost begin to cry. I don't know why—it's just that I felt so melancholic and sorry, as if I'd done something wrong.

So on Friday, I walked my blonde home and, the next day, I went over to Anya's. And, as soon as I walked into her apartment, I felt a sense of relief. It was like I was back home.

As I'm telling you this, I've poured everything into the frying pan, now I just need to scoop it up carefully with a fork and pull it toward the middle so the omelet is, you know . . . multi-layered. You can also turn it over and fry it on both sides, but not everyone likes that.

Anyway, the things they write about in magazines really are helpful. But unfortunately, they don't write about everything. There's the eternal scenario where the guy wants to fuck a girl, but she wants a relationship from him. But sometimes the reverse happens, right?

In short, we had a real romance that spring. Like, we called each other every night, held hands, and all the rest. I'm not going to talk about the sex—the springtime must have had an effect on Anya, too. We won't go into detail here—I warned you.

To be honest, it never made a difference to me whether my girlfriend was a shopgirl or, say, a manager. My buddies couldn't care less who I sleep with—and I'm choosing a girlfriend for myself, not for my buddies, right?

Then, Anya and I decided to go on vacation together. I chose an "all-inclusive" resort in Turkey, five stars, totally sick. I suggested we go together. At first, she was happy, but a few weeks later, she said: I can't make it work, I have no one to leave Gosha with.

Gosha is her son. An awful brat, I've only met him once, we all went to a café together. I almost died from the kind of stunts he pulled. I remember thinking: what if people thought this was my kid? In short, Gosha and I didn't get along very well.

So when Anya said she had no one to leave Gosha with, I suddenly remembered that my mom also never took a vacation by herself. She was always staying at girlfriends' dachas. Honestly, who'd wants to go to the seaside with their kid—everyone's dancing and kissing and all you can do is watch your son so that he doesn't drown by accident. I thought about this and began to feel so sorry for my mom that I almost cried. I love my mom very much. Although we rarely see each other.

Anyway, I called Anya and said: what the hell, the three of us should go together.

It's only a shame that I couldn't, of course, afford the all-inclusive, five-star resort for the three of us. But we still had a great vacation. Every time I looked at Gosha, I thought how happy I would've been if someone took me to the seaside when I was a boy. That's why I felt that everything that I was doing with Gosha, whether it was playing, swimming, or whatever else, I was doing for my younger self.

So you can say that Anya and I went on vacation by ourselves, but there were two versions of me there, a little one and a big one.

There. And now I have to put the omelet on a plate and slice a fresh tomato as garnish. It'll look nice, let me do it now, I'm almost done with the story, I can squeeze it in.

One time, the bosses sent me to a special seminar for salespeople—obviously, in error, because I wasn't planning on selling anything. Anyway, at the seminar, they told us that the best way to manipulate a client is to distort his field of selection. Say, offer two options, pretending that the other three didn't exist. I think this is called *cheating someone out of their money* and seems rather despicable. I'm mentioning this because I realized why men's magazines say nothing about married men.

It's a similar con. It's supposed to make the reader think he's only choosing between one woman and another, and not at all between a woman and a wife. Because if the reader gets married, he won't be reading these magazines anymore, and will instead subscribe to *Happy Parents* or an automobile publication.

That's why men's magazines don't say anything about how to propose to your girlfriend and why I had to improvise.

I think it turned out awesome! Obviously, Anya said she'll think about it—I would have been amazed if she started yelling: *Yes, darling, I dreamed about this for so long!*

We got back to Moscow and fell back into our routine, as if I'd never said anything. So I thought I'd give her a nudge, invite her over. Anyway, yesterday, I cleaned up my lair and, later on, we tumbled in here.

I think she liked it here. In the evening, she played on the computer, we drank tea, fucked, and then fell asleep.

At night, everything went beautifully as well. Maybe even better than usual. Although the usual is also very good.

In the morning, I wake up and see Anya sitting there with her eyes red, as if she's been crying. I ask: what's wrong, Anya? Is something wrong? And she answers:

"No, everything is perfect. It's just that, when we were having sex, I suddenly saw Grandpa and Grandma. When they were young. It was as if they were also . . . making love . . . in some dorm, on a cot, a long time ago. And last night, I even dreamed of them."

I ask her: *So why are you crying?* And she says to me:

"I suddenly realized that they loved each other their whole lives."

And she sniffled poignantly, like a child. Then I took her hand and said:

"Listen, I know everything about myself: I'm the most average guy, a run-of-the-mill, conventional person. My entire life, I was taught how to build a career and make money, then I was taught how to spend that money, how to meet women, how to dress, how to go on vacation. I was taught all kinds of crap, but nobody taught me how to love. Not my mom, not my grandma, or grandpa. They don't write about it in magazines, don't talk about it on the radio. I understand that I'm probably not very good at this. But my love is my own. It doesn't come from the magazines, it doesn't come from books, it wasn't taught to me by family or school. And I don't have anything else that's unique to offer—just this love. You are extraordinary and wonderful, you are beautiful and strong, your entire life, you've done all the things that I'm afraid to even think about. I know that you deserve better, but see, I don't have anything besides this love of mine, besides the most banal phrases like 'I'm only happy when I'm with you,' or 'I don't know what I'd do without you,' but these are just phrases, just words, and I don't know what we'd have to do so we can love each other our whole lives, but let's try, at least, maybe we'll end up like your grandma and grandpa, or end up different, because it'll be our love and no one else's . . ."

And I'm saying all this to Anya, getting choked up, almost crying, not really understanding what's come over me, and she looks at me in shock, as if she's seeing me for the first time, then gives me a long kiss and says, catching her breath: *I'm starving. Can you make breakfast?*

So now I'm standing in the kitchen, making an omelet, trying to figure out what Anya's answer was. Was it a *no* or was it a *yes*?

102.

1935. THE FATE OF A METRO BUILDER

There once lived a man in the Metro builders' dormitory, in a vast, far-away city unrivalled by any other in the world.

Day and night, red stars twinkled over the city's towers.

And, of course, this city was called Moscow.

Moscow is a beautiful city.

The man was building a Metro in Moscow, an underground railway. His wife also worked on the Metro construction project, in the women's Komsomol brigade.

The man's name was Mikhail and his wife's name was Marfa. She was a cheerful, beautiful young woman. Six months ago, she had come to the sixth division with the other Komsomol girls to work as a concrete-layer and there was nothing there yet: a vacant lot! It was dark and dirty, with rocks and puddles. The division superintendent—a kind and simple man—came by and said:

"First, we'll need to build a shaft, and then we can go down in it. For now, whip up a pantry, girls!"

Marfa tightened the kerchief around her head and, together with her girlfriends, built a pantry, then a cafeteria, a mechanical workshop, and a changing room. They were especially eager to build a changing room because there was no place for them to change and they had to go home in their boilersuits. On the tram, people would laugh at them and call them "fluffies."

"No worries," said Marfa, "we'll build the Metro and everyone will forget the tram! Plenty more room underground!"

Marfa worked a lot and her workload didn't diminish.

Mikhail also worked a lot: he was building alternative bridges for trams. First, their work revolved around a cut-and-cover tunnel, then, they worked within the circumference of Arbat Street and didn't go back to the dormitory for days. He and Marfa saw each other only a few times a week: either she would have a night shift or he would. Now and then, their days off would overlap, and then they'd go strolling around Moscow, go to the Central Park of Culture and Leisure in the summer and the Dinamo skating rink in the winter.

Schoolchildren from all around Moscow, laborers, and white-collar workers who weren't occupied by production activities at that hour skated to waltz music on the great oval field that had been made into an ice rink. Mikhail and Marfa spun around with everyone else, enjoying the fresh air.

By the skate rental window, a tall, upright man called Mikhail by name. Black service shirt, breeches, boots, and a few gray streaks on his temples like a spiderweb.

"Mitya!" Mikhail exclaimed and they embraced. "Well, brother, what are you doing and where? Wait, you haven't even met my wife. Dmitry, meet Marfa, Marfa, meet Dmitry, we were together at the workers' school, I told you about him."

Marfa smiled and extended a firm hand to Dmitry.

The three of them sat together in their little dormitory room, Marfa brought the tea-kettle and sliced the bread, and Dmitry poured vodka in the glasses. They toasted to their meeting, and Dmitry asked:

"Well, brother, tell me, where did you find this beauty of a wife?"

"At the construction site, where else," Mikhail burst out laughing. "Two years ago, they were building the hotel *Moskva*, that's where we met. We got married right away, I even took her last name, so now I'm a Melnikov. And how have you been? Tell us where you live, where you work."

"Oh, brother, don't ask me. I'm currently the director of a textile shop. Sales is a grisly business. Tell me about yourself instead. What's it like underground?"

Mikhail laughed:

"It's a prodigious mess. No one knows which cable goes where. Pipes, water drains—no blueprints, no drafts, nothing. We requested them from the archives, looked for them ourselves, but it's no use. Now, before we can drive piles into the ground, we have to dig wells to figure out what's down there. Or else we'll rupture a cable and two thousand Moscow residents will be left without a telephone. My father once told me that

Ivan the Terrible's library was hidden underground. I'll tell you one thing, if Ivan the Terrible's people worked the way they're working at the city council, Ivan himself wouldn't have found his library."

Dmitry wiped his sweaty, shaven head with his handkerchief, and Marfa noticed a narrow scar running across his round skull.

"What's that?" she asked.

"Wrangel," Dmitry said matter-of-factly. "When they chased us out of Crimea, they marked me, I barely escaped. It was a good time nonetheless, a simple time: we were here, they were there, draw your saber and—charge! I always felt sorry for you, Misha, you were young and didn't get a chance to fight. Ah, I hope a new war will break out soon—then I'll leave this shop and go to the front. See for yourself: what kind of merchant would I make?"

"And how did you end up at the shop?" Mikhail asked.

"The same way you ended up at the construction site," Dmitry laughed. "The party sent me."

They sat up until late. Dmitry reminisced about how he and his friends had battled Kolchak and Wrangel, about how they fought for a happy future, for the mighty and beautiful Soviet nation.

It's good when things are good, Marfa thought. People become kind, sociable.

That sunlit spring was strongly redolent of thunderstorms, wars, and freshly-poured cement.

One time, Mikhail came to his work shift and saw a hundred and fifty workers sitting in the changing room, waiting for something. They had just started timbering and were supposed to be vigilantly watching the fortifications, making sure they wouldn't collapse.

"What happened, guys?" Mikhail asked.

"The bitumen is burning on the first lot somewhere," a young, shaggy-haired man replied. "The fumes are so bad that it's impossible to work. They're locating the fire now, then we'll put it out and go down in the shaft again."

The tenth shaft was burning, the pneumatic foundation section. They decided to let out all the air. The smoke thinned out and the workers went back in the shaft, but the fire didn't let up. They had to pump cement solution behind the lining, where the wood and insulation burned.

Mikhail returned to his brigade and said:

"We have to set up a pump in the pneumatic foundation. It's heavy and dangerous work: there are still fumes, but we'll wear masks. Yermakov, Sidorenko, and Ostapov will go . . ."

Mikhail looked in the workers' faces and called out their last names one by one.

"What about me?" asked a heavyset, thirty-year-old man.

"You stay here," Mikhail said. "You have two children. If you die of poisoning, there'll be no one left to feed them."

A few hours later, the pump was set up, they poured cement solution in the drilled openings, and the fire began to die down.

"There's a singer who lives in the building next to the foundation pit," Mikhail recounted. "She comes home every evening and sings. The guys even send a delegate over from us to ask if she could sing some more. It's easier for us to work to music."

Marfa began to laugh:

"Like on holidays!"

"Right, like on holidays," Mikhail agreed, grew pensive, then said: "You know what I always miss in the winter? A holiday with a Christmas tree and a carnival. We always had a big tree at home with ornaments, a big star . . ."

"When Grandma was alive," Marfa said, "we went to church on Christmas . . . Then Grandma died, I left for Moscow, and . . . before you brought it up, the holiday never even crossed my mind."

Mikhail patted his wife's fair hair and kissed her tenderly behind the ear.

They almost never reminisced about the way they used to live before they met. They didn't have any living family, and it was like their lives had only started a few years ago, here in Moscow. Only once in a while, late at night, when the stars began to shine in the distant sky, Mikhail would remember his father, a gray-haired, prematurely old man. All that remained of him was a gold, antique ring he had given his son a long time ago.

Mikhail never took it off.

That night, when Mikhail and Marfa lay embracing on their narrow bed, he said slowly and seriously:

"I often think that if my father were still alive, he would have been happy for us. He would've liked you. I think that this is the kind of wife—and life—he would have wanted for me. After all, he had deliberately sent me to the workers' school, and in the last year of his life kept repeating that we had to live like workers and peasants. That must be why he died, he couldn't become a different kind of man—after all, he was a professor, a mathematician, a linguist."

"Darling, what's a linguist?" Marfa asked sleepily.

"An expert in various languages," Mikhail replied. "We had an immense library in every language. Father knew a lot, much more than I do, he understood a lot more than I do. Were he still alive, what would he say about this Metro initiative?"

"And what could he say?" Marfa marveled. "So many people in this city that there's no room for everyone on the ground. So we're going underground."

"Underground . . ." Mikhail repeats after her. "Underground and underwater, like the city of Kitezh and Altantis. Father told me about Shambhala—a secret city somewhere in India. I think it's also underground. There are magicians living there who possess secret knowledge. When father was alive, various people from the Joint State Political Directorate came around to talk to him about Shambhala. They were organizing some sort of expeditions . . . perhaps, when they couldn't find Shambhala in India, they decided to build it under Moscow. I always think there must be a secret meaning behind all these grandiose construction sites, these five-year plans. My father would have easily guessed it, but I can't. And I have a real need for this meaning, you know?"

Mikhail touched his wife on the shoulder and Marfa pressed against him even tighter.

"Are you asleep?"

"Hrrm," Marfa purred, "almost. I'm sorry, I still don't quite understand what you're talking about. You're very smart and I love you."

"My darling, I love you too," Mikhail replied, and held Marfa closer.

As he fell asleep, he thought to himself that, as long as he had love in his life, it wouldn't be hard for him at all to get by without secret meanings.

One time, Comrade Kaganovich went down in the shaft where Marfa worked. He wanted to see how the Komsomol shock brigade was working. When he saw Marfa, he was surprised:

"You have women working here?"

"Yes," Marfa replied. "I, Melnikova, came here with the Komsomol."

Comrade Kaganovich asked:

"What are you doing hammering?"

"What do you think, Comrade Kaganovich?" Marfa flared up. "That I came here to sweep with a broom?"

Afterward, she was summoned by the division superintendent, who said that Comrade Kaganovich made a special note about the Komsomol brigade's precise and thorough work. They expressed their gratitude to the whole brigade and gave out Metro-building badges in honor of Comrade Kaganovich's review.

That evening the proud Marfa walked home. All around her, Moscow reverberated and sparkled. Goggle-eyed automobiles, heavy-duty trucks, jangling trams, and dusty buses raced so close to her in the square, but didn't graze her; it was like they were guarding Marfa because she was walking and thinking about what mattered most.

Pilots take the airways.

Captains swim across blue seas.

Metro builders descend underground.

Everything was in its right place and Marfa, too, was in her right place. And that made her feel calm and happy.

Back home, she found Dmitry. He was unusually somber. Mikhail was listening to him closely and seriously, but the men's conversation died down as soon Marfa walked in.

"The man's in trouble," Mikhail said after Dmitry left. "There was an unaccounted-for expense at the shop. Mitya liked to say he was a terrible merchant, so someone embezzled the money and now he has to answer for it."

"What a misfortune," Marfa said. "What's he going to do?"

"He'll try to figure it out," Mikhail said gravely, "find the thief . . . he's got a week left, then the shop will be audited. He said that if they don't find the money, he'll have to go on trial."

"Maybe you can think of something?" Marfa asked and gave her husband a concerned, loving look. "I know you're smart, I believe in you."

Mikhail smiled and said:

"I'm not as smart as that. But I'll try."

At the Palace of the Soviets station, they were carrying out the decorative work. Everyone was slowed down by the master marble cutters, who kept missing deadlines. On a board that rated the brigades' work, there was a turtle drawn next to the marble cutters. As for Marfa's brigade, it never received a ranking lower that an airplane or an automobile.

"What sort of a pace is this?" the shift supervisor grumbled at them. "It's shameful to be moving like a turtle when you're building a metropolitan railway system! It's like you're working at a cemetery!"

"But we've worked at the cemetery our whole lives," they retorted.

This was in fact the case: in the past, the marble cutters made tombstones. The brigade was immediately reinforced with young Komsomol members, and the work went at full blast: the Palace of the Soviets station was finished in just six months.

On the frosty night of January 31, 1935, the head of the sixth division came out to the workers and officially confirmed that they were allowed to remove the heated enclosure from the completed above-ground ticket hall.

Marfa finished her shift at midnight, but her whole brigade stayed late to dismantle the enclosure.

"We built it and built it, what do you mean, we won't get to see the result?" someone said. "Fiddlesticks!"

The ticket hall exterior, which was enclosed by chipboard and lit by the harsh, almost blinding light of the January moon, resembled a large, makeshift circus tent.

Along with her brigade comrades, Marfa secured steel wires to the chipboard slabs. Then, a few dozen workers grabbed the wires by their ends. Like during a village holiday, Marfa thought—and, at that moment, the enormous wall of the enclosure began to slowly tilt, and when it reached a critical angle, fell with a thud and a clatter on the ground. Marfa hurried with everyone to load wooden planks and chipboard onto the trucks.

By three o'clock in the morning, the building was freed from its tattered winter garb.

The rumor that the Palace of the Soviets was finished spread like wildfire through all the metropolitan's divisions. Workers from all around the city poured onto Gogol Boulevard, and Marfa wasn't surprised at all when she heard Mikhail call her name.

They stood side by side, watching the first rays of the cold winter sun illuminate the airy, semi-spherical building.

"How splendid," Marfa whispered.

Mikhail wrapped his arms around her shoulders.

More and more people joined them. Men and women from Marfa's brigade, Yermakov, Sidorenko, and Osipov, shaft-men, plate-layers, and marble cutters. The square gradually filled with people, many of them regular Muscovites, students, workers, and Red Army soldiers.

Suddenly the crowd began to cheer and applaud. The chairman of the Moscow Soviet of People's Deputies, Comrade Bulganin, had come to congratulate the workers of the sixth division. He wanted to shake hands with the leading female workers personally, and the division superintendent drew Marfa toward him.

"Misha," she yelled out, "I'll be right back, don't leave!"

But how could she be right back? As if you could find someone in a crowd like that! Comrade Bulganin was long gone by now, but the crowd still didn't disperse. Marfa began to elbow her way out when she suddenly heard a familiar voice beside her, agitated and joyous:

"This is just the beginning! We will vanquish nature, melt the polar ices, build palaces for working people everywhere! We'll surround the continents with warm currents, make the Arctic seas produce billions of kilowatts of electricity, grow trees a kilometer tall . . ."

"Hello, Mitya!" Marfa said, and Dmitry rushed to her, kissing her on both cheeks.

"A holiday, what a holiday!" he repeated.

They held hands and made their way out of the crowd, helping each other.

"Misha's here too," Marfa said. "Let's wait a bit, maybe he'll see us."

"Yes, yes," Dmitry said excitedly. "Let's stand out here. Back in the Civil War days, I could only dream we'd live to see a day like this! That they'd take down the churches, build people's palaces, that our country would become great and mighty!"

Marfa smiled broadly and joyfully, then asked:

"How are you doing? Misha said you had trouble at the shop."

Dmitry hugged her impulsively:

"My dear Marfa! Didn't Misha tell you? It's all over, I don't work there anymore. I'm going back to the military. There is still fire in my belly! I leave for the Far East in a week."

"And the cash shortage?" Marfa asked very softly. "Did you find the money?"

"You're completely in the dark!" Dmitry exclaimed in astonishment. "Misha helped me, he brought the money and I put it in the register. But I promised to pay it back, don't you worry, I'll send everything back from my unit. So that's what Misha's like, he didn't even brag to you! And he saved me!" And Dmitry exuberantly shook his head.

When Marfa returned to their tiny dormitory room, Mikhail was already there. Marfa stuck her face in his big palms, in the familiar smell of underground dust, cement and metal, sweat and the male body. All that was missing was her husband's ring, which he usually wore on his finger . . .

A half-hour later, Mikhail was lying on the narrow bed, watching the still-undressed Marfa trying to light the kerosene stove. She had the beautiful body of a young working-class woman.

"We're out of kerosene," she said and sat down on the bed. She took her husband's hand and patted his orphaned finger. "Mitya is your friend, right? You couldn't have acted otherwise, right?"

"Yes," Mikhail nodded intently, "it just feels so strange, I can always sense it when I'm not wearing the ring. My finger feels so bare."

At that moment, Marfa silently took her mother's ring off her index finger and handed it to her husband.

"Try it on," she said.

Mikhail smiled—the difference was too great between an antique gold ornament and a cheap village trinket—but carefully took the ring from Marfa's hand and put it on.

"As if it were melded to my finger. Let's say our two rings merged into one, alright?"

"Of course," Marfa replied.

She climbed under the blanket again and lay still pressing against Mikhail.

"You know," he said, "when we were at the square, I kept thinking about my father. Too bad he's not alive today. He would have liked all this. An underground city, a Metro, marble arches, crowds of people on the streets. At the time, he thought that the end of the world was upon us, the new Noah's Flood. That we needed to grow out our fins, become underwater creatures, which is why he sent me to the workers' school. He thought that a new Dark Age had arrived, barbarism, the end of the arts and sciences. That there would be no more theaters or palaces. But it turned out this was only the beginning, that there is no flood, only a torrential rain, a spring shower. You can take cover under an umbrella, wait it out, then, go on living. Get married, have children, then, grandchildren. Live honestly and with dignity, live well. As if nothing happened. I think that if my father had known all that, he wouldn't have died back then, in '29."

Mikhail's voice breaks.

"I really miss him, almost always, all the time," and Marfa realizes

Mikhail is crying. Whereupon she sits up in bed, places her husband's head on her bosom and begins to rock him like an infant. He says through his sobs: "Thank you, thank you, I'm only happy when I'm with you, I don't know what I'd do without you," and many other words people say when they love someone, words destined for their beloved alone.

Soon they will fall asleep, fall asleep worn out by nighttime work and their lovemaking, fall asleep pressed against each other, feeling the warmth of each other's bodies, inhaling the scents of the great construction site and their love—and even in his sleep, Mikhail will now and again run his thumb over his new ring, gradually getting used to it.

Many years later, he will himself forget whose ring is on his finger and tell his children and grandchildren about the inscription in Sanskrit, tell them that he inherited the ring from his father, a mathematician and linguist. Not long before his death, he'll give the ring to Nikita and, ultimately, it will come to fit snugly around Anya-Elvira's finger, as if it were melded to it. But all that will happen in seventy years and, at present, Mikhail is sleeping with his arms around his wife and the tears in his eyes are drying. He is sleeping and dreaming that millions of people are entering the Metro's marble ticket halls, filling its spacious trains, going to work and school and hurrying toward their happiness. Of course, everyone has his own understanding of happiness, but, collectively, people know and understand that you have to live honestly, work hard, love each other deeply, and keep safe this vast, happy city called Moscow.

103.

THE SACRIFICE

Every clan has its secret domain, its sanctuary, which outsiders do not know about. Here, you can lick your wounds and gather your strength. Here, space is malleable and time is unhurried. This is a stationary point and a battlefield, the eye of a cyclone and the epicenter of an explosion.

Our family estate is a dark forest lake hidden in a thick grove. We are the only ones who can find our way to it, the only ones familiar with its dark taste, the only ones who swim in these waters, plunging to the bottom, summoning the underwater creatures. This is our family's gift, it's in our blood, which is as dark as nighttime lake water, our blood, which swooshes like a mill wheel inside our temples.

A secret sanctuary, a forest landmark, a family treasure. Sometimes a lake, sometimes a mill pond, sometimes a deep end. Dark water, a mill wheel, rotten snags on the bottom.

Usually, we come here alone. Today, we have met here for the first time.

We look at the reflections of our faces in the black mirror coated with ripples, inhale the moist, musty air with our nostrils, and glance around as if none of us has ever been here before.

The forest surrounds us like a jagged wall, looming over our backs like a spruce picket fence. The round disc of the moon hangs in the sky, replicating the contours of the lake at our feet.

"Good afternoon," Anya says.

"Hello," Nikita replies.

"Hi," Moreukhov waves his hand.

We are small children in the thick forest of eternity. Two Hansels and one Gretel.

We know what we have to do.

"So," Nikita says, "it probably doesn't make sense to wait for Rimma. Shall we begin?"

"Yes, probably," Anya sighs.

She was still hoping to meet her cousin here.

"Yep," Moreukhov says. "Let's figure it out, just the three of us."

We take each other's hands. Moreukhov's damp fingers, Nikita's firm grip, Anya's slender palm. As he presses it, Nikita involuntarily thinks of Masha—she loves to fall asleep holding his hand.

Space is malleable here, which is how we're able to hold hands as we gather around the forest lake in a round-dance. We know just one thing: that we shouldn't break the circle.

Slowly, we begin to move. Nikita sets the pace—quickening, uneven, breathless. In a midnight round-dance, we spin around the black forest mirror, the moon a pale stain in the middle.

We spin faster and faster.

There it is, our water cycle, our circular forest road. Water, vapor, rain, and snow; sublimation, evaporation, condensation, and freezing; the eternal water cycle, the wheel of Saṃsāra, of births and deaths, funerals and christenings.

We've almost worn ourselves out, we're out of breath. And now the second wind will kick in, Anya thinks. It's like a bender, Moreukhov thinks—the most important thing is not to stop while you've still got the strength. Nikita tries not to think at all and, instead, calls to mind the phantasmagorical vision of Dasha's orgasm. For some reason, Nikita knows that that's what's most important right now.

Sweat streams down their faces, salty drops fall in the dark water, feet glide along the clay banks, Nikita's grip weakens, Moreukhov's wet fingers are about to slip out of Anya's hand, *we'll break through*, she tells herself, *we'll swim up to the surface*, and, for the first time, the plural forms of these verbs begin to make sense: we're the ones who'll break through, we'll swim up to the surface, together, the three of us.

Maybe we really did get a second wind, maybe we really did find the right pace, but a powerful, resonant sound rose and lingered in the night air—hollow, guttural, and inhuman. It seemed to emanate from the depths of the lake and, at the same time, burst forth from our lungs in a triumphant moan.

The dark water became covered with ripples, the reflected disc of the moon split in half, and black waves touched our feet. The water whirled in time with our round-dance, coiled into a funnel, twisted into a spiral, seethed, gurgled, and bubbled—and it was there, at the very center of the lake, that the moving, quivering, and rising began.

We know who is coming up to the surface now. We know him. We've already met him.

The chthonic beast, an ancient deity, a deep-water monster, a near-bottom god, an octopus, a water creature. Slimy tentacles, rotten seaweed, a saucer on his head that's as white and round as the moon in the sky.

We stop and hold each other's hands tighter. Already, the waves are coming up to our chests, the monster is thrashing from side to side, trying to break the circle and break out of it.

How, on the deep-sea monster's birthday, we baked a pie from clay, Moreukhov says through his teeth, and we begin to squat and raise our interlinked arms as if we're doing a children's round dance. The dark waves beat against our faces and it's as if the circle will be broken any minute.

"Listen," Anya yells, "calm down, don't get angry, we'll do everything by the book. We acknowledge your power, we have brought you offerings, forgive us for troubling your peace and summoning you. The time has come for us to give, the time has come for our cleansing, and we are asking for your help, your support."

And Anya falls to her knees. A sudden, guttural squawk tears her mouth open. The supersonic shriek of a V-2 rocket, the whistle of a sniper's bullet, the rustle of the wings of the last angel, death in flight—and when the last note freezes over the forest, the lake grows still and the water lies down at our feet again. The monster levitates in the middle of the lake and only dark streams of water run down its smooth skin.

"I offer you my freedom," Anya says. "I offer you my solitude, my deliberate self reliance. I do this for myself, for my son, Gosha, for all of my relatives, for the benefit of all living beings."

Moreukhov is the second to go down on his knees. He leans his head over the dark water and vomits with desperate abandon. The vomit spews out of his mouth in a fountain—in the moonlight, it looks as if someone is throwing a handful of silver coins in the water.

"I offer you my faith," Moreukhov says, "my faith that I have chosen my own fate, the pride that I have taken in this choice, my pridefulness, my self-assurance. I do this for myself, for my grandfather Grigoriy, for everyone who has perished because of him, for the benefit of all living beings."

Nikita is the last to go down on his knees. In his hands is a heap of yellowish-red leaves, which he throws in the dark water; they rock on the waves like specks of yellow light, like red blood stains.

"I offer you my youth," Nikita says, "my desire to stop time, my heart-rending love for Dasha, my unrealized project with Kostya, everything I've lived through this past year. I do this for myself, for my wife Masha, for Grandfather Makar's *second Russia*, for the benefit of all living beings."

And at that moment, the water creature's saucer erupts into a ruby color and the drops of water on its skin begin to glow and change, pulsating and radiating every color of the rainbow; and now the colors flow into each other as if someone is blending paint or turning a kaleidoscope.

The nighttime forest explodes into a rainbow and the water at our feet blooms into fireworks.

"The blessing," one of us says, "the blessing has been received."

Then there's a light and the water twists into a funnel again while the iridescent octopus plunges into the lake, returning to its deep-water, near-bottom kingdom. The water settles and only a few yellow leaves lie motionless atop the black mirror that reflects the moon and our bowed faces.

Silently, we rise from our knees and let go of each other's hands. Don't ask why we didn't do this earlier. Space is malleable here or maybe, we grew out new pairs of hands during the sacrifice. We don't know ourselves.

Our time is up, it's time to go, and we start to say our goodbyes.

"Best of luck," Nikita says.

"I'll see you around," Moreukhov says.

"Drop by sometime," Anya says.

We throw a parting glance at the calm waters of the forest lake. There it is, our secret domain, our family estate, our sanctuary, our family treasure.

At that moment, Moreukhov turns to Nikita.

"Listen," he says, "I have a request for you. I know that your Masha is a medium, that she takes in human souls, the souls of the dead. I have two relatives over there from my mother's side. A little girl, Polina, and a woman, Lida. Exactly the kind that come to your Masha: no children, no heirs. But if it weren't for them, I wouldn't have come into this world. Put in a good word for them to your Masha, I owe it to them. Let her take them in if she can, alright?"

"I'll ask," Nikita answers, "but it's Masha's decision, not mine."

We part ways. The dark circle of the lake, the light circle of the moon. A stationary point, a battlefield, the eye of a cyclone, the epicenter of an explosion.

104.

SOMETHING VERY IMPORTANT

Moscow is a beautiful city, Nikita thinks. Especially from a taxi window. Especially in a brightly lit tunnel. Drunk and exhausted, he is on his way home, and still cannot choose between the two women he loves.

A few pencil strokes and another sheet of paper flies to the floor. Moreukhov sips his beer and draws one sketch after another. Gulag convicts, the haggard faces of peasants, a telephone muffled with a pillow, a dusty Moscow sunset, a starry sky over a salt steppe, a boy in the library, horsemen in the Asian mountains, a man and a woman in a shooting gallery, a black car by the entrance of Hotel Metropol, a scared boy with a pistol in his hand, a young woman under a white parasol, three children on a railroad embankment, a line formed along a brick wall, a rocket soars to the sky, an old man stands by a mill pond, two people lie embracing on a narrow bed, underwater monsters swim between snags, drowned corpses swell in the dark water, rotten brushwood, underwater stumps . . . Sheet by sheet, sketch by sketch. It's been many years since he's drawn like this.

Moreukhov is drawing and his fear rises up inside him. Soon, he'll face underwater reptiles, crayfish sinking their claws into living flesh, scaly hands embracing and clasping, and dark water closing in over his head. The beer will run out, the gin and tonic too, and the dead, 40 proof water will rush into his lungs.

Outside, it's raining. Streams of water are running down the window pane as if the room were a submarine compartment. Andrey, Anya asks, why do you need a computer? I have my games here, he replies, boys like shooting games, you know that. Show me one, Anya asks, I like shooting games too—and it's as if the monitor fills up with water and a barrel sight appears. Okay, Andrey says, press here, here, and here. First, test out the aiming function and I'll go put on the teakettle. Sure, Anya nods. Here, here, and here. Got it.

So they rise up from the depths—scaly, scabby water creatures with horns, bifurcated fishtails, and bared fangs. She sees octopus beaks, the long whiskers of burbots, the bulging eyes of fish, and the blue faces of the drowned.

Underwater monsters from Moreukhov's nightmares.

Anya shoots again and again, Nikita's riding in a taxi, outside it's raining. Moreukhov collects the sheets of paper off the floor—monsters, water creatures, drowned bodies—he looks at them as if he's saying good-bye, throws them in the bathtub, and sets them on fire. Fire, Moreukhov says, is stronger than water.

And when the last sheet of paper turns to ash, Anya stands up. Done, she says. Wow, Andrey marvels, I see that you're a real sniper.

Anya feels she has accomplished something very important.

And she hugs Andrey, they drink tea, and, perhaps, lie down in bed again, where, for the first time, Anya feels not like a swimmer, but like the water, and Andrey immerses himself in her and swims, while Nikita is still riding in the taxi and Moreukhov takes out a fresh sheet of paper, drawing a picture, then another, then the first one again, scratching it out and starting over—and, the next thing you know, the three of them slip out of the beautiful city of Moscow to bring their offerings to the bank of a dark forest lake. When they return, there's a finished drawing before Moreukhov—a man and a woman sitting at a café table; she seems a bit astonished and he's looking off to the side.

This is Nikita saying goodbye to Dasha.

It's not sad to sacrifice a romantic love—after all, a love affair doesn't need to be a happy one. It's excruciatingly painful, but, still, not sad. Nikita imagines how, many years later, Dasha's memories will become faded and forgotten—and she'll be a bit sad, but still find it pleasant to reminisce about a time when she was so young, loved a married man, they made a beautiful couple, and then it all ended.

He'll take Dasha's hand and hesitate to kiss it goodbye.

But that will be tomorrow.

Today, in a half-hour, Nikita will be seated next to Masha, holding her hand, saying: "Everything will be alright, you'll see. We'll go to America together and everything will work out"—and, for the first time in six months, he'll actually believe what he's saying.

Marriages are made in heaven, which means that every marriage has a sacred meaning. Nikita and Masha will stay together forever—like two people, like a man and a woman, like Grandpa Makar's two Russias: the ones who survived and the ones who perished.

But that will be in a half-hour.

In fifteen minutes, Nikita will make a decision: he'll stay with Masha, he'll go to America with her, and do everything possible so they can have a child. He'll say goodbye to Dasha for good, refuse Kostya's proposal, and keep his mid-sized business. He'll never have millions.

What can you do—you can't have everything, so you have to choose what's important.

But that will happen in fifteen minutes.

In ten minutes, Nikita will imagine how, many years later, he'll be drinking vodka with his son in old age, saying: *Regardless of how much I loved Dasha, I always knew I'd be with your mother for life, I don't even know why. You have to understand, it can happen to anyone once. Why aren't you saying anything, son? Say something!* and his son will say: *I understand everything, Dad. It's fine, don't worry.*

At present, Nikita knows this is what he must do. Even if his son replies differently. Even if he never has a son at all.

And right when Nikita walks into the apartment, Moreukhov puts pencil to paper one last time. He knows he has just accomplished something very important. Moreukhov leans over the drawing and examines it: a middle-aged man sits on the floor and next to him, slumped in a deep armchair as if she's dead, is his wife.

EPILOGUE
FISHIE

(the 2000s: birth)

Gosha (born 2002) and Sasha (born 2005)
cousins thrice removed

105.

THANK YOU, THANK YOU!

She pictures her belly as an enormous, round aquarium and in it, there is a big, cute fish turning from side to side. It keeps poking its head or tail against the glass and, sometimes, brushing its fin across it. It's swimming. Contented and happy.

Needless to say, there's no fish inside her, not even a tail, which disappeared in the eighth week, they checked everything on the ultrasound, it's a normal baby, she just doesn't know if it's a boy or a girl, doesn't want to know, let it be a surprise. Milka was told the wrong gender anyway, so I shouldn't get worked up about it, right? I don't care if it's a boy or a girl. Let it be a fishie while it's still swimming in there. My fishie is swimming and sucking its finger. So what if fish don't have fingers, it's a magical fish.

Of course, let it be a fishie. A fishie, as well as a bunny, a kitty, a mousie, a breadcrumb, my baby, my sweet thing, my golden nugget, my precious darling. Lena is sitting there purring tender words, patting her not-so-big belly, waiting for the fishie to flip its tail. It's nice when the father-to-be also puts his hand on the belly—*Can you feel him kicking, dear? See, he recognizes you!*—but Lena is sitting alone or, if she's lucky, with Milka. She's currently staying at Milka's house in the suburbs outside Moscow: in July, Milka went back to Moscow and Lena immediately started going to a maternity clinic, seeing doctors, taking classes for pregnant women, doing tests and screenings, daily walks . . .

They're strolling in a familiar grove. Lena laughs: I've rarely been here sober! Milka's drinking a Corona and giggling: tough it out, you're lucky that you don't smoke!

The summer passes and presently, Lena is strolling in the yellowish-red suburban forest, alone, but not really alone. She pats her belly and says: Sit still, fishie, it's too early for you to come out, swim around for at least another three weeks, or better yet, five, like you're supposed to.

Lena tries to guess if it's a boy or a girl. If it's a boy, let him take after my brother. Intelligent, talented, doesn't chase too much after girls, doesn't drink vodka, doesn't do drugs. What will I name him? I'll decide as soon as the baby is born because, over the past year, I've developed a dislike for all male names. And if it's a girl? I'll name the girl Mila, if Milka doesn't object.

I hope the girl takes after me. Long legs, pert breasts, small nose, narrow eyes. Me—and my mom. She would have been so glad! If she were still alive, I would have probably called her every day. They say that pregnant women *feel particularly close* to their mothers. But I never got the chance, I never got to experience a particularly close relationship with my mom, only a normal close one, like we had our whole lives.

Lena strolls down a broad forest path and pats her large belly; the leaves have wilted, the temperatures have fallen, and the autumn wind's blowing. Fishie-fishie, how are you doing there? You're not cold, right? Let me put my hand here so you can poke against it, okay? Like this, yes.

I'll give you the best education, in the summer, I'll take you to the seaside, make sure you get exercise . . . Bunny, do you want to exercise? You're keeping quiet. That means you don't really want to. I see, you're taking after your mom.

Milka has gone away for two weeks and loaned me her driver and the keys to her house. Of course, I can go to Moscow, but what would I do there? God forbid I get carsick, although I don't think I have morning sickness, knock on wood. It's still better here—I'll lounge around, watch TV. Milka has a *luxurious* living room: a big-screen TV, a home theater, a fluffy white carpet. You're lying there, clicking the remote, looking for a melodrama so you could have a good cry. You're on the verge of tears anyway, like you're supposed to be, probably. Like when you have PMS.

Naturally, her water broke smack in the middle of the *luxurious* carpet. Lena didn't even get scared, she said very calmly to herself: *So our aquarium broke, hold on now, Fishie, hold on now, Lena*, she called the driver, laid down in the backseat, and called the doctor: "I'm on my way to see you, my water broke," she said calmly, without panicking—and began to swear only when she found out that her doctor was out of town today, of all days. She grumbled: "Send my regards to your conference!" and hung up, then, decided: I'll call Milka and share the happy news about the carpet. I so enjoyed saying *my water broke*. At one point, I thought I wouldn't have to . . . ow, ow, ow.

So far, it's just as they said: a five-minute interval between contractions about one minute long. It's not too painful, it's pretty tolerable, especially if you drive safely. Hey, don't speed, I'm not giving birth right this second!

Listen, babe, I have news for you. You're not a fishie anymore, you're probably a bunny. Or a kitty or a little mole . . . who else lives in burrows? So, hold on, little one, alright? Just a few more hours and we'll see each other. My precious, my darling, please wait till the maternity clinic and then, come out quickly, agreed? Ow, ouch, now it really does hurt!

How am I supposed to breathe? Deeply with my chest and my nose? Inhale—exhale, inhale—exhale . . . and the intervals are getting shorter, what is this, ow, Mommy! Inhale—exhale, inhale—exhale . . . what, are we there already? Oh boy, I think I got here in time, it's not scary anymore, ow, motherfucker, ow, Mommy, it's not scary but it is painful.

Yes, I'm forty-five, yes, I'm not married, no, I don't want a cesarean. The doctor said there's no reason I should have one. No, I'm telling you, age is not a reason! O—O—O—O—O—O—O—O—O—O! Doggy style, doggy style, I know, come on, let's go, take me to the delivery room! Alright, I'll walk.

Listen, babe, we're already in the right place. Now Mom will lie down more comfortably and you can get out. So are you a girl or a boy? We'll find out soon, ow, ow, my little one, wait a bit longer, not so fast, A—A—A—A—A—A—A—A, motherfucker, where the hell is everyone! How did it go? Four inhales, six exhales. It's some kind of yoga. F—f—f—f, h—h—h—h—h—h. And now, doggy style, doggy style, it hurts so bad, Mommy!

What do you mean—lie down for an hour? Isn't it supposed to start right now, aren't I . . . No—no—no, I won't be able to bear it! A—A—A—A—A—A—A—A, who was the bitch who said there's no such thing as painful natural processes? I wonder if she's given birth herself? F—f—f—f, h—h—h—h—h—h.

Most women are normal, Lord, I'm the only moron. Why the hell am I giving birth? I have no man, no mother, I'm all alone in this city, my best friend is outside my wireless network, and my gynecologist is away at a conference. I'm all by myself, I mean, I'm sorry, bunny, it's just the two of us, but ow ow ow, just don't get mad O—O—O—O—O—O—O, that's not what I meant. F—f—f—f, h—h—h—h—h—h and again f—f—f—f, h—h—h—h—h—h.

My fishie, I mean, crap, my birdie, my bunny, my mousie, how are you doing there? We'll see each other very, very soon, Mom is waiting for you, Mom loves you, just be more careful there, alright? Just a second, A—A—A—A—A, it hurts so bad, Mommy, where have they all gone, I'm about to give birth.

Lord, how do I sneak out of here, huh? Let it give birth to itself and I'll come back for it later, alright? I'm such an idiot, forty-five years old and I needed this too! Alone, no man, no friend, Mom, Mom, Mommy, It hurts so bad, if only I'd known how badly it would hurt, I wouldn't have . . . ow, ouch, Mom, Mommy, do something! What did you always tell me? I don't remember, I haven't seen you for so many years, eight, almost nine, dear God, A—A—A—A—A—A—A, what, what? Not to be afraid of anything? Okay, Mom, okay, I won't be afraid. You think everything's fine? It's like this for everyone? And it was the same for you? When you had my brother or me? The both of us? Alright, I won't be afraid and I'll tell my child not to be either.

My sweetheart, my little nestling, my precious fox cub, just don't be afraid. Grandma said, don't be afraid and everything will go well. I'm doing completely fine, it just hurts a lot, Mommy, but I'm not afraid, damn it, I'm not fucking afraid of anything, so babe, don't be fucking afraid.

What are you saying, Mom? That everything will be alright? Yes, I know that everything will be alright. And later on, too? Post-delivery? He'll grow up healthy? And happy? What do you mean, *it depends*? Okay, okay, if you don't know, then why are you saying it? I'm not arguing with you, it just hurts so bad, A—A—A—A—A—A—A—A—A—A—A— A—A, Mom, can you call them? Oh, forgive me, I said a foolish thing and, anyway, thank you for coming, I wasn't expecting it at all, I feel a lot better, thank you. I'm really not scared anymore, everything's fine. Is your hand that cold or do I have a fever? It's always like this? Well, alright. Wait, don't leave so soon, tell me something. I didn't even ask you: how are you doing over there? What do you mean, *it depends*? Alright, alright, I got it: I'll find out for myself when I . . . um . . . grow up, but that won't be soon, right? After all, I have a child now, I'm a mom, I have things to do here, don't I?

Mom, I'm not going to die right now, right???

No, I wasn't asking you, where the hell were you, you've all gone nuts, what am I paying you A—A—A—A—A—A—A—A— A—A—A sorry A—A—A—A—A—A—A—A—A—A I wanted to say, what the fuck am I paying you for?

And now, I should push, right? Finally! A—A—A—A—A—A—A—A What do you mean, don't scream, I can't not scream, it hurts! Okay, okay, I'll try.

Listen to me, babe. You and I aren't afraid of anything, we're doing well. Just a bit longer and it'll be all over. Lord, how I want to see you, my little kiddo, I'm going to push and you come out, come on! Oh God, it hurts so bad, Lord, A—A, no, I'm not screaming, I'm just pushing this way, come on, my little one, come on!

Touch? Touch what? The little head? No, I don't want to, let's speed this up or else I'll die right now, come on now, babe, come on, my bunny, come on, come on, hurry up and climb out faster, dear God, oh God, oh God, oh God, I'm so happy, show me, show me. Yes, I can see it's a girl. Is she alright? Is everything okay? You're sure everything's okay?

And Lena cries from happiness, wow, the fishie turned out to be a little girl, and the obstetrician places this little girl on Lena's breast, she's all wet, completely clean, just wet, and smells delicious as she stares with her big eyes. Lena kisses her and cries and cries, repeating, *thank you, thank you,* imploring: let everything turn out well for her, let her be happy and not *it depends,* but always, always-always, like I was today, and grow up to be beautiful and smart and choose normal guys for herself, Lord, make it so she chooses normal guys for herself, not like I did my whole life, upon my soul, I beg you, let her choose normal ones, have their children and, if she needs me, I'll be there to give birth with her, I'll even come from *over there,* like my mom did today, if only everything turned out well for her, my mousie, my bunny, my fishie, my God, she's so beautiful, tell me, doctor, isn't she beautiful? My Sasha, Sashenka, my tiny tot.

Well, yeah, I wanted a Milka and I got a Sashka. I looked at her and immediately saw it: a real Sasha, a typical baby Alexandra, my beloved bunny, my precious fishie.

106.

2005. THE GREAT GAME.

The story of any family is simple: men and women were born, lived, and died; they made love, gave birth to new children, and ultimately gave us life.

All the rest is minor explicitation. Men toiled at the great construction sites, lived under false documents, worked at the NKVD, served out their prison camp sentences, launched rockets, killed, and informed on people. Women raised children, worked in factories, were philologists, housewives, and killers. Their offspring became salesgirls and secretaries, businessmen, artists, and alcoholics, but still remained a part of the Great Game.

The Great Game brings together everyone who is bound by blood, their forebears and offspring, their deceased parents and unborn children.

The Great Game is a carpet with an intricate pattern whose every curlicue replicates the entire drawing and fully comprises that drawing in it.

The Great Game is a vast net. You can get tangled up in it like a fish, you can rock in it like in a hammock, you can fall into it like into a safety net. Every knot is a human life.

The awareness that you're participating in the Great Game is the best thing that can happen to someone. If you're a part of the Game, then you're not worried about happiness, wealth, or love. The Great Game gives you the strength to make a choice.

A curlicue sprouts in the carpet pattern, but that curlicue cannot determine where to grow. It cannot do so until it realizes that it's a part of the drawing and that the drawing is infinite and beautiful. It cannot do so until it realizes that the entire drawing is replicated within any one of its details.

A family history is simple: our children will judge us and our grandchildren will forgive us. All that is left for us to do is remember. Remember that we are a part of the net, a part of the pattern, a part of the Great Game. We have gained strength from this, we did what we had to do in the face of inevitable judgment and forgiveness.

At present, what happens to us down the road doesn't matter anymore. We have inscribed our fate into the infinite pattern—we've lifted a family curse, made a sacrifice, and been united in holy matrimony.

It doesn't matter what will happen to us down the road, but it is possible to visualize a happy ending for every one of us—even if it can only be seen hazily, as if through the thickness of water, like a sunken city that keeps coming up to the surface and sinking to the bottom again.

107.

HAPPY ENDING

One night, Rimma is jolted awake. She is lying under a bedsheet while
the cool air of a Moscow summer night drifts in from the window. The
clock is ticking and the DVD-player light is blinking. She dreamed that
she flew up over her bed, looked down, and saw that it was neatly made,
as if no one had slept in it. She dreamed of a rental apartment, clean and
sterile. A pair of stockings and a Japanese school uniform hung from
the back of a chair. Very neatly folded. She dreamed of an office desk,
immaculate and untouched. She dreamed of the empty Moscow streets
where she once strolled, dreamed of a dead, deserted city. She dreamed
of cemeteries with neat rows of gravestones unmarked by either names
or dates. She dreamed of artificial flowers blooming on plastic trees.
She dreamed of the even light of square windows, the yellowish light of
streetlamps, the moon's reflection on still water.

She laid under the bedsheet and thought that, at long last, she didn't
have a body.

They're having breakfast together. Masha is wearing her nightshirt and
Nikita is naked from the waist up, wearing only his jeans. He always gets
up first—Masha likes to sleep in a bit.

The cheese on the toast has slightly melted—it tastes even better that
way. Nikita eats it and washes it down with hot coffee.

"Kostya called," he says, "he invited us over for the weekend. Should
we go?"

"Let's," Masha answers, "I haven't seen him in a while. You know, he's
kind of grown on me over the years."

"He's certainly grown on me!" Nikita replies with his mouth full, and Masha continues:

"At first, I was terribly irritated by his endless string of girls. I couldn't understand how Ksenia put up with it."

Nikita wants to say that Kostya has tempered his appetite lately, but instead says nothing, and smears jam on another piece of toast: it's probably not right to discuss your friend's lovers with your wife.

"And then I realized," Masha says, "that Ksenia simply doesn't notice."

"You mean, she pretends not to notice?" Nikita says.

"No, she just doesn't allow herself to notice. You know, the way I did back in the day. After all, you probably had a lover, you know, a long time ago, before we went to America. Some energetic young woman."

Nikita freezes, then, carefully swallows his coffee. What should he say? "No, what do you mean, darling, I've only ever loved you"? Deny everything, as a rule? Or pretend to be insulted? Say: "What makes you think that?" Yes, that's exactly what I'll say.

"I think you were really in love with her, unlike Kostya with his models," Masha says, and what really irks Nikita is how calmly she says it. *Ha! who cares, big deal, my husband fell in love with another woman.*

"What makes you think that?" he asks.

"I don't know," Masha replies. "After all, I'm an intuitive woman. I must have sensed it. Maybe it was the smell. No shower can wash away another person's sweat."

And she smiles, while Nikita suddenly remembers the moisture that covered Dasha's body, the woman from the deep end, the deep-water scream, the unexpected word during orgasm, the silvery taste of her kiss, a solitary man howling in a car, Masha's withered frame in an antique armchair, the doctors' blue scrubs, the smell of hospitals—and for a second, it all comes back to him, as if Nikita has accidentally fallen into his personal, autonomous time zone, his inner cache, his private archive, his hidden trunk—for a second, the air is still and the coffee loses its taste, while in his chest beats a lump of emptiness in place of a heart. Masha's voice carries to him from somewhere far away: *At the time, I had other things on my mind, but now I understand how much you loved her*—and Nikita takes Masha's hand and says:

"You know, right now, I can't even imagine loving anyone except you. Just now, you said: 'energetic young woman'—and for a second, I thought that everything suddenly vanished somewhere, that we vanished, and I was sitting in some other kitchen with an energetic young woman—and you won't believe how frightened I was." Whereupon Masha gets up, Nikita nestles his head between her breasts, she cradles his head like an infant's, and he mumbles something along the lines of: *thank you, thank you* and *I'm only happy when I'm with you and I don't know what I would do without you,* and maybe even sobs, but at that moment, his cell phone rings, Nikita picks up and Masha hears the driver's voice: "Nikita Vasilyevich, I dropped off the kids, I'm waiting by the entrance," Nikita looks at his watch and says: "Yikes, sorry, I'm running late," runs to get dressed, grabs his briefcase, and, after he's already opened the door, comes back, kisses her one more time and says: *I love you, little one*—and Masha smiles back. Nikita thinks of this smile as he goes downstairs. Masha picks up the jeans Nikita dropped on the floor, goes to the bathroom, grabs some of the children's things from the hamper, turns on the washing machine, washes the dishes, and calls the babysitter, all while continuing to smile.

At sunrise, the foam on the beach gravel resembles the flames on a Tibetan thangka—Anya had seen one at Vika's place at some point. Gosha tests the water with his foot and says:

"Brrr, it's cold!"

"It only seems that way at first," Anya replies and walks ahead of them into the sea. The cool morning air touches her feet, her knees, her hips . . . and when it climbs up to her belly, Anya dives in and swims down the sunny trail, fully enveloped in the golden glow, inhale after inhale, splash after splash, then, turns onto her back and lies still, rocking on the waves, merging with the sea and the morning sun. Then she hears snorting, spitting, and splattering, as if two paddleboats are making their way—and when Anya opens her eyes, she sees her men racing toward her covered in white foam and splashes—good Lord, how ineptly they swim!

Anya laughs: *After me, boys!* and dashes forward again, inhale after inhale, splash after splash, not forgetting to look back to see if Gosha and Andrey are doing alright and haven't fallen behind—and there's no one watching from the deserted shore how the three black dots slowly and triumphantly swim toward the distant horizon in the golden glow.

At first, he sat around with Dimon, who brought some new Hong Kong film, and felt uncomfortable explaining that new Hong Kong cinema couldn't hold a candle to the classic Hong Kong films of the eighties. Moreukhov told him he conceived a new graphic art series called *Conversations with God.*

"You know," he said, "when I was younger and I still drank a lot, I used to love talking to God. You're standing in a snowbank or something, vomiting and talking to God. That hasn't happened in a while, to tell you the truth, I've even started to get bored. So I recently remembered this and realized that I can't for the life of me recall what we talked about. What I said to Him, what He said to me—I don't remember a thing. You know, it's probably because each time I was too shaken by the fact that I was talking to Him, and didn't at all listen to what I was being told. And then I came up with this series: the drawings of the places where all this took place. Building entrance. Forest clearing. A couple of vacant lots that aren't there anymore. My room, at long last. You could say that it's a series of Troparyovo landscapes—if you can consider a drawing of my room a landscape."

Dimon yelled out: *Genius!* and promised to curate the exhibit and make sure to hang this text by the entrance because it was such a powerful conceptual gesture—the city as a meeting place between the artist and God—and Moreukhov laughed it off, refilled Dimon's teacup, and asked: *Have you even once spoken with God? Or only with the editor in chief?*

Then, Moreukhov walked Dimon to the Metro, they discussed Letov's new album, Moreukhov kept attempting to sing *like a little river fishie swimming to the ocean for no reason at all,* and Dimon jokingly pretended to be scared as dusk fell over Troparyovo. They parted by the Yugo-Zapadnaya Metro stop, slapping each other on the shoulder and agreeing to call each other next week—and presently, Moreukhov is walking home, his chest filled with the summer air, muttering some song about the sad dwellers of the earth, and, rather than heading straight home, he turns off into a forest clearing, passes the eponymous store, and descends into the forest, which is completely empty and silent and somewhat unseasonably dark.

Moreukhov is singing to himself and telling himself: *I'll take a turn and then go home and draw before I go to sleep,* after all, he wants a holiday, an adventure, and what's more, it's Troparyovo, nighttime, summer. Moreukhov walks through the forest, thinking he can't remember being here during his benders, but remembers perfectly how he used to stroll here as a boy, yes, that's right, there was a gazebo around here, he even made out in it with Sonya Sphilman, by the way, he needs to track down her email and write to her, see how she's doing over there. Wow, the gaze-bo's in its old place, although over the years it had been torn down and then rebuilt, and Moreukhov walks up to it, where a flock of teenagers is sitting at present, that's good, the young generation has replaced us, there's a lot we could tell them if they asked, but no one asks Moreukhov anything—on the contrary, they're eyeing him with hostility, as in, what do you want, and he comes closer, wants to say something along the lines of: "Everything's fine, guys, I'm not here to see you," when, all of a sudden, a female figure runs out and hurtles toward Moreukhov, not so much screaming as squeaking: "Help, help!," but at that moment, they drag her back in and the sound stops.

Whereupon Moreukhov approaches with an unhurried, cinematic gait and says something like: "Leave the girl alone and get the fuck out of here, now!," then, grabs someone's arm, twists it, finishes him off with a kick, punches someone else in the teeth, in the gut, retreats, attacks . . . a broken bottle in his right hand, fury in his eyes, flashbacks of drunken fights . . . he manages to yell one more time: "Get the fuck out of here, now!" when, suddenly, it gets hot and wet, then, again and again, and he falls and hears, as if through a fog, "Fuck, what have you done? Come on, we're peacing out!," the stomping of feet and then, silence.

Moreukhov gets up, staggers, and falls down again, feeling a mon-strous pain in his stomach, as if his intestines are being wound around a fist, it hurts so bad, Lord, it hurts so bad, I think I'm going to die right now, Lord, but if You can hear me, everything I said was true, I remem-bered it and will repeat it to You: thank You for the rustle of angel wings, for the frosty air, for the first swig, for the blue sky, for the black branches, for all the women I've had, for the movies and music, for Dimon and Vitalik, for the life I've lived, and the death I await. Take me away from here, Lord, if that's what You want, and fucking stop all this now, it hurts, Lord, it hurts so bad! Then, a female face leans over him, like the face of an angel, and a tender voice says: "Hang on, hang on just a bit, I've already called an ambulance, just don't die, please don't die," and Moreukhov closes his eyes and whispers: "That's funny . . . sober," and at that moment, a bloody bubble bursts on his lips and darkness sets in.

Then, six walk toward him: a blindfolded fencing teacher, a hun-gover customs agent with a machine gun, a New York hitman in dark sunglasses, a private detective in a Stetson hat, a baldheaded gun-slinger with a Colt-45, and a nonchalant Chinese man with a match between his teeth and a pistol in each hand. They bend over Moreukhov and say: "You did great, man, you didn't screw up! Welcome to the club, we're glad to see you, get up, let's go, what are you lying there for?" And Moreukhov gets up and asks: "Do they serve drinks here?" They smile in reply and Yul Brynner says:

"Yup."

108.

DARK WATER

In the morning, come out of the house, walk down the familiar streets, don't veer off course, keep walking until everything you've known in this life is behind you. Don't look back, keep walking, and the road will bring you to a dark forest as in a fairy tale. Don't be afraid, go in. Stop and listen—you can hear the water gurgling and the mill working. Walk toward the sound and you'll come out on the bank.

The forest encircles it like a jagged wall, the mill wheel hums, and dark streams run down the vanes, tell me, who sits in the pond? Who lives in this deep end, in this water?

Come closer, don't be afraid.

You brought a stick? A knotty branch with a hook on its end? Or maybe, an empty bottle, car keys, a toy sword? A black cat, a black rooster, a treat, a gift for those who live in the water? Perhaps, like the Brave Little Raccoon from the cartoon, you want to give them a smile, be friends with them?

Well, then, why don't you give it a try?

Bring offerings, toss in a black rooster, give away a black cat. Enter the water and the cold will touch your feet, then, your knees, hips, and belly. Dive in when it reaches your chest.

You can see them swim by one by one, do you recognize them? An old man with a gray beard, a suicidal man with a gun, a woman with a flat face waiting for the trumpet to start playing, followed by Makar and Mikhail, Nastya and Marfa, Grandma Olga, and behind her, Aunt Lida, Polina in the form of a withered angel, scraps of flesh, human flesh, in the form of fish schools: torn, minced, tattered; shriveled from hunger, scattered by explosions, pulverized by bullets.

They swim by slowly, one after another, as if filmed in slow motion.

The miller-sorcerer didn't want to die, he thrashed against the threshold and bit through his tongue, his arms were contorted by pain and blood came out of his mouth; he was the custodian of the inheritance and couldn't die until he gave it away.

He didn't want to die because he was a sorcerer? Who wants to die?

February 4, 2005, Alexander Melnikov, Uncle Sasha, Papa Sasha, Sashka, Sashenka, there he is gasping for breath, turning blue, catching the air with his mouth like a fish . . . What does he want to pass on, and to whom? He doesn't want to die either, he is also grasping for his life, clinging to it, freezing, turning numb, and swimming.

Don't be afraid, swim. Let the fish play in your hair, let the seaweed grow over with your beard and all that river moss sway between your legs.

Don't be afraid, swim with us, breathe our water, play our games, wait for the swimmer and make your way over, sink your teeth into him, grab him by the hair, hold him tighter, drag him down, become a tender death for him, a playful dolphin, a mermaid, a banana fish.

And what if he breaks free, swims up to the surface, comes out on shore—what then? Nothing. He won't remember a thing, he won't say anything. And if he does, no one will believe him.

The dead swim alongside us, the living dead and the dead dead, they reach out their hands, come out of the water at night, cling to the living and ask: who will bury your dead?

Our dead swim alongside us, we can't bury them ourselves.

The dead have their own inheritances: sorcerers' gifts, golden rings, family secrets, skeletons in the underwater closet. Dive in here, collect them, don't be afraid.

Don't be afraid of the dark water, open your lungs and learn how to breathe here, it's not hard.

Don't be afraid of rotten snags, they rotted a long time ago and are lying still, touch them and they'll fall apart.

Don't be afraid of toothy fish, they swim by and scatter in all directions like frightened spawn.

Don't be afraid of underwater monsters, we're the monsters. The monster-leviathans, the wondrous wonders, the marvelous marvels, the moist moisture, the deathly death, the fleshly flesh, flesh of my flesh, ashes to ashes, primogenitors, great-grandfathers and ancestors, old men and old women, men and women, boys and girls; we swim here in the dark water, in the forest deep end, in the forgotten history, in family legends, in untold dreams; our lungs are awash with the past, in our ears is the rushing of water, our eyes look blindly forward. Here, we swim, we swim . . .

Pour dark water in a crystal shot glass and drink the whole thing, to your health and their memory, to the living and dead, to the underwater creatures, to the people on earth, to ancient gods. And in farewell, toss a coin in the deep end, toss it so you'll return, so you'll recognize this water; recognize it when the icy cold touches your feet, then, your knees, hips, and chest. At that moment, you'll recall that you've already been here, you've gone swimming with us, you know that it's not so scary underwater.

It's not scary, no, it's not scary at all.

2005–2009, Moscow

CPSIA information can be obtained
at www.ICGtesting.com
Printed in the USA
JSHW080409061022
31288JS00003B/3